THE OLD MANOR HOUSE

THE OLD MANOR HOUSE

Charlotte Smith

edited by Jacqueline M. Labbe

broadview literary texts

National Library of Canada Cataloguing in Publication Data

Smith, Charlotte, 1749–1806
    The old manor house / Charlotte Smith ; edited by Jacqueline M. Labbe.

(Broadview literary texts)
Includes bibliographical references.
ISBN 1-55111-213-2

I. Labbe, Jacqueline M., 1965– II. Title. III. Series.

PR3688.S405 2002   823'.6   C2002-902938-4

Broadview Press Ltd. is an independent, international publishing house, incorporated in 1985. Broadview believes in shared ownership, both with its employees and with the general public; since the year 2000 Broadview shares have traded publicly on the Toronto Venture Exchange under the symbol BDP.

We welcome comments and suggestions regarding any aspect of our publications–please feel free to contact us at the addresses below or at broadview@broadviewpress.com.

North America
PO Box 1243, Peterborough, Ontario, Canada K9J 7H5
3576 California Road, Orchard Park, NY, USA 14127
Tel: (705) 743-8990; Fax: (705) 743-8353
email: customerservice@broadviewpress.com

UK, Ireland, and continental Europe
Thomas Lyster Ltd., Units 3 & 4a, Old Boundary Way
Burscough Road, Ormskirk
Lancashire, L39 2YW
Tel: (01695) 575112; Fax: (01695) 570120
email: books@tlyster.co.uk

Australia and New Zealand
UNIREPS, University of New South Wales
Sydney, NSW, 2052
Tel: 61 2 9664 0999; Fax: 61 2 9664 5420
email: info.press@unsw.edu.au

www.broadviewpress.com

Broadview Press Ltd. gratefully acknowledges the financial support of the Government of Canada through the Book Publishing Industry Development Program for our publishing activities.

Series editor: Professor L.W. Conolly
Advisory editor for this volume: Colleen Franklin

PRINTED IN CANADA

Contents

Acknowledgements

For introducing me to Charlotte Smith, I must thank Stuart Curran, whose groundbreaking graduate classes at the University of Pennsylvania in the early 1990s on Romantic-period women writers opened vistas of literary possibilities. That Smith is now being regarded as one of the most important and interesting authors in the enlarged Romantic canon is due to his example.

I am very grateful to Emma Clery, Lisa Vargo, Julie Schaffer, Peter Mack, and Derek Hughes for their patience in answering my many questions as I began (and completed) this edition. The staff in the Rare Book Reading Room and in Reprographic Services at the British Library were invariably helpful. Don LePan at Broadview was a model of encouragement, and Barbara Conolly and Leonard Conolly models of patience.

As always, however, my deepest thanks go to Rod Jones, whose support and unflagging ability to feel interest in my work, even when my own has evaporated, is beyond price.

Jacqueline M. Labbe
Coventry, England

For India Rose

Introduction

Biographical Sketch

Charlotte Turner Smith—poet, novelist, translator—is generally agreed upon by critics to have been born on 4 May 1749. The place is more open to question—for some, it is London, for others, Stoke-next-Guildford in Surrey.[1] Her family was prosperous: her father Nicholas Turner owned two country residences (Stoke Place and Bignor Park, Sussex) as well as a London townhouse in King Street, near St. James Square. Her mother, Ann or Anna Towers, had brought a dowry of £1000 to the marriage, a sum which prompts Loraine Fletcher, in her recent biography, to state that Smith's parents must have married for love, and "were an attractive couple."[2] Smith was the oldest of three, and her mother died giving birth to her only brother Nicholas in 1751. Brought up in the country by her maternal aunt, Lucy Towers, Smith spent her childhood mainly at Bignor Park, "my ci devant paternal house" as she called it,[3] and also at Stoke Place and at school in Chichester. Like Wordsworth was to do, Smith developed a deep attachment to her rural surroundings; "an early worshipper at Nature's shrine,"[4] she incorporates her love for natural beauty and her affinity with the South Downs of Sussex into much of her writing, especially her poetry, while her novels abound with superbly realized natural description. A decade before Wordsworth, Smith wrote with what modern scholars would call a Romantic feeling for landscape and Nature, and indeed her works had a signal affect on Wordsworth himself.[5]

Smith's education seems to have been limited to the usual cultivation of skills and talents thought necessary for a young gentlewoman:

---

[1]   See Loraine Fletcher, *Charlotte Smith, A Critical Biography* (Basingstoke: Macmillan, 1998) p. 11; Rufus Paul Turner, "Charlotte Smith 1749–1806: New Light on her Life and Literary Career" (Diss. U of Southern California, 1966): 16–17. This uncertainty reflects the perennial problem that information on too many women writers—even the most famous ones—is often lacking.

[2]   Fletcher, 11.

[3]   Letter to Samuel Rose, in Turner, 17.

[4]   "Beachy Head," l. 346, in Curran, 231.

[5]   While the two met only once, in 1791 when Wordsworth visited her in Brighton to obtain a letter of introduction to Helen Maria Williams in Paris, much of his most familiar poetry bears her stamp: "Tintern Abbey"; several of the poems in *Lyrical Ballads*; many of his sonnets. For remarks on these affinities, see Labbe, "*Beachy Head*," *A Companion to Romanticism*, ed. Duncan Wu (Oxford: Blackwell, 1998): 204–10.

while at school she learned music, dancing, drawing, and French, and experimented with writing poetry. By the age of eight, she and her siblings had moved from the country to London to continue their fashionable education. In novels of sensibility by such authors as Jane Austen, Fanny Burney, and Smith herself, a country education encourages virtue and simplicity, artlessness and charm—characteristics represented as emblematic of a heroine's purity. In more satirical fiction, a country education produces a bumpkin, a simpleton. Certainly, Smith's privileged upbringing indicated an eventual entrance into "society," and for this to be successful, some city experience was necessary. Despite her affection for the country, then, Smith's family followed the dictates of fashion, and she was placed at a popular school in Kensington. From there, she was removed at the age of twelve, according to some to take her place in society, according to others to save the school fees: her father, foreshadowing the profligacy of her future husband, was by 1761 deeply in debt, obliged to sell Stoke Place to pay his creditors.

This did not, however, affect Smith's debut into society, where from the ages of twelve to fourteen she shone as a young woman of fashion, wit, and means; as her sister notes, "as if foreseeing how short would be the period of her youthful pleasures, she pursued them with the avidity natural to her lively character; and though her father was sometimes disposed to check her love of dissipation[1] he always suffered himself to be disarmed by a few sighs or tears."[2] Although she was writing some poetry, and even sent some work to *The Lady's Magazine*, at this point she was an average teenager: in the language of her day, giddy and thoughtless. Her father's financial troubles were not apparent in the luxurious lifestyle she enjoyed, and she was encouraged to make her mark on society in a thoroughly conventional way; the eventual goal was, of course, marriage to a suitable partner, hopefully for love, as her parents had done.

Nicholas Turner's debts, however, forced a solution which led to the event that transformed Smith into a writer. When she was fifteen, her father married the heiress Henrietta Meriton, whose £20,000 and property would rescue him from ruin. The usual solution to the problem of stepmother-stepdaughter friction was to find a husband for the daughter, and so Benjamin Smith, the son of a London merchant with extensive property in the West Indies and interests in the East Indies, was

---

[1]   In this case, probably referring to late nights and balls rather than to anything more serious.

[2]   Fletcher, 19.

chosen. Before she turned sixteen, Smith was married, in an exchange she later in life characterized as a sale, herself "a legal prostitute."[1] Even as Smith had been brought up privileged and pampered, so too her husband; never able to settle at a job, self-indulgent to an extreme, and convinced of his entitlement to a life of ease, within only a few years he was plagued by debts his wealthy father was unable or unwilling to settle. It was due to Benjamin's unreliability that his father composed a will intended to allow his fortune to bypass his son entirely and go straight to his grandchildren; I will return to the issue of the will.

Smith and her husband lived together for twenty years, and between 1765 and 1785 she bore twelve children, nine of whom survived their infancy. During this time they moved frequently to escape creditors, once all the way to France (1784), while in 1783 she spent several months with Benjamin in the King's Bench, where he was imprisoned for debt. Smith saw her lifestyle change drastically from that of the fashionable lady to that of the always-pressed, always needy wife. Even after 1787, when she finally formally separated from her profligate, abusive and unfaithful husband (divorce was not an option without money and position), she was always subject to his financial demands. As Benjamin's wife, Smith was legally his possession, and as such all her earnings, all her property was, by law, his.[2] Her status in law was that of the *feme covert* [*sic*], the "covered woman," subordinate in all ways to her husband. Although this was intended to protect women from what the eighteenth century saw as their constitutional weakness, plainly it worked to benefit the husband; indeed, when Benjamin finally died in 1806 (only a few months before Smith herself), she wrote to a friend, "You mention havg [*sic*] seen in the papers, the death of Mr. Smith…. *Will you my dear Madam tell me, for it is very material to me to know, whether there was any addition to that circumstance & what?*"[3] Smith needs to know the facts since Benjamin's death makes a "material" difference to her—it will *de facto* change her material conditions for the better.

Smith's marriage, then, was defined by Benjamin's irresponsibility and brutality. However, it served to create Charlotte Smith the writer; her hardships and need meant that what at first was merely a pastime became her profession. Smith began publishing to make money. While in the King's Bench, she completed her *Elegiac Sonnets*, a series of irregular—that is,

---

1   Fletcher, 25.
2   For an invaluable discussion of the position of the married woman in eighteenth-century law, see Susan Staves, *Married Women's Separate Property in England, 1660–1833* (Cambridge: Harvard UP, 1990). See also Appendix C.
3   Letter to Sarah Rose, March 20, 1806; in Turner, 23.

non-Petrarchan—sonnets exploring the nature of grief, isolation, alienation, and exile, and using a dominating first-person persona so tangible that readers did not hesitate to name it as Smith. An instant success, the *Sonnets* generated both cash and reputation for Smith, and confirmed for her that poetry could regain her the status her marriage had cost her. To this end, she took the unusual step of signing her title page with both her full name and a residence—"Bignor Park, in Sussex." Although the estate was in no way hers—it belonged to her brother as the male heir—clearly in this first publication Smith sought to establish her credentials, not as the wife of Benjamin, but as originating from her family estate; not as a resident of a cell in debtor's prison, but as the inhabitant of a country house; and finally, not as "Mrs." but as "Charlotte Smith," a self-naming that rejects her status as *feme covert* in an open and declaratory gesture towards individuality.

Over the next twenty years, Smith published eight editions of *Elegiac Sonnets*, the two major Romantic poems *The Emigrants* (1793) and "Beachy Head" (1807), poems and books for children, a translation of *Manon Lescaut*, and ten novels, of which *The Old Manor House* is considered her best for its depth of characterization and assured handling of plot, as well as its expansive and affecting natural description. She wrote poetry to uphold her sense of self and to pursue the individuality her culture withheld from the married woman, and she wrote novels and other prose works to bring in the money necessary to support her children, most of whom were grown but all of whom drew on her resources: for school fees, dowries, military commissions. Smith never forgot she was a gentlewoman, and could never conceive of bringing up her children as anything other than genteel. And so, "chained to her desk like a slave to his oar, with no other means of subsistence for herself and her numerous children, with a broken constitution, unequal to the severe labour enjoined by her necessity,"[1] she wrote steadily from 1784 to her death on 28 October 1806.

Themes

The Old Manor House tells the story of the love between Orlando Somerive and Monimia Morysine, a young servant in the house of Orlando's elderly relative Mrs. Rayland.[2] However, it is more than a

---

[1] Cowper, in Ehrenpreis, xii.

[2] For later readers, this is the part of the plot that seemed essential; for instance, a mid-nineteenth-century edition in the editor's possession entitles the novel *The Old Manor House: or, Monimia and Orlando* (London: John Lofts, n.d.).

simple romance, as the action turns on the inheritance of Rayland Hall. The Somerives and the Raylands are related, but Mrs. Rayland's pride forbids her from seeing the Somerives as her equals; they are descended from a marriage between her aunt and a "mere yeoman." While Orlando strikes her as a true Rayland, he must also conceal his relationship with Monimia, as Mrs. Rayland would never accept such an unequal marriage. In the novel's course Orlando must leave to fight in the American Revolution (both to gain Mrs. Rayland's favour and to make a livelihood as a soldier), and upon his return he finds his father and Mrs. Rayland dead, his brother in debtor's prison, his mother and sisters distraught, Monimia missing, and most importantly, Rayland Hall in the hands of a clergyman who has obtained it by conniving to hide a will in Orlando's favour. Smith thus weaves together romance, politics, and the law to produce a novel that is as much about the disbursement of property as it is about the progress of a romance.

Smith wrote the novel from August 1792 to January 1793, just as the French Revolution was entering its violent stage.[1] An earlier novel, *Desmond* (1792), had been openly sympathetic to the Revolution, for which she had received some strong criticism. *The Old Manor House*, set in the 1770s, allows her to factor in a liberal politics without being overtly political. During August and September 1792, Smith was a visitor at William Hayley's Eartham villa, along with the poet William Cowper and his companion Mrs. Unwin, and the painter George Romney. It was here that she wrote the first volume of the novel, writing during the day and reading aloud her work to her fellow guests in the evening, to their great approval. Indeed, such was the impression she made that she gained the sympathy and respect of all three. This was a "rare halcyon interlude," as Ehrenpreis terms it;[2] by October she was back at her "oar." Critics have often determined that Volumes II to IV of the novel reflect the haste and worry of their author, and that the incongruities of plot and the seemingly hasty conclusion are due to her rushed writing (the novel was finished by early January 1793). However, this seems an unnecessarily harsh judgement. Certainly the first volume is the most leisured of the four, but then it also explores the relaxed setting of Orlando's youth, as the favourite of Mrs. Rayland. As the events of his life become more complicated, and more rushed, so too does the style of plotting and narrative. Smith uses form to shadow content; the novel is not *about* ease and

---

[1] See Appendix D for contextualizing material about the French Revolution.
[2] Ehrenpreis, "Introduction" to *The Old Manor House*, xi.

order and balance; therefore, it is not written in such a manner. Smith thus uses the pressure on her to her novel's advantage: it absolutely reflects not only her authorial situation, but also Orlando's character, and as he disintegrates, so too does the novel's pace. Form and function collude in a meaningful way. The problem for many readers, however, is that this technique is usually considered a much more modern development than that in train in the late eighteenth century; however, as I will indicate in the discussion of Smith's use of metaphor at the end of this introduction, Smith is in many ways a thoroughly modern novelist.

She is also a novelist who makes use of what is familiar to her. For instance, there are many points of congruence between events in *The Old Manor House* and Smith's life and affinities. The natural landscape of the south of England, for instance, that plays such a major part in her poetry, and for which she developed such an affection when a child, is essential to the affect of the novel. From its opening—"In an old Manor House in one of the most southern counties of England"—landscape is established as emotive and necessary to the plot's development. In his many treks from his family home at West Wolverton to the estate of the Manor House, Rayland Hall, Orlando Somerive frequently uses the natural scene to chart his emotional development: moonlit vs. dark nights, winter vs. spring—all allow Orlando to explain himself to himself. Once in America, Orlando uses the grandeur and sublimity of the landscape to question England's characterization of the colonists as "rebels." Even Smith's notorious mistake —locating savannahs in New York State and allowing Canada to bloom with magnolias—bespeaks a desire to see the New World as inherently more welcoming and naturally lovely than the Old. As Rufus Paul Turner also notes, landscape in *The Old Manor House* "subserves the story, dovetailing with and aiding mood and incident, as well as characterization."[1] When Orlando finally finds his missing love Monimia in a cottage deep in the woods, it is not only the fairy-tale, pastoral nature of the setting that affects the plot, but also the suggestion that Monimia, unlike most of the other characters, is thoroughly at home in nature, that the landscape itself has welcomed her, taken her in, and protects her. While Smith does not transform nature into "Mother Nature" as thoroughly as does, for instance, Wordsworth, she nonetheless uses the natural as a metaphor for the uncorrupted, the pure: Monimia is a child of nature in that she has remained almost wholly untouched by corrupt culture.

---

[1] Turner, 127.

In other ways, too, Monimia resembles a child of nature: she has no direct familial origins. We are told that Mrs. Rayland's housekeeper Mrs. Lennard has taken in her orphan grand-niece, the daughter of Mrs. Lennard's sister's daughter: "such at least was the history given in Mrs. Rayland's family of an infant girl, which at about four years old had been ... taken, as it was said, from nurse, at a distant part of the county." The narrator's sceptical tone is matched by that of the other characters in the novel, particularly Orlando's father, who continually refers to Monimia as Mrs. Lennard's "supposed" niece (the clear implication is that Monimia is in fact illegitimate, though her parentage is less clear. Mrs. Lennard would seem too old to be her mother). That Mrs. Lennard mistreats Monimia throughout the novel, placing her in the household as a lower servant, restricting her movements, eventually shutting her up first in her tower bedroom and then in Mrs. Lennard's own closet, finally simply sending her away and forgetting all about her, points to the housekeeper's position as, among other things, a bad mother (or mother-figure). Mr. Somerive, too, parents badly: he desperately wants Orlando to recover the Somerive family favour with Mrs. Rayland, and therefore teaches Orlando to be a sycophant and to please Mrs. Rayland above all else. He even attempts, like Smith's own father, to marry off both his daughter Isabella and Orlando himself to patently unsuitable, albeit rich, partners. Finally, his continual disparagement of Monimia,[1] his assumption that since she occupies a servant's role she must perforce be scheming and corrupt, show him to be tainted by the same worldly considerations and conventional world-views of most of the other (unsympathetic) characters. His weak fathering, vacillation, and untrustworthy judgement mirror that of Nicholas Turner; Orlando can find no adequate support in such a father. His mother, too, is weak, unable to cope with the failure of the family fortunes, and utterly debilitated by Mr. Somerive's death.[2] Indeed, when confronted with her son Orlando returned from war, her belief that he had been killed prevents her for some time from accepting the reality of his return. That Orlando subsequently delays telling her of his marriage to Monimia—a plot-point which has struck many readers as improbable—reiterates his understanding of her incapacity. For the two central characters, then,

[1] That is, until he meets Monimia, at which point he acknowledges her beauty, though not, however, her virtue; see Volume III, Chapter VIII.

[2] Smith's own renowned strength as a mother provides an ironic contrast with her character's ineptitude.

bad parenting defines and to a large extent constructs the trajectory of their love affair.

Mrs. Rayland herself both embodies and suffers from bad parenting. We learn in the first paragraph that family pride has created the situation the novel explores—who is the rightful heir to Rayland Hall:

> Mrs. Rayland was the only survivor of the three co-heiresses of Sir Hildebrand Rayland; one of the first of those to whom the title of Baronet had been granted by James the First. The name had been before of great antiquity in the county—and the last baronet having only daughters to share his extensive possessions, these ladies had been educated with such very high ideas of their own importance, that they could never be prevailed upon to lessen, by sharing it with any of those numerous suitors, who for the first forty or fifty years of their lives surrounded them; ... [T]he second, Mrs. Grace, saw herself at the advanced age of sixty-nine sole inheritor of the fortunes of her house, without any near relation, or indeed any relation at all whom she chose to consider as entitled to possess it after her death.

As with so many novels of the period,[1] parental responsibility and education are entwined; a bad or improper or useless education is invariably the result of parental inattention or inadequacy. Trained to regard herself as sufficient company (and in this way gaining a self-confidence and independence paradoxically denied to the properly-educated literary heroine—and Smith is aware of the paradox), Mrs. Rayland consequently finds herself unable to commit her property—a metonym for herself—to any one heir for most of the novel, and exercises the power property and wealth give her to maintain the dependence the Somerive family is too weak, collectively, to reject. Like perpetual minors, they await Mrs. Rayland's favours, while she, the parent unwilling to license independence, enjoys her dominance. Thus the family remains bound together, each generation inadequate to the needs of the other, each distrustful and resentful of the claims made by the other.

The issue at the heart of *The Old Manor House*, however, is property: who owns it, who claims it, who deserves it, and it is ineluctably tied up with the issue of parenting. Many of Smith's writings, novels and

---

1   See, for instance, Eliza Fenwick, *Secresy* (1795), Elizabeth Inchbald, *A Simple Story* (1791), and Jane Austen, *Northanger Abbey* (1818).

poems, explore the theme of inheritance, partly because Smith herself was embroiled in a lawsuit over a will for more than thirty years. When it became clear to her father-in-law Richard Smith that her husband Benjamin was untrustworthy and a wastrel,[1] he composed a will in which he attempted to bypass his son—his legal heir—and leave his fortune directly to his grandchildren. Will-making in the eighteenth century was notoriously difficult; even lawyers had trouble deciphering documents wrapped up in ornate and labyrinthine jargon.[2] Richard Smith drew up the will on his own, creating a testament filled with contradictions and irresolvable ambiguities.[3] The result was a fortune forever out of reach, a constant irritant to a woman already disinherited by her sex from any share in her own family's property (Bignor Park). Richard Smith, ironically, recognized Smith's suitability to manage the family fortune by naming her as one of the will's executors, another example of his well-meaning ignorance of the law; as Mary Hays noted in 1800,

> Mr. Smith's father died in 1776, an irreparable loss for her, towards whom he had always expressed particular affection, and of whom his opinion was such, that he appointed her, with his widow and his son, executrix to his will; a measure which her being a wife rendered ineffectual as to any present power. His will, though fortunately it provided for all her children then born, was complex and confused; and the trustees, who were also appointed, refusing to act, great inconvenience ensued, and whoever was to blame, Mrs. Smith and her children, now nine in number, were finally the victims.[4]

Almost all of Smith's readers during her lifetime and after have noted what Anna Letitia Barbauld calls her "bitter and querulous tone of complaint" but which Hays calls "that tincture of sadness which has

---

[1] As Turner relates, Richard Smith's will declares "… I have reason to believe that my Son does not intend to keep up the business after my death but purposes if he has power to do it to call in all the debts due from the correspondents to my Estate and undoubtedly as he seems totally bent upon the purchase of lands would be for investing the money all that way" (28).

[2] See Appendix C.

[3] So much so that Fletcher (338) is not alone in comparing its long journey through Chancery to the Jarndyce and Jarndyce case in Charles Dickens's *Bleak House*.

[4] Mary Hays, "Mrs. Charlotte Smith," *British Public Characters*, ed. Richard Phillips (1800–01): 48–49.

excited in every feeling heart so lively an interest."[1] Smith took the unusual step, for a respectable woman of her time, of publicizing her situation and apportioning blame. She did not accept the validity of a legal system that disenfranchised her doubly: for being a woman and being married. Egerton Brydges, another contemporary, is more sympathetic than most commentators to her strategy:

> It is probable that the quickness of Mrs. Smith's penetration, and the boldness of her temper impelled her sometimes to speak unwelcome truths to some of the people concerned in her affairs, who were generally accustomed to secure themselves by the glare of their riches from too near an inspection. This might be imprudent in point of self-interest; but surely it neither detracted from her virtue, nor from her claims to respect and admiration.[2]

His words show an awareness of Smith's bind, the conflicting demands of the proprieties and of self-respect and self-sufficiency.

This unending tangle over a will clearly informs *The Old Manor House*, described by Barbauld as revolving around Mrs. Rayland, the "best drawn character ... a wealthy old lady who keeps all her relations in constant dependence, and will not be persuaded to name an heir."[3] Indeed, the final volume centres on Orlando's search for a lost will, and his legal challenge to a will that has disinherited his family. Smith builds into her novel her knowledge of the unreliability of a legal system designed to facilitate the passage of property from male heir to male heir and to maintain a patriarchal status quo. She opens the novel deep in the unjustifiable uncertainty occasioned by an unmarried female landowner, and dramatizes the exigencies this creates, in a plotline that could be read as validating the need for a strict male primogeniture, but that more logically, given Smith's own situation, works instead to expose the law's inability to cope with the notion of a Mrs. Rayland. Rather than promoting convention, *The Old Manor House* charts the cost—to families, individuals, and relationships—of relying on convention.

---

[1]   Barbauld, Introduction to *The Old Manor House*, *The British Novelists, with an Essay and Prefaces Biographical and Critical*, vol. 36 (London: Rivington, 1810) ii. Hays, 47.

[2]   Egerton Brydges, "Memoir of Mrs. Charlotte Smith," *Censura Literaria, Containing Titles, Abstracts and Opinions of Old English Books*, vol. vii (London: Longman, 1815) 251.

[3]   Barbauld, vii.

The Property Romance

Mrs. Rayland, the owner of the Old Manor House, Rayland Hall, is not, of course, married; her title is an "honorary" one, but nonetheless it raises the spectre of the married woman *with* property, an anomaly in British law during the eighteenth century, as Susan Staves makes clear. Mrs. Rayland is an unmarried heiress with a title ("Mrs.") that implies she is married. She is in charge of a great estate, and the sole determiner of its future. At the same time, her sex emphasizes that the Rayland family has all but died out: in the language of law, the male line has become "extinct." John Habakkuk says that "it is certainly the case that the chance of extinction was high in the late seventeenth and early eighteenth century."[1] He goes on to point out that "the development in the later seventeenth century of stricter and more elaborate forms of settlement, providing for even very remote contingencies, must therefore have tended to reduce the number of occasions when, on the failure of the direct male line, a property descended to the daughter." Despite these efforts, however, "it is clear...that throughout these centuries, there were a large number of heiresses and that they were common enough in the eighteenth century."[2] In the case of the Raylands, there has been a signal "failure of the direct male line": Sir Hildebrand Rayland has, as we have seen, succeeded in producing only three daughters, of which "Mrs. Rayland"—Grace—is the middle. Smith plays on the notion of male "failure" and male "extinction" when she tells us that none of the three daughters "could [ever] be prevailed upon to lessen [their importance] by sharing it with any of those numerous suitors, who for the first forty or fifty years of their lives surrounded them." Smith uses the term "importance," but of course the reality is that marriage would have seen the transfer of the Rayland estate to the ownership of the husband, and the final "extinction" of the Rayland line.[3] Habakkuk assumes that heiresses will marry, but he also makes it clear that "the estate as an entity, as the basis of a distinct landed family, disappeared as a result of her marriage."[4] In other words, if Mrs. Rayland were truly a wife she would

---

[1]   Habbakuk, "The Rise and Fall of English Landed Families, 1600–1800," *Transactions of the Royal Historical Society*, 5th series, 29 (1979): 189.

[2]   Habakkuk, 189, 190.

[3]   While the Rayland name could be taken as a condition of marriage, nonetheless the ownership of the estate would still pass to the new husband. The "real" Raylands would have lost their property.

[4]   Habakkuk, 192.

no longer have any testamentary power over her property—indeed, she would no longer *have* any property. Smith thus opens her property novel by side-stepping legal proprieties; the Rayland estate is simultaneously still available to the Rayland family, and held by the most vulnerable member of that family, a daughter. By giving Mrs. Rayland sole control over her property, Smith grants her autonomy and the freedom of choice that money and power bring a man.

Unfortunately, Mrs. Rayland also stands as an emblem of the corrupting nature of absolute power, both on the holder of power and those around her who hope to benefit from it. The Somerive family, the product of a romantic disregard for property, hope to regain their place in the Rayland line by means of their youngest son, Orlando, a character by turns romantic, naïve, and servile. Orlando, named after a Rayland ancestor, is deliberately placed in the female Rayland line of descent, whereas his older brother Philip, named after his father, is placed to carry on the Somerive name. Smith is very careful to let her readers know the genealogy of the Somerive family: Mrs. Rayland's aunt had "giv[en] herself to a ... mere yeoman," this aunt's son then marries a companion to the Rayland sisters instead of one of them (which would have kept the property neatly in the family), and *his* son marries a woman "who had nothing to recommend her but her beauty, simplicity, and goodness." The Somerives seem to have distinguished themselves by a lack of concern for their own financial advantages: their line of inheritance seems based on love rather than property. However, Smith suggests that this laudable disregard for the sordid realities of life have actually resulted in a weakened and morally uncertain family: Mr. Somerive is vacillating, by turns tyrannical and indulgent; Philip is venal and untrustworthy; and Orlando spends most of his time pandering to Mrs. Rayland's demands. In the male line we see, as the first pages of the novel suggests, failure and extinction.

Smith, then, opens her novel by contrasting romance—the love-matches of the Somerive family—and property—the perpetual single state of the Rayland sisters. She intermingles these in the person of Orlando, born to reconcile the families, named after a Rayland ancestor through "reluctantly obtained permission." As Joseph Bartolomeo points out, this "is tantamount to servile flattery; thus the exotic name derives from the most practical and mercenary of motives."[1] Romance is put to the service of inheritance hopes. As the narrator notes, Mr. Somerive is regarded by

---

[1]   Bartolomeo, "The Subversion of Romance in *The Old Manor House*," *Studies in English Literature* 33 (1993): 647.

the community as Mrs. Rayland's heir-at-law, that is, the default heir; but since she is the sole owner, on the deaths of her sisters, and in complete testamentary control, such considerations do not apply. In fact, Mrs. Rayland embodies the notion of "property as individual absolute dominion": "that sole and despotic dominion which one man [sic] claims and exercises over the external things of the world, in total exclusion of the rights of any other individual in the universe," as Blackstone phrased it.[1] Orlando, then, must relate to Mrs. Rayland not as heir presumptive, but rather, to coin a term, heir desirous, and his success depends on how well he inserts himself into her world of absolute dominion.

Blackstone, in discussing the property rights of "things," shows how certain conventions of English property law originated in feudalism. Under this system, "all lands were originally granted out by the sovereign.... The grantor was called the proprietor, or *lord*; being he who retained the dominion of ultimate property of the feud or fee: and the grantee [vassal] ... had only the use and possession.... Besides an oath of *fealty*, or profession of faith to the lord ... the vasal [sic] ... did usually *homage* to his lord...."[2] The vassal also does service, usually military. As this short sketch suggests, Mrs. Rayland operates under a feudal system, expecting fealty and homage from her vassal, Orlando, and encouraging him to enter the army to do his service and regain the military glory once embodied by his namesake Sir Orlando. In attending on Mrs. Rayland and obeying her summonses, Orlando also performs what Blackstone calls "knight-service." Orlando, playing the feudal game, accepts his position as "knight" wholeheartedly, even to the point of devoting his love to a lady in a tower: Monimia. Orlando, and his family, expect that he will be rewarded with property, under the rubric of Mrs. Rayland's feudal system. Mrs. Rayland certainly expects fealty and homage, and in order to extend the rights of the lord to Mrs. Rayland, a woman, Smith adapts the feudal system to recognize the usefulness of the Statute of Wills, 1544, under which property could be willed away from heirs-at-law by the "father"—in this case, the mother.

In the first few pages of the novel, then, Smith weaves together a complex web of law and custom; she embeds in Mrs. Rayland a concern for form and family that relies solely on assumptions of inbred "quality" rather than wealth: class detached from its splendid trappings. Mrs. Rayland displays a romantic attachment to a feudal system that privileged

---

[1]   Blackstone, 1. See also Appendix C.
[2]   Blackstone, 53.

the few and allowed for the absolute dominion of property. It is only property *law*, however, that allows Mrs. Rayland to indulge her desire for feudal domination, as it is only through the intervention of a will that she can dispose of her property as she wishes. At the same time, Smith shows how necessary money derived from property is to the continuation of this system. Although Mrs. Rayland may not recognize it, it is clear that those around her venerate her for her wealth rather than for the glory of her name, and this includes the Somerive family, romantically attached to the notion of regaining their financial standing through Orlando's wooing of Mrs. Rayland. To a certain degree, then, the real romance at the heart of *The Old Manor House* is that between Orlando, the vassal, and his Lady, Mrs. Rayland, whose colours he figuratively carries into battle when she pays for his soldier's uniform.

However, it is plain that for Orlando, at least, the romance revolves around the figure of Monimia, another orphan in a castle, under the control of her wicked stepmother (aunt, of course, but functioning as a mother-figure), imprisoned in a tower, forced into the Cinderella-like role of servant. For Orlando, Monimia satisfies the romantic yearnings that attendance on an *old* lady never could. Orlando believes entirely in his own romantic heritage: as much as he may be mocked, either maliciously or playfully, by his brother and his brother-in-law-to-be, for his name and his romantic ideals, Orlando himself is totally immersed in a world of romance which he sees as in a constant struggle with the "real" world. The novel's engagements with the genre chart Orlando's growing inability to control his romantic destiny and his increasing immersion in what Bartolomeo calls "melodrama."[1] Rayland Hall, however, never loses its place: it is instrumental in, first, concealing Orlando's and Monimia's romance, and then in exposing it.

In each of the novel's four volumes, the relationship between property and romance is transformed. Volume I is the most "fairy-tale" in its approach: the love Orlando feels for Monimia moves "insensibly" from sibling to sexual ("Orlando, who had loved her as a playfellow while they were both children, now began to feel a more tender and respectful affection for her; though unconscious himself that it was her beauty that awakened these sentiments"). However, it remains a secret: Orlando uses his knowledge of the passageways and forgotten byways of the Hall to pursue his object of "teaching" Monimia—both about life and about love. The

---

[1] See Bartolomeo, *passim*. See also Appendix C for more information about the ways in which the genre was a contested category during the period.

Hall colludes in their secret, protecting them from discovery and easing their night-time meetings with its thick walls and far-flung rooms (though later it seems to hinder them). For a time, theirs is a hidden romance, protected as long as they stay within the Hall. It is only when Monimia ventures out, to be seen and immediately desired by the villain Sir John Belgrave, that the world intrudes. In his argument with Sir John, Orlando reaches manhood; Monimia is prompted to declare her love; their romance becomes an open secret. Significantly, the threatened duel allows Orlando's two Ladies to merge, since Mrs. Rayland is convinced he has argued with Sir John on her behalf. Property and romance again collide.

Volume II opens with an epigraph from *A Midsummer Night's Dream* that reinforces the idea of romance interrupted by worldly concerns, and that foreshadows the move the plot makes from Rayland Hall to its environs:

> Ah me! for aught that I could ever read,
> Could ever hear from tale or history,
> The course of true love never did run smooth;
> But either it was different in blood,
> Or else misgrafted in respect of years,
> Or else it stood upon the choice of friends;
> Or, if there were a sympathy in choice,
> War, death, or sickness, did lay siege to it.

Romance, as uncertain as the identity of the heir to the Rayland estate, loses the protection of the Hall in this volume. Katharine Rogers says that the novel's "Romantic elements emphasize the disparity between the unworldly, unselfish hero and heroine and the sordid world they must live in,"[1] and in Volume II this is expressed in Orlando's quest for "something to do," and his figurative oath of fealty to Mrs. Rayland when he allows her wishes that he be a "gentleman" to override his father's desire that he take up a profession. We also witness Orlando's increasing fervour in his relationship with Monimia, and his increasing breaches of propriety in the name of romance. As the novel will make clear, while Monimia may well be "unselfish," Orlando's devotion to Mrs. Rayland—or at least to the idea of being her heir—continually clashes with his romantic duty to

---

[1] Rogers, "Romantic Aspirations, Restricted Possibilities: The Novels of Charlotte Smith," *Re-Visioning Romanticism: British Women Writers, 1776–1837*, eds. Carol Shiner Wilson and Joel Haefner (Philadelphia: U of Pennsylvania P, 1994): 85.

Monimia, resulting in increasingly selfish behaviour. As the romance moves into the open, it can no longer be reconciled with property; fealty to one is infidelity to the other. If Orlando were fully loyal to Monimia, Mrs. Rayland would surely cast him off; if he were fully loyal to Mrs. Rayland, he would cast Monimia off. Orlando is fully aware that as the "lord" in her fiefdom, Mrs. Rayland controls his choice of a wife: to marry without her consent would be to forfeit his place as her heir. This is made plain when Miss Hollybourne is proposed as a wife; despite her position as an heiress, Mrs. Rayland's disfavour is enough to stop it cold in a way that Orlando's expressed aversion could not. Property wins out over mere wealth, and Mrs. Rayland maintains her absolute dominion. By the end of Volume II, Orlando is about the leave the Hall altogether to perform his "service," his romance with Monimia has been revealed to a servant, and thanks to his fealty and homage to Mrs. Rayland, the property seems secured. That his romance and his inheritance are in direct opposition to each other is suggested by his wild and irrational behaviour at the thought of parting from Monimia. However, their contingency is also asserted by Monimia's continued incarceration in the Hall: she is emblematic of his hopes and expectations.

Volumes III and IV show the result of Orlando's desertion of his property, and also the outcome of his demonstration of service to Mrs. Rayland. His romance at this point contradicts itself: as a romance hero, and as Mrs. Rayland's vassal, his trials in America should prove his suitability both to inherit the property and win his ladylove. Instead, they lead directly to the temporary loss of both. His reported death encourages Mrs. Lennard, the "wicked stepmother" to Monimia's innocent orphan, to conspire to hide (though interestingly, not to destroy) the will in Orlando's favour, and to substitute an earlier one favouring herself; she also sends Monimia away, since she has lost the protection of her "knight." Mrs. Rayland, too, sinks under the blow of Orlando's loss, and her feudal fiefdom is destroyed despite her efforts at control. When Orlando returns, he finds that loss of property has resulted in a complete loss of identity: no one recognizes him and, once he has forced their acceptance of his return, he finds that his previous status was dependent not on his personal qualities but rather on his expectations. Romance is thus, to borrow Bartolomeo's word, "subverted." Since property embodies civic individuality, the loss of property involves the loss of individuality, and Orlando must spend the rest of the novel in search of that which had distinguished him: Mrs. Rayland's favour. Tellingly, Monimia is found rather easily, although Orlando *does* spend an inordinate amount of time imagining the worst about her, and their marriage is accomplished expediently through a quick elopement to Guernsey. Orlando's full energies are needed, not to find his heroine, but to recover his property. Romance is subsumed to property most directly when Orlando realizes how even romantic love is compromised by poverty: "the romantic theory, of sacrificing every consideration to love, produced, in the practice, only the painful consciousness of having injured its object." As long as the property remains elusive, the romance is not complete.

In the end, the romance is transported entirely to the property when Orlando penetrates the now-derelict Rayland Hall in search of the hidden will. Although he has only been absent about a year and a half, the place has fallen into near-ruin; even as the romance is disabled by the loss of property, so too the property is disabled by the loss of romance. Orlando reactivates both when he finds the will, hidden by Mrs. Lennard in another one of the cavities Rayland Hall contains (thus linking the will with Monimia: both are accessible to Orlando only through a stealth and an understanding of the Hall's hiding-places). As Bartolomeo and Rogers have noted, Orlando's fancy, "that the scene resembled one of those so often met with in old romances and fairy tales," confirms his addiction to romance rather than reality, but it also, of course, cements the link between romance and property. The "hand or head found swimming in blood, which it is the [hero's] business to restore to the inchanted owner," so potent a symbol of magic in a fairy tale, is Orlando's way of apprehending his own lost fortune, as vital to his existence as a hand or head; in recovering the will, Orlando recovers his own will to act, and he does so through the integration of property, individuality, and romance.

The Gothic image that accompanies the discovery of the will links up to an earlier Gothicized occurrence, the ghostly voice that terrifies Monimia in the chapel in Volume I. Both link, not to the actual supernatural, but to the worldly values of property. The will's significance has been suggested; the voice turns out to be that of a smuggler, who with his gang has been using Mrs. Rayland's cellars as a storage place. Smith uses Gothic imagery as simply another code for property; smuggling, after all, is nothing more than the theft of property and the evasion of taxes. Similarly, Orlando's experiences in America, while allowing him to perform his "service" for Mrs. Rayland, can also be linked to property: the war revolves around the colonists' refusal to participate in the feudal system, swearing fealty and performing homage in the form of taxes.[1]

---

[1]   See Appendix D for more examples of the colonists' rebellious behaviour.

When they revolt, they are in a sense robbing Britain of its colonies. When Orlando goes to fight against them, he is fighting *for* the feudal system.

And yet, in the end neither feudal loyalties, the absolute dominion of property ownership, nor even romance are vindicated. Orlando gets his property and his lady, but has not been shown to be a proper romance hero; if anyone, it is the timid Monimia who is shown to be most heroic. On the other hand, the very nature of property ownership and inheritance have come under scrutiny. Orlando's long submission to Mrs. Rayland and his dependence on her possible preference for him both creates and compromises his potential as a romantic hero: he is given the right setting, and a heroine, and yet his actions are suspect and his manner servile. Mrs. Rayland, while she challenges primogeniture and female subordination, is no better a caretaker of her wealth for her sex. Her devotion to feudalism and to the honour of her name nearly result in the total elimination of the Rayland line. Indeed, even once Orlando recovers his property, he becomes a Rayland only through a legal act, and *buys* a baronetcy—a money-based return to a title that, we were told at the novel's start, was "granted" by James I. In this way, the re-invigoration of the male line is achieved artificially, while the bloodline is mixed with Monimia's unknown genetic heritage: she is never, contrary to romantic tradition, revealed to be of noble blood, or even a true "lady." The happy ending is contained in the passing of property from the sterile female line to the fertile male line (Orlando, in the penultimate paragraph, has a son "to whom he gave his own name"); the romance is subverted to economics. In the words of Warwick, Orlando's brother-in-law, "Money, contrivance, and courage are all that is necessary." Orlando, by the favour of Grace, lives happily ever after in Rayland Hall, a model of the modern romance hero.

Narrative and Metaphoricity

Orlando's romance fantasy thus interacts with legal reality to construct the property romance, and his and Monimia's story relies both on the conventions of genre and the challenges of infusing genre with social commentary. This is, of course, also at work in the novel's use of the American Revolution. In part this allows Orlando to perform his knightly, martial role, as noted, but this plot device also functions to signal Smith's continued revolutionary sympathies. Although sometimes misread as politically conservative, Smith's politics are in sympathy with her challenges to gender stereotypes and the social power wielded by the legal system. But she was also a canny writer dependent on sales to support herself and her children. When her novel *Desmond* was censured for its sympathetic approach to the ideals of the French Revolution, she devised a narrative strategy in *The Old Manor House* that permitted liberal critiques of conservative governing while also shielding, to a certain extent, their applicability to the 1790s. The novel's main action is set between 1775-1779, and Orlando goes to fight, not the French, but the rebelling American colonists.[1] When the novel, then, condemns British shortsightedness, or its treatment of its soldiers, or its political naïveté, it merely participates in the general conclusion that the war with America had been badly run.[2] The very obviousness of the applicability of its sentiments to the conflict with France acted, paradoxically, to protect Smith; although Barbauld in 1810 could say that *The Old Manor House* "was written [*sic*] during the war with America; and the author takes occasion, as also in many other of her publications, to show the strain of her politics,"[3] in the 1790s readers and reviewers seemed to gloss over this point. *The Old Manor House* was read as a romance, rather than as a political novel. Its setting in the past, its love story plot, its Gothic-style machinery all function to promote the romance—the unreal—rather than the novel—the believable. As the reviews appended to this edition show, readers were variously charmed by astute characterization, impressed by strong plotting, and irritated by unlikely plot developments, but they were not, as they were with *Desmond*, unduly concerned by its liberal politics.[4] Clearly, by 1793 the events of 1775-1783 were the distant past.[5]

---

[1] "In September 1793, [Smith's son Charles], who served as an ensign in the twenty-fourth regiment, lost his leg [in the siege of] Dunkirk" (Hays, 63). Smith therefore is intensely aware of the personal costs war can bring. See Appendix D for contextualizing information about the effects of war.

[2] Smith saves her most pointed references to the contemporary situation for her few footnotes, as if banking on the fact that readers tend to skip the footnotes anyway. It is a Smithian technique to secrete rebellion in the footnote. For a thorough discussion of Smith's poetic footnotes, see Labbe, "'Transplanted into more congenial soil': Footnoting the Self in the Poetry of Charlotte Smith," *Mar(k)ing the Text: The Presentation of Meaning on the Literary Page*, eds. Joe Bray, Miriam Handley, and Anne Henry (Scolar Press, 2000): 71–86.

[3] Barbauld, vii.

[4] See Appendix A.

[5] Smith did not avoid the French Revolution after *Desmond*, however; her other 1793 publication, the long poem "The Emigrants," explores precisely the effect of the Revolution on the individual and uses the image of the exiled émigrés to plot her own alienation from an illiberal and gender-bound society. See Labbe, "The Exiled Self: Images of War in Charlotte Smith's 'The Emigrants'," *Romantic War: Studies in Conflict and Culture, 1789–1815*, ed. Philip Shaw (Scolar Press, 2000): 37–56.

Smith uses politics in *The Old Manor House* the way she uses the law: she puts it to the service of plot, and in so doing transforms both into metaphor, into representation. This is her great skill as a writer: along with her ability to paint Nature, to evoke landscape, to create convincing and nuanced characters, and more consistent than any of these, is her talent for exploring culture, for engaging with the abstracts relied on by society and revealing them as constructs, as conceits. By utilizing tropes of law, genre, politics, and gender, Smith exposes them *as* tropes, as the thematics whereby a culture defines, and confines, itself. This is evident as well in her frequent use of aspects of herself in her characters, her portrayals of *"the chicanery of the law, and the turpitude of many of its professors,"*[1] and her repeated appeals to her readers in her own voice embedded in works of fiction and the created scenario. She interweaves fact and fiction to produce works equally dependent on fantasy and reality, and hence questions the boundaries that separate the real and the artificial. However, she is not simply writing "factions," wherein the factual is dressed up like fiction. Rather, she is emphasizing the fictionality—the artifice—of what her culture considered natural: male primogeniture, for instance, or the notion of the *feme covert*, or patriotism. Once such concepts are used metaphorically, as they are throughout *The Old Manor House*, their fictionality—their artificial, manmade nature—becomes apparent.

In some ways this means that Smith writes allegory, a return to an earlier model of fictionality. But it goes further than this, making use of the developments in literary form throughout the eighteenth century. Her characters and plots are not solely representative of a moral, but rather, in their mixture, in their *metaphoricity*, to coin a term, they enact their own dependence on, and departures from, cultural mores and norms. *The Old Manor House*, and Smith's other writings, anticipate the "meta," the style of writing aware of its own status as text, as genre. Her fictionalized self and the fictionalization of culture create a thematics of artifice that work to underscore the constructedness of human experience. In a biographical sketch of 1799, seven years before her death, the *Lady's Monthly Museum* speculates that "we probably, as is often the case, owe [Smith's] labours to misfortune. And happy it were for every woman in narrow circumstances, if they had the same resource in talents as well cultivated, and exertions as indefatigable."[2] Dogged by misfortune,

---

[1]   Hays, 50.
[2]   *Lady's Monthly Museum* 2 (May 1799): 341.

keenly alive to her status in society, and one of the most significant novelists and poets of the Romantic period, Smith translated her experience and her frustrations into art, some two hundred years before the term "cultural studies" was invented.

Charlotte Turner Smith: A Brief Chronology

1749	Born 4 May to Nicholas Turner and Anna Towers Turner
1752	Death of Anna Towers Turner
1764	Nicholas Turner marries Henrietta Meriton
1765	Marries Benjamin Smith, 23 February
1766	Birth of first child, a son (name unknown)
1767	30 April: birth of second child, Benjamin, death of first son
1768	Birth of third child, William Towers
1769	April or May, birth of fourth child, Charlotte Mary
1770	July, birth of fifth child, Braithwaite
1771	October or November, birth of sixth child, Nicholas
1773	February, birth of seventh child, Charles
1774	June, birth of eighth child, Anna Augusta
1776	April, birth of ninth child, Lucy
1777	May, death of son Benjamin; September (?), birth of tenth child, Lionel
1782	Birth of eleventh child, Harriet
1783	Accompanies husband Benjamin to King's Bench debtor's prison
1784	*Elegiac Sonnets* published; Smith accompanies Benjamin to Normandy
1785	January (?), birth of twelfth child, George, in Normandy
1786	Death of Braithwaite; *Manon Lescaut* published (and immediately withdrawn)
1787	*The Romance of Real Life*; separates from Benjamin
1788	*Emmeline; or, The Orphan of the Castle*
1789	*Ethelinde; or The Recluse of the Lake*
1791	*Celestina. A Novel*
1792	*Desmond. A Novel.* Smith living in Brighton, where Wordsworth visits her
1793	*The Old Manor House*; *The Emigrants, a Poem, in Two Books*
1794	*The Wanderings of Warwick*; *The Banished Man*; Smith moves to Bath for her health
1795	*Rural Walks: in dialogues; intended for the use of Young Persons*; *Montalbert, a Novel*; 23 April, death of Anna Augusta, Smith's favourite daughter
1796	*A Narrative of the Loss of the Catherine, Venus and Piedmont*

Transports; *Rambles Further: a continuation of Rural Walks*; *Marchmont, a Novel*

1797   *Elegiac Sonnets, Volume II*; eighth edition of *Elegiac Sonnets, Volume I*; Smith lives in Oxford

1798   *Minor Morals, interspersed with sketches of natural history, historical anecdotes, and original stories* (for children); *The Young Philosopher* (a novel)

1799   Smith moves to London

1800–02   *The Letters of a Solitary Wanderer: containing narratives of various descriptions* (in five volumes); Smith in increasing ill health and moves frequently

1804   *Conversations Introducing Poetry: chiefly on subjects of Natural History. For the use of children and young persons*

1806   Death of husband Benjamin, February; *A History of England: From the earliest records to the Peace of Amiens in a series of letters to a young lady at school* (in three volumes: Volume 3 by Mary Hays); 28 October: dies at Tilford, near Farmham, Surrey. Buried at St John's, Stoke-next-Guildford near her daughter Anna Augusta

1807   *Beachy Head, with Other Poems*; *The Natural History of Birds, intended chiefly for young people*

A Note on the Text

The edition used is the second of 1793. After the novel was published in early 1793, Smith thoroughly revised the text for style and made many substantive improvements (see Ehrenpreis for a comprehensive list). For this edition, the text has been reproduced with its eighteenth-century spelling and punctuation intact (with the exception of some extraneous quotation marks within quotations), although some obvious printer's errors have been silently corrected. Eighteenth-century typography can give a good idea of the sound of the text, especially dialogue.

Smith often used footnotes to expand, in a different voice to that of her text's narrator, on issues she felt strongly about. Such footnotes in this text are marked with her initials in brackets.

The Old Manor House was popular well into the nineteenth century. The British Library catalogue lists editions of 1810, 1837, and 1878, as well as a French edition from 1816: *Le Testament de la vieille cousine. Traduit de l'anglaise sur le deuxième édition. Par Hortense de Céré-Barbé.* There is also an undated mid-nineteenth-century edition entitled *The Old Manor House; or, Monimia and Orlando*. Anne Ehrenpreis also lists editions from 1822 and 1847. After that, the next edition is Ehrenpreis's, 1969, based on the first 1793 edition and emended by Smith's changes for the second edition.

THE
OLD MANOR HOUSE

VOL. I.

Nè fune intorto crederò che stringa
Soma cosi, nè cosi legno chiodo,
Come la fe, che una bella alma cinga
Del suo tenace, indissolubil nodo.

ARIOSTO—Cant. xxi. Stanza I.[1]

---

[1] No load so tight is bound by twisted cord,
No wood is joined so firmly by a nail,
As faith a candid soul, true to its word,
For ever in strong bonds will tie and seal ...
(*Orlando Furioso*, tr. Barbara Reynolds [Harmondsworth: Penguin, 1975], p. 649).

By opening the novel with a quotation from *Orlando Furioso* in the original Italian, Smith accomplishes several things. She anchors her character Orlando in the romance tradition, ensuring that his world is that of fantasy (incidentally, Ariosto's Orlando suffers from hopeless love that leads eventually to his madness). She displays her own learning and knowledge of the classics of the romance genre. She gestures towards a conflict that in its own way was about property and ownership ("the defence of Europe by Charlemagne against Islam," Reynolds, p. 12), although in religious rather than financial terms. Finally, Ariosto used the conflict between Christianity and Islam as a cover for events in his own day, in the same way that Smith masks her critique of her government by setting her novel in the recent past.

THE OLD MANOR HOUSE.

CHAP. I.

In an old Manor House in one of the most southern counties of England, resided some few years since the last of a family that had for a long series of years possessed it. Mrs. Rayland was the only survivor of the three co-heiresses of Sir Hildebrand Rayland; one of the first of those to whom the title of Baronet had been granted by James the First. The name had been before of great antiquity in the county—and the last baronet having only daughters to share his extensive possessions, these ladies had been educated with such very high ideas of their own importance, that they could never be prevailed upon to lessen, by sharing it with any of those numerous suitors who for the first forty or fifty years of their lives surrounded them; and Mrs. Barbara the eldest, and Mrs. Catherine the youngest, died single—one at the age of seventy, and the other at that of sixty-eight: by which events the second, Mrs. Grace, saw herself at the advanced age of sixty-nine sole inheritor of the fortunes of her house, without any near relation, or indeed any relation at all whom she chose to consider as entitled to possess it after her death.

About four miles from the ancient and splendid seat she inhabited, dwelt the only person who could claim any affinity with the Rayland family: this was a gentleman of the name of Somerive; who was considered by the people of the country as heir at law, as he was the grandson of one of the sisters of Sir Hildebrand: but Mrs. Rayland herself, whose opinion was more material, since it was all at her own disposal, did not by any means seem to entertain the same idea.

The venerable lady, and her two sisters, had never beheld this their relation with the eyes of friendly interest; nor had they ever extended towards him that generous favour which they had so much the power to afford, and which could not have failed to prove very acceptable; since he had married early in life, and had a family of two sons and four daughters to support on the produce of an estate, which, though he farmed it himself, did not bring in a clear five hundred pounds a year.

Various reasons, or rather prejudices, had concurred to occasion this coolness on the part of the ladies towards their cousin.—Their aunt, who had married his ancestor, had, as they had always been taught, degraded herself extremely, by giving herself to a man who was a mere yeoman.—The son of this union had however been received and acknowledged as the cousin of the illustrious heiresses of the house of Rayland; but following most plebeian-like the unaspiring inclination of his own family, he had fallen in love with a young woman who lived with them as companion; when it was believed that, as he was a remarkably handsome man, he might have lifted his eyes with impunity to one of the ladies, his cousins: this occasioned an estrangement of many years, and had never been forgiven.—The recollection of it returned with acrimonious violence, when the son of this imprudent man imitated his father, five-and-twenty years afterwards, and married a woman who had nothing to recommend her but beauty, simplicity, and goodness.

However, notwithstanding the repeated causes of complaint which his luckless family of Somerive had given to the austere and opulent inhabitants of Rayland Hall, the elder lady had on her death-bed recollected, that, though debased by the alloy of unworthy alliances, they carried in their veins a portion of that blood which had circulated in those of the august personage Sir Orlando de Rayland her grandfather; and she therefore recommended Mr. Somerive and his family, but particularly his youngest son (who was named, by reluctantly obtained permission, after Sir Orlando), to the consideration of her sisters, and even gave to Mr. Somerive himself a legacy of five hundred pounds; a gift which her sisters took so much amiss (though they possessed between them a yearly income of near twice five thousand) that it had nearly rendered her injunction abortive; and they treated the whole family for some time afterwards with the greatest coolness, and even rudeness; as if to convince them, that though Mrs. Rayland had thus acknowledged their relationship, it gave them no claim whatever on the future kindness of her surviving sisters.

For some years afterwards the dinners, to which in great form the whole family were invited twice a year, were entirely omitted, and none of them admitted to the honour of visiting at the Hall, but Orlando, then a child of nine or ten years old; and even his introduction was principally owing to the favour of an old lady, the widow of a clergyman, who was among the ancient friends of the family, that still enjoyed the privilege of being regularly sent for in the old family coach, once a year; a custom which, originating in the days of Sir Hildebrand, was still retained.

This lady was a woman of sense and benevolence, and had often attempted to do kind offices to the Somerive family with their rich maiden relations; but the height of her success amounted to no more than obtaining a renewal of the very little notice that had ever been taken of them, after those capricious fits of coldness which sometimes happened; and once, some time after the death of the elder Mrs. Rayland, bringing Orlando to the Hall in her hand (whom she had met by chance fishing in a stream that ran through their domain), without being chidden for encouraging an idle child to catch minnows, or for leading him all dirty and wet into their parlour, at a time when the best embroidered chairs, done by the hands of Dame Gertrude Rayland, were actually unpapered, and uncovered for the reception of company.

There was indeed in the figure, face and manner of the infant Orlando, something so irresistible, that if Mesdames Alecto, Tisiphone, and Megara[1] had seen him, they would probably have been softened in his favour— And this something, had always so pleaded for him with the three equally formidable ladies his relations, that notwithstanding the opposition of their favourite maid, who was in person and feature well worthy to make the fourth in such a group, and the tales of their old and confidential butler, who did not admire the introduction of any competitor whatever, Orlando had always been in some degree of favour—even when his father, mother and sisters were shut out, and his elder brother entirely disclaimed as a wild and incorrigible boy, who had been caught in the fact of hunting divers cats, and shooting one of their guinea hens—Orlando, though not at all less wild than his brother, and too artless to conceal his vivacity, was still endured—A new half-crown was presented to him on every return to school, together with abundance of excellent advice; and if any one observed that he was a remarkably handsome boy, the ladies never contradicted it; though, when the same observation was made as to the rest of the family, it was declared to be most absurd, and utterly unfounded in truth.—To the beauty indeed of any female the ladies of Rayland Hall had a particular objection, but that of the Miss Somerives was above all obnoxious to them—Nor could they ever forget the error the grandfather of these children had committed in marrying for her beauty the young woman, whose poverty having reduced her to be their humble companion, they had considered as an inferior being, and had treated with supercilious insolence and contempt.—To those therefore to whom her unlucky beauty was transmitted, they bore irreconcileable enmity, even in the second generation; and had any one been artful enough to have suggested that Orlando was like his grandmother, it would probably have occasioned the loss of even the slight share of favour he possessed.

When Orlando was about twelve years old, the younger of the three

---

[1] In classical Greek mythology, the Furies, also akin to the Fates, and as such the directors of Orlando's fortunes.

antique heiresses died: she left not however even a small legacy to the Somerive family, but gave every thing she possessed to her surviving sister. Yet even by this lady, though the coldest and most unsociable tempered of the three, Orlando was not entirely forgotten—she left him the bible she always used in her closet, and ten pounds to buy mourning; the other members of his family were not even named.

One only of the Mrs. Raylands now remained; a woman who, except regularly keeping up the payment of the annual alms, which had by her ancestors been given once a year to the poor of her parish, was never known to have done a voluntary kindness to any human being: and though she sometimes gave away money, it was never without making the wretched petitioner pay most dearly for it, by many a bitter humiliation—never, but when it was surely known, and her great goodness, her liberal donation to such and such people, were certainly related with exaggeration, at the two market-towns within four or five miles of her house.

With a very large income, and a great annual saving, her expences were regulated exactly by the customs of her family.—She lived, generally alone, at the Old Hall, which had not received the slightest alteration, either in its environs or its furniture, since it was embellished for the marriage of her father Sir Hildebrand, in 1698.

Twice a year, when courts were held for the manors, there were tenants feasts—and twice there was a grand dinner, to which none were admitted but a neighbouring nobleman, and the two or three titled people who resided within ten miles.—Twice too in the course of the year the family of Somerive were invited in form; but Mrs. Rayland generally took the same opportunity of asking the clergy of the surrounding country with their wives and daughters, the attorneys and apothecaries of the adjoining towns with theirs, as if to convince the Somerives that they were to expect no distinction on account of the kindred they claimed to the house of Rayland.—And indeed it was on these occasions that Mrs. Rayland seemed to take peculiar pleasure in mortifying Mrs. Somerive and her daughters, who dreaded these dinner days as those of the greatest penance; and who at Christmas, one of the periods of these formal dinners, had blest more than once the propitious snow; through which that important and magisterial personage, the body coachman of Mrs. Rayland, did not choose to venture himself, or the six sleek animals of which he was sole governor; for on these occasions it was the established rule to send for the family, with the same solemnity and the same parade that had been used ever since the first sullen and reluctant reconciliation between Sir Hildebrand and his sister; when she dared to deviate from the fastidious arrogance of her family, and to marry a man who farmed his own estate—and who, though long settled as a very respectable land owner, had not yet written Armiger after his name.[1]

But when the snow fell not, and the ways were passable; or when in summer no excuse was left, and the rheumatism of the elder, or the colds of the younger ladies could not be pleaded; the females of the family of Somerive were compelled to endure, in all their terrific and tedious forms, the grand dinners at the Hall. And though on these occasions the mother and the daughters endeavoured, by the simplicity of their dress, and the humility of their manners, to disarm the haughty dislike which Mrs. Rayland never took any pains to conceal, they never could obtain from her even as much common civility as she deigned to bestow on the ladies who were not connected with her; and Mr. Somerive had often been so much hurt by her supercilious behaviour towards his wife and daughters, that he had frequently resolved they should never again be exposed to endure it. But these resolutions his wife, hateful as the ceremony was to her, always contrived to prevail upon him to give up, rather than incur the hazard of injuring her family by an unpardonable offence against a capricious and ill-natured old woman, who, however oddly she behaved, was still by many people believed to intend giving all her fortune to those who had undoubtedly the best claim to it; others indeed thought, with more appearance of probability, that she would endow an hospital, or divide it among public charities.

When the young Orlando was at home, and accompanied his family in these visits, the austere visage of Mrs. Rayland was alone seen to relax into a smile—and as he grew older, this partiality was observed evidently to increase, insomuch that the neighbours observed, that whatever aversion the old Lady had to feminine beauty, she did not detest that which nature had very liberally bestowed on Orlando.—He was seventeen, and was not only one of the finest looking lads in that country, but had long since obtained all the knowledge he could acquire at a neighbouring grammar school; from whence his father now took him, and began to consider of plans for his future life.—The eldest son, who would, as the father fondly hoped, succeed to the Rayland estate, he had sent to Oxford, where he had been indulged in his natural turn to expence; and his father had suffered him to live rather suitably to what he expected than to what he was sure of.—In this Mr. Somerive had acted extremely wrong; but it was from motives so natural, that his error was rather

---

[1]   "Esquire, one entitled to bear heraldic arms" (*The Concise Oxford Dictionary*).

lamented than blamed.—An error however, and of the most dangerous tendency, he had now discovered it to be; young Somerive had violent passions, and an understanding very ill suited to their management.—He had early in life seized with avidity the idea, which servants and tenants were ready enough to communicate, that he must have the Rayland estate; and had very thoughtlessly expressed this to those who failed not to repeat it to their present mistress, tenacious of her power, and jealous of every attempt to encroach on her property.—He had besides trespassed on some remote corners of her manors; and her game-keeper had represented him as a terrible depredator among her partridges, pheasants, and hares. These offences, added to the cat-chafes, and tieing canisters to the tails of certain dogs, of which he had been convicted in the early part of his life, had made so deep an impression against him, that now, whenever he was at home, the family were never asked; and insensibly, from calling now and then to enquire after her while Mrs. Rayland lay ill of a violent fit of the gout, Orlando had been admitted to drink his tea at the Hall; then to dine there; and at last, as winter came on with stormy evenings and bad roads, he had been allowed to sleep in a little tapestry room, next to the old library at the end of the north wing—a division of the house so remote from that inhabited by the female part (or indeed by any part) of the family, that it could give no ideas of indecorum even to the iron prudery of Mrs. Rayland herself.

Though Orlando was of a temper which made it impossible for him to practise any of those arts by which the regard of such a woman could be secured; and though the degree of favour he had obtained was long rather a misery than a pleasure to him; his brother beheld the progress he made with jealousy and anger, and began to hate Orlando for having gained advantages of which he openly avowed his disdain and contempt.—As his expences, which his father could no longer support, had by this time obliged him to quit the university, he was now almost always at home; and his sneering reproaches, as well as his wild and unguarded conversation, rendered that home every day less pleasant to Orlando—while the quiet asylum he had obtained at the Hall, in a room adjoining to that where a great collection of books were never disturbed in their long slumber by any human being but himself, endeared to him the gloomy abode of the Sybil,[1] and reconciled him

---

[1] That is, Mrs. Rayland. Orlando compares her to the Sibyl, famous as a prophet and seer: again, a director of his Fate. A secondary meaning is sorceress or hag. Orlando sees Mrs. Rayland as both his benefactor and his tormentor.

to the penance he was still obliged to undergo; for he was now become passionately fond of reading, and thought the use of such a library cheaply earned by acting as a sort of chaplain, reading the psalms and lessons every day, and the service in very bad weather; with a sermon on Sunday evening. And he even gradually forgot his murmurings at being imprisoned on Sundays and on Fridays in the great old long-bottomed coach, while it was dragged in a most solemn pace either to the next parish church, which was indeed at but a short distance from the mansion, or to that of a neighbouring town, whither, on some propitious and sunny days of summer, the old lady loved to proceed in state, and to display to her rustic or more enlightened neighbours a specimen of the magnificence of the last century. But as history[1] must conceal no part of the truth, from partiality to the hero it celebrates, it must not be denied that the young Orlando had, though insensibly and almost unknown to himself, another motive for submitting with a good grace to pass much of his time in a way, for which, thinking, as he thought, the prospect of even boundless wealth could have made him no compensation.—To explain this, it may be necessary to describe the persons who from his ninth year, when he became first so distinguished by Mrs. Rayland, till his eighteenth, composed the household, of which he, during that period, occasionally made a part.

CHAP. II.

The confidential servant, or rather companion, and femme de charge of Mrs. Rayland, was a woman of nearly her own age, of the name of Lennard.—This person, who was as well as her mistress a spinster, had been well educated, and was the daughter of a merchant who lost the fruits of a long course of industry in the fatal year 1720.[2] He died of a broken heart, leaving his two daughters, who had been taught to expect high affluence, to the mercy of the world. Mrs. Rayland, whose pride was gratified in having about her the victim of unsuccessful trade, for which she had always a most profound contempt, received Mrs. Lennard

---

[1] Smith's narrator here identifies the novel as a "history"; in the taxonomy of literature, a history is superior to a mere romance.

[2] The year of the South Sea Bubble. Investors thought to make easy fortunes by sinking money into the South Sea Company, and most lost everything.

as her own servant. She was however so much superior to her mistress in understanding, that she soon governed her entirely; and while the mean pliability of her spirit made her submit to all the contemptuous and unworthy treatment, which the paltry pride of Mrs. Rayland had pleasure in inflicting, she secretly triumphed in the consciousness of superior abilities, and knew that she was in fact the mistress of the supercilious being whose wages she received.

Every year she became more and more necessary to Mrs. Rayland, who, after the death of both her sisters, made her not only governess of her house, but her companion. Her business was, to sit with her in her apartment when she had no company; to read the newspaper; to make tea; to let in and out the favourite dogs (the task of combing and washing them was transferred to a deputy); to collect and report at due seasons intelligence of all that happened in the neighbouring families; to give regular returns of the behaviour of all the servants, except the old butler and the old coachman, who had each a jurisdiction of their own; to take especial care that the footmen and helpers behaved respectfully to the maids (who were all chosen by herself, and exhibited such a group, as secured, better than her utmost vigilance, this decorous behaviour from the male part of the family; to keep the keys; to keep her mistress in good humour with herself, and as much as possible at a distance from the rest of the world, above all, from that part of it who might interfere with her present and future views; which certainly were to make herself amends for the former injustice of fortune, by securing to her own use a considerable portion of the great wealth possessed by Mrs. Rayland.

Of the accomplishment of this she might well entertain a reasonable hope; for she was some few years younger than her mistress (though she artfully added to her age, whenever she had occasion to speak of it), and was besides of a much better constitution, possessing one of those frames where a good deal of bone and no flesh seem to defy the gripe of disease. The sister of this Mrs. Lennard had experienced a very different destiny—She had been taken at the time of her father's misfortunes into the family of a nobleman; she had married the chaplain, and retired with him on a small living, where she died in a few years, leaving several children; among others a daughter, to whom report imputed uncommon beauty, and scandal a too intimate connexion with the noble patron of her father. Certain it is that, on his marriage, he gave her a sum of money, and she became the wife of a young attorney, who was a kind of steward, by whom she had three children; of which none survived their parents but a little girl born after her father's death, and whose birth occasioned that of her mother. To this little orphan, her great aunt Mrs. Lennard, who with all her starched prudery had a considerable share of odd romantic whim in her composition, had given the dramatic and uncommon name of Monimia[1]—Such at least was the history given in Mrs. Rayland's family of an infant girl, which at about four years old had been by the permission of her patroness taken, as it was said, from nurse, at a distant part of the county, and received by Mrs. Lennard at Rayland Hall; where she at first never appeared before the Lady but by accident, but was the inhabitant of the house-keeper's room, and under the immediate care of the still-room maid, who was a person much devoted to Mrs. Lennard.

Mrs. Rayland had an aversion to children, and had consented to the admission of this into her house, on no other condition, but that she should never hear it cry, or ever have any trouble about it.—Her companion easily engaged for that; as Rayland Hall was so large, that *les enfans trouvés*[2] at Paris might have been the inhabitants of one of its wings, without alarming a colony of ancient virgins at the other. The little Monimia, though she was described as having been

> "The child of misery, baptized in tears," LANGHORN.[3]

was not particularly disposed to disturb, by infantine expressions of distress, the chaste and silent solitudes of the Hall; for though her little fair countenance had at times something of a melancholy cast, there was more of sweetness than of sorrow in it; and if she ever shed tears, they were so mingled with smiles, that she might have sat to the painter of the Seasons for the representative of infant April.[4] Her beauty however was not likely to recommend her to the favour of her aunt's

---

[1] Monimia's "dramatic and uncommon name" derives from Thomas Otway's play *The Orphan* (1680), in which the orphan Monimia attracts the love of two brothers, Castalio and Polydore. She secretly marries Castalio (as Smith's Monimia will Orlando; see Volume 4), is tricked into sleeping with his twin Polydore, and eventually kills herself with poison after the brothers have committed suicide. Monimia's status as orphan is asserted through her name, as is her position as romance heroine, although Smith allows her Monimia to live.

[2] "Found children": that is, foundlings.

[3] Smith refers to John Langhorne's poem *The Country Justice* (1774). As with her name, Monimia's character is contextualized through literary allusion, although here Smith sets up the spectacle of suffering (the theme of Langhorne's poem) only to assert Monimia's difference.

[4] James Thomson (1700–1748) wrote *The Seasons* between 1726 and 1730. "Spring" was published in 1728.

affluent patroness; but as to recommend her was the design of Mrs. Lennard, she saw that a beauty of four or five years old would be much less obnoxious than one of fifteen, or even nine or ten; and therefore she contrived to introduce her by degrees; that when she grew older, her charms, by being long seen, might lose their power to offend.

She contrived that Mrs. Rayland might first see the little orphan as by chance; then she sent her in, when she knew her mistress was in good humour, with a basket of fruit, an early pine,[1] some preserves in brandy, or something or other which was acceptable to her Lady's palate; and on these occasions Monimia acquitted herself to a miracle; and presented her little offering, and made her little curtsey, with so much innocent grace, that Hecate[2] in the midst of her rites might have suspended her incantations to have admired her. At six years old she had so much won upon the heart of Mrs. Rayland, that she became a frequent guest in the parlour, and saved her aunt the trouble of opening the door for Bella, and Pompey, and Julie.[3] From the tenderness of her nature she became an admirable nurse for the frequent litters of kittens, with which two favourite cats continually increased the family of her protectress; and the numerous daily applications from robins and sparrows under the windows, were never so well attended to as since Monimia was entrusted with the care of answering their demands.

But her name—Monimia—was an incessant occasion of reproach— "Why," said Mrs. Rayland, "why would you, Lennard, give the child such a name? As the girl will have nothing, why put such romantic notions in her head, as may perhaps prevent her getting her bread honestly?—Monimia! I protest I don't love even to repeat the name; it puts me so in mind of a very hateful play, which I remember shocked me so when I was a mere girl, that I have always detested the name. Monimia!— 'tis so very unlike a Christian's name, that if the child is much about me, I must insist upon having her called Mary."

To this Mrs. Lennard of course consented, excusing herself for the romantic impropriety of which her Lady accused her, by saying, that

---

[1]   "Pine" is short for "pineapple."

[2]   Hecate is the "goddess of ghosts, witchcraft, and black magic; in art, she was often represented as a figure with three bodies, or a figure with three heads" (Saad Elkhadem, *York Companion to Themes and Motifs of World Literature*, Fredericton, CA: York Press, 1981, p. 100). Given that Mrs. Rayland represents one of three original sisters, Hecate's triple figuration is significant.

[3]   Probably the names of Mrs. Rayland's dogs, given that Smith also shows Monimia's responsibilities for the Hall's cats and birds.

she understood Monimia signified an orphan, a person left alone and deserted; and therefore had given it to a child who was an orphan from her birth—but that, as it was displeasing, she should at least never be called so. The little girl then was Mary in the parlour; but among the servants, and with the people around the house, she was still Monimia.

Among those who fondly adhered to her original name was Orlando; who, when he first became a frequent visitor as a school-boy at the Hall, stole often into the still-room to play with the little girl, who was three years younger than himself—and insensibly grew as fond of her as of one of his sisters. Mrs. Lennard always checked this innocent mirth; and when she found it impossible wholly to prevent two children who were in the same house from playing with each other, she took every possible precaution to prevent her Lady's ever seeing them together; and threatened the severest punishment to the little Monimia, if she at any time even spoke to Master Somerive, when in the presence of Mrs. Rayland.—But nothing could be so irksome to a healthy and lively child of nine or ten years old, as the sort of confinement to which Monimia was condemned in consequence of her admission to the parlour; where she was hardly ever suffered to speak, but sat at a distant window, where, whether it was winter or summer, she was to remain no otherwise distinguished from a statue than by being employed in making the household linen, and sometimes in spinning it with a little wheel which Mrs. Rayland, who piqued herself upon following the notable maxims of her mother, had bought for her, and at which she kept her closely employed when there was no other work to do.—When any company came, then and then only she was dismissed; but this happened very rarely; and many many hours poor Monimia vainly prayed for the sight of a coach or chaise at the end of the long avenue, which was to her the blessed signal of transient liberty.

Her dress, the expence of which Mrs. Rayland very graciously took upon herself, was such as indicated to all who saw her, at once the charity and prudence of her patroness, who repeatedly told her visitors, that she had taken the orphan niece of her old servant Lennard, not with any view of making her a gentlewoman, but to bring her up to get her bread honestly; and therefore she had directed her to be dressed, not in gauzes and flounces, like the flirting girls she saw so tawdry at church, but in a plain stuff; not flaring without a cap, which she thought monstrously indecent for a female at any age, but in a plain cap, and a clean white apron, that she might never be encouraged to vanity by any kind of finery that did not become her situation.—Monimia, though dressed like a parish girl, or in a way very little superior, was observed by the visitors who happened to see her, and to whom this harangue was made, to be so very pretty, that nothing could conceal or diminish her beauty. Her dark stuff gown gave new lustre to her lovely complexion; and her thick muslin cap could not confine her luxuriant dark hair. Her shape was symmetry itself, and her motions so graceful, that it was impossible to behold her, even attached to her humble employment at the wheel, without acknowledging that no art could give what nature had bestowed upon her.[1]

Orlando, who had loved her as a playfellow while they were both children, now began to feel a more tender and more respectful affection for her; though unconscious himself that it was her beauty that awakened these sentiments. On the last of his holidays, before he entirely left school, the vigilance of Mrs. Lennard was redoubled, and she so contrived to confine Monimia, that their romping was at an end, and they hardly ever saw each other, except by mere chance, at a distance, or now and then at dinner, when Monimia was suffered to dine at table; an honour which she was not always allowed, but which Mrs. Lennard cautiously avoided entirely suspending when Orlando was at the Hall, as there was nothing she seemed to dread so much as alarming Mrs. Rayland with any idea of Orlando's noticing her niece. This however never happened at the time to occur to the old Lady; not only because Mrs. Lennard took such pains to lead her imagination from any such probability, but because she considered them both as mere children, and Monimia as a servant.

It was however at this time that a trifling incident had nearly awakened such suspicions, and occasioned such displeasure, as it would have been very difficult to have subdued or appeased. Mrs. Rayland had been long confined by a fit of the gout; and the warm weather of Whitsuntide[2] had only just enabled her to walk, leaning on a crutch on one side, and on Mrs. Lennard on the other, in a long gallery which reached the whole

---

[1]   Smith appeals to the romantic convention that the heroine is usually a princess or other highborn maiden, often disguised as a servant or a pauper, or sometimes switched at birth. Monimia, however, is never unmasked as anything other than a servant, although Mr. Somerive, among others, suspects her of being Mrs. Lennard's illegitimate daughter (given Mrs. Lennard's age, however, this is unlikely; what is more important is Monimia's assumed illegitimacy). In this way, Smith makes use of, while also undercutting, the expectations of genre; she also undermines the assumption that a servant can never be as well-bred as a genteel lady.

[2]   "Whitsuntide" refers to the period of Whitsunday (the seventh Sunday after Easter Day) and the days immediately following.

length of the south wing, and which was hung with a great number of family pictures.—Mrs. Rayland had peculiar satisfaction in relating the history of the heroes and dames of her family, who were represented by these portraits.—Sir Roger De Coverley[1] never went over the account of his ancestors with more correctness or more delight. Indeed, the reflections of Mrs. Rayland were uninterrupted by any of those little blemishes in the history of her progenitors, that somewhat bewildered the good knight; for she boasted that not one of the Rayland family had ever condescended to degrade himself by trade; and that the marriage of Mrs. Somerive, her aunt, was the only instance in which a daughter of the Raylands had stooped to an inferior alliance—The little withered figure, bent down with age and infirmity, and the last of a race which she was thus arrogantly boasting—a race which in a few years, perhaps a few months, might be no more remembered—was a ridiculous instance of human folly and human vanity, at which Lennard had sense enough to smile internally, while she affected to listen with interest to stories which she had heard repeated for near forty years. It was in the midst of her attention to an anecdote which generally closed the relation of a speech made by Queen Anne to the last Lady Rayland on her having no son, that a sudden and violent bounce towards the middle of the gallery occasioned an interruption of the story, and equal amazement in the Lady and her confidante; who both turning round, not very nimbly indeed, demanded of Monimia, who had been sitting in one of the old-fashioned bow-windows of which the casement was open, what was the matter?

Monimia, covered with blushes, and in a sort of scuffle to conceal something with her feet, replied hesitating and trembling, that she did not know.

Mrs. Lennard, who probably guessed the truth, declared loudly that she would immediately find out.—But it was not the work of a moment to set her Lady safely on one of the leathern settees, while she herself hastened to the window to discover, if possible, who had from the court below thrown in the something that had thus alarmed them. Before she reached the window, therefore, the court was clear; and Monimia had recovered from her confusion, and went on with her work.

---

[1] Sir Roger de Coverley features in a number of issues of *The Spectator* (1 March 1711 to 6 December 1712), a daily periodical mainly written by Joseph Addison and Richard Steele. Sir Roger, a member of the fictitious Spectator Club, represents the landed gentry. He is, like Mrs. Rayland, overly concerned with lineage.

Mrs. Lennard now thought proper to give another turn to the incident. She said, it must have been some accidental noise, from the wainscot's cracking in dry weather—"though I could have sworn at the moment," cried she, "that something very hard, like a stone or a stick, had been thrown into the room. However, to be sure, I must have been mistaken, for certainly there is nobody in the court: and really one does recollect hearing in this gallery very odd noises, which, if one was superstitious, might sometimes make one uneasy.[1]—Many of the neighbours some years ago used to say to me, that they wondered I was not afraid of crossing it of a night by myself, when you, Ma'am, used to sleep in the worked bedchamber, and I lay over the house-keeper's room. But I used to say, that you had such an understanding, that I should offend you by shewing any foolish fears; and that all the noble family that owned this house time out of mind, were such honourable persons, that none of them could be supposed likely to walk after their decease, as the spirits of wicked persons are said to do. But, however, they used to answer in reply to that, that some of your ancestors, Ma'am, had hid great sums of money and valuable jewels in this house, to save it from the wicked rebels in the time of the blessed Martyr;[2] and that it was to reveal these treasures that the appearances of spirits had been seen, and strange noises heard about the house."

This speech was so exactly calculated to please the Lady to whom it was addressed, that it almost obliterated the recollection of the little alarm she had felt, and blunted the spirit of enquiry, which the twinges of the gout also contributed to diminish; and fortunately the arrival of the apothecary, who was that moment announced, and whose visits were always a matter of importance, left her no longer any time to interrogate Monimia. But Mrs. Lennard, having led her down to her great chair, and seen her safely in conference with her physical friend, returned hastily to the gallery, where Monimia still remained demurely at work; and peremptorily insisted on knowing what it was that had bounced into the room, and struck against the picture of Sir Hildebrand himself; who in armour, and on a white horse whose flanks were overshadowed by his stupendous wig, pranced over the great gilt

---

[1] Here, Smith introduces the "fake Gothic": she describes scenes that, in another novel, might well be supernatural, but in *The Old Manor House* are merely covering up natural, although often illegal, activity (for instance, smuggling). Throughout the novel, the Gothic is never more than a trope by which characters express fear, or through which Smith conveys characters' inadequacies.

[2] Charles I, beheaded in 1649.

chimney-piece, just as he appeared at the head of a county association in 1707.

Monimia was a poor dissembler, and had never in her life been guilty of a falsehood. She was as little capable of disguising as of denying the truth; and the menaces of her aunt frightened her into an immediate confession, that it was Mr. Orlando, who, passing through the court to go to cricket in the park, had seen her sitting at the window, and, "not thinking any harm," had thrown up his ball "only in play," to make her jump; but that it had unluckily gone through the window, and hit against the picture.

"And what became of it afterwards?" angrily demanded Mrs. Lennard.

"It bounded," answered the innocent culprit—"it bounded across the floor, and I rolled it away with my feet, under the chairs."

"And how dared you," exclaimed the aunt, "how dared you, artful little hussey, conceal the truth from me? how dared you encourage any such abominable doings? —A pretty thing indeed to have happen!— Suppose the good-for-nothing boy had hit my Lady or me upon the head or breast, as it was a mercy he did not—there would have been a fine story!—Or suppose he had broke the windows, shattered the panes, and cut us with the glass!—or what if he had beat the stained glass of my Lady's coat of arms, up at top there, all to smash—what d'ye think would have become of you, you worthless little puss? what punishment would have been bad enough for you?"

"My dear aunt," said the weeping Monimia, "how could I help it? I am sure I did not know what Mr. Orlando was going to do; I saw him but a moment before; and you know that, if I *had* known he intended to throw the ball up, I dared not have spoken to him to have prevented it."

"Have spoken to him, indeed!—No, I think not; and remember this, girl, that you have come off well this time, and I sha'n't say any thing of the matter to my Lady; but if I ever catch you speaking to that wicked boy, or even daring to look at him, I will turn you out of doors that moment—and let this teach you that I am in earnest." Having thus said, she gave the terrified trembling girl a violent blow,[1] or what was in her language a good box on the ear, which forcing her head against the stone window-frame almost stunned her; she then repeated it on the lovely neck of her victim, where the marks of her fingers were to be traced many days afterwards; and flounced out of the room, and,

---

[1]   Monimia often suffers physically: at the hands of Mrs. Lennard; through the presumption of Sir John Belgrave; because of Orlando's wild and inconsistent behaviour; and due to her own anxiety.

composing herself, went down to give her share of information, as to her Lady's complaint, to the apothecary.

The unhappy Monimia, who had felt ever since her earliest recollection the misery of her situation, was never so sensible of it as at this moment. The work fell from her hands—she laid her head on a marble slab, that was on one side of the bow window, and gave way to an agony of grief.—Her cap had fallen from her head, and her fine hair concealed her face, which resting on her arms was bathed in tears.—Sobs, that seemed to rend her heart, were the only expression of sorrow she was able to utter; she heard, she saw nothing—but was suddenly startled by something touching her hand as it hung lifelessly over the table. She looked up—and beheld, with mingled emotions of surprise and fear, Orlando Somerive; who, with tears in his eyes, and in a faltering whisper, conjured her to tell him what was the matter.—The threat so recently uttered yet vibrated in her ears—and her terror, lest her aunt should return and find Orlando there, was so great, that, without knowing what she did, she started up and ran towards the door; from whence she would have fled, disordered as she was, down stairs, and through the very room where Mrs. Rayland, her aunt, and the apothecary were in conference, if Orlando, with superior strength and agility, had not thrown himself before her, and, setting his back against the door, insisted upon knowing the cause of her tears before he suffered her to stir.

Gasping for breath, trembling and inarticulately she tried to relate the effects of his indiscretion, and that therefore her aunt had threatened and struck her. Orlando, whose temper was naturally warm, and whose generous spirit revolted from every kind of injustice, felt at once his indignation excited by this act of oppression, and his anger that Mrs. Lennard should arraign him for a childish frolic, and thence take occasion so unworthily to treat an innocent girl; and being too rash to reflect on consequences, he declared that he would go instantly into the parlour, confess to Mrs. Rayland what he had done, and appeal against the tyranny and cruelty of her woman.

It was now the turn of poor Monimia to entreat and implore; and she threw herself half frantic on her knees before him, and besought him rather to kill her, than to expose her to the terrors and distress such a step would inevitably plunge her into.—"Indeed, dear Orlando," cried she, "you would not be heard against my aunt. Mrs. Rayland, if she forgave you, would never forgive me; but I should be immediately turned out of the house with disgrace; and I have no friend, no relation in the world but my aunt, and must beg my bread. But it is not so much that," added she, while sobs broke her utterance, "it is not so much *that* I care for—*I* am so unfortunate that it does not signify what becomes of me: I can work in the fields, or can go through any hardship; but Mrs. Rayland will be very angry with you, and will not suffer you to come to the Hall again, and I shall—never—never see you any more!"

This speech, unguarded and simple as it was, had more effect on Orlando than the most studied eloquence. He took the weeping, trembling Monimia up in his arms, seated her in a chair; and drying her eyes, he besought her to be comforted, and to assure herself, that whatever he might feel, he would do nothing that should give her pain.—"Oh! go then, for Heaven's sake go from hence instantly!" replied Monimia.— "If my aunt should come to look for me, as it is very likely she will, we should be both undone!"

"Good God!" exclaimed Orlando, "why should it be so?—why are we never to meet? and what harm to any one is done by my friendship for you, Monimia?"

"Alas!" answered she, every moment more and more apprehensive of the arrival of her aunt, "alas! Orlando, I know not; I am sure that it was once, before my aunt was so enraged at it, all the comfort I had in the world; but now it is my greatest misery, because I dare not even look at you when I happen to meet you.—Yet I am sure I mean no hurt to any body; nor can it do my cruel aunt any harm, that you pity a poor orphan who has no friend upon earth."

"*I will,* however," replied he warmly, "pity and love you too—love you as well as I do any of my sisters—even the sister I love best—and I should hate myself if I did not. But, dear Monimia, tell me, if I cannot see you in the day-time, is it possible for you to walk out of an evening, when these old women are in bed?—When I am not at the Hall they would suspect nothing; and I should not mind walking from home, after our people are in bed, to meet you for half an hour any where about these grounds."

Ignorant of the decorum required by the world, and innocent, even to infantine simplicity, as Monimia was, at the age of something more than fourteen, she had that natural rectitude of understanding, that at once told her these clandestine meetings would be wrong.[1] "Ah no; Mr. Orlando!" said she sighing, "that must not be; for if it should be known—"

---

[1] The novel opens in the year 1775, at which time Monimia is identified as 'something more than 14"; it closes in 1779, making Monimia just 18. Not only is she a servant, she is also, at the novel's start, and even in the terms of the mid-eighteenth century, a child. Smith herself was hurried into marriage at the age of 15 (she would have been 15 in 1775).

"It cannot, it shall not be known," cried he, eagerly interrupting her.

"But it is impossible, my good friend, if it were not wrong; for you remember that to-day is Saturday, and your school begins on Monday."

"Curse on the school! I had indeed forgot it.—Well, but promise me then, Monimia, promise me that you will make yourself easy now; and that when I come from school entirely, which I shall do at Christmas, we shall contrive to meet sometimes, and to read together, as we used to do, the Fairy Tales and the Arabian Nights, last year, and the year before.—Will you promise me, Monimia?"[1]

Monimia, whose apprehensions every moment increased, and who even fancied she heard the rustle of Mrs. Lennard's gown upon the private stair-case that led down from the gallery, was ready to promise any thing.—"Oh! yes, yes, Orlando!—I promise—do but go now, and we shall not perhaps be so unhappy: my aunt may not be so very ill-humoured when you come home again."

"And say you will not cry any more now!"

"I will not, indeed I will not—but for God's sake go!—I'm sure I hear somebody."

"There is nobody indeed; but I will go, to make you easy."—He then, trembling as much as she did, hastily kissed the hand he held; and gliding on tip-toe to the other end of the gallery, went through the apartments that led down the great stair-case, and taking a circuit round another part of the house, entered the room where Mrs. Rayland was sitting, as if he had been just come from cricket in the park.

He had not left the gallery a moment before Mrs. Lennard came to look for Monimia, whom she found in greater agitation than she had left her, and still drowned in tears. She again began in the severest terms to reprove her; and as the sobs and sighs of the suffering girl deprived her of the power of answering her invectives, she violently seized her arm; and, dragging rather than leading her to her own room, she bade her instantly undress and go to bed—"that you may not," said she, "expose your odious blubbered face."

Poor Monimia was extremely willing to obey.—She sat down and began to undress, listening as patiently as she could to the violent scolding which her indefatigable aunt still kept up against her; who having at length exhausted her breath, bounced out and locked the door.

---

[1]   Orlando's and Monimia's relationship is to a great extent modelled on the romances they have read together; Orlando, especially, views life through a romantic lens, conditioned by textual expectations. Smith alludes to the common belief that too much romance-reading unfitted the reader for real life, although the reader in that case is more usually female.

Monimia, then left alone, again began to indulge her tears; but her room was in a turret[1] over a sort of lumber-room, where the game-keeper kept his nets and his rods, and where Orlando used to deposit his bow, his cricket bats, and other instruments of sport, with which he was indulged with playing in the park. She now heard him come in, with one of the servants; for such an effect had his voice, that she could distinguish it amid a thousand others, and when it did not seem to be audible to any one else.—Though she could not now distinguish the words, she heard him discoursing as if he seemed to be bidding the place farewell for that time. She got upon a chair (for the long narrow window was so far from the ground that she could not see through it as she stood); and she perceived Orlando cross the park on foot, and slowly and reluctantly walk towards that part of it that was next to his father's house. She continued to look at him till a wood, through which he had to pass, concealed him from her view. She then retired to her bed, and shed tears. Orlando left his home the next day, for his last half-year at the school (having that evening taken leave of Mrs. Rayland); and it was six months before Monimia saw him again.

CHAP. III.

However trifling the incident was that is related in the foregoing chapter, it so much alarmed the prudent sagacity of Mrs. Lennard, that when, on the following Christmas, Mr. Orlando returned to his occasional visits at the Hall, she took more care than before to prevent any possibility of his ever having an opportunity of meeting Monimia alone; and, as much as she could without being remarked by her Lady, from seeing her at all. But while she took these precautions, she began to think them useless. Orlando was no longer the giddy boy, eager at his childish sports, and watching with impatience for a game of blindman's buff in the servants' hall, or a romp with any one who would play with him. Orlando was a young man as uncommonly grave, as he was tall and handsome. There was something more than gravity, there was dejection in his manner; but

---

[1] Monimia's turret-room further enhances her fairy-tale/romance-heroine status. Like Rapunzel or Sleeping Beauty, she waits in her tower. Smith emphasizes, and ironizes, this when she later has Orlando break through into Monimia's room through an old, covered door in the wall at the head of her bed.

it served only to make him more interesting. He now slept oftener than before at the Hall, but he was seen there less; and passed whole days in his own room, or rather in the library; where, as this quiet and studious temper recommended him more than ever to Mrs. Rayland, she allowed him to have a fire, to the great comfort and benefit of the books, which had been without that advantage for many years.

Mrs. Lennard, who now beheld him with peculiar favour, though she had formerly done him ill offices, seemed willing to oblige him in everything but in allowing him ever to converse with her niece, who was seldom suffered to appear in the parlour, but was kept to work in her own room. Mrs. Rayland's increasing infirmities, though not such as threatened her life, threw the management of every thing about her more immediately into the hands of Mrs. Lennard; and, occupied by the care of her own health, Mrs. Rayland's attention to what was passing around her was less every day, and the imbecility of age hourly more perceptible. She therefore made no remark on this change of system; but if she happened to want Monimia, or, as she chose to call her, Mary. She sent for her, and dismissed her when her service was performed, without any farther enquiry as to how she afterwards passed her time.

Orlando, however, though he had, since his last return, never spoken a word to Monimia, and though, in their few and short meetings, the presence of Mrs. Lennard prevented their exchanging even a look, was no longer at a loss to discriminate those sentiments which he felt for the beautiful orphan, whose charms, which had made almost in infancy an impression on his heart, were now opening to a perfection even beyond their early promise. Her imprisonment, the harshness of her aunt towards her, and her desolate situation, contributed to raise in his heart all that the most tender pity could add to the ardency of a first passion. Naturally of a warm and sanguine temper, the sort of reading he had lately pursued, his situation, his very name, all added something to the romantic enthusiasm of his character;[1] but in the midst of the fairy dreams which he indulged, reason too often stepped in to poison his enjoyments, and represented to him, that he was without fortune, and without possession—that far from seeing at present any probability of ever being able to offer an establishment to the unfortunate Monimia, he had to procure one for

---

[1] Orlando's "romantic enthusiasm" is his strongest character trait. Smith makes sure to show its ramifications when she portrays Orlando as constantly at the mercy of his emotional responses to situations: wild, frenzied, despairing, ineffectual. In this way she calls into question the romance itself.

himself. It was now he first felt an earnest wish, that the hopes of his relations had sometimes encouraged might be realized, and that some part of the great wealth of the Rayland family might be his; but with this he had no new reason to flatter himself; for Mrs. Rayland, though she seemed to become every day more fond of his company, never took any notice of the necessity there was, that now in his nineteenth year he should fix upon some plan for his future establishment in the world.

This necessity however lay heavy on the heart of his father, who had long felt with anguish, that the misconduct of his eldest son had rendered it impossible for him to do justice to his younger. With a small income and a large family, he had never, though he lived as economically as possible, been able to lay by much money; and what he had saved, in the hope of accumulating small fortunes for his daughters, had been paid away for his eldest son in the first two years of his residence at Oxford; the third had nearly devoured the five hundred pounds legacy given to his family by the elder Mrs. Rayland; and the first half-year after he left the university, and which he passed between London and his father's house, entirely exhausted that resource; while Mr. Somerive in vain represented to him, that, in continuing such a career, he must see the estate mortgaged, which was the sole dependence of his family now, and *his* sole dependence hereafter.

So deep, and often so fatal, are early impressions in minds where reason slowly and feebly combats the influence of passion, that though nothing was more certain than that Mrs. Rayland's fortune was entirely at her own disposal, and nothing more evident than her dislike to him, he never could be persuaded that, as he was the heir at law, he should not possess the greater part of the estate; and he was accustomed, in his orgies among his companions, to drink "to their propitious meeting at the Hall, when the old girl should be in Abraham's bosom,"[1] and not unfrequently "to her speedy departure." He settled with himself the alterations he should make, and the stud he should collect; proposed to refit in excellent style the old kennel, and to restore to Rayland Hall the praise it had formerly boasted, of having the best pack of fox-hounds within three counties. When it was represented that the possibility of executing these plans was very uncertain, since the old lady certainly preferred Orlando, he answered—"Oh! damn it, that's not what I'm afraid of—No, no; the old hag has been, thanks to my fortunate stars, brought up in good old-fashioned notions, and knows that the first-born

---

[1] That is, dead. The term "Abraham's bosom" appears in the Gospel of St. Luke, verse 19.

son is in all Christian countries the head of the house, and that the rest must scramble through the world as well as they can—As for my solemn brother, you see nature and fortune have designed him for a parson. The tabby may like him for a chaplain, and means to qualify him by one of her livings for the petticoats; but take my word for it, that however she may set her weazen face against it, just to impose upon the world, she likes at the bottom of her heart a young fellow of spirit—and you'll see me master of the Hall. Egad, how I'll make her old hoards spin again! Down go those woods that are now every year the worse for standing. Whenever I hear she's fairly off, the squirrels will have notice to quit."

It was in vain that the mild and paternal arguments of Mr. Somerive himself, or the tears and tender remonstrances of his wife, were employed, whenever their son would give them an opportunity, to counteract this unfortunate prepossession. He by degrees began to absent himself more and more from home; and when he was there, his hours were such as put any conversation on serious topics out of their power. He was never indeed sullen, for that was not his disposition; but he was so thoughtless, so volatile, and so prepossessed that he had a right to do as other young men did with whom he had been accustomed to associate, that his father gave up as hopeless every attempt to bring him to his senses.

The greater the uneasiness to which Mr. Somerive was thus subject by the conduct of his eldest son, the more solicitous he became for the future establishment of the younger. But he knew not how to proceed to obtain it. He had now no longer the means of sending him to the university, of which he had sometimes thought, in the hope that Mrs. Rayland might, if he were qualified for orders, give him one of the livings of which she was patroness; nor could he, exhausted as his savings were by the indiscretion of his eldest son, command money enough to purchase him a commission, which he once intended.[1] Sometimes he fancied that, if he were to apply to Mrs. Rayland, she would assist in securing an establishment in future for one about whom she appeared so much interested at present; but he oftener apprehended, from the oddity and caprice of her temper, that any attempt to procure more certain and permanent favours for Orlando, might occasion her to deprive him of what he now possessed.

---

[1] "Livings": the tenancy of a parish vicarage and its ministry was in the gift of the landlord of the area. A commission signified an officer's rank in the armed forces. As the younger son, Orlando can only choose the priesthood, the military, or the law and remain a gentleman. Both the priesthood and the law required a university education.

Mrs. Somerive, though a woman of an excellent understanding, had contracted such an awe of the old lady, that she was positively against speaking to her about her son; while maternal partiality, which was indeed well justified by the good qualities and handsome person of Orlando, continually suggested to her that Mrs. Rayland's prepossession in his favour, if left to take its course, would finally make him the heir of at least great part of her property.

Thus his father, from uncertainty how to act for the best, suffered weeks and months to pass away, in which he could not determine to act at all; and as more than half those weeks and months were passed at the Hall, his mother fondly flattered herself, that he was making rapid advances in securing to his family the possessions they had so good a claim to.

Neither of them saw the danger to which they exposed him, of losing himself in an imprudent and even fatal attachment to a young woman, while they supposed him wholly given up to acquire the favour of an old one; for in fact Mrs. Lennard had so artfully kept her niece out of sight, that neither of them knew her—they barely knew that there was a young person in the house who was considered in the light of a servant; but whether she was well or ill looking, it had never occurred to them to enquire, because they never supposed her more acquainted with their son than any other of the female domestics.

Poor Orlando, however, was cherishing a passion, which had taken entire possession of his heart before he was conscious that he had one, and which the restraints that every way surrounded him served only to inflame. Monimia now appeared in his eyes, what she really was, infinitely more lovely than ever. She was on his account a prisoner, for he learned that when he was not in the country she was allowed more liberty. She was friendless, and harshly treated; and, with a form and face that he thought would do honour to the highest rank of society, she seemed to be condemned to perpetual servitude, and he feared to perpetual ignorance; for he knew that Mrs. Rayland had, with the absurd prejudice of narrow minds, declared against her being taught any thing but the plainest domestic duties, and the plainest work. She had, however, taught herself, with very little aid from her aunt, to read; and lately, since she had been so much alone, she had tried to write; but she had not always materials, and was frequently compelled to hide those she contrived to obtain: so that her progress in this was slow, and made only by snatches, as the ill humour of her aunt allowed or forbade her to make these laudable attempts at improvement.

Her apartment was still in the turret that terminated one wing of the house, and Orlando had been at the Hall the greater part of a fortnight, without their having exchanged a single word. They had indeed met only twice by mere accident, in the presence of the lady of the mansion and of Mrs. Lennard; once when she crossed the hall when he was leading the lady to her chair out of the gallery; and a second time when she was sent for on an accession of gout, to assist in adjusting the flannels and cushions, which Mrs. Rayland declared she managed better than any body.

As she knelt to perform this operation, Orlando, who was reading a practical discourse on faith in opposition to good works, was surprised by her beautiful figure in her simple stuff gown, which had such an effect on his imagination that he no longer knew what he was reading; but, after half a dozen blunders in less than half a dozen lines, he became so conscious of his confusion that he could not proceed at all, but, affecting to be seized with a violent cough, got up and went out. Again, however, this symptom escaped Mrs. Rayland, who, tho' she read good books as a matter of form, and to impress people with an idea of her piety and understanding, cared very little about their purport, and was just then more occupied with the care of her foot than with abstract reasonings on the efficacy of faith.

In the mean time Monimia, who blushed if she even beheld the shadow of Orlando at a distance, and whose heart beat at the sound of his voice, as if it would escape from her bosom, had never an opportunity of hearing it, unless he accidentally spoke to some person in the room under hers, where she knew he often went, and particularly at this season, which was near the end of February, when the ponds were drawn, and the nets and poles in frequent use: but the door by which this room opened to the court was on the other side. Monimia had only one high long window in a very thick wall that looked into the park: whenever therefore, as she sat alone in her turret, she heard any person in the room beneath her, she listened with an anxious and palpitating heart, and at length fancied that she could distinguish the step of Orlando from that of the game-keeper or any of the other servants.

If she was thus attentive to him, without any other motive than to enjoy the pleasure of fancying he was near her, Orlando was on his side studying how to obtain an opportunity of seeing her; not in the intention of communicating to her those sentiments which he now too well understood, but in the hope of finding means to make her amends for the injustice of fortune. If there was any dependence to be placed on expression of countenance, the animation and intelligence that were visible in the soft features of Monimia promised an excellent under-standing. What pity that it should not be cultivated! What delight to be her preceptor, and, in despite of the malignity of fortune, to render her mind as lovely as her form! This project got so entirely the possession of Orlando's imagination, that he thought, he dreamed of nothing else; and, however difficult, or even impracticable it seemed, he determined to undertake it.[1]

Mrs. Lennard slept at some distance; but there was no other way of Monimia's going into any part of the house but by a passage which led through her room; for every other avenue was closed up, and the last thing she did every night was to lock the door of the room where her niece lay, and to take away the key.

The window was equally well secured, for it was in effect only a loop; and of this, narrow as it was, the small square of the casement that opened was secured by iron bars. The Raylands had been eminent royalists in the civil wars, and Rayland Hall had held out against a party of Fairfax's army that had closely besieged it.[2] Great part of the house retained the same appearance of defensive strength which had then been given it; and no knight of romance ever had so many real difficulties to encounter in achieving the deliverance of his princess, as Orlando had in finding the means merely to converse with the little imprisoned orphan.[3] Months passed away, in which his most watchful diligence served only to prove that these difficulties were almost insurmountable; nor would he perhaps, with all the enthusiasm of love and romance, have ever conquered them, if chance had not befriended him.

Mrs. Rayland had given him, under restrictions that he should use it only while he was at the Hall, a very fine colt, which was of a breed of racers, the property of the Raylands, and very eminent in the days

---

[1]   This reference to Galatea (Pygmalion's ideal sculpted woman, who comes to life) shows Orlando's continuing inability to see Monimia as anything other than his intended romance heroine. Later references to her as Miranda (from Shakespeare's *The Tempest*) and as a hidden gem further her identity as a fictional construct rather than a "real" character. This, however, reflects Orlando's mindset, which Smith always undercuts.

[2]   The war between the Royalists (loyal to Charles I) and the Cavaliers (loyal to Cromwell), 1642–1649. "Fairfax" is probably Thomas Fairfax (1612–71), 3rd Baron Fairfax, parliamen-tarian general during the Civil War. His father, Ferdinando (2nd Baron Fairfax, 1584–1648), also commanded parliamentary forces. Neither ventured as far south as Rayland Hall is meant to be, however.

[3]   Orlando sees the Hall as built in part to keep him from Monimia; this is one way in which Smith uses the property of the Hall both to separate the two and to figure their deter-mination to be together.

of Sir Hildebrand. Out of respect to its ancient prowess, the breed was still kept up, though the descendants no longer emulated the honours of their progenitors on the turf: but the produce was generally sold by the coachman who had the management of the stable, and who was supposed to have profited very considerably by his dealings.

Orlando, highly gratified by this mark of Mrs. Rayland's favour, undertook to break the young horse himself, and to give it among other accomplishments that of leaping. There was no leaping-bar about the grounds; but in the lumber-room on the ground floor of one of the turrets he had seen the timber of one that had formerly stood in the park. To this place, therefore, he repaired; and in removing the large posts, which were very little injured by time, some other slabs of wood, boards, and pieces of scaffolding were moved also, and Orlando saw that they had concealed a door, formerly boarded up, but of which the boards were now broken and decayed; he forced away a piece of the rotten wood, and saw a flight of broken stone steps, just wide enough to admit one person with difficulty. His heart bounded with transport: he knew that this stair-case must lead to the top of the turret, and consequently wind round the room occupied by Monimia, which it was probable had a communication also with the stairs. But, unable to determine in a moment how he should avail himself, or acquaint her, of this fortunate discovery, and trembling lest it should be known, and his hopes at once destroyed, he hastily replaced the spars of wood that had concealed the door, before the return of the gardener and the under game-keeper, who had been assisting him in his operations about the leaping-bar; and hastily following them to the spot where they were putting it up, he affected to be interested in its completion, while his mind was really occupied only by plans for seeing without fear of discovery his adored Monimia.

CHAP. IV.

Love rendered Orlando so politic, that he determined rather to defer the happiness he hoped for, in gaining unmolested access to Monimia for two or three days, than to risk by precipitancy the delightful secret of the concealed door, and to watch the motion of the dragon whose unwearied vigilance might at once render it useless. He therefore set himself to observe the hours when Mrs. Lennard was most certainly engaged about her mistress; and he found, that as she indulged very freely in the pleasures of a good table, of which she was herself directress, she became frequently unwilling to encounter much exertion after dinner; and generally left Monimia (who either did not dine below, or retired with the table-cloth) unmolested till six o'clock, when, if he was not there, she was called down to make tea.

These hours therefore seemed most propitious for the experiment he must of necessity make, which was to ascend the stair-case, and seek for the door that probably, though now blocked up, had originally led from it into the room inhabited by Monimia; from whence, as it was perhaps only boarded up, he hoped to make her hear, and to prevail upon her to assist in forcing a passage through it.

He knew Mrs. Lennard was less upon the *qui vive?*[1] when he was not about the house; and therefore, the evening before that when he intended to put his project in execution, he took leave of Mrs. Rayland, and told her that he was going home for a few days, when with her permission he would return. Mrs. Rayland, who now thought the house melancholy without him, bade him come back to the Hall as soon as he could, which he promised with a beating heart, and departed.

The next day, however, having taken the precaution to get a letter of compliment from his father to Mrs. Rayland, the better to account for his quick return, if to account for it should be necessary, he set out on foot after dinner; and as he arrived at Rayland Hall just as the servants of that family were eating theirs, which was always a long and momentous business, he had the good fortune not to meet any one, but to enter the lower room of the turret; and as he had often the key, he now locked the door, and listening very attentively heard Monimia walking above, and convinced himself that she was alone.

As silently as he could he removed the planks and timber that concealed the door; and having so placed them that, without discovering the aperture, they leaned so hollow from the wall that he could get under them, he tore away the remaining impediments that obstructed him, and entered the low stair-case, of which about fourteen broken and decayed steps led, as he expected, to another door which was also boarded up, and then wound up to the top of the turret. He stopped a moment and listened; he distinctly heard Monimia sigh deeply, and open a drawer. He considered a moment what way of accosting her would be least likely to alarm her too suddenly, and at length he determined to speak.

---

[1] I.e., "who goes there?"

After another pause, and finding all was silent in her room, he tapped softly against the boarded door: and lowering his voice he called, "Monimia, Monimia!"

The affrighted girl exclaimed, "Good God! who is there? who speaks?" "Be not affrighted," replied he, speaking louder, "it is Orlando," "Orlando! and from whence, dear sir, do you speak?" "I know not, for I cannot tell what part of your room this door opens to; tell me, where do you hear the sound I now make?" "Against the head of my bed." "Cannot you then remove the bed, and see if there is not a door?" "I can," replied Monimia, "if my trembling does not prevent me, for my bed goes upon casters; but indeed I tremble so! if my aunt should come!" "She will not come," replied Orlando impatiently: "do not give way to groundless fears, Monimia; but, if ever you had any friendship for me, exert yourself now, to procure the only opportunity we shall ever have of meeting—remove your bed, and see what is behind it."

Monimia, trembling and amazed as she was, found in the midst of her alarm a sensation of joy that was undescribable. It lent her strength to remove the bed, which it was not difficult to do; but the room was hung with old-fashioned glazed linen, when many years before it had been fitted up as a bed-chamber: this kind of arras entirely hid the door. "Ah!" cried Monimia, "there is no door, Mr. Orlando. The hangings are just the same here as about the rest of the room." "Cut them," cried he, "with your scissors, and you will find there is a door." "But if my aunt should discover that they are cut?" "Oh heavens," exclaimed Orlando, "if you are thus apprehensive, Monimia, we shall never meet; but if you have any regard for me"—The adjuration was too powerful: Monimia forgot the dread of her aunt in the superior dread of offending Orlando. She took her scissors, and, cutting the hangings, which through time were little more than tinder, discovered the door, which was very thin, and only nailed up, strengthened on the outside by a few slight deals across it. Orlando, who, like another Pyramus,[1] watched with a beating heart the breach through which he now saw the light, forced away these slight barriers with very little difficulty; and then, setting his foot against the door, it gave way, and the remnant of tattered hanging made no resistance. He found himself in the room with Monimia, who from mingled emotions of pleasure and fear could hardly breathe. "At length," cried he, "I have found you, Monimia! at length I have got to

---

[1]   As most famously satirized in Shakespeare's *A Midsummer Night's Dream*, Pyramus could only approach his lover Thisbe through a very small hole in a wall.

you." "But we shall both be utterly ruined," interrupted she, "if my aunt should happen to come: speak low, for heaven's sake, speak low. I should die upon the spot, if she should happen to find you here."

"Let us consider," said Orlando, "how we may meet for the future. I do not mean to stay now; but you see this door gives us always an opportunity of seeing each other." "But how shall I dare?" cried the trembling Monimia: "my aunt watches me so narrowly, that I am never secure of being alone a moment: even now, perhaps, she may be coming."

So great was the terror which this idea impressed on the timid Monimia, that Orlando saw there was no time to be lost in settling their more secure meetings. "Have you," said he, "have you, Monimia, courage enough to make use of this door, to come down into the study to me when we are sure all the house is quiet? You know there is a passage to that end of the house, without crossing either of the great courts or any of the apartments, by going through the old chapel, and nobody can hear you. I only propose this, because I suppose you are afraid of letting me come up here."

"Oh! either is very wrong," replied she, "and I shall be sadly blamed."

"Well, then, Monimia, I am deceived, cruelly deceived. I did believe that you had some regard for me, and I protest to heaven that I mean nothing but the purest friendship towards you. I want you to read, which I know you have now no opportunity of doing. I would find proper books for you; for you may one day have occasion for more knowledge than you can acquire in the way in which you now live. Perhaps clandestine meetings might not be right in any other case; but, persecuted as you are, Monimia, we must meet clandestinely, or not meet at all. Alas! my dear friend, it may not be long that I may be here to ask this favour of you, or to request you to oblige me for your own good. My father is considering how to settle me in life."

"To settle you!" said Monimia, faintly.

"Yes—I mean, to put me into some profession in the world; and whatever it is, it will of course carry me quite away from hence. As soon as it is determined upon, therefore, Monimia, I shall go—and perhaps we shall never meet again: yet you now refuse to grant me the only happiness that possibly my destiny will ever suffer me to taste—I mean that of being of some little service to you. What harm can there really be, Monimia, in what I request? Have we not lived from children together, like brother and sister? and why should we give up the sweet and innocent pleasure of loving each other, because your aunt is of a temper so detestably severe and suspicious?"

"Indeed I know not," said Monimia, whose tears now streamed down her cheeks; "but I know, Orlando, that I cannot refuse what you ask; for, indeed, I do not believe you would desire me to act wrong."

"No, I would die first."

"Tell me then, what would you have me do? I tremble so that I am really ready to sink, lest my aunt should come: tell me, dear Orlando, what would you have me do?"

"Replace your bed as soon as I am gone, and I will take care that no signs shall remain below of the discovery I have made. As soon as the family are all in bed, and you are sure your aunt is gone for the night, I will come up and fetch you into the study; where, whenever I am here, we can read for an hour or two every night: tell me, Monimia, do you agree to this?"

"I do," replied she; "and now, dear Orlando, go; it will soon be tea-time, my aunt will come to call me."

"You will be ready then to-night, Monimia?"

"To-night?"

"Yes; for why should we lose an hour, when perhaps so few are left me? When I am gone to some distant part of the world, you may be sorry for me, Monimia, and repent that when we could see each other you refused."

The idea of his going, perhaps for ever, was insupportable, and the timid doubts of Monimia vanished before it. She thought at that moment, that to pass one hour with him were well worth any risk— even though her aunt should discover and kill her. She hesitated there-fore no longer, but promised to be ready in the evening, and to listen for his signal. Having thus gained his point, Orlando no longer refused to quit her, but returned by his propitious stair-case; and replacing the boards, at its entrance below, as nearly as possible as he found them, he went out unseen by any body; and going back to the road which led through the park, he walked hastily across that part of it that was imme-diately before the windows of the apartment where Mrs. Rayland sat; and then went into the house, and sent up, as was his custom, to know if he might be admitted. She ordered him to be shewn up, and received him with pleasure; for she just then was in a very ill humour, and wanted somebody in whom she could find a patient listener, while she related the cause of it, and declaimed against the persons who had occa-sioned it—which was thus:

The estates in this country were very large, and that possessed by the house of Rayland yielded in extent to none, but was equal to that of its nearest neighbour, a nobleman, who owned a great extent of country which immediately adjoined to the manors and farms of Mrs. Rayland, and on which there was also a fine old house, situated in the midst of the domain, at the distance of about five miles from Rayland Hall; the estates divided by a river, which was the joint property of both.

Lord Carloraine, the last possessor of this property, was a man very far advanced in life. Many years had passed since the world in which he had lived had disappeared; and being no longer able or desirous to take part in what was passing about a court, to him wholly uninteresting, and being a widower without children, he had retired above thirty years before to his paternal seat; where he lived in splendid uniformity, receiving only the nobility of the county and the baronets (whom he considered as forming an order that made a very proper barrier between the peerage and the squirality),[1] with all the massive dignity and magnificent dulness that their fathers and grandfathers had been entertained with since the beginning of the century. Filled with high ideas of the consequence of ancient blood, he suffered no consideration to interfere with his respect for all who had that advantage to boast; while, for the upstart rich men of the present day, he felt the most ineffable contempt; and while such were, in neighbouring counties, seen to figure away on recently acquired fortunes, Lord Carloraine used to pique himself upon the inviolability of that part of the world where he lived—and say, that very fortunately for the morals and manners of the country, it had not been chosen by nabobs and contractors[2] for the display of their wealth and taste. And that none such might gain any footing in the neighbourhood, he purchased every farm that was to be sold; and contrived to be so much of a despot himself, that those who were only beginning to be great, shunned his established greatness as inimical to their own.

Mrs. Rayland perfectly agreed with him in these sentiments; and had the most profound respect for a nobleman, who acknowledged, proud as he was of his own family, that it had no other superiority over that of Rayland, than in possessing an higher title. He had been, though a much younger man, acquainted with the late Sir Hildebrand; and

---

[1] The nobility, or peerage, of the county would consist of titled aristocrats. Baronets were called "Sir" but did not otherwise have a title, and sat in the House of Commons rather than the House of Lords. The squirality would consist of the local landed gentlemen: property owners, but without titles.

[2] "Nabobs and contractors": derogatory terms for the nouveau riche, like Stockton's family. "Nabob" originally referred to a deputy governor in the Mogul empire in India, and then came to signify a man whose wealth was made in India.

whenever Mrs. Rayland and Lord Carloraine met, which they did in cumbrous state twice or thrice a year, their whole conversation consisted of eulogiums on the days that were passed, in expressing their dislike of all that was now acting in a degenerate world, and their contempt of the actors.

But the winter preceding the period of which this history is relating the events, had carried off this ancient and noble friend at the age of ninety-six, to the regret of nobody so much as of Mrs. Rayland. His estate fell to the grandson of his only sister, a man of three-and-twenty, who was as completely the nobleman of the present day, as his uncle had been the representative of those who lived in the reign of George the First.[1] He cared nothing for the ancient honours of his family; and would not have passed a fortnight in the gloomy solitude of his uncle's castle, to have been master of six times its revenue. His paternal property and parliamentary interest[2] lay in a northern county; and therefore, as ready money was a greater object to him than land in another part of England, he offered the estate of Lord Carloraine to sale, as soon as it came into his possession; and in a few months it was bought by the son of a rich merchant—a young man, lately of age, of the name of Stockton; whose father having had very lucrative contracts in that war which terminated in 1763,[3] had left his son a minor with a fortune, which at the end of a ten years minority amounted to little short of half a million.

The purchase of Carloraine Castle by such a man had given Mrs. Rayland inexpressible concern and mortification, which every circumstance that came to her knowledge had contributed to increase. She had already heard enough to foresee all the inconveniencies of this exchange of neighbours; on which she dwelt continually, yet seemed to take strange pains to irritate her own uneasiness by daily enquiries into the alterations and proceedings of Mr. Stockton; who, even before the purchase was generally known to be completed, had begun, under the auspices of modern taste, to new model everything. He came down to Carloraine Castle twice or thrice a week, every time with a new set of company; almost every one of his visitors was willing to assist him in his plan of improvements, and he listened to them all—so that what was built up to-day, was pulled down to-morrow. All the workmen, such as bricklayers, &c. &c. in the neighbourhood, for many miles, were engaged

---

[1]   George I reigned from 1714–27.

[2]   A landed gentleman of sufficient property had an automatic seat in Parliament.

[3]   The French and Indian War, 1757–63.

to work at the Castle; and the delicacies which used to be supplied by the neighbouring country, and in which Mrs. Rayland had usually a preference, were now offered first to "his honour, 'Squire Stockton:"— and his honour's servants, to whom the regulation of his house was entrusted, were so willing to do credit to their master's large fortune, that they gave London prices for every thing: the vicinity of affluent luxury was thus severely felt by those to whom it was of much more real consequence than to Mrs. Rayland.

To her, however, this circumstance was particularly grating. She complained bitterly to every body she saw, that poultry, if she had by any accident occasion to buy it, was doubled in price; that the prime sea fish was carried to the Castle; and more money demanded for the refuse than she was accustomed to give for the finest. But with the beginning of September more aggravating offences began also. An army of sportsmen came down to the Castle, who had no respect for the hitherto inviolate manors, nor for the preserved grounds around Rayland Hall, which not even the game-keepers ever alarmed with a hostile sound. Her park—even her park, where no profane foot had ever been suffered to enter, was now invaded; and on the second of September, the day of which the occurrences have been here related, five young men and two servants, with a whole kennel of pointers, had crossed the park, and killed three brace of partridges within its enclosure, laughing at the threats, and threatening in their turns the keepers, who had attempted to oppose them.

No injury or affront that could be devised could have made so deep an impression on Mrs. Rayland's mind, as such a trespass. She was yet in the first paroxysm of her displeasure, though the occasion of it happened early in the morning, when Orlando was admitted; whose mind, attuned to the harmonizing hope of being indulged with the frequent sight of Monimia, was but little in unison with the petulant and querulous complaints of Mrs. Rayland; while she for above an hour held forth with unwearied invective against the new inhabitant of Carloraine. "These," cried she, "these are modern gentlemen!—Gentlemen! a disgrace to the name!—City apprentices, that used to live soberly at their shops, are turned sportsmen, forsooth, and have the impudence to call themselves gentlemen. I hear, and I suppose 'tis true enough, that Mr. Philip Somerive thinks proper to be acquainted with this mushroom fellow— and to be one of his party!—Pray, child, can you tell me—is it true?"

"I believe, madam, my brother has some acquaintance, but I fancy only a slight acquaintance, with Mr. Stockton."

"Oh! I have very little curiosity—I dare say he is one of the set, and it is very fit he should. 'Birds of a feather, you know, flock together.' But this I assure you, Mr. Orlando—take this from me—that if you should ever think proper to know that person, that Stockton, your visits here will from that time be dispensed with."

Orlando, conscious that he had never exchanged a word with any inhabitant or visitant of Carloraine, and conscious too that all his wishes were centred in what the Hall contained, assured Mrs. Rayland with equal warmth and sincerity, that he never had, nor ever would have, any connexion with the people who assembled there. "So far from my wishing to hold with such people any friendly converse, I shall hardly be able to refrain from remonstrating with them on their very improper and unhandsome manner of acting towards you, madam; and if I meet them on your grounds, I shall, unless you forbid me, very freely tell them my opinion of their conduct."

Mrs. Rayland had never in her life been so pleased with Orlando as she was at that moment. The readiness with which he entered into her injuries, and the spirit with which he undertook to check the aggressors, placed him higher in her favour than he had ever yet been; but her way of testifying this her satisfaction, consisted in what of all others was at this moment the most mortifying; for she invited him to stay to supper in her apartment, which was a favour she hardly did him twice a year. Orlando, wretched as it made him, could not make any excuse to escape; and it was near an hour later than usual, before Mrs. Rayland, retiring, dismissed Orlando to watch for the silence of the house, which was a signal for his going to the beloved turret.

CHAP. V.

The clock in the servants' hall struck twelve, and was answered by that in the north gallery. With yet deeper tone the hour was re-echoed from the great clock in the cupola over the stables; when Orlando, listening a moment to hear if all was quiet, proceeded through an arched passage which led from the library to the chapel, and then through the chapel itself, whose principal entrance was from a porch which opened to a sort of triangular court on the back of the house next the park. He had previously unbarred the chapel door, which was slightly secured by an iron rod: the lock had long since been rusted by time, and the key lost;

for, since the death of Sir Hildebrand, who was buried with his ancestors in the chancel, the ladies his daughters had found themselves too much affected to enter the chapel (which was also the church of the small parish of Rayland), and had removed the parochial service to that of the next parish, within a mile: and as both belonged to them, the livings were united, and the people of either were content to say their prayers wherever their ladies chose to appoint.

Orlando, till he found it opened his way to Monimia, without going through or near any inhabited part of the house, had never explored the chapel; but the night before that on which the experiment was to be made, he had taken care to see that in his passage through it he had no impediment to fear; for of those superstition might have raised to deter a weaker mind, or one engaged in a less animating cause, he was insensible.

He now, having convinced himself that all the family were retired, walked softly through the aisle; and having without any difficulty opened the door of the porch, that adjoined the pavement round the east or back front, he stepped with light feet along it, entered the lower room of the turret which was nearly opposite, and ascended, still as silently as he could, the narrow stair-case.

"Monimia! Monimia!" cried he in a half whisper, "Monimia, are you ready?" "I am," replied a low and tremulous voice. "Remove the hangings, then," said Orlando. Slowly the faltering hands of the trembling girl removed them. Orlando eagerly received her as she came through the door-way. "Are you here at last?" cried he vehemently. "Shall I be at liberty at last to see you? But how cold you are! how you tremble!" "Ah! Mr. Orlando," answered Monimia, half shrinking from him, "ah! I am so certain that all this is wrong, I so dread a discovery, that it is impossible to conquer my terrors: besides, I have recollected that one of the windows of my aunt's closet up stairs looks this way. If she should be in it, if she should see us!"

"How can she be in it without a light? She hardly sits there in the dark for her amusement. You know it is impossible she can have any suspicion; yet you torment yourself, and destroy all my happiness by your timidity. Ah, Monimia! you are cruel to me." "I would not be cruel to you for a thousand worlds, Orlando, you know I would not. But, if I were to die, I cannot conquer my terrors. I tremble too with cold as well as with fright; for I have waited so long past my hour of going to bed, that I am half frozen."

"And yet you are not glad to see me, Monimia, when at last I am come?"

"Indeed I am glad, Orlando; but hush! hark, surely I heard a noise. Listen a moment, for heaven's sake, before we go down."

"It is nothing," said Orlando, after a pause, "it is nothing, upon my soul, but the wind that rushes up the narrow stair-case to the top of the tower."

"Speak low, however," replied Monimia, as she gave him her cold tremulous hand to lead her slowly down the ruined steps; "speak very low; or rather let us be quite silent, for you remember what an echo there is in the court."

They then proceeded silently along the flag-stones that surrounded the court opening on one side to the park, and entered the porch of the chapel; where when Monimia arrived, she seemed so near fainting, that, as they were now sheltered from all observation, Orlando entreated her to sit down on one of the thick old worm-eaten wooden benches that were fixed on either side.

Unable to support herself, Orlando made her lean against him, as endeavouring to re-assure her, he besought her to conquer an alarm, "for which," said he, "Monimia, I cannot account. What do you fear, my sweet friend? Do you already repent having entrusted yourself with me?"

"Oh! no indeed," sighed Monimia, "but the chapel!" "What of the chapel?" cried Orlando impatiently. "It is haunted, you know, every night, by the spirit of one of the Lady Raylands, who I know not how long ago died for love, and whose ghost now sits every night in the chancel, and sometimes walks round the house, and particularly along the galleries, at midnight, groaning and lamenting her fate."

Orlando, laughing at her simplicity, cried, "And who, my dear Monimia, who has violated thy natural good sense by teaching thee these ridiculous stories? Believe me, none of the Lady Raylands, as you called them, ever died for love; indeed I never heard that any of them ever were in love but my grandmother, who saved herself the absurdity of dying, by marrying the man she liked, in despite of the opposing pride of her family; and as she was very happy, and never repented her disobedience, I do not believe her spirit walks: or if it should, Monimia, if it were possible that it should, could you not face a ghost with me for your protector?"

"Any living creature I should not fear, Orlando, if you were with me; but there is something so dreadful in the idea of a spirit!"

"This is not a place," said Orlando with quickness, "this is not a place to argue with your prejudices, Monimia, for you seem half dead with cold; but come, I beseech you, into the library, where there is a fire, and trust to my arm to defend you from all supernatural beings at least, on the way."

He then drew her arm within his, and pushed open the door of the chapel. When Monimia felt the cold damp that environed her as he shut it after them, and found herself in such a place, without any other light than what was afforded by two gothic windows half blocked with stone work, and almost all the rest by stained glass, at mid-night, in a night of September, she again shuddered and shrunk back: but Orlando again encouraging her, and ridiculing her fears, she moved on, and passing the stone passage, he at length seated her safely by the study fire, which he now replenished with wood. As she was still pale and trembling, he brought her a glass of wine (of which Mrs. Rayland allowed him whatever he chose), which he insisted on her drinking, and then, seating himself by her, enquired with a gay smile, how she did after her encounter with the lady who died for love?

"You think me ridiculous, Orlando, and perhaps I am so; but my aunt has often told me, that ghosts always appeared to people who were doing wrong, to reproach them; and, alas! Orlando, I am too sensible that I am not doing right."

"Curse on her prudish falsehood!" cried the impetuous Orlando. "If ghosts, as you call them, were always on the watch to persecute evil doers, I believe from my soul that *she* would have been beset by those of all the Raylands that are packed together in the chancel."

Such was the awe of her aunt in which Monimia had been brought up, that the little respect and vehement manner in which Orlando spoke of her, had in it additional terror. She did not speak; she was not able: but the tears which had till then trembled in her eyes now stole down her cheeks. Orlando was tempted to kiss them away before they reached her bosom; but he remembered that she was wholly in his power, and that he owed her more respect than it would have been necessary to have shewn even in public.

"Let us talk no more of your old aunt," re-assumed Orlando; "but tell me, Monimia, all that has happened in these long, long months of absence."

"Happened, Mr. Orlando!" repeated Monimia.

"Nay," interrupted he, "let me not be *Mr.* Orlando, my lovely friend, but call me Orlando, and try to fancy me your brother. Tell me, Monimia, how have you passed your time since I was allowed to see you last? What an age it is ago! Have you practised your writing, Monimia, and has Lennard allowed you the use of any books?"

"A few I got at by the assistance of Betty Richards, who has the key of this room to clean it when you are absent, Orlando; but if my aunt had found it out, she would never have forgiven either of us. I was forced therefore to hide the books she took out for me with the greatest care, and to read only by snatches. And as to writing, I have done a little of it because you desired me; but it has been very difficult; for my aunt Lennard never would allow me to have pens and ink; and Betty Richards has given me these too by stealth, when she was able to procure them, as if they were for herself, of Mr. Pattenson the butler, who was always very kind to her about such things, till a week or two ago; when he was so cross at her asking for more paper, that we thought it better to let alone applying to him again for some time."

"The old thief was jealous, I suppose," answered Orlando. "I believe he was," said Monimia; "for he has a liking, I fancy, to Betty, though to be sure he is old enough to be her father."

Orlando was now struck with an apprehension which had never before occurred to him: he feared that, in the gratitude of her unadulterated heart for the kindness she received from this Betty Richards, she might betray to her the secret of their nocturnal visits; and he knew that the love of gossiping, the love of finery, the love of nice morsels which the butler had it in his power to give, or even the love of shewing she was entrusted with a secret, were any of them sufficient to overset all the fidelity which this girl (the under house-maid) might either feel or profess to feel for Monimia.

Against this therefore it was necessary to put her on her guard; which Orlando endeavoured to do in the most impressive manner possible, and even urged her with warmth to give him her solemn promise that she never would entrust this servant with any secret, or mention to her his name on any account whatever.

"Indeed, Orlando," replied Monimia, when he had finished this warm exhortation, "indeed you need not be uneasy or anxious about it; for there is one reason that, if I had no other, would never permit me to tell this poor girl that I meet you unknown to my aunt."

"And what is that?"

"It is, that Betty is, like myself, a very friendless orphan, a poor girl that my aunt has taken from the parish; and as I know very well that all our meetings will one day or other be discovered, it would entirely ruin her, and occasion the loss of her place and her character, if Betty were supposed to know any thing about it; therefore you may be assured, Orlando, that she never shall: for whatever misery it may be my fate to suffer myself, I shall not so much mind, as I should being the cause of ruining and injuring another person, especially a friendless girl, who has always been as kind to me as her situation allowed her to be."

Enchanted with her native rectitude of heart and generosity of spirit, Orlando rapturously exclaimed, "Charming girl! how every sentence you utter, every sentiment of your pure and innocent mind delight me! No, Monimia, I am very sure that such a security as you have given me is of equal force, perhaps superior as it ought to be, even to your faith to me—superior, Monimia, to the wish which I am sure you have, to spare me any sort of unhappiness." The fine eyes of Monimia were swimming in tears, as, tenderly pressing her hand between his, Orlando said this. "You do me justice," said she in a faltering voice, "and I thank you. I do not know, Orlando, why I should be ashamed to say that I love you better than any body else in the world; for indeed who is there in it that I have to love? If you were gone, it would be all a desert to me; for, though I hope I am grateful, and not undutiful to my aunt Lennard, I find I do not love her as I love you. But indeed I do believe she would not have me feel affection for any body; for she is always telling me, that it is the most disgraceful and odious thing imaginable, for a young woman, dependent as I am, to think about any person, man, woman, or child; and that, if I would not be an undone and disgraced creature, I must mind nothing but praying to God, which I hope I never neglected, and learning to earn my bread by my hands. And then she tells me continually how much I owe her for taking me into her Lady's family, and what a wicked wretch I should be if I were ungrateful."

"Don't tell me any more about your aunt, do not, I entreat you," cried Orlando impatiently. "I should be sorry to say any thing that should stain, even with the most remote suspicion of ingratitude, that unadulterated mind. But—I cannot—no, it is impossible to resist saying, that, like all other usurped authority, the power of your aunt is maintained by unjust means, and supported by prejudices, which if once looked at by the eye of reason would fall. So slender is the hold of tyranny, my Monimia!"

"Dear Orlando," said Monimia smiling through her tears, "you talk what is by me very little understood." "No!" replied he, "she has taken care to fetter you in as much ignorance as possible; but your mind rises above the obscurity with which she would surround it. She has however brought in supernatural aid; and, fearful of not being able to keep you in sufficient awe by her terrific self, she has called forth all the deceased ladies of the Rayland family, and gentlemen too for aught I know, and beset you with spirits and hobgoblins if you dare to walk about the house."

"Ah! Orlando," answered Monimia timidly, and throwing round the room a half fearful glance, "I do believe you injure my aunt Lennard in that notion; for I am almost sure she believes what she tells me."

"Pooh!" replied he, "she has too much sense. A good bottle of Barbadoes water, or ratafia,[1] would call your pious aunt in the darkest night, and just as the clock strikes twelve, into the very chancel of the chapel itself, or even into the vaults under it."

"Do not laugh at such things, Orlando; do not, pray! unless you are very sure they are all foolish and superstitious fancies. I assure you, Orlando, that having been used to walk about this great old rambling house by myself, at all times of the day, and sometimes, when you have not been here, late of a night, I cannot have been much used to indulge fear; for, frightened or not frightened, I must have gone if my Lady or my aunt had ordered me. But though I am not the least afraid, or used not to be afraid, when I was assured in my own heart that I had never done or intended any harm, yet I have seen and heard—"

"Nay then, Monimia, tell me what you have seen and heard," cried he, fixing his eyes eagerly on her face, and pulling his chair nearer to hers, "and let us draw round the fire and have a discourse upon apparitions."

"You will laugh at me, Orlando," said she, looking smilingly and yet grave; "but what I have to tell you is true nevertheless."

"Tell it then, Monimia—If any proofs have power to make me a convert, they must be yours."

"Well then, Orlando, I assure you it is no fancy, but absolutely true, that some time last February, at which time my aunt was very ill by the fall she had down stairs, she used to intrust me with the keys, and to send me about the house for things she wanted. You know that when Mr. Pattenson is out, she always insists upon having the keys of the great cellars, as well as all the rest, left with her; and that, after quarrelling some years about it, she has got the better; and, though he will not give her his keys, has my Lady's leave to have keys of her own, which she always takes particular pleasure in using when he is out (which he happened to be that night at the christening of Mr. Butterworth's child), whether she really wants the things she sends for or no. It was a terrible stormy night, and very dark, when my aunt, who was but just got well enough to sit in my Lady's room, took it into her head, after every body was gone to bed, but Betty Richards and I, that she wanted some

---

[1] Barbadoes-water is a fruit cordial flavoured with orange- and lemon-peel. Ratafia is a cordial or liqueur flavoured with fruits like peaches, apricots, and cherries (or their kernels), and almonds. Smith had a personal interest in the West Indies; her son Lionel later became the Governor of, first, Barbados, and then Jamaica (1832–39), and was an ardent and effective supporter of emancipation.

hot shrub and water.[1] She sent me to look for shrub in her closet, where I believe she knew there was none; and when I came back to say there was none, she bade me go into the east-wing cellar, which goes, you know, under the house, towards this end of it, and fetch half a dozen bottles; and she gave me the key and a basket. I stood trembling with fear; for had I been sure of being killed even at that moment, I am very certain I could not have determined to venture alone."

"What is the foolish girl afraid of?" said my aunt. "Of going alone so far, Ma'am," said I, "at this time of night."

"And is not *this* time of night," said my aunt angrily, "or is not *any* time of night, or any time of day, the same thing to *you?* Idiot!—and do you dare to affect any choice, how and when you shall obey my commands?"

"Oh! no indeed, my dear dear aunt," answered I trembling, "no indeed; but remember—remember, before you are so angry with me, that an hundred and an hundred times you have told me, that all the galleries and passages about this house are haunted; and that you have yourself seen strange sights and heard frightful noises, though you never would tell me what they were: how shall I, my dear aunt, encounter that which has terrified you?—Pray, forgive me! or, if you will not, inflict upon me any punishment you please: only be assured, my dear dear aunt, that, terrible as your anger is to your poor girl, she had rather endure it than go into those passages and vaults alone."

"Why, thou art a driveller, a perfect idiot," answered Mrs. Lennard, "and art fit only for a cap and bells, clean straw, and a whirligig.[2]—Apparitions, you stupid fool! But tell me, will you go for what I want, if this other moppet, who looks as white as a cheese-curd, will go with you?"

"The offer of going with Betsy Richards had somehow quite a charm with it, compared with the terrors of going alone; and therefore I readily agreed to the proposal, flattering myself that Betsy would refuse, and that I should be so excused.

"But poor Betsy had, like myself, a most terrible awe of my aunt, whom ever since she could remember she had been taught to fear. "To be sure, I will go," said poor Betsy; "to be certain, I will go, if madam she desires it; though for certain—"

---

[1]   Shrub is made with orange or lemon juice (or other citrus fruit), sugar, and rum (or other spirits). Hot shrub and water is therefore a form of hot toddy.

[2]   A whirligig is a large cage suspended so as to turn on a pivot, used as punishment for, among others, camp-following prostitutes: Mrs. Lennard insinuates that Monimia is both mad and sexually loose. The word also means a "fickle, inconstant, giddy or flighty person" (*OED*).

"None of your ifs, you silly baggage! but here, take the candle; and do you, you nonsensical ninnyhammer, take the basket, and fetch instantly what I want. The old shrub stands in a bin, quite at the lower end of the farthest arched vault, next the chapel wing: put your hands elbow deep in the saw-dust, and you will feel it; bring half a dozen bottles, and mind you take care of your candle—for the whole family of Rayland are piled up in their velvet coffins within two or three feet of you; and it would be a very unhandsome thing to set their old dry bones in a blaze on their own premises."

"Neither Betsy nor I dared answer; for, as my aunt spoke these last words, she waved her hands for us to go. After we were out of hearing, I, who held Betsy fast by the arm, expressed my apprehension at what had passed. I did this more particularly, because I had never heard my aunt talk so freely before. Betsy, frightened as she was at the thought of the expedition we were undertaking, could not help tittering at the surprise I expressed, and said, "Lord! why, the old woman has been sitting so long after supper with madam, that she has been taking care to keep the cold out of her stomach:"—meaning that Mrs. Lennard had been drinking too much, which till then I had never any notion of. "I am sure," replied I to my trembling companion, as we went down the cellar stairs, and were frightened by the echo of our feet, "I am sure, Betsy, we want something to keep the cold of fear out of *ours*.—Do I tremble as much as you do, and do I look as pale?" "Oh! hush," said she, "hush! I shall drop if I hear a voice—it sounds so among these hollow doors." Her teeth chattered in her head, and she held the candle in her hand so unsteadily that I was afraid it would have gone out. In this manner we proceeded to the bottom of the stairs, which you know are very long, and had got half a dozen paces along the passage, which is, you may remember, very high and narrow and long, when we heard a loud rushing noise at the other end of it. Something came sweep along; but Betsy let fall the candle, and fell herself against the wall, where I endeavoured in vain to support her. She sunk quite down; and, as I stooped to assist her, somebody certainly brushed by me. I know not what I heard afterwards, for fear deprived me of my senses. This, however, lasted but a moment; for, my recollection returning, I was sensible that whatever there was to hurt us, we should do more wisely to endeavour to return back to my aunt's room than to remain in that dismal place. With great difficulty, by rubbing her hands within mine, and reasoning with her as soon as she seemed able to hear it, I prevailed upon Betsy Richards to try to walk. The apprehension that this frightful apparition might return (which she whispered me had the figure of a tall man in a white or light-coloured gown), had more effect upon her than any thing I could say; and she consented to try to return up the stairs. It was so dark, however, that we were obliged to feel our way with our hands; and I own I every moment expected to put them against the frightful figure which my companion had seen."

"But you were wrong there," said the incredulous Orlando; "for if it were a ghost, Monimia, you know a ghost is only air, and of course you could not have touched it.—But tell me how your aunt received you."

"It was, I am sure, almost half an hour before we got back, more dead than alive, to the oak parlour. She asked us very impatiently, what we had been so long about? but neither of us was presently able to answer. She saw how it was by our faces, but very sharply bade us tell her that moment what was the matter. Betsy had then more courage than I had; for I was more afraid of my aunt, if possible, than of the ghost, and so she related as well as she could all she saw or fancied she saw. Mrs. Lennard was extremely angry with us both, and scolded us for a quarter of an hour; which I thought was a little unreasonable towards me, since she was angry with me now for being afraid of the very things she had been teaching me to fear. However, as there was no chance of persuading us to make another attempt that night, and she was disabled by lameness from going herself, she was forced to be content with some other of the cordials she had in her closet; and afterwards she rather wished to have the story hushed up and forgotten, for somehow or other that key of the cellar was never found after that night. The basket and the candle remained where they were dropped; yet the key, which was a very great heavy key, and which I had in my hand, was gone; and Mr. Pattenson would have made such a racket about it, that my aunt, as she had another, let the story drop, and contrived an excuse a week or two afterwards, when she was able to get about herself, to have the lock changed."

"And this is all the reason you have, my Monimia, from your own observation, to believe in spirits?" said Orlando.

"All!" replied she, "and is it not then enough?"

"Not quite, I fear, to convince the scepticism of the present day. I do not, however, wish to prejudice your mind on the other side, by bringing arguments against the possibility of their existence; but I will give your reason an opportunity of deciding for itself. Against to-morrow night, when we shall meet again, I will look out and mark for you all those stories of supernatural appearances that are related by the most reasonable people, and are the best authenticated. You shall fairly enquire whether any of those visits of the dead were ever found to be of any use to the living. We are told that they have been seen (as is reported of that vision which Clarendon tells of),[1] to warn the persons to whom they appeared, or some others to whom they were to repeat their mission, of impending danger. But the danger, however foretold, has never been avoided; and shall we therefore believe, that an all-wise and all-powerful Being shall suffer a general law of nature to be so uselessly violated, and shall make the dead restless, only to terrify the living?"

"Oh! but in cases of murder you know what spectres have appeared!"

"Yes, Monimia, to the conscience of the guilty; but even that is not always ready to raise hideous shadows to persecute the sanguinary monsters who are stained with crimes; for if it were, Monimia, I am afraid not one of our kings or heroes could have slept in their beds."

"And yet," said Monimia shuddering, "and yet Orlando, you sometimes talk of being a soldier!"

"Ah! my sweet friend," replied Orlando, "I have no choice, but must be what they would have me. Yet believe me, Monimia, if I had a choice, it would be to pass all my life in some quiet retirement with you. We should not want either of us to be very rich, for we should certainly be very happy."

To this poor Monimia felt herself quite unable to answer; but sighing deeply, from the fear that it could never be, she tried to turn the discourse: "Is it not very late, Orlando," said she, "and had I not better go?"

"If you insist upon going yet, I shall be half tempted to let you travel through the chapel alone," replied he smiling, "and, to revenge myself for your desertion, expose you to meet the tall man in the white dress." He then led the conversation to other subjects, gave her some books he had selected for her reading, and some materials for writing; and, after insisting upon her promise to meet him the next night, he consented that she should return to her turret. As, with his arm round her waist, he conducted her through the chapel, and still found her tremble, he gently reproached her with it. "Ah!" said she, "Orlando, you are surely unreasonable, if you expect me to be as courageous as you are!" "Not at all," answered he; "for you may derive your confidence from the same source, and say, as I do, *I fear no evil angel, and have offended no good one.*"

---

[1] Ehrenpreis notes that "the Duke of Buckingham was warned of his impending death by a person to whom the ghost of the Duke's father had appeared in a dream (Clarendon, *History of the Rebellion*, Book I, paragraphs 89–93)" (p. 537). Underlying Orlando's exemplary tale are references both to the English civil wars and the American Revolution, to which Orlando will be sent.

Monimia promised to do all she could towards conquering her apprehensions. They were by this time arrived at the door of her chamber, where tenderly kissing her hand, he again bade her good night, or rather good morning, for it was near three o'clock; and waiting till he heard the door safely concealed by her bed, and hearing that all was secure, he turned to his own room, and went to rest in spirits disposed to indulge delicious dreams of happiness to come.

CHAP. VI.

Another and another evening Orlando attended at the turret, and the apprehensions of Monimia decreased in proportion as her reason, aided by her confidence in him, taught her that there was in reality little to fear from the interposition of supernatural agency. The dread of being discovered by people in the house, however, still interrupted the hours which passed with imperceptible rapidity while they were together. This might happen a thousand ways, which Monimia was ingenious in finding out; while Orlando was sometimes successful, and sometimes failed, in ridiculing those apprehensions which he could not always help sharing.

The mind of the innocent Monimia had been till now like that of Miranda in her desert island.[1] To her, the world that was past, and that which was now passing, were alike unknown; and all the impressions that her infant understanding had received, tended only to confirm the artificial influence which her aunt endeavoured to establish over her imagination. Her poverty, her dependence, the necessity of her earning a subsistence by daily labour, had been the only lessons she had been taught; and the only hope held out to her, that of passing through life in an obscure service.

But she had learned now that, abject and poor as she was, she was an object of affection to Orlando, who seemed in her eyes the representation of divinity. The reading he had directed her to pursue, had assisted in teaching her some degree of self-value. She found that to be poor was not disgraceful in the eye of Heaven, or in the eyes of the good upon earth; and that the great Teacher of that religion which she had been bid to profess, though very little instructed in it, was himself poor, and the

---

[1] Miranda is the innocent daughter of Prospero in Shakespeare's *The Tempest*. When she is first introduced, she has never seen a man besides her father.

advocate and friend of poverty. In addition to all this knowledge, so suddenly acquired, she had lately made another discovery. Her aunt had always told her that she was a very plain girl, had a bad person, and was barely fit to be seen; but since the marriage of the servant who had lived at the Hall during the infancy of Monimia, Betty Richards, the under house-maid, had been ordered to do the little that Monimia was allowed to have done in her room. Mrs. Lennard had taken her from the parish officers as an apprentice; and having long seen her only in her coarse gown and nailed shoes, and observed in her manner only a great deal of rustic simplicity, had not the least idea that under that semblance she concealed the cunning and the vanity of a country coquette; and that the first week she passed in Mrs. Rayland's family had called forth these latent qualities. She was a ruddy, shewy girl, with a large but rather a good figure; and her face was no sooner washed, and her hair combed over a roll, than she became an object which attracted the attention of the great Mr. Pattenson himself; who, proceeding in the usual way by which he had won the favour of so many of the subaltern nymphs in Mrs. Rayland's kitchen, began to make her many presents, and to talk of her beauty; and as she could not forbear repeating all these extravagant expressions of his admiration, Monimia could as little help reflecting, though she was some-how humbled as she made the comparison, that if Betty was so hand-some, she could not herself be so ugly as her aunt had always represented her. The fineries which her new friend received Monimia beheld with-out any wish to enjoy such herself; though on Betty, a poor girl bred in a work-house, they had a most intoxicating effect. They were given under the strictest injunctions of secrecy, which was tolerably well observed towards the rest of the house; and the finery, which at first consisted only of beads and ribbands, was reserved for Sunday afternoons, and put on at a friend's cottage near a distant church. But it was not in female nature to conceal these acquisitions from Monimia; and it was in her drawers that they were often deposited, when there was reason to apprehend that the little deal box, which had till lately been amply sufficient for the check apron and linsey-woolsey gown of Betty, might not safely conceal the ribbands "colour of emperors' eyes,"[1] the flowered shawls, the bugle neck-laces, and caps with new edging to them, which she now possessed.

Sometimes, when Betty obtained leave to go out, and thought that, Mrs. Lennard being engaged with her Lady, and the other servants gone

---

[1] Ehrenpreis speculates that Smith refers to "the 'eyes' of the Emperor moth" (p. 537). The quotation remains unidentified.

different ways, she should escape unnoticed across the park, she persuaded Monimia, who knew not how to refuse her any thing, to let her dress at her little glass; and there the progress of rural coquetry had full power to display itself. She tried on her various topknots, disposed her hair in a thousand fanciful ways, and called to Monimia for her opinion, which of them was most becoming; appealing for the authority of these variations to a certain pocket-book, presented her also from the same quarter, which represented in one of its leaves "six young ladies in the most fashionable head-dresses for 1776."[1]

Monimia, with all her ingenuous simplicity, had sense enough to smile at the ridiculous vanity of the girl; and to know, that her accepting all this finery from the old butler was quite wrong. But she felt also that to reprove her for it would look like envy, and that to remonstrate would probably be vain. She contented herself therefore with keeping as much out of her confidence as she could; and had reasons enough of her own, which were continually strengthened by the exhortations of Orlando, for keeping her from being a too frequent visitor in her room.

But the remarks she made upon all this, and upon numberless circumstances in the house which Betty related to her, no longer left her in her original ignorance. In a great house there are among the servants as many cabals, and as many schemes, as among the leaders of a great nation; and few exhibited a greater variety of interests than did the family of Mrs. Rayland. Mrs. Lennard at once hated, feared, and courted Pattenson, who having been taken a boy from the plough, had been gradually promoted till he became the favourite footman of the elder Mrs. Rayland, who, on the death of an old man who had long occupied that post, made him butler; where he was supposed to have accumulated in the course of five-and-twenty years a great deal of money, was known to have several sums out at interest, and had bought two or three small farms in the county, with the approbation of his Lady, whose favour had never once failed him, though various attempts had been made to injure him in her opinion by complaints of his amours. Though he was a perfect Turk in morals,[2] and though in his advanced life he rather indulged than corrected this propensity to libertinism, he had hitherto contrived to escape his Lady's wrath; and indeed knew that

---

[1] This sets the main plot's action as commencing in 1776, the year of the Declaration of Independence.

[2] Late eighteenth-century Britain considered the Turks to be inherently licentious and immoral, and used as evidence the harem and the widely-held assumption that Islam did not believe women to have souls.

nobody but Mrs. Lennard or the old coachman had, among the domestics, interest enough to shake her good opinion of him; and of both the one and the other, though aware that neither of them bore him any good will, he was tolerably secure.

How the prudent and guarded Mrs. Lennard came to be in his power was never fully understood; but in his power she certainly felt herself: for though they were in habits of frequent squabbling about trifles, which indeed with the Lady seemed necessary to break the tedious uniformity of her life, yet whenever she found Mr. Pattenson really angry, she, albeit unused to the condescending mood,[1] began to palliate and apologize—and peace was generally made over some nice thing, and some fine old wine, by way of a *petit souper* in Mr. Pattenson's parlour, after Mrs. Rayland was gone to bed.

The old coachman, who was the other favourite servant, was always a third in these peace-making meetings. He was a man grown unwieldy from excess of good living, and more than seventy years old; but he possessed an infinite deal of cunning, and knew how to get and how to keep money, with which it was his ambition to portion his two daughters, and to marry them to gentlemen; and his dealings in contraband goods, as Rayland Hall was only eight miles from the coast, his having the management of the great farms in hand, and his concern in buying and selling horses, were together supposed to have rendered this object of ambition an easy attainment. Of deeper sagacity than the other two, he foresaw that the time could not be far distant when Rayland Hall, and all the wealth that belonged to it, must change its possessor. It was a plan of Mrs. Lennard and Pattenson to enjoy and to secure all they could now, and to be well assured of a very considerable legacy hereafter. But old Snelcraft had farther hopes; and for that reason, though he had at first opposed as much as he could the reception of Orlando, and since expressed displeasure towards him, he of late had in his head floating visions of the probability there was that, if Orlando came to the estate, he might marry his favourite daughter, Miss Patty Snelcraft, who would have such a fine fortune, and was, as her father believed, the very extract of all beauty. Ridiculous and chimerical as such a project was, the old man, in the dotage of his purse-proud vanity, believed it not only possible but probable: for, though he knew that Mrs. Rayland would have disinherited her own son for entertaining such an idea for a moment, yet he saw that Mr. Orlando had no pride at all; and he was

---

[1]   *Othello*, V.ii.359: "Albeit unused to the melting mood."

pretty sure, from the arrangements that he believed were made as to money, that, great as the sum of ready money would perhaps be that Mrs. Rayland might leave behind her, none of it would be suffered to go to Mr. Orlando. Miss Patty Snelcraft was, as this precious plan got more entirely the possession of her father's imagination, taken from a boarding-school at a neighbouring town, and one luckless day brought to church in all the finery which she had there been accustomed to wear. But the effect was very far from that her parents intended, who expected that Madam would have sent for her to the Hall, as she used to do at breaking up, and have commended her beauty and elegance; instead of which, Mrs. Rayland no sooner arrived at home than she sent for Robin, as she still called her old servant, who now was seldom able to mount the box himself, and asked if it was possible that the tawdry thing she had seen with his wife was his daughter? He answered in all humility that it was his eldest daughter, who, as she had now finished her learning, he had taken home from boarding-school.

"Finished her learning!" exclaimed the old lady; "and is that what she has learned, to dress herself out like a stage-player, like a mountebank's doxy? Upon my word, Robin, I am sorry for you. I thought you and your wife had more sense. What! is that a dress for a sober girl, who ought to be a help to her mother, and to take care of her father in his old age?"

"She does, Ma'am, do both, I'll assure you," answered Robin, terribly stung by this reproof, "and is a very good and dutiful child. And as to her fineries, Ma'am, and such like, you are sensible that I'm not myself no judge of them there things; and my wife I believe thought, that seeing how by your goodness and my long and faithful service we are well to pass, for our condition and circumstances and such like, there would not be no offence whatsumdever in dressing our poor girls, being we have but two, a little dessent and neat, just to shew that one is no beggar after having served in such a good family so many years."

The lady, a little softened by this speech, which was made in almost a crying tone of voice, replied, "Well well, good Robin, I know how to make allowances; but do you and your wife learn for the future to make a more modest use of the means you are blessed with, and never encourage your girls to vanity and extravagance. Here's Mary here, Lennard's niece, whom I give leave to be in the house (Monimia stood waiting all this time with the chocolate, which the old lady always swallowed as soon as she came in from her devotions), she, I assure you, comes of parents that many people would call genteel; and yet you see, as it has pleased Providence to make her a dependant and a servant, I never suffer her to stick herself out in feathers and flowers like a May-day girl."

The lecture ended, and the old coachman withdrew, extremely discontent that his Patty had been compared to the house-keeper's niece, who was, as he muttered to himself, a mere pauper; and Monimia was not at all flattered by being brought forward as a comparison for Miss Snelcraft, whom the servants, and particularly Betty, had been turning into ridicule for her awkward finery and airs of consequence—nor did the expression, that she was born of parents whom some people would call genteel, at all sweeten the bitterness of this comparison. Monimia, who had before in the course of the day received a severe mortification from her aunt, in being refused leave to go to church, now, as soon as her service in waiting on Mrs. Rayland with the chocolate was performed, withdrew to her own room, and indulged her tears. At length she recollected that, though all the rest of the world might despise and contemn her, the heart of Orlando was hers; she was secure of his affection; he would repeat it to her at night, when he had promised to fetch her to his room: and these reflections dried her eyes, and dissipated her sorrows: they even lent her force to bear, without betraying her impatience, the intrusion of Betty Richards, who soon after asked leave to come in. "Oh, laud! my dear miss," cried she, as soon as she entered the room, "how we be shut up in this here old place like two little singing-birds in a cage!—I've been trying to persuade old Jenny to let me take her turn this a'ternoon to go to church, and have promised to give her two turns for one; but the cross old witch says indeed she chooses to go herself.—Oh lud lud! I'd give a little finger to go."[1]

"And why are you so eager to go to-day, Betty, more than any other afternoon?"

"Oh gad!" replied the girl, "for five hundred reasons:—first, because it's so early that I could get away to West Wolverton church with all the ease in the world, and 'tis such a sweet afternoon, and winter will be here now soon; besides that—but you must not tell for an hundred pounds—my good old fat sweetheart brought me home last night the most beautifullest bonnet, such as the milliner told him was worn by the tip-top quality in Lonnon—and I die to wear it, and to go to West Wolverton church in it this very afternoon; for at ours, you know, I dares as well jump into the fire as put it on."

---

[1] Betty shows her ill-breeding and inherent inferiority (rather than a purely class-bound one) in her oaths: "laud" and "lud" (Lord), "gad" (God), "Lord," and later "Gemini."

"But why do your bonnet and your piety conspire to carry you so far just this very evening, Betty," said Monimia smiling, "when both East Wolverton and "Bartonwick have an evening church, and are not much more than half as far?"

"Oh! thereby hangs a tale—What! You hadn't heard then, I suppose, of all the great doings at West Wolverton?"

This was the name of the village in which was situated the house of Mr. Somerive.—"Great doings!" repeated Monimia, changing colour; "no, I have heard of nothing."

"Why then you must know, Miss, that Mr. Orlando, who was not here last night—

(Monimia knew it well, for they had agreed two nights before not to meet till the present evening)—

"Mr. Orlando, I say, came over about an hour ago, just as my Lady came from church, and after walking backwards and forwards in his melancholy fashion, with a book in his hand, upon the broad pavement in the chapel court, which really oft-times rives one's very heart to see him, he went away to his study. For my part, I was sitting in the window up stairs for a moment, for I had just been making up my Lady's fire before she came from church—when all of a sudden I saw John Dickman, 'Squire Somerive's groom, come riding up; so down I went to speak to him. He gave me a letter, which I carried in to Orlando, who seemed monstrous surprised at it, as he was but that minute as 'twere come from home; and when I went back to the kitchen John told me, he was ordered to wait for his young master—for that Madam Somerive's brother, the London merchant, was come down, with some of his family, sons and daughters, and the gentleman from some part beyond sea, who was to marry the eldest Miss Somerive, for he had got his father's consent, and the wedding was to take place out of hand. And so," added Betty, who had almost talked herself out of breath, "and so, as Mr. Phil. is out, gone as he always is upon a visit to they newcomers up at Castle, the 'Squire he ordered John to fetch *our* Orlando out of hand home to entertain all this grand company."

"And he went!" said Monimia in a faint voice, who had changed colour a dozen times during this narration.

"Oh, Lord! yes, to be sure he went," replied Betty; yet somehow he look'd to me as if he had rather of stay'd; and hung about for some time, as thof unwilling to go. Lord! sir, said I, as I went to shut up his windows before he lock'd the study door—Lord, how strange it is that you are not like other young men, and never cares nothing for company and such like! He only sighed, a sweet creature!—when I'm sure, if all the grand lords and dukes, and even the King, and the Prince of Wales, and the Archbishop of Osnabig,[1] and all his majesty's court, were to be collected together, there's not one of them to be compared to young 'Squire Orlando—Lord! what would I give to see all these gentlefolks together at West Wolverton church, and that dear sweet Orlando out-shining them all!"

"And that was the reason," said Monimia in a still fainter voice, "that you are satisfied with no church but West Wolverton? But after all, Betty, pray are you sure these ladies and gentlemen will be there?"

"As sure as five pence—for John Dickman told me so. Oh! that I could but go!—for Orlando, you know, Miss, who is the sweetest temper'd good-naturdest creatur in all England, would never tell if he saw one ever so smartly drest:—No, egollys! he's more like to give one some trifle or other to help one out, than to blab to get one anger."

"Has he ever given you any thing, Betty?" said Monimia, in a voice the tremor of which she could not disguise; for, mingled with number-less other sensations, something like a half-formed jealousy and suspicious apprehension now entered her heart—"tell me, Betty, what has he ever given you?"

"Why I assure you," replied the girl pertly, "not above a month ago neither, after he had been here for almost a fort-night, he called me to him as I was a dusting of them there guns and arrows and what d'yecallums, as hangs over the chimney in that parlour as you goes through to get to his study—And so, says he, Betty, you've a good deal of trouble in cleaning of my room and making my fire, and perhaps your lady may not recollect it, and so may not make you a consideration for it; and there-fore, Betty, I beg you'll accept this, and I wish I had it in my power to do better.—And if you'll believe me, Miss, it was a brand new crown, quite new, a crown piece they told me it was. I would have given any thing not to have changed it, but to have laid it up as a keepsake—But there!—I had not money enough without it to buy my new cotton gown, when Alexander Macgill the Scotchman called here; and so away went my poor dear crown, though I had leverer have parted with one of my fingers."

"You did right, however," said Monimia coldly; "the gown you wanted, and the crown, I dare say, Mr. Orlando meant you should use."

"I suppose he did, a dear sweet creature!—Lord a mercy! what would I give to have a peep at his sweet face this afternoon! I'll tell you what, Miss, though you cannot go to church, nor I neither, we might ten to

---

[1]   "Osnabig" is a variant of "Osnabrück." It also describes a coarse linen originally made in Osnabrück: even when describing Orlando, Betty's mind focuses on clothes.

one see these gentlefolks ride by, if we could but steal up to the upper park, and so through the little common. 'Tis not much better than three miles, and we might not be miss'd."

"No," said Monimia drily, "I shall run no such risk indeed of making my aunt angry; and besides, what would Mr. Somerive, or Mr. Orlando, or any other of them think if they saw us there?"

"Hang their thoughts!" replied Betty; "what would it signify to us what any body thought, if we pleased ourselves? I'll go and see how the land lays, and if the two old girls have done their dinner, and are set down together to take their afternoon's dose."

"Do not come back then, Betty," said Monimia; "for I certainly will not go out without leave, and you know it's nonsense to ask it—therefore, if you like it, go; but I assure you I shall not."

Having thus released herself from her importunate visitor, Monimia sat down to consider all she had told her. That Orlando should quit the house without telling her, gave her at first extreme pain; yet a moment's reflection convinced her that, unless he had made a confidante of Betty, of which she now saw all the danger, there was no possible way of his conveying to her intelligence of the sudden summons he had received from his father; for Mrs. Lennard was at home, and had shut herself up in her own room to do twenty little services which she frequently chose to have performed on Sunday mornings. A thousand doubts now arose in the mind of Monimia, whether he would be able to call for her at night; a thousand apprehensions lest the people he was with, particularly his uncle's daughters, whom he had said were very pretty women, should estrange his thoughts from her, and rob her of his affections. These fears were so acute, that she was trying to drive them from her, when Betty returned, and, finding the door of her room fastened, tapped softly at it, and cried, "Miss, miss! who will refuse to go to the park now!"

"You have not surely got leave!"

"No, nor I have not asked it; but the old ladies are hard set in to their good things. Madam has had a gouty feel in her stomach all day, she says, and that's always a symptom for a double dose; and as to your aunt, she has been ailing too, and will not flinch her share, you know very well."

Monimia, alarmed at the loud whisper, had opened the door before the end of this speech, and let in her unwelcome companion, who now repeated, that every body was safely bestowed who could interrupt them; and that, as it was still very early, they might have a good chance of seeing some of these comers, and above all Orlando, in their evening ride. But Monimia, who was displeased with the familiar way in which the girl named Orlando, and knew that he would object to her walking with her, assumed a virtue when she had it not; and though she believed they might safely go the way she proposed, and return before the hour when it was likely her aunt would want her; though she would have given half the world only for the chance of seeing Orlando at a distance, she positively refused—and had the resolution to see Betty set out by herself, with her new "most beautifullest" bonnet pinned under her petticoat, which she proposed putting on when she got clear of the house; and then Monimia, forcing her attention from what had the last few hours engaged it, sat down to the sort of lesson which Orlando had last marked for her, and which she had promised to make herself mistress of before she saw him again;—though, alas! while she read, the idea of the superior advantages enjoyed by the Miss Woodfords, his cousins, their beauty, and the probability there was that one of them might be intended for him, too frequently distracted her thoughts, and impeded her good intentions.

CHAP. VII.

The day had been unusually warm; but towards evening a thunderstorm came on, and, as it grew later, a tempest of wind, with heavy and continual rain.

Betty, sulky that Monimia refused, and still more sulky that she had got nothing by her long walk, but nearly spoiling all her finery, had not come to Monimia's room any more; but she received, at the usual hour, the usual summons for tea. She thought both Mrs. Lennard and her aunt uncommonly peevish and tedious, and that the sermon one was reading, while the other fell a sleep, was most unreasonably long. At length she was dismissed, and, retiring to her turret, began to listen to the wind that howled in tremendous gusts among the trees, and to the rain falling in torrents, the rushing of which was redoubled by the leaden pipes that from the roof of her turret threw the water in columns on the pavement below. Would Orlando come? Through such a tempest it were hardly to be wished he should. Having been absent all day, there would be no fire in his room, he would be drenched with rain, and half dead with cold. Monimia then could not desire he should come; yet she felt, in despite of her reason, that she should be very unhappy if he did not; for, though so many causes might combine to detain him, her humble ideas of herself, and the pictures she had made of the beauty and attractions of the Miss Woodfords, added another which rendered her wretched. "Alas!" cried she, "Orlando among them will be too happy to think of me; and it is quite ridiculous to suppose that he will quit these ladies, to come through the storm almost five miles to poor Monimia. No, no! Orlando will not come."

Still however she could not determine to go to bed, at least till the hour was past for which he had made the appointment. At the usual time her aunt, who now frequently omitted to come herself, sent Betty for her candle, and her door was locked as usual, for that was a ceremony which either in person or proxy was always performed. But Monimia now no longer passed the long interval between half after nine o' clock and the hour when Orlando usually called her, in darkness; for he had furnished her with the means of procuring a light, and with small wax candles. One of these she now lit, and endeavoured to sit down to read—but the violence of the wind, which she fancied every moment increased, and the flashes of lightning which she saw through her narrow casement, to which there was no shutter, distracted her attention; and she could only sit in miserable anxiety, listening to the various noises which in such a tempestuous night are heard around an old building, and especially such a part of it as she inhabited; where, around the octagon tower or turret, the wind roared with violence from every point; while, in the long passages which led from thence to her aunt's apartments, it seemed yet more enraged, from being confined. She now traversed her small room with fearful steps; now sat down on her bed, near the door, that she might the more readily hear Orlando if he should come; and now got on a chair, and opened her casement to observe if there seemed any probability of the storm's abating; but still, though the thunder had ceased, the clouds, driven against each other by violent and varying gusts of wind, produced vivid flashes of lightening, which suddenly illuminated the whole park. But Orlando came not, and it was now near an hour past his usual time. Again the poor anxious Monimia, now half despairing of his coming, and trying to persuade herself that she did not wish he should come, traversed her room—again went to her window. Another and another hour passed: amidst the heavy gusts and mournful howlings of the wind, she had counted the clock, that, with a more than usually hollow sound, told twelve, one, two—Orlando certainly did not mean to come—no! it was unreasonable to suppose he would; unreasonable to flatter herself that he would quit a cheerful circle of his relations, to traverse the extensive commons and lanes, and all the park, that lay between West Wolverton and the Hall, in such a night, when no person would think of going out but on life and death. Yet, while she thus argued with herself, a few tears involuntarily stole from her eyes; and as she gave up all hopes of his coming, and lay down in her clothes on the bed (for she had not the resolution to undress herself), she sighed deeply, and said to herself: "And yet, if it had been me who was expected, I do not believe any storm could have hindered me from trying to see Orlando! and I am sure no company would.—Yet he is quite in the right, I know, and I do not blame him."

She could not, however fatigued and weary, close her eyes for some time. The clock at length struck three; and soon after, wearied with watching and anxiety, she fell into unquiet repose.

Suddenly, without being conscious how long she had indulged it, she started from her sleep, and fancied she heard the well-known signal: she listened a moment; it was repeated. Trembling with joy, yet equally agitated by fear, she arose and answered it; and removing the impediments that were between them, and again lighting her candle, Orlando stepped into the room.

His clothes and his hair were streaming with water, and he said hastily, as he came through the hangings, "You had given me over, my Monimia, had you not?"—"Long ago," replied she, with an apprehensive countenance, which yet was lightened up with pleasure. "And now I am come, Monimia," reassumed he, "you must suffer me to remain here, for I cannot get into my own room: the chapel doors, you know, are fastened within side, and by the usual way at this hour of the night it is impossible. I can stay but a moment; but I could not bear to be so many hours without seeing you; and besides, I had no means of letting you know why I went so suddenly from hence, and I fear you have been unhappy."

"I should have been unhappy indeed, if Betty, who heard it from the servant who came for you, had not told me as a piece of news, that company had arrived unexpectedly at West Wolverton.—And in such a night, Orlando, was it possible to expect you could leave them to come so far? How good it is of you!—And yet you will suffer, I fear, from your wet clothes. Good God! what can I do to prevent your suffering?"

"Be not uneasy about that, my angel friend," replied Orlando; "such trifles I never attend to, and never suffer from; if you will let me sit down here with you, I will take off my great coat, and my other clothes are not so very wet. At this hour there will surely be nothing to apprehend from my staying here."

"I hope not," said Monimia, "I hope not, if we speak low. The wind is so high, that any trifling noise could hardly be heard by my aunt if she were upon the watch, which I hope she is not." "You are generous to indulge me," answered Orlando, "and I must be a monster to dream of injuring such innocence and candour. But, Monimia, there are a thousand uneasy thoughts continually crowding upon me about you. This Betty Richards—I am afraid she is a bad girl; I am sure she is an artful one; and there is an alliance of some sort or other between her and the old butler: you will never trust her, Monimia?"

"Never indeed," replied Monimia; "for though she is of late much thrown in my way since my aunt has become more indolent from her accident, I never willingly am with her; nor do I indeed like her so well as I used to do."

"Continue to keep yourself then from much intimacy, Monimia; for the conversation of such a girl, to a mind pure and unsullied like yours, is to be dreaded. It is coarse at least, if not vicious; and if it be not dangerous, is at all events improper. Discourage therefore her talking to you as much as you can, even about the tittle tattle of the house." Monimia most readily promised to obey him:—and then observing that he looked at her with a peculiar expression of uneasiness in his countenance, she said, "But is that all, Orlando? Is there not something else that gives you concern?" "Yes," replied he; "I will not conceal from you that there are many things. This wedding of my sister's, though I most sincerely rejoice that she is likely to be happily settled, seems to teem with troubles for me."

Monimia turned pale, but only clasped her hands together as she sat by him, and did not interrupt him. He went on.

"My uncle Woodford piques himself extremely upon having brought about this marriage; for the father of the young man (a merchant at Corke in very great business) for some time positively refused his consent, because of Philippa's want of fortune. My uncle, you know, or rather you do not know, is just the reverse of my mother, and is as bustling and spirited as she is mild and tranquil. Having got his money himself, he has no notion that any thing but money is worth thinking about, and that the money is best that is made in trade; and therefore, as he has only one son, who does not choose to take up his business, but is studying at the Temple,[1] he has adopted a notion, that it would be

---

[1] The Temple was one of the Inns of Court which held the main lawyers' premises. Prospective lawyers lived and studied here.

much better for me to go with him to London, and learn his business of a wine merchant, to which I may succeed."

"And marry one of your cousins," said Monimia in a faint voice, "who are, you have told me, such pretty women?" "If that is part of his plan," answered Orlando, "my Monimia, he has kept it to himself.—But I do not believe it is, as one of them is engaged, and the other would not think me either smart enough or rich enough. Whatever may be Mr. Woodford's plan, however, that part of it will certainly never take effect; nor indeed will any of it, for I feel a total disinclination to it."

"Why then are you so distrest, Orlando, at the proposal?"

"Because I see it makes my father restless—not exactly the proposal, so much as the conversation my uncle has held with him.—He has been declaiming against the folly of my dreaming away my time in waiting for a legacy from Mrs. Rayland; which after all, said he, the whimsical old woman may not give him—and what if she does? If she acts as she ought, the estate, you know, brother Somerive, ought to be your eldest son Phil's; and if she gives the rest of your family three or four thousand pounds each, what will that do for your youngest son? Why, not give him salt to his porridge."

"Dear papa," said Maria, "what an expression!"—"Well, well, child," answered my uncle, "I can't stand to pick my words, when I am as anxious about a thing as I am about this—I say, and every man who knows the world will agree with me—I say, that a fine young fellow like my nephew here ought not to waste his life nailed to the gouty chair of a peevish old woman, who ten to one dies and bilks him at last. Let him be put into some way of doing for himself—every man who knows the world will agree with me—let him be put into some way of doing for himself; and then, if Mrs. Rayland has a mind to be a friend to him, take my word for it she'll do it so much the sooner. I'm sure of it, for I've remarked it in my dealings among mankind, and every man who knows the world will agree with me, that people are always more ready to help those who are in a way of doing well, than those that hang about helpless. If Orlando here was in a way of getting forward in the world, why you'd see that the old girl would be twice as kind to him—or, if she was not, why he need not so much care."

"I found," continued Orlando, "that this discourse, though my father did not perfectly assent to the justice of all its arguments, made a deep impression on his mind, which had long been disturbed by the difficulty of finding for me some proper line of conduct for my future establishment: and the determination is, that Mrs. Rayland is to be applied to for her opinion as to my sister's marriage, by way of compliment; and in regard to me, by way of sounding her intentions. It appears to me to be all very bad policy; and I foresee nothing but vexation, perhaps my removal from hence."

Orlando paused a moment; and Monimia, with a deep and tremulous sigh, repeated, "From hence!—Alas! Orlando, I have foreseen that the happiness I have so little a while enjoyed of seeing you would not last long!"

"I know not," replied he. "I may be too easily alarmed; but, with the bustle and fuss my uncle makes about every thing he pursues, he seldom fails of carrying his point; and he is now elated with his success over the prudent and worldly-minded Mr. Fitz-Owen, and believes his interposition would every where prove as infallible as it has done in hurrying up this marriage for Philippa."

"Do you think it then too much hurried?" said Monimia.

"I hardly know," replied he, "how to think it otherwise. Mr. Fitz-Owen is a very young man: he only saw Philippa half a dozen times when she was in town last spring with my uncle; and he has insisted upon this match with as much vehemence as he could have done had he known all her good qualities."

"That," said Monimia, "is a very grave reflection. If Philippa has the good qualities of which the gentleman is ignorant, the discovery that beauty is her least perfection will increase his happiness."

"But what does she know of *him*, Monimia? What opportunity can she have had to judge of a man with whom she is engaged to pass her life? Surely the acquaintance of a fortnight is very insufficient to form her judgment of a character on which the happiness of her whole life is to depend. Mr. Fitz-Owen may be a very good-tempered and worthy man; but, as he is the native of another country, it is impossible we should know whether he is or no. However, I keep all these reflections to myself; for the affair is settled, and my father seems pleased with it. Philippa too seems to become attached to Mr. Fitz-Owen. There is something very flattering to a young woman in the attention and perseverance he has shewn. He has a good person, and she really I believe likes him."

"But you do not, Orlando?"

"I do not dislike him—I only wish I knew more of his temper; and I wish too that my bustling busy uncle had not contrived to connect my affairs with those of this wedding, and to hurry every thing with a precipitation that hardly gives one time to breathe. It was only on Thursday evening that Fitz-Owen arrived from Dublin with his father's consent: on Friday he delivered his credentials; and on Saturday the impetuous Mr. Woodford whirled him, with his own daughters and his officious self, down to us, where he pursues his plan with the same vehemence; for he has already settled with my father, that the letter to Mrs. Rayland is to be written to-morrow, and on Wednesday Philippa and Isabella, and, if Mrs. Rayland consents, I also, return with them to London," (Monimia shuddered, and checked an involuntary emotion she felt to implore Heaven aloud that Mrs. Rayland might be inexorably averse to this scheme), "where," continued Orlando, "the marriage is to take place as soon as the usual forms can be gone through—Philippa is to set off to Ireland with her husband, and Isabella is to remain the winter with the Woodfords; my uncle being sure, he says, of getting her married as well as he has done Philly."

"Alas! Orlando, you will go then; for Mrs. Rayland, however she may dislike such a proposal, will not, I am afraid, oppose it: there is something so odd in her temper, that, though she is offended if her advice is not asked, she will seldom give it when it is, especially if she believes any other person has been consulted first."

"I understand her perfectly, my Monimia, and I see nothing but vexation gathering for me in every quarter. Alas! it is not one of the least, that, while these people remain, my father expects me to stay at home; though, as my brother is so good as to promise to come hither to-morrow, I think I might be spared."

"And has your brother," said Monimia, "been consulted on this plan of your going into business with your uncle?"

"Oh, yes! It was opened to him after dinner, while I had left the room a moment to consider by what means I could get to you; and I found him eagerly promoting it for reasons which I heartily forgive, while I thank God I feel myself incapable of harbouring such sentiments towards him, could we change situations. I must follow my destiny, Monimia, whatever it may be; for I must not make my poor father, and still less my mother, unhappy. They have too many uneasy hours about Philip; and while the marriage of Philippa gives them some satisfaction, it shall not be embittered by any opposition of mine to what they may think right for me—and yet I own, Monimia, I own, that to go with Mr. Woodford, to be confined to that sort of business, would make me most completely wretched." He said this in a tone of voice so expressive of despondence, that Monimia, oppressed as she was before, could conceal the anguish she felt no longer. Still, however, she tried to check the excess of her sorrow, while he tenderly soothed her, assuring her that, whatever might be his fate, he should love her to the end of his life; and if he thought that the drudgery of a few years at any business, however irksome to him, would enable him to pass the rest of his life in moderate competence with her, he would submit to it, not only as a duty, but as a blessing. "And now, my Monimia, let us consider how we can meet to-morrow night—by that time something may more decidedly be known.—I will come then early in the morning, before this letter, of which I dread the event, is sent; and, under pretence of enquiring how Mrs. Rayland does, and then of going into the study for some of my clothes, which I often leave there, I can open the chapel door, and prepare every thing for our going to the study the next evening; for to live without seeing you, Monimia, is impossible, and I fear to meet here often might be too hazardous."

"It would indeed," replied Monimia, "and even now I have been in misery the whole time—Yet it was so late, Orlando, before you came!"

"It was two o'clock before I could leave the company; for my uncle is a man who loves to sit long over his wine, to tell what he thinks good stories, and call for toasts and songs, suffering nobody to quit the room as long as they can distinguish the glass from the candle. My father, very little used to this sort of conviviality, was tired, and left us to manage him as we could.—My brother would have remained with him till now, I dare say, most willingly; but he had promised to be at Stockton's, with whom he now almost entirely lives, to a great hunting party this morning; and he dashed through the rain about one o'clock. Fitz-Owen got extremely drunk, and was extremely noisy; and I found there was no way for me to escape but by feigning to be in the same situation; by which stratagem I was at length released; and flew, Monimia, with impatience to thee, dear source of all the happiness I have, or ever hope to have, on earth!"

It was now so near the dawn of day, that Monimia besought him to consider the danger there was, if he staid longer, of being observed in his departure by the labourers coming to their work. Orlando owned there was something to fear, yet felt unusually reluctant to go, and lingered till the break of day was very visible through the casement. He then tore himself away, and escaped from the turret without observation; but in crossing the park he was seen at a distance by the footman, who was up on some scheme of his own. As great rewards were offered for the detection of poachers, and the fellow concluded Orlando to be one, he hastily called one of the grooms; and they went round together to another part of the park, by which they thought this intruder must pass; and, as Orlando was mounting the stile, he was amazed to find himself suddenly collared by one man, and rudely seized by the arm by another. His uncommon strength and activity enabled him to disengage himself instantly from both. They as instantly discovered their mistake, and with a thousand apologies returned to the house: but this unlucky rencounter was afterwards talked of in the family; and though the conjectures to which it gave rise were remote from the truth, they yet failed not to disturb the tranquillity of the young lovers.

CHAP. VIII.

Mr. Somerive, after many debates with himself, and many conversations with his wife, at length determined to write to Mrs. Rayland: it was indeed necessary to pay her the compliment of consulting her on the marriage of his daughter; and he thought it not an improper opportunity to try what were her intentions in regard to Orlando, by hinting that an occasion now offered to establish him advantageously in trade.

The arguments of Mr. Woodford had not on this point so much influence as to prevent his fearing the experiment he was about to make; but the conduct of his eldest son, which nothing could restrain, made him look forward with fear to the future. He found his own health very much injured, by the uneasiness he had lately undergone; and he knew that should he die, the only dependance of his wife and his unmarried daughters must be on Orlando, and on the friendship of Woodford. To put his son therefore into business with his wife's brother was certainly a very desirable plan, if Mrs. Rayland did not intend better to provide for him; and it was certainly time to know whether she had or had not any such intentions in his favour.

The letter then which Orlando so dreaded, was written, after great precautions in choosing the words. It requested her approbation of his eldest daughter's marriage with Mr. Fitz-Owen, the only son of an eminent merchant at Corke; and said, that as Orlando was now of an age in which it became necessary to think of his future establishment, thoughts were entertained of putting him into business with his uncle; but that nothing would be concluded upon without the entire approbation of Mrs. Rayland, to whose notice and protection he was so much obliged.

A servant was sent with this letter about noon. It was received and read in due form, and a verbal message returned, that Mrs. Rayland would at her leisure write an answer, and send one of her own servants with it.

On this occasion Mrs. Rayland talked to Lennard—not to consult her, for it was an affair in which she thought herself alone competent to judge—but to give vent to her spleen, and to express her dislike of all people in trade, and particularly of poor Mrs. Somerive. "Those vulgar mundungus folks," said she, "will not suffer the family to better by their chance connection with a gentleman—Let them marry their girls, if they will, to dealers and chapmen; I shall never interfere: they are all like the mother, and may make good tradesmen's wives; though, if Mr. Somerive had not, like his foolish father, had a low taste, his daughters might have married men of family, who would have been proud to be allied, though distantly, to ours. As it is, they must carry their cherry cheeks to a lower market—I shall never oppose it. But for Orlando, there was something of an air of good blood about him, that almost made me doubt at times his birth by his mother's side. However, if he gets these buying and selling notions in his head, and chooses his mother's low origin should continue to be remembered, I have done. I suppose he's got among them—a fine flashy set of tradesfolks—and enters into their amusements and views; and if so, *I* shall never disturb him, let him go his own way; only I shall not choose to have a shop-keeper an inmate at Rayland Hall."

Monimia, who was called down a moment before to assist in cutting out linen, was present during this harangue, for they considered her as a mere cypher. She found herself terribly affected by the opening of it; but when it proceeded to speak of Orlando, she measured four times instead of two, notched a piece of Irish cloth in the wrong place, and was beginning to use her scissors the wrong way, when a severe look from Mrs. Lennard, who snatched it out of her hand, with "What are you about, mope?" restored her to her recollection. She begged pardon; and another look from her aunt bade her beware that she did not offend a second time—when Mrs. Rayland thus went on:

"After a taste for *such* company, this place must be very dull: drinking and jollity, I suppose, are soon learned. And so Mr. Orlando has not been here these two days! Mighty well; he is his own master—Lennard! he has not called this morning, has he?"

Monimia, by a glance of her eye, saw him at that moment pensively and dejectedly crossing the park on foot. She dared not however say so; but finding herself quite unequal to the misery of being present at an interview, in which she foresaw that, in consequence of this fatal letter, he would be forbidden the house, and seeing that her aunt determined she *should* stay, she hung her foot as if by accident in the long roll of linen that was on the ground, and, in pretending to disengage it, fell with some violence against an old heavy gilt leather screen that went across one side of the large room, and ran the sharp-pointed scissors, with which she was cutting the linen, into her arm a little above the wrist.

Her aunt, however, did not perceive it, till the blood streamed from her arm, round which, without any complaint, she wrapped her handkerchief. The paleness and faintness, which she could not disguise, were accounted for when Mrs. Lennard saw the handkerchief bathed in blood. Monimia, who was actually sinking to the earth, though not from the wound, was then dismissed, while Betty was called to take care of the careless girl, and ordered to put some Friar's balsam[1] to the cut; and she just tottered out of one door as Orlando, after sending up for permission, entered at the other. This was fortunate; for, had he beheld her in such a situation, and had she at that moment seen him, their intelligence could hardly have been concealed. The looks Mrs. Lennard had cast on her, when she first appeared confused, had impressed her with terror, and, she fancied, menaced all that was dreadful. With difficulty, and leaning on Betty's arm, she reached her turret; where, under pretence that the accident of having hurt her arm had turned her sick, she begged a glass of water, and lay down, being otherwise unable to conceal from Betty the agitation of her spirits, and the terror she was in for the reception of Orlando.

Mrs. Rayland, instead of the kindness she was used to shew him, now received him with the most cold and repulsive formality. "Your servant, Mr. Orlando—Please to take a chair," was all she said; and in the manner of her saying it, Orlando saw abundant cause to fear that his father's letter had undone him with Mrs. Rayland.

"I find we are to lose you, Sir!—you are going to turn merchant, or shopkeeper!"

"Not, Madam," replied Orlando, "if you think my doing so a wrong measure."

"Oh! Sir, I never pretend to dictate. Every one knows their own affairs best; and by all means *you* ought to follow your father's orders and your own inclinations."

"Alas, dear Madam!" replied Orlando, with a sort of spirited humility that well became him, "my father's orders would, I believe, in this case be given with reluctance; and though *I* should obey them, it would be with reluctance indeed!"

---

[1] "Friar's balsam" is a tincture of benzoin compound used to treat skin ulcers and other wounds.

"What, Sir! (relaxing a little of her vinegar aspect) is it not your own desire then that you should be put apprentice or journeyman to this person, this brother of your mother's? I thought, for my part, that finding perhaps, like your brother and other gay young men, that the country was very dull, you chose probably to figure in London; for it is trades people now that can best afford to shew away, as witness the newcomers at poor Lord Carloraine's fine place—those what d'ye callums—they were trades-people—yet nobody can attempt to live as they do. If such things can be done by trade, no wonder young men are eager to begin. The Hall, Mr. Orlando, must be a dull place, when once you have got these fine doings in your head."

"Madam," said Orlando trembling, for he now found that his fate depended on the event of this dialogue—"Madam, I have always avoided the meanness of adulation, nor will I use it now; you ought to despise me if I did; and I know you have generosity enough to have bestowed all the favours I have received from you, without expecting me to sacrifice my integrity or my freedom."

Mrs. Rayland did not very clearly comprehend this sentence. It was partly complimentary, and therefore to her taste; but the words *sacrifice* and *freedom,* at the end, on which a strong emphasis was laid, sounded a little like rebellion. She therefore screwed up her visage to its former asperity, and answered: "No, indeed, Sir, *I* expect no sacrifices from any body; and as to freedom—every body is free to do as they like best in their own affairs, as I told you before."

"You will not then, Madam, suspect me of meanness unworthy equally of my respect for you and what I owe myself, if I declare to you, that I have no wish to enter into trade, for which I am very certain I have no talents; and that, though I must obey my father if he insists upon it, yet I shall be very unhappy, and had rather, infinitely rather, if you will have the goodness to permit it, remain at home, with the advantage of being allowed sometimes, in paying my respects to you, to have, as I have had for some months, the use of your library; where I hope I am qualifying myself for one of the liberal professions against the time when my father can find an opportunity to place me in one: and in the mean time, I call God to witness, that, to associate with such people as Mr. Stockton, or to emulate his splendour, is so far from being my wish, that to be compelled to do it would be the greatest punishment that could be inflicted upon me."

"I believe, cousin Orlando, I believe—and I am pleased to see it—you have some understanding; and indeed, young man, I think too well of you to wish to see you a tradesman." "Cousin Orlando," were, he well knew, words that always portended good humour, and were never used but on days of high favour. They now sounded most soothingly in the ears of Orlando.—"Will you then, Madam, be so very good, when you take the trouble to answer my father's letter, to express your sentiments on this matter? and I am sure he will then press it no farther."

"I shall tell him, child," replied she, "that I think you may do better; and for the present, as you are not idle, that you may go on with your studies at the Hall."

Orlando, in raptures at having carried his point, thanked his venerable cousin a thousand times. He never thought her so reasonable before: she never fancied him so much like her grandfather Sir Orlando; and so many civilities passed between them, that, before they parted, she gave him a bank-note of ten pounds, and he was admitted to the honour of kissing her hands. In this excellent humour, which Mrs. Lennard did not discourage, he left her, went into the study to secure his admittance in the evening, and to recover himself of the extreme perturbation he was in, before he returned to the party with whom he was to dine at home.

Mrs. Rayland then having called for her writing materials, which seldom saw the sun, and being placed in form at her rose-wood writing-box, lined with green velvet and mounted in silver, produced, at the end of four hours, the following letter, piquing herself on spelling as her father spelt, and disdaining those idle novelties by which a few superfluous letters are saved.

Rayland Hall, 12th day of September, A.D. 1776.

"Sir, my kinsman,

"I have received youre letter, and am oblidged by your taking the troubbel to informe me of youre famely affairs, to the wich I am a sinceer goode wisher. In respecte to youre daughter Philippa must begge to be excused from giving my opinion, not haveing the pleasure to know the gentleman, and being from my retired life no judge of the personnes charactere, who are remote and in bisness, as I understande this personne is; wherefore I can onleye thereupon saie, that doubtlesse you, being as you are a goode and carefulle father, will take due care and precaution that youre daughtere shall not, by her marriage, be exposed to the mischances of becoming reduced by bankruptcies and other accidents, whereby peopel in trade are oft times grate sufferers—But your care herein for your daughter's securitye is not to be questionned. Furthermore, respecting youre youngest sonne, Mr. Orlando, he is very certainelye at youre disposal also, and you are, it may be, the most competent judge of that which is fitting to bee done for his future goode and advantage. I wish him very well; he seeming to me to be a sober, promising, and well conditioned youthe; and such a one as, were I his neerer relation, I shoulde thinke a pitye to put to a trade. I am at present alwaies glad of his companie at the Hall, and willinge to give anye littel encourragement to his desier of learninge in the liberal sciences fitting for a gentleman, the wich his entring on a shoppe or warehouse would destroye and put an ende to. However that may bee, I saie again, that you, being his father, are to be sure the propperest personne to determine for him, and he is dutiefullie inclined, and willinge to obey you. Yet by the discourse I have had with him there-upponne, it doth not appeare that the youthe himself is inclined to become a dealer, as you purpose.

"Heartilie recommending you in my prayers to the Disposer of all goode giftes, and hoping he will directe you in all thinges for the well-doing of your famely, I remaine,

Sir, my kinsman,
youre well-wisher
and humbel servant,
GRACE RAYLANDE."

This letter was received at Wolverton while Mr. Somerive, his two sons, Mr. Woodford and Mr. Fitz-Owen were yet over their wine. The anxious father opened it with a palpitating heart, nor were the younger part of the audience less solicitous to know its contents. As there were none of them towards whom secrecy was absolutely necessary, though it might have been more prudent, Mr. Somerive, at the request of his eldest son, put it across the table to him—who, with that thoughtless indiscretion which marked his character, read it aloud, with comments serving to turn into ridicule the writer, and the sentiments it contained. The description of Orlando—under that of a sober, promising, and well-conditioned youth—was read with a burst of laughter; while the slighting way in which trade was mentioned, and the contempt thrown on shopkeepers, under which Mrs. Rayland seemed to describe wine merchants and every person in business, raised the indignation of Mr. Woodford and Mr. Fitz-Owen, who both agreed in declaring that the opinion of such an old crone was not worth consulting; that she was in a perfect dotage, as well from pride as old age; and that it was a conde-scension in Mr. Somerive to have consulted her at all. Orlando, however, saw all this with concern mingled with joy. He was pretty sure, from the countenance of his father, which he solicitously watched as he perused the letter, that the part of it which related to himself was kinder than he expected; that it had turned the fluctuating and unde-cided opinion of his father in his favour; and that he should not now, by being sent with his uncle Woodford, be condemned to the double misery of quitting Monimia, and associating with persons whose manners and ideas were so different from his own, that it was a perpet-ual punishment for him to be in their company. The displeasure of his brother at the partiality Mrs. Rayland expressed for him was easily accounted for; and Orlando had long accustomed himself to bear his rough jokes, and even his sarcastic reproaches, which he vented when-ever they met, without much uneasiness.

As soon as Mr. Somerive could disengage himself from his company, he withdrew to consult with his wife on the purport of Mrs. Rayland's letter, and made a sign to Orlando to follow him in a few moments.— He did so, and found his father and mother in consultation in the garden. The mother, whose heart was half broken at the idea of parting with her daughter so suddenly, was weeping with joy to find that Orlando would not yet leave her: flattering herself, from the purport of the letter, that the affluent fortune of Mrs. Rayland would at last centre with Orlando, and putting the most favourable construction on every expression that related to him, she agreed with Mr. Somerive, that noth-ing would be so imprudent as to think of removing him; and it was even determined, that Mr. Somerive should that evening write to her again, thanking her for her advice about his daughter, and leaving the future fate of Orlando wholly to her disposal; that Orlando should himself carry the letter, and ask leave to take his former apartments for some time—only returning once again to Wolverton to take leave of his eldest sister, whom he was to see no more before she went to Ireland—and of his second sister Isabella, who was to accompany her to London, and to pass some time with her uncle and aunt Woodford.

Never did Orlando obey his father with more alacrity than on this occasion; and on his return Mrs. Rayland never received him more kindly. He was now again invited to partake of her supper: without putting much force on himself, he shewed her exactly that sort of atten-tion which was the most agreeable to her, and appeared grateful with-out being servile. At length he was dismissed; and, when the house was perfectly quiet, he flew to Monimia, who accompanied him to the study; and when he related how much more happily the events of the day had passed than he had at its beginning expected, she shed tears of delight; and the sweet sensations of hope, which they now dared to indulge more than there ever yet appeared reason to indulge them, made this one of the happiest evenings they had ever passed together.

The following day Orlando returned to the house of his father, and found that, in regard to some parts of his family, a new arrangement had taken place. Mrs. Somerive, as the hour approached for her two eldest daughters to leave her—one to be separated from her perhaps for years, and to enter into another family—found herself so much affected, that her husband, who was very indulgent to her, agreed she should accompany the party to London, be present at the wedding of her daughter, and return in a fortnight, bringing Isabella back with her, if the idea of leaving her was at the end of that time uneasy to her. This being settled, Orlando took leave of his mother and sisters that evening: the former rejoicing that he would remain in the country; and the latter, but particularly the eldest, lamenting their separation with many tears: for Orlando, who was tenderly attentive to his sisters, was fondly beloved by them all; though to Selina, the third, who was a year younger than himself, he was more attached than to the rest.

Pensively he returned back to the Hall after this melancholy parting: it was the first time the family had been thus separated; for, except the unhappy eccentricities of his eldest son, the union of Mr. Somerive's children, and the promise they all gave of excellence, had hitherto made him amends for much of the difficulty he found in supporting them. But Orlando saw that the hour was now come when his father felt equal pain for the fate of those who were about to be what is called established in the world, and for those whom he knew not how to establish, or, in case of his death, to provide for. All that filial tenderness and good sense could suggest to his ingenuous and generous mind, he said to console his father; but with infinite concern he observed, that the wounds inflicted by the profligacy of his brother festered more deeply every day, and that all he could do had too little power to assuage the constant pain arising from this source; from which, though his father did not complain, Orlando thought it but too evident that his health was gradually impaired.

Against the uneasiness these observations gave him he found the only respite in his books, to which he assiduously applied himself—and in his evening conferences with Monimia, who every hour became more dear to him, and whose personal charms seemed every hour heightened by the progress of her understanding. As the nights became longer, and more obscure, they met earlier, and with less apprehension of detection; and as Mrs. Lennard seemed to become more and more remiss in her office of duenna,[1] the opportunities they had of seeing each other in the course of the day (though they rarely ventured to hold any conversation) sweetened the tedious hours between their meetings.

Thus almost a fortnight passed after the departure of Mrs. Somerive and her daughters for London; Orlando remaining constantly at the Hall, except dining occasionally with his father, or riding over in a morning to enquire after him, Mrs. Rayland seeming every day more fond of his company; and every body about the house, even the old servants, who had hitherto had such an ascendancy, appearing to consider him as the future master of the domain, where he was now invested with powers he had never before enjoyed. The game-keeper was ordered to suffer no other person to have the liberty of shooting on the extensive manors, and Mrs. Rayland was pleased when the game that was brought to the table was killed by Orlando; while, whatever diminution of consequence the confidential servants might suffer by this growing fondness of their mistress for him, there was something in his manner so fascinating, that their jealousy and anger were insensibly converted into attachment; and all, even the austere Mrs. Lennard herself, seemed to wish him well; except Mr. Pattenson, who, in proportion as he became in favour with others, appeared to dislike him.— Orlando had some time before remarked his rudeness, and often fancied that he watched him, and had some suspicion of his evening conferences with Monimia—yet if he had, it was more likely he would speak of what he knew, than secretly resent what he had in fact nothing to do with: but some resentment he appeared to harbour; and, whenever he met Orlando, surveyed him with looks which expressed anger, scorn, and apprehension. Orlando, conscious of never having injured him, and fearful only in one point, endeavoured to guard against any mischief he could do by discovering his evening visits to the turret, or those of Monimia to the library; and, for the rest, despised his wrath too much to attempt appeasing or resenting it.

Mrs. Lennard, to whom the constant residence of Orlando at the Hall might be supposed to be disagreeable, was much more civil to him, now that he was a fine young man, than ever she had been during his childhood; to her he was always extremely obliging; and though he disdained to stoop to the meanness of flattering Mrs. Rayland, where money might

---

[1]   "Elderly woman acting as governess and companion in charge of girls; chaperon" (*The Concise Oxford Dictionary*).

be supposed to be his sole object, he did not think it equally unworthy to use a little art to promote the interest of his love. Mrs. Lennard was remarkably open to two sorts of adulation—She loved to be thought a woman of sense, and to hear how fine her person must have been in her younger days. She was even now accustomed to say, that though not so well to *meet*, she was still well to *follow*; for she fancied her tall perpendicular figure exhibited still a great deal of dignity and grace. These foibles were so evident, and, whenever she was not with Mrs. Rayland, she took so little pains to conceal them, that Orlando, who thought it too probable that on her the future happiness of his life depended, believed it not wrong to take advantage of them to acquire her favour; and he succeeded so well by adroitly administering now and then a little well-timed flattery, that Mrs. Lennard not only held him in high esteem, but endeavoured to secure his, by cultivating the graces he had remarked. She entered on a new course of reading, and a little modernised her appearance. To have made too many and too rapid improvements in the latter respect, would have been attended with the hazard of displeasing Mrs. Rayland; hers therefore were confined to that sort of emendations which she was not likely to perceive.

It happened that, in the progress of these refinements, Mrs. Lennard had occasion for some articles which Betty Richards (who was a very great favourite, from the assiduity which she affected in her service particularly) was commissioned to buy. The place she was to go to was rather a large village than a town, and was about three miles and a half from the Hall; the way to it leading partly through the park, and partly through some hanging woods and coppices which belonged to Mrs. Rayland. Monimia happened to be in the room when Mrs. Lennard was giving Betty this commission for the next morning; and as her aunt had promised her a few articles for herself, for which she had immediate occasion, she ventured to solicit leave to go with Betty to make these purchases.

"Dear Madam," said she, "do indulge me this once. I have hardly been out of the park twice in my life; and though I have no desire to go any where when you disapprove of it, surely there can be no harm in my walking to such a place with Betty, just to buy what you are so good as to allow me. We shall not be gone above two hours and a half, for I will go as early as you please in the morning."

Mrs. Lennard, who happened to be in a better humour than usual when this request was made, agreed to it, under some restrictions. She said, that if Monimia *did* go, she must be back by nine o'clock at the very latest, and not go into any house but that of the universal dealer with whom her business was; that she must make no acquaintance, and enter into conversation with nobody. To all this Monimia most willingly agreed; and she believed that Orlando, whom she determined to consult in the evening, would not object to her going, on such an occasion, so little a way, whatever dislike he had to her associating much with Betty.

To Orlando, therefore, she communicated her design as soon as they met, who did not seem much pleased with it; but, to a matter apparently so trifling, he was ashamed of making any serious opposition, when she said that she really wanted the articles her aunt had given her leave to buy, which no other opportunity might afford her. He therefore, after expressing his hopes that she would continue upon her guard against Betty, whom he told her he saw more and more cause to mistrust and dislike, consented to the little expedition she meditated, and directed her the nearest way through the woods and the preserved pheasant-grounds of Mrs. Rayland. "I shall be out with my gun to-morrow," said he; "but I suppose I must not venture to meet you as if it were by chance?"

"I think," answered Monimia, "you had better not. Were we to meet, it would perhaps look like design; and as we could not venture to enter into conversation, it is hardly worth the risk of Betty's talking about it, since we should only just pass each other in the woods."

"I believe," replied Orlando, "it will be better not; especially as I told Mrs. Rayland at dinner yesterday, and while your aunt was present, that I should walk with my gun to my father's, and try to round his lands for some game to send up to my mother and sister."

Mrs. Lennard had probably recollected this circumstance when she so easily gave Monimia the permission she asked, her walk lying quite on the opposite side of the country. It was agreed, therefore, that Orlando should not incur any suspicion of a correspondence between them, by changing his plan for the next day; and after that was settled, Orlando read to her a letter he had that day received from his mother. It related to the marriage of Philippa, and her immediate departure for Ireland—described the state of her own mind on bidding adieu to her daughter—and said, that Mr. Woodford had insisted on her staying another week in town to recover her spirits; which however she should rather do to indulge Isabella, who had never been in town before, with the sight of the play-houses and other public places; for that *her* own spirits would be infinitely more relieved by collecting around her the rest of her children. "But," added she, while a tear had blistered the paper where the sentence was written, "why do I thus fondly flatter myself, and forget that your brother, my Orlando, is almost a stranger to us, and is, I much fear, by his thoughtless conduct, slowly destroying the invaluable life of your dear father? Alas! while I remember this, I know not how I should support myself if I did not find comfort in thinking of you."

Orlando's tears, while he read this letter, fell where the paper was marked by those of this beloved parent. The delightful visions he had been indulging but the moment before, disappeared; and he hardly dared think of Monimia, if it must be at the expence of wounding the peace and destroying the hopes of his parents. One look, however, from her, the sound of her voice as she soothingly spoke of his mother, dissipated these mournful thoughts; and, as he led her to her turret, he fancied that, if his mother could see her, she would love her as much as he did, and be happy to add to the family she wished to collect around her, so amiable and interesting a creature.

CHAP. IX.

Early on the following morning, Monimia, awaking from her short repose, prepared herself for her little journey, which, unused as she was to go farther than about the park, or in the walled gardens, was to her an event of some importance. The best dress she had was a white gown, which she put on to make her appearance in the village, with a little straw hat tied under her chin with blue ribband. Her fine hair, which she had never attempted to distort with irons, or change by powder, was arranged only by the hands of nature; and a black gauze handkerchief, which her aunt had given her from her own wardrobe, was tied over her shoulders. Nothing could be more simple than her whole appearance; but nothing could conceal the beautiful symmetry of her figure, or lessen the grace which accompanied her motions. Her companion Betty, as eager as she was for the walk, entered her room before she was quite ready, dressed in all the finery she dared shew at home, while she reserved her most splendid ornaments to put on at the park stile, and to be restored to her pocket at the same place on their return.

It was a clear morning in the middle of October when they set out. They happily executed their commissions; but Betty had so much to say, so many things to look at, and so many wishes for the pretty things she saw—and the man and his wife, who kept the shop, were so glad to see the *ladies*, as they called them both, and so willing to shew all the newest things from the next provincial town, as very fashionable, and pressed them so earnestly to go into their parlour, and eat some cake and drink some of their currant wine, that Betty had quite forgot Mrs. Lennard's injunction to return at nine o'clock; nor could the repeated remonstrances of Monimia prevail upon her to leave the house till the clock struck eleven. Monimia, very much alarmed, and fearing that her aunt would, in consequence of this disobedience, never allow her to go out again, then prevailed upon her companion to set out; and to save as much time as they could, they walked as fast as possible up the path which led from the village, through a copse that clothed the steep acclivity of a hill, which, at the end of about three quarters of a mile, led to Mrs. Rayland's woods. They passed with equal speed through the first of these woods, the path still ascending; but when they came to the second, Monimia, from unusual exertion, from the heat (for the sun had yet great power and force), and the apprehensions of her aunt's anger, was quite exhausted, and begged Betty to let her rest a moment on the steps of the stile; to which she, who feared Mrs. Lennard's displeasure much less than Monimia, readily assented.

"Lord, Miss," cried she, as they sat down, "how frighted you be at nothing! Why, what can your aunt do, child? She can't kill you; and as for a few angry words, I've no notion of minding 'em, not I: 'tis hard indeed if one's to be always a slave, and never dares to stir ever so little;—one might as well be a negur."

"I would not for the world," answered Monimia, "offend my aunt when she is kind to me; and it was very good in her to give me money to buy these things, and to let me go for them."

"I see no mighty matter of goodness in it," cried the other: "who is to provide for you, if she does not, who is your own natural relation? Egollys! Miss, if I was you, I should be very apt to shew her the difference. Why, very often she uses you like a dog, and I'm sure she makes you work like a servant. There's Mr. Pattenson always a-telling me, that handsome girls have no occasion to be drudges as I be, or as I have been; for that in London they may make their fortunes, and live like the finest ladies of the land."[1]—Thus she ran on, while Monimia, hardly hearing, and not at all attending to her conversation, sat silent, considering how extraordinary Orlando would think it, if by any accident he should know she was out so long—and trying to recover her breath that they might proceed—when suddenly several spaniels ran out of the

---

[1] Betty, apparently unwittingly, expresses a wish to be a high-class prostitute, or a courtesan.

wood, a pheasant flew up near them, and the report of two guns was heard so near that Monimia started in some degree of terror; while Betty, whose nerves were much stronger, clapped her hands, and, laughing aloud, cried: "Oh jingo! if here ben't some gentlemen shooting—let's stay and see who they be!"

"No, no!" said Monimia, "let us go."

She then arose to walk on; but the voices of the persons who were shooting were now heard immediately before them, and she turned pale when she thought she distinguished that of Orlando. Instantaneously, however, the sportsmen broke out of the thick underwood into the path before them, and Monimia beheld a young man, whom, from his distant resemblance to Orlando, she immediately knew to be his elder brother. With him were two other gentlemen, and a servant who carried their nets. "Oh ho!" cried the elder Somerive; "what have we here! two cursed pretty wenches—hey, Stockton? Here's a brace of birds that it may be worth while to mark, damme!" He then approached Monimia, who shrunk back terrified behind her companion; while Betty, far from feeling any apprehension, advanced with a curtsey and a giggle, and "Pray, Sir, let us pass."

"Not so quickly, my little dear," said Mr. Stockton; "I am a new comer into this country, and have a great inclination to be acquainted with all my pretty neighbours—By Heaven, you are as handsome as an angel—Pray, my dear, where do you live?"

"With Mrs. Rayland, Sir," said Betty, dropping another curtsey; "and I beg your honour will not stop us, for my Lady will be very angry."

"Damn her anger," cried Stockton; "does she think to shut up all the beauty in the country in her old fortification? If she's angry, you pretty little rogue, leave her to vent it on her jolly favourite butler, that fellow who looks like the confessor to the convent, and do you come to me—I keep open house for the reception of all pretty damsels in distress—and bring your companion here with you."

He then looked forward towards Monimia, and saw her in an agony of tears; for the conversation of Philip Somerive and his companion, to whom he gave the title of Sir John, had terrified her so much that she could no longer command herself.—"Why, what the devil's the matter?" cried Stockton. "Why, Sir John—why, Somerive, what have you said to that sweet girl?"

"We've been asking her who she is," replied Sir John; "and it seems she does not know."

"You are the housekeeper's niece, are you not?" said Somerive.

"Tell me, my dear," addressing himself to Betty, "is not this little simpleton, that falls a-crying so prettily, the reputed niece[1] of that old formal piece of hypocrisy, Lennard? Come, tell us—you have more sense than to cry because one asks a civil question."

"Lord, Sir," replied Betty, "to be sure you are such another wild gentleman that I don't at all wonder you've frighted our Miss, who, poor thing! has scarcely ever been out of our house all her life.—Yes, Sir, 'tis Miss Monimee, Sir, Madam Lennard's kinswoman; and I hope, Sir, you'll please to give us leave to pass, for we shall have a great deal of anger for being out so much longer than Madam Lennard she gived us leave to stay."

"Tell us then," said Sir John, taking both Monimia's hands, which she in vain endeavoured to disengage from his grasp—"tell us where and when we can see you again, and then you shall go."—"Yes," cried Stockton, addressing himself to Betty, "tell us, my dear girl, when can we see you again?" "We shall not easily relinquish the acquaintance," interrupted Somerive; "and if you are to be met with only at the Hall, I shall contrive to get into favour again with that immortal old frump, and I can tell you that's no small compliment."

"Oh! dear Sir," giggled Betty, "I vow and declare you put me all in a twitter with your wild ways. Indeed, Sir, you can't see us no where; for, as to Miss, she never goes out, not at all.—For my share, to be sure, I now and tan be at church, and such like; but for all that, it's morrally impossible for us to see you nohow at all."

"Well then," cried Stockton, "we'll have a kiss a-piece somehow at all, now we do see you."

"Yes, yes," said Somerive, "that we will."

"Well, gentlemen," replied Betty, "I am sure this is very rude behaviour (Lord, Miss, why d'ye cry so? I warrant they won't do no harm); and if you insist upon it, I hope you'll let us go then."

"Yes," answered Somerive, "we'll let you go then."

Betty went through the ceremony without making many difficulties; but when Stockton advanced towards Monimia, to whom Sir John had all this time been making professions of violent love, she retreated from him; and her alarm was so evidently unaffected that Sir John stopped him.—"Don't, Stockton," cried he; "Miss is apparently very new to the world, and we have distressed her." "Well, well," answered Stockton, "we

---

[1]   This is one of the many references to Monimia's assumed illegitimate status. The character who most persists in this is Mr. Somerive, Orlando's father.

won't distress her then. Come, Somerive, we shall meet these charming girls some other time; I see you are taking care of that," for he continued whispering Betty; "so let us now go on to beat the wood." Somerive, who seemed to have made, during his momentary conversation, some arrangement with Betty, now agreed to his; and, as he passed Monimia, looked earnestly under her hat, and said in a half whisper, "Upon my honour! that sober well-conditioned young man, Mr. Orlando, has a fine time of it—these are his studies at the Hall!" Poor Monimia, sinking with terror and confusion, now endeavoured to disengage herself from Sir John, and to follow Betty, who, making more half-curtseys, and looking smilingly after the gentlemen, was walking on; but he, who had attached himself to Monimia, was not so easily shaken off. He told Stockton and Somerive, that he should go home another way, and should shoot no more. "Good morrow, therefore," added he, "I shall wait upon these ladies through the woods; and as you do not want Ned (speaking of his servant), he may as well go with me and take home the birds." To this the other two assenting departed; while Sir John, giving his servant a hint to enter into conversation with Betty, and discover as much as he could relative to Monimia, again joined her, though she had walked forward as quickly as possible, and desired her, as he said she seemed tired, to accept of his arm. Monimia, more terrified every step she took, and dreading lest he should insist upon following her to the Hall, now acquired courage to entreat that he would leave her; while he, regardless of the distress so evident in her countenance, endeavoured to prevail upon her to listen to him; and in this manner they had proceeded nearly to the part of the woods which open directly into the park, when suddenly, at a sharp turn of the path, Orlando, with his gun upon his shoulder, stood before them.

Amazement and indignation were pictured in his countenance when he beheld a stranger walking close to Monimia, and seeming to have his arm round her waist. Thrown totally off guard by an appearance so sudden and so extraordinary, he cried, "Pray, who is this gentleman?— Pray, what does this mean!" Betty, who had been detained some paces behind, now approached; and Orlando, recollecting himself, took no other notice of Monimia, who would, had she dared, have flown to him for protection; but slightly touching his hat, he advanced to Sir John, and said, "I suppose, Sir, you have Mrs. Rayland's permission to shoot in these preserved grounds?"

"I always shoot, Sir," answered Sir John haughtily, "in all grounds that happen to suit me, whether they are preserved or no, and take no trouble to ask leave of any body."

"Then, Sir," said Orlando with quickness, "you must allow me to say that you do a very unhandsome thing."

"And I," rejoined the other, "say, whether you allow it or no, that you are a very impertinent fellow."

The blood rushed into the face of Orlando: and even the pale and terrified countenance of Monimia, who caught hold of Betty for support, did not deter him from resenting this insolence. "Who are you," cried he, seizing Sir John by the collar, "that thus dare to insult me?"

"And who are you, scoundrel," answered his antagonist, endeavouring to disengage himself, "who dare to behave with such confounded impudence to a man of my consequence?"

"Curse on your consequence!" exclaimed the enraged Orlando, throwing him violently from him: "If you are a gentleman, which I doubt, give me an opportunity of telling you properly who I am."

"*If* I am a gentleman?" cried the other. "Am I questioned by a park-keeper? or by some dirty valet?"

Sir John, who was quite the modern man of fashion, did not much approve of the specimen Orlando had given him of athletic powers:— he liked him still less when he replied—"My name is Somerive—my usual residence at West Wolverton, or Rayland Hall. Now, Sir, as you speak neither to a park-keeper nor a valet, you must tell me from whom I have received this brutal insult."

"My servant will tell you," replied he; "and, if you are likely to forget his information, you shall hear it properly from me to-morrow. In the mean time, my dear girl," added he, turning familiarly to Monimia, "let us leave this fierce drawcansir to watch the old Lady's pheasants; and as you seem much alarmed by his ridiculous fury, let me have the pleasure of seeing you safe home."

He would then have taken the arm of the trembling Monimia within his; but she shrunk from him, and would have passed on. He still insisted, however, on being permitted to attend her home; when Orlando, quite unable to command himself, sprung forward, and, seizing the arm of Monimia, cried, "This young Lady, being under the protection of Mrs. Rayland, is under mine; and I insist on her not being troubled with your impertinent familiarity. Come, Madam, if you will give me leave, I will conduct you to your aunt." He then, without waiting for any farther reply, walked hastily away; while Sir John, filled with rage and contempt, bade his servant follow him, and inform him that the person whom he had thus grossly affronted was Sir John Berkely Belgrave, baronet, of Belgrave Park in Suffolk, brother-in-law to the Earl of Glenlyon of

Scotland, and member of parliament. Orlando heard this list of dignities with contemptuous coolness; and then, as he continued to walk on, bade the servant tell his master, Sir John Berkely Belgrave, of Belgrave Park in Suffolk, brother-in-law to the Earl of Glenlyon of Scotland, and member of parliament, that he expected to hear from him.

They were no sooner out of sight, than Orlando, addressing himself to Betty (for Monimia was quite unable to answer him), said: "Where did you meet this man? and how came you to be with him?"

"Lord," said Betty, pertly, "how could we help it? and pray where was the harm? For my part, I always speak to gentlefolks that speak to me; I've no notion of sitting mum chance, when gentlemen are so civil as to speak genteel to one. Here's a fuss, indeed, about nothing! And so you've gone and made a fine piece of work, and had a mind for to have fit that baron knight—I suppose there will be a pretty to do!"

"But where did you meet him?" repeated Orlando impatiently.

"Don't bite one's nose off," said Betty: "Gemini! what a passion you put yourself into—Met him!—why we met him, and two more very obliging civil gentlemen as I ever wish to see; your brother was one of them, and what then? I'm sure it's wast ridiculous to quarrel and fall out about a few nasty pheasants with all the gentlefolks about. That's the reason that Mistress never has nobody come to see her at the Hall; and one may as well live in a prison. I'm quite sick of it, for my share."

As nothing but mutterings were to be obtained from Betty, Orlando no longer questioned her; but as his first emotion of something like anger mingled with vexation towards Monimia had now subsided, he said to her, in a low and mournful voice, "This is all very disagreeable; would to God you had never gone this unlucky walk!"

"Would to God I never had! for now I see nothing but misery will arise from it. But let us part here:" (they were now in the park) "it is quite enough for me to have gone through what has passed within this hour; there is no occasion to add to my terror, by letting my aunt see us together. I thought I should suffer enough by being so late home; but, good God! what is *that* fear in comparison of what I suffer now about this quarrel?"

"The quarrel, as you call it, will be of no consequence, Monimia: I shall probably hear no more of it;—or, if I do, Mrs. Rayland will not be displeased at my having spoken to these men, who have so long impertinently trespassed on her manors."

"But who," said Monimia, "who shall ensure your safety, Orlando, if you *do* hear more of it?"

"I must take my chance about that. Do not, my Monimia," whispered he, "make yourself uneasy about it: I shall see you at night; and now, perhaps, it will be better to part." He then said aloud, that Betty might hear, who was a few paces behind, "Since you seem now to be delivered from the persecution of this impertinent stranger, I wish you a good morning." Orlando then walked another way, as if pursuing his diversion of shooting; and Betty joining Monimia, they proceeded together towards the house.

As they went, Betty, who was very much displeased with Orlando, because he seemed to have given all that attention to Monimia which she had herself a great inclination to monopolize, began again to exclaim against the folly of his having driven away and quarrelled with a baron knight, as she emphatically termed it. "Why one would have thof," cried she, "actually that the gentleman, who is in my mind a pretty gentleman, had done some great harm. If Mr. Orlando had been your sweetheart, Miss, he couldn't have brustled up in a greater passion."

"My sweetheart!" said Monimia faintly; "how can he be my sweetheart, when you know, Betty, I have hardly exchanged ten words with him in my whole life?"

"Well, Miss, you nid not colour so about it—Lord, I suppose people have had sweethearts before now; and the better's their luck:—not that I say Mr. Orlando is yours, for I knows to the contrary."

"I believe," said Monimia, making an effort to command herself, "I believe, Betty, it will be as well, on many accounts, not to say any thing about all this at home. If this unlucky quarrel should go any farther, which I hope it will not, it will make my aunt very angry if she knows we were present at it;—and, upon the whole, I wish you would make a resolution not to speak of it."

"Not I," answered Betty, "I shan't speak of it, not I.—I'm none of your blabs—and scorn to say any thing to make mischief;—besides, we shall have anger enough for staying so much later than we were bid to stay. Yes; we shall have a fine rattle; and there stands Madam Lennard at the window, watching for us." They were now near the house, and poor Monimia, looking up, saw her aunt indeed watching their return. She trembled so much, that she could hardly find strength to get into the house; where as soon as Betty arrived she was hastening to the kitchen; but Monimia finding it impossible to meet, alone, the first rage of her aunt, entreated her to go up stairs.

"Do not leave me, dear Betty," said the timid Monimia; "I am in such terror already, that if my aunt is very violent against me, I really believe

I shall die on the spot. You have more courage than I have—for Heaven's sake, do not leave me."

"I don't know any good I can do," replied Betty; "but however, if I must go, I must." They then ascended the stairs together, and entered the room where Mrs. Lennard waited for them in the disposition of an hungry tigress who has long been disappointed of her prey. She scolded with such vehemence for near half an hour, that she absolutely exhausted every form of invective and reproach which her very fertile genius, and the vocabulary of Billingsgate,[1] could furnish her with; and then taking Monimia rudely by the arm, she led her to her turret, and locked her in, protesting that, so far from ever suffering her to go junketing out again to the village, she should not leave her room for a week. With this threat she left her weeping niece, and turned the key upon her: but Monimia, somewhat relieved by her departure, felt with secret delight that it was not in her power to confine her—and that at night she should see Orlando. Yet the danger he had run into recurred to her with redoubled force; and never did she pass such miserable hours as those that intervened between her aunt's fierce remonstrance, and that when she expected the signal from Orlando.

CHAP. X.

The unfortunate rencontre which promised to produce so much uneasiness, was occasioned by the impatience of Orlando at Monimia's long absence. He had gone early in the morning to his father's, as he had the preceding evening proposed: and returning about ten o'clock, anxious to know if Monimia was come back from her walk, he enquired among the servants for Betty; and was told that she was not yet come home from the village, whither Mrs. Lennard had sent her early in the morning. "What do you want with Betty, sir?" said Pattenson, who heard the enquiry. "To make the fire up in my room," replied Orlando. "Any other of the maids can do that as well, I suppose," answered the butler, sullenly; and then, from his manner, Orlando was first struck with the idea, that

---

[1]   Billingsgate, a fishmarket near one of the gates to the original City of London (now confined to the centre of modern London), and noted for the strong and uncouth language of its merchants. Mrs. Lennard exposes her inherent vulgarity and ill-breeding: Smith is calling her a fishwife.

Pattenson, being an admirer of Betty, was apprehensive of his acquiring too much of her favour. This observation was a great relief to him, and dissipated the fears he had long entertained, that the old butler suspected his stolen interviews with Monimia.

Uneasy, however, at her staying so much later than the hour when he knew she was ordered to return, he could not forbear making a circuit round the wood-walks of the park, where he could not be observed, and passing towards the preserved pheasant-grounds, through which her path lay; where he had not waited long before the appearance of Monimia, attended by Sir John Belgrave, produced the alarming conversation which the last chapter related.

When Orlando parted from Monimia, and began cooly to consider what had happened, he felt no other uneasiness than that which arose from his apprehension that her name might be brought in question; for he was a stranger to all personal fear, and was totally indifferent to the resentment of Sir John Belgrave, which he thought it probable he might think it wise to lay aside; for he did not appear to be one of those who are eager to acquire fame by personal danger. However that might be, Orlando's principal concern was, how to appease the fears of Monimia; and as early as it was safe to go to the turret, he repaired thither; but this happened almost an hour later than usual. Pattenson had visitors, some tradesmen from a neighbouring town, to sup with him; and Orlando, who was upon the watch, had the mortification to hear them singing in the butler's room at half after eleven, and to find it near one o'clock when they betook themselves to their horses, and departed. It was yet near half an hour longer before the lights about the house were extinguished, and all was quiet.

The night, dark and tempestuous, added to the gloomy appearance of all that surrounded Monimia; while her imagination, filled with images of horror, represented to her, that his delay was owing to the consequences of his morning's adventure; and these apprehensions, added to the fatigue and anxiety she had gone through during the day, almost overcame her before the well known, long wished for signal was heard.

At length, Orlando had safely placed her by the fire, and began to speak as cheerfully as he could of what had passed;[1] but he saw her pale, dejected, and ready to sink—her eyes swollen with weeping—and her

---

[1] Although Orlando speaks lightly, his words suggest that in many ways *The Old Manor House* functions as an "anti-romance" as much as a romance: the episodes that require Orlando to act the hero are consistently undercut and shown to be derived from misunderstandings and (most frequently) Orlando's personal inadequacies. In other words, the romance ideology rests on flawed, even false, assumptions.

whole frame languid, depressed by the uneasy circumstances of the day, and the uneasy suspense of the night. For the latter he easily accounted; and he endeavoured to dissipate her dread as to the consequences of the former. "This fine gentleman," said he, "who could persecute with his insulting attentions a young and defenceless woman, my Monimia, can never have much proper and steady courage; or, if he has, he will, if he has a shadow of understanding, be ashamed of exerting it in such a cause. Besides, after all the applications that have with great civility been made to Mr. Stockton, entreating him to forbear, either by himself, his friends, or servants, trespassing on those woods, where Mrs. Rayland is so fond of preserving the game, nothing can be more ungentleman-like than to persist in it: it looks like taking advantage of Mrs. Rayland's being without any man about her who has a right to enforce her wishes, which, whether capricious and absurd or no, should surely be respected. I feel myself perfectly justified for having spoken as I did, and only regret that you were present. Relate to me, Monimia, what passed before I met you. Did not Betty say, that my brother was one of the people who were with this Sir John Belgrave?"

Monimia then related all that had passed, as well as the alarm she had been in had allowed her to observe it; and in the behaviour of his brother, particularly in the speech he had made to Monimia as he passed her, Orlando found more cause of vexation than in any other circumstance of the morning. He foresaw that the beauty of Monimia, which had hitherto been quite unobserved, would now become the topic of common conversation; his father and his family would be alarmed, and his stay at the Hall imputed to motives very different from his love of solitude and study. Hitherto Monimia had seemed a beautiful and unique gem, of which none but himself had discovered the concealment, or knew the value. He had visited it with fonder idolatry, from alone possessing the knowledge where it was hid. But now half his happiness seemed to be destroyed, since his treasure was discovered, and particularly by his brother, who was so loose in his principles, and so unfeeling in his conduct. As these painful reflections passed through his mind, he sat a while silent and dejected, till, being awakened from his mournful reverie by a deep sigh from Monima, he saw her face bathed in tears. "Ah! Orlando," said she, in a tremulous voice, "I see that you feel as I do. All our little happiness is destroyed; perhaps this is the last night we shall ever meet: something tells me, that the consequence of this luckless day will be our eternal separation." The sobs that swelled her bosom as she said this impeded her utterance. Orlando, with more than usual tenderness, endeavoured to sooth and re-assure her—when suddenly, as he hung fondly over her, speaking to her in a low voice, she started, and said, in a whisper, "Hush, hush—for heaven's sake—I hear a noise in the chapel." Orlando listened a moment. "No—it is only the wind, which is very high to-night." But listening again a moment, he thought, as she did, that it was something more; and before he had time to imagine what it might be, the old heavy lock of the study door, that opened from the passage to the chapel, was moved slowly; the door as slowly opened, and at it a human face just appeared. Starting up, Orlando, whose fears were ever alive for Monimia, blew out the single candle which stood at some distance from them; and then springing towards the door he demanded fiercely who was there. Monimia, whose terror almost annihilated her faculties, would have thrown herself into his arms, and there have waited the discovery which appeared more dreadful than death: but he was instantly gone, and pursued through the chapel a man, whom however he could not overtake, and who seemed at the door to vanish—though the night was so dark, that it was impossible to distinguish any object whatever. Through the chapel he had heard the sound of feet; but when he got to the porch, and from thence listened for the same sound to direct his pursuit along the flag-stones, it was heard no more. All was profoundly silent, unless the stillness was interrupted by the howling of the wind round the old buildings.

Orlando, after a moment's pause, was disposed to fasten the chapel door before he returned; but he recollected that perhaps he might enclose an enemy within it, or impede the escape of his Monimia to her turret. Uncertain therefore what to do, but too certain of the agonizing fears to which he had left her exposed, he hastily went back; and securing that door which led from the chapel to the passage as well as he could (for there was no key to it, and only a small rusty bar), and then fastening the door of the study, he approached, by the light of the wood fire which was nearly extinguished, the fainting Monimia, who, unable to support herself, had sunk on the ground, and rested her head on the old tapestry chair on which she had been sitting.

Orlando found her cold, and almost insensible; and it was some moments before he could restore her to her speech. Terror had deprived her of the power of shedding tears; nor had she the strength to sit up: but when he had placed her in her chair, he was compelled to support her, while he endeavoured to make light of a circumstance that overwhelmed him with alarm for her, and with vexation beyond what he had ever yet experienced.

They had both distinctly beheld the face, though neither had the least idea to whom it belonged. Orlando had as distinctly heard the footsteps along the hollow ground of the chapel; it was not therefore one of those supernatural beings, to whose existence Monimia had been taught to give credit. Orlando would willingly have sheltered himself under such a prejudice, had it been possible; for all the ghosts in the Red Sea would have terrified him less than the discovery of Monimia by any of the family; yet, that such a discovery was made, he could not doubt; and the more he thought of even its immediate conse-quences, and the impossibility there might be to reconvey his lovely trembling charge to her own room, the greater his distraction became; while all he could make Monimia say, was, "Dearest Orlando, let me stay and die here! A few hours longer of such extreme pain, as I at this moment suffer, will certainly kill me; and if I die in your presence, my death will be happier than my life *has* been, or than now it ever can be."

Orlando being thus under the necessity of conquering his own extreme disquiet, that he might appease hers, began to make various conjectures as to this man, tending to encourage the hope that it was some accidental intruder, and not one whose business was to discover her. "But even if the villain came with that design," said he, "I do not believe he could distin-guish you, so instantly I blew out the candle: or, if he saw a female figure, he could not know it to be you; it might as well be any other woman." These suppositions had little power to quiet the fears with which Monimia was tormented; but when Orlando seemed so deeply affected by her situation; when he declared to her that he was unequal to the sight of her terror; and that not even the discovery they dreaded could make him so wretched as seeing her in such a situation; she made an effort to recover herself, and at length succeeded so well as to regain the power of consulting with him, as to what was best to be done.

It was now early morning, but still very dark, with rain and wind. It was however time to consider of Monimia's return; for within two hours the servants would be up, and in even less time the labourers in the gardens would come to their work. It was at length agreed, that Orlando should go through the chapel first, and try if he could discover any traces of their alarming visitor; and if, after his reconnoitring, all appeared safe, that Monimia should return as usual to her apartment.

Orlando then, directing her to fasten herself the study door within side, went through the chapel with a candle in his hand, which he shaded with his hat to prevent the light being seen from the windows. He looked carefully among the broken boards which had once formed two or three pews, and then went into the chancel, but saw nothing. He passed through the porch, leaving his candle behind the door on one of the benches, but nobody appeared: and by the very faint light of the first dawn, on a stormy October morning, which served only to make "the darkness visible,"[1] he could just see round the whole chapel court, and was satisfied nobody was there. Thus convinced, he returned to Monimia; assured her that the wretch, whoever he was, was gone; and that there seemed to be no danger in her returning to her apartment. He endeavoured again to persuade her that her alarm, however just, would end without any of the consequences they dreaded; made her swallow a large glass of wine; and then taking one of her hands in his, he put his other arm round her waist; and with uncertain steps himself, while through fear *her* feet almost refused to move, they proceeded slowly and lightly through the chapel; neither of them spoke; Monimia hardly breathed; when arriving about the middle of it, they were struck motionless by a sudden and loud crash, which seemed to proceed from the chancel; and a deep hollow voice pronounced the words, "Now—now."

There was a heavy stone font in the middle of the chapel, with a sort of bench under it. Orlando, unable at once to support and defend Monimia, placed her on this bench; and imploring her to take courage, he darted forward into the chancel, from whence he was sure the voice had issued, and cried aloud, "Who is there? Speak this moment. Who are you?"

The words re-echoed through the vaulted chancel, but no answer was returned: again, and in a yet louder voice, he repeated them, and again listened to hear if any reply was made. A slight and indistinct noise, like the shutting a distant door, and a low murmur which soon died away, left every thing in profound silence. He remained however yet an instant listening, while Monimia, resting against the stone a cheek almost as cold, was petrified with excess of fear; and in the dread pause between Orlando's question and his awaiting an answer, the old banners which hung over her head, waving and rustling with the current of air, seemed to repeat the whispers of some terrific and invisible being, foretelling woe and destruction; while the same wind by which these fragments were agitated hummed sullenly among the helmets and gauntlets, trophies of the prowess of former Sir Orlandos and Sir Hildebrands, which were suspended from the pillars of the chapel.

---

[1] Milton, *Paradise Lost*, I. 63.

When Orlando returned to her, he found her more dead than alive. He soothed, he supported her, and earnestly besought her to exert herself against the fear that oppressed her.

"What shall we do, Monimia?" said he. "For my own part, rather than see you suffer thus, I will take you in my hand, and declare at once to these people, whoever they are, that we cannot live apart. And should we, by such an avowal, forfeit the protection of our friends, what is there in that so very dreadful? I am young and strong, and well able to work in any way for a subsistence for us both. Tell me, Monimia, should you fear poverty, if we could but live together!"

"No," replied Monimia, acquiring courage from this excess of tenderness in her lover—"no, Orlando, I should be too happy to be allowed to beg with you round the world." "What then have we to fear?" whispered he. "Come, let us go and face these people, if, as their expression "Now" seems to intimate, they are waiting for us without. In the chapel they are not, however the sound seemed to come from thence. I fear they way-lay us at the door. But if we are thus prepared against the worst that can befall us, why should we shrink now, only to be exposed a second time to alarms that seem to threaten your life, from your extreme timidity? Tell me, Monimia, have you courage to brave the discovery at once, which sooner or later must be made?"

"I *have* courage," answered she; "let us go while I am able." She arose, but could hardly stand. Orlando however led her forward, listening still every step they took. They heard nothing either in the chapel or in the porch; and being now on the pavement without, they stopped and looked around them, expecting that the person or persons whose words had alarmed them would appear; but there was nobody to be seen, yet it was now light enough to discern every part of the court. "This is wonderful," said Orlando; "but since there seems to be nothing to prevent it, let me see you, my Monimia, safe to your room; and let me hope to have the comfort of knowing, that, after the fatigues and terrors of such a day and night, you obtain some repose." "How can you know it, Orlando," answered she, "since it will be madness, if we escape now, to think of venturing a meeting to-morrow night?" "I would not have you venture it; but, Monimia, I have thought of a way, by which I can hear from you and write to you in the course of the day, which, under our present circumstances, must be an infinite satisfaction. As I have at all hours access to the turret, I can put a letter at your door behind your bed; and there you can deposit an answer." To this expedient Monimia readily assented. Without any alarm they passed the rest of their short walk. Monimia promised to go immediately to bed, and to endeavour to compose herself; and Orlando, having seen her secured in her turret, returned to the chapel, determined to discover, if possible, what it was that had so cruelly alarmed them. Again he went over every part, but could discover nothing. He then determined to go round the house; and resolute not to spare any wretch who might be lurking about it with evil designs, he went into a large unin-habited parlour that opened into the study from the body of the house, where, over the chimney, several sorts of arms were disposed, which for many years had never been used. He took down an hanger, and a pair of horse pistols; both were somewhat injured by neglect, and of the latter he knew he could make no use till they had been cleaned; but drawing the hanger from its scabbard, he sallied forth in eager expectation of finding some means to discover, and at least to terrify from future intrusion, the man he had seen and heard; but after wandering round the house, through the gardens, and even over the adjoining offices, for above an hour, he saw nothing that could lead him to guess who it could be. The work-men and servants were all at their usual employments. He talked to some of them, but observed no consciousness of any thing extraordinary in any of them. He then returned, not less uneasy than before his search. Sometimes the idea of Sir John Belgrave presented itself; but that he should have ventured to visit the Hall at such an hour, he soon rejected as an impossibility. Had Mrs. Rayland discovered his intelligence with Monimia, she would have signified her displeasure openly and at once. At length he supposed it might be his brother. This, as Philip Somerive knew the house, appeared the least improbable of all his conjectures. But still it was hardly to be supposed that he would leave his jovial companions on such a night for the pleasure of persecuting him, when so many other means were now in his power, by which he might disturb the happiness of Orlando. Dissatisfied with every supposition, but becoming every instant more restless and anxious, he waited with impatience for the customary time of visiting Mrs. Rayland. It came, and she behaved to him just as usual. Some hours, therefore, were still passed in fruitless conjectures and tormenting suspense.

CHAP. XI.

Orlando left Mrs. Rayland about twelve o'clock, convinced that, what-ever discovery had been made, she was yet perfectly unacquainted with it. He thought it best to tell her as much of what had happened the preceding day, as he was sure she would not disapprove: he therefore mentioned to her, in the presence of Lennard, who seemed as ignorant of any misadventure as she was, that he had gone round the park with his gun, after his return from his father's in the morning, and, hearing several shot fired in the copses, he had followed the sound. "I met, madam," said he, "Mrs. Lennard's niece and your servant Betty, and almost at the same moment a gentleman shooting, and a servant following him with several pheasants. I thought it necessary to speak to him; and we had rather high words. I found he had two companions with him, whom I did not see: Stockton himself was one of them (Orlando always carefully avoided naming his brother). The man to whom I spoke, was, I found from his servant, a baronet."

"A baronet, child!" said Mrs. Rayland; "impossible! at least if he is, it must be one of the new-made baronets: these, as well as new-created lords, spring up like mushrooms, from nobody knows where every year. A man of family could not behave so. This person is some enriched tradesman, who has bought his title. Belgrave!—Belgrave!—I don't recollect the name. No; he cannot be a man of any family."[1]

Orlando saw that Mrs. Rayland had not the least idea of the circumstances likely to follow his dialogue with Sir John Belgrave, and only dwelt upon the improbability that a man whose title was above two years old, could commit so great an indecorum as he had been guilty of. Unwilling, therefore, to awaken in her mind those apprehensions of future consequences, of which she seemed quite ignorant, he soon after turned the discourse; and, leaving her and Mrs. Lennard both in perfect good humour, he returned to his study, and sat down to give Monimia the satisfaction of knowing, that, to whomsoever the affright of the preceding evening was owing, Mrs. Rayland and her aunt had certainly no share in it, and as yet no suspicion of their intercourse.

He had been employed thus near half an hour, and had just finished his letter, when Betty bounced into his room.

"There's one without vants to speak to you," cried she: pouting and sullenly she spoke; and then, shutting the door as hastily as she had opened it, was going: but Orlando, following her, said, "Betty! who is it? If the person has a letter for me, let it be sent in; if not, beg to know his name." (A letter or a message from Sir John Belgrave was what he expected.)

---

[1]   Mrs. Rayland shows her allegiance to the idea of breeding as dependent on birth: only the longevity of a title validates it. In addition, by calling Orlando "child," she both emphasizes his dependent status and places him as her "childe": her noble page.

"I shan't carry none of your messages, indeed," replied the girl: "but I suppose the person without is your father; I never see him but once or twice, but I'm pretty sure 'tis he."

"Good God!" exclaimed Orlando; "and why, then, if you knew him, would you let my father wait without?"

"'Twas no business of mine, Mr. Orlando, to shew him in; and besides folks sometimes has *company* with them in their rooms, you know; and then an old father may be one too many, Mr. Orlando."

"What do you mean by that?" cried Orlando eagerly.

"Nay, never mind what I means—I knows what I knows; but I think you mid as well take care not to get other folks into bad bread, that are as innocent as the child unborn."

"I insist upon your telling me," said Orlando, seizing her hand—"I insist, nay I implore you, *dear* Betty, to tell me—"

At this moment the old butler appeared at the door of the parlour in which they were standing; and seeing Orlando apparently interceding with Betty, he said roughly,

"Instead of pulling the wenches about, and behaving in this rakish sort of way in *my* mistress's house, it would be more becoming of you to go speak to your father, who is waiting in the stable-yard."

"You are impertinent, Mr. Pattenson!" answered Orlando; "and I beg you will understand that impertinence from any one I am not disposed to endure."

Orlando then went hastily out—Pattenson muttering as he passed, "I don't know how you'll help yourself."

In the stable-yard Orlando found Mr. Somerive. He had not dismounted, having made it a rule for many years never to enter Mrs. Rayland's house unless he was invited. Orlando saw by his countenance that he was under great concern; and respectfully approaching him, he said,

"Dear Sir, is all well at home? Is my mother returned? Is she well?"

"Your mother is not returned, Orlando," replied Mr. Somerive in a grave and melancholy tone; "but she is well, and all is well at home."

"I hope then, Sir, that I owe this visit merely to your kindness. Will you get off your horse, and come in?—I have a fire in the library—or shall I let Mrs. Rayland know you are here?"

"Neither the one nor the other," replied Mr. Somerive. "But get your horse immediately, and come with me; I have business with you."

"I have only slippers on, Sir; will you walk in while I put on my boots?"

"You will not need them—I shall not detain you long. Your horse is already saddled by my desire—You have your hat, and therefore hasten to follow me."

Orlando would have given half a world to have had an opportunity of depositing his letter to Monimia, which he had put hastily into his pocket; but there was now no possibility of escaping to do it; and in the hope that his father would soon dismiss him, yet foreseeing that what he had to say was of a very painful nature, he mounted his horse, which one of the grooms brought out, and followed his father across the park. Mr. Somerive was silent till they had got at some distance from the house. Orlando rode by his side a foot pace. He observed that his father sighed deeply two or three times, and at length said: "Orlando, I desire you will give me a faithful detail of all that passed yesterday."

The events of the night dwelt more upon his mind than those of the day; and believing therefore that his father alluded to them, he blushed deeply, and repeated, "All that passed yesterday, Sir?"

"Yes," replied the father; "you certainly don't mean to affect misunderstanding me. You have got into a quarrel with one of the guests of Mr. Stockton: I have heard of it from one quarter; let me now have your account of it."

"That is very easily given, my dear Sir," answered Orlando, relieved by finding that the adventures of the night were not meant. "I met a gentleman shooting in those woods, where, you know, it has been for years the particular whim of Mrs. Rayland, as it was, they tell me, of her father, to preserve the pheasants. You know that Mr. Stockton has often been entreated to forbear; and you will allow that it is unhandsome to persist in doing what is offensive to a defenceless woman; therefore, upon meeting this Sir John Some-thing, with his servant carrying a net full of birds, I spoke to him on the impropriety of his shooting in those woods, and indeed almost within the park. He answered me very insolently, and I collared him; after which some rather high words passed between us. He sent his servant after me with his address; and I expected to have heard farther from him to-day."

"And was that all, Orlando?" said Mr. Somerive, looking steadily, and somewhat sternly, in his face.

"That was all that passed, Sir," replied Orlando hesitating, and blushing again.

"And was there no other person present when this quarrel happened? Was there no other cause for your displeasure against this gentleman, than what arose from his having killed these birds? Orlando, I used in your infancy and early youth to have the firmest reliance on your veracity; shall

I have the infinite mortification *now* to find myself mistaken?"

"No, Sir," answered Orlando, "nor now, nor ever; I have no reason to be ashamed of saying the truth, when called upon—though I should—"

"Come, come, Orlando!" cried his father; "you would not tell it, if you could, without being guilty of the meanness of a direct falsehood, conceal it. There were two young women present; and you thought it necessary to resent the behaviour of this Sir John Belgrave to one of them."

"Yes, I thought him very impertinent. The young woman was terrified, and I considered myself bound to protect her from him. I am sure, Sir, you would yourself have done the same thing."

"Perhaps I might. You are acquainted then with this girl, for whom you exercised your chivalry?"

"Certainly," said Orlando, again blushing so much that his father could not but perceive it—"certainly I am—am acquainted with her; that is—I know her to be sure, a little;—indeed, as I live so much under the same roof, it would be odd, and strange, if I did not."

"Very odd and strange indeed, Orlando," replied Mr. Somerive drily—"very odd and very strange;—especially as your brother tells me that the damsel is remarkably handsome."

"Well, Sir," cried Orlando with quickness, "admitting it to be so: does my brother think to do me an ill office with you, by telling you that I admire beauty; or that I defended a woman, for whom, if she had been ugly, I should equally have interposed, from the impudent persecutions of a coxcomb?"

"I do not believe that your brother intended to do you an ill office. On the contrary, he came to me this morning, at an hour when a visit from him was very unexpected, to tell me that he was very uneasy at the resentment expressed by Sir John Belgrave; and to desire I would prevent this disagreeable affair from going farther, by prevailing on you to make some proper apology."

"And if that was my brother's sole intention, I see no necessity for his having named the lady; there was otherwise ground enough for the quarrel, if a quarrel it can be called. However, I heartily forgive Philip; and am only sorry that he thinks he has cause to do me every disservice in his power."

"Do you call his anxiety for your safety a disservice? He hopes to prevent any risk of it, by telling me what has happened, and procuring, before it is too late, an apology."

Orlando checked his tears: "And does my father really think," said he, "that I *ought* to make an apology?"

"If the affair passed as Philip represented it to me, I think you ought; for you seem by that account to have been the aggressor."

"No, Sir," cried Orlando: "in every thing else your commands should be my law; but here I hope you will not lay them upon me, because I feel that, for the first time in my life, I must disobey them."

"And your mother," said Mr. Somerive, "your mother, on her return, is to hear that you are engaged in a duel; that you have either killed a man, who is a stranger to you, for the sake of a few paltry pheasants, or have yourself fallen? Oh rash and headlong boy!—if you did not feel deeper resentment than what a trespass on Mrs. Rayland's grounds occasioned, you would not thus have engaged in a dispute so alarming. I greatly fear your attachment to that girl."

Orlando, without denying or assenting to the truth of this accusation, related distinctly the very words that had passed.—"You see, Sir," continued he, "that it was about no girl the quarrel began; for, upon my soul! these were the very words."

"I think still," said his father, "that it is a very foolish affair; and, should Sir John Belgrave insist upon it, that you ought to make an excuse."

"Never," said Orlando; "and do not, dear Sir, do not, I conjure you, lay me under the cruel necessity of disobeying you. You cannot, with all the spirit you possess yourself, desire me to act like a coward; you must despise me if I did: and even my dear, my tender mother would blush for her son, if she thought him afraid of any man when he is conscious of a good cause."

"What is to be done, then?" cried Somerive in great perplexity. "You will certainly receive a challenge, Orlando."

"And then I must certainly accept it. But indeed, dear Sir, you are needlessly distressed: if this warlike Sir John must vindice his injured honour by firing a brace of pistols at me, I have as good a chance as he has; and at all events, if I fall, you will be delivered from the anxiety of providing for me, and I shall die lamented, which is better than to live disgraced. But after all (seeing his father's distress increase), I am much mistaken if this most magnanimous baronet had not rather let it alone— A few hours will determine it; and before my mother's return, whom I should be very sorry to terrify, it will be over, one way or other."

"You will not then, Orlando, settle it by an apology?"

"Never, indeed, my dear Sir."

"Nor give me your word that there is no attachment between you and this girl, this niece of Lennard's?"

"Why, my dear father," replied Orlando gaily, "if I am to be shot by

Sir John Belgrave, my attachments are of little consequence; it will therefore be time enough to talk of that when I find myself alive after our meeting."

"Young man," said Somerive, with more sternness than he almost ever shewed towards Orlando before, "you were once accustomed to obey implicitly all my commands.—At hardly twenty, it is rather early to throw off all parental authority. But I see that the expectations you have formed of possessing the Rayland estate, have made you fancy yourself independent."

"Pardon me, dear Sir! if I say you greatly mistake me. If I were to-morrow to find myself, by Mrs. Rayland's will, the owner of this property, which is of all things the most unlikely, I should not be at all more independent than I am now; for, while my father lived, I should be conscious that he alone had a right to the Rayland estate; nor should I then consider myself otherwise than as a dependant on his bounty."

"There is no contending with you, Orlando," said Mr. Somerive, bursting into tears, "I cannot bear this!—You must do, my son, as your own sense and spirit dictate; and I must leave the event to Heaven, to whose protection I commit you!—Yet remember your mother, Orlando: remember your sisters, whose protector you will, I trust, live to be; and do not, more rashly than these unlucky circumstances require, risk a life so precious to us all."

Orlando threw himself off his horse, and, seizing his father's hand, bathed it with his tears. Neither of them spoke for some moments. At length Orlando, recovering himself, said: "My father! I would die rather than offend you—If I could, or if I can without cowardice and meanness evade a meeting which may give you pain, I will. In the mean time let us say nothing about this squabble to alarm my mother, if she returns, as you say you expect she will, to-morrow. If any thing happens worth your knowing, you shall instantly hear of it: and in the mean time let me entreat you not to make yourself uneasy; for I am well convinced all will end without any of those distressing events which your imagination has painted."

Mr. Somerive shook his head and sighed. As he found nothing could be done with Orlando, he had determined to try to put a stop to the further progress of the affair, by his own interposition with Sir John Belgrave; and therefore, bidding Orlando tenderly adieu, he told him to go back to the Hall, while he himself went to his own house to consider how he might best ward off the impending evil from a son whom he every day found more cause to love and admire. He saw too evidently that Orlando had an affection for Mrs. Lennard's niece; for which, though it might be productive of the loss of Mrs. Rayland's favour, he knew not how to blame him. But these discoveries added new bitterness to the reflections he often made on the situation of Orlando; with which, notwithstanding the flattering prospect held out by Mrs. Rayland's late behaviour to him, his father could not be satisfied while it remained in such uncertainty. The anxiety however that he felt for the immediate circumstances, suspended his solicitude for those which were to come. A few hours might perhaps terminate that life, about the future disposition of which he was so continually meditating.

Orlando, deeply concerned at the distress of his father, and too much confirmed in his opinion of his brother's treachery and malice, returned to the Hall filled with disquiet. He had now much to add to his letter to Monimia, for he resolved to keep nothing a secret from her; and he went impatiently into his own room to finish his letter, when, upon the table, he found the following billet:

"SIR,

"As I find, on enquiry, you are by birth a gentleman, you cannot believe I can pass over the very extraordinary language and conduct you chose to make use of yesterday. Yet, in consideration of your youth, and of your relationship to Mr. Somerive, the friend of *my* friend Stockton, I shall no otherwise notice it than by desiring you will write such an apology as it becomes you to make, and me to receive. I am, Sir,
                    "Your humble servant,

Carloraine Castle,   "J.B.BELGRAVE."
Oct, 18, 1776.

To this letter, which Orlando was told was delivered a few moments before by a servant who waited, he, without hesitation, returned the following answer:

"SIR,

"Not conscious of any impropriety in my conduct, I shall assuredly make no apology for it; and I beg that neither your indulgence to my youth, or my relationship to Mr. Philip Somerive, may prevent your naming any other satisfaction which your honour may require, and which I am immediately ready to give.
                    "I am, Sir,

"Your humble servant,

Rayland Hall,   "ORLANDO SOMERIVE."
Oct. 18, 1776.

Having dispatched this billet, he continued very coolly to conclude
his letter to Monimia; and this last circumstance was the only one he
concealed from her. Having done it, he went to the turret, and softly
mounted the stair-case, flattering himself that, if he heard no noise, and
could be quite secure that no person was with her, he might venture to
see Monimia for a few moments. He listened therefore, impatiently;
but, to his infinite mortification, heard Betty talking with more than
her usual volubility; and as his name was repeated, he could not help
attending to her harangue.

"Oh! to be sure," said she, in answer to something Monimia had said;
"to be sure, I warrant Orlando is a saint and an angel in your eyes—but
I know something."

"Tell me Betty," said Monimia tremulously, "tell me what you know."

"Why I know—that though he looks as if butter wouldn't melt in
his mouth, cheese won't choke him. I can tell you what, Miss, he's slyer
than his brother, but not a bit gooder—What's more, he lets women
into his room at night."

"Women!" cried Monimia, "what women? How should he do that?
and who should they be?"

"That's more than I can tell; but some hussy or other he does let in,
I tell you, for I know they as have seen her. There's Pattenson has been
mad as fury with me, saying as how it was me; and all I can say won't
persuade him to the contrary.—Egollys! if it had been me, I should not
have gone to have denied it, in spite of Pattenson; but he's as mad as a
dog, and won't hear nothing I can say, but swears he'll tell my Lady—
though I can bring Jenny to prove that, at that very time as he says I
was sitting along with 'Squire Orlando in his own study, I was fast asleep
up stairs—And so if Pattenson does make a noise about it, Jenny offers
to take her bible oath before the Justice."

"I think," said Monimia, acquiring a little courage from the hope she
now entertained that she had not been distinguished, "I think it is much
better to say nothing about it."

"So I tells him," answered Betty; "but he is so crazy anger'd with me
that he won't hear nothing I can say—and there to be sure I own I
should like to know who this puss is."

"Why," replied Monimia, "what can it signify, Betty, to you?"

"It signifies to every body, I think, Miss, especially to us poor servants, who may lose our characters. You see that I'm blamed about it already, and Pattenson is always a telling me that Mr. Orlando has a liking for me, and that I keeps him company.—Not I, I'm sure!—but it is very hard to be brought into such a quandary as this, when one's quite as 'twere as innocent as can be. I'd give my ears to see this slut."

"Why, who did ever see her?" enquired Monimia.

"Oh! that's neither here nor there—she was seen, and that's enough."

"I think it's impertinent in any body to pry into Mr. Orlando's room, and I dare say it is all a mistake—"

"Please the Lord, I'll find out the mistake," said Betty, "and, I warrant, know who this dear friend of Orlando's is before I'm two days older— and I know somebody else that won't be sorry to know."

"Who is that?"

"Why his brother—a dear sweet man—He came up to our house last night, Miss, after 'twas dark, on purpose to speak to me. I won't tell you half he said; but he's a noble generous gentleman, and has a more genteeler taste too than Orlando; and for my share, I think he's as handsome."

Monimia now seemed to let the discourse drop, and to be considering what she ought to do. Orlando waited yet a little, in hopes that Betty would go, and that he might have an opportunity of seeing Monimia: but immediately the dinner bell rang; and as he now generally dined with Mrs. Rayland, he was afraid of being enquired for, and retired silently to his room, somewhat earlier, from the strong reason he now had to believe, that, whoever it was whose curiosity brought them the preceding evening to his door, they were actuated by no suspicion in regard to Monimia, and that they had not even distinguished her countenance and figure; and he meditated how to prevent any suspicion concerning her—content to be accused himself of any other folly or error, if Monimia could but escape.

CHAP. XII.

It was probable that Sir John Belgrave's messenger would immediately return, fixing the time and place where he would meet Orlando, who debated with himself whether he should send the billet he had received, and that he expected, to his father. He had not yet determined how he ought to act, and was traversing the flagstones which went around the house considering of it, when his father's servant appeared, and delivered to him the following letter:

"My dear Orlando,

"I have just seen Sir John Belgrave at Mr. Stockton's, who, on my account, as this affair really gives me great pain, is willing to drop any farther resentment, if you will only say to me, that you are sorry for your rashness. I entreat you to gratify me in this—I will not say I command you, because I hope that I need not; but this unlucky business *must* be settled before the return of your mother, from whom I have to-day heard that she will be at home to-morrow with Isabella, since she cannot determine to leave her in London.—I have also a letter from my old friend General Tracy, of whom you recollect hearing me speak as one of my early friends. He is much acquainted with your uncle Woodford, and has been very obliging in promoting his interest among his connections, which are with people of the first rank.—Having met your mother and sisters at Mr. Woodford's, he has renewed that friendship which time and distance, and our different modes of life, have for some years interrupted; and as he is fond of field sports, and your mother has said how happy I shall be to see him, he intends coming hither to-morrow for ten days or a fortnight, and brings your mother and Isabella down in his post chaise. This intelligence has put Selina, who is now my house-keeper, into some little hurry, as you know we are little used to company; and it prevents my coming to you myself, as I should otherwise have done.—But I repeat, Orlando, that this uneasiness must be removed from my mind. Write to me therefore such a letter as I may shew to this Sir John Belgrave, and let us hear no more of it. I beg that you will inform Mrs. Rayland that I expect company, and that you will obtain her leave to be here to-morrow to receive them. Robert waits for your answer, which I am persuaded will be satisfactory to

"Your affectionate father,

"P. SOMERIVE."

To this letter, which was extremely distressing to Orlando, since it imposed upon him what he had he thought with propriety refused, he knew not what to answer. To suffer his father to say to Sir John Belgrave that he was sorry for what had passed, seemed to him even more humiliating than to say it himself—he could not bear to owe his safety to his father's fears; yet it gave him infinite pain to disobey him, and was the first time in his life that he had been tempted to act for himself, in opposition to his father; and the apprehensions of what his mother would feel were still more distressing to him; yet his high spirit could not stoop to apologize for what he knew was not wrong, nor to say he was concerned for having acted as he should certainly act again were the same occasion to arise. After much and uneasy deliberation, he at length dispatched to his father the following lines:

"My dear Sir,

"Again I must entreat your pardon for the disobedience I am compelled to be guilty of. Indeed it is impossible for me, highly as I honour your commands, and greatly as I feel the value of your tenderness, quite impossible for me to make any apology to Sir John Belgrave: for, were I to say that I am sorry for what passed, I should say what is false, which surely my father will never insist upon. It would grieve my very soul to alarm my mother; but surely there is no necessity for her knowing any thing of this silly business. As you expect General Tracy to-morrow, of whose military character I have often heard you speak with applause, I entreat that you will rather entrust him with the affair, and ask him whether I ought, all circumstances fairly related, to make the submission required of me; and as I am sure I may leave it to him to decide for me, I promise that I will abide by his determination, and will not till then meet Sir John Belgrave if he should in the mean time send me an appointment; though even this delay is, I own, incompatible with my ideas of that spirit which, in a proper cause, should be exerted by a son of yours. Let this promise, however, of a reference to General Tracy make you easy at present, my dear and honoured Sir! and be assured in every other instance of the obedience, and in every instance of the affection, of your

"Orlando."

Rayland Hall,
Oct. 20th, 1776.

Having dispatched this letter, Orlando dismissed the affair of Sir John Belgrave from his mind for the present, and gave all his thoughts to Monimia. The circumstance of the man's appearing at his door, though much less alarming than it seemed at first, was yet such as threatened to put an end to all those delicious conversations which had so long been the charm of his existence. Not to have an opportunity of seeing Monimia, was death to him; yet to see her, were she exposed to such terrors as she had undergone at their last interview, was impossible. In order to turn all suspicion from her, he would very willingly have been suspected of a *penchant* for Betty, and have encouraged her flippant forwardness; but that, as it awakened the envy and jealousy of Pattenson, was likely to put him upon the watch, and to bring on the very evil he dreaded. During the day, indeed, he had now frequent opportunities of seeing Monimia, who was now, unless under her aunt's displeasure, less rigorously confined than formerly; but those interviews were never but in the presence of a third person; and after what his father had said, and what had happened on the alarming evening, he was compelled to be more than ever cautious. Tormented by uncertainty, and perplexed by apprehensions, he passed a wretched afternoon; impatiently waiting till he could ascend the turret, and at least, if he could not see Monimia, obtain a letter from her. The hour at length came when he believed every one in the house were occupied with their own affairs; and having excused himself from drinking tea with Mrs. Rayland, under the pretence of being busied in writing for his father, he stole softly to the room under that of Monimia, and from thence up the stairs.

He listened, fearful of again hearing the indefatigable clack of Betty; but every thing was profoundly silent. The letter, which he had deposited there, was gone; but there was no answer. He feared Monimia was ill—the terror, the fatigue of the preceding night, had been too much for her. It was dreadful to be within two or three paces of her, and yet not dare to enquire.

Still listening some time in breathless anxiety, he at length determined to tap gently at the door; for he was pretty well convinced she was alone. Monimia, who was really ill, had lain down; but, starting at the well-known signal, she approached close to the door, and said, "Orlando! Gracious Heaven! are you there?"

"Yes, yes!" replied he; "is it impossible you can admit me for a moment? I am miserable, and shall hardly keep my senses if I cannot see you."

Monimia, without replying, moved her bed and admitted him. It was already dark, but she had a candle on her table, and Orlando was shocked to see how ill she looked. He spoke of it tenderly to her: she assured him it was only owing to her having been so much fatigued and frightened, and that a night's rest, if she could obtain it, would entirely restore her. "But you must not stay, Orlando!" said she— "indeed you must not!"

"Why?" answered he—"Is not your door fastened? Who is likely to interrupt us?"

"My aunt or Betty," replied she; "for, though my aunt is at her tea, there is no being secure of her. I have said I am ill, in which it can hardly be said I am guilty of a falsehood; and as I am under her displeasure on account of my unluckily staying beyond her orders, yet she may perhaps be seized with some whim, and even the voice of Betty would terrify me to death."

Orlando, promising to go, yet finding it impossible to tear himself from her, began to speak of what he had heard from Betty in the morning, while he waited at the door of Monimia's room after depositing his letter. "You see, my angel," said he, "you see you are not suspected; and that the impertinent brute, whoever it was that dared intrude upon us, did not distinguish you. Make yourself easy therefore, I conjure you, and let us think no more of this alarm, for which, though I cannot yet discover how, I am sure I shall in a few days be able to account."

"But I shall never again have courage to venture to your room, Orlando."

"You will," replied he, "surely, when I am able to convince you that such an interruption will happen no more, and till then I do not wish you to venture."

"Hush, dearest Orlando!" whispered Monimia; "speak very low! I heard the door at the end of the passage open."

They both listened; and instantly Betty, by attempting to open the door, convinced them their fears were not groundless.—"Lud, Miss," cried she, pushing against the door, "what have you lock'd yourself in for? Open the door—I want to speak to you."

"Don't speak!" whispered Orlando: "let me out as softly as you can, and then tell her you were sleeping."

"She has the ears of a mole," said Monimia, "and I shall be undone,"

Quickly and softly, however, as her trembling hands would let her, she assisted in Orlando's evasion—Betty still thumping at the door— "I must come in, Miss, this minute."

"I am laid down for my headach," replied Monimia as soon as Orlando was gone: "It is strange that I can never have any repose! I was just asleep, Betty, and should be very glad not to be disturbed."

"Glad or not glad," replied the other, "I must come in. 'Tis an odd thing, I think, for people to push their chairs and tables about in their sleep! If you can do that, I suppose you can open the door?"

Monimia now opened the door, and tremulously asked Betty, who flounced into the room, what was the matter?

"Matter!" said she—"why there's a fine to do below—There's your favourite young 'Squire; he, as never does no wrong, has got into a fine scrape—just as I thought!"

"Good God!" replied she, in a voice hardly articulate, "tell me what you mean."

"Why this great gentleman, as he affronted so, has determined to kill him outright—He have been writing to him about it this morning; and Orlando, he is so stomachful, he won't ask the gentleman's pardon, and so now they be to fight."

"And how," said Monimia, speaking with difficulty, "how did you hear all this?"

"Why, from Sir John's own man, a smart servant as ever I see, who is just come with a letter to fix the time and place where they be to meet; and he have been telling us how it is to be: and so my mistress she have heard of it, and there'll be a fine to do I can tell you. They have been going for to find young 'Squire Orlando, but he is out somewhere or another. Mistress is in a fine quandary, but she says how Orlando was quite in the right."

Betty having thus unburthened herself of news which she was so anxious to tell, returned to see a little more of the smart servant; but not till Orlando, who had heard enough at the beginning of her conversation, had flown down to receive a letter which he had long expected, and now prepared to answer; though he was convinced that, by the bustle Sir John Belgrave chose to make, there was very little probability that he desired to be very much in earnest. The anxious night that this would occasion to his Monimia was his chief concern. He determined to attempt seeing her again, in hopes to alleviate her uneasiness; but he was first compelled to attend to Mrs. Rayland, who sent for him, and to whom he now related what had passed before, and read the letter which he had just received from Sir John Belgrave, which ran thus:

"Sir,
"In consideration of your respectable father, I did hope that you might have spared me the disagreeable task of chastising your improper behaviour. I shall be, on Thursday at twelve o'clock, in the meadow adjoining to West Wolverton, with a brace of pistols, of which you shall take your choice.
I am, Sir,
   your humble servant,

   John Berkely Belgrave."

Carloraine Castle,
Oct. 20th, 1776.

To this billet Orlando answered thus—

"SIR,

"I WILL assuredly attend you at the time and place appointed; and
have only to regret, that the persons to whom this affair has most
unnecessarily been communicated, have so long an interval of uneasiness thus imposed upon them. I am, Sir,
        your humble servant,

            ORLANDO SOMERIVE."

Rayland Hall,
Oct. 20th, 1776.

Mrs. Rayland, who entered into this business with an earnestness of
which she seemed on most occasions incapable, approved of his letter,
and admired the spirit he exerted in a cause which she considered as
her own. Her fears for his safety seemed to be absorbed in the pleasure
she felt in having a champion who was so ready to take up her quarrel
against those whose inroads had long disturbed her, and whom she
hoped to mortify and humble.

Orlando, therefore, never was so high in her favour; but his own
heart was torn with anguish, in reflecting on the situation of Monimia.
As soon as the house was quiet he returned to the turret, made desperate by reflecting on her distress, and thinking it better to hazard a
discovery than to leave her a whole night in solicitude so alarming.

Monimia, who little expected his return, admitted him as soon as
she heard his signal. He found her in that state of mind which allows
not the sufferer to shed tears; pale, and almost petrified, she sat on the
side of her bed, with clasped hands and fixed eyes, while he related to
her the whole of a transaction which he wished he could have
concealed from her till the event could be known. But it was long
before he could persuade her that the danger was infinitely less than it
appeared. It was evident that Sir John Belgrave, by postponing to
Thursday what he might as well have settled on Wednesday, had no
objection to the interference of the family he had taken care to alarm;
and rather wished to have the honour of appearing a man of nice
honour and dauntless courage at little expence, than to run the hazard

of maintaining that character by needless rashness. When Orlando therefore had represented his conduct in the ridiculous light it deserved, and shewn her how probable it was that his father and General Tracy would contrive to prevent a meeting, the fears of Monimia were in some degree subdued; and at day-break Orlando left her, having insisted on her promising to endeavour to sleep, and to make herself as easy as under such circumstances was possible.

END OF THE FIRST VOLUME.

VOL. II

Ah me! for aught that I could ever read,
Could ever hear from tale or history,
The course of true love never did run smooth;
But either it was different in blood,
Or else misgrafted in respect of years,
Or else it stood upon the choice of friends;
Or, if there were sympathy in choice,
War, death, or sickness, did lay siege to it.

SHAKSP. Midsummer Night's Dream.

CHAP. I.

On the following morning Orlando received an early summons from his father, requesting him to be at home by two o'clock, when his mother, his sister, and General Tracy were expected; for, as the General travelled with his own four horses, which were very fine ones, and of which he was particularly fond, the ladies had agreed to remain one night on the road, and reach home early the second day; though the journey was otherwise easily performed in one, West Wolverton being only about sixty-five miles from London.

Orlando having informed Mrs. Rayland of the reason of his absence; having seen Monimia for a moment, again whispered to her to be less apprehensive for his safety, and promising to see her at night, he proceeded to obey his father. On his arrival, he found him walking with the General on the grass plot before the door; and, springing from his horse, paid his duty to him, was introduced in form to the General, and then eagerly asked for his mother and his sister.

They were within; and Orlando, flying to them, was surprised by his mother's throwing her arms around him, and falling into an agony of tears, in which his three sisters, who stood around her, accompanied her. He entreated an explanation; and learned from Isabella, who alone was able to speak, that the servants had been telling them, instantly on their arrival at home, that he was about to fight a duel, in which it was the opinion of the informers that he must certainly be killed.

Orlando, execrating the folly of the servants, or rather the paltry conduct of Sir John Belgrave, who had apparently made all this bustle on purpose, endeavoured to re-assure and console his mother; but her alarm for his safety was too great to allow her to listen patiently to any thing he could say, since the fact of his having received and accepted a challenge from Sir John Belgrave he did not attempt to deny. The anxious mother, now that she saw him before her, thought only of preventing the meeting which might deprive her of that comfort for ever. She seemed afraid of his stirring from her sight, as if Sir John Belgrave had lurked in every corner of the house; and desired he would remain with her in her own room, while she sent Isabella to entreat that Mr. Somerive would come to her.

When he saw her, her tears and agitation sufficiently explained to him, that those whom he had expressly ordered to be silent had found it impossible to obey him. To Selina and Emma, the two youngest girls, who had remained at home, it had been known almost as soon as to himself, but he had enjoined them to conceal it from their mother; and knew that, whatever it cost them to be silent on such a subject, neither of them would disobey him. It was, however, too late, or at least useless, to declaim against the folly of those who *had*; and he found sufficient employment in appeasing the distress of his wife and daughters, while he sent Orlando to entertain the General.

General Tracy was the second brother of a noble family; and, having entered very young into the army, had passed through the inferior ranks with that rapidity which interest always secures. At five-and-thirty he had a regiment; and as some of the fortunes of uncles and aunts had centred in him, he was now, at near sixty, a man of very large fortune, and seemed to want nothing to complete his happiness, but the power of persuading others, as he had almost persuaded himself, that he was but five-and-thirty still.

To effect this, and maintain that favour which he had always been in among the ladies, was the great object of his life. His person had been celebrated for beauty; and he desired to preserve a pre-eminence, which was in his opinion superior to any fame he could derive from his bravery in the field, or his ability in the senate, where he had long been a member, certainly voting with the minister of the day. He had a place about the court, at which he was a constant attendant, and where the softness and elegance of his manners, the pliability of his political attachments, and his very considerable interest and property, rendered him a great favourite.—All the time he could spare from his duty there, he seemed to devote to the service of those fashionable women who give the ton,[1] and whose favour he disputed with the rising heroes of the fashionable world. But he felt in reality only disgust and satiety in their company; and had no taste but for youth and beauty, of which he was continually in search—and with his fortune his search could not be unsuccessful. He had no scruples to deter him from decoying any young woman whom he liked, that chance might throw into his power; but he usually avoided with care any scheme which was likely to be interrupted by the unpleasant remonstrances of a father or a brother, and generally pursued only the indigent and the defenceless.

As he purchased his wine of Mr. Woodford, he had occasionally been at his house. His daughters were rather handsome, and very lively girls; and though they did not come exactly under the description of those whose

---

[1] That is, the "tone": they set the style for fashionable London.

preference the General could without much trouble secure, he found himself pleased with their company, because they were greatly flattered by the admiration of such a fashionable man, and never so happy as when the General sent his superb coach for them, and gallanted them to some public place, or drove them in his phaeton through Hyde Park to Kensington Gardens. Their father, who thought more of the good customer which the General was himself, and the great families he had recommended him to, than of any necessity for reserve in his daughters, encouraged this acquaintance (which their mother was as well pleased with as the young women) till the neighbourhood talked loudly of their indiscretion, and till the youngest Miss Woodford, who was his peculiar favourite, was declared by many ladies to have considerably injured her reputation. This she herself considered only as a testimony of their envy, and her own superior attractions; and the more she heard of their maligant remarks, the more eagerly she endeavoured to shew her contempt of their opinion, and her power over the General, who, on the return of the family to town after their visit to West Wolverton, was more than usual at the house. But thither he was no longer attracted by the charms of Miss Eliza Woodford. The moment he beheld Isabella Somerive, he had no eyes for any other person; and though he soon learned that she was in a situation of life which placed her above those temptations which he generally found infallible, and had a father and two brothers to protect her, the impression she had made was such that he could not determine to lose sight of her; and as the discovery of the preference he gave her had made both her cousins very little desirous of her company in London during the winter, where she seemed too likely to rob them of all their conquests, he found she was to return home with her mother—and thither he resolved to follow her.

An opportunity of introducing himself into the family of Somerive was easily obtained, when he recollected that, in the preceding war, Somerive, in whose own county there was at that time no militia, had, being then an active man, procured a commission in that of a neighbouring county, and served in a camp then formed for the defence of the coast, where he himself was a captain. They had at that time been frequently together, and afterwards kept up some degree of intimacy, till Somerive's marriage fixing him wholly in retirement, the gay and fashionable soldier thought of him no more.

The General, however, no sooner knew who the visitors at Woodford's were, than he most assiduously and successfully paid his court to Mrs. Somerive; talked to her continually of her husband, whose merits he affected to remember with infinite regard, and for whose interest he appeared to feel the warmest concern. It was a theme of which Mrs. Somerive, who adored her husband, was never weary; and while General Tracy so pathetically lamented the interruption of their friendship, nothing was more natural than her entreaties to him that he would renew it.

That was the point he had laboured to gain, and he accepted the invitation she gave him, adding the opportunity of the shooting season to his other inducements, the better to colour so unexpected a visit. He had found it convenient to pretend a great passion for field sports—partly because it was fashionable, and partly because it shewed that his powers of enduring fatigue were equal to the youthful appearance he assumed; and to support this, he now and then went through, what was to him most miserable drudgery, that of a day's hunting or shooting; but he more usually contrived, when he was at the houses of his friends for these purposes, to sprain his ancle in the first excursion he made, or to hurt himself by the recoil of his gun: and by such methods he generally managed to be left without suspicion at home with the ladies; with whom he was so universal a favourite, and to whom he had so many ways of recommending himself, by deciding on their dress, reading to them books of entertainment, and relating anecdotes collected in the higher circles where he moved in the winter, that he found no loss of attention from the progress of years—a progress indeed which he took the utmost pains to conceal. His clothes, which were always made by the most eminent taylor, were cut with as much care as those of the most celebrated beauty on her first appearance at court; and he had several contrivances, of his own invention, to make them fit with advantage to his person. His hands were more delicate than those of any lady; and though he could not so totally baffle the inexorable hands of time as to escape a few wrinkles, he still maintained a considerable share of the bloom of youth, not without suspicion of Olympian dew, cold cream, and Spanish wool.[1] Certain it is that he was very long at his toilet every day, to which no person, not even his valet-de-chambre, was admitted. With all this he was a man of the most undoubted bravery; and had not only served in Germany with great credit, but had been engaged in several affairs of honour, in which he had always acquitted himself with courage and propriety. Such was the man who was now, from no very honourable motives, become an inmate in the house of Mr. Somerive.

---

[1] According to Ehrenpreis, Olympian dew was "a preparation to make the eyes glisten" (p. 537). Spanish wool was a variety of rouge, and may also refer to the wool used to apply it, while cold cream was, and still is, facial cleanser and moisturizer.

When Mr. Somerive had appeased the distress into which his wife was thrown by the intelligence she had so abruptly received about Orlando, and had prevailed upon her to compose herself and appear at dinner, he returned back to his friend, whom he found in conversation with Orlando; and he determined that he would, over their wine, relate to him what had passed between Sir John Belgrave and his son (who had put Sir John's last letter into his hands), and take the General's opinion as to what was fit to be done.

Dinner was announced, and the ladies of the family appeared;—the mother, with swollen eyes, which she could not a moment keep from Orlando; and the daughters appearing to sympathize with her, particularly Selina, who was fondly attached to Orlando, and who, from the terror in which she saw her mother, having caught redoubled apprehension, could hardly command her tears; and though the General failed not to compliment her on her beauty, which even exceeded that of her sister, and to speak in the warmest terms to Mr. and Mrs. Somerive of their lovely family, Selina heeded him not. He observed that Isabella was less insensible of his studied eulogiums, and from thence drew a favourable omen. Emma, the youngest of the girls, was only between twelve and thirteen.

As soon as the table-cloth was removed, Mrs. Somerive, under pretence of being a good deal fatigued with her journey, and somewhat indisposed, withdrew with her daughters: Mr. Somerive soon after gave Orlando a hint to go also; and then he opened to General Tracy the affair which lay so heavy on his heart, and entreated his advice how to act.

"I am glad," answered the General, "to learn the cause of Mrs. Somerive's concern, which was so evident at dinner, as well as that of her amiable daughters, that I was afraid some very disagreeable incident had happened in the family."

"And is not," said Mr. Somerive, "what I have related disagreeable enough?"

"No, upon my honour! I see nothing in it but what is rather a matter of exultation. Your son is one of the finest and most spirited young men I ever saw. If he was a son of my own, I should rejoice that he had acted so properly, and be very proud of him."

"But you would not risk his life, surely?" said Mr. Somerive.

"Why, as to that," replied the General, "in these cases there is some little risk, to be sure; but I should never check a lad of spirit. I know Belgrave," added he, smiling.

"And what is his reputation for courage?" enquired Mr. Somerive.

"Oh! he is quite the fine man of the day," answered the General carelessly.—"He will fight, if he must—but I believe is quite as willing to let it alone."

"It will break my wife's heart," said Mr. Somerive dejectedly, and amazed at the different light in which two people, from their different modes of life, consider the same object; "it will certainly break my wife's heart, if any evil befalls Orlando."

General Tracy now saw that an opportunity offered by which he might confer an obligation on the family, which must secure their endless gratitude, and he resolved to embrace it.

"If it makes you all so uneasy," replied he, after a moment's pause, "and especially if her fears make Mrs. Somerive so very wretched, suppose we try what can be done to put an end to the affair without a meeting. I dare say Belgrave will easily be induced, on the slightest apology, to drop the affair entirely."

"But even the slightest apology Orlando will not be persuaded to make," said Mr. Somerive.

"He is right," answered the General; "and I honour him for his resolution. It is a thousand pities," continued he, again pausing, "that such a gloriously spirited young fellow should waste his life in seclusion, waiting on the caprices of an old woman—What do you intend to do with him?"

"That," said Somerive, "is what I have long been in doubt about. I had thoughts once of putting him into trade; but to that project Mrs. Rayland's objections, and Orlando's little inclination to follow it, put an end."

"I am glad they did; for it would have been a sad sacrifice, I think, to have set so fine a young man down to a compting-house desk for the rest of his life."

"And at other times," re-assumed Mr. Somerive, "I have thought of the church. Mrs. Rayland has very considerable patronage; but though I have hinted very frequently to her my wishes on this subject, she never would understand me, to give me any assurance that she would secure him a living; or made any offer of assistance to support him at the university, which she knows that it is quite impossible for me, circumstanced as I am at present, to do."

"She was in the right of it," cried the General. "The old lady has more sagacity than I suspected, and knows that it would be absolutely a sin to make him a parson, and bury all that sense and spirit in a country vicarage. Why, my good friend, do you not put your son into the army?— that seems to be the profession for which nature has designed him."

"Because," answered Somerive, "I have, in the first place, no money to buy him a commission; and, if I had, there are two great objections to it:—it would half kill his mother, and take him out of the way of Mrs. Rayland, which appears to be very impolitic."

"What if a commission were found for him," said General Tracy, "do you think the other objections ought to weigh much? Consider of it, my good friend; and if you think such a plan would be eligible, and the young man himself likes it, perhaps it may be in my power to be of some use to you."

Mr. Somerive warmly expressed his gratitude for the interest that his friend seemed to take in the welfare of his Orlando; and then, after a short silence, said: "But, my dear General, we forget, while we are planning schemes for the future life of Orlando, it may be terminated to-morrow."

"Well," replied he, "since I see you cannot conquer your alarm about this matter, and as I am still more concerned for Mrs. Somerive, I will go over early in the morning to Belgrave, who has wisely appointed the meeting at twelve o'clock, and somehow or other we will get it settled.—If I say to the doughty baronet, that his honour will suffer nothing by dropping it, I am pretty well assured that he will be content to let it go no farther. Make yourself easy therefore, and go tell your wife that I will take care of her little boy, while I pay my respects to the young ladies whom I see walking in the garden."

Somerive, whose heart was agonized by the distress of his wife, hastened to relieve her; and the General went off at a quick march to overtake the three Miss Somerives, to whom he related some part of the conversation that had passed between him and their father, and the task he had undertaken of settling the affair with Sir John Belgrave.

The sensible hearts of these charming girls were filled with the liveliest emotions towards the General, who, if he could save their brother from danger, which their timidity had dreadfully magnified, they believed would be entitled to their everlasting gratitude. The brilliant eyes of Isabella sparkled with pleasure, while the softer blue eyes of Selina were turned towards him filled with tears of pleasure; and little Emma longed to embrace him, as she used to do her father when he had granted any of her infantine requests. While every one alternately expressed her thanks, Tracy whispered to Isabella, by whose side he was walking: "To give the slightest pleasure to my lovely Isabella, I would do infinitely more; and, rather than she should be alarmed, take myself the chance of Sir John Belgrave's fire."

Isabella, too ignorant of the ways of the world to be either offended or alarmed by such a speech, and naturally pleased by flattery and admiration, smiled on the enamoured General in a manner so fascinating as overpaid him for all the trouble he had taken or proposed to take: and while he meditated against his old friend the greatest injury he could commit, he reconciled himself to it, by determining to do such services to the other part of the family, as would more than compensate for the inroads he might make on its peace by carrying off Isabella; for to carry her off he was resolved, if his art could effect it. His eagerness, however, to serve Orlando, had another motive than this of retribution. He foresaw that so spirited a young man might prevent, or, not being able to do that, would very seriously resent his designs upon a sister; the character of the elder brother, of which he had by this time formed a pretty clear idea, left him little to apprehend from him; but the fiery and impetuous Orlando would, he thought, be much better out of the way.

His conversation with the Miss Somerives now took a gayer turn; and so happy did he feel himself with three such nymphs around him, that he regretted the summons which called them in to attend the tea-table.

Mrs. Somerive, who had now been long in conference with her husband, and afterwards with Orlando, appeared much more cheerful than at dinner, and surveyed the General with those looks of complacency which expressed how much she was obliged to him for the interference he had promised. The evening passed off pleasantly. Orlando staid to supper; but then told his father, that he had some business to do for Mrs. Rayland early the next day (which was true), and therefore he would return to the Hall that evening. Mr. Somerive, who still felt a dread which he could not conquer, entreated him to give his word of honour, that he would not throw himself in the way of Sir John Belgrave till the hour of that gentleman's appointment. This Orlando (who was ignorant of the plans in agitation to prevent that appointment from taking place at all) thought himself obliged to comply with: on which condition his father, though reluctantly, suffered him at midnight to mount his horse and return to Rayland Hall, where he had desired Betty to sit up for him; fearful of entering through the chapel, lest his doing so should lead to those suspicions he was so desirous of avoiding. As soon as he left his father's door, he put his horse into a gallop, impatient to be with Monimia; and as he crossed the park, he saw a light in her turret, and pleased himself with the idea of her fondly expecting his arrival.

CHAP. II.

Orlando, on his entering the servant's hall, found Betty waiting for him as she had promised. "Lord, Sir," cried she as soon as he appeared, "I thoft as you'd never come! Why it's almost half past one o'clock, and I be frighted out of my seven senses sitting up so all alone."

"I beg your pardon, dear Betty!" replied he; "but I could not get away sooner. I'll never detain you so long again; and now suffer me to make you what amends I can, by desiring your acceptance of this." He presented her with a crown, which she looked at a moment, and then, archly leering at him, said, "Humph! if you give folks a crown for sitting up for you in the kitchen, I suppose they as bides with you in your study have double price."

"Come, come, Betty," said Orlando, impatient to escape from her troublesome enquiries, "let me hear no more of such nonsense. I have nobody ever in my study, as you know very well. It is very late—I wish you a good night."

He then, without attending to her further, as she seemed still disposed to talk, took his candle, and went to his own apartment; where, after waiting about a quarter of an hour, till he thought her retired, and the whole house quiet, he took his way to the turret.

Monimia had long expected him, and now received him with joy, chastised by the fear which she felt on enquiring into the events of the day. Orlando related to her all that he thought would give her pleasure, and endeavoured that she should understand the affair of the next day settled, for he would not violate truth by positively asserting it; and Monimia, apprehensive of teasing him by her enquiries, stifled, as much as she could, the pain she endured from this uncertainty. This she found it better to do, as she observed Orlando to be restless and dissatisfied: he complained of the misery he underwent in his frequent absences, and of the unworthy excuses he was compelled to make. He expressed impatiently the long unhappiness he had in prospect, if he could never see her but thus clandestinely, and risking every moment her fame and her peace. Monimia, however, soothed him, by bidding him remember how lately it was that they both thought themselves too happy to meet upon any terms; and would very fain have inspired him with hopes that they might soon look forward to fairer prospects—hopes which he had often tried to give her. But, alas! she could not communicate what she did not feel; and whichever way they cast their eyes, all was despair as to their ever being united with the consent of those friends on whom they were totally dependant.

Orlando, most solicitous for the peace of Monimia, had never been betrayed before into these murmurings in her presence, forgetting the threatening aspect of the future, while he enjoyed the happiness that was present. But all that had passed during the day had assisted in making him discontented. His mother's tears and distress, the tender fears of his sisters, and the less evident, but more heavy anxiety which he saw oppressed his father, all contributed to convince him that, in being of so much consequence to his family, he lost the privilege of pleasing himself; that his duty and his inclination must be fore ever at variance; and that, if he could resign the hopes of being settled in affluence by Mrs. Rayland, he still could not marry Monimia without making his family unhappy—unless indeed he had the means of providing for her, of which at present there appeared not the least probability. Mrs. Rayland seemed likely to live for many years; or, if she died, it was very uncertain whether she would give him more than a trifling legacy. When he reflected on his situation, he became ashamed of thus spending his life, of wasting the best of his days in the hope of that which might never happen; while Monimia, almost a prisoner in her little apartment, passed the day in servitude, and divided the night between uneasy expectation, hazardous conference, and fruitless tears.

It was these thoughts that gave to Orlando that air of impatience and anxiety which, even in the presence of Monimia, he could not so far conquer but that she observed it before he broke through the restraint he had hitherto imposed on himself, and indulged those fears which he had so often entreated her to check.

At length, however, the hope she affected to feel, the charm of finding himself so fondly beloved, and that his Monimia was prepared to meet any destiny with him, restored him to that temper which he was in when he proposed to brave the discovery of their attachment. With difficulty she persuaded him to leave her about three o'clock. He glided softly down stairs; and when he came out of the lower room of the turret, he found the night so very dark that could not see his hand. He knew the way, however, so well, that he walked slowly but fearlessly on, and had nearly reached the chapel-door when he found his feet suddenly entangled; and before he could either disengage himself, or discover what it was that thus impeded his way, somebody ran against him, whom he seized, and loudly demanded to know who it was.

"And who are you?" replied a deep surly voice: "let me go, or it shall be the worst day's work you ever did in your life."

Orlando, now convinced that he had taken the fellow who had so insolently intruded upon him, and so cruelly alarmed Monimia, felt himself provoked to punish him for his past insolence, and deter him from repeating it: he therefore firmly grasped his prisoner, who seemed a very stout fellow, and who struggled violently for his release—so violently indeed, that Orlando, exerting all his strength, threw him down, but, in doing so, the rope which he had at first trod upon being in the way, he fell also: still, however, he held his antagonist fast, and, kneeling upon him, said resolutely, "Whoever you are, I will detain you here till daylight, unless you instantly tell me your name and business."

"Curse your strength!" replied the fallen foe; "if I was not a little boozy, I'd be d——d before you should have the better of me."

"Who are you?" again repeated Orlando.

"Why, who the plague should I be," cried the man, "but Jonas Wilkins!—Ah, Master Orlando, I knows you too now well enough;—come, Sir, let a body go. I know you'd scorn to do a poor man no harm."

"Jonas Wilkins!" exclaimed Orlando, who knew that to be the name of an outlawed smuggler, famous for his resolution, and the fears in which he was held by the Custom-house officers—"Jonas Wilkins! And pray," enquired Orlando, releasing him, "what may have brought you here, Mr. Jonas Wilkins?"

"Why, I'll tell you," replied the fellow, "for I knows you to be a kind-hearted gentleman, and won't hurt me. The truth of the matter then is—the butler of this here house, Master Patterson, is engaged a little matter in our business; and when we gets a cargo, he stows it in Madam's cellars, which lays alongside the house, and he have the means to open that door there in the wall, under that there old fig-tree, which nobody knows nothing about. So here we brings our goods, until such time as we can carry it safely up the country, and we comes on dark nights to take it away."

"And you were here on Monday night, were you not, and came into my room through the chapel?"

"Yes, that I did, sure enough. Aha, Master Orlando! I think we've cotch'd one another."

"If that be the case," replied Orlando, "it would have been well if we had kept one another's secrets. Why did you speak of having seen one in my room?"

"Egad! old Pattenson was down in the cellar himself, for we were helping up some heavy goods that night. I don't know what a devil ail'd me, but I thought I'd just give a look into your room, where, you must know, before you comed to live, we used now-and-then to put a few kegs or so upon a pinch—and, d—n it, there was you with a pretty girl. Ah, Master Orlando! who'd think you was such a sly one?"

"Well, but," said Orlando, "what occasion was there, Jonas, for your telling Pattenson?"

"To tease the old son of a b——," answered Jonas. "Why, don't you know that he's after Betty Richards, and as jealous as poison? So I made him believe 'twas she."

"You made him believe!"

"Aye, for it might be she or another!—Curse me if I saw who it was! for you blow'd out the candle, whisk! in a minute."

Orlando, heartily glad to hear this, pursued his enquiry further. "Pray," resumed he, "tell me why some person a little while after cried out, "Now! now!"

"Why, we thought that all was quiet; and as I and a comrade of mine was waiting for the goods, we were going to heave them up, and that was the signal; but you were plaguy quick-eared, and began to holla after us, so we were forced to let the job alone till to-night, and Pattenson let us out through the t'other part of the house. We've done the business now, and my comrades they be all off with the goods—I only staid to gather up our tools, because I be going another way."

Orlando, now finding himself thus unexpectedly relieved from the difficulty of accounting for the circumstance of the night of alarm, was far from resenting the resistance his new acquaintance had made, or heeding the pain he felt from some bruises which he had received in the struggle; but being rather pleased at this rencontre, and wishing to know how far the trade of the worshipful Mr. Pattenson was likely to impede his future meetings with Monimia, he invited Jonas into his room, and told him he could give him, late as it was, a glass of wine.

Jonas accepted his invitation, but desired he might stay to coil up his ropes, which he deposited in the porch, and then followed Orlando, who had taken his hanger from the chimney where it usually hung, and put his pistols, which were both loaded, by him. These precautions were not meant against his guest, whom he did not suspect of any immediate intention to injure him, but to let him see that he was prepared against intrusion, from whatever motive it might be made, at any other time.

When the man made his appearance, Orlando, prepared as he was for the sight of a ruffian, felt something like horror. His dark countenance shaded by two immense black eyebrows, his shaggy hair, and the fierce and wild expression of his eyes, gave a complete idea of one of Shakespeare's well-painted assassins; while, in contemplating his athletic form, Orlando wondered how he had been able a moment to detain him. He wore a dirty round frock, stained with ochre, which looked like blood, and over it one of those thick great coats which the vulgar call rascal-wrappers. Orlando poured him out a tumbler of wine, and bade him sit down. The fellow obeyed, drank of his wine, and then, after surveying the room, said, turning with a sly look to Orlando, "What, master, she ben't here then to-night?"

"Pooh, pooh!" cried Orlando, "let's forget that, good Jonas!—Your eyes deceived you—there was nobody here: and I assure you it was well you disappeared as you did, or you would have paid for your peeping," shewing one of his pistols.

"Aye, aye," answered Jonas, "you've got a pair of bulldogs, I see! And I," added he, pulling a pocket-pistol from under his frock, "I've a terrier or two about me; and 'twas ten to one, Mr. Orlando, if I had not a given a pretty good guess who it was, that I had not taken you for an officer, and treated you with more sugar-plums than would have sat easy upon your stomach."

"We are good friends now, however," said Orlando; "so drink, Jonas, to our better acquaintance."

He then gave him another full tumbler of wine, and began to question him on his exploits. He found him one of those daring and desperate men, who, knowing they are to expect no mercy, disclaim all hope, and resolutely prey upon the society which has shaken them off. He had been drinking before Orlando met him; and now the wine with which Orlando plied him, and the voice of kindness with which he spoke to him, contributed to open his heart. Jonas disclosed to Orlando all their manoeuvres, and it was not without astonishment that he found both Snelcraft, the coachman, and Pattenson so deeply engaged among the smugglers, and deriving very considerable sums from the shelter they afforded them, and the participation of their illicit gains. Orlando found that during the whole winter, in weather when no other vessels kept the sea, these adventurous men pursued their voyages, and carried their cargoes throughout the country in weather when "one's enemy's dog"[1] would hardly be turned from the door.

Orlando, after some consideration on the means of escaping that

---

[1]   *King Lear*, IV.vii.36.

interruption which this combination among the servants in the house seemed to threaten, told the man, as if in confidence, that under the restraint he was in, in Mrs. Rayland's house, he sometimes found it convenient to go out after the family were in bed, to meet at a neighbouring town some friends whom Mrs. Rayland disliked he should see; "and therefore," said he, "I wish, Jonas, that, as I should not wish to interrupt you, you would give me some signal on those nights when you are at work in the cellar."

This the smuggler readily promised, and they agreed upon the sign which should signify the importation or exportation of the merchandise of Mr. Pattenson from the cellars of his mistress.

Orlando, possessing this secret, flattered himself that his very extraordinary acquaintance would keep his word, and that the communication between the study and the apartment of Monimia might once more be open, without making her liable to those terrors from which she had suffered so much.

The man, whom Orlando continued to behold with a mixture of horror and pity, was now nearly overcome with the wine he had drank, and began to tell long prosing stories of his escapes and his exploits, in which he related instances of dauntless courage, tarnished, however, by brutish ferocity. At length Orlando reminded him that day was fast approaching, and saw him out of the chapel-door, repeating his assurances that nothing of what he had himself that night discovered should transpire. Orlando then fastened the chapel and the other doors, and betook himself to his repose—thinking less about the meeting that was to take place, as he believed, on the morrow, than on the recent discovery he had made, which nearly quieted his terrors in regard to Monimia's having been seen; and he impatiently longed for an opportunity to communicate to her the satisfaction which he hoped she would derive from this assurance.

The late hour at which he had gone to bed, and the fatigue of mind he had experienced the preceding day, occasioned it to be later than usual when Orlando awoke. He started up; and recollecting that he had some writing to finish for Mrs. Rayland, and that he was to meet Sir John Belgrave at twelve o'clock, he hastened to dress himself, and had hardly done so before he received a summons to attend his father, who waited for him as usual in the stable-yard.

He found Mr. Somerive again on horseback, and easily understood that his purpose was to keep him from his appointment, to which, however, he was positively determined to go. While his father, in a peculiar strain of dejection and concern, was yet talking to him, as he leaned on the horse, Mrs. Lennard saw them from one of the windows; and having acquainted her Lady, she, contrary to her usual reserved treatment of Mr. Somerive, sent down a very civil message, requesting his company with Orlando to breakfast.

This invitation, so flattering, because so unusual, was of course accepted. Somerive knew that Mrs. Rayland was acquainted with the affair which hung over him with an aspect so threatening, and hoped that she would unite with him in persuading Orlando to those concessions which might yet afford the means of evading it, if the General's interposition should fail; instead of which, he found her elated with the idea of punishing the audacity of Sir John, fearless of any danger which in the attempt might happen to Orlando, and piquing herself on the supposition that in him had revived a spark of that martial and dauntless spirit which she had been taught to believe characterized the men of her family. She seemed surprised, and somewhat offended, at the alarm Mr. Somerive expressed; and hinted, in no very equivocal terms, that this timidity was the effect of that mixture of plebeian blood, from the alloy of which only Orlando, of all the family, seemed exempt; while Mr. Somerive, in his turn, beheld, with a degree of horror and disgust, a woman who, to gratify her pride, or revenge her quarrel, on so trifling a subject, was ready to promote perhaps the death of one for whom she had appeared to feel some degree of affection.

With views and opinions so different, their conference was not likely to be either very long or very satisfactory. Mr. Somerive knew that when Mrs. Rayland had once taken up an opinion, argument against it offended, but never convinced her; and that in proportion as her reasoning was feeble, her resolution was firm. Thus baffled in his hopes of her effectual interposition, and seeing that Orlando was bent upon keeping his appointment, of which the hour was now at hand, Mr. Somerive sat awhile silent, mortified and wretched—hoping, yet fearing, for the success of the General's interposition, and considering what he should do if it failed.

He had just determined to obtain a warrant immediately, and to put both parties under arrest, when a servant brought to him the following letter:

"MY DEAR SIR,

"I am now with Sir John Belgrave; and as I know the very natural and tender solicitude which you and your amiable family are under, I lose not a moment in doing myself the pleasure to assure you that Sir John consents to give the matter up, and that without any concessions from your son that may be derogatory to his honour. If Sir John allows me to say that he is sorry for what has passed, it can surely not be too much for Mr. Orlando to make to him the same concession. I have great satisfaction in communicating to you the success of my sincere endeavours to be serviceable, and have the honour to be,

"My dear Sir,

"Your most devoted servant,

"Charles-Ferdinand Tracy."

Mr. Somerive read this billet with a beating heart, apprehensive that the interposition of Mrs. Rayland would prevent making even the slight apology which General Tracy dictated; and seeing him restless, and meditating how to escape, he hastily bade Mrs. Rayland good morning, and ordering, in a more peremptory voice than he generally assumed, Orlando to follow him, he left the room; and, as soon as he was alone with his son, put into his hands the letter he had received, at the same time telling him that he must be obeyed in the command he laid upon him, to make immediately the concession required.

Orlando, convinced that he ought to do so, after the appeal he had himself consented to make to the General, assured his father of his obedience. They found, on enquiry, that General Tracy's servant had been sent first to West Wolverton; from whence Mrs. Somerive had, in the most terrifying state of suspense, hastened him to Rayland Hall, where he now waited. Orlando therefore attended his father into his own room; where being furnished with pen and ink, Mr. Somerive wrote to the General in those terms that appeared requisite, and to which Orlando did not object. The letter was then instantly dispatched by the servant; and thus ended an affair which had so much disturbed the peace of the Somerive family, and threatened consequences still more painful. Somerive now ordered his son to return to Mrs. Rayland, shew her the General's letter, and inform her that the business was ended as much to his honour, as her highest notions of what was due to a descendant of Sir Hildebrand (whose blood was less alloyed than that of the rest of his family) could exact. Somerive said this with some degree of asperity; for, though pleased with the partiality of Mrs. Rayland for Orlando, he could not but feel the contempt she expressed towards himself. He told Orlando he expected him to dinner, and then returned home; his mind relieved from an intolerable load, and his heart swelling with gratitude towards his excellent friend, General Tracy.

CHAP. III.

Every one of the party who met at dinner at Mr. Somerive's was ready to worship the General, except Orlando, who still felt himself dissatisfied, and much disposed to enquire by what conversation an accommodation had been so easily brought about. This enquiry, however, he, at his father's request, forbore to make, and the General was perfectly satisfied with the gratitude expressed by the rest of the family; and in the distant but polite behaviour of Orlando, saw, what confirmed him in his original idea, that it would be much better if he was out of the way.—The charms of Isabella had now such an ascendancy in the General's imagination, that he determined nothing should impede his designs; and he believed that the straitened circumstances of Somerive, of which he was no longer ignorant, would give him the means of obtaining his daughter.[1]

Somerive had indeed communicated to him, as a friend, the uneasy situation of his affairs, and deplored the conduct of his eldest son. At their next conference, therefore, alone, Tracy contrived, without forcing the conversation, to bring it round to that point; and when Somerive spoke of the distress which arose from the misconduct of his son Philip, the General took occasion to say, "It is indeed, my friend, a circumstance extremely to be lamented, and, in my opinion, renders the situation of your youngest son much more critical.—I heartily wish he was in some profession. Have you considered what I said to you about the army?— I believe I could be of very material service to you in that line."

"Dear General," exclaimed Somerive, "how much I feel myself indebted to you! Yes, I certainly have thought of it; and the result of my reflections is, that if his mother consented, if Mrs. Rayland did not object—"

"My good friend," interrupted the General, "can a man of your understanding, when the well-doing of such a son is in question, think that these *ifs* should have any weight?—Mrs. Somerive, all tender as she is, has too much sense to indulge her fondness at the expence of her son's establishment; and as to Mrs. Rayland—I have not, indeed, the honour to know her—but the only question seems to be, will she, or

---

[1] General Tracy's attitude makes plain one of the underlying concerns of *The Old Manor House*: that courtship and commerce are inextricably mixed. For the same reason, Monimia's and Orlando's relationship revolves around the possibility that Orlando will inherit Rayland Hall.

will she not, provide for Orlando?—*If* she will, why will she not say so? If she will not, are not you doing your son an irreparable injury in suffering him to waste in fruitless expectation the best of his days?"

"It is very difficult," replied Mr. Somerive, after musing a moment, "very difficult to know how to act: Mrs. Rayland has a temper so peculiar, that if she is once offended, it is for ever. Perhaps, however, since I see she piques herself on the military honours of her family, perhaps she may not be displeased at Orlando's entering on the profession of arms. She seemed much more eager to promote than to check his ardour in this affair with Sir John Belgrave; and as the British nation is now engaged in a quarrel with people whom she considers as the descendants of the Regicides,[1] against whom her ancestors drew their swords, it is not, I think, very unlikely that she might approve of her young favourite's making his first essay in arms against those whom she terms the Rebels of America."

"As to that," answered the General coldly, "it may be very well, in starting the idea, to give her that notion; but, in fact, this campaign will end the unworthy contest.—Of this I have the most positive assurances from my military friends on the spot, as well as the firmest reliance on the measures adopted by Ministers; and I am convinced that those wretched, ragged fellows, without discipline, money, clothes, or arms, will be unable longer to struggle for their chimerical liberty. Probably they are by this time crushed; and, therefore, as no more troops will be sent out, your son will not, if you adopt this plan, be separated from his family, and may still occasionally visit this capricious old gentlewoman, who, unless she differs much from the rest of her sex, of all ages and descriptions, will not like a handsome young fellow the less for having a cockade in his hat."

"Ah, General!" returned Somerive smiling, "I fancy your own experience among the women well justifies that remark. Since you really are so sure that Orlando would not be sent abroad, which will make a great difference certainly in his mother's feelings on this point, and perhaps in those of Mrs. Rayland, I will take an immediate opportunity of speaking of it to my wife, and we will consider of the safest method of taking Mrs. Rayland's opinion upon it. As to Orlando himself, there can be little doubt of his concurrence;—at least I hope not. And there are

---

[1] Since the American colonists are rebelling against their British ruler, as the Puritans did in the English Civil War, Mrs. Rayland sees them as allied with the earlier group who succeeded in beheading a king (hence regicide).

other reasons, my friend, besides those that I have named to you, why his present situation is utterly improper, and why it seems to me that he cannot too soon be removed from it."

Mr. Somerive, in speaking thus, was thinking of Monimia, who, ever since he had first heard her described, had occurred to him continually. The necessity there was for attending immediately to the affair of the threatened duel, had hitherto prevented his speaking of her to Orlando, in that serious manner which he thought the affair merited: but he had repeatedly touched on it; and finding Orlando shrink from the investigation, he laid in wait for an occasion to probe him more deeply—an occasion which, perceiving his father sought it, Orlando as solicitously endeavoured to avoid giving him, by contriving to be always busied in attending on his sisters or his mother; but while he thus got out of the way of his father, he was very much in that of the General, who could hardly ever get an opportunity of whispering to Isabella those sentiments which daily acquired new force. For, the week following that when the affair with Sir John Belgrave was settled, Orlando could find no excuse for returning to Rayland Hall of a night: he was therefore reduced to the necessity of going thither after his own family were in bed; and as the way through the chapel was not open to him, he could only see Monimia in her own room, and their meetings were therefore very short, and so hazardous, that the impatience and discontent of Orlando could no longer be repressed or concealed.

The greater his attachment to Monimia became (and every hour it seemed to gather strength), the more terrible appeared her situation, and his own. They were both so young that he thought he might easily obtain an establishment, and that the noon of their lives might pass in felicity together, were he, instead of remaining in a state of uncertain dependence, to be allowed to go forth into the world. Sanguine and romantic in the extreme, and feeling within himself talents which he was denied the power of exercising, his mind expatiated on visionary prospects, which he believed might easily be realized. When to provide for passing his life with Monimia was in question, every thing seemed possible; and as he heard much of the rapid fortunes made in India, and had never considered, or perhaps heard of the means by which they were acquired, he fancied that an appointment there would put him in the high road to happiness; and various were the projects of this and of many other kinds, on which his thoughts continually dwelt.

General Tracy, who had long read mankind, easily penetrated into the mind of a man so new to the world as Orlando; and though he saw that his young friend did not greatly esteem him, he was not by that observation deterred from conciliating as much as possible his good opinion, till at length Orlando communicated his discontent at being at his time of life so inactive and useless; and the General, having brought him to that confession, started the scheme he had before proposed only to his father, of procuring him a commission, and lending him all the interest which he was known to possess, to promote his fortune in the army.

A proposal so friendly, and so much adapted to the warm and ardent temper of Orlando, was acknowledged with gratitude, and without farther consideration embraced, on condition that his family did not oppose it. The General told him, that it was in consequence of his father's apparent inclinations that he had at first thought of it; that his mother had certainly too much sense to reject such an advantageous offer for him; "especially," added he, "as from the present state of the war, there is not the least likelihood of your being sent abroad.—You know best, however, my dear Sir," continued the General, with something on his countenance between a smile and a sneer—"you know best how far your campaigns against the game on the Rayland manors may answer better than the services of a soldier, or whether the old lady's hands can bestow a more fruitful prize than the barren laurels you may gather in bearing arms for your country."[1]

There was in this speech something that conveyed to Orlando an idea that he was despised; and that there was meanness in his attending on Mrs. Rayland like a legacy hunter—of all characters the most despicable. The blood that rushed into his cheeks, spoke the painful sensations this impression brought with it. He could not, however, express them with propriety to a man whose only purpose seemed to be that of befriending him, by rousing him from indolence, and even from a species of servitude. The General saw that what he said had the effect he wished; and Orlando left him, determined to avail himself of the opportunity that now offered for obtaining what he believed would be a degree of independence. He began to consider how he might prevail on Mrs. Rayland to assist, instead of opposing this scheme; and how he might thus obtain a certain portion of liberty, without offending one to whom gratitude and interest contributed to attach him. A deep and

---

[1]   General Tracy alludes to another of the novel's tropes: that Orlando's attendance on Mrs. Rayland constitutes a romantic attachment to what she represents—property, and his potential to inherit.

painful sigh, raised by the reflection of the misery of parting from Monimia, followed the resolution he adopted; but he recollected that by no other means he could remove the cruel obstacles between them, and that resolution became confirmed.

He had not yet, however, the courage to communicate to her the probability there was that they must soon part. Their short conferences, in every one of which they incurred the hazard of discovery, passed, on her side, in mournful presentiments of future sorrow, which she yet endeavoured to conceal; and on his, in trying, now to console her, and now in acknowledging that there was but too much cause for her fears: projects were considered, however, for their future meetings with less risk. She told him, that during the time he was so much at home, her aunt confined her less strictly through the day: that in proportion as she found herself become more necessary to Mrs. Rayland, and more secure of a great provision after her death, Mrs. Lennard became more indolent, and more addicted to her own gratifications. Betty, who was a very great favourite, had little else to do than to wait upon her; and employment in which Monimia herself was often engaged, though she was now more usually employed about the person of Mrs. Rayland, who found her so tender and attentive that she began to look upon her with some degree of complacency. This task, while it added a heavy link to her fetters, she yet went through, not only with patience, but with pleasure; for she hoped that by making herself useful to Mrs. Rayland, she might not only have more frequent opportunities of seeing Orlando during the winter, which she imagined he would pass at the Hall, but perhaps obtain from her such a share of recollection at her death, as might remove the necessity of an entire dependence on Mrs. Lennard; a dependence which some late observations had made her believe as precarious as she felt it to be painful.

In consequence of General Tracy's visit to Sir John Belgrave at the house of Mr. Stockton, he received from the master of it an invitation, which he accepted; Mr. Stockton first waiting upon him at West Wolverton—Sir John, and Philip Somerive, with several others of the late visitants at the Castle, were gone into Scotland on a shooting party; but Mr. Stockton had a succession of visiters.—His magnificent style of living, which it was known he had a fortune to support, attracted not only all his London friends by turns to his house, but from every part of the country acquaintance had poured in upon him; acquaintance who desired nothing better, in the way of entertainment, than his French cook and his well-furnished cellars afforded them.—The Clergy were his very constant guests; and he loved to have two or three of them always about him, at whom he might lanch those shafts of wit which he had picked up here and there, and which consisted of common-place jokes upon religion; well knowing, that with these select few (orthodox as they were), the excellence of the entertainment he gave them secured their silence and complaisance.

The General, who was in manners really a man of fashion, was by no means delighted with the gross and noisy society he found at Stockton's: but he saw that if he would escape suspicion, he must not make his visit at Somerive's too long; and, therefore, was glad to be assured that there was an house in the immediate neighbourhood, where he might remain a fortnight or three weeks, after prudence dictated his departure from that of Mr. Somerive; which he now feared must happen before his hopes with Isabella were successful, for he found it much more difficult to obtain any degree of favour, than his own vanity and her giddiness had at first led him to suppose.

Isabella Somerive was not naturally a coquette: but she had a greater flow of spirits than any of her family, except her elder brother, whom she greatly resembled in the thoughtless vivacity of his disposition; from her sex and education, what was in him attended with dangerous errors, was in her only wild but innocent gaiety, becoming enough to youth, health and beauty. Of that beauty she had early learned the value: she had heard it praised at home, and found her father and mother were pleased to hear of it. But during her short stay in London she had been intoxicated with the incense that was offered her; and, notwithstanding the good humour inherent in her disposition, she failed not to enjoy, with some degree of feminine triumph, the preference that was given her over her cousins, whose admirers seemed all disposed to desert them on the first appearance of this rustic beauty; and she felt, too, the pleasure of retaliation for all the airs of consequence which the Miss Woodfords had assumed in their visits to West Wolverton, from their superior knowledge of fashions, public places, and great people. But, above all, Isabella was delighted by the preference given her by a judge so discerning as General Tracy—whose taste in beauty was so universally allowed, that his admiration had given eminence to several pretty women, who would never otherwise have been noticed. Far however from thinking of him as a lover, Isabella, who was, with all her vivacity, as innocent as little Emma herself, considered him merely as her father's friend, and would have applied to him for advice, in as much expectation of receiving it with disinterested wisdom, as her father himself. The fine speeches he took every opportunity of making, she believed partly arose from habit, and were partly proofs of his admiration; which she thought perfectly harmless, though it sometimes struck her as ridiculous. And in conversation with her sisters, and sometimes with her mother, she laughingly called the General—her old beau—her venerable admirer, and said she wished he was thirty years younger. Mrs. Somerive sometimes checked her; but oftener smiled at the description she gave of the General's solemn gallantry, and of the trouble she knew his toilet cost him; "which really," cried she, "grieves one's very heart. Poor man! it must be excessively fatiguing; and after all, I think he would be a thousand times more agreeable, if he could be persuaded to appear as my father and other men do, of the same age.—Instead of putting on toupees and curls, which it requires so much art and time to make fit snug and look natural, how preferable would a good comfortable wig be to his poor old head! which I am sure must ache sadly every day, before Beaumielle[1] has patched up the gaps that time has made!—and, besides, I know he is always in fear of some of this borrowed chevelure's coming off, and disgracing him; I have absolutely seen him nervous about it."—"Dear Isabella," said Mrs. Somerive, who was present at this description, "how you run on! The General, I dare say, has no false hair; and if he has, how does it materially differ from a wig!"

"Oh mamma!" replied her daughter, "I believe it differs so much in the General's opinion, that he had rather have his head cut off than his hair. A wig! I have seen him shudder at the idea."

"You have seen him!" said Mrs. Somerive: "pray when?"

"The other day, when he rode out with us. There was a terrible high wind, and I knew the ancient beau would be ten times more discomposed by it than we were—So, as soon as we got upon the downs, I set off with a brisk canter directly against it; and the poor dear General was obliged, you know, to follow us."—

"Well?"

"Well—and so he buttoned up the cape of his great coat round his ears, and set off after us; but as ill fortune would have it, this cape, I suppose, loosened the strings of his curls, and the wind blew so unmercifully that he did not hear of their defection from his ears; but as he came gallopping up to me and Selina, who were a good way before him, these ill behaved curls deserted, and were flying, like two small birds tied

---

[1] Ehrenpreis speculates that Beaumielle was a cosmetic, and notes that "various preparations with a honey base ["mielle"] were used to promote hair growth" (p. 538). A chevelure is a wig.

by the leg, half a yard behind him; and if he had been commander of a town suddenly blown up by the enemy, he could not have looked more amazed and dismayed, than he did when I called out to him—General! General! your curls are flying away!—He put up his hand to his two ears alternately, and finding it too true that these cowardly curls had left their post, and were retained only by a bit of black twist, he gave them a twitch, and thrust them into his pocket—while he said most dolorously, "Ever since that fever I got last year by overheating myself walking with the King at Windsor, I have lost my hair in some degree; and till it is restored I am under the necessity of wearing these awkward contrivances.""Dear General," said I, as if I pitied his distress, "I am afraid you will catch cold without them. Had you not better wrap a handker-chief about your head? I am sure you must feel a difference—I am in pain for you!—It is, indeed, an awkward contrivance; and I should think you would find more comfortable and certain accommodation in a wig."

"A wig!" exclaimed he—"a military man in a wig!—like a turtle-eating cit,[1] or a Stock-Exchange broker!—Impossible!—No! lovely Isabella, you can never suppose I ought to make myself such a figure; and I assure you I have, when not hurt by illness, a very tolerable head of hair."

"For your time of life, General!" said I,—This completed the poor good man's dismay; and he set about assuring me, that the military hard-ships he had gone through in the younger part of his life, and perhaps a little irregularity since, made him look at least fifteen years older than he was, and so went on making such fine speeches as he thinks becom-ing in so *young* a man."

"Upon my word, Isabella," remarked Mrs. Somerive, "you will offend the General by all this flippancy; and your father, I assure you, would not be at all pleased if you should."

"No, indeed, my dear mamma!" answered she, "there is no danger of my offending him. The rattling speeches I make to him, and even my turning him into ridicule when only Selina and I are by, is so far from offending him, that he seems to like it.—Does not he, Selina?"

"It is not right, however, in my opinion," said Selina.

"Why not if you please, my Lady Graveairs?"[2]

---

[1] "Cit" was short for "City", the financial centre of London, and also used to designate those who worked in trade in the City. "Turtle" is short for turtle soup, a delicacy associated by the General with the vulgar. General Tracy denies wearing a wig because of its incon-gruity with his military status; it is a marker of low breeding and vanity and hence only suited to the self-important *nouveau riche*.

[2] A character in Colley Cibber's 1704 play *The Careless Husband*.

"Because I do not think a person's age," replied Selina, "a proper subject of ridicule."

"No," answered Isabella—"not if they do not make it so, by attempting to appear young; but how is it possible to help laughing at a man who fancies that, at sixty, he can pass of six-and-twenty?"

"If it is the General's foible," said Mrs. Somerive gravely, "it seems to be the only one; and it makes him happy, and hurts nobody. He is so worthy a man that it is immaterial whether he is sixty or six-and-twenty; and if he has the weakness to prefer being thought the latter, which, however, Isabella you know is not true, he should not be rudely reminded that nobody else thinks so."

"Well, if this worthy man will flirt with and make love to girls young enough to be his grand-daughters, I must laugh, if it *be* wrong," cried Isabella.

"Make love!" exclaimed Mrs. Somerive: "What do you mean, child?"

"Why—only, mamma, that if he were a young man, the marvellously fine speeches he studies would seem like love-making speeches. I told him the other day, that since he thought me so very charming a creature, I wished he would persuade his nephew to be of the same opinion, for there would be some sense in that."

"His nephew!—Who is his nephew?" enquired her mother.

"I never saw him," replied Isabella; "but Eliza Woodford has often, and says he is the most elegant and the handsomest young man about town."

"Do you mean," said Mrs. Somerive, "the son of his elder brother, Lord Taymouth?"

"Oh! not at all—he is a miserable looking mortal:—No, this nephew, as Eliza tells me, is the only son of his sister, Lady Something Tracy, who married a Mr. Warwick, who, though a gentleman, her family thought was a match so much beneath her, that they never forgave her; and as she and her husband both died early, this young man, who was their only child, and had a very small fortune, was brought up by the General, who means to make him his heir."

"He is a good creature," said Mrs. Somerive; "and every thing I hear increases my esteem for him."

"You would consent then, my dear mamma," replied Isabella, "to my having Captain Warwick?"

"Alas!" answered her mother mournfully, "Captain Warwick, my dear girl, heir to the fortune of General Tracy, will never, I fear, *ask* my consent. Young women without fortune, though their merit be indisputable, are not likely now to marry at all; very unlikely, indeed, to meet with such high fortune."

"I don't see that at all," cried Isabella. "Selina and Emma may determine to die old maids if they please; but, for my part, I'll try, as long as I am young and good looking, for a husband; and as to this Warwick, I am bent upon setting my cap at him without mercy, if his uncle would but give me an opportunity. That he will not do; for though he is so good to him, and gives him such an handsome allowance, he hardly ever sees him; and has bought him a company in another regiment, rather than have him in his own, and so he is sent off to America—and—"

"You have no chance then," interrupted Mrs. Somerive, "of trying your power, Isabella?"

"No!" cried she; "but it is excellent sport to teize his uncle about him, who always avoids talking of him, just like a coquettish Mamma, who hates to hear that Miss is tall and handsome."

Mrs. Somerive, again gently reproving her daughter for speaking thus of the General, put an end to the conversation by sending her daughters away to dress for dinner; while she meditated alone on what her husband had that morning said to her on the subject of Orlando's entering the army. He had now, for the first time, explained to her all the reasons he had for wishing his son removed from Rayland Hall; and had communicated the principal of these, his suspicions of an attachment to Monimia. Mrs. Somerive felt all the truth of what her husband urged in favour of this plan; and, particularly uneasy at the information he had given her about Monimia, she now tried to reason herself out of those fears for his personal safety, which yet led her to wish he might remain, on whatever terms, near her and his family.

CHAP. IV.

The family of Somerive was almost the only one in the country, or at least within five and twenty miles, who had not waited on Mr. Stockton after his purchasing the estates of Lord Carloraine. For this Mr. Somerive had several reasons. Though he disdained any mean compliances with the caprices of Mrs. Rayland, he thought it wrong to connect himself with a man who, on his first appearance in the country, had offended her unhandsomely enough; and he knew it would not only be impolitic in regard to her, but to the economy of his own family. His servants, plain and laborious, were at present content with their portion of work and of wages; but were they once introduced into such a servants hall as that of the Castle, where the same profusion reigned as was customary in the parlour, he knew they would immediately become discontented, and of course troublesome and useless. The people whom he found were generally assembled at the Castle, most of them young men, celebrated for their dissolute manners, were not such as he wished to have introduced to his daughters. And these causes co-operating to make him wish to avoid every acquaintance with Mr. Stockton, he had taken some pains to prevail on his eldest son to avoid it also; but Philip Somerive, who had some slight knowledge of Stockton in London, hastened, in spite of his father's remonstrances, to renew and strengthen it as soon as he settled in the neighbourhood, and was very soon more at Stockton's than at home. The simple economy of his father's house appeared to him a total deprivation of all that a gentleman ought to enjoy; and when contrasted with the voluptuous epicurism that reigned in the splendid mansion of his new friend, he had not the courage to return to it oftener than want of money compelled him to do: and he forgot that to these temporary gratifications he was sacrificing the peace of his father, his mother, and his sisters; and laying up for himself all the miseries of indigence, and all the meannesses of dependence.

It was here he confirmed, by indulgence, that passion for play which he had acquired at college. The party at Carloraine Castle passed whole nights in gaming, where young Somerive often lost, but, alas! sometimes won; and in the triumph of his success, the pain and inconvenience of his ill fortune was forgotten. He learned some of those modes of ascertaining the matter, which he saw so happily practised by others; and, after some time, became, in some measure, one of the initiated, and had, in consequence, seldom occasion to apply to his father for money—therefore he seldom went near him: sometimes whole months therefore passed, during which his family never saw him, though they knew that much of his time was passed with Mr. Stockton, whom this circumstance contributed to render odious to Mr. Somerive.

After the acquaintance, however, commenced between Stockton and the General, Somerive found it very difficult to keep the same distance; and Stockton, who had a great inclination to see Somerive's handsome daughters, of whom he had heard so much, was so importunately civil, while General Tracy, on the other hand, promoted the acquaintance so warmly, that Somerive and Orlando engaged to dine with Stockton on one of those days when he had invited half the country. The latter went with extreme reluctance; not only because what he had heard of the man himself, and of the people who surrounded him, gave no favourable idea of the society; but because he thought it wrong to hazard offending Mrs. Rayland, in a point which, to pursue, afforded no pleasure either to his father or himself. Neither of these reasons for denial, however, could be urged to the General, who he thought already despised him for his assiduity about the old lady; and as his father had been induced to consent, Orlando could not refuse to accompany him.

The table was furnished with all that modern luxury has invented, or money could purchase: the greatest variety of expensive wines, and a superb dessert, finished a repast, at which were collected a group as various as their entertainment, though not so well chosen. The beginning of the dinner was passed in that sort of talk which relates solely to eating: when that exercise was relaxed, something like an attempt at conversation was made. The last news from America was discussed; but as they all agreed in one sentiment—that the rebellious colonists ought to be extirpated—there was no room for argument, and the discourse soon languished; and then again revived on topics nearer home—game, poachers, and turnpikes:[1] the wine had by that time circulated enough to give their conversation, if conversation it might be called, another turn. They grew noisy and offensive; and Orlando, who was never before among such a set of people, nor had ever in his life heard such language, was unable to conceal his disgust, though he only shewed it by silence, and by passing from him the bottle which he saw had so affected the little understanding that the majority of the company had possessed.

This was at length perceived by Mr. Stockton, who, accustomed to indulge himself in what he fancied shrewd sayings, and to expect that every man not so rich as himself should submit to be his butt, began to attack Orlando on the score of his being a milk-sop, and living always in the lap of the old lady at the Hall.—To this Orlando answered with good humour, perfectly indifferent what such a man as Stockton thought of him; but the latter seeing how well he bore this first attack, could not resist the temptation of pursuing his blow. "Why, damn it now!" cried he, "we know very well, Sir Rowland (that was the name which Philip Somerive gave to his brother in derision), we know very well that you are no more of a saint than your neighbours; and that though you are in waiting on an old woman all day, you makes yourself amends at night

---

[1]   The most likely meaning for "turnpike" in this context is a barrier across a road, stream, or path, usually to stop passage until a toll was paid. Ehrenpreis defines "turnpike" as "wire snares used by poachers" (p. 538), but the *OED* cites the first use of this meaning as being in 1879. However, such a meaning would make sense, and it is certainly possible that Smith uses it in this way, despite the *OED*.

with a young one—aye, and a devilish pretty wench she is too as ever I saw.—Egad! Belgrave was half mad about her for a week, and had a mind to have stormed the tower where this dulcinea[1] lives, notwithstanding its being guarded by the fierce Sir Rowland.—I don't know her name.—Tell me, Sir Knight, how is your goddess called? and by the Lord we'll drink her health in a bumper!"

Mr. Somerive, who saw in the changes of Orlando's expressive countenance, that his answer would inevitably bring on another quarrel, arose hastily, and, addressing himself to Mr. Stockton, while he commanded Orlando to be silent, he said, "After what passed, Mr. Stockton, in regard to Sir John Belgrave and my son, this mention of the affair can only be considered as an insult to us both. If that be your purpose, some other place than your own house should have been found for it. We will now quit it, in order to give you an opportunity of pursuing your design, without adding the breach of the laws of hospitality to those of decency and good manners."

Somerive then taking Orlando by the arm, insisted on his going with him; while the General, and some other men in the room, who were yet in possession of their senses, got round Stockton, who was very drunk, and represented how wrong it was to renew the conversation on Sir John Belgrave; an affair which had been settled with so much difficulty, and had threatened such serious consequences. The profession, birth, and riches of General Tracy, gave him great authority in the opinion of even the wealthy and insolent Stockton himself; and as he loved his ease, even beyond the indulgence of his purse-proud arrogance, he saw at once, that in gratifying the one, he had, more than he intended, risked the other. He therefore sent one of his dependents to apologize to the two Somerives, who had already left the room: General Tracy too went to assure them of Stockton's concern for what had passed; excused it by alledging his inebriety, and declared that he should think both Mr. Somerive and his son wrong to take any further notice of the idle words of a man who was himself convinced of their impropriety. "We will talk of all this at our leisure, dear General," replied the elder Somerive: "at present you must allow me to take Orlando from an house, into which I am heartily concerned that either of us ever entered."

"I will go with you, my dear friend," cried the General; "but first allow me to return to poor Stockton, who is extremely concerned for what has happened, and to tell him—"

---

[1] See note 2, p. 199.

"Any thing you please from yourself, Sir," said Orlando interrupting him; "but nothing from me, unless it be—"

"Leave the matter to *me*, Orlando," cried Somerive sternly. "You know, General," added he, addressing himself to his friend, "how little it can be my wish to have this ridiculous matter go any farther; but as I never yet bore a premeditated insult myself, so I will not ask Orlando to do it, be the consequence what they may."

"Good God!" exclaimed the General, "this was no premeditated insult; it was merely the folly of a man in a condition which disarms resentment, even from those of the most quick feelings."

"He must tell me so himself, then," said Orlando.

"I will undertake that he shall," answered the General; "and so you leave the house satisfied, I hope?"

To this the elder Somerive answered drily: "Blessed are the peace-makers, my good General!" and then, leaving him to return, if he pleased, to his new friends, he mounted his horse, which, with that of Orlando's, his servants had brought to the door, and they proceeded homeward together.

This was the opportunity of speaking to Orlando, that his father had been some days watching for; and the scene that had just passed, awakening all his fears about Monimia, was an additional motive to him not to neglect it.

Orlando, whose heart was bursting with indignation at the insult offered to her name, rode silently by his side, expecting, with a mixture of concern and confusion, that his father would again press him on his attachment. He was studying, without being able to determine, how he should answer. He had never been guilty of a falsehood; and could he now reconcile himself to the meanness of attempting one, he believed it would be fruitless; yet, to betray the tender, trusting, timid Monimia— to acknowledge their clandestine meetings, which his father might not be persuaded were innocent—and to render himself liable to be forbidden ever again to see her—how was it possible to determine on risking it, by an avowal of the truth? There was not much time for this painful debate. Mr. Somerive put his horse into a walk, and then said, in that grave and earnest manner which alway affected his son—

"You see, Orlando, all the mischief to which this boyish and indiscreet love of yours has exposed, not only yourself, but the young woman who is, unluckily for her, the object of it."

"Love, Sir!" said Orlando, not knowing very well what to say.

"Nay, Sir," cried Somerive more sternly, "don't affect ignorance; you have been playing the fool with that young girl that Lennard passes for her niece. Answer me honestly—have you not?"

"No, Sir—never."

"Have a care, young man—I can pardon the follies of youth, but premeditated falsehood I never will forgive."

"Be so good then, my dear father, to explain precisely your meaning; and when I perfectly understand the charge, I will answer it as truly as if I were on oath."

"The girl is handsome?" said Somerive.

"Certainly," answered Orlando.

"And you have informed her of it, no doubt?"

"Pardon me, Sir, I never have; and I believe she is at this moment unconscious of it."

"Really! that is wonderful.—She is employed, I think, in the house as a kind of under housekeeper."

"No, Sir; but she sometimes undertakes part of her aunt's business when she is engaged or indisposed, and sometimes attends Mrs. Rayland."

"And lives, I suppose, as Lennard does, in the parlour with the Lady?"

"Very rarely, Sir, and as a matter of great favour, she dines there; rather oftener, though still not regularly, is allowed to drink tea in the parlour."

"Humph!—and at other times, I suppose, she takes her seat at the table allowed Snelcraft and Pattenson: the latter worthy man is celebrated, I think, for his various and successful amours under the roof of my very pious kinswoman. This poor girl, I suppose, is in the way of adding to the trophies of that excellent and faithful servant. Upon my word, Orlando, you may find him a very formidable rival."

"Gracious Heaven, Sir!" cried Orlando, who could not bear even the supposition, " what mistaken notions you have formed of Monimia!"

"Monimia!" exclaimed Somerive, who, serious as the matter was, could not help smiling: "Monimia!—why thou art far gone, my poor boy, since thou hast found such a name for thy nymph—Monimia! I must be allowed, since we are talking plainly of the matter, to call her Mary."

"You may call her what you please, Sir," replied Orlando very impatiently, "so as you do justice to her innocence and goodness. Suffer me to speak, Sir," added he, finding his father about to interrupt him—"suffer me to declare to you, that not one of your own daughters, my sisters, whom I so tenderly love, are more innocent, or more worthy of respect and esteem, and, let me add, of admiration, than this young woman."

"Indeed! is that your opinion?—Pray, Orlando, what means have you had of being so well informed of all these perfections, which you are so willing to put in comparison with those of your own family?"

"Continual experience, amounting to perfect conviction."

"Truly that is marvellous, considering this young person, according to your own account a servant, so seldom drinks tea, and so much seldomer dines with Mrs. Rayland, where, I suppose, she is not allowed any great share of the conversation, even when she *is* admitted;—though you are willing to put her on a level with your sisters, I suppose you hardly so practised this levelling principle on yourself, as to pursue your studies of this miracle to the table of the great Snelcraft, and greater Patteson."

"No, Sir," retorted Orlando warmly; "nor does Monimia ever sit at that table."

"May I then ask, without offending this lady, whose nom de guerre is I find *settled* to be Monimia—where you have seen enough of her to form a judgment so much in her favour?"

"That may be done by seeing her once. You yourself, my dear father!" added Orlando extremely moved, "if you were once to see her, would not blame me for what I have said. Indeed you would not: you would own that she is all I have described."

"Poor boy!" cried Mr. Somerive with a deep sigh; "at your age I remember thinking just the same of a very handsome girl. I too have had my Monimia! my Celinda, my Leonara; and many were the heart-aches these beauties gave me. I should, therefore," continued he, in a more solemn tone—"I should, therefore, my dear Orlando! pass over this juvenile passion, and not even enquire about it, if, from the peculiarity of your situation, and that of the young woman, as well as from your tendency to romantic quixotism, which perhaps I have too much encouraged, I did not fear that it may end more seriously. She is very pretty! and you are very young, and very much in love!—If she is innocent—"

"*If!* Good God, Sir, what shall I say to convince you of it?"

"Nothing, Orlando; speak simply the truth, and I will attend to you: allow me to finish the sentence—If she is innocent and amiable, as you *believe* her to be, you would not certainly destroy that innocence? you would not render her unamiable?"

"Not for a million of worlds!" cried Orlando eagerly.

"Well, then, Orlando, in order to reconcile your honour with that love which it seems you do not affect to deny, it follows that you would marry her?"

"Most undoubtedly, Sir, I would."

"To throw yourself out for ever from every hope of favour on the part of Mrs. Rayland; and, while you render your own family miserable, to entail poverty for life on the woman you love, and her children?"

"I know it all but too well: permit me, however, Sir, to say, that as to my family, *I* do not see why they should make themselves miserable about it, since the morals, the manners, the person of my wife, could be no disgrace to them; and if I chose to work for her, surely I have a right to live with whom I please."

"To work!" cried Somerive angrily. "How work?—you who are in no profession, and could not even support yourself?"

"Pardon me, Sir," answered Orlando, "and let it not offend you, if I say, that a young man of almost one and twenty, six feet high, and in perfect health, must be a very contemptible wretch, indeed, if he is unable to obtain a provision for himself, and to provide for his wife."[1]

"Wild and ridiculous!" exclaimed Somerive. "If you were twelve feet high, and had as many hands as Briareus,[2] how could you employ them? you who have been brought up to nothing, who know nothing—"

"That, Sir, is my misfortune—surely not my fault."

"I allow it. It is a misfortune to which I see other misfortunes are annexed, if a remedy be not instantly found. I perceive, Orlando, that this matter, on which it is plain you have thought deeply, is likely to be even more serious than I apprehended. I must find a profession for you, which shall take you out of a situation so hazardous. I understood General Tracy, that if a commission could be obtained, you expressed no disinclination to enter the army?"

"Certainly I do not.—And let my readiness, or rather my eagerness to embrace that offer convince you, Sir, that whatever may be my future hopes, I do not mean to involve Monimia in my present difficulties, nor to aspire to happiness till I have earned it. Put me, Sir, instantly to the proof. Procure for me a commission, or send me out a volunteer. You shall not see me shrink from any task you may impose on me. But, in return, I expect not to be compelled to resign the hope that will alone animate me—I love Monimia passionately; I shall always love her; and I will not promise to resign her for ever."

"I shall leave all that to time and absence," answered Somerive; "and

---

[1]   Orlando, then, is nearly twenty-one, a good four or five years older than Monimia (although Smith notes that Orlando is only three years older in Chapter II, this does not seem to work out, if Monimia is fourteen or fifteen in 1775, and Orlando is twenty in 1776. The age debate is muddied further if we remember that in Chapter I, Orlando is said to be "now seventeen" and only a few paragraphs later eighteen).

[2]   "Many-handed person [Greek mythology]" (*The Concise Oxford Dictionary*).

insist on nothing but that you will join with me in prevailing on Mrs. Rayland to hear of your entering into the army without dissatisfaction. Though I wish you to have the means of being in some degree independent, it were folly to forfeit needlessly your expectations from her. Try, therefore, so to manage this as to obtain her consent."

"Mrs. Rayland will not, I really believe, oppose it," said Orlando.

"Try her," answered his father; "on your sincerity in doing so I shall rely: and remember Orlando, that if from any other artful quarter attempts are made to persuade her against consenting to this plan, I have only to inform her of your curious plan of marrying her housekeeper's niece, and put her upon enquiring into the intrigue you are carrying on, and you would be banished for ever from Rayland Hall."

"There would be as little wisdom in that, Sir," said Orlando with great warmth, "as there is truth in imputing an intrigue or art to Monimia. However, you are to do as you please."

"And you, Sir," retorted Somerive warmly, "seem to think yourself authorised to say what you please.—Let not my indulgence, which has ruined your brother, and now I see is likely to be your destruction; let not my indulgence hitherto, lead you to depend too much upon it. You shall find, Sir, that if you are ungrateful and undutiful, I can be harsh, and can make myself obeyed. But here, for the present, I desire to end the discourse. We are near home, and I will not have your mother made uneasy, either by the report of what happened to-day at dinner, or by any knowledge of your folly, which has not yet reached her. I shall go immediately to my study; and I recommend it to you to go to your own room, and not appear to-night; for your mother, you know well, is so accustomed to penetrate into my thoughts and yours, that she will not fail to perceive that something is wrong—and she shall not be rendered unhappy."

Orlando, most willing to obey his father in this respect, made no other answer than wishing him a good night; and as soon as he dismounted at home, he retired to his own room, and, with mingled sensations of resentment and sorrow, of anger and despondency, began to reflect on what had passed during the day. The insolent language used by Stockton stung him to the soul. He saw too evidently, that his nightly meetings with Monimia were suspected, if not known—known to the unprincipled and profligate Stockton, who had put the most odious construction on the conduct of the innocent Monimia. Yet he was compelled also to allow, that whatever might be the suspicions of opinions concerning her, he could not avenge or defend her, without being too well assured that consequences must ensure still more fatal to her. If their intercourse was once suspected by Mrs. Rayland, he knew that Monimia would be dismissed with disgrace; that she would probably be abandoned by her aunt, and thrown upon the world, where he had not the power of protecting her from poverty, though he might guard her from insult. The only comfort he had was, that his father, when his interrogatories seemed most hardly to press him to declare how and where he met Monimia, had been diverted to other discourse; that he had, therefore, not been reduced either to tell him a falsehood, or to betray the secret of the door which admitted him to the turret; a secret of which he yet hoped to avail himself, in the interval that must occur between the time of his returning to the Hall and his departure for the army, which he now saw was certain. He felt no wish more ardent than that of reconciling his Monimia to his going, exchanging with her mutual vows of eternal affection, and setting forth in the certainty of her remaining under the protection of Mrs. Lennard, and in the hope that he should return in a situation that might enable him to ask her hand, and to render her subsequent life as happy as the fondest love and competent fortune could make it. But Orlando saw too plainly, that if his evening conferences were known to his father, he would, at whatever risk of ruining him for ever with Mrs. Rayland, put an end to them; and therefore, as more caution than ever was requisite, he determined, for one night, to refrain from the short and dangerous indulgence he had snatched by travelling from Wolverton to the Hall in the middle of the night; and, though Monimia expected him, to forbear seeing her till the next evening, when he hoped to have arranged in his mind what it was the most necessary to say, to make her submit with composure to their separation. Then too he hoped to know something certain of this commission, of which the General hourly expected intelligence from London; and that he should not, by speaking with uncertainty, add suspense to the other uneasy sensations he must inflict on Monimia. He flattered himself also, that he should hear of the General's having fixed the day of his departure. He had now been a fortnight at West Wolverton; and though his stay seemed, the more it was prolonged, to yield to the rest of the family encreased satisfaction, Orlando, whom it detained from the Hall, began to think it the most tedious and unconscionable visit that ever one friend paid to another; and, far from suspecting the real motive, thought with astonishment on General Tracy's living so long among people so unlike his usual associates, and so much out of his way.

CHAP. V.

To reconcile Monimia to his departure, to hide from her the anguish of his own heart at the knowledge that he must go, were no light tasks to Orlando: they were such as all his courage, all his sense of propriety, were nearly unequal to. What would become of her when he was gone? From his earliest remembrance, the certainty of seeing Monimia at the Hall had constituted his principal happiness: yet *he* had many other amusements abroad; he had many relations whom he loved, and who tenderly loved him; he had several pursuits to engage his mind, and several amusements to occupy his time.—Monimia! alas! what had Monimia? Almost alone in the world, *she* had no connection but her aunt, whose reluctant kindness and cold friendship answered but ill to the affectionate temper of the lovely girl, who would have been attached to her, all repulsive as her manners were, from gratitude, and because she believed her the only relation, if Mrs. Lennard had given her leave.—But, selfish, narrow minded, and overbearing, it was impossible for Monimia to love her; and she once remarked, when she stole for five minutes (while her aunt attended Mrs. Rayland to a morning visit) into the garden with Orlando, that she resembled a passion-flower, that having once been supported by a sort of espalier, the wood had decayed, and, nothing being put in its place, the plant crept along the ground, withering, from the dampness to which it was exposed. "See," cried Monimia, "this plant resembles me! It seems abandoned to its fate." Orlando remembered what he then said to drive from her mind such gloomy ideas; but now they were about to be verified. If Monimia was to him all that hitherto sweetened his existence, he was at least as necessary to hers; and a thousand painful fears assailed his heart, as to what she must feel at parting, and what would be her fate when he was gone.

No overture on the affair of his accepting a commission had yet been made to Mrs. Rayland. Mr. Somerive wished Orlando to manage it himself.—Orlando, conscious that much depended upon it, and unwilling to take any decisive step, however necessary, as long as he could avoid it, had still put it off from hour to hour; saying, what was indeed true, that he was now so seldom at the Hall at hours when it was proper to speak of business, that he had found no opportunity.

The next day, however, but one after the dinner at Stockton's, the family were much surprised by the unexpected return of Philip Somerive; who, arriving late in the evening, told his father and mother that he was come, with their permission, to pass some months at home. Tenderly anxious about him as they all were, and ever flattering themselves that a change of conduct would restore him to them, his family received him with such expressions as evinced that they were ready to kill the fatted calf:[1] Orlando felt even more pleasure than the rest at his return; and the younger, unlike the elder brother in the parable, murmured not that there was joy and feasting when he who had been lost was found. Yet this did not arise altogether from the disinterested generosity of his nature. He would at any time have rejoiced that his brother's appearance gave comfort to the hearts of his father and his mother: he now doubly rejoiced, because the presence of Philip Somerive at home dismissed Orlando, almost as a matter of course, to the Hall. He had at this time inhabited the apartment set aside for his brother; his own was occupied by the servant of the General, who was too fine a gentleman to be sent into the attic story. West Wolverton house was not a large one; and Orlando, not so well disguising his impatience as he attempted to do, said to his mother as soon as tea was over, that he knew his stay that night must be attended with some inconveniencies and removals, and therefore he would, with her permission and his father's, go back to the Hall. Mrs. Somerive immediately assented, and said, "And you had better, if your father pleases, set out directly, Orlando, or you will not have your bed aired; and I am sure that little tapestry room where you sleep, as it is on the ground floor, and has windows only to the north, and those windows only long old-fashioned casements, must be horribly damp."

"If you will have the goodness then to say to my father that I am gone, and why gone so early," said Orlando, "it will be better than my disturbing the company with the ceremony of—Good-night!"

To this Mrs. Somerive assenting, Orlando left the room to get his horse; but as he passed through the hall, he met his sister Selina. "Good-night, sweet girl!" said he kissing her hand as he passed her.

"Whither are you going, then, Orlando?" enquired she.

"To the Hall—You know there is no convenient room for me now; and since Philip is come back, I am less wanted."

At this moment Mr. Somerive passed through the hall, and catching some of these words, he put the same question to Orlando; who answered, "that his mother had agreed to his going to the Hall, to make room for his brother; and promised, Sir, to name it to you," added he.

---

[1]   Smith alludes to the Biblical story of the prodigal son, whose return prompts his father to kill the fatted calf to celebrate; this in turn sparks the resentment of the younger, dutiful son.

Mr. Somerive paused a moment—"To the Hall," said he, "Orlando! You are in great haste, I see. Surely you might have staid to supper, as you have not seen your brother so long."

Orlando then gave his mother's reason for his going earlier. "That," said his father gravely, "is a very good reason for your mother; and *you*, I have no doubt, have some of still greater weight:—but remember, Orlando," continued he more sternly, "remember I will not be *trifled* with. Go—I wish you a good-night, and as much repose as your *conscience* will let you taste when you render your father unhappy!"

Mr. Somerive then passed on; and Selina, who had hardly ever in her life heard him speak as if half angry to her brother Orlando, remained amazed and trembling, clinging to his arm. "Good God!" cried she as soon as her father had shut the parlour door, "what is all this, my dear brother? what does my father mean?"

"Can you, Selina," said Orlando in a low and mournful voice—"can you be very faithful, very guarded on a point where my life depends on secrecy? Can you, Selina, be secret as the grave, if I trust you?"

"Can you doubt it?" answered the still more alarmed Selina.—"Well then, to-morrow, perhaps—for to-morrow I must be here again—to-morrow, Selina, if I obtain permission from another person yet more interested than I am, I will perhaps tell you. In the mean time adieu, my dear sister!—If you hear Philip mention me at supper to my father, try to remember what he says."

Orlando then hastened away, fearful of being detained; and as the weather was serene, he determined to go on foot, that, if he found all quiet round the apartment of Monimia, he might glide up for a moment to apprise her that they might without interruption meet in his study that evening. There was a late moon, and the night promised to be beautifully clear; he knew therefore that there was little or no hazard of brandy and tea-merchants being abroad: and as to the hint dropt by Stockton, which had at first given him so much pain, he now fancied it was merely the random folly of a drunkard, and that he knew nothing of Monimia but what he might have collected from Philip Somerive after their first unlucky meeting in the woods.

Had he now taken his horse, he must of necessity have made his return known to the stable-servants at the Hall, before he could have a moment's conversation with Monimia: he proceeded therefore quickly on foot, meditating as he went on what had just passed with his father and his sister.

He had often thought of entrusting Selina with the secret of his passion for Monimia. He had often wished they were known to each other. Equally innocent, amiable, and gentle, with a perfect resemblance in temper and in years,[1] he believed that they would fondly love each other; and that if he could see them attached, it would be the happiest circumstance of his life. He hoped too, that the society and the soothing sweetness of Selina would be a source of comfort to his Monimia when he was far from her. But how he could bring them together, he had yet no idea—Selina being never admitted but on days of ceremony at Rayland Hall; and Monimia being so nearly a prisoner, that the unlucky excursion which occasioned them all so much trouble, was almost the first, and was, in consequence of her stay, which had given so much offence, likely to be the last her aunt would allow her to make. He proposed, however, to consult Monimia upon it, and consider whether some safe means of their meeting could be found.

Between that gate of the park that lay towards West Wolverton, and the house, there were two paths. The upper one was over an eminence where the park paling enclosed part of the down, under which it spread a verdant bosom, with coppices and tall woods interspersed. The other path, which in winter or in wet seasons was inconvenient, wound down a declivity, where the furze and fern were shaded by a few old hawthorns and self-sown firs: out of the hill several streams were filtered, which uniting at its foot, formed a large and clear pond of near twenty acres, fed by several imperceptible currents from other eminences which sheltered that side of the park; and the bason between the hills and the higher parts of it being thus filled, the water found its way over a stony boundary, where it was passable by a foot bridge unless in time of floods; and from thence fell into a lower part of the ground, where it formed a considerable river; and, winding among willows and poplars for near a mile, again spread into a still larger lake, on the edge of which was a mill, and opposite, without the park paling, wild heaths, where the ground was sandy, broken, and irregular, still however marked by plantations made on it by the Rayland family. It was along the lower road, which went through woods to the edge of what was called the upper pond, that Orlando took his way. Just as he arrived at the water, from the deep gloom of the tall firs through which he passed, the moon appeared behind the opposite coppices, and threw her long line of trembling radiance on the water. It was a cold but clear

---

[1] Ehrenpreis (538, n. to p. 159) notes that this is not strictly true, as Monimia is meant to be three years younger than Orlando, and we are told in Chapter VIII, Vol. I that Selina is one year younger than he. However, as indicated in note 1, p. 175, Smith is less than precise about her characters' age differences, although she takes better care with dates.

evening, and, though early in November, the trees were not yet entirely stripped of their discoloured leaves:—a low wind sounded hollow through the firs and stone-pines over his head, and then faintly sighed among the reeds that crowded into the water: no other sound was heard, but, at distant intervals, the cry of the wild fowl concealed among them, or the dull murmur of the current, which was now low. Orlando had hardly ever felt himself so impressed with those feelings which inspire poetic effusions:— Nature appeared to pause, and to ask the turbulent and troubled heart of man, whether his silly pursuits were worth the toil he undertook for them? Peace and tranquillity seemed here to have retired to a transient abode; and Orlando, as slowly he traversed the narrow path over ground made hollow by the roots of these old trees, stepped as lightly as if he feared to disturb them. Insensibly he began to compare this scene, the scenes he every day saw of rural beauty and rural content, with those into which his destiny was about to lead him—"Oh, Monimia!" sighed he, "why cannot I remain with thee in this my native country? How happy should I be to be allowed to cultivate one of the smallest of those farms which belong to the Rayland estate, and, comprising in thy society and that of my family all my felicity, have no wish but to live and die without reading that great book which they call the World!—Alas! shall I ever understand its language? shall I ever become an adept in the principles it teaches? and shall I be happier if I do?—But they tell me that a young man should not be idle! that he must be something, a lawyer or a soldier! and yet, to assist men in ruining each other, and spoiling the simple dignity of justice, seems the business of the first; and to learn the art of destroying honourably our fellow-men, the whole concern of the second.—There are, however, other professions, it is true—I might be a clergyman, and remain here with little to do but to ride twenty or thirty miles of a Sunday, to execute, with the hurry of a postman, the duties I should have sworn to fulfill: and can I conscientiously do what I see done every day? Impossible!—I might too be a merchant: but that I have no talents for a profession, honourable as I allow it to be, where the mind is continually chained to the calculation of profit and loss; and if I am to enter into active life, let it be rather in any line than that which shall confine my activity to a compting-house—For then, Monimia! I must equally leave thee, and live among those who value nothing but money, and who would ridicule a passion like mine."—He paused, and again looked around him. "How beautiful a scene!" continued he; "I would that Monimia were here to enjoy it!—But never am I allowed to point out to her these lovely prospects, never permitted to cultivate that pure and elegant taste which she has received from nature;

and I am now about to tell her that we are to part never perhaps to meet more!—Yet the die is cast: I have promised—nay, I ought to obey my father—and I go—" A deep and mournful reverie succeeded, as, walking onward, his rapid imagination described to him all the sad possibilities that might arise between him and his happiness. In this desponding temper, but without meeting any one to interrupt him in his intended visit to Monimia, he reached the turret, and softly and silently ascended the staircase. He took the usual precautions to ascertain that Monimia was alone; and then, being admitted for a moment to speak to her, he assured her that she might, without any danger, venture to his room that evening. He told her he had much to say to her—much, on which their future happiness depended, to offer to her consideration; and therefore he besought her to divest herself of her fears, and to oblige him. Monimia, confiding entirely in him, promised to be ready; and Orlando, then going through the servants' hall, as if he had that moment arrived from West Wolverton, desired Betty to make up his fire and prepare his bed, saying, that he was come back to his own apartments, on the arrival of his brother at home. He then enquired of Pattenson, if he thought Mrs. Rayland could be spoken to that evening? "I know nothing of the matter," answered the old butler in a very sullen tone; "you may ask the women-folks, as you're always a-dangling after them.—When I saw Madam last, she was not in a way very like to be troubled with company to-night."

Orlando, angry and disgusted by this rudeness, now enquired of the cook, who, though she rivalled in person and features the dame Leonarda of Gil Blas,[1] was a great admirer of beauty in others, and had always beheld Orlando with partial eyes. "Is Mrs. Rayland ill, then, Martha?" said he. "Not that I knows on," replied the woman—"Only a few twinges of the gout about her feet, much as ordinary, that makes her, I reckon, a little peevish: and I understood that Madam was a little out of sorts at hearing nothing of you yesterday; and they've been a-telling her as how you dined out with them there gentlefolks at the Castle, as Madam hates worse than any varmint."

"So," thought Orlando, "I am at length become of consequence enough to be missed if I am longer absent than usual! but the officious malice of whoever it was that related our dinner party yesterday, had

---

[1] Gil Blas (1715–35), by Alain-Rene Lesage, was one of the most influential foreign novels of the eighteenth century. A comic picaresque novel, it was translated by Tobias Smollett in 1749. Leonarda is "the old cook in the robbers' cave, who had 'an enormous chin turning up, an immense nose turning down,' an olive complexion, and purple eyes" (Ehrenpreis, p. 538).

probably spoiled my reception.—Can you tell me, Martha, whether your lady is likely to see me to-night, if I send up for leave?"

"Lord! I'll answer for't," answered the cook; "ifackins, I believe Madam, if she was fairly left to herself, is always as glad to see you as can be—I'll go up now, if you please, and let her know you be here."

This courteous offer Orlando readily accepted; and in a few moments Martha returned. "Well, Martha, may I go up?" enquired he. "Yes, you may," replied Martha; "but Madam's not in one of her sugar-plum humours, I can tell you.—She've got the gout in her foot, and she've got some vagaries in her head about your going to visit her innimies: you'll have a few sour looks, I doubt—but, Lord! Master Orlando, you've such a good-looking pleasant countenance, that I'll defy the witch of Endor[1] to be anger'd long with you."

Then, thanking his ambassadress for the trouble she had taken, and being somewhat encouraged by her opinion of the powers of his countenance, he walked up stairs.

He tapped at the door, as was his custom; and was, by the shrill sharp voice of Mrs. Lennard, directed to come in. He was struck, on entering the room, by the sight of Monimia, who stood near the fire watching the moment when a saucepan, in which some medicine Mrs. Rayland was causing to be made, should be ready to remove. Without, however, noticing her, he approached his venerable cousin, in whose countenance, which seemed to have gained no additional sweetness, he did not read a very favourable answer to his enquiry of—how she found herself?

"No matter how," replied she with abrupt asperity; "if it had been any consequence to you, you would have asked yesterday, I suppose."

"I was detained all day by my father, Madam; and I do most truly assure you (and never was any declaration more sincere than this of Orlando), that I was very unhappy at being detained all day from the Hall."

"Humph!" cried Mrs. Rayland, "your new friends no doubt made you amends. I thought, Sir, you had known that when people go *there*, I never desire to see them *here*, not I. I wish, if you like such acquaintance, you had taken the hint. But perhaps you thought that you might

---

[1] In the Old Testament, the Witch of Endor "conjures up Samuel for [a] distressed Saul" (1 Samuel 28:3–25; see Laurence Urdang and Frederick G. Ruffner, Jr., *Allusions: Cultural, Literary, Biblical, and Historical: A Thematic Dictionary*. Detroit: Gale Research Company, 1982, p. 390). Martha seems to be using the image to signify a permanently angry personage. The *OED* cites a colloquial use of the term to mean a bewitching person or a medium, but the first usage is given as 1819. As in note 1, p. 170, however, this is not necessarily definitive.

take to your brother's courses, and no harm done. For my part, I shall wash my hands of any concern about it, let what will be the end on't."

Orlando now began with calmness, yet without any thing like sycophant submission, to account for his father's having been led by the entreaties of General Tracy, to whom he thought himself much obliged, to break through a resolution he had taken never to visit at Carloraine Castle:—"a resolution," added Orlando, "that he now heartily wishes he had adhered to, as he found the society such as he neither approves for me, or can endure for himself. I assure you, Madam, he never intends to repeat the experiment, which nothing but his wishes to oblige the General made him consent to now."

"Well," said Mrs. Rayland, a little appeased, "it is very wonderful to me that General Tracy, a man of family, can associate with these low bred upstarts—people who always will give one the notion of having got into the coaches they were designed to drive—But so goes this world! Money does every thing—money destroys all distinctions!—Your Creoles and your East-India people[1] over-run every body—Money, money does every thing."

"There is one thing, however, Madam," answered Orlando, "that it does not seem to have done—It does not appear to me to have given to this Mr. Stockton, either the mind or the manners of a gentleman."

"Indeed, child!" cried the old lady: "Well, I am glad that you learn to distinguish.—Poor wretch! I've heard that his father walked up out of Yorkshire without shoes, and was taken by some rich packer to clean his warehouse, and go on errands. Well, so it is in trade!—So you think him vulgar and ill-bred?—But I suppose you had a very profuse entertainment: can you remember the dishes?"

Orlando could with difficulty help smiling at the pains Mrs. Rayland took to feed her disquiet, by obtaining minute particulars of the man whose ostentatious display of wealth so continually offended her. He assured her, however, that he was, in regard to the variety of ornaments of a table, so little of an adept, that, though he knew there was both turtle and venison, he could not tell the name of any other dish. "But I believe, Madam," said he, "there was almost every thing that at this time of the year comes to table, dressed every way that could be imagined."

"Kickshaws, and French frippery, spoiling wholesome dishes. If I had

---

[1] Mrs. Rayland refers again to the nouveau riche: those whose wealth derives from the West Indies (the Creoles) and those who made millions in India in association with the East India Company.

my health," cried Mrs. Rayland as if animated anew with a truly British spirit—"if I had my health, I would ask the favour of General Tracy to dine at Rayland Hall. Indeed I would request his company to the tenants' feast at my own table, and shew him, if he is too young a man to remember it, what an old English table was, when we were too wise to run after foreign gewgaws, and were content with the best of every thing dressed in the English fashion by English people."

Orlando had a thousand reasons to promote a plan as unexpected as it was desirable. Besides the hope he had that the conversation of the General might reconcile Mrs. Rayland to a plan for his independence, and engage her to contribute to its being advantageously carried into execution, he was amused with the idea of seeing together two such originals as Mrs. Rayland and General Tracy; and he knew, that as the latter was a *man of family*, and so very polite, he should not risk their mutually disliking each other by bringing them together: or at least that, if such a circumstance should happen, those manners, which both piqued themselves on possessing, would prevent their shewing it.—For these, and for many other reasons, he eagerly seized on the hint Mrs. Rayland had dropped. "Dear Madam," cried he, "I heartily hope you *will* be well enough. The General would be greatly flattered by such a distinction! I know that nothing would oblige him so much. When is the tenants' feast to be? I wish, if it is fixed, you would permit me to be your messenger to-morrow, and to carry him an invitation."

"Truly, child," replied Mrs. Rayland, whose anger seemed to be quite evaporated, "I am so out of the use of having company, that I don't know well what to say to it. I find my people have fixed the tenants' feast for Thursday next, that is, this day week; and if I were sure of being quite well—Lennard, what do you think of the matter?"

Lennard, who loved nothing better than great dinners, in which she was of so much consequence, answered, "Why, indeed, Ma'am, I think you'll be quite well enough—nay, I could venture to say so positively. Your foot is getting better apace; and in other respects, when you have been free from pain for a while, I have not know you better these many years."

"Well, Orlando, then," resumed the old lady, "we'll consider of it, and let you know to-morrow.—You have taken to your bed below again, I find?"

"I have, Madam, with your permission."

"Well, then, you may come and breakfast with me; and, for to-night, order what you please for your supper in your own room."

Orlando, rejoiced to be thus reconciled, now wished her a good-night, and retired; casting, as he went, a melancholy glance toward

Monimia, who, quite unnoticed by either of the ladies, had stood the whole time with her eyes fixed on the fire, and her beautiful arms exposed to its scorching heat, while she was employed in watching the important preparation that was boiling. But Monimia herself, far from feeling her situation, would have undergone infinitely more inconvenience, for as many hours as she now had done minutes, to have enjoyed the satisfaction of hearing Orlando's voice, even when his words were not addressed to her, and of observing the favour he was in with Mrs. Rayland; whose anger, however she seemed desirous of cherishing it, was put to flight on the first apology of her young favourite.[1]

CHAP. VI.

The meeting of the evening promised to be undisturbed. It was long since Orlando had seen his Monimia quietly seated by the fire in the Study; and now that he was once more to enjoy that happiness, he could not determine to embitter it by speaking of the probability there was that he was soon to leave her, and enter on a new mode of life. He could, when they were actually together, the less resolve to speak of this, as Monimia appeared in unusual spirits; and from what she had observed of Mrs. Rayland's behaviour to him, in the interview at which she had been present, she found reason for forming more sanguine hopes than she had ever yet indulged, that their delicious visions were not chimerical; and that Orlando, if not master of Rayland Hall, would yet be amply provided for by the favour of its present possessor.

Instead, therefore, of destroying these flattering visions, which lent to the lovely features of Monimia the most cheerful animation, he endeavoured to divest his own mind of the painful reflections it had of late entertained; and instead of talking of what *was* to happen, he wished to fortify the mind of Monimia against whatever *might* happen, by giving her a taste for reading, and cultivating her excellent understanding. The books he had given her, the extracts she had made from them,

---

[1] Mrs. Rayland's inability to stay angry shows how romantically involved she is with Orlando; further, Smith links Monimia's desire to hear her beloved's voice with Mrs. Rayland's evident pleasure in doing so. When, in Chapter IX of Volume II, Mrs. Rayland asserts that Orlando is "yet too young" to think of marrying, Smith implies that Mrs. Rayland feels jealous possession: "Mrs. Rayland answered rather coldly, 'I believe Mr. Orlando has no thoughts of marrying.—He is yet too young.'"

and her remarks, afforded them conversation, and gave to Orlando exquisite delight. He had animated the lovely statue, and, like another Prometheus, seemed to have drawn his fire from heaven. The ignorance and the prejudices in which Monimia had been brought up, now gave way to such instruction as she derived from Addison and other celebrated moralists.[1] She understood, and had peculiar pleasure in reading the poets, which Orlando had selected for her; and when she repeated, in a fascinating voice, some of the passages she particularly admired, Orlando was inspired with the most ardent wish to become a poet himself.

Very different was the way in which his elder brother passed this evening. Tormented with fear and remorse, that unfortunate young man had returned to his long-deserted home, for no other reason than because he had, during his northern expedition, lost to his companions every guinea that he could by any means raise, and had besides contracted with them a very considerable debt of honour. He knew not how to apply to his father, whom he had already impoverished; yet his pride would not let him return to Mr. Stockton's, whither some of the party were again gone, till he had the means of satisfying their demands against him. In this emergency he came home, in hopes of finding some pretence to procure the money of his mother, whom he believed he could persuade to borrow it for him of her brother Mr. Woodford, as she had done a less considerable sum once before; or at all events to gain a few days, in which he might consider what to do.

It was to the dejection he felt on the awkward circumstances to which he had reduced himself, that the gravity and steadiness of manner was owing, which his father took for contrition and reformation. It lasted, however, no longer than till the next evening, when, after tea, Mrs. Somerive as usual, in order to amuse the General, proposed cards— Mr. Somerive, however, having a person with him upon business from whom he could not disengage himself, and Orlando having returned to Rayland Hall immediately after dinner, there was not enough to make a whist table (as none of the young ladies played), and therefore young Somerive proposed to the General to sit down to piquet.[2]

---

[1] Smith again alludes to the story of Pygmalion and Galatea: see note 1, p. 61. Prometheus stole fire from Zeus and so "enlightened" humankind; he was condemned to the everlasting torment of having his liver daily torn from him by an eagle. Joseph Addison (1672–1719) was considered to be a pre-eminent formulator of ideas of taste and intellectual rigour (see notes 1, p. 49, and 1, p. 502).

[2] Piquet: a card game.

To this proposal he of course consented, and, either from chance or design, the General lost every party, and had presently paid to his antagonist twelve guineas. Animated by this success, especially as it was against a man who was known to be in habits of playing at the first clubs, Philip Somerive again proposed playing after supper. Fortune continued to be propitious; and when his father, mother and sisters retired, at a later hour than ordinary, he still continued at table, where he was now a winner of about fifty guineas.

They were no sooner out of his way, than the true spirit of gaming, which their presence had checked, broke out.

"This is poor piddling work, General!" exclaimed he: "Do you not think hazard[1] a better thing?"

The General answered coolly, that it certainly was; "but," added he, "I suppose my good host would think his house polluted by having the necessary instruments in it. He has no other dice, I dare swear, than those in the back-gammon table."

"Oh! as to that," answered young Somerive, "I am always provided with an apparatus in case of emergency—there is no travelling without such a resource—I have the pretty creatures up stairs. What say you, General—shall we waste an hour with them?"

"With all my heart," replied Tracy. "Let us see if you are as much befriended by chance, as you have been by skill."

Young Somerive now produced from his travelling portmanteau a box and dice: he put a green cloth over the table, that the rattling of them might not be heard in the house; and then telling the servants that none need sit up but the General's servant, they began to play, and continued at it till morning broke, with various success—But on quitting it, Somerive found himself a very considerable gainer, and retired to his bed flushed with the hope that the General, all veteran as he appeared, and calmly as he played, was a pigeon, from whose wings he might pluck the feathers which were wanting to repair his own.

The General, who only wanted a study of his character, and to whom hundreds were as nothing when he had any favourite project in view, was now perfectly assured that, by losing money to him, or by supplying him with it when he lost to others, this young man would become wholly subservient to his wishes, however contrary to honour or conscience. He did not dislike play, though he never regularly pursued it; and had one of those cool heads in such matters, which had prevented his ever suffering

---

[1] A game at dice in which the chances are complicated by arbitrary rules (*OED*).

by it. He had generally been a winner, and particularly in betting:—he frequented, when he was in London, all the houses where high play is carried on; and was so much accustomed to see thousands paid and received at these places as matters of course, that he held the trifle he had paid to Philip Somerive the evening before as not worth remembering. It was therefore with some surprise that he heard Mr. Somerive, who had called him apart the next morning, express in very forcible terms, his great concern that his son had won so large a sum of him. If the General felt any concern, it was that Philip should have been unguarded enough to speak of it. He soon, however, learned that Mr. Somerive alluded solely to the fifty guineas he had won at piquet, and that of the subsequent transactions of the evening he knew nothing. This therefore he carefully concealed, and, assuring Mr. Somerive that he had almost forgot they played at all, conjured him not to be uneasy about it.

"I know, my dear General," said Somerive, "I know perfectly well that this is a mere trifle to you; but to my son it may, nay it will have the worst consequence. He is, I see with an aching heart, too much devoted to play—Success only nourishes this ruinous passion—And distressed as I have been, and indeed am, by his conduct, I should rather have paid an hundred pounds for him than have seen him win fifty."

The General endeavoured to quiet, on this head, the apprehensions of the unhappy father, by telling him that he saw nothing in the young man that was not at his age, and with his prospects, very excusable. "It is surely," said he, "hazardous, my good friend, to check your son too much. If home is rendered utterly unpleasant to him, his volatility seeks resource abroad; and there you know how many designing people beset a young man of his expectations."

"Good God!" exclaimed Somerive, "*what are* his expectations? He has impressed you, I see, my dear Sir, with the same idea which has in fact undone him, and will undo us all. What expectations has he that can in the least be relied upon, unless it be of this small estate, which he is already dismembering, and which will soon disappear—ah! very soon indeed, in the hands of a gamester."

"Tie it up, then," said the General.

"I cannot," answered Somerive; "for it is entailed,[1] and, except my wife's jointure of a hundred a year, which with difficulty I contrived to settle upon her, he may dissipate it all, and I have no doubt but he will."

---

[1] Entailment meant that an estate had to descend to the nearest male relative. This is most famously explored in Jane Austen's *Pride and Prejudice* (1813).

"You judge, I think, too hardly of him. Something is surely to be forgiven him, who has always been told that he must be heir to the great property of the Raylands, and possess one of the largest landed estates in the county."

"O! would to heaven he never had been told so!" said Mr. Somerive with a deep sigh. "If ever, my dear General, he should talk to you about it, pray endeavour to wean him from expectations so ruinous, and, I think, so fallacious. It is true that I am heir at law to all the estates of Sir Orlando Rayland my grandfather, in default of Sir Hildebrand's daughters having issue, but not if the survivor of them disposes it by will, for the whole is hers without any restriction; and there is not the least chance of her dying *without* a will, for I know she is *never* without one: and the people who surround her take especial care that her own family shall be excluded from it."[1]

"You do not then suppose," said the General, "you do not believe it possible that these people, by whom I conclude you mean those old servants of whom I have heard you speak, have interest enough with her to secure to themselves so large a property as Mrs. Rayland possesses. I should think it more likely that though she will probably give them considerable legacies, she will leave the estate to the next heir; her pride will urge her to this, perhaps, on the condition of his taking the name of Rayland."

"I fear, not," answered Mr. Somerive. "She has a very singular temper, and has always been taught that the sister of *her* father Sir Hildebrand disgraced herself by marrying my father. She has on a thousand occasions given me to understand, that the small portion of the Rayland blood which I have the honour to boast, is much debased by having mingled with that of a plebeian; and that the blood of my children being still a degree farther removed from the Raylands, she cannot consider them as belonging to the family, which is in her opinion extinct—She means therefore to perpetuate its remembrance by the only method in which she believes she can do it worthily; and, after giving her servants considerable legacies—perhaps something to Orlando—to have recourse to the common refuge of posthumous pride, and, with her large landed estates, to endow an hospital, which shall be called after her name."

---

[1]   Mr. Somerive points out that Mrs. Rayland, as an unmarried woman, owns her property outright (a widow would essentially hold the property in trust for her nearest male relative). Smith relies heavily on the legal loophole that allowed the claim of an heir at law to be superceded by testament. See Appendix C for more information.

The General exclaimed loudly against such a method of settling her property; but, after hearing on what Mr. Somerive founded his opinion, he agreed that it seemed but too probable. "And yet," added he, "it appears to be more the interest of these servants, by whom you say she is governed, that the estate should descend to an individual—particularly that of the old housekeeper, who, from what I can make out of the scraps I have picked up here and there about this Monimia, seems to have a plan of drawing in your youngest son to marry her; and of course it must be her wish that *he* should be Mrs. Rayland's heir."

"I have not discovered," replied Somerive, "in all I have collected from Orlando, that the aunt is at all privy to their attachment. But that indeed may be her art—She possesses more than almost any woman I ever knew; and had she much less, she must know that the bare suspicion of such an intrigue, on the part of Mrs. Rayland, would occasion the disgrace of Orlando—the expulsion of the girl from the house—and perhaps the ruin of herself, if the least idea occurred of her being their counsel."

"Upon the whole, then, my friend," cried the General, "I think that the putting Orlando into some profession immediately seems the only prudent measure you can take. This will probably ascertain Mrs. Rayland's intentions, if they are in his favour; and, if they are not, will remove him from a situation which appears in my mind a thousand times more likely to ruin him for life, than even those imprudences of which you complain in his brother: for be assured, my dear Sir, a young fellow is never so completely ruined as when he has married foolishly—Every other folly is retrievable; but an engagement of that sort blasts a man's fortune for ever: and the wisest thing he can do afterwards is to hang himself."

Though Mr. Somerive, who was not a "man of the world," and who had experienced many years of happiness with a woman whom he married for love, was by no means of Tracy's opinion as to marriages of affection in general, he saw the variety of evils such a marriage would bring on Orlando, in as strong a light as his friend could represent them. He therefore entirely acquiesced in the necessity of his being removed from Rayland Hall; and waited with impatience for Orlando's account of what had passed in that conference which he had undertaken to hold with the old lady, on the subject of his entering the army.

Just as he parted from General Tracy, who about an hour and a half before dinner retired to his toilet, Orlando appeared on horseback. His father met him; and bidding him join him in the garden as soon as he had put his horse in the stable, he walked thither—Orlando in a moment attended him. "Well," said Mr. Somerive gravely, "have you had an opportunity of conversing with Mrs. Rayland on this matter? I have it every hour more at heart, and am determined that you shall be removed from your present situation, unless, what is not to be expected, she signifies her positive resolution to make you very ample amends for your loss of time, and gives me assurances of it."

Orlando, in this peremptory determination of his father, fancied he saw the machinations of his brother to get him away from the Hall; but, without expressing any part of the pain such a suspicion gave him, he answered, "You know, my dear Sir, that in our last conference on this subject, I assured you of what I now desire to repeat, that I live only to obey you; but I have had no opportunity of speaking to Mrs. Rayland on this subject; for when I saw her on the first evening of my return to the Hall, it was with great difficulty I could appease the anger she felt at our having dined with Stockton."

"She knew it then?"

"Oh, yes!—Lennard and Pattenson take care she shall know every thing. At length, however, I had the good fortune, not only to obtain a remission of my offence, but to engage her to invite our family and the General to dine at her table on Thursday, when the tenants' feast is to be held at the Hall. Mrs. Rayland piques herself on shewing the General, whom she respects as a man of family, a specimen of old English hospitality, in opposition to the modern profusion of the Castle—and her desire to obtain his suffrage in favour of the ancient mode of living at Rayland Hall, has performed what no other consideration would have effected. This unexpected project entered her head the moment I had described our visit; and all yesterday was passed in considering about it, and debating with Lennard whether she should be well enough. To-day it is decided that she shall, and I am sent with the invitation, which certainly you and my mother and sisters will accept; and I suppose General Tracy will oblige us by going also."

"Of that there can be no doubt," replied Mr. Somerive.

"I thought, therefore," added Orlando, "that you and the General might have an opportunity, during the course of the day, of introducing the conversation relative to my entering the army; and that it would be perhaps better than my abruptly disclosing what may, in some of her humours, appear to Mrs. Rayland as a desire on my part to quit her."

"You have certainly given my ancient cousin love powder, Orlando," said Mr. Somerive smiling; "for I never heard that, even in her younger days, she shewed for any body as much affection as she lately has done to you."

"And yet," replied Orlando, "I am almost certain that it goes no farther than a little present kindness, or perhaps a small legacy."

Mr. Somerive, feeling that this was too probable, and was indeed what he had just before been repeating to General Tracy, sighed deeply—and bidding Orlando go with his message of invitation to his mother and sisters, he sent up the card to the General; and then went on his usual circuit round his farm, desiring Orlando to stay dinner.

CHAP. VII.

Orlando returned to Rayland Hall in the evening, carrying with him the most polite answer from General Tracy; and, from his own family, assurances of the grateful pleasure with which they accepted Mrs. Rayland's invitation for the following Thursday. Poor Monimia too, though she was to have no other part in this festivity than to assist her aunt in preparing for it, heard with satisfaction from Orlando that it was fixed, because she believed that this unusual civility towards his family and their guest was an indubitable mark of Mrs. Rayland's increasing affection for him.

Orlando, however, who from his father's last conversation, and from his persuasion that Mrs. Rayland would not oppose it, saw that his departure was certain, and would soon happen, thought it cruel to encourage the flattering impressions which the soft heart of Monimia so readily received, and which he had himself taught her to cherish when they were apparently much less likely to be realised. He therefore, when they met this evening, renewed, what he had sometimes distantly touched upon before, the probability that he must soon enter the army, and quit, at least for a time, the spot which, while she remained on it, contained all that gave value to his life. The tender, timid Monimia, in whose idea every kind of danger was attendant on the name of soldier, was thunderstruck with this intelligence: and it was not till Orlando had tried every argument to sooth and console her, that she was able to shed tears. "Could we hope, my Monimia," said he when he found her composed enough to listen to him—"could we hope to continue as we are, and to converse thus undiscovered for years to come, tell me if there is not too much bitter mingled with the few transient moments of happiness, to make us reasonably *wish* to continue it? When we meet, is it not always in fear and apprehension? and are we not ever liable to the same alarm as that from which you suffered so cruelly three weeks since?—Alas! even now we are in the power of an unprincipled ruffian, who, though he appeared willing to engage for mutual secrecy, may, in a fit of drunkenness, betray us; or, through mere insolence, tell—because he has the power of telling. He did not see you; but he knows, and indeed so does Pattenson, that somebody was with me; and the very jealousy that misleads the old rogue Pattenson, will perhaps make him watch and discover us. I need not, Monimia, describe all I should suffer for you if that were to happen; nothing would remain for us but to fly together: and surely I need not add, that if I did not fear to expose you, my angel, to the miseries of poverty, I would, without hazarding a discovery, fly to-morrow; but I am, you know, under age, and we could not marry in England. If I was thus to disoblige my father, he would abandon me for ever, and from Mrs. Rayland I could expect nothing. Such is the melancholy train of thought I have been compelled to admit in reflecting on our present situation. Perhaps the line of life that is proposed for me is the only one that we can with hope look forward to for the future."—He paused a moment: Monimia stifled the sobs that convulsed her bosom; she could not speak, but sat with her handkerchief to her eyes, and her head resting on her hand, while he proceeded—"It is certain that I must tear myself from you; that I must enter on a new scene of life, and perhaps encounter some difficulties and hardships: but would you not despise a man of my age, who would not so purchase independence? If I have a profession, I shall have something on which to depend, if Mrs. Rayland will not, and my father cannot provide for me; something on which, if I have tolerable fortune, I may in a few years be enabled to support my Monimia. Can I, ought I with such hopes to hesitate?"

"I allow," replied Monimia with a deep sigh—"I allow that you ought not."

"While General Tracy lives," resumed Orlando, "he will be my friend; at least such are his promises to my father. He assures him that he will make a point of my speedy promotion; and his interest is certainly such as leaves no doubt of his having the power to do it."

"Ah, Orlando!" said Monimia in a low and broken voice, "you speak only of the good, and forget or conceal the evil. What if you are maimed, or killed? What then becomes of Monimia, who could not die too, but must live perhaps the most desolate and miserable creature upon earth?"

"General Tracy," replied Orlando, "has assured my father, that the regiment in which he means to procure me a commission, and for which they are now recruiting, is about to be immediately recalled from America, where the war must very soon terminate in favour of England, and that therefore I shall certainly not be sent abroad: he even says, that as soon as I have my commission, it is highly probable that I shall be ordered into this country on a recruiting party, and may take up my quarters for two or three months in this neighbourhood."

These reasonable arguments, joined to the flattering hope that Orlando might, though he entered on a profession by which he would, she believed, become independent, still remain in England, and even be occasionally in his native county, added to the conviction that they could not long continue to see each other without being discovered, reconciled Monimia to the thoughts of his accepting the commission offered to him by the General; and she became more calm, and able to talk of it with some degree of composure. Orlando, on their parting for that time, besought her to assure him that she would make herself easy, and learn to think of his destination rather as a matter of satisfaction than apprehension. Monimia promised all he desired: but she was no sooner alone than her apprehensions again returned, and the sad possibilities that she had before enumerated recurred in all their terrors to her imagination. To these many were added of which she dared not speak to Orlando; the fears that he might forget her; and that when once entered on new scenes, and among all the beauty, elegance, and accomplishments which she read of in magazines and newspapers, the humble Monimia would be remembered no longer. This seemed to her so probable, and was so distressing to her heart, that she thought she could better endure almost every other evil. Sleep refused to banish these cruel ideas from her mind; and the morning broke, and called her from her restless bed to her task of attending on her aunt in the house-keeper's room, before she could find any comfort in any of her reflections, unless it was the hope that Mrs. Rayland might oppose the scheme of sending Orlando away, since Monimia persuaded herself that she every day became fonder of his company.

Monimia appeared before her aunt so pale, from want of sleep, and from the acute uneasiness she had undergone, that Mrs. Lennard, notwithstanding her usual insensibility, took notice of it.

"Hey-day, girl!" cried she, "why, what's the matter now? Why you look, I protest, as if you had been up all night! Pray what have you been about?"

"About, aunt!" said Monimia, while a faint blush, excited by fear and consciousness, wavered a moment on her cheek—"I have been about nothing."

"That is what you generally are about, I think," replied Mrs. Lennard harshly. "But I suppose you have been sitting up after some nonsense or other—with your books or your writing. I shall put an end to Madam Betty's career, I promise you; I know she lets you have candles, and gets books for you out of the Study, though I have time after time forbidden her to do any such thing."

Monimia, willing to let it be thought that Betty did do so, rather than excite any other suspicion by denying it, only said mildly—"I hope, dear aunt, there is no harm in my trying to improve myself, if I do not therefore neglect what you order me to do?"

"Improve yourself!—Yes, truly, a pretty improvement—Your chalky face and padded eyes are mighty improvements: and I'd be glad to know what good your reading does you, but to give you a hankering after what you've no right to expect? An improved lady will be above helping me, I suppose, very soon."

"When I *am*, my dear aunt," answered Monimia, "it will be time enough for you to forbid my reading; but, till then, pray don't be angry if I endeavour to obtain a little common instruction."

"Don't be impertinent," exclaimed Mrs. Lennard; "don't be insolent—for if you are, Miss, this house is no place for you.—I see already the blessed effects of your reading—you fancy yourself a person of consequence: but I shall take care to put an end to it; for, if Betty supplies you with candles, I'll discharge her."

"She has *not* indeed, my dear aunt," said Monimia, whose generous mind could not bear that another should suffer for her.

"She has not!—what has she not?" enquired Mrs. Lennard.

"She has not lately supplied me with candles," replied Monimia.

"How is it, then," cried Mrs. Lennard, fixing on her a stern and enquiring eye, "that light is sometimes, aye and very lately too, seen from your window, at hours when your own candle is taken away, and when you ought to be in bed?"

To this Monimia could answer nothing, but that it was true she had now and then saved a piece of wax candle herself; but, in order to put an end to an enquiry which had already made her tremble with the most cruel apprehensions, she endeavoured less to account for what *had* happened, and which she could not deny, than to appease her aunt by very earnest assurances that what offended her should happen no more, and that, since she so much disliked her reading of a night, she would never again practise it.

Mrs. Lennard seemed to be somewhat satisfied by these protestations—

though, while Monimia was with many tears repeating them, her fierce eyes were fixed on the countenance of her trembling niece with a look of questioning doubt, which made Monimia shrink with dread—for it seemed to intimate that more was suspected than was expressed.

At length, however, she condescended to appear pacified; and summoning Betty and another of the maid-servants, she gave them their employments in preparing for the grand dinner: then ordering Monimia to take her share, and the superintendence of the whole, she returned to the parlour; and poor Monimia, glad to be relieved from her presence, proceeded as cheerfully in her task as her melancholy reflections on what had passed with Orlando the preceding night, and her newly-awakened dread of her aunt's suspicions, would allow her to do.

Mr. Somerive was much at a loss to know how to act in regard to his eldest son: fondly flattering himself that this beloved son had seen the dangerous errors of his former conduct, he could not bear the idea of shewing any resentment at what was past, or that, by his being left out of the party going to Rayland Hall, he should be considered as an exile from the favour of Mrs. Rayland; yet, to let him go without an invitation, he knew, would give offence, and he knew not how to set about obtaining one. Orlando, who passed a few moments with him in the course of the preceding Wednesday, saw his father's uneasiness, because he had felt something of the same kind himself about his brother; and he generously, though without making any merit of it, undertook to remove this source of vexation, by engaging Mrs. Rayland to invite him. This was an arduous task, as the old Lady had not seen him for more than two years, and during that time had heard only evil reports of his conduct. The offence he had given her by associating with the Stockton set, and even joining in those trespasses of which she believed she had so much reason to complain, had embittered her mind against him, even more than his gaieties and extravagance:—yet Orlando, by assuring Mrs. Rayland that he was now sensible of his error, that he was come home with a resolution to remain with his family, and that it would discourage him in the career of reformation if she did not seem ready to forgive, and again consider him as a part of it, so flattered her self-consequence, and soothed her resentment, that she agreed to receive Philip as one of her guests, and commissioned Orlando to carry an invitation to his brother: nor could she, with all her natural severity of temper, and little sensibility to great or generous actions, help being affected by the noble disinterestedness of her young favourite, who thus laboured to reconcile to her a brother who would have been considered by most young men as a formidable rival in her favour, and have been assiduously kept at the distance to which he had thrown himself. This exalted goodness of heart she put down immediately to the account of the Rayland blood; and in praising Orlando to Mrs. Lennard, to whom she now often spoke of him with pleasure, she remarked, that he every day became more and more like the Rayland family—"What fine eyes the young man has!" cried she; "and how they flashed fire when he was pleading for that sad brother of his with so much earnestness!—And then when I seemed willing to oblige him, what a fine countenance! I could almost have fancied it was my grandfather's picture walked out of its frame, if it had not been for the difference of dress!"[1]

Mrs. Lennard assented, and encouraged every favourable idea her Mistress entertained of Orlando; but all this while a mine was proceeding against him, of which the success would inevitably ruin all his hopes.

This originated in the jealousy of Pattenson, who, whatever favour he obtained by dint of presents and money from his coquettish dulcinea,[2] could never divest himself of his apprehensions that Orlando was a successful rival. This cruel fear had taken possession of his mind long before the discovery of Jonas Wilkins; and notwithstanding the girl's solemn protestations that she was in her own bed at the time she was accused of being with Orlando in his Study, and the offers of the woman who lived in the same room to confirm this by her *Bible oath*, Pattenson could never be persuaded but that it was Betty herself; because, having not the slightest suspicion of Monimia, who was, he knew, locked in by her aunt every night, he believed that it was impossible it could be any other person. Betty, in order to tease him, sometimes affected to be conscious that the accusation was true, while she persisted in denying it; and Orlando rather encouraged than repressed a notion that prevented any conjectures which might have glanced towards Monimia.

For three weeks, therefore, this uneasy suspicion had corroded the bosom of the amorous though venerable Mr. Pattenson, who, greatly as he loved his ease, resigned it to the gratification of his revenge; and who

---

[1]   For Mrs. Rayland, Orlando stands as a descendant of the Raylands alone (untainted by Somerive ancestry), and as such will be the most suitable heir.

[2]   "Idolized and idealized mistress" (*The Concise Oxford Dictionary*): derived from Miguel Cervantes, *Don Quixote* (1605, second part 1615), wherein Dulcinea is Don Quixote's mistress. *Don Quixote* is a classic romance text, but it also dramatizes the imaginary nature of the romance: its hero is the classic deluded hero whose implicit belief in tales of chivalry results in his madness and eventual death. While the passage here refers to Pattenson's bewitchment by Betty, the relevance to Orlando's attachment to the romance is also clear.

determined to detect Betty, and in doing so thought he should have an opportunity of ruining Orlando with his Lady, and thus getting out of his way a rival who might one day be his Master; and whom he hated, not only on account of his love, but of his interest; for so highly had he been in favour with all three ladies, that each had, in dying, given him a very considerable legacy, and recommended him to the survivor; and he did not doubt but that, on the decease of his present Mistress, he should find his property inferior to that of few gentlemen in the county.

The gradual increase, therefore, of the favour shewn to Orlando did not at all please him; but his attempts to injure him with Mrs. Rayland had never succeeded, and began to be displeasing to her. Still, however, he knew that, if Orlando were detected of an intrigue with one of her women-servants, it was an offence which Mrs. Rayland would never pardon; and though this discovery would certainly occasion the discharge of the fair Helen for whom he sighed, Pattenson was sure that Orlando could not take her into his protection for want of money; while, being dismissed without a character by the two inexorable vestals, his Lady and her companion, the girl would be glad to make terms with him; and he was quite rich enough to undertake to keep her in some of the neighbouring towns, till she might be supplanted by some newer object.

Such were the speculations of the politic Pattenson; but, like many other politicians, he pursued, among the many crooked paths before him, that which led him from his purpose. Instead of watching Orlando, he set himself to watch Betty, who never went in even with a message to him in his Study without Pattenson following her; and on the night he engaged her to sit up for him, the butler was concealed in a closet within the servants' hall, and heard all their conversation; and though what then passed tended directly to prove to Pattenson that he was in an error, he persuaded himself that they suspected his concealment, and had agreed upon what they should say to mislead him.

Instead, therefore, of rejoicing to find his suspicions were not confirmed, he was only irritated to find that his attempts to detect the supposed lovers were baffled; and he redoubled his vigilance in watching Betty, and engaged one of the footmen in the same office. This was the same man who had seen Orlando cross the park one morning at a very early and unusual hour, and who then taking him at a distance for a poacher, had pursued and stopped him; circumstances which the fellow, who was the mere creature of Pattenson, had afterwards related to him, with conjectures as to the reason of Orlando's appearance that had helped to raise higher those suspicions Pattenson had before entertained.

That Mrs. Rayland had determined to have company at her own table, and particularly the family of Somerive, on the day of the tenants' feast, was a terrible vexation to Pattenson—who, instead of presiding like the master of the house in the hall, would now be only the butler at the side-board in the great dining-room; and to chagrin for the consequence he thus lost, was added the mortification of knowing that while he should be busied in attending on his Lady up stairs, Orlando, who on these occasions, which happened twice a year, always mingled with the young farmers, would have all the *ladies* of the hall to himself.

It had been the custom of the house, time immemorial, for the land-lord, receiving his Michaelmas rents,[1] to give the most numerously-attended entertainments of the year, and to allow the tenants's sons and daughters, their friends, and the servants of the family, to have a fiddle in the great hall. The Mrs. Raylands, notwithstanding the state in which they had been educated, had been always, during their youth, led to the company by their father, and, accompanied by Lady Rayland, had each gone down one dance with some neighbouring gentleman who was invited on purpose, or with the chaplain of the family. Those days, though long since past, with almost all the witnesses of their festivity, were still recollected by Mrs. Rayland with some degree of pleasure; and as she adhered most scrupulously to old customs, however unlike her usual mode of life, this sort of rustic ball given to the tenants had always been kept up, except in those two years that were marked by the death of two of the ladies.—Mrs. Lennard and Mr. Pattenson, who had long presided at them, loved the gaiety of the scene, and the consequence they had in it, as they were considered as the master and mistress of the feast; for though Mrs. Rayland once used to go down to honour it with her presence for ten minutes, she had now left off that custom, from age and infirmity; and her servants, to whom it was attended with some trouble and loss of time, had persuaded her that she was always ill after such an exertion. It was, there-fore, usual with her to sup on this anniversary somewhat earlier than ordi-nary, and to go to her bed, dismissing Lennard to her post of mistress of the revel, with a strict charge to her to watch assiduously against the intru-sion of drunkenness or impropriety; to see that all the guests withdrew in due season, and quite sober; and to settle every thing after their departure for the decorum and tranquillity of the next day.

---

[1] Michaelmas: feast of St. Michael, on 29 September: a quarter-day (that is, the end of the third quarter of the year) on which landlords received the rents on their properties from their tenants.

Mrs. Lennard had in general adhered to these good rules, though she thought herself at liberty a little to vary from them in the detail. Thus she deemed it no breach of the regularity her Lady recommended, if she acceded to the earnest solicitations of a handsome young farmer, who, as she was persuaded, left the buxom damsel his partner, purely for the gratification of going down a dance with her; though it sometimes happened that her interest in the renewal of a lease, or some building wanting on the farm, for which she could effectually intercede, were more powerful motives than even the honour or the pleasure thus obtained—notwithstanding Mrs. Lennard's assertion, which was probably true, that she had learned to dance of the dancing-master who taught the first Duke of Cumberland and *all* the Princesses, and that she was celebrated for her excellence in that accomplishment, particularly her great agility in the rigadoon.

This rigadoon,[1] like all early and pleasing acquirements, was still recollected with gratitude for the fame it had obtained for her; and notwithstanding the lapse of years, and some rheumatic complaints, she could occasionally introduce some of its original graces into her country dance. It is true she never performed above one or two at most; but what she *did*, she piqued herself upon executing with a degree of spirit, which made all the operators in cotillon steps, and allemands, "hide their diminished" heels.[2] But, now alas! a fall she got a few months before, and the cruel and cowardly attack of the rheumatism on the limb while it was in a disabled state, had put an end to the exhibition of this rigadoon step for ever. Yet, with the true spirit of perseverance, Mrs. Lennard, though she danced no more, loved to overlook the dancers, and not having the same reasons as Pattenson had to dislike the party proposed, had with all her interest promoted it—feeling, probably, that the pleasure she resigned in the country-dance "with her rigadoon step,"[3] would be amply made up to her in appearing no longer as only house keeper and attendant, but in the capacity of a companion and friend to Mrs. Rayland; for, now her Lady was so infirm, she was introduced in that character whatever company might be in the house. Far as she was advanced in years, to adorn her person was her foible; and she reflected with some pleasure on the smart and well-fancied dress with which she intended, on this impor-

---

[1] Rigadoon: lively dance for two persons; cotillon: general name for a dance; allemand: any one of several German dances; a country dance figure.

[2] *Paradise Lost*, IV. 35. In the poem, the stars hide their diminished "heads."

[3] Ehrenpreis identifies the quotation as from *Tatler* 34 (28 June 1709). *The Tatler*, founded by Richard Steele, ran from 1709 to 1711. It was followed by *The Spectator* (see note 1, p. 49).

tant Thursday, to astonish and outshine the Somerive family. Of this vanity, however, poor Monimia was the victim; for, after many debates about what she should wear, Mrs. Lennard found something to do to every article of her dress. These alterations were entrusted to Monimia; and at night when Orlando sought her, as usual, in the hope that he might pass an hour with her in her own room, he found her not only indulged with candles, which had been so lately prohibited, but weeping over a task which she doubted whether it would be possible for her to finish, in the time assigned her, to her aunt's satisfaction.

Orlando had a particular interest in her appearing to advantage the next day; for, though he knew she would not be allowed, nor did he wish her to be seen among the guests, he had imagined a project to introduce her and his sister Selina to each other while every other person was engaged. The more he reflected on this scheme, the more practicable it appeared, and the more it flattered his imagination. He, therefore, could not bear to think that, between fatigue and fretting, the beauty he had said so much of to Selina should not be seen in all its brilliancy. "You shall not," said he, "Monimia, go with me to-night, but you shall go to bed; and if those cursed things must be done, you may finish them in the morning."

"Ah, no!" replied Monimia, wiping away the tears, which on so slight an occasion she was ashamed of letting him see—"no, Orlando, not so—I must neither pass these next four or five hours with you, or in my bed; but must sit up and finish this: for I am very sure that, with the dawn of the morning, my aunt, without considering how little time she has allowed me for this business, will summon me to that which must go forward in the house-keeper's room; and that, to-morrow, I shall have the jellies and syllabubs to make, to give out everything to the cook, and to help in all the made dishes: perhaps I shall never sit down ten minutes from the time I get up till dinner is sent in: and therefore what I have to do of this sort, must be done to-night."

"Curse on the ridiculous, ostentatious old woman!" exclaimed Orlando. "I cannot bear to think of your being so fatigued!"

"Do not," said Monimia with an angelic smile—"do not let us, my dear friend, be rendered uneasy by trifles, when it is but too probable that we shall have so many real sorrows so soon to contend with. What is the loss of a few hours rest? and of how many hours have not I voluntarily deprived myself! Besides," added she, seeing him gaze on her with a look of deep concern, "to finish the whole is not so great an effort as I foolishly, from low spirits, owing perhaps to thinking too much on the conversation of last night, as first represented it to myself. However, Orlando, instead of my going down to your room, I must sit here."

"And I must not remain with you?" cried he.

"A little while you may," replied Monimia; "but speak low—I shall not do my millinery the worse for your sitting by me, if you will but be calm and reasonable."

They then began to consult on the proposed meeting of the next day. Monimia trembled as it was talked of; yet pleasure was mingled with the apprehension with which she thought of being made acquainted with any of his relations, particularly with his beloved Selina, whom he represented as a second self. It was settled, after some little debate on the subject, that when every part of the family were engaged in the hall, Monimia should, at an hour fixed upon, find her way in the dark to the Study; not through the chapel, but by the usual way through the house; and that Selina should be brought there by her brother immediately afterwards, where they might remain half an hour unsuspected, and with much less hazard than in Monimia's room. This being arranged, Orlando entreated her to spare herself as much as possible; and having extorted a promise from her, that when she found herself fatigued she would endeavour to sleep, he reluctantly left her.

CHAP. VIII.

Monimia, secure of the tenderest affection of her lover, bore, without more repining, the little hardships to which her situation exposed her:—but her mind looked forward, in mournful anticipation, to the time when she should no longer hear that soothing voice lending her courage against every transient evil; no longer receive continual assurances of the ardour and generosity of his attachment; and find in his disinterested love, his attentive friendship, sufficient consolation against her uncertain or uneasy destiny.

To obey him, was the first wish of her life; she therefore endeavoured to drive from her mind the melancholy reflections that prevented her repose, and put off the finishing her work till the next day. As soon as it glimmered through her casement, she arose to her task; which having soon finished, she awaited with a lightened heart the other orders of her aunt.

The whole house was in a bustle—and Mrs. Rayland not only in unusual health, but as anxious for the splendour and excellence of the entertainment, as if she had a deeper design than merely to outshine the newer elegancies of Carloraine Castle. All the operations of Mrs. Lennard and her attendants succeeded happily. By half after two all the guests were assembled: by half after three all the tables groaned under the weight of venison and beef. About seventy people were assembled in the hall. In the dining-parlour the party consisted of General Tracy, who was placed at Mrs. Rayland's right hand; on her left Mrs. Hollybourn, the wife of the archdeacon of that district, a lady of a most precise, and indeed formidable demeanour: opposite to her, and next to Mrs. Somerive, sat the Doctor himself, a dignified clergyman, of profound erudition, very severe morals, and very formal manners; who was the most orthodox of men, never spoke but in sentences equally learned and indisputable, and held almost all the rest of the world in as low estimation as he considered highly his own family, and above all himself.

Between her mother and Mr. Somerive, on the other side, was placed their only daughter and heiress, Miss Ann-Jane-Eliza Hollybourn, who, equally resembling her father and her mother, was the pride and delight of both: possessing something of each of their personal perfections, she was considered by them a model of loveliness; and her mind was adorned with all that money could purchase. The wainscot complexion of her Mamma was set off by the yellow eyebrows and hair of the Doctor. His little pug nose divested of its mulberry hue, which, on the countenance of his daughter, was pronounced to be *le petit nez retroussé*, united with the thin lips drawn up to make a little mouth, which were peculiar to "his better half," as he facetiously called his wife. The worthy archdeacon's short legs detracted less from the height of his amiable daughter, as she had the long waist of her mother, fine sugar-loaf shoulders that were pronounced to be *extremely genteel*, and a head which looked as if the back of it had by some accident been flattened, since it formed a perpendicular line with her back. To dignify with mental acquirements this epitome of human loveliness, all that education could do had been lavished; masters for drawing, painting, music, French, and dancing, had been assembled around her as soon as she could speak; she learned Latin from her father at a very early period, and could read any easy sentence in Greek; was learned in astronomy, knew something of mathematics, and, in relief of these more abstruse studies, read Italian and Spanish. Having never heard any thing but her own praises, she really believed herself a miracle of knowledge and accomplishments; and it must be owned, that an audience less partial than those before whom she generally performed, might have allowed that she performed very long concertos, and solos without end, with infinite correctness, and much execution. Then she made most inveterate likenesses of many of her acquaintance; and painted landscapes, where very green trees were reflected in very blue water. Her French was most grammatically correct, though the accent was somewhat defective; and she knew all manner of history—could tell the dates of the most execrable actions of the most execrable of human beings—and never had occasion to consult, so happy was her memory, Trusler's Chronology.[1] As it was believed, so it was asserted by the Doctor and his wife, that their daughter was the most accomplished woman of her age and country; and by most of their acquaintance it was taken for granted. The gentlemen, however, whom all these elegancies were probably designed to attract, seemed by no means struck with them: some of them, who had approached her on the suggestion of her being an heiress, had declared that her fortune made no amends for her want of beauty; and others had been alarmed by the acquisitions which went so much beyond those they had made themselves. Thus, at six-and-twenty (though the lady and her parents, for some reasons of their own, called her no more than twenty-two), Miss Hollybourn was yet unmarried! for, of those lovers who had offered, some had been rejected by the Doctor, and some by herself. She affected a great indifference, and talked of the pleasures of pursuing knowledge in an elegant retirement. But it was observed, that whenever any young men of present fortune, or of future expectation, were in the country, Dr. Hollybourn's family returned the visits of the ladies to whom these gentlemen belonged, with unusual punctuality.

While they were in this part of the world, they always dined once or twice at Rayland Hall, where the Doctor was well received as a most pious worthy man, his Lady as a very good kind of woman, and Miss as a mighty pretty sort of a young person. Of late the whole family had risen into higher favour; for the Doctor was the only clergyman in the country around who had resisted the good entertainment so profusely given at Carloraine Castle, and had refused to visit a man who kept a mistress. He had even gone farther, and preached a sermon which all his congregation said pointed immediately at Mr. Stockton; but as Mr. Stockton did not hear it, and having heard it would not have cared for it, the reproof only edified his hearers, and raised the Doctor in the esteem of the Lady of the Hall.

---

[1] According to Ehrenpreis, John Trusler, *Chronology: or, a Concise View of the Annals of England* (1769), p. 538.

The lower part of the table was filled by the four Miss Somerives and their two brothers; Orlando, at the request of Mrs. Rayland, taking his seat at the bottom.

The plenty and excellence of the table, which was furnished almost entirely from the park, farm, warren, gardens, and ponds of Rayland Hall, were highly commended by the guests, and by none with more zeal than the General and the Doctor, who vied with each other in applying that sort of flattery of which their venerable hostess was most susceptible. The General spoke in terms of the highest respect of her ancient family, and of the figure made in history by the name of Rayland. The Doctor, while he did justice to the excellent dishes before him, launched out in very sincere praise of the domain which produced them: the beautiful park which, he averred, fed the very best venison in the country; the woods abounding in game; the extensive ponds, whose living streams contained all manner of fish; the rich meadows below, that fatted such exquisite beef; the fine sheep walks on the downs above, which sent to table mutton that rivalled the Welch mutton itself!—then, such gardens for fruit! such convenient poultry yards!—Mrs. Rayland, who loved to hear her place praised, could have listened to such eulogiums for ever; and seemed totally to have forgotten that, according to the course of nature, she should be mistress of these good things but a very little time longer, and that, when a little space in the chancel of the adjoining church would be all she could occupy, they must pass into the possession of another.

Who that other was to be, appeared an enquiry which the Doctor had much at heart. From some late circumstances he had reason to suppose that Orlando would be the fortunate possessor of all the excellent accommodations which impressed him with so much veneration:—but he now saw the elder brother again received, and when he considered the advantages which primogeniture might give him in the mind of Mrs. Rayland, he doubted to which of the Somerives it would be politic to pay court.

Some ideas were floating in his mind, that whichever of these young men became master of Rayland Hall, could not fail to be a very proper match for the most accomplished Miss Hollybourn. It was certain that he had always reckoned upon a title for her; but such a deficiency might easily be made up by the successor to such a fortune. What so easy as to change a name by the King's most gracious license? and to renew the old title of Baronet, which had been so long in the family?—Sir Philip Rayland! Sir Orlando Rayland! either sounded extremely well.

Both were very well looking young men, and the youngest remarkably handsome. The more the Doctor considered the project, the more feasible it appeared; and he now began to study the chances, which he thought he could do from Mrs. Rayland's behaviour.

A very little observation determined him in favour of Orlando. He saw that Mrs. Rayland seemed to look upon him as her son, while towards his brother her manners were cold and stately. When dinner was over, the gentlemen, after a short stay over their wine, followed the ladies to another apartment. General Tracy was, at the desire of Mrs. Rayland, shewn into the gallery of portraits by Orlando—and the young ladies, at the request of Miss Hollybourn, who had never seen all the pictures in the house, were permitted by their mother to be of the party; while Philip Somerive, who went out under pretence of accompanying them, slipped away as soon as he left the drawing-room, and went after his own imagination.

It was now dark, and these portraits were to be shewn by candle-light to General Tracy, who cared not a straw if the whole race of Raylands had been swept from the memory of mankind; though he had, partly by guess, and partly from recollection, been incessantly talking to Mrs. Rayland about the glory of her ancestors. By this he perceived he had made a very unexpected progress in her favour; which he would by no means forfeit by shewing any indifference to her proposal of visiting the representations of the eminent men in whose praise he had been so eloquent. But a much stronger inducement was his hope to find an opportunity of speaking to Isabella, while he pretended to contemplate with admiration the picture of her great-grandfather.

But this hope was rendered abortive by the presence of Miss Hollybourn, who leaning on Isabella's arm, continued to question Orlando as to the history of every portrait, and then made her remarks upon it—sometimes addressing herself to the General, and sometimes to Orlando, who were equally weary of her, and who would both have given the world for her absence; for Orlando dreaded her detaining him beyond the time that he had fixed for the meeting between his sister Selina and Monimia; and the General detested her for being in the way when he fancied he could otherwise, by some means or other, have enjoyed that notice from Isabella which he found it so difficult to obtain in the house of Mr. Somerive; where, since he had spoke more plainly of his passion, she had not only shunned him, but had assured him that she would repeat his conversation to her father. Twice, therefore, he had been forced to apologize, and turn off his professions as a joke, because he could never find her long enough alone to allow of his using those arguments that he thought must be successful; and he had been eagerly solicitous to accept the invitation from Mrs. Rayland, because he hoped that in such a great house, in a day of universal festivity, such an opportunity would be found.

Miss Hollybourn, having sufficiently shewn her knowledge both in painting and history, and imagining her auditors were amazed and edified by both, requested to know if the house did not furnish many other portraits of remarkable persons, or pictures by eminent hands. Orlando answered coldly, that there were some in other parts of the house, but none particularly worthy her attention. She desired, however, he would have the goodness to shew her round that suit of rooms. It was the side of the house formerly set apart for company, but now was very rarely inhabited. The furniture was rich, but old fashioned:—the beds were of cut velvet or damask, with high testers, some of them with gilt cornices:—the chairs were worked, or of coloured velvets, fringed with silk and gold, and had gilt feet:—fine japanned cabinets, beautiful pieces of china, large glasses, and some valuable pictures, were to be seen in every room, which, though now so rarely inhabited, were kept in great order; and the oak floors were so nicely waxed, that to move upon them was more like skating than walking.

Miss Hollybourn had something to say on every object she beheld. One bespoke the grandeur, another the taste, a third the antiquity of the family who were owners of the mansion; but still, among all this common-place declamation, it was easy to see that the most amiable moveable in it at present was, in her opinion, the handsome, interesting Orlando.

General Tracy, accustomed to study the fair, perceived this immediately. He perceived, too, that Orlando disliked her as much as she seemed charmed with him, and that therefore this rich heiress would not be the means of preventing the plan they had in agitation from taking effect. He therefore ventured to say to him, when he had an opportunity as they descended the great stair-case—"You are a fortunate man, Sir!"

"Fortunate, Sir!" said Orlando, who had nothing in his head but his intended meeting with Monimia—"How do you mean fortunate?"

"Nay," replied the General, "most young men would, I believe, think it fortunate to be so highly approved of by such a young lady!"

"What lady, Sir!" cried Orlando, in increased alarm, and still thinking of Monimia.

"Miss Hollybourn," replied the General—"the accomplished Miss Hollybourn."

"Miss Hollybourn!" exclaimed Orlando with a contemptuous look; yet recollecting that he had no right to despise her, whether the General's conjecture was just or not, he added, "The approbation of *such* a young lady is certainly what I neither desire nor deserve."

This passed as they waited on the stair-case, while Miss Hollybourn explained to the two Miss Somerives the Loves of Cupid and Psyche, which were painted on the wall; though the picture was so little illuminated by the two wax-candles, carried by Orlando and a servant, that nothing but her passion to display her universal knowledge, could have induced her to attempt clearing up the obscurity in which the wavering and unequal light involved a story not very clearly told by the painter. At length the dissertation finished; and the whole party returned to the drawing-room, where they found the good Doctor had supported the conversation during their absence. In about half an hour afterwards Mr. Pattenson came in great form to announce that the tenants were assembled in the hall, and requested to know if their Lady was well enough to oblige them with her presence during their first dance. This was the established etiquette. Mrs. Rayland answered, that she would be there; and then addressing herself to her company, she said, "That it had always been her custom in the time of Sir Hildebrand, her father, to lead down, with her dear deceased sisters, the first dance at the tenants' feast; that the custom had been long since laid aside; but if any of the friends whom I have now the pleasure of seeing assembled, will condescend to go down a dance with the tenantry and domestics—"

The General and the Doctor eagerly interrupted her—

"I am not a dancing man, Madam," cried the General: "I never was fond of dancing. How much I now, in looking at that beautiful group of young ladies, have cause to regret it! and much I shall envy the young men, who no doubt will take advantage of such an opportunity."

"I, Madam," cried the Doctor, quitting his seat and waddling to her, "am neither by nature or profession a dancing man; but to shew you how much I honour so excellent a custom, there is my substitute (pointing to his daughter), and I will venture to say that few men ever boasted a better."

Mrs. Rayland, then looking round the room, said, "Mr. Orlando Somerive, you will have the honour of beginning the dance with Miss Hollybourn."

Orlando, who would have heard of an impending earthquake with as much pleasure, hesitated, and said, "My brother, Madam—my brother has a superior claim to that happiness."

"No, no, child!" cried Mrs. Rayland; "not at all—you are, *as it were*, at home here, and therefore I will have you begin. Besides, I don't see your brother:—when he returns, he may take your eldest sister; and the two youngest ladies may dance together, for I suppose you will all choose to dance."

Mrs. Somerive assented for her daughters, and said, "Perhaps, Madam, Philip is already below."

"However that may be," replied Mrs. Rayland coldly, "it is quite time to begin; the people are, no doubt, impatient. Therefore, if you General Tracy, and you Dr. Hollybourn, and you Mr. Somerive, will have the kindness to see the ladies to the hall, my people will help me thither in a few moments."

The man of war, and the man of peace, now declared how happy they should esteem themselves to be permitted the honour of being her attendants; but she told them, only Pattenson and Lennard had been used to it, and again desired they would conduct the other ladies. The General, under the cruel necessity of offering his hand to Mrs. Somerive, or Mrs. Hollybourn, cast a wistful look towards Isabella, and took the hand of the latter on seeing Mrs. Somerive conducted by the Doctor; while Orlando, with a heavy heart, led Miss Hollybourn, and his sisters followed. It was now within a quarter of an hour of the time that he had hoped to meet his Monimia; and he saw himself tied down to an engagement from which he feared there was little hope of escaping in time. Philip, to whom he most earnestly wished to transfer the little coveted honour designed him by his partner, appeared not; and poor Orlando stood awaiting his arrival at the head of fifteen or sixteen couple who were going to dance, execrating his ill fortune, which seemed to have brought this odious heiress on purpose to disappoint him of the exquisite pleasure with which he had on this night fondly flattered himself—that of forming a lasting and tender friendship between the sister he so fondly loved, and his adored Monimia.

CHAP. IX.

At length Mrs. Rayland was seated at the upper end of the hall, near the fire—the General placed himself by her, and the Doctor strutted round her—the other ladies were opposite; and the dance began.

Poor Orlando, whose heart beat not responsive to the music, made, however, an effort to conceal his vexation. His partner, who had learned for many years of the most celebrated master, exerted all her knowledge of the art, and displayed all her graces to attract him; while he, hardly conscious of her existence, proceeded mechanically in the dance; and so little penetration had the spectators, that his absence, or distaste to what he was about, was wholly unperceived, while Mrs. Rayland could not help observing to the Doctor how well Orlando performed—"Is he not," said she, "a fine young man?"

"Indeed he is, Madam," replied the Doctor, who had now the opening he so long wished for; "a very fine young man, I think;" and he became an inch higher as he spoke. "I think indeed that this island produces not a finer couple than *your* kinsman, Madam, and the *daughter* of your humble servant."

Mrs. Rayland, who loved not female beauty, whether real or imaginary, did not so warmly assent to this as the Doctor expected; who, not discouraged, squatted himself down in the place the General had that moment vacated (who could not forbear walking after Isabella down the dance), and thus proceeded:

"I assure you, dear Madam, I have often spoken most highly in praise of your sagacity and discernment in electing the young Orlando as your favourite and *protegé.* He is a fine young man—good, prudent and sensible; and, I am sure, grateful for your bounty. I dare say that he will do well; for, under your auspices, there are few men even of consideration and fortune, who, having daughters, would not be proud of an alliance with him."

Mrs. Rayland answered rather coldly, "I believe Mr. Orlando has no thoughts of marrying—He is yet too young."

"He is young, to be sure, Madam; but, for my own part, I must observe, that early marriages founded, as no doubt his would be, alike on prudence and inclination, generally turn out happily. As to my own girl, undone as I and Mrs. Hollybourn must to be sure feel without her, I declare to you that, though she is so young, I should not hesitate to dispose of her to a man of even her own age, if I were convinced that he was a prudent, sober young man, unlike those sad examples of folly and extravagance that we see before our eyes every day; a young man who had had a virtuous education, which in my opinion is a private one; a young man of family and of good expectations—I say, Madam, that on such a one, though his present fortune be unequal to Miss Hollybourn's expectations, I should not hesitate, young as she is, and living as I do only by gazing on her, to bestow her with twenty thousand pounds down, and—I will say nothing of future expectations—I am, I bless the Father of all mercies, in a prosperous fortune—I have seventeen hundred a year in church preferment; my own property, which I have realised in land, is somewhat above twelve hundred. When I have given my girl her little marriage portion, I have still something handsome in the three per cents, and in India stock a trifle more. My brother-in-law, the bishop, has no children, and my daughter will inherit the greatest part of his fortune. So you see, Madam, that, to say nothing of her personal and mental accomplishments, which to be sure it ill becomes *a father* to insist upon—I say, reckoning only her pecuniary advantages, there are few better matches in England."

The Doctor, who knew that Mrs. Rayland loved money, imagined she could not fail of being attracted by this history of his wealth, nor misunderstand his meaning in giving it: but he had for once mistaken his ground. Mrs. Rayland, though she loved her own money, loved nobody the better for having or affecting to have as much. She knew that, rich as Doctor Hollybourn now was, he began his classical career as a servitor at Oxford; and that his "brother-in-law the bishop," from whose *nepotism* his wealth and consequence had been in great measure derived, was the son of an innkeeper. Though she always spoke highly of his piety, and his high-church principles, she had ever contemned his efforts to make himself be considered a man of family: nor did she feel much disposed to encourage any scheme to make Orlando independent of her by marriage, still less an attempt to extort from her a decision concerning him; which, whatever her real sentiments might be, she was not of a temper to declare. For all these reasons she heard the conversation of Doctor Hollybourn very coldly, and only said, "that to be sure Miss was a very accomplished young lady; and, having such a fine fortune, might expect to marry in high life."

Still the Doctor was not repulsed; and, fancying that he had not yet spoken plain enough, he went on to enlarge on his notions of happiness, and on his views for his daughter. High life, he said, in the common acceptation of the word, was not his ambition. It was real domestic happiness, and not unnecessary and unmeaning splendour, he desired for his dear girl—a good husband untainted with the vices and false philosophy of a dissolute age—an handsome country residence, where she might be received into an ancient and religious family—were rather his objects. "A title," added he, "a title has its advantages no doubt, and especially if it be an ancient title, one that brings to mind the deeds of the glorious defenders of our country—men who have shed their honourable blood in defence of the Church of England, and their King—who bled in the cause for which Laud and his sainted master died![1] When I hear such names, and see their posterity flourishing, I rejoice—When I learn that such families, the honour of degenerate England, are likely to be extinct, my heart is grieved. And how should I be thankful, how feel myself elevated, if *my* daughter, marrying into such a family, should restore it, while *my* interest might obtain a renewal in her posterity of the fading honours of an illustrious race!"

This was speaking at once pompously and plainly. But Mrs. Rayland was more offended by the air of consequence assumed by the Doctor, than flattered by the fine things he said of her family; and she so little concealed her displeasure, that Mrs. Somerive, long weary of the parading and supercilious conversation of Mrs. Hollybourn, and who saw, by the Doctor's frequently looking towards Orlando, that the discourse was about him, and that Mrs. Rayland was displeased with it, arose and came towards them: she said something to Mrs. Rayland merely with a view to break the discourse, which was, however, immediately done much better by the General, who, afraid of being too particular, now left Isabella; and returning to the seat Doctor Hollybourn had seized, he cried, "Come, come, my good Doctor, we soldiers are a little proud of our favour with the ladies, and we do not patiently see ourselves displaced by you churchmen. I shall not relinquish my seat by my excellent hostess."

The Doctor then got up; and fancying, from the softness and sweetness of Mrs. Somerive's manner, that he should in her meet a willing auditor, and perhaps the very best he could find for a scheme which acquired every moment new charms in his imagination, he asked if he should attend her to the other end of the room to look at the dancers; to which, as she was extremely restless and uneasy by the long absence of her eldest son, whom she every moment hoped to see enter, she readily assented.

The General then took possession of the post the Doctor had quitted; and being more used to every kind of approach, he made infinitely more progress with Mrs. Rayland, in obtaining her consent to Orlando's entering the army, than the Doctor had effected for his scheme, not with standing the splendour of his fortune, the accomplishments of his daughter, or his mention of "his brother the bishop."

In the mean time the poor young man, who was rendered by Mrs. Rayland's favour an object sought for by the divine, and by his own spirit

---

[1] Doctor Hollybourn appeals to Mrs. Rayland's family's royalist leanings by referring to the executions of the Archbishop Laud and Charles I in this fawning way.

an object of dread to the soldier, was half distracted, and knew not what he was about. It was now past the hour when he had promised Monimia to bring Selina to her; for, not expecting the unwelcome addition of the Hollybourn family, he concluded that, after going down a dance with one of the buxom daughters of the principal tenant, he could have slipped away at the end of it; and whispering his mother that he was going to shew Selina some of his drawings, and how he had ornamented his little tapestry room, that he might account for her absence, he should have had an uninterrupted hour with his most beloved sister and his Monimia.

Instead of this he now found himself fixed for the whole night to Miss Hollybourn; who had already declared that she found herself in such a humour for dancing, and that really the whole set was so much more tolerable than she expected, that she should not very soon wish to sit down. Poor Orlando, who had no excuse to offer for quitting her, had no hope but in the arrival of his brother, to whom he flattered himself he might resign this unenvied honour at least for one dance: but even this hope was very uncertain; for Philip might perhaps return no more to the room, or if he did, might be unwilling to accept the felicity of dancing with Miss Hollybourn, for he was not of a humour to put himself out of the way for any one; and, as he very seldom danced at all, would now, if he did join the dancers, much more probably select for his partner one of the handsome daughters of the tenants, with whom he could be more at home.

Thus the time which Orlando expected to have passed in so different a manner wore away. In vain he looked towards the door—no brother arrived to succour him. The second dance was already at an end; and Isabella, who had, with her mother's permission, accepted the hand of a rich young farmer, while Selina and Emma danced together, had already called a third, and was flying down with a spirit and gaiety which quite enchanted her ancient lover; while Orlando, who on account of Miss Hollybourn still kept a place near the top, was preparing with an heavy heart to follow her, when his father, with an expression of extreme concern on his countenance, approached, and asked him if he knew where his brother was?

"No, Sir, indeed I do not," answered Orlando; "I cannot even guess—but, for God's sake, give me leave to go look for him. I see you are very uneasy at his absence."

"I am indeed," replied Mr. Somerive, "and your mother much more so."

"Let me go, dear Sir, then," said Orlando eagerly.

"No, no," answered his father:—"Go down this dance, and take no notice—if then he does not come, go see if you can find him. I have been in search of him myself, but to no purpose. I fancied he might be in your room. I went to the library door, for I could have sworn I heard somebody walking there; but the door was locked, and I called and knocked at it in vain. If Philip was there, he had some reason—no good one, I fear—for not answering."

Orlando, now ready to sink into the earth, yet unable to fly from his intolerable task, began the dance, after having been twice called upon by his partner; but thinking only of the terror Monimia must have been in, while, shut up in the library, she heard his father at the door, and over-whelmed with vexation at being thus detained from her, he could no longer command that portion of attention that was requisite even to the figure of the dance. But having blundered four or five times, turned the wrong women, and run against the men, then missed his time, and put every body out, he said in a hurrying way to Miss Hollybourn, who began to be much discomposed by his mistakes—"I really beg a thousand pardons, but Isabella's dance is so extremely difficult I cannot go down it—I shall only distress you, Madam, by my blunders; had we not better go to the bottom?"

"Dear Sir," cried the lady bridling, "I can find no such difficulty in it. If you would only take the trouble to attend a moment, I am sure I could explain it to you so that you *could* not make a mistake.—Now only observe—We first pass between the second and third couples—and I lead out the two gentlemen, and you the two ladies—then meet and alle-mande—then *le moulin*[1] at bottom—then I turn the third gentleman—then you—"

Orlando, unable to command himself, said, still more confusedly, "No, upon my honour, I shall never do it. I am very sorry to disappoint you, Madam; and wish I could for this dance recommended you another partner." He then bowed, and was walking away, when she bounced after him.

"You don't imagine there is any other person here," cried she, biting the end of her fan—"I hope you don't imagine there is any body else here with whom *I* shall dance!"

"Pardon me, Madam," said Orlando, taking her hand; "here is my elder brother, who has even a better right to that honour than I have." At this moment his eyes were gratified by the sight of Philip, to whom he, with-out waiting for Miss Hollybourn's answer, led her, and cried, "Dear Phil,

---

[1]   According to Ehrenpreis, "a figure in which the women join their right hands, give their left to their partners, make a complete turn, and balance" (p. 538).

here am I in the most awkward distress imaginable; Miss Hollybourn wishes to dance this dance down, and I am so stupid I cannot do the figure. I am sure you will be very happy to supply my place."

Philip, who was never much disposed to sacrifice his own pleasure to the gratification of others, and who had schemes of his own on foot, answered with less than his usual ceremony (for he was never more polite for having drank a good deal):

"A-hey, Sir Rowland! who told you so? How the devil should I, who am no dancer, execute what is too difficult for so perfect a caperer as thou art—Sir Knight?"[1]

Mortified beyond endurance at being thus rejected, Miss Hollybourn, disengaging her hand with an angry jerk from Orlando's, said haughtily— "Pray, Mr. Orlando, spare yourself this trouble; I am content to sit still." She then walked away; and Orlando, not giving himself time to consider what he did, said in a whisper to Philip—"If you have any compassion, my dear Phil, take her for this dance—I will be grateful, believe me, and I will not desire to punish you with her above half an hour."

"D—n her, a little carroty, pug-nosed moppet!" cried Philip, "as ugly and as insolent as the devil—why should I take the trouble to humour her?"

"It will oblige me beyond expression," answered Orlando; "it will oblige my father and mother."

Philip just then recollecting that he was upon his good behaviour, agreed, though with an ill grace; and Orlando eagerly carrying him up to Miss Hollybourn, who sat fanning herself and swelling at the top of the room, began a speech, in which he blundered worse than he had done in dancing; but Philip took it out of his hands, and said, "Madam, I am so much in an habit, in *this* house, of giving the *pas* to my brother here, Sir Rowland, that I really dared not aspire to the honour of your fair hand till I perfectly understood that he had relinquished it for the present dance; but as he has now explained himself, if you will allow me the bliss of being his double, I will acquit myself to the best of my poor abilities; and if you, charming Miss Hollybourn, will deign to instruct me, you shall find, that under so lovely a preceptress I shall make up in docility for deficiency of practice."

Miss Hollybourn had so little natural sense among all her acquirements, that this speech, which from its substance, and still more from

---

[1]   Here, as elsewhere, Smith uses the ne'er-do-well Philip to expose Orlando's romantic leanings as ineffectual pretension.

the manner of its delivery, was evidently meant in ridicule, seemed to her to be very polite, and made very much in earnest. She therefore, casting a look towards Orlando, much less sweet than those she had favoured him with towards the beginning of the evening, assented with a smirk to the proposal of his brother—and immediately joined the dancers; while Orlando, trembling lest some new interruption should again deprive him of the sight of Monimia, hastened to find Selina, to whom he beckoned, and whispered to her to come round another way, where he would meet her, that their going out together might not be remarked. He changed his mind about speaking to his mother, fearing least she should propose going too, if the object was only to shew Selina his room; and he thought it better to risk an enquiry after Selina, which perhaps might not be made, or, if it were, might easily be answered.

It was the custom on these occasions for the inferior servants not to come into the hall till the Lady and her company, if she happened to have any, were withdrawn. When the business of the dinner and tea tables was over, they became spectators from a railed gallery, which over the entrance to the hall made a communication between the principal apartments above. Here the upper house-maid, the footmen, and the cook had been stationed—Betty, most superb in red ribbands, not quite so long as the rest.

Monimia had been forbidden by Mrs. Lennard to appear at all during any part of the evening; an injunction which she was not at all disposed to disobey. She was far, therefore, from envying Betty, who came into her room all in a flutter, as soon as she was dressed, to shew her finery, and descant on the pleasure she expected in dancing when Madam was gone, and the gentlefolks, and boasting how many solicitations she had already had from the young men. Monimia, glad to get her out of the room, thought only of fulfilling her engagement with Orlando, and of the pleasure and comfort of being made known to one of his sisters; yet her timidity and diffidence made her fear this interview as much as she wished it. Unconscious of the interesting sweetness of her countenance, and the simple graces of her form, she feared lest Selina might think her brother's affection ill placed, and blame his attachment to an object of so little merit. Under these impressions, she would have given herself all the advantages that dress afforded; but her scanty wardrobe left her very little choice, and she had no means of varying her appearance from what it usually was—a white muslin gown being the utmost of her finery. She took care, however, to dispose her hair in the most becoming manner she could; and having finished her little toilet, she descended with a palpitating heart and a light step to the part of the house through which she was to pass in going to the Study. It was now empty, for all the servants were in the gallery, waiting the departure of their Lady, to join the festivity of the night; and Monimia glided through the north wing, which was never at any time inhabited, and without any misadventure reached the Study, where she waited in trembling suspense the arrival of Orlando and Selina.

Every body being engaged in the middle of the house, that part of it was as silent as if there was no bustle in the other, except the distant sound of the music in the great hall, to which Monimia, with the door of the Study a-jar, involuntarily listened; when she was suddenly alarmed by a voice in the adjoining parlour, talking and laughing, and apparently romping, and a man's voice answering in a half whisper, and begging of the first person, whom she knew to be Betty, to be more quiet. As her being discovered in Orlando's Study would have ruined her peace for ever, she shut-to the door as softly as she could, and turned the key. The conversation between the two people without appeared to be so animated, that she flattered herself they did not hear her; but as she still remained listening at the door, hardly daring to breathe, her terror was increased by hearing them approach and attempt to open it. "Egad! it is locked," cried a voice which Monimia then first discovered to be young Somerive:—"Does Sir Rowland always lock his door?'

"Generally he does," replied the other, "but I dare say among the house keys there's one that will open it—yet, hang it, don't let us try. He'll come perhaps, and that you know will be very disagreeable."

"He come!" said Philip—"No, no, he's safe enough—He dares as well jump into the fire as quit the post where the old woman has placed him—Come, come—see if there's no other key will open this door. Besides, as to his coming, what should he come here for? 'Tis more likely, if he can get away, he'll go to visit Miss in the turret."

"Lord!" cried Betty, "how you have that notion stuffed into your head—when I tell you again and again, he no more meets Miss, as you calls her, than the child unborn. Sure I should know—She! a poor innocent silly thing! I don't believe he takes any account of her—But hush! Oh gemini! who's there?"

The voice of the elder Somerive was now heard, calling aloud in the passage leading to the parlour they were in for his eldest son. "Philip!" cried he, "Philip!—where are you?"

"'Tis my father," said Philip—"Cannot we get out without meeting him?"

"Oh yes," replied Betty; "follow me, and don't speak for all the world."

She then opened another door which led out into the garden, which, as Orlando usually came in that way, was seldom locked; and as all this had passed in the dark, they glided away unperceived—not a moment however before Mr. Somerive, entering with a candle the room they had quitted, gave a new alarm to the terrified Monimia. Mr. Somerive, who had heard the footsteps of the fugitives as they left the parlour, imagined somebody was walking in the Study—He therefore tried the door, on the other side of which poor Monimia still stood trembling, and again loudly called on Philip Somerive; entreating him, if he was there, to answer him, and representing all the ill consequences of his thus disappearing abruptly, after having been received into an house where he had before given offence, but where it was so material for him to be thought well of. No answer however was returned; and at length Monimia heard Mr. Somerive close his fruitless remonstrance with a deep sigh, and depart.

These repeated alarms now seemed to subside, and a dead silence ensured, but still Orlando came not.—Monimia, not daring to have a candle lest the light should be discerned under the door, sat down in the window-seat which was the nearest to it to listen for his arrival, though doubting from what his brother had said whether he would arrive at all. The large old library, half furnished with books and half hung with tapestry, and where the little light afforded by a waning moon gleamed faintly through the upper parts of the high casements which the window-shutters did not reach, was perhaps the most gloomy apartment that fancy could imagine. Monimia looked round her, and shuddered—The affright she had undergone in the chapel, though it was explained, still dwelt upon a mind which had so early been rendered liable to the terrors of superstition; and she looked towards the door that opened to the passage of the chapel, fancying some hideous spectre would appear at it: or she reasoned herself out of such an idea, only to give way to one more horrid; and figured to herself that the ruffian whom Orlando had described to her, and whose name was held in dread by the whole country, might enter at it as he had once done before. Against this apprehension she might have been secured by satisfying herself that the door was locked; but she had not the courage to cross the room.

Sitting therefore and listening to every sound, she again distinguished the music in the great hall, which, as the wind swelled or fell, floated through the rest of the house; and she could not help contrasting that scene of festive mirth with her dark and gloomy solitude:—"How happy," said she, "are the Miss Somerives, and this other young lady! They, under the sanction of their parents, are gaily enjoying an innocent and agreeable amusement; while I, a poor unprotected being, wander about in darkness and in dread, and, though I do nothing wrong, undergo the terrors and alarms of guilt.—But, do I not act wrong? Alas! I am afraid I do—It *must* be wrong to carry on a clandestine correspondence, to meet by stealth a young man whom his friends would discard were they to know he met me at all—It must surely be wrong to incur imputations from which, if once they are believed, it is impossible I can ever be vindicated—wrong to let Orlando hazard, for me, the loss of Mrs. Rayland's favour—and wrong to put myself in the way of being believed no better than the servant, of whose light conduct I have seen so many instances, besides that which this moment happened, of her privately meeting Mr. Philip Somerive. How could I bear to be thought of by others as I think of her! and yet I seem to act as culpably. Oh Orlando! surely if you thought of this, you, who are so generous, so anxious for my happiness, would never expose me to it. Yet we must meet thus, or never meet at all!—and could I bear to be deprived of seeing him for the little, the very little time that is yet to pass before he is sent from hence—never—never perhaps to return?"

This sad idea filled her eyes with tears; and she was not recovered from the agony into which it threw her, when she again heard footsteps in the parlour—Somebody trode lightly along. Monimia listened, and fancied there was more than one person—Immediately the lock was turned; and the door being fastened, a voice, which she recognised with joy for that of Orlando, said, in a half-whisper: "Monimia! are you not there? It is Selina and I—open the door therefore without apprehension."–Monimia remembered, with affright, that the voices of the two brothers bore a great resemblance to each other, and she again hesitated. But Orlando speaking louder, and her recollecting that his brother could not know that Selina was to accompany him, she, though with trembling apprehension, turned the key, and Orlando and his sister appeared.

"Let me," cried he, as he put Monimia into the arms of Selina—"let me unite in bonds of everlasting friendship the two loveliest and most beloved of beings!" Selina tried to say, "Whoever is dear to Orlando is so to me, and I rejoice in thus being allowed to say so." But, though she had innocently studied the sentence, she was too much confused to make it articulate; and Monimia was quite unable to speak at all. In a moment, however, Orlando, attempting to hide the uneasy flutter of his own thoughts, approached them with a candle which he had lit at the embers of his fire; and, reminding them how short their interview must be, bade them both sit down—"and let us," added he, "endeavour to enjoy moments so brief and so precious."

CHAP. X.

Selina, as timid, and almost as new to the world as Monimia herself, was too much terrified at the risk Orlando ran, and at what she herself hazarded, to be soon composed. She could hardly, indeed, have been in greater trepidation had she escaped from the company to have met a lover of her own. Her eyes, however, were occupied in examining the face and figure of Monimia; and no feminine envy induced her to deny the existence of that beauty or sweetness of which Orlando had said so much. She even thought Monimia more lovely than her brother had described her, yet she saw her to little advantage; for, the alarming situation she had been in for almost an hour and a half, the apprehension lest Orlando should not come, the reflections which arose while she waited for him, and the emotion with which she now for the first time beheld his sister, had robbed her fair cheeks of their tender bloom; her eyes were swollen, and her voice was faltering and faint. Orlando seated her near Selina, and, sitting down by them, threw one arm round each of them; and, looking with a smile on both, said, "Why, what silent girls you are!—Selina! is it thus you greet your new friend? You who will talk to me of her for an hour, and never ceased soliciting of me to contrive this unhoped for meeting?—And you, Monimia! Come, come, I must have you more conversable.—Let us consider, my dear girls, how you may meet hereafter; for, without accomplishing that, the present meeting will only serve to tantalize us all."

The tears, which she had for a moment restrained, again filled the eyes of Monimia.—But, turning them tenderly on Orlando, she sighing said, "Ah! how can I hope your sister Selina, amiable and indulgent as she seems, will again incur, for me, hazard which I see now makes her tremble, and fears which I myself can hardly endure?—Indeed, Orlando, if you did but know what I have suffered since I waited here in expectation of your coming!"—"I know it," cried Orlando, imagining she alluded to his father's having been at the door of the Study— "But luckily you had taken the precaution to lock the door; which I, little suspecting that this part of the house would be visited, had neglected to desire. So, as my father neither saw nor suspected any thing but that my brother was in this room, there is no harm done, nor any thing to fear."

Monimia sighed, but thought it was improper, before Selina, to repeat the dialogue that she had heard between Mr. Philip Somerive and his female companion. She was far, however, from believing there was nothing to fear; and their short conference was to her embittered with the dread of a discovery, which she could not conquer. Selina, trusting to the judgment of her brother, and desirous of obliging him, succeeded better in conquering the restraint she had at first felt; and, charmed with the vice, the manner and person of Monimia, she eagerly entered into his views, and talked over the means by which they might sometimes meet, if, as was too probable, invincible obstacles continued to be opposed to their seeing each other by the consent of Mr. and Mrs. Somerive—that of Mrs. Rayland could not be asked, and that of Mrs. Lennard they were sure would not be granted.

In this conversation Orlando spoke of what was to happen when he was gone, in terms that signified how certain he was that he should go. Monimia's heart sunk as he repeated, "When *I* am not here, I cannot see that there can be any objection to your openly seeing my sisters.— "Alas!" thought she, "what wretched company shall we then be to each other! yet to see the sisters of Orlando will always be a comfort to me." Selina too heard with extreme pain the frequent mention he made of his departure; and having, from many observations she had made on the behaviour of General Tracy, during his residence of almost five weeks in her father's house, conceived a very unfavourable opinion of him— her dislike amounted almost to detestation when she considered him as being the principal mover of the plan which was thus to rob her of her beloved brother. Whatever she thought of his conduct in other respects, she had the prudence to keep to herself, and affected to dislike him only on account of Orlando.

Among the various little schemes which were considered for the future acquaintance of Selina and Monimia, none seemed sufficiently safe to be adopted without farther consideration; but Orlando prom- ised to think of them all, and to acquaint them both with the result of his reflections. It was by this time necessary to part—Orlando proposed leading his sister back to the room, and carrying her immediately to his mother, to tell her that she had been in his apartment, that any surprize excited by her absence might be ended with farther enquiry; while

Monimia hoped to find her way back to her own room, as safely as she had before traversed the house in her way from it.

They were then reluctantly bidding adieu, when they were thunderstruck by an attempt from without to force open the door. Orlando, thrown for a moment entirely off his guard, turned pale; and, casting towards Monimia a look of anguish and terror, he cried, "Who can it be? what shall we do?"—The tender timid Monimia had at this instant more presence of mind than he had: "Let me go," said she, "into your bed-chamber—there I can lock myself in: then ask who it is; and, if it is one who has a right to enquire into your actions, open the door, and let him see you are sitting here with your sister."[1] There was not a moment to deliberate, for the person without still tried to open the door. Orlando waved his hand to Monimia to execute her project:— she glided away, and shut after her the door, which was hung on both sides with tapestry and shut without noise, while Orlando demanded, in a loud and angry voice, who was at the door, and what was their business? At first a feigned voice answered, "Open the door, good friends, and you shall know our business." Orlando answered, "I shall not open it till I know to whom;"—and then a violent burst of laughter discovered it to be Philip—who cried, "Soho! have I caught you, Sir Roland? Is this my good, pious and immaculate brother?" "What folly is this!" said Orlando angrily as he opened the door—"and is it not strange that I cannot sit a moment in my own room with Selina, but you must break in upon us like a drunken constable?" "Gently, Sir Knight!" answered Philip Somerive as he staggered into the room— "fair and softly, if you please! no hard words to your elders, most valorous chevalier!—Selina is it?—By this light so it is! Well—I did not think, my good brother, you were so eager to put off your precious bargain upon me, only for the pleasure of a *tête-à-tête* with our little simple Selina. I thought you had very different game in view—Egad, I'm not clear now that I have been mistaken—Heh, child!" added he turning to Selina, "are you very sure you are not a blind? why, my dear little whey face, what makes you look so pale?"

"Your strange behaviour, brother," said Selina, who tried to collect spirit enough to speak without betraying the agitation she was thrown into. "Come, come, child!" replied he, "lectured as I am on all hands, I

---

[1]   Monimia's "presence of mind" shows her to be less caught up in the romance than is Orlando. Again, Smith suggests that to be immersed in the (property) romance is to be unfitted for life, and provides another example of Orlando's inadequacy.

shall not let babes and sucklings preach to me. Your mamma, miss, won't be very well pleased, I can tell you, if she does not find you with the other misses; they are just going away, I believe. The old woman is gone up to her apartment, and the misses are ordered off. There's the General, like my mother's gentleman-usher, hunting the fair bevy together, and there will be a hue and cry after you in a moment."—"Very well!" answered Selina; "Mamma will not be angry when she knows I am only with Orlando." "And I," said Orlando, "shall take care of her back; therefore you need not, Philip, be under any concern about her."

"Well, then," cried this tormentor, "as I am cursed tired, my dear knight, and have got a devilish headach, prithee, when thou art gone, lend me thy apartment for half an hour's quiet. I've promised George Green and half a dozen more of them, to meet them by and by in Pattenson's room, and make out the night according to good old custom; and if I get a nap while the sober party, the cats and their kittens, are trundling off, I shall escape all the plaguy formality of "Wish you good night, dear ma'am!—hope you'll catch no cold!—shall be glad to hear you got home safe!—most agreeable evening indeed!—wish we may meet here this time twelvemonth!"—and such mawkish cant; and I shall be as fresh as morning to meet the good fellows by and by—So, come, Sir Rowly, lend me your bed for a little. I'll send in pretty Betty," added he leering, "to make it for you before you come to bed."

Orlando, fearing, from this strange proposal, his brother was aware how impossible it was for him to grant it, now looked more confused than ever, and said very peevishly, "You are so drunk now, Philip, that it will be much wiser and more decent for you to go home directly—I at least will have nothing to do with your stay. Come, Selina, let us go—Philip, I will follow you."

"No, indeed you will not!" replied he, setting himself down by the fire. "If you won't lend me your bed, you will at least let me have a chair."

"I will leave nobody in my room," said Orlando warmly.

"What! hast got any bank-notes? has thy old woman given thee a little hoard? Egad she has!—I've a good mind to rummage, that I may know what brotherly help thou couldst give in case of a bad run."

"This is insupportable!" cried Orlando:—"What shall I do with him?" whispered he to Selina. Poor Selina, unable to advise, was in as great consternation as the half distracted Orlando, who walked about the room a moment, considering by what means he could disengage himself from this troublesome visitor; but unable to think of any, he was beginning, in mere despair, to expostulate with him anew, when the approach of other persons was heard in the parlour; and Mr. Somerive himself, apparently in great displeasure, entered the Library.

"Orlando!" cried he, "Philip! Selina! what is all this? to what purpose are ye all here?—Selina; your mother is much amazed at your absence."

Orlando, then collecting his scattered thoughts, related, that he had merely brought Selina thither for a few moments to shew her his apartments, which she had never seen; and that while they were sitting quietly together, Philip, "whose situation, Sir, you see," said he, "came in, and I could not prevail upon him to leave us, or to suffer us to return altogether to the company."

Mr. Somerive, now speaking with an air of authority and concern to his eldest son, received only an account of his request to Orlando, which, he insisted upon it, was a very reasonable one. "You are indeed," said his father, "fit only to go to bed; but it must not be in Mrs. Rayland's house— you must come, Sir, with me."

Young Somerive then arose to obey; for his father, when he was present, and had resolution to be peremptory, still retained some power over him. He staggered however so much that he was unable to proceed. Mr. Somerive bade Orlando assist him, which he was willing enough to do; but as Philip leaned upon him he whispered, "Sir Knight! if I can give the reverend senior the slip, I will still have my nap, and finish the evening with those joyous souls; d—me if I don't!"

This threat terrified Orlando more than ever: he knew how likely it was to be executed; and therefore, in the hope that he might be able presently to return and release Monimia, whose longer absence from her room might be attended with the most alarming consequences, he hastily determined to lock the Study door, and thus convince his brother that his scheme of returning thither, to which he saw he adhered either with the stupid obstinacy of intoxication, or disguising under its appearance, knowledge more destructive, was impracticable. He therefore, as soon as they were all out of the room, locked the door, and, saying aloud he had done so, he proceeded before his father, with a candle in his hand, to the apartment where Mrs. Rayland, much fatigued with the exertions of the evening, was taking leave of her guests. Philip, who seemed by no means in a condition to appear before her, had been consigned, in the way, to the care of one of the men-servants, who had seated him by the fire in a passage-parlour, where he was in a few moments fast asleep.

Mrs. Somerive, to whom Selina's absence was easily accounted for, gently chid her for not saying whither she was going; and the long ceremonies of good-night on all hands being at length over, Orlando handed to her coach the nymph whom he had, in her opinion, so ungallantly forsaken. He found her so much hurt at being made over to his brother, who probably had not acquitted himself to her satisfaction, that he found it necessary to apologize, at which however he was extremely awkward, assuring her, with much hesitation, that he was not aware that she would so soon quit the dancing-room, and that he flattered himself with the expectation of being honoured with her hand in a dance, where he could acquit himself in a manner more worthy so excellent a partner.

The Lady received his excuses with coldness and disdain; but the Doctor, who heard, seemed more willing to accept them in good part. "I never suspected, Sir," cried the consequential Divine, "that, with your understanding, you could fail to appreciate the Lady whose hand you held—It is not the fond partiality of the father, but common candour, which leads me to say, that of equals she has few in merit, superiors none. I hope we shall meet here again, Mr. Orlando; and that we shall see you, with good Mr. and Mrs. Somerive, and their fine family, at Comber Park. Good Mrs. Rayland, I heartily hope, that most worthy lady, who bears her years surprisingly well, will be able, before the winter's rigorous advances lay an embargo on valetudinarians; I say, I hope my excellent old friend will fix on some day to grace our poor abode, and sacrifice with us to the hospitable deities."

Orlando bowed his assent to a speech which he began to fear would last all night.—No effort of his, however, could have stopped the stream of the Doctor's eloquence, when once it began to flow; but fortunately Mrs. Hollybourn found it cold, and said peevishly, "Dear Doctor! you keep Ann in a thorough air—Pray consider—she has been dancing, and I tremble for the effects of such a current of air—"

Blessings on your care! thought Orlando, who was in the most extreme uneasiness all this time, lest Monimia, who he knew could not escape from his room, should be missed in her own. The parade, however, that was yet made before this family were seated in their carriage, took up several minutes more; and even when Orlando had at length the satisfaction to see them driven from the door, he was compelled to attend to the disposal of his father, his mother, his four sisters, and the General, who could not for some time settle how they should return—the General being solicitous to take two of the young ladies in his post chaise; to which Mrs. Somerive very peremptorily objected, to the amazement of her husband, who, not having the least idea of her motives, cried, "Bless me, my dear! it will be better surely to put any two of the girls under the care of General Tracy, than to crowd him with me and Philip, who, if we can find him, is not, I fear, in a state to travel without incommoding his companions."—"Well, then," replied Mrs. Somerive, frightened at having said more than she intended, "I will have the pleasure of going in the General's carriage, and Emma can sit between us without inconvenience." In this arrangement the General was obliged to acquiesce, and even to appear pleased with it, though it baffled the schemes he had been laying for the whole evening. This second carriage then departed; and now Orlando, who could well have left his sisters in the care of his father, would have flown to his imprisoned Monimia—But a new difficulty arose; his brother, for whom search had been making, as well in the room where he had been left sleeping, as in every other part of the house that had been opened for company, was no-where to be found.

The Somerive family had all taken their leave of Mrs. Rayland, and waited in a parlour near the hall. Mr. Somerive now expressed great alarm at the ill success of those inquiries that had been made after his eldest son. "Perhaps, Sir," said Orlando,—"perhaps my brother, finding himself, when he awoke, unfit to appear, is gone home on foot." Orlando had indeed very different conjectures; and, in the whole tenor of his behaviour that evening, found reason to fear that he had but too positive information relative to Monimia, and was determined to detect her. This apprehension, and the dread of her being missed by her aunt, who would in all probability visit her room as soon as the company were dispersed, gave to Orlando's manner such wildness and confusion as increased the distress of his father. Orlando repeated, "I am persuaded, Sir, Philip is gone home—I dare say you may yourself return quite easy."

"Are you so easy yourself then?" answered Mr. Somerive—"I think not, Orlando, from your countenance. Even admitting that my son has walked homeward, and will not commit any impropriety which shall expose him, or injure him in the opinion of Mrs. Rayland, is there nothing to fear for the safety of a man who has such a road to travel, in such a state?"

"Let me, Sir, go then, and seek for him on that road; and do you, I entreat you, return home and make yourself easy. A longer delay will not only alarm my mother, but occasion enquiries on the part of Mrs. Rayland, who will probably hear of it by her servants;—nor can it indeed answer any purpose, since every search that can be made has already been made within the house."

"Have you the key of your own apartment?"

"I have, Sir," replied Orlando, trembling lest his father was about to ask for it. "I locked the door of the Study when we all left it together."

"He cannot therefore be there," said Mr. Somerive, musing—"I cannot conjecture where he can be!"

"Pray, Sir," cried Orlando, "pray be composed, and suffer me to go the parkway homeward—I am persuaded my brother is safe."

"He does not indeed," said Mr. Somerive with a deep sigh—"he does not deserve the solicitude I feel for him. Orlando, on you I depend for finding and conducting him home."

Orlando solemnly assured his father and his sisters that he would do so; and as their remaining longer at the Hall contributed nothing towards relieving their uneasiness, they at length determined to go.

When they were gone, Orlando hoped that the alarms of the night were over, and that Mrs. Lennard, as the tenants and all the servants were still dancing in the hall, would not have time to think of the usual ceremony of locking Monimia's door at ten o'clock. It was now however twelve.

With a palpitating heart then he went to find her. She was still locked in his bedchamber, where, half distracted by fears of every kind, she had had sufficient time to reflect on all the hazards she incurred by these clandestine meetings with Orlando; and sometimes determined, if she escaped detection this time, never to be prevailed upon to venture it again.—Then the sad recollection, that he would soon cease to ask it, and that, if she did not meet him thus, she must relinquish the pleasure of ever speaking to him at all, shook the resolution which fear and prudence united to produce;—and she almost wished, dreadful as it would at the moment be, that a discovery might compel them to the expedient Orlando once named—that of their flying together, and trusting to Providence for the rest.

CHAP. XI.

Orlando found Monimia alarmed and dejected; but hardly giving himself time to re-assure her, and account for his long absence, he besought her to hasten to her room—"I hope," said he, "and believe the house is quite uninhabited on this side still, for all the servants are in the hall. My brother is missing, and I have promised my father to find him and conduct him home. What a task! for I know not where to look for him: not a moment must be lost, since my family are in such cruel alarms. However, I will wait here, my Monimia, till I think you are safe in your turret, and then set out—I know not whither—on this search."

Monimia hastened to do as he desired. "But is Betty," said she, "in the hall? I have reasons, which I have not now time to explain, for believing they are together." "I know not," answered Orlando, whose fears every moment increased; "I care not what happens if you are but once in safety."

Monimia then with light and timid steps passed through the adjoining parlour. She found all that end of the house deserted, and regained the long passage which led from her turret to the apartment of her aunt. All was quiet, and she flattered herself that Mrs. Lennard, occupied by the attention necessary to be shewn to the guests, had for once omitted the ceremony of locking the doors of that part of the house, and particularly hers, at the usual hour. In this hope she tripped along the passage, and had just reached the door of her own room, when Mrs. Lennard, with a candle in her hand, appeared at the other end. There was no hope of escape— She stood trembling, unable to open the lock, which she held in her hand; while her aunt with a hasty step and an angry countenance advanced towards her—"Hey-day, Madam!" cried Mrs. Lennard, "pray, what makes you here? so dressed, too, I assure you! I thought I had ordered you not to leave your room. Pr'ythee, Miss, where have you been? and how have you dared to disobey my orders?"

"Dear aunt," cried the affrighted Monimia, in a voice almost inarticulate through fear—"Dear aunt! be not so very angry—Every year till now you were so good as to give me leave to go into the hall-gallery to look at the dancers for a quarter of an hour. I dressed myself in hopes that some time in the evening I should see you to ask leave—it grew very late, you did not come to my room, and so—"

"And so, hussey, you left it without, did you?"—Monimia, unwilling to advance another direct falsehood, remained silent; and Mrs. Lennard, fixing her fierce enquiring eyes upon her, said sternly, "Monimia, there is something in your conduct which I do not understand—I suspect that you are a very wicked girl—I have had hints given me more than once, that you are imposing upon me, and ruining yourself."

"How can I impose upon you, Madam?" said Monimia, who, believing the crisis of her fate was now approaching, tried to collect a little spirit—"How can I impose upon you? Do you not always confine me to my room, and have I any means of leaving it without your consent?"

"That is what I am determined to discover," cried Mrs. Lennard— (Monimia became paler than before)—"You have a false key, or you have some other means of getting out—However, it is not at present a time to enquire into this. Go now, Madam, to your room, and to your bed. Having seen you here is enough to convince me, that the intelligence I have had given me is not without grounds. Come, Miss, as you may perhaps choose to set out again—if you have, as I suspect, the means of opening the door—I shall wait here till you are in bed, and take away the candle."

Monimia, who dreaded nothing so much as that Orlando might ascend the secret stairs, in order to enquire if she was safe, while her aunt was yet with her, hastened to undress herself; and as she feared that, if all were silent in her room, Orlando might speak without the door, which would inevitably discover them at once, she wished, for the first time in her life, that the copious stream of eloquence with which the pleasure of scolding always supplied Mrs. Lennard might now continue in full force—she therefore contrived to say something which she imagined would produce this, and she succeeded. Provoked at Monimia's attempt to excuse or defend herself, and impatient at being kept from the party below, in which she considered herself, now that her lady and the guests were withdrawn, as the first figure, Mrs. Lennard spared not her lungs, nor was she very nice in the choice of those epithets which most forcibly expressed her anger against her niece. In the midst of this harangue, Orlando, impatient to know whether Monimia was safe, and unable to set out in search of his brother till he had obtained this satisfaction, softly ascended the narrow stairs, and in a moment was convinced that all their escapes, during this perilous evening, had ended in a complete discovery of their intelligence; for to nothing less could he impute the fury in which Mrs. Lennard appeared to be. Under this impression, his spirits and temper quite exhausted by the various perverse accidents that had within a few hours befallen him—irritated by frequent disappointment, and indignant at the insults to which he believed Monimia was at the moment exposed, he was on the point of bursting into the room, declaring his affection for her, and meeting at once the invectives of her aunt, the renunciation of all his hopes from Mrs. Rayland, and the displeasure of his own family. He blamed himself for not having before taken a step which, whatever might be its future consequence, would at least be decisive, and save Monimia from those cruel alarms and distressing conflicts to which his love had so long made her liable. But at the moment that his hand was lifted to execute this rash purpose, the storm within seemed to abate: he heard Mrs. Lennard say—"I assure you, that the very next time I see or hear the least grounds for believing you are carrying on such a correspondence, that day shall be the last of your stay under this roof." This gave Orlando hope that they might not be absolutely discovered; and at the same moment the idea of his father made more unhappy, and deploring the fate that gave him two sons equally careless of their duty—of his beloved and affectionate mother weeping at the disobedience of her children—arose forcibly to check his precipitate resolution. He hesitated; he listened; Mrs. Lennard spoke lower, but still in a tone of remonstrance and reproach. He determined to wait to speak to Monimia after her departure, but she seemed not likely to depart; and as he attentively listened to what he could not now very exactly distinguish, the terms in which she expressed her indignation, he heard several voices calling him in the park. This was a new alarm—To issue from the lower part of the turret at such an hour, when it was impossible he could have any business there, was not to be thought of: yet the door was not closed, and he believed it not improbable that the people who were he apprehended in search of his brother, might at length seek *him* there; as his intoxication, when he was missing, might lead them to imagine that he might have gone into some of the buildings and have fallen asleep. He descended therefore, and waited at the door. The voices were now at a distance; and apparently being near the apartment of Mrs. Rayland, the persons who had before called aloud were afraid of disturbing her. He seized this opportunity of escaping; and, following the sound, which was still heard at intervals, he met at length the groom and the under footman, who told him that Mr. Philip Somerive had returned about a quarter of an hour before into the room, where he was now so extremely riotous that he had got into a quarrel with one of the young farmers; that he had stripped to box; and that every interposition of theirs only served to enrage him more. They therefore besought Orlando to return into the hall, that he might appease and prevail upon his brother to go home; for that their Lady, already alarmed by the noise, had sent down orders to have the house immediately shut up, and for the people to depart. A thousand times during the course of this evening had poor Orlando execrated his own folly, that had thus brought his brother into an house, where, while he had been such an unceasing torment to him, he had probably effectually ruined himself. But there was now not a moment to give way to these repentant reflections. He hastened therefore into the room, where his brother, awakened from the stupor of drunkenness into its most extravagant phrensy, had taken some offence at a young man of the company, and was now withheld only by the united strength of three stout farmers from fighting. Orlando for some time argued and implored in vain. The fury of Philip only changed its object, and was directed against him. But with his opponent, whose blunt English spirit was not, as he declared, "at all disposed to yield tamely to

the insults of any 'squire, no not the biggest 'squire in the king's dominions," the cool reasoning of Orlando had more effect. He soothed then
this justly offended rustic, and, promising that Philip should hereafter
acknowledge the impropriety of his behaviour, he prevailed on him to
depart with Pattenson and some other of the men into another room;
and then his brother being almost exhausted, and relapsing again into
stupidity, Orlando wished to conduct him home. This was however, on
consideration, found to be impossible; for he was equally unable to ride
or walk, even with the assistance which Orlando was very ready to lend
him. In this dilemma nothing remained but to put him into his own bed;
where, being at a great distance from Mrs. Rayland, there was no probability of her knowing the state to which his intemperance had reduced
him. This then he determined to do. Pattenson and a party of the men
who were in habits of drinking had already withdrawn: the women were
huddling away to their respective homes; and Orlando, with the help of
the groom, carried off the almost senseless Philip to his own bed-chamber, where he left him on his bed; and then, harassed and unhappy as he
was, fatigued with all that had happened, and torn to pieces with anxiety about Monimia, he yet had another task to perform, which he felt,
however painful, to be necessary—and this was, to walk to West
Wolverton, that, by his account of Philip, he might quiet the fears of his
father as to his personal safety.

He arrived there, quite worn out with uneasiness; and the pale countenance and dishevelled hair with which he entered the parlour, seemed
to confirm all the fears with which the unfortunate Somerive had been
tormented on account of his eldest son. He found him walking backwards
and forwards in the parlour, listening to every noise; and he had passed the
whole interval in this manner, except that he had now and then gone up
stairs to his wife, whom he had prevailed upon to go to bed, to persuade
her to mitigate those fears under which he was himself agonized. At this
juncture the appearance of Orlando, whose looks seemed to speak only
of some sad catastrophe, deprived his father for a moment of the power
of asking what intelligence he brought; and when he could speak, it was
only to say—"Orlando! your brother?"—"He is safe, dear Sir," answered
Orlando;"pray be not thus alarmed." "Relate, then," cried Mr. Somerive
in an eager voice, "relate where he is—wretched boy!"—"Indeed, Sir,"
said Orlando extremely shocked at the look and manner of his father,"you
consider this matter more seriously than it deserves, and are more alarmed
than the occasion seems to require." He then related what had happened,
softening however his brother's folly as much as he could; and assured his

father that he would take care Philip should return in the morning, and that Mrs. Rayland should be kept ignorant of the confusion his intemperance had occasioned.

"You are a noble and excellent creature, Orlando," cried Somerive, with a sigh as if his heart would break; "but God knows what will become of your unhappy brother. This relapse into debauchery, so degrading, awakens all my fears—fears, which a little subsided on his unexpected return home. But it is not an hour, my dear boy, to detain you with the misery that I see awaits us all. Since you have given up your bed to Philip, I desire you will take one here, while I hasten to quiet the anxiety which has almost overcome your poor mother, who imagined nothing less than that her son was drowned, or that some other horrid calamity had befallen him."

Mr. Somerive then departed; and Orlando, though somewhat comforted by having the power to relieve the sad solicitude of his parents, was infinitely too uneasy to feel any inclination to sleep, though he was so greatly fatigued. It was by this time day-light; and, after some reflection, he resolved to return back to the Hall, and to await in the library the hour when he should be delivered from the unwelcome inmate whom he had been compelled to admit. Every other anxiety however that assailed him was unfelt, when he thought of the situation in which he had left Monimia. The harsh tones in which the threats of Mrs. Lennard were delivered still rung in his ears; and his fancy represented the lovely victim of her ill humour drowned in tears, yielding to despair, and perhaps recollecting with anguish and regret the moments she had given to his importunate love. It was broad day by the time he returned to the Hall, and the workmen and gardeners were dispersed about the house. He dared not therefore indulge himself with another visit to the turret; but having with some difficulty obtained admittance from the tired and sleepy servants, he wrapped himself in his great coat, and sat down in the Study, where he easily discovered, by the loud snoring from the adjoining room, that Philip was sleeping away the effects of the powerful draughts of the preceding night. Orlando, half tempted to envy the state of forgetfulness into which he had fallen, occupied himself in reflecting on the strange and perverse accidents of the evening, in which he and Monimia had trembled so often on the brink of discovery—perhaps were discovered, just at the time when they had flattered themselves with the hope that they might the more securely meet. He revolved all that was likely to happen if Mrs. Lennard was really acquainted with their correspondence; and hesitated not to resolve, in that case, to go to his father, to declare his affection for Monimia, and to rescue her from the tyranny of her aunt, whatever might ensue. On the other hand, if their acquaintance yet remained doubtful, or only suspected, he saw that prudence and duty, his tenderness for Monimia, and his affection for his father, equally dictated their present separation; and that, to whichever of these he listened, they agreed in pointing out his leaving Monimia now, to acquire some establishment which might give them at least a probability, without the breach of any duty, of being happily united hereafter. There was something humiliating to his ingenuous mind, in all the arts and prevarications which their clandestine correspondence compelled him to use himself, and to teach the innocent Monimia. A thousand times he wished that he had been born the son of a day-labourer; that his parents, entertaining for him no views of ambition, had left him to pursue his own inclinations. A thousand times he lamented that Monimia was not circumstanced like Miss Hollybourn, that he might openly have addressed her: and the image of the arrogant heiress arose with redoubled disgust to his mind, when he compared her situation with that of his desolate orphan Monimia. More than three hours passed away while these thoughts were fluctuating in his mind. At the end of that time he was aroused by the entrance of Betty, who pertly demanded if he did not choose any breakfast?

He desired to have it brought. To which the girl replied, "Perhaps you had rather breakfast with the old women?"—"Whom do you mean?" enquired Orlando.

"Mean!" answered she; "why, who should I mean, but mistress, and mother Lennard? There's no other old woman in the house as I knows on, nor there had not need. They've been enquiring after you."

"After me?"

"Yes," replied Betty. "And Madam I suppose will tie you on to her apron-string soon, for she is never easy without you. Upon my word, Mr. Orlando, you look a little rakish though, I think, for such a *sober* young gentleman, and considering too that you did not demean yourself with dancing as you used to do with us servants, after the gentlefolks were gone. I warrant however that you did not pass the time at prayers."

"You give your tongue strange license," said Orlando, who endeavoured to conceal his vexation, for he imagined that all alluded to Monimia. "However, do tell me, if Mrs. Rayland wishes me to breakfast with her?"

"I knows nothing about her wishes," replied the girl; "I only knows that Lennard have been asking every servant in the house about you, and cross-questioning one so that I suppose she thoft I had got you locked up in my cupboard, as they say she used for to have the men-folk in her younger days in the housekeeper's store-room.[1] The old woman and the oven for that! Set a thief to catch a thief!"

"I do desire," said Orlando, "that you would have done with all this, and tell me whether Mrs. Lennard expects me at breakfast? However," added he, pausing, "I will alter my dress, and wait upon her at all events; and do be so good as to prepare in the mean time some breakfast for my brother."

Betty then left him apparently with pleasure to execute this last commission; and Orlando, after changing his clothes, went to Mrs. Lennard's room to enquire whether Mrs. Rayland wished to speak to him, and at what time he might wait upon her. This however was not his only motive; he thought he should immediately discern by Mrs. Lennard's reception of him, whether his fears of a partial or an entire discovery were well founded. He fortunately found Mrs. Lennard in the housekeeper's room; and, accosting her with his usual interesting address, he enquired how Mrs. Rayland did after the fatigues of the evening, how she was herself, and whether he might at any time that morning make a personal enquiry after Mrs. Rayland?

The sage housekeeper received his civilities with great coldness, and answered, even with some asperity, that Mrs. Rayland was much better than ever she could have expected after so much company. "As to your enquiring after her, Sir," added she, "I don't know indeed how that may be; perhaps (fixing on him her penetrating eyes) there are *other* people in the house after whom you would *rather* ask."

Orlando, whose conscious blood rose into his cheeks at this speech, felt them glow, and the sensation increased his confusion. "No," replied he, hesitating. "No, certainly you cannot....suppose....that there is any body....that I....that I wish to enquire after more than Mrs. Rayland....I was much afraid that the fatigue would be too much for her."

"There are other people," replied the lady, "who were fatigued also. I must beg the favour of you, Mr. Orlando, not to interfere with my niece. I suppose it was by your desire or contrivance that she took the liberty of leaving her room last night, contrary to my positive orders."

Orlando, a little recovered from his consternation, endeavoured to laugh this off, and was proving to Mrs. Lennard that it was impossible for *him* to have occasioned this disobedience, when a summons came

---

[1]   This hint at Mrs. Lennard's racy past lends credence to the idea that Monimia may well be her illegitimate daughter.

for her to attend Mrs. Rayland; and "I was ordered, Sir," said the footman, "to desire you would come up also, if you were about the house."

Mrs. Lennard now stalked away with great dignity, and Orlando followed her, more than ever alarmed for Monimia.

CHAP. XII.

Instead of the reproaches Orlando expected to hear, Mrs. Rayland received him, if not with so much cordial kindness as usual, at least without any appearance of anger. After the usual compliments on his part, and some enquiries on hers, whether all those who were immediately her guests had gone as soon as they left her, Mrs. Lennard withdrew, and Orlando was left alone with the old Lady, and again trembled lest some remonstrances were to be made; for his mind was so entirely occupied by that subject, that he forgot it was possible for the attention of others to be differently engaged.

His apprehensions increased, when Mrs. Rayland, after a solemn silence, thus began:

"I believe, Mr. Orlando, I have given you abundant proof that I esteem you above the rest of my kinsman's family."

Orlando bowed, and would have said that he was sensible of and grateful for her kindness; he could make nothing of the sentence—but blushed, and faltered while Mrs. Rayland went on.

"Your father has once or twice proposed sending you out into the world, and has consulted me upon the occasion. I suppose you are not unacquainted with the plan he has lately thought proper to propose for you."

Orlando, relieved by hearing that her discourse did not tend whither he feared it would, said that he knew General Tracy had offered his father to procure him a commission; "an offer, Madam," continued he, "of which I waited to hear your opinion before I myself ventured to form any wishes on the subject."

This was carrying his complaisance farther than he had ever yet done. But, confused and apprehensive as he was, he said any thing which might turn the discourse from what he most dreaded, without having his mind enough at liberty to enquire rigorously into the truth or propriety of what he uttered; and even the independent spirit he had always prided himself on supporting, was lost amid his fears for Monimia.

Mrs. Rayland looked at him steadily for a moment—

"You are ready then," said she, "to follow any line of life, Orlando, which your friends approve?"

"I am, Madam! and always have been."

"And you do not dislike the army?"

"Very far from it, Madam."

"I have been accustomed from my youth," reassumed the old Lady after another pause, "to consider the profession of arms as one of those which is the least derogatory to the name of a gentleman."

"It is honourable, Madam, to any name."

"My grandfather," continued Mrs. Rayland, "after whom you were by the permission of our family called——my grandfather, I say, Sir Orlando Rayland, appeared with distinguished honour in the service of his master in 1685, against the rebel Monmouth, though not of the religion of King James. My father Sir Hildebrand distinguished himself under Marlborough, when he was a younger brother, and saw much service in Flanders. Of remoter ancestors, I could tell you of Raylands who bled in the civil wars; we were always Lancastrians, and lost very great property by our adherence to that unhappy family during the reigns of Edward the Fourth and Richard the Third. My great great grandfather, who was also called Orlando ..."

Mrs. Rayland had soon totally forgotten the young hero who was before her, while she ran over the names and exploits of heroes past; and, lost in their loyalty and their prowess, she forgot that hardly any other record of them remained upon earth than what her memory and their pictures in the gallery above afforded. Orlando, however, heard her not only with patience but with pleasure. In recurring thus to them when the question of his professional choice was before her, it appeared that she had somehow associated the idea of his future welfare with that of their past consequence; and besides the satisfaction this discovery afforded him, he began to hope that his fears of any discovery were quite groundless.

Mrs. Rayland having at length completed the catalogue of the warriors of her family, and having no more to say, returned to the subject which had given rise to this discussion.—"Therefore, young kinsman, I say that, if this worthy General Tracy will favour you with his counte-nance, if your father and your relations approve of it, and if you yourself are disposed for the profession of arms, I shall be glad not only to give you some assistance towards setting out, but to aid you from time to time in such means of promotion as the General may point out to me."

Orlando, who now found the whole affair decided, felt one pang at the certainty which presented itself, that he must quit, soon quit his beloved Monimia; it was severe, but momentary: and with equal warmth and sincerity he thanked Mrs. Rayland for her goodness, and assured her that he was ready to avail himself of her generous intentions in his favour.

"But are you sure, Mr. Orlando," added Mrs. Rayland interrupting his acknowledgements—"are you quite sure that no unworthy connection, no improper attachment here, will make the departure for your regiment disagreeable to you?"

The blood that had so often been the treacherous emissary of conscience before, now flew to the cheeks of Orlando; indeed his whole countenance changed so much that Mrs. Rayland, though not very clear-sighted, perceived it. Her brow took that severe look which it almost always lost in the presence of her young favourite—"I see," cried she, observing Orlando still hesitate—"I see that I have not been misinformed."

Every thing seemed to depend on the presence of mind which he was at this moment able to exert. He recovered himself, and said, in a firm and calm tone, "I know not, Madam, what information you have received; but this I know, and do most solemnly assure you, that I have no unworthy connection, no improper attachment—and," added he, animated by reflecting that his love for the innocent, amiable Monimia was neither, "and when you discover that I deceive you, I am content to relinquish your favour for ever."

"Indeed you will lose it," answered Mrs. Rayland, a little relaxing of her severity;—"and that I may still have the pleasure of supposing you worthy my good opinion, and that well disposed young man which I have always wished to find you, your leaving this place a while may not be amiss. I know how to make some allowance for the arts of wicked girls; but I shall take care that no such person disgraces my family for the future. In regard to you, cousin, I hope you are above any such unworthy thoughts. It must be my business to give proper directions for the rest, and for the due regulations of my family. You will prepare, cousin, for your commission, which the worthy General tells me he expects every day; he assures me it is worth upwards of four hundred pounds. Your father is very happy in having met with a real friend."—Orlando, thunderstruck by a speech which he believed related to Monimia, stood like a statue. It was fortunate for him that Mrs. Rayland, after the words wicked girls, continued to speak; for, had she not done so, Orlando would infallibly have betrayed himself by entering into a warm defence of Monimia; he would indeed have confessed, without reserve, their long attachment, and frequent interviews: but the rest of her speech, and the entrance of Mrs. Lennard, for whom she rang just as she concluded it, gave him time to recollect himself: yet when Mrs. Rayland, in her usual way, dismissed him, he doubted whether his honour and his love did not call upon him to come to an immediate explanation. The consideration and kindness which Mrs. Rayland expressed for him, so unlike the usual prudish asperity of her disposition, were offensive and hateful to him when he believed she acquitted him at the expence of Monimia. He hastened however to his own apartment, because it was necessary to see what was become of his brother. It was some alleviation to his confusion and distress to find Philip was gone; and he sat down, endeavouring to collect his thoughts, and to determine on what was to be done.

That Monimia was on his account to be dismissed from the house of Mrs. Rayland, and the protection of her only relation, the circumstances of the preceding night, added to what he had just heard, left him but little reason to doubt. What then was to become of her? and how could he make her any reparation for the injury he had done her, but by instantly declaring the truth, and relinquishing all prospect of future prosperity, from which she must be excluded?—Desperate as he felt this step to be, he was in a state of mind that urged him to decide on any thing that might bring their fate to a crisis: and, believing himself finally determined, he started up from this short counsel with himself, and was going hastily to the apartment of Mrs. Rayland, when at the door he was stopped by Betty, who, with her hat on, and a small bundle in her hand, dropped him a curtsey, and said, with an arch smile, "I'm come to take my leave of you, 'Squire, and to wish you well."

"Whither are you going then, Betty?" said Orlando.

"Lord, Sir," cried the girl, "you're such another hard-hearted gentleman!—What! I warrant you don't know that Madam have sent me down my wages, with orders to go out of her house directly, and all upon your account."

"Upon my account!"—"Pattenson it seems have been telling more false lies to Madam. He won't believe ever since that night that somebody was seen in your room—I don't know who, not I—but that you and I be too great: Madam Lennard would never hear on't till to-day; but now they've found out, by laying their old noddles together, that I was out of the house last night, and they says 'twas along a you. Knowing my own innocence, I bears it all; for I be clear of the charge, as you know very well: I wish every body could say as much; but I know what I know."

Orlando now instantly comprehended that it was of Betty Mrs. Rayland had spoken, and not of the innocent Monimia, whom his own rash impatience was again on the point of betraying. Sensible of his good fortune in having been thus prevented, he was still confused and agitated. "Whatever you know, Betty," said he, "of me, I am at least very sorry you have, by any mistake relative to me, lost your place, and Mrs. Lennard's favour."

"As to *her* favour," answered the girl pertly, "I values it no more than that; and she had better keep her tongue within her teeth about me, I can tell her that; and as for places, there's more in the world. One should have a fine time on't, indeed, to pass all one's life in this here old dungeon, among rats, and ghosts, and old women. However, young 'Squire, I advises you, as a friend, to take more care for the future: some people are very sly; but for my part I scorn to betray 'um—but mayhap the next housemaid mid'nt be so willing as I have been to bear the blame for things she's as innocent of as the child unborn."

"I cannot tell to what you allude," replied Orlando in a hurried voice; "but this I know, that if I have done you any injury, I am very sorry for it, and willing to make you any reparation in my power." He then took a guinea from his pocket—"Accept of this," cried he, "and be assured I shall on any future occasion be happy to serve you."—The girl took the guinea, but without expressing any gratitude either for that, or his apparent wishes to make her what amends he could for the loss of her place:—she flippantly told him, she hoped, for all Madam's injustice, and the malice of her enemies, she had *friends* who not let her be beholden to nobody—She then left the house.

Orlando, thus relieved from the most acute uneasiness he had ever suffered, returned to his room. He most ardently wished to communicate to Monimia the joy he felt in finding that the suspicions excited by so many awkward circumstances, had by some means or other fallen upon this servant; and apparently without doing her any injury, which would have considerably lessened his satisfaction. Far from regretting her dismission, she seemed pleased with having had an opportunity given her to be dismissed; and Orlando, who had long known her to be a very improper associate for Monimia, found many reasons to be glad of her departure. That she knew, or very strongly suspected their meetings, seemed very evident; she was much less dangerous any where than within the house—and as to what she might say without, which might be prejudicial to the character of Monimia, he determined to prevent the ill effects of that where it might be most prejudicial, by confessing, before he left the country, the very extent of his fault to his father, who already suspected so much of the truth.

However earnestly he wished to speak to Monimia, and however uneasy the idea of her suspense and dejection made him, he could find no opportunity of speaking to her during the morning, without hazard, which he had too recently suffered for, so immediately to incur again. Though Mrs. Lennard had artfully made Betty the victim, there was still reason to believe she was not without suspicions; and to irritate or increase them now, would be to preclude himself from the last pleasure he was likely to taste during the rest of his short residence at the Hall— the pleasure of soothing his beloved Monimia, and, at the few interviews which they might yet obtain, reconciling her soft heart to the necessity of that separation that was so soon to happen.

He was summoned to dinner with Mrs. Rayland, who seemed pleased to find he was still at the Hall. Never did the old Lady appear in such good humour with him, or so relaxed from the starch prudery of her usual character.—She gave way to her love of telling anecdotes and stories of her own family; and, pleased with the attention Orlando gave to her narratives, she hinted to him, though still with great ambiguity, that it would be his own fault if he was not one day or other the representative of a family so illustrious. She then spoke of his elder brother with anger and contempt, which Orlando generously tried to soften; of his mother with her usual coldness and dislike; and of his sisters as good, pretty-behaved girls—"that is, I mean, the two youngest. As to Miss Belle—she's a London lady already: I protest it hurts me to see young women so bold—but she has been cried up for a beauty. 'Tis vanity ruins all girls—no good is ever to be expected from them when once they get conceited notions into their heads of being handsome."

Orlando undertook the defence of his sister with more zeal than prudence; but Mrs. Rayland, though not to be convinced that Isabella was not a vain coquet, which indeed her unguarded gaiety gave the old Lady very good reason to believe, was however in a humour to be pleased with all Orlando said. Her attachment to him had been long insensibly increasing; and though, like another Elizabeth, she could not bear openly to acknowledge her successor, she was as little proof as the royal ancient virgin, against the attractions of an amiable and handsome young man, whom she loved to consider as the child of her bounty, and the creature of her smiles. Though determined to keep him dependent during her life, and even to send him out a soldier of fortune, she really meant to give him, at her death, the whole of her landed property; and the machinations of Pattenson, whose jealousy and avarice alike excited his hatred to Orlando, had hitherto had an effect so different from what he expected, that he found his politics entirely baffled, and that he was more likely to lose, by farther attempts, his Lady's regard, than to shake that she entertained for the young favourite.

A few years before, the very suspicion of an intrigue would have shut for ever the doors of Rayland Hall against the supposed delinquent; but now the attempts to impute such to Orlando had ended in nothing but the dismissing a servant—a circumstance proving at once, that though some credit was given to the accusation, no resentment towards him was entertained.

Mrs. Lennard, who had more sense and more art than Pattenson, and who had opportunities more closely to observe her Lady, had long seen the progress of her affection for Orlando, and long ceased to counteract it.—She was not weak enough to imagine, as Pattenson did, that such great property as Mrs. Rayland possessed would be divided among her servants—but she knew that she should herself possess a very considerable legacy; and she thought it better that Orlando should inherit the bulk of the fortune, than either his father, who had always considered the old servants about her as his enemies, or any public charity—to some of which Mrs. Rayland had, in former fits of ill humour, expressed an intention to leave the Rayland estate.

Mrs. Rayland had, in common with many old people, a strange aversion to speaking of her will, or of what was to happen after her death; and far advanced as she was in life, she talked of future years as if she believed herself immortal. Mrs. Lennard had, however, once seen part of a will—with which, in respect to herself, she had great reason to be satisfied. She knew that Mrs. Rayland had lately made another, to which she was not a witness;—for such was the peculiarity of her Lady in this respect, that she had sent for a lawyer and witnesses from London, that none of the neighbouring attornies, or even her confidential servants, might know its contents. Mrs. Lennard did not doubt but that Orlando was in this made heir of almost all the landed property; but she had no reason, from Mrs. Rayland's behaviour to her, to apprehend that this new will was at all prejudicial to herself.

Still, however, it was not her interest to encourage the affection which many circumstances gave her reason to believe Orlando entertained for her niece. She knew that, if the rashness of youth and passion should urge them to marry, it would not only ruin Orlando, who would then be a beggar; but that she should herself be accused of having promoted this fatal indiscretion, and lose her own advantages without obtaining any for her niece, whom she by no means wished to see independent of her, even if independence could thus have been obtained; and whom she treated with redoubled rigour, when she found reason to believe that Orlando felt for her that attachment which she had from their childhood foreseen and attempted to prevent.

The more Orlando gained on the favour of Mrs. Rayland, the more apprehensive Mrs. Lennard became of his affection for Monimia: she had however persuaded herself, that, with the precautions she took, their clandestinely meeting or carrying on any correspondence was impracticable; and, satisfied that Monimia was confined to her room, her vigilance had now and then slumbered. But it awakened by the late reports that obtained in the house and about the country; reports which originated in the gossip of Orlando's nocturnal visitor; of his being missing at unusual hours, and from Betty's hints. When, therefore, Pattenson's jealousy was so far roused as to urge him to speak to his Lady of a supposed intimacy between Orlando and this his faithless favourite, Mrs. Lennard let it make its impression; and Betty's pertness, who had before agreed with Philip Somerive to take the first opportunity of going off to him, gave her a pretence immediately to discharge her. Mrs. Rayland, content to part with her favourite Orlando, because she thought it for his advantage to see something of the world in an honourable profession—and because she believed, if youth and idleness had concurred with the art of the girl with whom he was accused, to lead him into any improper connection, this was the best way to break it—determined on his departure with satisfaction, since the General assured her there was at present no probability of his leaving England.

Mrs. Lennard, who thought herself fortunate in having all the suspicions fall on Betty, kept as a profound secret those she entertained herself relative to Monimia, whom she resolved narrowly to watch till Orlando was gone. And Pattenson, glad that the young minion was to go, as he termed it, for a soldier, reconciled himself by that reflection to the failure of his original plan, which had been totally to ruin him with Mrs. Rayland. As to the loss of his fair one, he knew she would not remove far; and that resentment for his accusations would not make her long relentless, while he had presents and money to offer her.

Such were, at this juncture, the politics of Rayland Hall.

CHAP. XIII.

The house of West Wolverton too had its politicians; but none of them were so content with their past operations, or future prospects, as the venerable group last described.

Isabella, wild and coquettish as she was, could no longer affect to misunderstand the language with which General Tracy ventured to address her. For some time, however, she attempted to laugh it off; but at length resolved, by the counsel of Selina, to speak to her mother, and entreat that, if the General remained any longer their guest, she might not be so often left to hear professions so insulting, which the presence of her sisters did not always restrain. Mrs. Somerive, whose heart was half broken by the behaviour of Philip, and who saw, with inexpressible anguish, the ravage which the uneasiness arising from that source was hourly making on the constitution of her husband, had been fondly flattering herself, during the first weeks of the General's visit, that in him Mr. Somerive had found a sincere friend, and their children a powerful protector. The solicitude he expressed for Orlando, and the consideration with which he treated Philip, made her sanguinely believe that he would provide for one, and possibly reclaim the other. The sums which the latter had won from him at play—Mrs. Somerive, who knew nothing of their nightly gambling, supposed the General had lent him; when her heart, overflowing with gratitude towards this generous friend, was suddenly struck with the intelligence Isabella gave her.

She at first fancied the vanity of Isabella might have given meaning to his expressions which they were never meant to convey; but, upon questioning her and Selina repeatedly, and from the observations she made the two following days, she was convinced that their representations of his behaviour were just. This cruel certainty she determined however to conceal from her husband, and to guard, by her own prudent watchfulness, against the artifices of the General, without bringing on a rupture between him and Somerive that might be attended with consequences she sickened to think of.

The General, however, who paid her the most assiduous court, was soon sensible of a change in her manners; for she was incapable of the dissimulation which people of the world so successfully practise. From hence, and from the behaviour of Isabella, the General found that a longer stay would betray his insidious designs without contributing at all to their success, and he prepared to go; yet could not bear to relinquish for ever his hopes of gaining Isabella, with whom he was more in love than ever. He lingered, therefore, notwithstanding all the discouragement he received; and Somerive, who believed him the best and most sincere friend that ever man had, communicated to him all his affairs, and all his anxiety—by which the General perceived plainly, he was in such a state of mind as must hasten him to the grave; and he had learned that, impressed with ideas of his (the General's) friendship for all his family, he had made him executor, and trusted the welfare of his wife and daughters entirely to him and to Orlando.

Though Tracy therefore could neither give up his pursuit, nor succeed in it at present, he believed that the death of the father, the indigence to which the whole family would be reduced, and the absence of Orlando, would together make easy the project of obtaining Isabella for a mistress, and that patience and dissimulation alone were necessary to keep up his influence in the family, till they should be wholly in his power. He determined, therefore, to check himself; to make no more professions with which Isabella could be offended, but to express his contrition that he had said what she construed into want of respect; to hint remotely at honourable intentions; and thus, without engaging himself, or, as the fashionable phrase is, committing himself, to retain his influence over the whole family, as well as over the father; and to be assured that, whenever he chose to return, he should be received with pleasure. As to any suspicion that Isabella might think him of an age so disproportionate as to hear even his honourable offers with disdain and ridicule, it never occurred to the General; and he was pretty well assured, from the pecuniary circumstances of the family, that every other member of it would receive the remotest hint of an intended alliance with transport. The behaviour of Mrs. Somerive, on the evening of the tenants' ball, convinced him that Isabella had not merely threatened when she protested she would speak to her mother of his behaviour; and he found that though Mr. Somerive, whenever he talked of going, pressed his stay, it was time to depart.

The messenger, who was sent to the post town on the following evening for letters, brought to General Tracy a large pacquet, arrived that day by the stage. On opening it, it was found to contain the commission of an ensign for Orlando Somerive, executed in due form, from the War Office. This he hastened to offer, with a florid speech, to Mrs. Somerive; who had hardly recovered from the emotions with which the sight of it, and his peculiar and studied manner of presenting it, occasioned, when Orlando, anxious to know at what time his brother had got home, and how his mother and sisters were after the fatigue and uneasiness of the night before, arrived.

On his first entrance, he enquired eagerly after his brother.—"Your brother!" cried Mr. Somerive; "he is not at home, Orlando, nor have we seen him since last night:—believing he was with you, and indeed supposing it possible that he was not well enough to leave your apartment, I made myself tolerably easy about him.—But when did he leave you? and where is he now?"

Orlando replied, that he had left his bed about eleven o'clock; and then, to quiet the uneasiness which he saw this unexpected absence gave to them all, he added, "But he is gone, I dare say, to Mr. Stockton's, where he has talked some time of intending to pass a day or two, and probably will not return home till to-morrow or next day."

"Gone to Mr. Stockton's!" exclaimed Mrs. Somerive—"What! without linen or change of clothes, though there is an house full of company?"

Mr. Somerive, who saw how much his wife was alarmed and affected, endeavoured to speak lightly of the absence of her son—"You know, my love," said he, "that Philip does not pique himself on being a beau; and that the party at Mr. Stockton's are only men. He can probably borrow any linen he wants of his friends; and as he means to be at home so soon, and has no servant with him, perhaps preferred doing so to the trouble of sending home for his own." Mrs. Somerive sighed, and cast a desponding look on her husband, who added, "But come, my dear Bella, you and I have something to say to Orlando—we will go all together into my study for a few moments, and the girls will have tea ready against our return."—So saying, he took his wife's hand, and, Orlando following them, they left the room.

Mrs. Somerive was no sooner released from the restraint which the presence of the General imposed, than she threw herself into a chair, and fell into an agony of tears. Her husband gently chid her for emotion which he endeavoured to persuade her was much beyond the occasion; and, having succeeded in rendering her somewhat more calm, he told Orlando that his commission was arrived, and enquired whether any conversation had passed between him and Mrs. Rayland in consequence of what had been held between her and General Tracy the preceding evening? Orlando related it all as nearly as he could recollect it, save only that sentence which related to some fancied attachment; and Mr. Somerive received, with great pleasure, what appeared to him equal to a confirmation of the most sanguine hopes he had ever entertained on his son's behalf.—Mrs. Somerive however was less elated: she could not comprehend how Mrs.

Rayland, if she had so much affection for Orlando, could not only bear to part with him, but promote his departure; or how, if she meant to make him her heir, she could determine to send him out in the world a soldier of fortune. The representations of her husband, however, and the content which Orlando expressed, reconciled her by degrees to what she could not now recall. She gave him, but not without many tears, the commission with which General Tracy had just presented her—but as she tried to give him her blessing with it, she relapsed into convulsive sorrow. Mr. Somerive found it would only distress her to return to the parlour; he therefore bade Orlando lead his mother to her own room, while he, returning to where his daughters were sitting with General Tracy, bade them go to her, and send their brother down to the parlour.

Orlando, on his entrance, addressed himself to Tracy, whom he thanked in the most graceful terms. The General answered his compliment with politeness, and the three gentlemen then began to discourse of the departure of Orlando for that party of his regiment that were in England, which Tracy told him could not properly be deferred longer than till the following week. He advised therefore that Orlando should set out for London on the following Monday—"when," said he, "as I shall go thither myself, I can have the pleasure of giving you a place in my post-chaise."

Mr. Somerive, while he expressed regret that the General was to leave him so soon (though his stay had been prolonged to almost six weeks), yet embraced this offer with avidity. He foresaw, that in the equipment of Orlando, of which Mrs. Rayland was, he understood, to defray the expence, the directions of such a friend could not fail of being extremely useful, and that his instructions might in a thousand more material instances be of advantage to him.—It was therefore settled among them, that, on the evening of the following Sunday, Orlando should take leave of his ancient benefactress, and repair to his father's house, to be ready to attend General Tracy to town the next morning.

Orlando was now impatient to return to the Hall—He hoped to have a few moments conversation with Monimia that evening; alas! only one more was to intervene before his departure: and the painful task of reconciling her to his going so soon and of taking a long—long leave, seemed to require an age!—His restlessness became so evident that his father noticed it—"You will stay here to-night, Orlando?" said he. "No, Sir," answered his son; "I wish with your leave to return to the Hall.—Mrs. Rayland often asks for me at breakfast, and you will allow that just at this period I should not seem in the slightest degree to neglect her."—"You are right in returning," said Mr. Somerive, fixing his eyes steadily on those of his son, "if that is your *only* motive."—Orlando, not able to bear the penetrating looks of his father, turned away, and said hastily—"Besides, Sir, I wish to enquire after my brother—for, however I affected before my mother to believe he was at Stockton's, I assure you I do not know he is there, nor have I any guess about him but what makes me uneasy."—"Go, then," replied his father with a deep sigh—"but remember, Orlando, that from *you* I expect sincerity."—"And you shall not be disappointed, Sir," answered Orlando warmly; "before I take my leave of you, and ask your last blessing, my heart shall be laid open to you, which I would rather pierce with my own hand than suffer it to harbour ingratitude or dissimulation towards so good a father."—Tears were in the eyes of the father and the son.—"Orlando!" said Somerive in a faltering voice, "go to your mother before you leave the house, and give her all the comfort you can— the absence of your brother overwhelms her with fear and distress; and before we see you to-morrow, my son—for I suppose we shall see you ..."

"Certainly, Sir! at any time you name."

"Make that convenient to yourself, Orlando; only, before we do see you, endeavour to find your brother, and persuade him to return, or at least bring us some news of him."

Orlando promised he would; and then went to his mother, who had by this time reasoned herself into a more calm state of mind. Having taken leave of her and his sisters for the night, he set out on foot to return to the Hall.

The night was overcast and gloomy; chill and hollow the wind whistled among the leafless trees, or groaned amid the thick firs in the dark and silent wood;—the water-falls murmured hollow in the blast, and only the owl's cry broke those dull and melancholy sounds, which seemed to say—"Orlando, you will revisit these scenes no more!" He endeavoured to reason himself out of these comfortless presages. He tried to figure to himself the happier days, that never seemed so likely as now to be his, and at no very remote period. Though Mrs. Rayland was, from peculiarity of temper, averse to naming her successor, she was not at all likely to hold out hopes she never meant to realize, and certainly she never gave any so strong as what her conversation of that morning had offered. He endeavoured therefore to persuade himself, that the time was not very far distant when, if he was not actually the possessor of Rayland Hall, he should at least have a competency as should enable him to settle in this his native country with his beloved Monimia. He tried to animate his drooping spirits with the idea that, in the profession into which he was now entering, he might find the means of accelerating this happy period: But then the frightful interval that must intervene occurred to him, with all the possibilities that might happen in it; and the destitute state of Monimia, the ill health of his father (which, though he did not complain, was visible to every body), the unhappy misconduct of his brother, threatening the ruin and dispersion of his family, and the possibility that Mrs. Rayland might disappoint the expectations she had raised, all combined to sink and depress him, and again to lend to the well-known paths he was traversing, horrors not their own, while every object repeated—"Orlando will revisit these scenes no more!"

By the time he reached that part of the park from whence the house was visible at a distance, it was quite dark, and, had he not almost instinctively known his way, he could not have discerned it—for no light glimmered from the Gothic windows of the Hall, not even in that part of the house inhabited by the servants; and Orlando imagined that most of them, fatigued the night before, were gone earlier than usual to bed. He fixed his eyes earnestly on Monimia's turret:—all was dark; and he doubted whether her aunt had not removed her, in consequence of the suspicions that originated in the circumstances of the preceding evening. This apprehension made his spirits sink still more heavily; and when he was within an hundred yards of the house, he stopped, and gazed mournfully on the place, which perhaps no longer contained the object of his affection.

There is hardly a sensation more painful than the blank that strikes on the heart, when, instead of the light we expect streaming from some beloved spot where our affections are fondly fixed, all is silent and dark.—Ah! how often in life we feel this yet stronger, when the friend on whom we rely becomes suddenly cold and repulsive! Orlando, who was passionately fond of poetry, recollected the simply descriptive stanza in the ballad of Hardyknute:

> "Theirs nae licht in my lady's bowir,
> Theirs nae licht in the hall;
> Nae blink shynes round my fairly fair—"

And, like the dismayed hero of the song,

> "Black feir he felt, but what to fear
> He wist not zit with dreid."[1]

---

[1]   Ehrenpreis identifies these lines as from the last two stanzas of the ballad by Elizabeth, Lady Wardlaw (1719) (p. 538).

Quiet as every thing appeared round the house, he knew it was earlier than the hour when Mrs. Lennard usually locked the door of Monimia's apartment for the night; it *was* possible that she might have detained her niece in her own room longer than was her general custom.

In hopes that he might see the light at length glimmer through the casement, which would assure him Monimia was there, he determined to watch for it a little longer, where he might not be himself observed.

It was indeed so very dark that he was sure it was impossible for any one to discern him from the house, or at least to distinguish his figure from that of the deer who were feeding around him. He sat down therefore on the turf; but the dreary moments passed, and still no light appeared—though Orlando was sure that if a light was in the room he must see it, because of the want of shutters towards the upper part of the long window. A thousand conjectures disturbed him, and grew, as time wore away, more and more painful. Perhaps Monimia was indisposed, and had gone early to bed; perhaps the alarms she had suffered the preceding evening, and uneasiness at his not having seen her, might have overcome her tender spirits, and, together with the harsh reproaches of her aunt, have rendered her really ill. His warm and rapid imagination now represented her sinking under anguish of mind which she dared not communicate—and tenderly reproaching him for being the cause of all her sufferings. It was he who had disturbed the innocent serenity of her bosom—and persuaded her to grant him interviews, with which she continually reproached herself. Or, if this was not the case, if her lovely frame was not overwhelmed by sickness arising from sorrow, perhaps she was more strictly confined in some part of the house where it would be impossible for him to see her; from whence it would be equally impossible for her to escape to him, to indulge him in the last sad pleasure of a parting interview. This last conjecture appeared highly probable, from what Mrs. Lennard had said to him in the morning; and he found it too intolerable, even while it was but conjecture, to be supported with patience. The great clock now struck eleven: every vibration seemed to fall on his heart.—He traversed yet a little longer the turf immediately under the windows of the turret; and at length saw a light from the servants' hall, whither he went, hoping, yet fearing, to gain some intelligence which he dreaded to ask. He entered, however; but found only Pattenson there, who was putting out the fire. It was in vain Orlando addressed him with great civility. The sulky old butler, who imputed to him the alacrity with which his favourite nymph had left the house, looked at him with a countenance cloudy and indignant, and deigned not even to give him the candle he asked for.—"There are candles, if you want them!" was all he could obtain from him. He enquired if Mrs. Rayland was gone to her room? if he could speak to Mrs. Lennard? To which Patteson, turning sullenly away, replied, "The women's side of the house has been shut up these two hours—you'll hardly get any admittance to make your flummering speeches to any on 'em to-night."— Orlando, already irritated by vexation, was so much provoked at this insolence, that he was tempted to knock down the consequential Mr. Patteson; but he fortunately recollected that he was an old man, and a servant, and that it was unworthy of him to strike such a person, whatever might be the provocation. He could not however help expressing his anger for this insult, in terms stronger than he usually allowed himself; and then, half frantic, went to his own room, merely because he knew not what to do to obtain some intelligence of Monimia.

After a moment's consideration, he went through the chapel, and to the lower room of the turret. If Mrs. Lennard had discovered the door of communication, he thought he should perceive it by some means or other—but all below was as he left it:—he then mounted the stairs, and listened at the door behind Monimia's bed, but all was profoundly silent. He ventured to tap softly at the door, their usual signal, which Monimia never failed, when she was alone, to answer instantly; but now no answer was returned. He spoke—but no soft voice, in tremulous whispers, replied. Again he rapped, and spoke louder; but still all was dead silence around him.—Yet he waited a moment or two—lost in distracting conjectures—Monimia was certainly not in her room— what then was become of her, or whither was she gone? He felt as if he should never see her more, though it was impossible to suppose she was removed from the house. At length he returned to his own apartment again, more wretched than he left it;—and not seeing any probability of discovering that night what could thus have robbed him of the sight of Monimia, he went to his bed—but not to sleep, though he had suffered so many hours of mental and bodily fatigue. He watched the earliest dawn of light; and as soon as he could discern the objects about the park, he dressed himself and went out—walking slowly round the house, and looking up at all the windows, in hopes that if Monimia was as restless as he was, she might appear at that of the room she was confined in, in the expectation of seeing him. But he made his melancholy tour repeatedly in vain. He then returned to his own room, furnished himself with materials for shooting, and went into the kitchen under pretence of drying some powder; that, while he watched it carefully himself, he might have an excuse for staying to talk a little with the cook. This woman, whose admiration of Orlando's beauty had made her much his friend, was willing enough to gossip with him, and talked much of Betty's being so suddenly discharged, declaimed against her, and hinted that it was pity such a young 'squire should under-value himself so as to take a liking to such a tawdry trollop.—Orlando, who cared very little what was thought of him in regard to Betty, rather humoured than denied the oblique charge; but endeavoured to lead the conversation towards Mrs. Lennard, whom she called a covetous cross old frump; "and as for that," added the woman, "she uses that sweet child, her niece as they call her, no better than a dog."

"Why, how does she use her?" cried Orlando faltering and in a hurried voice: "What! has she lately done any thing?"

"Not as I knows on; but I knows she is always rating her, so as the poor young thing have no peace of her life—and if she offer for to come to speak to any of us sarvants, there's a rare to-do!—Fine airs truly for mother Lennard to give herself—as if her niece was a bit better than we be!—If she's so proud that she won't let the girl speak to no sarvants, I think she mid as well not make her work like one—which I'm sure she does, and shuts her up like as a felon in jail."

"Where," said Orlando, "does she shut her up?"

"Why, in her own room, don't she? From morning to night, and from one year's end to another, she's lock'd up in that there place, that's just for all the world like a belfry."

"And is she there now?" cried Orlando eagerly.

"Yes," replied the cook, "I suppose so—I think, 'squire, instead of running after such a drab as Bet, you'd better help Miss out of her cage."

This was said merely at random; but Orlando's confusion was evident. He found that whatever removal Mrs. Lennard had projected and executed for her niece, she had not communicated her intentions, or the motives of them, to this servant, and probably not to any of the others.—His distracting suspense was now almost insupportable. He had promised his father to enquire after Philip; he was under the necessity of seeing Mrs. Rayland; and must pass some part of the day with his family. Thus circumstanced, it was impossible, unless he gained some immediate intelligence of Monimia, that he could acquaint her with the decision made in the course of the preceding day in regard to his departure for London—impossible to contrive a meeting, on which his hopes had so long dwelt, when he might reconcile her to his going, and offer her those vows of everlasting attachment which he meant most religiously to keep. It now occurred to him, that he would take his gun, and fire it on the side of the house that was next Mrs. Lennard's apartment, in hopes that Monimia might come to the window for the chance of seeing if it was he who fired.—Retiring therefore hastily from the kitchen, without seeming to attend to the raillery of the servant with whom he had been talking, he said there was a hawk about the park, which he had seen early that morning strike a young hare; and that he would endeavour to shoot it. He went then almost under the windows of Mrs. Lennard's room, and fired repeatedly, without obtaining what he wished for. At length he saw through the casement the figure of Monimia. He clasped his hands together, as if to entreat her stay, and to express the anguish he laboured under. She looked fearfully behind her, as if dreading her aunt—and then beckoned to him to approach. He flew under the window—she opened the casement, and said, while fear made her voice almost inarticulate, "My aunt suspects us, and has removed me into her closet—Come after it is dark under the window, and I will tell you farther."

"Gracious Heaven!" exclaimed Orlando, "I go from hence on Monday, and we shall meet then no more."

"I dare not stay," cried the trembling Monimia—"Pray, come as soon as it is dark!"

"To what purpose," exclaimed Orlando, "if I am only to see you thus? By Heaven I shall lose my senses!"

"Oh! if you knew," said Monimia, "what I have suffered, you would not terrify me now—For mercy's sake, go!" She then shut the window; and Orlando, not caring and hardly knowing what he did, went again round the house—half tempted to turn the mouth of his gun against himself. The wildness and distraction of his countenance struck one of the under keepers, who, believing he was really in pursuit of some bird of prey, came to offer his assistance. The impatience however of Orlando's answers, so unlike his general obliging manners, convinced the fellow that the report he had heard in the family was true, and that Orlando was in despair, because handsome Betty, as she was called among the servants, had left the family on his account. The young man loved Orlando, as did indeed every creature who approached him; and he now endeavoured to console him—"If I was you, Sir," said he, as he walked after him, "I would not take this to heart so much." "What!" cried Orlando peevishly, "take what to heart?"—"Why about this young woman," answered the keeper: "to be sure you parted, but perhaps all's for the best; who knows?"

Orlando, whose head and heart were full of Monimia, imagined that it was of her the man spoke; and turning hastily to him, he said in an eager, yet angry way—

"What is it you mean, Jacob, and what is for the best?"

"Nay, Sir," answered Jacob, "I only say, that worse might have come of it; for to my knowledge there have been a deal said, and the talk of the country sure enough it have been. There was t'other night at the Three Horse Shoes—there was three or four of us of the Hall, and John Dutton and Richard Williams at Mill, and Stokes and Smith, and some more—and so they were speaking of this here young body; and Stokes, who is a free spoken man, he said, says he"—"What scoundrel," exclaimed Orlando, enraged and thrown wholly off his guard, "what infamous lying scoundrel shall dare to traduce her?—I will tear the soul out of any rascal, who shall breathe even a suspicion against Monimia."

"Monimia, Sir!" cried the man, who was thunderstruck by the violence of Orlando, "Lord, I was speaking of Betty—she as went away this morning because of your keeping company with her—I'm sure, Sir, I never thought no harm of Miss Monimmy, nor scarce ever see her twice in my life."

Orlando now repented him of his rashness.—"Well, well," said he—"I believe you, Jacob—I'm sure you would not say or think any harm of an innocent young lady, especially, Jacob, if you thought it would displease me, and do me a great deal of harm."—Jacob now most earnestly protested not only his unwillingness to offend, but his desire to oblige his honour.—Orlando, whose spirits were yet in such a tumult, that he could not arrange the ideas that crowded on his mind, now bade Jacob follow him into his study. Unwilling as he had always been to put Monimia into the power of servants, he knew that something decisive must be hazarded, or that he must resign all hopes of seeing her before he went: he was the less scrupulous, as he was so soon to go, and he hoped he could make it this young man's interest to be faithful to him.—It occurred to him, that even when he was gone, some person must be in his confidence, who would receive, and deliver to Monimia, the letters which he knew he dared not direct to her at the Hall. This mistake therefore, which had for a moment vexed and confused him, he now thought a fortunate circumstance, and without farther reflection, disclosed to this young man his long affection for Monimia; the difficulties he was in at the present moment about seeing her; and his wish to find some means of corresponding with her hereafter. Jacob entered into his situation with an appearance of intelligence and interest with which Orlando was well satisfied. They agreed upon a plan for the evening—by which Orlando hoped to procure an interview with Monimia, instead of merely seeing her at the window; and elated with his hope, he forgot the hazard and impropriety of the means he had used to obtain it.

Having however talked over and settled every thing with his new confident, he went to pay his compliments to Mrs. Rayland, to whom he reported the arrival of his commission, and whom he found in the same disposition as when he last saw her—Then having obtained her leave to dine at his father's, he set out in pursuit of his brother, in hopes of carrying some intelligence to his family that might dissipate their uneasiness, of which his own did not render him unmindful. He rode therefore to Mr. Stockton's, where he learned from the servants, that Mr. Philip Somerive had been there about one o'clock; that he had borrowed linen of their master, with whom he staid till after a late dinner, and then had set out in a post-chaise, as he said, for London. This was information but little likely to quiet the uneasiness of his father and his family—with a heavy heart, therefore, Orlando proceeded to give it. Mr. Somerive received it with a deep sigh, but without any comment; his wife with tears; while the General, from whom they concealed nothing, endeavoured to console them by speaking light of it. "I am persuaded," said he, "my good friends, that your extreme solicitude and anxiety for your children often carry you beyond the line that dispassionate reason would mark for your conduct towards them."— Then addressing himself in his insinuating way to Mrs. Somerive, he added—"For example, now, my dear good friend—you no sooner hear that it is right for you to part with your younger son for the army, than you imagine that he will be killed. No sooner is your elder missing upon one of those little excursions, which a young man of high spirit, without any present employment, very naturally indulges himself in; than you figure to yourself I know not what evil consequence. Believe me, Orlando will not sleep in the bed of honour, nor our more eccentric Philip be devoured by the Philistines. Make yourselves easy, therefore, I beg of you. Your son is gone to London for four or five days perhaps—what then?—Here is your other son going with me—and we will make it our business to see Philip, if you will but make yourselves easy—and I dare say you will have him with you again, before you eat your Christmas dinner, safe and sound."

Mr. Somerive, who saw from sad experience the departure of Philip in a very different light, would not however dwell longer on a subject so affecting and so useless. It was of no avail to discuss now the reasons he had to dread the conduct of his eldest son, in this unexpected absence; nor did he wonder, for he had often seen it in others, at the composure with which General Tracy argued against the indulgence of uneasiness, which he himself could never feel; and he repeated to himself, as he longed to say to his friend, that it is easy to recommend patience with an untouched or insensible heart; patience in evils, that either can never reach the preacher, or which he is incapable of feeling.—Some lines of Shakespeare, applicable to the General's remonstrance, and the uneasy state of his thoughts, occurred to him as he walked into the garden to conceal those thoughts from his wife.

> "No, no! 'tis all men's office to speak patience
> To those that wring under a load of sorrow;
> But no man's virtue or sufficiency
> To be so moral, when he shall endure
> The like himself. Therefore give me no comfort."[1]

END OF THE SECOND VOLUME.

---

[1] *Much Ado About Nothing*, V.i.27–31. Smith amends Shakespeare's word "counsel" to "comfort."

VOL. III.

War is a game, which were their subjects wise,
Kings should not play at. Nations would do well
T'extort their truncheons from the puny hands
Of heroes, whose infirm and baby minds
Are gratified with mischief, and who spoil,
Because men suffer it, their toy the world.

COWPER.[1]

---

[1] *The Task* (1785), V. 187–192. William Cowper (1731–1800) was one of Smith's most admired contemporaries, not the least by Smith herself. She dedicated her long poem *The Emigrants* (1793) to him, describing him as "one of the few, who, at the present period, rescue [Britain] from the imputation of having degenerated in Poetical talents …" (see Curran, p. 133).

CHAP. I.

Orlando could not, though he attempted it, conceal the anguish of his heart during the day; for though he had arranged with his new confident the means of seeing Monimia, it was far from certain these plans would succeed; or, could he be content with the means which he had used, however desirable the end—Monimia, who, while she yielded to his earnest entrèaties, had always felt, from the natural rectitude of her under-standing, the impropriety of their clandestine correspondence, would, he feared, be more than ever sensible of her indiscretion, when she found that servant was entrusted with it—and on thinking over what had passed between him and the under keeper, he found more reason to entertain a good opinion of his acuteness than of his integrity.—When to these reflections were added the certainty of his immediate departure, and the uncertainty of his return; the mournful looks of his mother, who could not behold him without tears; the deep, but more silent sorrow marked on the countenance of his father, and the pensive expression of regret on those of his sisters; he could with difficulty go through the forms of a melancholy dinner, at which the General in vain attempted to call off the attention of his hosts to subjects of common conversation, and to divert them from private misery by those public topics which then interested none of them. The expulsion of the Americans from the province of Canada, which had happened the preceding August; and the victory gained by the British fleet near Crown Point against a small number of their gondolas and galleys, in the course of the following October, successes of which exaggerated official accounts were just received, were matters whereon the General triumphantly descanted, and on which he obtained more attention from his audience, because he asserted very posi-tively that, in consequence of these amazing advantages, the whole conti-nent of America would submit, and the troops of course return as soon as they had chastised the insolent colonists sufficiently for their rebel-lion.—Orlando then, he assured his family, was not at all likely to join his regiment, which would almost immediately be ordered home; but would be the safe soldier of peace, and perhaps return to them in a few weeks, no otherwise altered than by his military air and a cockade. The only smile that was seen the whole day on the faces of any of the family was visible on that of Mrs. Somerive, on the General's description of an American flight, though none had a more tender heart or a more liberal mind: but having heard only one side of the question, and having no time or inclination to investigate political matters, she now believed that the Americans were a set of rebellious exiles, who refused, on false pretences, "the tribute to Caesar,"[1] which she had been taught by scriptural authority ought to be paid. Thus considering them, she rejoiced in their defeat, and was insensible of their misery; though, had not the new profession of Orlando called forth her fears for him, she would probably never have thought upon the subject at all—a subject with which, at that time, men not in parliament and their families supposed they had nothing to do. They saw not the impossibility of enforcing in another country the very imposts to which, unrepresented, they would not themselves have submitted. Elate with national pride, they had learned by the successes of the preceding war to look with contempt on the inhabitants of every other part of the globe; and even on their colonists, men of their own country—little imagining that, from their spirited resistance,

> "The child would rue that was unborn
> The *taxing* of that day."[2]

At length the hour arrived when Orlando obtained permission to return to the Hall: he told his father, that as he meant to take leave of Mrs. Rayland that night, in order to pass the greater part of Sunday with his family, it was necessary to pay her this last compliment. Mr. Somerive acceded to the necessity he urged; but, at parting from him, fixed his eyes on those of his son, with a look which expressed solicitude, sorrow, and pity. It questioned his sincerity, and yet seemed not to reproach him. Orlando could not bear it: he hurried away, and rode as speedily as he could to the Hall; where he sent up for leave to wait on Mrs. Rayland to tea, and then went in search of Jacob, who easily found a pretence for attending him in his Study. Orlando with a palpitating heart questioned him: "Have you," cried he, "discovered any means by which I can obtain access to Monimia, or get her down stairs, without the knowledge of Mrs. Lennard?"

---

[1] From the Gospel of St. Mark, 12.17. Mrs. Rayland expects the colonists to pay willingly a tithe, which, as landlord, she also expects from her tenants.

[2] Smith slightly rewrites lines from *The Ballad of Chevy Chase* (15th century): "The child may rue that is unborne/ The hunting of that day!" The ballad focuses on a feud between the families of Percy and Douglas. In the subsequent battle, both Percy and Douglas are killed. Smith comments on the futility and uselessness of war and by implication describes Britain and America as related; her substitution of "taxing" for "hunting" shows her awareness of the root cause of the American Revolution: taxation without representation.

"Faith, Sir," answered the man, "'tis no easy task as your honour have set me, I can tell you—However, I've contrived to speak to Miss—"

"Have you?" cried Orlando eagerly: "there's an excellent fellow. And what does she say?"

"Aye, Sir," replied Jacob, "that's the thing. She was in a sad twitter when she know'd you had told me, and said it was impossible to do what you desired—for the room where she sleeps is a closet within Madam Lennard's, hardly big enough to hold a bed: but it is an impossible thing to get out of a night after Madam's in bed, by reason that her room doors are locked; and for the window, it is barred up with a long iron bar; so that if Miss had courage to get down a ladder, she could not get out—or if she did, she could never get back again. Her aunt, she says, finds her being there vastly inconvenient; and, as soon as you are gone, reckons to send her back to her own room."

"I shall be driven out of my senses," exclaimed Orlando, as he traversed the room: "if I cannot see her before I go, I shall be distracted—How did you obtain admittance to her? Cannot I speak to her by the same means?"—"Why hardly; for you must know that I was forced to get one of the maids to help me. The new house-maid that Madam have hired this morning upon trial, is an old acquaintance of mine; I gave her an item of the matter, and so she contrived to take me up to mend the window-shutter, which she had broke on purpose; and bid me I should take a hammer and nails, and make a clatter if Madam Lennard came. I took care to make my job long enough; and when the old house-keeper ax'd me what I was a doing, I had an excuse you know pat, and it passed off very well; and not only so, but she said to me, says she—"When you have done that job, Jacob, I wish you would just look at the wainscot under the window, and under them there drawers of mine; for it's as rotten as touchwood, and the rats are for ever coming in," says she; and says she, "I never saw the like of this old house—it will tumble about our ears, I reckon, one day or 'nother, and yet my lady is always repairing it," says she; "but the wainscoting of this here end of the wing," says she, "has been up above an hundred years; and we may patch it, and patch it, and yet be never the nearer: but, for my part, I suppose it will last my time," says she."

Orlando no sooner heard that another person, the new house-maid, had been incautiously admitted to participate a secret which he had hitherto so anxiously guarded, than his vexation conquered the pleasure he had for a moment indulged, in learning that it was possible for another, and therefore for him, to see Monimia. To the latter part of the game-keeper's oration he could not attend, occupied with the idea of the new uneasiness this circumstance must give to Monimia; and agitated by innumerable fears and anxieties, he remained a moment silent after his companion had ceased to speak, and then said—"She told you, I think, that after I was gone, her aunt would suffer her to return to her former apartment?"

"Yes, that was what she said."

"Well, then, I will go. Indeed I am going by day-break to-morrow. Nay, I am going from this house to-night; and therefore I shall take leave of Mrs. Rayland this evening." He paused a moment, and then added, "I suppose it is possible to convey a letter to Monimia, though I despair of seeing her?"

"O Lord! yes, Sir, that you may do for certain; for I told her, that if she would let down a letter for you by a string at seven o'clock, I would be there to take it; and you might send her one back the same way."

"What is it o'clock now?" cried Orlando.

"Almost six, Sir."

"It is time then for me to go to my appointment with Mrs. Rayland, whose tea I am afraid is ready. Do you be punctual to seven o'clock; and, if I can escape, I will be with you at the window. But I beseech you, Jacob, to remember, that all the obligation I shall owe you on this occasion will be cancelled, if you are not secret. I wish you had not mentioned this matter to any other person, especially to a woman—You know they are not to be trusted."

"Aye! that I know well enough; they'll cackle, I know they will, if life and death depended upon it: but, Lord! Sir, how a-name of fortune was I to get at Miss, unless I had done so? and I do believe Nanny is as trusty as most."

It was equally useless to argue on the necessity of the measure, or the discretion of Nanny. The die was cast; and to meet Monimia safely after so much hazard had been incurred, was all that it would now answer any purpose to think of. Orlando, during his short conference with his own thoughts, had determined to take that night his last leave of Mrs. Rayland, and to say to her before Mrs. Lennard, that he was to set out the next morning early, with General Tracy, for London. He hoped, by thus acting, to persuade the aunt of Monimia that she might safely send her back to her former apartment; and that by making an appointment with her for Sunday, when he would by the people at the Hall be believed on his way to London, he should enjoy without inter-ruption the melancholy pleasure of bidding her adieu, and settling the safest method for their future correspondence.

For this purpose he wrote to her; and sealing the letter, he put it into his pocket and repaired to Mrs. Rayland; who, understanding he was come to take his leave, received him with great solemnity, yet not with less kindness than usual.

Her conversation consisted chiefly of good advice. She declaimed against the vitiated state of modern manners, and related how much better things were in her time. She warned him to beware of the gamesters and bad women, who, she said, were the ruin of all young people; and gave him, though obliquely, to understand, that his future favour with her depended on his behaviour in this his first appearance in life.

With her the age of chivalry did not seem to be passed; for she appeared to consider Orlando as a Damoisell, now about to make his first essay in arms.[1] Indeed, while she talked much of modern immorality and dissipation, she knew very little of modern manners, seldom seeing any of those people who are what is called people of the world; and forming her ideas of what was passing in it, only from newspapers and the Lady's Magazine, or some such publication, which excited only wonder and disgust—while her recollection came to her relief, and carried her back to those days she herself remembered—and with still greater pleasure to the relations her father had given of what passed in his. The freedom of modern life suited so ill with the solemnity of respect that was shown towards her in her youth, that she shrunk from the uneasiness it gave her, and made around her a world of her own: of which when Orlando became an inhabitant, all that regarded him was assimilated to her own antediluvian notions.

In answer to her long and sage lecture, Orlando assured her, and with great sincerity, that he had no wishes that were not centered in the spot and neighbourhood he was about to leave: that, new as he was to the world, he yet believed it would offer him no objects that could a moment detach his affections from his family and friends. There was so much earnestness, and something so impressive in the manner of his saying this, as not only enforced belief, but sensibly affected Mrs. Rayland. She almost repented that she had ever consented to his going; but to detain him now without acknowledgeing him as her heir (which she had determined never to do), was not to be thought of; and General Tracy had succeeded in convincing her, not only that it was a justice due to her young rela-

---

[1]   A damoisell, more usually spelled "damoiseau," is a young noble not yet made a knight. While both forms are archaic, Smith uses a spelling that not only indicates Mrs. Rayland's attachment to a feudal system, but also threatens to make Orlando over in Mrs. Rayland's image: that is, transform him into a "damsel."

tion to give him an opportunity of seeing more of mankind; but that, as he would not quit England, he would enjoy all the advantages of an honourable profession, without losing the advantage of her protection. Without giving implicit credit to the tales by which Pattenson attempted to prejudice him in her favour, she thought enough of them to let them influence in some degree her determination; and she believed that, if he had formed any improper attachment, nothing was so likely to break it as sending him from the country, and into scenes of life which would, she supposed, occupy his mind without injuring his morals.

It seemed as if towards the close of her life Mrs. Rayland had acquired, instead of losing, her sensibility; for she, who had hardly loved any body, now found that she could not without pain part from Orlando. She felt her pride and pleasure equally interested in exerting towards him that generosity, which from the rest of his family she had withheld; and the apparent dejection of his spirits, the reluctance with which he left the Hall, made him appear to her more worthy than ever of her favour. When therefore she had exhausted every topic of advice she could think of, and received from the manly simplicity of his answers, all the assurances that words could give of his gratefully receiving it, she presented him with a bank-note of two hundred and fifty pounds; which she told him was for the purpose of purchasing what he would have occasion for on his first entrance into the army. She had, however, so little idea of modern expences, that she really considered this as a very great sum, and such as it was an amazing effort of generosity to part with: yet, while she made this exertion, her kindness towards him was so far from being exhausted, that she told him he should find her always his banker, so long as he continued to give her reason to think of him as she thought now.

Orlando kissed the hand of his ancient benefactress; but the tears were in his eyes, and he was unable to speak. He tried, however, to thank her for this last, and for all her former favours to him: but the words were inarticulate; and the old lady herself, "albeit unused to the melting mood,"[1] was now so much affected, that she could only faintly utter the blessing she gave him. "You had better not say any more, Sir," said Mrs. Lennard, who seemed disposed to weep too—"much better not, for indeed it will make my lady quite out of spirits." Orlando, very willing to shorten such a scene, turned to Mrs. Lennard, towards whom in

---

[1] *Othello*, V.ii.359. See also note 1, p. 84. Both Mrs. Lennard and Mrs. Rayland have *Othello*—the tragic romance—as their emotional reference point.

a few hurried words he expressed his thanks for her past kindness, and his wishes for her health and happiness; and then hastened away, his heart oppressed by the scene that had passed, yet bearing tumultuously with the thoughts of that which was to come.

He hardly dared, however, give himself time to think. He had told Mrs. Rayland a falsehood, for which his ingenuous heart already smote him. He was about to act in direct violation of all he had promised, and all she expected of him. He knew that, were he detected lingering about the house, after what he had just said of his intentions of leaving it immediately, he should lose for ever all the advantage of that favour which Mrs. Rayland now so openly avowed for him; and that, if his attachment to Monimia were known, it would excite more anger and resentment than almost any of the errors against which she had been warning him. But all these considerations, strongly as they ought to have operated against any other indiscreet indulgence, were powerless when put in competition with his tender affection for Monimia; and to leave her without being able to speak to her and console her, was what he could not for a moment have endured to think of, if poverty, disgrace, and exile from every other human being had been the alternatives.

On entering his room, he found it wanted only a few moments of seven. He glided therefore round the house, and found his punctual confident already waiting for the signal. "We need not both be here," said Orlando: "Go, Jacob, and wait for me in my room: I have asked leave for you to go with me to-night to carry a portmanteau to West Wolverton." Jacob obeyed; and Orlando, almost breathless with fear lest he should be disappointed in this his forlorn hope, waited under the window.

The casement at length softly opened, and Monimia appeared at it. He spoke to her, and bade her let down the string for a letter, "on the success of which," said he, "more than my life depends.—Read it then, Monimia, read it quickly, and give me an answer."

The trembling girl, whose hurry of spirits alone supported her, now hastened away with the letter; and, in an instant, threw down a piece of paper on which she had written with a pencil—"If I am suffered to go back to my own room to-night, I will be ready on the usual signal; but, if I am not, I cannot write. If I am not, farewell, Orlando—farewell for ever; for I shall be too wretched to make it possible for me to live. Remember, dear Orlando, your poor friend! and may you be very happy, whatever becomes of me! Go, now, for heaven's sake!—I am sure my aunt will be here in a few moments: and all depends upon her believing you gone."

As it was too dark for Orlando to discern these words, he was compelled to go back to his own room to read them. The doubt they left upon his mind distracted him; but it was a doubt which, if he attempted to remove it, would become a certainty that would destroy this faint ray of hope. He went back, however, to the window, in hopes that he might yet speak one word to Monimia; but he saw that there was now another candle in the room; and, retiring a little farther so as to be able to see more of it, he distinctly saw Mrs. Lennard walking in the room, and apparently busied in the usual occupations to which she dedicated Saturday nights. To stay, therefore, was not only useless but dangerous; and he thought it better to make a great bustle in going, that all the inhabitants of the Hall might be apprised of his absence. He sent Jacob into the kitchen to give some farther orders about forwarding his trunks and baggage to the next market-town, as they were to be sent to London by the waggon; and then, mournfully and reluctantly, prepared to leave the room where he had passed so many happy hours—the room where his mind first tasted the charms of literature, and his heart of love. It was indeed possible that he might once more revisit it, once more that evening with Monimia; but it was also possible, perhaps most probable, that he might not see her again.

A thousand painful reflections presented themselves. He left her exposed to numberless inconveniencies; and his late rashness, had, perhaps, added to them by putting her into the power of servants. Yet he might be denied an opportunity to put her upon her guard against any of the circumstances he foresaw, or even to settle how she might receive his letters.

He traversed the library, yielding to these tormenting thoughts; and, by the light of the solitary candle he had set down in the window seat, every thing appeared gloomy and terrific. Every object and every sound seemed to repeat the sentence that constantly occurred to him— "Orlando will revisit this house no more!" It is difficult to say how long he would have indulged this mournful reverie (notwithstanding his resolution just before taken to quit the house with as much noise as possible), if he had not been alarmed by the sound of a female step in the adjoining parlour. He started. It was perhaps Monimia! He flew to the door; and there, with too evident marks of disappointment in his countenance, he discovered it to be Mrs. Lennard herself, who, with a candle in her hand, and much perpendicular dignity in her air, stalked into the Study—"I am glad, Mr. Orlando, you are not yet gone, for I have a message from my Lady." Orlando would have faced a cannon with less trepidation than he waited for this message, which his conscience told him might relate to Monimia. It proved, however, to be only that he would give to Lennard the keys of the rooms; and that she might see the window safe and barred. To this, though it disappointed him wholly of his hopes of meeting Monimia there, it was impossible to object. The cautious house-keeper, therefore, barricaded every avenue to this apartment, without forgetting the door that led to the chapel; and then formally enquiring if Orlando had taken out every thing he wished to have, to which he answered Yes (as his boxes had been moved the preceding day), she said she would follow him; and he left the room with an additional pang, while Mrs. Lennard locked the door and marched solemnly after him.

Towards the middle of the great parlour, through which they were passing, he stopped, and said in a voice that betrayed his emotion— "You will be so good, dear Madam, to assure Mrs. Rayland of my grateful respects, and to accept yourself a repetition of my good wishes."

"Thank you, Sir," answered the lady, "I am sure I wish you very well: but now, Mr. Orlando, since we part friends—"

"I hope we *always* were friends, Madam," said Orlando, attempting to smile, and turn the discourse, which he feared tended to the subject he most dreaded.

"I hope so too, Sir; but I must say, that I am afraid in regard to that girl, my niece, there has been some wrong doings. It was not right in you, Mr. Orlando, I must say, to hold a secret correspondence with her, which I am very sure you did by means of that sad slut Betty, who latterly has been always giving me hints of it: but I, who did not think Monimia so cunning and artful, did not understand them; and, even to this day, I cannot imagine how you contrived so often to talk to her out of the window, without being seen or heard. However, it's all over now, I hope; and I am willing to let it be forgot as a childish frolic. When you return here, Sir, you will by that time have seen too much of the world to think about such a chit as Monimia—if, indeed, she should happen to be here so long."

Orlando, divided between his joy to find that the real avenue by which they had conversed was unknown, and the pain the last hint gave him, knew not what to reply; but, confused and hesitating, he stammered out a sentence which Mrs. Lennard did not give him time to finish—"Come, come, Mr. Orlando," said she, "I know you are above any false representations: besides, I assure you, you cannot take an old bird with chaff—However, as I said before, there is an end of the matter—I shall take care of young Madam here; and I dare say you will find plenty of ladies where you are going, better worth looking after."

Orlando, utterly unable to answer this raillery, now wished her once more health and happiness; and said (again vainly attempting to appear unconcerned)—"I really do not love to contradict ladies, my dear Mrs. Lennard! so you must have your own way, however your suspicions may wrong me." He then hastened away to mount his horse, with which Jacob waited for him at the door of the servants' hall that opened towards the stables:—but as he passed through, he found all the servants assembled at it to take leave of him. Even Pattenson was there; but, by the expression of his air and manner, with very different sentiments from the rest—for they all testified their concern; while the old butler, with a contemptuous sneer on his countenance, appeared to be delighted by his departure.

At once flattered and pained by the good wishes and prayers for his prosperity with which they crowded around him, while most of the women shed tears, Orlando spoke kindly to each of them, assured them that he should rejoice in any good that might befal them; "But," added he, "I hope, my kind friends, we do not part for a great length of time, and that on my return I shall find you all here, unless any of you lasses should be carried off by good husbands." Then again wishing them all well, he mounted his horse; and Jacob following, he rode away from the Hall—but not with a design of going to the house of his father; he rather meant to linger about the woods till the hour when he thought there was a chance of his finding Monimia once more in the turret.

CHAP. II.

Orlando, already repenting, though he hardly knew why, that he had told the game-keeper so much, was very unwilling to entrust him with more. He had not so exactly described the way of his communication with Monimia, as to enable any other person to find it; and he wished rather to recall than to increase the confidence he had placed in a man of whom he knew very little, and who might perhaps make an ill use of his confidence. A new difficulty therefore arose: he knew not what to do with Jacob and the horses, which he now repented that he had used. If he sent them on to his father's, it would be suspected by a family who were every hour looking out for him, that he had staid behind with Monimia: if he left them in the wood, the man would probably be discontented; and if he sent them to an alehouse near the mill at the extremity of the park, Pattenson (who was the great friend and patron of the man who kept it) or some of the other servants might be there, whose enquiries could neither be satisfied nor evaded. Determined however as he was to open his heart to his father before his last adieu, he, after some deliberation, resolved to send them home; and he thought the enquiries his father would make, would give him a good opportunity to put an end (at least as far as he could) to a mystery of which he felt ashamed, as unworthy of himself, and of the object of his affection.—Thus resolved, he told the game-keeper he meant to return back to the Hall, in the hope of seeing Monimia for five minutes; and that he should go to West Wolverton with his horse and portmanteau, whither he would himself follow in about two hours, as he should tell his father, if he asked after him, on hearing or seeing the horses arrive without him.

The man obeyed; and Orlando, making a circuit through the woods, in order to return to the Hall by the least frequented way, and to have as little of the open part of the park to cross as possible, arrived once more at the mansion which he had so lately quitted as for the last time.—He walked very slowly on purpose; and his thoughts were such as brought with them only dejection and sorrow.

He could not help recollecting with regret, those hours, now gone for ever, when, in his early youth, he traversed these paths—happy in the present, and thoughtless of the future;—when he had no passion to torment, no fears for its object to depress him; but went to Monimia with the same simple eagerness as any of his sisters or his other playfellows, and was unconscious that the rest of their lives would be embittered with anxiety and disappointment—perhaps remorse.—Orlando already felt something like it: with the most candid and ingenuous temper he had lived some time in a course of deception—he had taught it to the innocent, unsuspecting Monimia, and had sullied the native candour and integrity of her character. The sophistry by which he had formerly prevailed upon her to consent to their clandestine meetings, now seemed mean and contemptible; but perhaps, in thinking thus, Orlando was too much like other transgressors, who repent because they can sin no more.

He thought himself, however, firmly determined that, had he staid at the Hall, he would, at whatever hazard, act with more openness; but as he was going from it, there could be no harm in this last adieu. In writing to Monimia there could be nothing wrong, especially as he meant not to make a secret of it to his father and Selina, nor indeed to any of his own family: while the peculiarities of Mrs. Rayland, and the watchful malignity of Mrs. Lennard, seemed fully to justify his not revealing to them what would be so hazardous to Monimia and to himself.

Amid these disquieting and contradictory reflections, he at last reached the Hall. It was the darkest of December nights, but calm and still. Orlando walked slowly round the house, which, save a glimmering light from the window of Mrs. Lennard's room, bore no appearance of being inhabited. His longing eyes, which had anxiously watched for some consoling beam from the turret, whither they had so often been turned with transport, now sought for the propitious ray in vain. Still it was possible Monimia might be there, but, from her aunt's late suspicions, deprived of a light. As the house seemed perfectly quiet, he ventured up to the well-known door, and, listening awhile, tapped at it; no answer was given!—he repeated the signal louder; still no delicious sounds were heard in return!—and, convinced at length that his project had wholly failed, and Monimia was still a prisoner, he became half frantic, from the reflection that he had hazarded their secret in vain: he had in vain imagined a finesse, and asserted a falsehood, and perhaps must at last go without seeing her, his heart torn at once by his own sufferings and by the idea of hers.

In stepping back to return down the stairs, when after a long stay all hope had forsaken him, his foot struck something before him, which seemed to be a parcel: as not a ray of light entered the place where he was, he felt for this with his hands, and, at length finding it, he discovered it to be a small book: it was tied with a packthread; and Orlando immediately supposed, what was indeed the truth, that Monimia, not being permitted to return that evening to sleep in her former apartment, had, however, on some pretence or other entered it, and deposited at the door that book, which contained a letter. He opened the book with trembling hands, and found what he expected by the seal; but to read it was impossible, where he had no means of procuring light: he therefore put it into his pocket as eagerly as if he was afraid somebody would take it from him, and then ran towards home; where, hardly feeling the ground as he went, he arrived, in a state of mind so uneasy and confused, that he no longer was capable of caution or reserve; but hastening into the kitchen, where he first perceived a light, he snatched up a candle without speaking, and was hurrying with it to his own room, when his father, who had been anxiously watching his arrival, opened the door through which he was preparing to pass up stairs; and seeing him pale and breathless, his eyes wild, and his hair dishevelled, he concluded that something very terrible had happened to his brother.—The rash, unthinking ,and vehement character of Philip, his wild profusion, and unsettled principles, had of late so harassed the imagination of his father, that he now thought only of his committing suicide; and the sudden appearance of Orlando, in such an agitated state, struck him with the idea that this fatal event had happened—"Almighty God!" cried he, as he seized the arm of Orlando, who, muttering something, would have passed to his room—"Almighty God! what I have dreaded has happened."—Orlando, who thought at that moment only of Monimia, and was impatient at every interruption, was, however, so struck with this exclamation, and with the look of anguish that accompanied it, that he stopped, and, with terror equal to that with which he had been addressed, cried, "What, my dear Sir! for Heaven's sake what has happened? My mother, my sisters!"—"Oh, your brother!" interrupted Mr. Somerive—"tell me the worst at once, it cannot be more dreadful than my fears represent it."—"Indeed, Sir, I know nothing of my brother; nothing has happened to him that I know of—I hope you have heard nothing?"

"No!" cried Mr. Somerive, a little recovering from his apprehension. "Speak low, Orlando; I would not for the world alarm your mother, who is in bed:—but your looks, your haste, your staying out, and your sudden appearance, gave me I know not what idea, that some dreadful accident had happened to poor Philip."

"Dear Sir," replied Orlando, "you will really destroy yourself, if you give way to such horrible apprehensions; Philip, I am persuaded, is well.—Pray compose yourself; I am extremely sorry I alarmed you, and be you will make yourself easy."

"Ah! Orlando," said Mr. Somerive as he sat down in the parlour, whither he desired his son to follow him—"ah, Orlando! you relieve me from one misery only to plunge me into another, less insupportable indeed, but still most painful to me.—What is the meaning, my dear boy, of these haggard looks, of this disordered manner, of these late walks, and this breathless return? Some mystery hangs over your actions, which cannot but be injurious, since those actions, were they not such as your own conscience condemns, need not be concealed from your family—from your father!"

"They shall not, Sir!" replied Orlando warmly—"I will not leave you in doubt about my conduct; you will find nothing in it that need make you blush for your son: spare me but this one night, and to-morrow there shall not be a wish of my heart concealed from you."

"Alas, poor boy!" said Mr. Somerive tenderly, "I guess but too much of them already:—but, Orlando, I depend upon your integrity; I have never known it deceive me. Go, therefore, now—and let me not see to-morrow that wild and unsettled look, that pale countenance, and so many symptoms of suffering, which I, my son, see but too plainly, and yet dare hardly say I pity, for fear I should encourage what I ought to condemn." Then, with a deep sigh, he added, "Good night, dear Orlando! I will go and endeavour to compose myself, or at least conceal from your mother the uneasiness that devours me.—Ah, my child! many and many nights I do not close my eyes: the sad image of Philip, bringing ruin on himself, on my wife, and on my poor girls, haunts me eternally; and then, Orlando, when my expectation rests on you, when I think that I have another son who will protect and support them when I am gone—for I feel that I shall not live long—then the apprehension of some fatal entanglement that will ruin all our hopes, comes over my heavy heart; and I see nothing for my wife, and my dear girls, but poverty and despair."

"Oh! this is too much," cried Orlando; "I cannot indeed bear it—What shall I say—what shall I swear, to quiet these distracting apprehensions?— Good God, Sir! what have I ever done, what selfish actions have I ever been guilty of, which could lead my father to suppose that, to gratify myself, I would abandon my dear—my affectionate mother, or forget the interest of my sweet sisters?"—"Nay, Orlando, you never have given me reason for such a supposition; but let us talk of it no more—once more, good night!" Orlando then kissed his father's hand, and left him. Eagerly he tore open the letter, which had already, from his excessive impatience, occasioned to him so much pain. It contained these few words:—

"My aunt refused to let me return to my former room this night, and you well know I dared not press it; I could obtain no more than permission to go thither for half an hour to put it to rights, as she has told me I shall go back to it to-morrow; and I use that opportunity to leave this letter, inclosed in a book, which I hope you will not miss. Orlando, if you go to-morrow, we shall meet no more!—But as you mentioned not setting out till Monday morning, I flatter myself that if that is so, you will not go without seeing me: at all events I will be in the great pond-wood between four and five to-morrow evening; and will wait on the old bench not far from the boat house. I will not say what I shall suffer till you come, if indeed you do come: but be not uneasy for me, for my aunt will have no doubt of your being quite out of the country by to-morrow, and therefore will let me go out to walk without any questions. If you can come, I shall not expect to find an answer at my door.—If you cannot—But, indeed, Orlando, my trembling hand, and the tears that fall upon the paper, prevent my saying any more. I cannot write a farewell to you!—But if I never should see you again, do not forget me, Orlando!—And may God bless you, and make you happy!"

The paper was indeed blistered, and some of the words almost obliterated, by the tears that had mingled with the ink. Orlando kissed these marks of tender sensibility a thousand and a thousand times: he laid the precious paper to his heart, and believed the talisman abated its throbbing; then took it to read again, and endeavoured to calm his spirits with the assurance that he should meet the adored writer of it, and repeat an hundred times protestations of tenderness which he never felt more forcibly than now. But as soon as his disquieting apprehensions about Monimia, and his fears of not seeing her, were appeased, the scene he had just passed through with his father recurred with more acute pain to his mind: he had promised to reveal the secret which was already suspected; but, though he firmly adhered to this resolution, surely his father would not insist upon his promise to give up all thoughts of Monimia—That he felt to be a promise which he could not make—his whole heart recoiled from it. Ah! why was it thus impossible to reconcile his duty and his love; and why should his attachment to Monimia be inconsistent with the attention his family would have a right to—if—if his father should die?—The very idea of his father's death was insupportable; and yet he was going from him, and could not watch his health, or contribute to his comfort. Thus wretched Orlando tried in vain to sleep—his blood throbbed tumultuously in his veins; his heart seemed too big for his bosom; by carrying his thoughts to the dreadful parting of the next day, he was rendered incapable of tasting any present repose; and day appeared before his troubled thoughts had so wearied his frame as to allow him to fall into unquiet slumber. Even in his short and disturbed sleep, tormenting visions assailed him—he saw the funeral of his father, who yet appeared living, or at least appearing to him, though dead—and pointing with one hand to his mother and his sisters, while with the other he waved him away from Monimia, who, at a distance, seemed to sit dejected and alone, in a wild and dreary scene, where birds of prey screamed around her—from which she endeavoured to escape towards Orlando, and held out her hands to him for help in vain. A repetition of these unformed horrors took away all inclination to sleep. At seven o'clock Orlando left his bed, more dejected than ever he felt before; and dreading the dialogue that must ensue, he joined his father, who was walking, melancholy and alone, in the garden.

CHAP. III.

Somerive received his son with tenderness; but his dejection was but too visible. Orlando approached him with apprehension, and his voice trembled as he spoke the salutation of the morning. They traversed a long gravel walk twice before either of them spoke again. At length Mr. Somerive asked Orlando, if he had seen his mother and sisters? He answered, that he believed they had not yet left their chambers; and another painful silence ensued, which neither of them seemed to have resolution to break.

At length Mr. Somerive said, "This, Orlando, is the last day we shall pass together for some time—let it not be clouded by dissimulation on your part; it shall not be so with remonstrance on mine: but my advice you will hear, since indeed, my son, it is for your sake, not my own, I give it—I shall soon be out of the reach of all the evils of this world!"

"Do not talk so, dear Sir!" exclaimed Orlando, seizing his father's hand; "do not, I beseech you!—Such gloomy presentiments will over-cloud this day with more pain for me, than your severest remonstrance. Pray think more cheerfully; you are yet but in the middle of life; you have a constitution naturally good; and you may yet many years see around you a family who idolize their father."

"No, Orlando!" cried Somerive interrupting him, "it will not be. Your brother, on whom my first hopes were fixed, he has inflicted the wound which, from long irritation, is become incurable; and where—alas! Where is this family so fondly beloved?—Philip is gone! for I see that nothing can save him—My eldest daughter is married into another kingdom, where I can never see her—And you, Orlando, you are now going from me: I am not superstitious, but I feel something like an assurance that we part to-day for ever; or if I am so favoured by Providence as to embrace you again, will you be the same after having entered the world; will you bring back to me the excellent heart, the ingenuous temper, the integrity of principle that has hitherto made me glory in my son?"

Orlando, who expected a very different opening to this conversation, warmly repeated his protestations, that nothing should make him forget the duty he owed his father—the affection he felt for his family. "Ah, Sir!" cried he, "if you knew how little is to be apprehended from the world, where the whole heart is already absorbed in attachment, contracted in the early dawn of life, and interwoven with the very existence, you would not feel these fears, nor wound me with these doubts."

"*I* have lived near fifty years, Orlando; you have not yet finished your twenty-first. I have seen, though passing in obscurity much of my time—I have seen young men set out in life uncorrupted, and apparently endowed with every noble principle that could render them honours to their country or their families; yet, in a very few years, I have seen them, either hardened by ambition, or degraded by debauchery, not unfrequently combining both; and if they have interest, pursuing the one only as the means of indulging in the other."

"It is very true, Sir," answered Orlando:"but the ambition of a soldier is surely glorious ambition; it leads to honour through hardship and danger; and he who follows his profession earnestly, can have little time for the sallies of irregularity."

"You are to be a soldier of *peace*, Orlando; but I will do you justice, I do not believe you will disappoint my hopes by becoming a gamester or a libertine."

"No, Sir!" said Orlando vehemently."To be the first I have no inclination, and for the second you have a security which I am sure you will believe infallible—I promised you last night that I would open my whole heart to you; dare I now then solicit your patience while I acquit myself of what I hold to be an indispensable duty, and speak with that sincerity to you, which I have reproached myself for ever neglecting to observe, though indeed it was not always possible?"

"I attend," said Mr. Somerive in a grave and low voice:"I would not, Orlando, touch upon this subject, because I wished to see if you had candour and resolution to speak when you might have evaded it."

Orlando, whose momentary courage already failed him, now half repented that he had said so much—now shrunk from the unworthy idea of concealing any thing. He began then in a low and tremulous tone; and while his heart throbbed with a thousand painful emotions; he related to his father the whole progress of his passion, even from his first recollection of the time when he began to love Monimia better than any of his sisters; when, in going to the Hall, he thought more of seeing her than of the amusements in which he was indulged, and often refused to ride out on a horse Mrs. Rayland allowed him occasionally to have when he was about eleven years old, or to go to play with the men in the park; because, at the hours when these recreations were offered him, he had opportunities of sitting with Monimia, who was employed by her aunt to pick cowslips from their stalks, to collect rose leaves, or dry flowers and herbs in the housekeeper's room. He concealed nothing from his father that happened in the progress of his love; and as his timidity gradually vanished, he spoke of her with all the enthusiasm and all the tenderness of passion. His father sighed more deeply than he did as he proceeded in his story; when he ceased speaking, remained a moment silent; and then, with another long-drawn sigh, he said, "I have always suspected something of this sort; but my conjectures were short of the truth.—If I had known, Orlando, that the Hall contained so dangerous an inmate, not all the hopes that have been raised by Mrs. Rayland's partiality to you, should have induced me to have suffered your residence there."

"Good God! Sir," exclaimed the young man, "can you call an angel dangerous? Oh say rather that my Monimia will prove to me a guardian seraph!—In thinking of her, I find my mind elevated, and purified—I live only for her—I wish only to live worthy of her."

"Just now, Orlando, you talked of living only for your family—for your mother—for your sisters; and now this angel is the only object of your future life!—An angel! every idle boy that reads ballads or writes them, every scribbler that sends his rhymes to a magazine, calls the nymph who inspires him an angel; and such an angel is this Monimia of yours! and from such sort of reading you have learned to fancy yourself in love with her. The niece of Lennard is the last person in the world whom I would wish you to elect, and ..."

"And why the niece of Lennard, Sir?" said Orlando somewhat impatiently—"surely my father is too liberal to confound their merits. Poor Monimia! She is indeed the niece of Lennard; but, believe me, she does not in any instance resemble her—And what is her birth? does it render her less amiable, less lovely?"

"Oh, softly!" cried Somerive, interrupting him in his turn, "I have not the least doubt, Orlando, but that you could prove in a moment that this seraphic damsel is not only the most perfect of human beings, but the better for belonging to a woman who has always stood between me and the countenance of my relation; a woman who, in all probability, will finally rob me of my birth-right.—Unhappy, ill-starred boy! Do you not see that, by this misplaced attachment, you have put it into the power of Mrs. Lennard to destroy all the hopes you have been cherishing? Do you not see that you have put yourself upon her mercy? that, under pretence of not knowing of this clandestine love, she has suffered it to go on? secure of being able to ruin you at any time with her Lady by discovering it, and making a merit of her own disinterested conduct."

Orlando felt that there was too much truth in this observation; but the greater those hazards were that he incurred for Monimia, the dearer she became to him.

"Well, Sir," said he, "and if Mrs. Rayland's favour can be held only by the sacrifice of every honest affection, I will disclaim it. Why should she discard me for loving an amiable, beautiful girl, who—?"

"Nay, nay!" cried his father impatiently—"Why has she invincible pride, and obstinate prejudice? Why has she always held me at a distance, because my father, though her only relation, was the son of a man who could distinctly count no more than two generations? Why has she always expressed her detestation of the memory of *my* mother, whom fortune reduced to be her companion? Why has she ever despised *your* mother, because she was the daughter of a man in trade? It is of no use to inveigh against, or investigate the cause of all these supercilious distinctions in the mind of our old cousin: we know that, unluckily for us, they exist; and we know they are invincible. How do you think a woman so haughty and arrogant would like to hear that the young man she has been distinguishing by her favour, and to whom there is some reason to think she may make up the injustice she has done his family, has engaged himself to marry one of her domestics; a girl brought up in her house through charity, the daughter of a nobleman's steward, and the niece of her housekeeper?"

"If such are her prejudices, Sir," exclaimed Orlando warmly, "that I must make myself eternally wretched lest I should offend them, I had rather, much rather, give up for ever all those hopes, of which the reality would be too dearly purchased, if the best part of my life, and all that can render it valuable, is to be the price. I thank General Tracy more than ever for giving me a commission, which, little as it will afford me, and weak as my hopes are of preferment, will at least render me in some degree independent."

"I am obliged to General Tracy too," said Mr. Somerive, "for you will now be taken out of the most perilous situation that it is possible for a young man of your temper and imagination to be in. If Lennard is satisfied with having got you out of the house (for I doubt not but it was she who so much accelerated your going), it will be well;—a little more knowledge of the world will cure you of this romantic passion. I hope you are not engaged to this girl?"

"Engaged, Sir!"

"Aye, Orlando—engaged?"

"If I give you no more trouble, Sir," said Orlando dejectedly, "with what you are pleased to term my romantic passion, I must be forgiven if I answer no questions as to my future conduct; it shall not be such as shall disgrace my family, or give you any *reasonable* cause of uneasiness."

The emphasis laid on the word reasonable did not at all please Mr. Somerive—"You must give me leave, Sir," said he rather sternly, "to judge of the reasonableness of my feelings myself: you evade my question, after all your professions of sincerity. Good God! what a fate is mine! One of my sons is lost to me; the other is going to throw himself away, if not as unworthily, at least more irrecoverably:—your brother may be reclaimed by time and affection; but an unfortunate marriage, contracted so early in life, is certainly ruin."[1]

This speech was ill calculated to appease the concern and impatience with which Orlando found that his father, generally so considerate and indulgent, suffered his dislike to Mrs. Lennard to stifle every generous and liberal sentiment of his heart; and he was on the point of answering with more warmth than he ever in his life ventured to use, when fortunately, to save him from repentance, which would instantly have followed if he had given his father greater pain, the General joined them, and, after a few common compliments, they were met, as they walked towards the house, by Mrs. Somerive with a summons to breakfast. Though the interposition of the General had a little relieved both, the enquiring eyes of Mrs. Somerive were not easily evaded or deceived: she saw, and trembled to see, the emotions that shook the soul of her husband; while, on the expressive features of Orlando, disquiet and anguish, mingled with something of disappointment and resentment, were too visibly to be traced by paternal solicitude. The presence of the General, however, and of the three girls, prevented her speaking of what so much affected her; by degrees the clouds upon her husband's brow seemed less heavy; but Orlando was pensive and silent: the attempts he evidently made to shake off his concern, were quite ineffectual; and as soon as his hasty breakfast was over, he took his hat, and, turning to his mother, enquired whether the dinner hour was as usual (for on Sundays the family were sometimes accustomed to dine earlier): she answered that it was; and Orlando, then slightly bowing to the rest, was leaving the room, when his father cried, "I thought you were to pass this last day of your stay in the country with us, Orlando!"—"I shall be back to dinner, Sir," replied he as he shut the door.—Somerive, who, in the dread of his losing Mrs. Rayland's favour, and in his hatred to Mrs. Lennard, had spoken of Monimia with more asperity than he felt, was now convinced that harshness would have little influence on the warm impetuous spirit of his son; that he would have

---

[1]   This example of Mr. Somerive's rashness and selfishness illustrates his inability to differentiate between Mrs. Rayland's dependents; it also shows his self-interest, usually repressed.

done better to have trusted to mildness and persuasion, and to have treated him in this instance, as he had hitherto always done, rather with the gentleness of a friend, than the authority of a parent.

Stung with regret, anguish, and disappointment, Orlando wandered away from the house, hardly knowing why, or whither he was going. Instead of obtaining for Monimia his father's protection, and the countenance of his family during his absence, with which he had fondly flattered himself, he had heard what almost amounted to a prohibition against thinking of her any more; and his own candour and sincerity, to which he had been taught so religiously to adhere, had apparently done him more mischief than the hints which his brother had thrown out, who had (as he lately learned from Selina) never ceased attempting, during his last visit at home, to impress his father and mother with a notion, that Orlando had not only a correspondence, but a correspondence of the most criminal nature, with Mrs. Lennard's niece. Mrs. Somerive, always unwilling to see the faults of one son, or to hear of the supposed faults of another, had sometimes evaded, and appeared, when she was forced to hear it, quite indifferent to this information; while Somerive, whatever credit he might give to the existence of what he thought such a foolish and boyish inclination, discouraged this invidious disposition in his eldest son; and though he sometimes felt a good deal alarmed about Orlando, he thought so contemptibly of Mrs. Lennard, because he had learned early in life to despise and dislike her, that he could hardly imagine it possible for a relation of hers to make a lasting impression on a young man of so much taste and spirit. He was however often uneasy, and particularly after the dinner party at Stockton's, on this subject; but, upon enquiry, he could not find that Monimia was a girl likely long to captivate his son, or to engage him in a serious attachment. Some persons told him, indeed, that she was a pretty girl; others, that she was a handsome girl; but more, that there was not any thing very extraordinary in her: while from other quarters he heard that her aunt treated her like a common servant, except that she never sat in the kitchen or the servants' hall; and that she hardly ever was seen by any of the family, being employed in attending Mrs. Rayland only when she was sick, and at other times in waiting upon or working for Mrs. Lennard in her own room. Somerive therefore thought, that whatever childish affection his son might have felt for her, could hardly have any serious termination, or any that could injure him with Mrs. Rayland; and if now and then, on remarking some peculiarity in Orlando's conduct or looks, he recollected Philip's wild assertions about this "fair maid of the Hall," as he was accustomed in ridicule to call her, the hope that such childish love would be forgotten, and the idea he had taken up that Mrs. Lennard kept her niece quite out of Orlando's way, and treated her as a mere servant, quieted his alarms; for which indeed he had no remedy, for he could not either object to any person whom Mrs. Rayland chose should inhabit her house, or remove Orlando from it till the present period, when he had her consent and assistance.

But to whatever motives the conduct of Mr. Somerive was really owing, Orlando had seen it in that view only that was the most flattering to his sanguine hopes: they now appeared to be destroyed for ever, and he saw only despair before him. Far from being allowed to ask his mother's permission for Selina to see his Monimia, he dared not name her again, lest he should receive an injunction which the certainty of immediate death would not compel him to obey; and his projected confession that he was going in the evening to meet her for the last time, he now had not courage to make; yet he could not disguise it; for, since the General's residence in this family, their simplicity of living, and their hours, had been entirely changed; and instead of dining at three, as had been always their custom, they now called it four: but it was often, in compliance with the General's habits, near an hour later; five was the hour Monimia named in her note; it was perhaps the only one in which she had a chance of escaping: therefore, whatever might be the displeasure it occasioned to his father and his family, whatever might be their conjectures and remarks, he must either fail returning to dine with them, or break away perhaps before the removal of the table cloth; to do the former would have been less uneasy to himself, but he feared it would be more offensive to his family. Resolutely determined to see Monimia at all events, he fixed upon the latter; but as he could bear no more of his father's displeasure than what he was sure (he thought) of hearing when he returned from his last dear interview, he could not resolve to go back to the house, but continued walking, almost mechanically, towards Rayland Hall, forgetting, in the extreme agitation of his spirits, how very material it was that he should not be seen after he had taken his last leave of Mrs. Rayland, and she believed him gone out of the country.

This never occurred to him till, under a hollow sand cliff that bounded one side of the great pond, near the mill, on the verge of the park, he suddenly heard the rattle of a carriage, and, looking behind him, saw Mrs. Rayland's coach stopping at the gate, within two hundred yards of him. He then recollected the contemptible figure he should make, and the irreparable injury it would do him with her, if he were detected in a falsehood, accompanied too with apparent ingratitude; but it was almost too late to escape, for on one side was the water, and on the other a high and almost perpendicular bank, that in some places hung over the road:—he had not, however, a moment's time to deliberate; but, seizing one of the roots that grew out of the sides, he sprang up, not without some hazard of pulling the crumbling loose soil, of which the bank was formed, upon him:—two steps brought him to the top, where, however, he would have been in a more exposed situation than below, if the holly, hazle, broom, and branches of pollard oaks that clothed the top of the eminence, had not afforded him a friendly concealment:—he threw himself among them; and then, perfectly sure that he could not be seen, he peeped among the withered leaves of the oak and the thicker green of the holly, and saw very distinctly the carriage approach, in which, with a palpitating heart, he perceived Monimia sitting backwards with her aunt, while Mrs. Rayland alone occupied the opposite seat. He then recollected, that this was the day on which Mrs. Rayland usually went in state to the church of a neighbouring parish; a ceremony that was performed four times a year, when the weather did not forbid it. He was amazed at his own thoughtless indiscretion; and saw that he owed his escape from its consequences to a mere accident. On these occasions a footman went behind, and Mr. Pattenson rode in great form by the coach side. It happened that the man behind the coach had been ordered by his Lady, at the church-door, to call with a message upon her tenant the miller, whom not being immediately able to find, he staid while he was enquired for; and Pattenson was under the necessity of dismounting to open the gate, which, as he was extremely unwieldy, and rode a spirited and well fed horse, was by no means the work of a moment. Orlando, after his apprehensions were at an end, found in this little incident something from which he drew a favourable omen; he was pleased to see that, in consequence of his supposed absence, Monimia was indulged with a greater degree of liberty, and appeared much in favour with Mrs. Rayland and her aunt: and it seemed as if destiny, however remotely, was determined to favour him; for in this last, as well as in innumerable preceding instances, he had trembled on the very brink of detection, and yet he had hitherto escaped; at least he had reason to rest assured that Mrs. Rayland suspected nothing, and was far from imagining that her young kinsman was devotedly attached to her little, humble Mary.

CHAP. IV.

Sufficiently punished by the alarm he had been in for his indiscretion, Orlando no longer ventured to appear where any of the tenants or servants of the hall might probably meet him; but, as he was afraid of returning to the house of his father till the whole family were assembled, lest he should hear more of the reproof he could so ill bear, he lingered about the coppices; and as a chain of them led to a sharp eminence clothed with wood, that overlooked a part of the park, where, among the venerable trees scattered around it, the Hall-house appeared, he sat himself down on an old seat which had been placed here for the prospect afforded by this woody knoll, and indulged reflections which, though far from pleasant, were mournfully soothing. He recollected that, in this copse, but a few years before, he had once been permitted with some other children to accompany Monimia in gathering the nuts with which it abounded—How gay and happy they were then! how unconscious of evils to come!—Under that tuft of hazle Monimia sat, while he threw the fruit into her lap; and there he pursued a squirrel for her, which escaped up that old beech tree!—The letters carved by the rustics, whose Sunday's walk in summer sometimes led them to this bench, remained: he remembered them well; and, for the first time in his life, felt disposed to take his share of this species of fame;[1] and, with his knife, he engraved on that part of this covered seat which had suffered least from

> —"The sylvan pen
> Of rural lovers,"[2]

the words—"Orlando, 9th December 1776"—flattering himself that this rude memorial might be seen by Monimia, and draw from her soft bosom one sigh more of tender recollection, in his absence.

---

[1]   So admirably described in the exquisite poem of the Task, where he speaks of the alcove
         ——"Impres'd
      "By rural carvers, who with knives deface
      "The pannels, leaving an obscure, rude name,
      "In characters uncouth, and spelt amiss." [CS]
      The Task, I.280. Smith again shows her admiration for Cowper's poem.
[2]   Thomson [CS]. James Thomson (1700–48), *The Seasons* (1726–30), "Summer" (1727), l. 1364. Like *The Task*, *The Seasons* is a staple of the genre of meditative blank verse (unrhymed iambic pentameter).

Thus passed the time till the hour nearly approached when he believed the whole family would be together, and when he should therefore escape any farther conversation with his father. He made his way towards home, over hedges and through the most pathless part of this woody country; and, entering the house by the kitchen, he enquired for his mother and sisters. The servants answered, that their mistress was ill, and had lain down on the bed; but that the young ladies were in the parlour.

Concerned for his mother, whom he fondly loved, Orlando hastened into the common parlour, where he saw Isabella leaning her head on her hand, in which was an handkerchief, and Selina hanging over her, her eyes streaming with tears. Orlando, imputing all this to his mother's illness, enquired eagerly how she did, and how she so suddenly became ill? Selina, in answer, exclaimed, "O dearest Orlando! how glad I am you are come back! we have been wishing and seeking for you."

"But, my mother!" cried Orlando, "my dear mother!"

"She is only very much agitated," replied Selina, "and I hope will be better presently: but Isabella—"

"What, for God's sake, has happened to you?" said he, interrupting one sister, and addressing his hurried enquiry to the other.

"Tell him, Selina," said Isabella, "and ask him how he would act if he were situated as I am?—I will go to my own room."

"What is all this, my dear girl?" said Orlando as soon as she had left the room: "Isabella seems less affected than you are!"

Selina then related to him, that soon after breakfast her Father and General Tracy had walked out together, at the desire of the latter; where the General had opened his intention of offering himself to Isabella as an husband—of making very great settlements if she accepted of him—and, in short, said Selina, "he made the proposal appear so advantageous to my father, that the disparity of age seemed by no means a sufficient objection against accepting it:—he therefore referred the General wholly to Isabella herself, with whom he conversed as soon as he returned home, representing his own situation, which certainly affords us all but a melancholy prospect, Orlando. He even told Belle, in regard to our circumstances, some particulars which have been owing to Philip's expences, that my father says he has not ventured to tell even to my mother, because they would half kill her.—It seems that we shall not have any provision in case of our poor father's death, as Philip has stripped him of all he had saved; and as this estate would be Philip's, we should not have, to support us all, above fourscore pounds a year, my mother's settlement; which, as she had so small a fortune, was all she would let my father settle upon her.—This, you know, is not twenty pounds a piece for us; and Isabella would not certainly be happy with such a pittance, if it were possible for her to live upon it: only, therefore, consider what a contrast the General's offers make—Besides the power such a match would give her to make our dear parents easy (which I own is the only circumstance that would shake my resolution were I in her place), she would be raised so much in rank! and have such a large fortune!—so much splendour round her! things which you know Belle has no dislike to, that I believe she will consent, though she has a hundred times ridiculed the General; and when he has been making love to her—"

"Making love to her!" said Orlando; "has he long made love to her?"

"I *think* he has," replied Selina. "I know very little how people make love; but I am sure if that was not making love, I cannot guess what is. Belle, at first, only laughed at him, and used to say such rude things about his wig and his false teeth, and the art he used to make himself look young, that I have wondered an hundred times how he bore it: but afterwards he grew more importunate, indeed I thought impertinent, and Belle threatened to speak to my father. As for my mother, we agreed to tell her the sort of language he held whenever he could get my sister alone, or with only me and Emma; and my poor mother, afraid of disobliging a man who she thought had been such a friend to you, and might be to the whole family, desired we would not tell my father, who would certainly have resented such behaviour, and contented herself with keeping us out of his way, and never suffering us to be out of her sight. So the poor General, not being able to succeed in carrying away Isabella on his own terms—"

"Curse on his insolent presumption!" cried Orlando passionately; "he never could dare to think of it."

"My mother," answered Selina, "believes he did:—but you see he repents of his evil intentions, and is determined to be generous and honest at last."

"And does my sister Belle accept of him then?"

"That is the matter now in debate. My father has represented the situation she will be in, if he dies and leaves her unmarried. She knows all the pecuniary advantages that attend such a situation as the General offers her: and the question only is, whether, as she has no attachment whatever, the charms of grandeur, the chance of being a Countess (for the General's elder brother has but one son, a poor puny boy), and being called the honourable Mrs. Tracy, are not sufficient temptations to make her forget that the husband who is to give her all these advantages is a good deal older than her father?"

"And how do you think the debate will terminate?" said Orlando.

"Isabella has been crying about it, as you see; and my mother's being so extremely affected made me cry; but I believe, Orlando, that the General need not despair. Isabella, however, has desired till this evening to consider of it; when she is to give him her answer herself. He said that he could not go to town and leave undecided a matter on which the whole happiness of his life depended: nor could he bear to be in the presence of the adored object, till the hour when this decision was to be made: so as soon as he had made his fine speeches, he mounted his horse, and is gone to dine at Stockton's."

"Selina," enquired Orlando, "tell me honestly, my sweet sister, what you would do, were you in Isabella's place."

"I am very glad I am not, Orlando; but I will tell you honestly as much as I know of my own heart—Were father to say to me, as he has said to my sister Belle, that to see me so opulently married would make his latter days easy, and save him from those hours of anguish that now torment him about the future fate of us all, I should certainly marry this old man, if he were ten thousand times more odious to me than he is. To make my father happy, Orlando, whom I now see often sinking under a weight of anxiety that is destroying him—to secure to our dear indulgent mother the comforts of affluence, if we should lose him—and to promote your interest, Orlando, and poor Philip's, and my sister's, I would throw myself alive into the fire; or, what would be to me much more hateful, I would marry a man whom I abhor."

The fine blue eyes of Selina, on which those of her brother were tenderly fixed, filled with tears as she said this—her voice failed her a moment—but her brother did not interrupt her and she went on—

"But were only myself in question: then, were I to see poverty and even servitude on one side, and General Tracy with his brother's coronet in one hand, and a settlement of ten thousand a year in the other, I do assure you that I should refuse him."

"Generous, charming girl!" cried Orlando; "I do believe you, my Selina; and I rejoice that you are not exposed to the alternative. Belle, though I love her dearly, has not, I know, quite your heart; and I hope does not so much dislike this man, if it is indeed so probable that she will accept of him—Besides, the situation in life which he can offer, has charms for her gayer and more ambitious mind, which my soft Selina cannot taste."

"What shall I say to my sister is your opinion, Orlando?"

"That she must consult her own heart, my dear; for I cannot, in such an affair, give any opinion. But now, Selina, as we shall not have half a moment longer together, tell me, could you contrive to go with me this evening to meet Monimia for the last time?" Selina, at first, started some objections—If they both went out together their design in going could hardly be concealed; and she should perhaps incur the displeasure of her father and mother, who would not be well content that Orlando, whom they probably wished to consult on the important affair in agitation, should quit them immediately after dinner. It was however, after some debate, settled that he should go first; and that Selina, to whom every thing was soon rendered easy that could contribute to the happiness of her beloved brother, should follow him; for she said that she might then perhaps not be missed; because it was often her custom to sit of an evening with Emma up stairs, as they had usually a great deal of work to do for themselves and their mother; and though this was not a day when they could make that excuse, yet their habit of doing so would make their absence little remarked on an evening when a business was in debate so momentous as Isabella's answer. The brother and sister had hardly settled their little plan of operations, before they were told the dinner was ready and on their entering the dining room the rest of the family were already assembled there.

Mrs. Somerive, though she had collected resolution to appear at dinner, could not conceal the agitation of her mind—Orlando so soon to leave her, and the fate of Isabella in suspense!—Her dread lest her daughter should sacrifice herself and be unhappy, opposed to her wishes that she might be established in such high affluence, made her mind a chaos of contending emotions; while Somerive himself, reading in her countenance all that passed in her heart, and knowing, even better than she did, how necessary such an alliance was to the preservation of all the family, was even more affected; but he had yet strength of mind enough to conceal it better, and to appear calm, though thoughtful and melancholy, frequently turning his eyes on Isabella, who seemed in a kind of elegant languor, the effect of her debate between duty and indifference; though, in fact, it had been held much more between aversion and vanity, in which the latter hardly needed the aid of any other consideration to come off conqueror.

In a family party so situated, there was not, of course, much conversation, and the dinner passed without any body's eating, though each pressed the other to eat, and affected to eat themselves.—Orlando hardly spoke three words, and those were addressed to his mother, the interesting concern of whose still beautiful countenance wounded his very soul. Distracted between the fear of adding to that concern by his abrupt departure, and of a failing in his appointment with Monimia, he believed this dinner, useless as it was, was the very longest he ever sat down to. Just as the table-cloth was removed, he heard the clock strike five; and, looking at his watch, which went by the great clock at the Hall, he found their own was ten minutes too slow.—Monimia then was waiting for him in the wood, listening to every noise, and accusing him of cruelty and delay! Before this idea, every other consideration vanished; and, starting up, without even attempting an excuse, he hurried away; nor had his father, who called to ask whither he was going—nor the more tender voice of his mother, who cried, "Orlando! my son! surely you will not leave us!" power to detain him a moment. He rushed out of the house, and ran, with the swiftness of an Indian, to the great-pond wood.

By the time he arrived there, it was almost dark; but he discerned between the stems of the tall firs the figure of Monimia sitting on the seat he had marked to her as the place of their meeting. Never before did he seem to love her so ardently as at that moment; his heart was softened by the thoughts of their immediate separation, while, oppressed with the occurrences of the day, it seemed ready to burst.—Breathless from the speed with which he ran, and hardly knowing what he did, he threw himself on his knees before her, and seizing her hands, bathed them with his tears.

The trembling girl, who had been there even earlier than her appointment, and who had, amid an hundred other fears, despaired of his coming, alarmed, and unable immediately to weep, hung over him, as with frantic gestures he spoke to her; and when she would have reproached him for the apprehensions in which he had left her, her words were inarticulate; and it was some time before either of them were able to congratulate the other that they thus met once more!

Alas! the bitter certainty that a long, long separation must soon follow, poisoned the pleasure of their meeting: neither knew how to speak of it, yet it was impossible for either to think of any thing else.

"You go to-morrow, Orlando?" said Monimia. "Yes," answered he; and then relating what had passed in regard to Isabella, he added, that perhaps if his sister determined to accept the offers of General Tracy, as he believed she would, it might be in some respects advantageous to him; "for I understand," said he, "that the enamoured old beau means, if his love is successful, to return in a few weeks—perhaps three weeks or a month, in order to carry off his young bride; and that he has hinted to my father, that from thence forward, considering me rather as his brother than his protegé, he shall not only procure leave of absence from the General of my regiment—(for I am not in his, but in that where his nephew, Captain Warwick, has a company)—but use his utmost endeavours to procure me immediate promotion. I own, Monimia, that though I think this marriage most preposterous, and that my sister Isabella is marrying merely for money; yet I am so weak, and I am afraid so selfish, that the idea of gaining by this alliance the advantage of seeing you, which I could not often do otherwise, makes me half forget the disparity of the ages, and overlook the absurdity of a man of sixty-five marrying a girl of twenty-one; indeed, whether I approved or disapproved it, would in this case make no difference; therefore, as I could not prevent the evil, if it be one, there is, I trust, no meanness in my availing myself of the good."

Monimia felt a weight, heavy as the hand of death, taken off her heart, when he told her they were, in consequence of this new family arrangement, likely so soon to meet again. Her mind, which had dwelt with horror on the idea of a separation for months, perhaps for years, was now relieved, by supposing it might not be for more than three weeks; and knowing nothing of military rules, she supposed that after the first forms of entering on his new profession were gone through, he might return to the Hall; and that if she could not, from that active watchfulness which her aunt might renew, see him every day, she should at least know that he was under the same roof, or within a few miles of her; to know even that he was in the same county, was a satisfaction; she should hear Mrs. Rayland speak of him, if she was herself deprived of the happiness of meeting him; she should see him in the park, and hear his voice speaking to others, if he was not allowed to speak to her. Perhaps Mrs. Lennard, convinced by this absence that her suspicions had been groundless, might less vigilantly oppose their future intercourse. All these hopes—for the hopes of a young and inexperienced mind, are sanguine and easily received—served so far to assuage the pain Monimia had felt on their first meeting, that she became soon able to converse with calmness; and not only quieted her own troubled spirits, but endeavoured to soothe and compose those of Orlando. Her voice had upon his heart the power of magic—deliciously soothing as it was, it excited that sort of painful pleasure which is only expressed by tears. From this state of tender sympathy they were soon awakened, by a voice calling at a distance for Orlando.—Monimia started, in terror; but her lover immediately appeased her fears, by telling her what his haste and the tumult of his mind had made him before omit, that he had appointed Selina to meet them. They now therefore (as it was so nearly dark that they could hardly distinguish their way) hastened together towards that part of the wood from whence the voice came; and they soon met the poor terrified Selina, who, almost speechless with fear, on finding herself so far from home alone, and in a night that threatened impenetrable darkness, trembled like a leaf, and said to Orlando, as he took her arm within his, that the whole world should not have bribed her to venture what she had now done for him.

He led again towards the bench by the boat-house, though Selina pressed him to return home as soon as he could.—"I tremble," said she, "and am terrified to death, lest I should be missed: my father indeed is never very angry; but just at this time I would not for the world add to the many causes of uneasiness which he has about the rest of us."—

"Nor would I," replied her brother; "no Selina, there is not in the world any sacrifice I would not make to both or either of my parents, except that of my affections for Monimia." He then, though both urged him to put an end to this interview, which seemed indeed only productive of needless pain, insisted upon their sitting down by him; and, holding their hands, which he kissed as he united them, he besought them to love each other when he was gone, and to consider each other as more than sisters! He told Monimia, it was in cover of his letters to Selina he proposed to write to her, and not by the means of the under gamekeeper, as he had once proposed; and he then enquired if they could not appoint some one day in the week when they might meet in that spot: "I shall then be present with you," said he, mournfully, "at least in imagination—yes, however distant my person may be, my soul will be here! I shall, in fancy at least, enjoy the delight of seeing together the two beings whom I most fondly love, and of knowing they are occupied with the thoughts of their poor Orlando! There is a story in one of the popular periodical publications, I believe in the Spectator,[1] of two lovers, who agreed at a certain hour to retire, each from their respective engagements, to look at the moon; the romantic satisfaction they enjoyed in knowing that the eyes of the person beloved were, at the moment they were gazing on it, fixed on the same planet, will by this means be

---

[1] Although Orlando cites *The Spectator*, the story he alludes to, as John Bender and Simon Stern note (*Tom Jones* [Oxford World's Classics, 1996], p. 898, n. to p. 378), does not mention the lovers looking at the moon. Instead, the scene repeats almost verbatim one from Book VIII, Chapter IX of Henry Fielding's (1707–54) novel *Tom Jones* (1749). Smith, perhaps unwittingly, reveals her debt to this novel (although it is possible to argue that she merely shows Orlando's faulty memory). Like Orlando, Tom becomes romantically involved with a servant; like Monimia, Tom is a foundling orphan, although his parentage is established by the novel's end (and Monimia's never is).

doubled to me; for I shall know that at such an hour on such a morning my Monimia and my Selina will be just in this place; I shall see
them—I shall see the eagerness with which Monimia will ask for news
of me—the pleasure with which Selina will give it.—Every object round
this spot will be present to me; and wherever I may be, however occupied in my duty, my soul will at that moment be particularly here."

Selina, not less anxious to gratify him in this romantic fancy than
Monimia herself, now named Monday, as the morning when this innocent assignation should be made; and gave as her reason for it, that on
that day her mother was less likely to miss her, from her being then
particularly engaged in settling her domestic concerns; and that as they
did not always certainly receive letters from the neighbouring post town,
except on Sundays, the morning of the following day of the week would
be that, in which it would be most likely she should have those that were
to be sent her for Monimia.

Poor Monimia, with a deep sigh, reflected, that if all this was necessary to soften a separation of only three weeks (for Orlando had again
assured her it would not be more), a longer would be quite insupportable to them both. The deep sound of the great clock at the Hall tolling
six, sullenly conveyed towards them by the water, roused her from her
momentary dread of future sorrow to a perfect sense of that which was
immediately before her. It was necessary to hasten this dreadful parting;
there was not a moment to lose; for at a quarter past six she was to be
in the parlour to make the tea for Mrs. Rayland and her aunt, and the
nearest way was near a mile to the house.—Falteringly she spoke to
Orlando of the danger of her stay—he heard her, but he could not
answer.—Selina, who was almost as fearful of being missed as she was,
repeated it.—"Come then," cried Orlando dejectedly, "since it must be
so, let us go."—He took one under each arm, and was moving towards
Rayland Hall, when Selina cried, "Dear brother! you will not go to the
Hall?"—"No," answered he; "but I will not suffer Monimia to go so far
alone; therefore we will see her safe in sight of the house, and then
return."—"We must be very quick then," said Selina.—"As quick as you
can walk, my sister;" answered he, still in extreme agitation: "for I care
not how soon the pain I endure at this moment is at an end—I suffer
the tortures of the damned!" The poor girls, terrified at the vehemence
with which he spoke, and the wild way in which he hurried on, made
no reply, and only exerted themselves to keep up with him. In silence
they ascended on a high stile, which in one place separated the park; and
in silence ascended the hill which arose behind the north front of the

house.—Monimia then desired him to stop—"We are now," said she, "within sight of the house, and there can be no danger for me."—"Within sight!" said Orlando: "How is that, my Monimia, when it is so dark that we are hardly within sight of each other?"—"No," replied she; "but what I mean is, that there is nothing to fear in my crossing the park alone."—"I shall go with you, however," said Orlando, "to the old thorn in the dell below."—"At the hazard," said Monimia, trembling, "of our being met by some of the servants at the Hall, or people going home from their Sunday's visits to them?"—"At the hazard," added Selina, "of terrifying and displeasing my father and mother?"—"At the hazard of every thing!" replied Orlando, with a degree of impetuosity which neither of them had courage farther to oppose. They again became silent; and as they continued to walk very fast, or rather to run, they presently reached the place which Orlando had himself named for their parting; where Monimia again stopped, and disengaging her arm from his before he could prevent her, she said, faintly, "And now, Orlando, God bless you!—dear, dear Selina!" She was quite unable to finish the sentence; but, turning, would have left them, when Orlando, throwing his arms round her, wildly pressed her to his bosom.—"Be not so much concerned," said she, trying gently to disengage herself; "remember you have told me we shall meet soon—very soon again: Orlando! if you really love me—if you pity me, do not, I implore you, detain me now."—"I will not," said he: "God forbid that I should injure you, dearest, loveliest—!" She was gone!—he stood a moment like a statue, while her white cloaths made her distinguishable through the gloom.—Selina then entreated him to hasten home—"No!" he said, dejectedly; "No, I must stay here till I hear the door, by which I know she will enter the house, shut after her; and then I shall be sure she is safe." Selina could not oppose this; it could indeed take up but a moment—"Hush!" cried Orlando, "do not speak; let us listen—ha! the door shuts! Well, Selina, I will now go back with you; and a thousand and a thousand times I thank you, my best Selina, for your indulgence to me."

They then hurried back the way they came, and with as much haste as the darkness of the night would permit: it was above three miles by the nearest path; and Orlando, occupied solely by the anguish of having parted with Monimia, uttered not a syllable; while Selina, excessively alarmed lest her mother should have missed her, felt her heart beat so much with apprehension, that it was with the utmost difficulty she could keep pace with him.

CHAP. V.

On their arrival, however, at the house, Selina was agreeably surprised to find, from little Emma, who was reading in the room they shared above stairs, that she had never been enquired for; that the General had arrived just before, to tea, which was, on his account, ordered later than usual; and that Isabella, who had been below ever since dinner, with her father and mother, was now, she believed, alone with the General, to whom she was to give her answer.

The palpitating heart of Selina then became quieter: she took off her hat and cloak, adjusted her hair, and prepared for the summons she expected to have to make the tea. Orlando a moment afterwards glided up to them; he said there had been no enquiries for Selina, and all was right.—"I went," said he, "as is my general custom when I come home, into my father's study, but I found nobody; and, from what I can gather from the servants, this important answer has been given, and our old brother is with his papa and mamma, and with his future bride; they are all settling the ceremony together."

"How can you laugh, Orlando," said Selina, "at any thing so serious?"

"Nay," replied he, assuming a levity he was far from feeling, "you would not have me cry, Selina! If Isabella is happy in this match, surely her family have reason to be glad of it; but one cannot help thinking of January and May!"[1] Selina had read but little, and knew not to what he alluded; nor had she the time to reply, for at that moment Mrs. Somerive looked in upon them; she smiled, as it seemed, through tears.—"Orlando," said she, "I am glad you are returned—Why did you leave us so abruptly after dinner? But come, my children, we wait for you below."—"And are we to find there a new relation, Madam?" said Orlando. "Is the General to compose hereafter a part of our family?"— "Your sister has decided that it shall be so," replied Mrs. Somerive, stifling a sigh; "and you, Orlando, will be pleased to see how much pleasure this alliance (notwithstanding there is certainly a too great disparity of years) gives to your dear father. The difference of age is indeed the only objection: in every other respect General Tracy is a match infinitely superior to what any of my daughters could have

---

[1] Smith alludes to Chaucer's "Merchant's Tale" from *The Canterbury Tales* (c. 1387). This Tale tells the story of an old man, January, who marries a young woman, May; it is the archetypal mismatch and ends with May cuckolding January under his very eyes.

pretensions to." Mrs. Somerive then led the way down stairs, and her children followed her.

During supper the General assumed, as well as he could, the triumphant air of a young successful lover. Isabella was silent, and affected resignation to the will of her parents; while her father looked at her with eyes in which doubt and concern were mingled with hope and satisfaction. It seemed as if he at once rejoiced in having his daughter so well established, and yet feared that to the dazzling advantages of rank and fortune she might sacrifice her happiness. None of the party seemed much disposed for conversation; and as the General and Orlando were to depart early the next morning, they separated sooner than usual: Mrs. Somerive in better spirits than she would have been, if the General had not assured her that he would himself bring Orlando down with him, when he returned to claim the happiness of becoming allied to her, and might call himself the most fortunate of men.

Calmed by these promises, of which she saw nothing that should impede the execution, she beheld her son depart on the following morning, without any of those paroxysms of grief which Orlando had so much dreaded, and which he was so ill able to bear. Before the travellers got into the chaise, in which they were to go post to London, the General demanded an audience of his future bride; and Orlando was at the same time closeted by his father, who enjoined him to preserve his morals, to attend to the cultivation of that good opinion with which the General honoured him (points which a little experience proved to be incompatible), and lastly, to make enquiry after his brother, and, if he could find him, to endeavour by every possible means to persuade him to return home.

Orlando promised to obey all these injunctions, to the utmost of his power; and glad to escape hearing any other charges, which he might have found it impossible to obey, he received the summons now sent him to attend the General with pleasure; for nothing is more painful than the sensations which arise at the moment of separation from such friends, even though the absence be but transient. The General had paid his compliments all round, and Orlando now embraced his family with tears in his eyes. His father wrung his hand, and once more gave him his blessing.—His mother could not utter the last adieu! but went back into the parlour with her daughters; while Orlando, seated by his military patron, left his paternal mansion as fast as four post-horses could carry him.

He was not disposed to talk; but as the distance increased between him and Monimia—between him and his family, all he held dear in the world! the depression of his spirits increased also; while his companion, as he approached the scene of his former habits, and thought of the raillery he should encounter upon his new system of reformation, became more silent and contemplative: the clamours of his mistresses, of whom he had now three upon his hands, and the ridicule of his friends, arose to his imagination in a very formidable light; but then the beauty, youth, and vivacity of Isabella Somerive seemed excuses for a much greater folly than he was about to commit. He recollected many of his acquaintance, whom he was willing to suppose much older than himself, who had married young women without half her attractions. He fancied, that he was weary of the dissipated life he had hitherto led; that as he would soon be no longer a young man, but be *declining towards* middle age, it was time to have somebody who would be truly attached to him; while his being married did not at all preclude him from gallantries, which he saw every body else pursue whether they were married or not. The greatest inconvenience he foresaw, was what arose from the precipitate affection he had shewn towards his nephew, Captain Warwick, the orphan son of his sister, whom he had taught to consider himself as heir to his fortune, who would be much mortified at the disappointment. However, he reconciled himself to this objection, by reflecting that it would be very hard indeed if his kindness to his nephew should prevent his gratifying himself; and by resolving to make young Warwick an immediate present of a thousand pounds, and to settle a very handsome income upon him after his death, that he might not be quite thrown out of those expectations to which he had been brought up, when the General should have a family of his own.

Nothing was farther from the General's intentions than to marry Isabella Somerive, even when he had first changed his battery, and pretended to her honourable love; but he found so little prospect of succeeding with her, even if all was to happen in her family as he had foreseen, and he felt it so impossible to live without her, that what he had begun with the most insidious designs, concluded at last in an honest, though an absurd one: and having once taken the resolution to commit matrimony, he endeavoured to reason himself out of every objection that pride, libertinism, or the fear of ridicule, continually raised against it. Isabella, whose heart was perfectly free from every impression in favour of any other man, had so behaved as to make the enamoured General believe, that only her charming reserve, owing to her rustic education, prevented her avowing her attachment to his person; though, on a thousand occasions previous to his serious declaration, she had placed his vanity and affectation of youth in the most ridiculous point of view, and had shewn him that she did not care a straw for him.

But such power has vanity in obscuring the best understandings, that her ancient lover really supposed he could inspire her with sincere affection for him. Still, however, he felt an awkward kind of sensation when he thought of the numberless gay young men with whom his blooming Isabella would be surrounded when she was his wife. Above all, he reflected with disquiet on his nephew, who was reckoned one of the handsomest men of the times—he was three-and-twenty; and the General felt no satisfaction in being called uncle—Uncle! it sounded so antique. Warwick, indeed, was never admitted to live with him; and he now repented that he had procured leave for him to come home from America, in consequence of a wound he received there, and heartily wished him back again; but his return thither was not, according the General's own account, very likely to happen. If the presence of Warwick at his own house in Grosvenor Place was not agreeable to him, that of Orlando was as little so; and though not for quite the same reason, for another very similar. Before the last conquest made by Isabella Somerive over the susceptible heart of General Tracy, at least a third of it had been possessed by a young woman, whom he had purchased of her mother, and whose assumed virtue and great attractions had induced him to admit her into his house, where she had reigned ever since very despotically. As he had not yet settled whether he should part with her or not, and acquired courage to tell her his intentions, she must, till he could make up his mind on this point, remain where she was; and, whatever might be his future resolution, he did not greatly like that the handsome, young Orlando should be introduced to her acquaintance. As he could not give this reason to Mr. Somerive for not asking Orlando to take up his abode in his house, he had sedulously avoided mentioning it at all. Orlando had never thought about it; but, occupied solely by what he had left, he considered not a matter so inconsequential as whither he was to go when he got to town. Tracy had once or twice led the conversation to topics which he thought would engage Orlando to say what he intended in this respect; but Orlando took no notice of it, till, at length, just as they crossed Fulham Bridge, Tracy said, "Mr. Somerive, shall my chaise and horses put you down in London?—You know I stop on this side the turnpike, at Hyde-Park Corner; but the chaise shall go with you wherever you please."

"I am much obliged to you, Sir," answered Orlando, who never till that moment recollected that the General had not invited him to his house—"but there is no sort of occasion to take your carriage.—I shall go," added he, "this evening to Mr. Woodford's."

That was a plan that the General did not quite approve of; he knew that, if his intended marriage was once known at that house, it would be instantly spread among his friends by means of the communication Woodford had with many of their families, which was a circumstance he was not yet prepared for. The ambition of Woodford himself, and the malice and disappointment of the two young ladies, would busy them all in circulating the report; and the General, in love as he was, and determined to marry, had not yet prepared himself to stand the ironical congratulations of his male of female friends, but particularly the latter, on his resolution of uniting himself in holy matrimony to the niece of his wine merchant. These thoughts made Orlando's intentions of going to Woodford's, which however he might easily have foreseen, very unpleasing to him; and he remained silent some time, considering how he might guard against the inconveniencies he apprehended.

His reasons for not giving him an apartment in his own house kept their ground; but he would very fain have prevented his going to Woodford's, at least till he had himself taken some means to parry the first burst of the ridicule he so much dreaded. He could not take one very obvious means to prevent the circulation of the news of his intended marriage, by requesting Orlando not to speak of it; for he had often remarked that he was quick-spirited, not without a considerable share of pride, and affectionate solicitude for the honour of his sisters; to affect, therefore, making a secret in London of what he had so openly avowed in the country, could hardly fail of awakening the high-spirited Orlando to some degree of resentment, if not of doubt in regard to the reality of his intentions. After a long debate on the subject, the General at last recollected that it was impossible to suppose Somerive himself would not write to a brother-in-law, whom he was so much accustomed to consult, on a subject so interesting and important; and that, therefore, any precautions he might take in regard to Orlando would be useless. It is true that his being by his intended marriage allied to his own wine-merchant, had given him many severe qualms, which a glance from the arch and bright eyes of Isabella had at once dissipated; but now, as he approached his townhouse, and saw those bright eyes no longer, these fits of half repentance, originating in pride and prejudice, recurred with more force; and when he arrived at his own door, he started from one of the reveries thus brought on, and again said to Orlando, "Shall my servants get you a hackney coach?"

There was something in the abrupt manner of asking this, which suddenly convinced Orlando that the General had no inclination to ask him into his house. Piqued by this observation, he answered coldly, that there was no occasion to trouble his servants, for that he should walk to the house of his uncle, and would send a porter for the small portmanteau he had in the chaise.—By this time the General's valet de chambre had opened the chaise-door, and Orlando, who was on that side, got out. He stopped; and the General, as he followed him, asked, in a low voice, some question of one of the footmen who had been left in town, and who came to the chaise-door also: to which question the man answered aloud, "No, Sir! she is gone out." The General, turning to Orlando, who was coolly wishing him a good evening, said—"You will certainly do me the favour to walk in?"

Orlando by this time comprehending that there was some lady usually resident with him who was not to be seen, and that he was only asked in because she was at this time absent, answered, that he would not then intrude upon him:—"but as I shall want the advantage of your instructions, Sir," said he, "on many things of which I am totally ignorant, I shall be obliged to you to tell me where I am to receive your orders."

There was a coldness, and indeed a haughtiness, in the manner of Orlando's saying this, that convinced the General he saw and was offended by the evident design he had himself formed of evading to give him an invitation. More disconcerted than he had almost ever felt in his life, he had again pressed him to go into the house, which Orlando again refused; and then saying he hoped to hear from him at Mr. Woodford's, when and *where* he might attend him for the purpose of receiving those instructions relative to his future proceedings which he had promised his father to give him, he again wished him a good evening, and walked away.

Orlando had never been in London but once when he was about sixteen, and had then only attended his mother on a visit for about a week in the spring, which she had passed with her brother. He remembered that he never was so happy as when they left it, and, on a fine evening of May, returned from the smoke of the Strand, in one of the streets of which Mr. Woodford lived, to his dear native county, where only there seemed to be any happiness for him. Since that time he had never felt a wish to revisit London; and in a melancholy mode he now proceeded along the streets, recollecting little more than his way from Piccadilly to the Strand. Every object wore a very different appearance from what they did when he saw them before. It was now a dreary, foggy evening in December, and just at the hour when the inhabitants of the part of the town he was in were at their desserts, so that hardly any carriages but a few straggling hackney-coaches and drays were rumbling over the pavement. As he passed Charing-Cross the bustle became more; and the farther he advanced, the throng of coaches coming out of the city, and going towards the play-houses from other parts of the town, deafened him with noise: but it was a mournful reflection, that, among all the human beings he saw around him, there was not one interested for him. While the dirt through which he waded, and the thickness of the air, filled him with disgust, his mind went back to the dear group at home: he saw them all assembled round the fire in the little parlour—his father trying to dissipate with a book the various anxieties that assailed him for his children, now and then communicating some remarkable occurrence to his wife as she sat at her work-table:—he saw Isabella employed in making some little smart article of dress, and fancying how well she should look in it—and Selina, while she and Emma were assisting his mother in completing some linen for him, more attentive to her father's reading, often asking questions and soliciting information.

But when he had finished this picture, his fancy, with more pain and more pleasure, fled to the lovely figure of his Monimia in her solitary turret, sighing over the tender recollection of those hours which would never perhaps return, sometimes wishing she had never known them, but oftener regretting that they were now at an end.—He saw her stepping cautiously into the library, whenever she could find it open, to take or replace some book which they had read together—she shed tears as she read over the well-known passages he had particularly pointed out to her—she dwelt on the pages where he had with a pencil marked some peculiar beauty in the poetry. He fancied he saw her take out the lock of his hair which he had given her in a little crystal locket, press it to her lips, and then imagining she heard the footsteps of her aunt, return it hastily into her bosom, and place it near her heart. A thousand tender images crowded on his mind; he quite forgot whither he was going, and was roused from this absent state of mind only by finding himself at Temple-Bar. Recalled then from the indulgence of his visionary happiness to the realities around him, he recollected that he had passed the street where his uncle lived: with some enquiries, however, he found his way back; and, on arriving at the house, he heard that Mr. Woodford was out, having dined in the city; and that his wife and her daughters were gone to the play with a party of friends who were to sup with them. He was told, however, by the maid-servant who let him in, that he was expected, and that a bed had been prepared for him by direction of her master, who had received notice of his intended arrival by a letter from the country the day before. Orlando could not help remarking to himself, that he was likely to have but a cool reception in an house, the inhabitants of which could not one of them stay at home to receive him; but he was new to the world, and his heart open to all the generous sympathies of humanity. He thought that relations loved one another as well in London as in the country; but he soon saw enough of these to make him resign, with perfect composure, a too strict adherence to old-fashioned claims of kindred.

CHAP. VI.

A moment's reflection recalled the confused and dissipated thoughts of Orlando back to the transactions of the day. He had never liked General Tracy much; and he now liked him less than ever, and regretted that Isabella was to be his wife. He almost doubted whether he ever meant to make her so; and the idea of any deception raised his indignation. But he had nobody to whom he could communicate his thoughts: and it was perhaps fortunate for him that he had not; for his open, unguarded temper, incapable of dissimulation, and despising it wherever it appeared, was very likely to have betrayed him into confidences with his uncle which would have hurt his father.

The moment, however, he saw Woodford, he shrunk into himself; and instead of remembering that he had not yet been at home to receive him, felt only concern that he was come home at all.

Warm from a city dinner, the boisterous manners of his uncle appeared particularly disgusting to Orlando, who had lately been accustomed to associate only with women, or with his father and the General; the conversation of the former of whom was pensively mild, and that of the latter so extremely courtly that he seemed always to fancy himself in the drawing-room. Orlando, therefore, was almost stunned with the halloo of his uncle on receiving him: he shook him, however, heartily by the hand, crying—"Well, my boy! I'm glad to see thee: though devilishly thou art bit, my little hero, to find that all that old Tabby's fine promises end in sending thee to carry a rag upon a pole, and get shot through the gizzard by the Yankies.—Aha! I was right, you see.—Take my word another time. I know the world, and never saw that waiting for such chances answered—A young fellow may wait till he is grey on one of those hags, and the devil a bit find himself the forwarder at last.—They never die; for o' my conscience I believe they have each of them as many lives as a cat: and when at last they have the conscience to turn the corner, it's ten to one but they bilk you after all.—No, no; take my advice another time—never depend upon them; 'tis better to shift for one's self."

"Well, Sir," said Orlando, whom this harangue equally tired and disgusted, "you see that I have followed your advice, by embracing a profession—"

"A profession!" cried Woodford with a contemptuous look; "and what a profession!—To be shot at for about five-and-thirty pounds a year! Hey? or how much is it? thereabouts, I believe.—A rare profession, when a man ties himself down to be at the command of about a dozen others!"—In this manner he ran on, nothing doubting the shrewdness of his remarks, and not meaning to be rude and brutal in making them: yet Orlando felt that he was both; nor was he much relieved by the change in the conversation that brought the General's intended match into discussion. Woodford was at once flattered by such an alliance, and mortified that his own daughters had missed it. He felt proud that he should boast of having *the Honourable* Lieutenant General Tracy as his nephew, but was vexed that he had not any share in bringing it about; and this contrariety of sensations found vent in the coarse raillery he uttered to Orlando, who was once or twice on the point of losing his temper, before the entrance of the ladies and their party from the play put an end to a dialogue so very disagreeable to him.[1]

Young Woodford, who, having quitted trade to study the law, was now a motley composition between a city buck and a pert Templar, accompanied his mother and sisters; which he took care to signify was a great favour, and not owing to his wish to oblige them—but to see how he liked a young woman they had with them from the city, and who was the only daughter of a rich broker of the tribe of Israel, who had, however, married a Christian, and was indifferent enough about his own religion to let his daughter be called a Christian also. Her fortune was supposed to be at least seventy thousand pounds; and Mr. Woodford had long been scheming to procure a match between her and his Jemmy:—to which Jemmy declared he would condescend, if he could but bring himself to like the girl. But he "thought her confoundedly ugly, and had no notion of sacrificing himself to money." The girl herself, just come from a boarding-school, her head full of

---

[1]   Orlando's entry into fashionable life recalls Evelina's similar meeting with vulgar City relatives: the "cits" referred to in note 1, p. 166 (see *Evelina*, by Frances Burney, 1778).

accomplishments and romance, was in great haste for a lover. Mr. James Woodford was reckoned, by some of his young acquaintance, a very smart, fashionable man; and Miss Cassado needed very little persuasion to fancy herself in love with him.

The intended husband of Maria Woodford, and a young man who seemed to have pretensions to the other sister, were the rest of the party; who, preceded by Mrs. Woodford, now appeared. The ladies of the family spoke with cool civility to Orlando—the younger Woodford with the air that he imagined a man of fashion would assume for the reception of his country cousin: but under this apparent contempt he concealed the mortification he felt from the observation that Orlando, who was always admired by the women, was much improved in his person since he last saw him.

With his two female cousins Orlando had never been a favourite, notwithstanding his acknowledged beauty; and that for no other reason, than because he had never paid to their charms the tribute of admiration they expected from every body. Eliza particularly disliked him, because he had refused a sort of proposal made by her father to give him her hand and a share of the business. But the young Jewess, who consulted only her eyes, immediately discovered, by their information, that this stranger was the sweetest, handsomest, most enchanting man in the world; and that James Woodford was nothing to him. She had her imagination filled with heroes of novels, and the figure and face of Orlando exactly corresponded with the ideas of perfection she had gathered from them; while the natural good-breeding which accompanied whatever he said, and that sort of pensive reserve he maintained in such a company, which gave to his manner peculiar softness, placed him at once among the dear interesting creatures with which her head was always full; and she either so little knew, or so little wished to conceal the impression he had made, that James Woodford and his mother perceived it, both with an accession of ill-humour which did not sweeten their manners towards Orlando.

At supper every body talked together; though their eagerness to be heard could not be justified by the importance of what they had to say, which was chiefly remarks on the players, criticism on their acting, or anecdotes of their lives, of which the younger Mr. Woodford had apparently a great fund. Orlando, who knew none of them, and for whose conversation there was no vacancy if he had been disposed to converse, sat a silent auditor of this edifying discourse; now wondering at the importance affixed to people and events which appeared to him of so little consequence—now comparing the noisy group in which he sat, with the dear circle at home, and his delicious *tête-à-têtes* with his soft and sensible Monimia—and not unfrequently looking with some degree of wonder on the rosy cheeks, disfigured forms, and disproportioned heads of the ladies—but especially on that of Mrs. Woodford, whose cheeks were as red, and whose plumage waved as formidably as that of any of the misses. He soon determined, that till he could finish his business about his commission, and prepare for his duty, he would take a lodging, and not remain where he was likely to find so little society to his taste, and where his reception was hardly civil.

Having taken this resolution for the morrow, he felt no other wish but that the disagreeable night would end; and totally neglected by every body but Miss Cassado, who now and then addressed herself to him in a sweet sentimental tone, he had disengaged his mind from the scene around him, and was picturing in his imagination the turret of Monimia. He saw her sleeping; and her innocent dreams were of him! Every piece of furniture in the room, the books, and the work that lay scattered about it, were present to him. It was the image only of Orlando that sat at the table of Mr. Woodford; the soul that animated that image was at Rayland-Hall.

But from this illusion he was startled by Woodford; who, giving him a smart blow on the shoulder with his open hand, cried, "Why, Captain! you are in the clouds! Hey-day! what pretty plump dairy-maid at the Hall is the object of this brown study? Never mind, my lad—a soldier finds a mistress wherever he goes; and though I dare swear thou hast broken a sixpence with her as a token of true love—she will not break her heart, I warrant her, while there's a sturdy young carter in the county of Sussex—Come, most magnanimous Captain, cheer up! We are going to drink in a bumper of such claret as thou hast not often tasted, Confusion to the Yankies, and that there may soon be not a drop of American blood in their rebellious hearts!—As thou art going to fight against them, thou wilt help us drink against them—Come; your glass, Sir, your glass! and when that toast has passed, I have another."

Orlando, who was more shocked and disgusted by every word his uncle spoke, now took his glass in silence; and Woodford, engaged in some of that conversation which he called roasting, with another of the young men, let him drink the wine without insisting on his repeating words, from which, almost ignorant as he was of the nature of the contest with America, his reason and humanity alike recoiled.

But he did not escape from the future toast with which his insupportable uncle had threatened him. When the whole company had drawn round the fire (for their supper was now concluded), and every glass was again by the order of Mr. Woodford *charged*—he, who in dining out, and in the liberal potations he had taken since he came home, had already swallowed more than was sufficient to elevate his robust spirits, stood up with his back to the fire in the middle of his family and his guests, and there gave a toast which had a very direct reference to General Tracy's marriage with his niece Isabella, in terms so very improper that Orlando, to whom it was particularly addressed, felt every principle of personal honour or general propriety insulted by it, and positively refused not only to drink it, but to stay in the room while it was drank. Being once roused, and feeling himself right, the vulgar ridicule of his uncle had as little effect as the more serious and angry remonstrance of his coxcomb cousin, who assured him, that only his little knowledge of the world, and rustic education, could cover him from the most serious resentment. A severe pang touched the sensible heart of Orlando, as he recollected that his beloved mother would be vexed at this difference between her brother and her son: but, when he related the cause, he was sure she would not blame, but commend him; and conscious of all the dignity of an unadulterated mind, scorning to stoop to even an unworthy expression because it was authorised by custom, or insisted upon by a relation, he took his hat, and, wishing the ladies good-night with great politeness, was leaving the house, when Woodford himself overtook him at the door, and apologised for his unguarded proposal, by which, however, he protested he meant not to offend him. On this apology, and on an assurance that he should hear no more of such offensive conversation, Orlando returned to the room, though fully determined to leave the house the next day.

The licentious and vulgar mirth, however, which Mr. Woodford chose to call conviviality, was at an end after this incident. James Woodford, already detesting Orlando, could hardly be civil to him; the lady of the house beheld him with a mixture of envy, contempt and terror: the misses, his cousins, felt only resentment and contempt: but the little Jessica, gone already an age in love, admired his spirit, and adored his beauty; and when her father's chariot, with an old Hilpah who acted as a sort of Duenna in it, came to fetch her home, she made a tolerably confident advance to engage the "brave pretty creature" to escort her home.[1] Orlando, however, either did not or would not understand her; and James

---

[1] "Jessica" was a slang term for a Jew, derived from Shakespeare's *The Merchant of Venice*: Shylock's daughter is called Jessica. Hilpah appears in the *Spectator* 584–85 (23/25 August 1714); she is an aged crone who nonetheless marries at 100 and again after being widowed at 160.

Woodford, piqued at the preference given to Orlando, which the lady was at no pains to conceal, suffered her to depart alone.

The rest of the party immediately separated: the young barrister retired to his chambers, hardly deigning to wish his country cousin good-night— Orlando, whose trouble no kindness from this family had the power to allay, as their neglect had no power to increase it, went to his room little disposed to sleep; fatigue of body and mind gave him up to a few hours of forgetfulness. At dawn of morning he awoke, and, as he knew it would be long before any of the servants rose in an house where night was converted into day, he dressed himself; and as the day was to be dedicated to business, and he wished to lose as little time as possible, he went to breakfast at a coffee-house, and left a note for his uncle, saying, in civil but cold terms, that, as he had so many affairs to transact in a very short time, he must keep very irregular hours, and therefore should be a troublesome inmate in a family; for which reason he should take a lodging near the part of the town where his engagements lay, and should only occasionally trespass upon him for a dinner.

From the coffee-house where he breakfasted he wrote to General Tracy, requesting his directions, as he determined not to call at his house. To this letter, however, he did not expect an answer till after one o'clock, as the General was seldom visible sooner; and he employed the long interval in writing to his family a short account of his safe arrival in London, and in pouring out his whole heart to Monimia in a letter, which he inclosed in one to his sister Selina.

General Tracy was in the mean time suffering, on one side, all the apprehensions of what would be thought and said, when his intended marriage should be known, by those whose interest it was to keep him single; and, on the other, from his fears of losing Isabella, his passion for whom absence did not promise to do much towards curing. Warwick had been returned from his recruiting party above a week, and had been several times in Grosvenor Place enquiring for his uncle; and the behaviour of the lady of the house towards her ancient lover was such as gave him great reason to suppose that his intended reform was suspected, if not known. Of this, however, he had no longer any doubt, when, going late in the evening after his arrival in town to the house he usually frequented in St. James's street, he was attacked upon this tender subject by all his old friends, and rallied without mercy. As he could not deny an affair of which they seemed so well acquainted with the particulars, he took at once the resolution to avow it; their ridicule then ceased, and Tracy returned home, glad that this first burst of laughter was over.

But much was yet to come of a more serious nature, against which he armed himself as well as he could, by reflecting that he had a very good right to please himself, and that neither Captain Warwick, nor any of those other persons to whom he had given a claim over him, had any other dependence than on his bounty. To the women on whom he had made settlements, he knew he must pay them; but whatever he had done for Warwick was entirely voluntary; and as his nephew had no other dependence, he would hardly, for his own sake, so behave as to cut himself off from a share of his future fortune because he could not have it all.

Armed with these reflections, he determined to end this disagreeable state at once, by telling Warwick what he intended for himself, and for him. And when his nephew, apprised of his being returned to London, waited on him the next morning at breakfast, Tracy, though he would rather have mounted a breach, plunged at once into the subject—informed Captain Warwick of his intention to marry, and of the immediate present, as well as future provision he intended for him.

Warwick, who had always feared his uncle's very youthful propensities would, as he advanced in life, betray him into the very folly he was now about to commit, received this intelligence with more concern than surprise. He was himself of the gayest and most inconsiderate disposition. In the height of health, youth, and spirits, the admiration of every woman he saw, and the life of every company he went into, his vanity did not allow him to suppose that he owed any part of that admiration to the prospect he had of being heir to General Tracy's wealth; and, imputing it all to his own merit, he fancied himself superior to the malice of fortune. There were many possibilities which, on a moment's reflection, weakened the blow which this intelligence seemed at first to give to his fairest hopes—His uncle might change his mind a day before it was executed—the young woman might jilt him—or, even if the marriage took place, he would probably have no children; and then he should himself be so little injured by this match, that it was not worth thinking about with any degree of concern.—The thousand pounds too, which his uncle promised him, was a douceur that considerably abated the bitterness of such intelligence; and Warwick, rather through the carelessness of his nature than from motives of prudence or policy, received this intelligence so much more calmly than Tracy expected, that his uncle appeared to be in a better humour with him than ever. This uneasy subject once discussed, Tracy proceeded to inform him, that the brother of his intended bride, for whom he had procured an Ensign's commission in his (Warwick's) regiment, though not in the same company, had accompanied him to

London, in order to equip himself for the service, and to join that part of the corps that were in England. While he was speaking, Orlando's note was brought in; and on Tracy hinting that such were his wishes, Captain Warwick immediately offered to go himself to the young soldier, and give him every assistance and information that could be useful to him.

Instead, therefore, of a written answer to his note, Orlando heard a gentleman enquiring for him in the coffee-room; and on his appearing, Captain Warwick, whose figure and address immediately prejudiced every body in his favour, introduced himself as the nephew of General Tracy.

If Orlando instantly conceived a favourable opinion of Warwick, *he* was yet more struck with his new acquaintance. From his uncle's account, and from what his own imagination added to it, he supposed that he was to be a temporary bear-leader to a tall straight-haired cub just come from school, who wanted a drill serjeant rather than a fashionable acquaintance: but when he saw, and only for a moment had conversed with Orlando, he perceived that he was one of those beings for whom education can do little, and whom nature has so highly favoured that nothing can be added by art. The two young men, thus highly pleased with each other, soon entered into conversation, with that unguarded familiarity which accompanies generous tempers in the candid days of youth. Orlando spoke his mind very freely on the absurdity of the match meditated by the venerable General; and Warwick as freely ridiculed it, while he could not help expressing some curiosity as to Isabella, whose charms had thus brought about what so many artful women of all descriptions had been trying at for the last thirty years at least. Orlando described his sister as he really thought her—a very handsome girl, full of spirit and vivacity, with a great deal of good humour—a good share of understanding, which did not, however, exempt her from being very vain, and somewhat of a coquette. It was on enquiries relative to her person, which he said must be extraordinary, that Warwick dwelt the most—"Really," said Orlando, "I have seen many women who are as handsome, some handsomer. For example, I think Selina, my third Sister, infinitely more beautiful, though I own to you she is not generally reckoned so."— "Upon my soul," replied Warwick, "your family, Somerive, must be a very dangerous one—I suppose, though, I am pretty secure; for my good old uncle, or *young* uncle—I cry him mercy!—will not let me have a peep, for the world, at this future aunt of mine!" Orlando was glad to see that Warwick received with so much *gaieté de coeur*, an event which would have raised in the minds of most other persons, so situated, inveterate enmity against his whole family. Warwick engaged him to dine at a tavern in Pall-Mall; and they then went out together, that Orlando might know where to find the tradesmen for whom he had occasion.

CHAP. VII.

For a young man of the temper and disposition of Orlando, there could not be a more dangerous companion than Captain Warwick. Indulged from his infancy, by his uncle, in every thing that did not interfere with his own pleasures, and having no parents to restrain him, Warwick never dreamed of checking himself in whatever gratified his passions or flattered his imagination. His spirit and vivacity recommended him to societies of men, where he learned to be an agreeable *debauché*, to drink without losing his reason, but not always to play without losing his money. His very fine person, and the softness of manners he could occasionally assume, endeared him to the women, among whom he was called the handsome Warwick, and with them lost his time—but hitherto without losing his heart. With all his acquired imperfections, he retained many inherent good qualities— He was humane, generous, and candid: his soldiers adored him; and his friends, amid all that fashionable dissipation in which most of them lived, were more attached to Warwick than fashionable men usually are to any body. Orlando, in the simplicity of his heart, thought him the man in the world most calculated to be his friend. Warwick was recruiting at Barnet; but, however, had obtained leave to be in London: and Orlando, who, after passing a few days with him, could less than ever endure the sort of society he found at Mr. Woodford's, took a lodging near Warwick's, and they became almost inseparable. The General, embarrassed between his love for Isabella Somerive, which he could not conquer, and his present connections, which he knew not how to break, passed in a state of mind by no means enviable the first week after his return to London; but the greatest torments he was to experience had not yet overtaken him, for the societies of fashionable women, among which he had been the oracle, were not yet assembled for the winter. He dreaded, when he met them, not only the loss of his consequence, but the scorn and ridicule he should be exposed to. He wished to be once married, when common civility would repress those sarcasms to which he knew he should be otherwise exposed; yet as the preparations necessary for this important event, which he assured Mr. Somerive he would hasten, were to be begun, his resolution failed: he wished he had not gone so far, but adhered to his former cruel plan, of waiting till the death of her father, and the distress and dispersion of her family, which that event threatened, had thrown her into a situation in which it was likely she might be tempted to accept his less honourable proposals. While the mind of the ancient lover thus fluctuated between the fear of losing her quite, and the reluctance he felt to resign his liberty to obtain her, Isabella discovered no impatience for his return; but waited for her promised dignities with tranquillity, which her father was far from sharing. The painful idea of sacrificing his daughter to mercenary considerations, was not more supportable than that of leaving her destitute, together with the rest of his family, of a comfortable subsistence; but, above all, the cruel desertion of his eldest son, of whom he had now heard nothing for many weeks, corroded his heart with unceasing torments; and those torments were increased by the necessity he imposed upon himself, of concealing them as much as possible from his wife.

The letters he received from Orlando were his only consolation; yet even these were embittered, by hearing, in every one of them, that all his enquiries after his brother had hitherto been fruitless. Warwick, who found great pleasure in his company, had, very early in their acquaintance, learned the source of that anxiety which often clouded the open countenance of his friend; and in hopes of meeting Philip Somerive, they had gone together, not only to public places, and to all parts of them which it was likely he might frequent, but to gaming-houses and taverns of the second class, where, from Orlando's description of his brother's style of conversation, Warwick thought it most likely he would be found: but they gained no intelligence of him; and the very research was not made with impunity by Warwick, who could seldom help engaging in any thing that was going forward. But Orlando's affection for his family, and for Monimia, secured him effectually from the infection of such societies—he had strength of mind enough to consider how much he owed to them and to himself, and to reflect how unpardonable his conduct must appear to his father, if, in undertaking to recover his brother, he should lose himself. These reflections, and an heart almost insensible of all pleasures but what derived from the hope of passing the summer of his life with Monimia, were antidotes even to the influence of Warwick's example, who often gaily rallied his country prejudices, but never seriously attempted to pervert his principles—and sometimes, in their more serious conversations, was candid enough to own that he should himself be a happier man if he did not, rather than incur the ridicule of those for whose opinion he felt only contempt, plunge into vices for which he had no taste, and call pursuits pleasurable, which, in fact, had no power to bestow pleasure.

Orlando had now been three weeks in London; for the plan of returning to pass his Christmas at Wolverton, which had been once proposed, had been given up. The General, contented with having introduced him to Captain Warwick, had seen no more of him since than common civility required, and was now gone to pass that space of time between the end of the old and the beginning of the new year, when it is very unfashionable to be in London, at the house of his brother, Lord Barhaven,[1] who usually remained at his northern residence till the end of January. The General had originally proposed to return to Somerive's house at this time; but not having yet recovered the doubting qualms which he had since felt, he thought a fortnight at his brother's, where he hoped and believed no idea of his intentions could yet have been heard, would give his arguments on both sides fair play, which now were so equally balanced: he should be alike removed from the fascinating charms of the blooming Isabella, and from those rivals who, in London, had many established claims on his heart and his pocket.—He should not, on one hand, be delighted with the spectacle of family happiness and domestic comfort, which the circle at Somerive's house offered to him; nor, on the other, dread the ridiculous light into which the wit of his London friends threw his intended marriage with a beautiful rustic, young enough to be his grand-daughter. For these reasons he wrote to Somerive, lamenting the necessity he was under to change his plan; and alleging that it was family engagements alone that impelled him to do so, but that as soon as they were fulfilled he should hasten on the wings of rapture to West Wolverton, he set out for the North.

Orlando continued another month in town without hearing of his return, or wishing to hear it for any other reason than because it would, he thought, be the signal of their going down together to the house of his father.—At the end of that time he became impatient—he had been now above six weeks absent, and the letters he had from his family, but still more those he less frequently received from Monimia, irritated this impatience. The anguish of mind that every week increased, while Mr. Somerive had no news of his eldest son, was by his letters forcibly expressed to Orlando, while his mother and his sisters gave him mournful accounts of his father's health. Mrs. Rayland's letters were, though very rare, the greatest alleviations to his uneasiness that Orlando received; for they were as expressive of kindness, and of increasing attachment for him,

---

[1]   As Ehrenpreis notes, "Mrs. Smith has forgotten that she has given Tracy's only brother the name of Lord Taymouth" (539, n. to p. 301). In terms of dates, we are now in early 1777.

as the reserve of her manner, and the formality of her style, would permit them to be; and it was a great and unusual degree of favour towards any one, that alone could urge her to write at all. The two letters he received from her, therefore, were considered by Orlando as being more unequivocal proofs of her settled affection for him, than any she had yet given.

Still the time that was to intervene before he should be permitted to return to the dear paternal spot, around which were assembled all the future hopes of his life, seemed insupportably long.—He was now in Hertfordshire with his men; and only occasionally obtained a few days to pass with his friend Warwick in London. In the tedious days he passed almost alone in a little country town, his resource was in books, and to such as he could attain he applied himself with more avidity than he had ever done at the Hall. Thus passed the month of February, and part of March. Mr. Somerive then believing, with great appearance of reason, that Tracy was trifling with his daughter, wrote to the General in such a way as must bring on a decision. In consequence of this, the General, still wavering, returned to London, from whence, and from his duty in Parliament, he had absented himself since the beginning of the session on pretence of ill health. On his arrival in town a circumstance awaited him, which called him back to his honest resolutions; for the young woman, on whom he had profusely lavished great sums of money, who was established in his house, and whose settlement he had lately increased in consequence of his proposed marriage, had quitted his house the evening before that on which she knew he was to return to it, leaving a letter, in which she turned him, and all her former professions of attachment to him, into ridicule. She took with her all the presents he had made her, to a very considerable amount—gave him the name of a person whom she had authorised to receive the annual sum he was to pay her—informed him she was gone to Italy with a young man of fashion, whom she named to him, and was his most obedient humble servant.

As the excessive vanity of the General had blinded him so far as to make him believe he was extremely beloved by this young woman, who had always laughed at and imposed upon him, he was thunderstruck by an incident so unexpected, and cruelly mortified to find, that while he was meditating how to soften to her the pain of parting, she was thinking only of flying from him with a younger lover. His resolutions in favour of matrimony, which pride and the dread of ridicule had at least suspended, now returned in all their force. He immediately wrote to Somerive, excusing, as plausibly as he could, his late apparent backwardness, and acquainted him that he only waited for the drafts of the settlements, which, as particular circumstances in his affairs rendered much attention to them necessary, his solicitor had promised to have drawn up, and laid before two of the most eminent counsel—all which he was assured would not take up above a fortnight, at the end of which time he should lay himself and his fortune at the feet of his adorable Isabella.

The General however, though he was now really in earnest, could not prevail on men of law to make a forced march in his favour; and the fortnight elapsed in queries and questions in which there seemed no other end to be obtained than that of increasing the fees of the gentlemen of the long robe, and the bill of attendance to the attorney. Somerive again thought himself trifled with; and the General, in order to convince him he was not, went down on a sudden to West Wolverton, where the charms of Isabella regained at once all their power; and after staying ten days, and renewing in the most solemn manner, his engagements with Somerive, he returned to London, to make the last preparations for his marriage, which was fixed to be within three weeks. As it had long been settled that Orlando was then to return home to be present at the celebration of these nuptials, he heard that all was at length settled, with a mixture of pleasure and pain.—The delight he felt at the idea of returning to friends so dear to him—above all of seeing his Monimia, was embittered by reflecting on the sacrifice his sister was about to make in this unequal marriage; nor could he reflect without regret on the injury it would do to the interest of his friend Warwick, who, however, spoke of it himself with philosophic gaiety.

It was near the end of April before the General, who now remained steady to his engagements, could prevail upon the tardy special pleader, the puzzling counsel, and the parchment-loving solicitor, to complete their parts in this intended contract. At last however the General, attended by two of them, set out for West Wolverton, and in a few days was followed by Orlando.

The day after his arrival was occupied till it was almost dark, with the ceremony of hearing these endless settlements read; and, as he was a party to them all, it was impossible to escape, even on pretence of the indisputably necessary visit to Mrs. Rayland; but the instant they were signed he flew eagerly to the Hall.[1]

---

[1] Orlando combines his "necessary visit" to Mrs. Rayland with his equally necessary visit to Monimia: again, the two women are merged in Orlando's romantic attachments to property and to love.

The sight of the many well-known objects on his way—every tree, every shrub, recalled to his mind a thousand pleasing ideas; and as he passed hastily through the fir wood, where in a dreary night of December he had last parted from Monimia, or at least passed a few agitated moments previous to their parting, he compared his present sensations with what he had at that time felt, and laughed at the superstitious impression given him then, and on some former occasions, by the gloom of the winter sky—when he fancied that, in the hollow murmur of the breeze, he heard, "Orlando will revisit these scenes no more!"

Every object, then wrapped in real and imaginary horrors, was now gay and joyous. It was a lovely glowing evening, towards the end of April.—The sun was set, but his beams still tinged with vivid colours the western clouds, and their reflection gave the water of the lake that warm and roseate hue which painting cannot reach.—The tender green of spring formed to this a lovely contrast; and, where the wood of ancient pines ceased, his path lay through a coppice of low under-wood and young self-planted firs—the ground under them thickly strewn with primroses and the earliest wild flowers of the year.

Hope and pleasure seemed to breathe around him—Hope and pleasure filled the heart and flashed in the eyes of Orlando; and perhaps the moment when he reached the door of the old Hall, though he was forced to stop a moment to recover his breath and recollection, was one of the happiest in his life.

It had been the established custom, from his first admission to the Hall, never to enter the apartment of Mrs. Rayland but on permission, but now, as he had informed her from London that he intended to be at the Hall in a few days, and had received an answer most cordially inviting him, his impatience would not permit him to wait for this cere-mony; and he hardly felt the ground beneath him, as he sprang up the stairs that led to her usual sitting parlour, and opening the door, saw, by the faint light which the old gothic casements afforded at that hour of the evening, Monimia sitting on the opposite window seat alone. He flew towards her, forgetting, at that moment, that the world contained any other being. Surprise and pleasure deprived her as much of her recollection as they had done her lover; but it returned sooner, and she entreated him to forbear those frantic expressions of tenderness which were so dangerous in such a place.—"Where are the old Ladies then?" cried he—"they are only walking in the gallery," replied Monimia, "as Mrs. Rayland was not well enough to go out to day—they will be back immediately."—"That cannot be," cried Orlando impatiently, "for you know how slow their progress is; but let us not lose a moment in talking of them.—Tell me, Monimia, can I see you at night as I used to do?—Are you still in your turret, with the same means of leaving it?—Tell me, Monimia, I must not—I cannot be refused."

"Ah, Orlando!" answered the faltering Monimia, "dearest Orlando! how often have I repented of those dangerous, those improper meetings; with how much difficulty we escaped, and how impossible it would have been for any other circumstance than your absence to have quieted the suspicions of my aunt!—And ought we now to renew this hazardous correspondence—ought we to incur again such danger?"—Orlando interrupted her: "Ought we!" exclaimed he. "Is that a question Monimia would have made after so long an absence, if Monimia was not changed!" "Changed, Orlando! can you think me changed?"—"Prove then that you are not," said he, again impatiently interrupting her: "let me see you to night; my leave of absence is only for a few days, till my sister is married, and I must not—I will not be trifled with."—"Oh, hush! hush!" whispered she, "there is a noise! they are coming from the gallery!—I had better not be found here with you."—"Promise then, Monimia—promise me, and you shall go.—I will hazard every thing, even an immediate discovery, if you refuse me." Monimia, trembling at his vehemence, then sighed her consent—and hardly knowing what she was about, gathered up the work that lay in the window seat, and softly left the room, while Orlando walked to the other end of it, assuming, as well as he was able, an air of unconcern; but before he had made a second turn Mrs. Rayland entered—and started at the sight of him, though she had expected him either that day or the next.

He approached her with all that affection which is inspired by gratitude; and as he respectfully kissed her hand, she expressed her pleasure at seeing him returned. He then paid his compliments to Mrs. Lennard, whose eyes he saw were thrown round the room for Monimia; she returned his civilities, however, with great good humour. Candles were ordered, and Mrs. Rayland invited him to supper, and to take up his residence at the Hall—favours which, with unfeigned pleasure, he accepted. The old Lady, who had now been accustomed to contemplate Orlando as a creature of her own forming, was pleased to fancy him improved, both in his person and his manners, during his short absence.—He had acquired a military air—he was more easy, but not less respectful; and she fancied that he resembled her grandfather's picture more than he used to do; but she expressed some surprise not to see him in uniform, which she said, in her time, all gentlemen of the army appeared in usually.

Orlando promised he would conform to what she thought right in that respect—not however without some apprehensions, that as he advanced in life she would propose to him, in order that he might be still more like Sir Orlando Rayland, whose portrait she wished him to resemble, to purchase a tie wig, and brandish a sword, of which the guard should be lost in an immense sleeve.

As Mrs. Rayland was not very well, having lately had an attack of the gout, to which she was in the spring particularly subject, she dismissed the young soldier early; and it was with inexpressible delight that Orlando took possession once more of his old apartments, which had been carefully prepared for him. It would not be easy to describe the subsequent meeting between him and Monimia, who suffered herself to be persuaded to renew that clandestine intercourse, which they had both so often condemned as wrong, and renounced as dangerous; but when Monimia could prevail upon him to talk less of his present happiness, and to be more reasonable, she related to him all that had passed during his absence.—Her life had, however, afforded very little variety, but was rather amended in regard to Mrs. Lennard's treatment of her, who employed her more than usual in attendance on Mrs. Rayland, in order to save herself trouble, gave her more liberty, and was rather less harsh towards her than formerly.— She related, that she was now often suffered to go to church, which had afforded her the opportunities she had snatched to meet Selina and correspond with him. Her aunt had apparently forgotten her suspicions and anger when he was no longer near the Hall; and the disappearance of Betty Richards, who was said to have gone off (according to her own assertions) to Philip Somerive, and was reported to be supported by him in London, had been the means of eradicating entirely from the mind of Mrs. Rayland all those suspicions which the gossip of the country, collected and repeated by the jealousy of the old butler, had made on her mind; and she now thought better of Orlando than if these doubts had never been raised.

Orlando, in collecting all this from Monimia, saw too clearly the reason why his brother had so carefully avoided him; and amid all the delight of which his heart was sensible in this conference, it felt a sharp pang, when he reflected how great an accession of pain this intelligence, which did not seem to have reached him yet, would give to the already wounded heart of his father.

Day unwelcomely appeared, and it was dangerous for Monimia to stay a moment longer.—Orlando conducted her safely back, extorting from her a promise that they should meet every night during the short time he was to stay. When he left her his spirits would not allow him to sleep.—The morning was delicious, and a thousand birds from the woods, on every side the park, seemed to hail his arrival. Again all the enchanting visions with which youth and hope had formerly soothed his mind re-appeared—never did they seem to him so likely to be realized. His sanguine imagination, no longer repressed by doubts of Mrs. Rayland's intentions towards him, which were now every thing but actually declared, represented to him the most bewitching scenes of future happiness. The only alloy was his brother's indiscretions and his father's health; but he believed he should be able to obviate the inconveniencies of the one, and to restore the other, when he should possess, what the course of nature rendered likely to be at no great distance, the property of Mrs. Rayland, which he meant to resign to his father for his life.

"Happy pliability of the human spirit!"[1] Happy that period, when youth, and health, and hope, unite to paint in brilliant colours the uncertain future—when no sad experience, no corrosive disappointment, throws dark hues over the animating landscape; or, if they do, are softened into those shades that only add to its beauty! Orlando would not distinguish, in that his fancy was busied in drawing, any but agreeable objects—Monimia infinitely more lovely, and, if possible, more beloved than ever, was the principal figure.—He saw her the adored mistress of that house, where she had been brought up in indigence, in obscurity, almost in servitude; this gem, which he alone had found, was set where nature certainly intended it to have been placed—it was to him, not only its discovery, but its lustre was owing—he saw it sparkle with genuine beauty, and illuminate his future days; and he repressed every thought which seemed to intimate the uncertainty of all he thus fondly anticipated, and even of life itself.

The cool tranquillity of morning, the freshness of the air, the beauty of the country whithersoever he turned his eyes, had not sufficient power to sooth and tranquillize his spirits—he believed a book which should for a moment carry him out of himself would do it more effectually; and returning to the library, he took from the shelves two or three small volumes of poetry which he had purchased, and retiring to an elevated spot in the park, which commanded a view of Monimia's turret, he attempted in vain to read; but the sensations he felt were so much under the influence of fancy, that they suddenly assumed a poetical form in the following verses:

---

[1] Ehrenpreis cites Laurence Sterne's humorous homage to sensibility, *A Sentimental Journey* (1768): "sweet pliability of man's spirit, that can at once surrender itself to illusions" (p. 539).

HYMN to LOVE and HOPE.[1]

Twin stars of light! whose blended rays
Illuminate the darkest road
Where fortune's roving exile strays,
When doubt and care the wanderer load,
And drive him far from joy's abode.

Propitious Love and smiling Hope!
Be you my guides, and guardian powers,
If, doom'd with adverse fate to cope,
I quit in Honour's rigid hours
These dear, these bliss-devoted towers.

Yet here, O still, most radiant! here
(Attend this prayer of fond concern)
To beauty's bosom life endear,
Presaging as ye brightly burn
The rapture of my blest return.

CHAP. VIII.

Three days, three happy days to Orlando, now passed rapidly away. Divided between his father's house and the Hall, and appearing to constitute the comfort of both, he was himself gay and cheerful, in the certainty that at night he should see Monimia. The charms of the season; the beauty of the country, to which he was attached as well from taste as habit; the tender affection of Monimia, which, though more guarded, was more lively than on their early acquaintance; the delight of knowing that his father's sorrows were soothed and suspended by his presence; and that his mother looked upon his attention to her as overpaying her for every other anxiety; all conspired to give value to his existence,

---

[1] By Smith. Unusually, this poem never appeared in any other of Smith's collected poetic works. Stuart Curran speculates that this is "because it is so closely tied to the particular situation of its putative author" (*The Poems of Charlotte Smith*, ed. Curran [Oxford: Oxford UP, 1993], 167), but this consideration did not stop Smith from incorporating Orlando's other effusions into her *Elegiac Sonnets*. Curran's edition entitles the poem "Hymn to love and life."

and to blunt the asperity of those reflections in regard to his brother, which now and then would interpose and give him momentary disquiet. He was not quite content about Isabella, who, through the air of gaiety she assumed, did not seem to be really so well pleased as she affected to appear. The fulsome fondness of her ancient military lover sometimes raised her ridicule, but oftener disgust, which Orlando saw with concern. But on these occasions he reflected that nothing in this world is without its alloy; and that so many advantages would accrue to his family by the marriage of Isabella, that as she did not seem herself averse to it, it was folly in him to think of it with concern.

On the morning of the fourth day after his arrival, he had just walked over from the Hall, where Mrs. Rayland had detained him to breakfast, and was engaged in conversation in the parlour with his father and the General, when a dark-coloured chariot, drawn by four sleek dock-tailed horses that might have matched the set at Rayland Hall, was seen to approach the house, followed by three servants in purple liveries.

Mr. Somerive expressed some surprise at this, as he had not the least recollection of the equipage: their enquiry, however, who it could be, was immediately answered by the appearance of Doctor Hollybourn; who, waddling out, enquired for Mr. Somerive, and was shewn into the room where he was sitting.

Mr. Somerive was so little accustomed to receive visits of civility from Doctor Hollybourn, or indeed any visits at all, that he was as much surprised at this as he could be at a matter of so little consequence. The very great condescension of the good Doctor, who bowed as low as his prominent stomach would let him, and whose speeches were interlarded by all kinds of flattery, Mr. Somerive accounted for by recollecting that the Doctor was extremely fond of the company of persons of title, and never so happy as when he could introduce some anecdote which related to his "brother the Bishop," or to some Right Honourable or Right Reverend Friend. He had, on the occasion of their meeting at Rayland Hall the preceding November, paid his court most assiduously to the General; and enlarged upon the beauty of his brother the Lord Barhaven's seats; all of which, he said, he had visited. Somerive now therefore concluded that it was to the report of his honourable guest, and of his intended alliance with the family, that he owed this very obliging visit; which, however, he began to think very tedious, and dreaded its lasting till the evening: when, at length, the good Doctor, after a pompous preface, said that he had an affair of some consequence to communicate to Mr. Somerive, on whose time he begged to trespass alone for ten minutes.

Somerive, who could not imagine what a man with whom he had so slight an acquaintance could have to say to him, immediately applied this unexpected circumstance to the idea always present to his mind. He fancied some ill had befallen his eldest son, and that one of his friends had commissioned this man of the church to break to him the horrid tidings; and then to pour into his wounded mind the consolation his profession enabled him to bestow.

In an agony not to be described, therefore, Somerive led the way into his Study; where the Doctor, after another flourishing preface, which Somerive in the confusion of his mind took for a preparatory discourse, offered to him for Orlando his daughter, the fair and accomplished heiress, to whom he declared he would give twenty thousand pounds down, with an engagement that at his death that sum should be trebled.

Though the proposal gave no great pleasure to Somerive, because he disliked Doctor Hollybourn, and was almost sure Orlando disliked his daughter; yet this conversation, so different from what he expected to hear, gave, while it relieved him from the most dreadful apprehensions, the appearance of joy to his countenance; he thanked the consequential Doctor for the honour he did his family, promised to communicate to Orlando the purport of their conference, and to wait upon him with an answer, or send Orlando on the following day. They then returned to the General and Orlando—the conversation turned on common topics; and the Doctor, though asked to stay dinner, withdrew with his usual dignity.

The General was now considered as part of the family; and before him Somerive, who had hardly yet recovered from his surprise, related to Orlando, as soon as he was gone, the purport of his visit.

Mr. Somerive seemed at first but little disposed to listen to proposals of such a nature from a man whom he had always rather disliked, and who now seemed to have made them, only because it was generally understood that Orlando was acknowledged as the intended heir to the great estates of the Rayland family.

Orlando very plainly declared his disinclination to hear of them; while the General, by no means accustomed to consider pecuniary advantages as matters to be slightly thought of, or hastily rejected, asked such questions as led Somerive to explain the particulars of Miss Hollybourn's fortune and expectations; after which he contrived to turn the conversation to indifferent matters for a few moments, and then walked away with Somerive, whom he very seriously advised to reconsider the matter before he suffered Orlando to throw from him this opportunity of becoming a man of fortune and independence.

The Doctor's proposal, however flattering it would have been to many young men, even though they declined accepting it, gave to Orlando no other pleasure than what for a moment arose in reflecting, that, in thus refusing an affluent fortune, he gave to Monimia an additional proof of his affection. His father, however, after his late conversation with the General, and some reflection alone, began to see this offer in a more favourable light than it had at first appeared to him; and notwithstanding the little inclination he felt for the family of Hollybourn, he was now of an age and under circumstances which gave to such a fortune as Orlando was now offered its full value in his opinion. His mind, already accustomed to contemplate the marriage of General Tracy with Isabella as a desirable event, more easily accommodated itself to think with approbation of another match equally dazzling, when opposed to the present uncertain situation of Orlando. After taking, therefore, some turns in his Study alone, he sent for his son, and entreated of him to forbear giving the Doctor an answer at least for two or three days.

Orlando, who had never hesitated himself what answer to give, imagined it impossible to give it too soon.—"Surely, Sir," said he, "as I cannot accept this good Doctor's very obliging proposals, it will be useless and uncivil to delay a moment saying so, which I will say in a letter in the least displeasing manner I can; but which, however, I must beg leave to do this evening."

"I be then that you will *not*," said Somerive in a more peremptory tone than he was accustomed to use—"In such an affair I will not act without consulting Mrs. Rayland."

"Mrs. Rayland, Sir," answered Orlando, "will, I am very sure, either not interfere, or, if she does, it will not be to recommend Miss Hollybourn."

"We will enquire that," replied his father coldly; "in the mean time you have my directions not to write to Dr. Hollybourn."

"Till when, Sir?"

"At least not till after I know Mrs. Rayland's opinion."

"All the opinions upon earth, Sir," cried Orlando, "will not make me change my resolutions."

"I thank you, however, Orlando," said Somerive, "for avowing how little deference you pay to mine."

"Dear Sir, it was only half an hour since you seemed as little disposed to listen to this unexpected overture as I am."

"I had not then thought of it properly. You are young, and rash enough to determine on the most important matters in ten minutes—

I am not; and therefore I again desire you will not write to Dr. Hollybourn this afternoon."

Orlando, a good deal hurt at this change in his father's sentiments, and dreading importunity on an affair of such a nature, then enquired if he might himself wait upon Mrs. Rayland?—Somerive answered, "You may, if you will at the same time deliver a letter from me in explanation, and say nothing yourself till that letter shall be read."

This Orlando promised, being pretty certain that Mrs. Rayland would be much less anxious for this connection than Mr. Somerive supposed, who now desired him to send his mother into the Study.— He obeyed; and left them to consult together on this unexpected offer, and to write to Mrs. Rayland, with whom he proposed dining, and had engaged to return to his father with her answer early in the evening.

Orlando now saw only persecution and trouble preparing for him at home during his short stay, for the tears and tenderness of his mother were infinitely more formidable to him than any other mode of interference.— To Selina, whom he called out to walk with him in the shrubbery, while this conference was holding, and this letter writing, he communicated all he felt. She had only tears to give him; for, to resist her father's commands, or even his wishes, seemed to her impossible. She trembled at the idea of Orlando's withstanding those wishes, yet knew enough of his invincible attachment to Monimia to be assured that he could never yield to them.

A servant at length brought to Orlando the letter to Mrs. Rayland for which he had waited, and he took his way to the Hall.

As he had promised his father not to speak upon it before Mrs. Rayland had read the contents, he sent it up by one of the footmen, with a message importing that he waited her commands.

In this uneasy interval he dared not go in search of Monimia, nor could he detach his thoughts a moment from the subject of a proposal which threatened to empoison the few days of delight which he had promised himself. Restless and anxious, he walked backwards and forwards in the Study with uncertain steps, now listening to every noise in hopes of receiving a summons to attend Mrs. Rayland; and now believing, from the delay, that she saw the proposal of Dr. Hollybourn in a favourable light, and was writing to his father to enforce its acceptance.

At length he was desired to walk up stairs; and, with a fluttering heart, he entered the apartment of Mrs. Rayland, who began by saying—"You know, I suppose, the contents of the letter my kinsman Mr. Somerive has taken the trouble to send me?" Orlando answered, that he certainly did.

"And pray, Sir, have you any wish to accept this offer? An offer!—The world methinks is strangely changed!—For a man to *offer* his daughter—is such an indecorum—In *my* time such a proceeding was unheard of—But however we live and learn!—I have heard that the way of these days is to send young women to market like cattle: but there is something perfectly shocking in it to me.—However, I suppose, to people of the world it is nothing new or extraordinary.—Pray, Sir, what are your intentions?"

Orlando immediately saw, and saw with inexpressible pleasure, that Mrs. Rayland was averse to the alliance with Dr. Hollybourn. He answered therefore—"My intentions, Madam, are to decline an offer which certainly lays me under great obligations to Dr. Hollybourn, but which the profession I have chosen, and my inability to offer Miss Hollybourn an heart such as her fortune and merit give her a right to expect, render it impossible for me to accept."

Mrs. Rayland, pleased to see that Orlando had no desire to become independent of her, or to force her to a positive declaration of her future intentions in regard to him, which she fancied his father wished to do by engaging her to give her sentiments on this proposal, now smiled very graciously upon him, and said, "I think you right, cousin Orlando.—Dr. Hollybourn is to be sure a very worthy man:—his daughter, they say, is a young person well brought up; and the fortune is very large, which first and last he can give her, besides what he is always telling me he is to expect from his brother the bishop.—But, you are yet a very young man, cousin; and in truth it seems to me to be time enough to think of marrying.—The *fortune* of this young woman is certainly very considerable: but, perhaps, not greater than at some time or other—(she hesitated as if afraid of saying too much)—I say, by the time your settling in life is advisable, perhaps you may not have occasion to make fortune an object in marrying, so much as a good family.—Dr. Hollybourn talks of *his* indeed, which is not well judged; for there *are* people who recollect both the Doctor and his brother, the bishop, in very humble stations compared to what they are now. God forbid, though, that I should despise them therefore! not at all; that is not my meaning—And to be sure *your* family, my cousin, has not of *itself* much pretensions to match with ancient blood—(and again she hesitated as fearing to betray her intentions too far)—I say, if ever you are in a situation to marry, I would advise that you think of a woman of a good family at least."

Orlando waited with impatience for the conclusion of this speech;

and then falteringly and eagerly asked of Mrs. Rayland, if she would have the goodness to put into writing her opinion on this subject?

This, however, she refused, as she said *she* would not appear to interfere in it upon any account.—"Will you then, Madam, take the trouble to see my father?—Will you allow him to wait upon you?—for he is so anxious for me, and, I believe, thinks this affair likely to be so agreeable to *you*, that he will be hardly easy unless he hears your sentiments."

Mrs. Rayland, drawing herself up, as was her way, said—"I shall be glad to see Mr. Somerive on any matter that relates to *you*, cousin, though on this occasion I own it seems very needless.—However, you have my leave to say, that I shall be ready to talk over this business with my kinsman, provided, as I said before, I am not supposed by Dr. Hollybourn or his family to interfere."

Orlando, impatient to have this affair concluded at once and for ever, now asked if his father might wait upon her that afternoon?—"When he pleased," was the answer;—and Orlando, fearing that if she was left long to consider of it she might change her mind as his father had done before, now ran to West Wolverton with the utmost speed, quite forgetting that he was to have dined with Mrs. Rayland, or that dining at all was necessary.

When he arrived there, he hastened to relate to his father and his mother, whom he found together, the purport of his conference with Mrs. Rayland; to whom Mr. Somerive agreed to go immediately after dinner, though he seemed visibly disappointed; while Mrs. Somerive, who had for a moment indulged herself with the hopes that her Orlando, instead of continuing in dependence on the caprice of Mrs. Rayland, and of being separated from her by an hazardous profession, might be placed at once in great affluence, and in the immediate neighbourhood, relinquished those hopes with a deep sigh, but said nothing to her son on a point where it would now be useless.

Mr. Somerive, finding the General was gone on a visit to Stockton's, from whence it was probable he would not return till half an hour after four, determined to hasten to Mrs. Rayland before dinner. He got on horseback, therefore; and, attended by Orlando, on their arrival at the Hall he expressed to his son some apprehensions that the lady of the house might be at dinner: but Orlando, whose impatience could brook no delay, declared, without a very strict enquiry into the hour, that it was not yet time, and that he was sure they might go to the parlour where she usually sat, as she had so positively said they might come at any time.

Somerive, almost as anxious for the conference as his son, though from very different motives, agreed then to proceed. Orlando would have sent up a servant, had he met one; but none happened to appear, and he walked before his father up the stairs, and, opening the door of Mrs. Rayland's sitting room, he saw her at table, with Mrs. Lennard on one side of it, and Monimia on the other. He would have retreated; but it was too late. He was already in the room—his father already at the table, apologising to Mrs. Rayland for his unseasonable intrusion. She received him with civility, but without any degree of kindness or warmth—desired he would take a chair and sit down, and then said to Monimia, who stood blushing and trembling, and not daring to look up—"Mary, you will withdraw, I have business with my kinsman."

"I beg I may not disturb any body," cried Mr. Somerive turning his eyes towards Monimia, and immediately comprehending who she was—"I beg I may be allowed to retire till dinner is over."—"No, Sir," answered Mrs. Rayland; "I shall be glad to hear your business now, and I will dismiss my people."

Mr. Somerive again looked at Monimia as she left the room, and he saw that Orlando was lost, if his being so depended upon his attachment; for the extreme beauty, sweetness and grace of Monimia, so unlike the cherry-cheeked coarse rustic which his fancy had represented her, amazed and grieved him. He felt at once, that a young man whose heart was devoted to her, could never think of Miss Hollybourn, and that he himself could not blame an attachment to an object so lovely, however imprudent, or however ruinous.

Mrs. Lennard now offered to withdraw; but her lady bade her finish her dinner, while poor Orlando cast a melancholy look after Monimia, and then on the seat she had left, which Mrs. Rayland desired him to take. The dinner was soon removed; and then Mr. Somerive, in a few words, repeated the purport of his letter. Mrs. Rayland, even more strongly than she had done to Orlando, expressed her wish that the offer of Dr. Hollybourn might be politely declined; and though she evaded giving her reasons for it, Somerive thought he saw them unequivocally, and that, though she studiously avoided declaring it, she had determined to put Orlando into a situation in which it would be not at all necessary that he should marry, for money, a woman to whom he was indifferent.

Mrs. Rayland had very little art; yet she fancied herself a profound politician, and never considered that, while she forbore positively or even remotely to give Orlando assurances of possessing her estate, her insisting upon the propriety of his marrying, whenever he did marry, a woman of *family*, was in effect declaring that she meant he should be the person who was to perpetuate hers, on which she put so high a value, and thus to efface, in the illustrious blood of his posterity, that alloy which the inferiority of the Somerives had mingled with that of the Raylands.

Somerive, convinced of this even from the pains she took to conceal it, yielded at once to her wishes, and assured her he would permit Orlando with great politeness to decline Dr. Hollybourn's proposal; yet as he continued to listen to her harangues upon *family*, he could not help looking significantly at Orlando—looks which his son perfectly understood to say, "How will this accord with your attachment to the young person who was this moment dismissed by Mrs. Rayland, as one of "her people?"

The old Lady, however, was hardly ever in so good a humour with her relations as she became after this affair was discussed; and Mr. Somerive never left the house so full of hopes that his family would be its possessors as he did after this interview, when he returned home in good spirits, though entirely relinquishing the idea of Orlando's becoming the nephew of a bishop.

Orlando himself, though impatient to write and dispatch the letter to Dr. Hollybourn, yet staid at the Hall to drink tea, by the desire of Mrs. Rayland, who gently chid him for deserting her at dinner. It was with more pain than pleasure that he heard Monimia sent for to make the tea, which had hardly happened twice within the last three years when he was in the house. Mrs. Lennard cast a look at him when her Lady ordered her niece to be called: but she could make no objection without raising those suspicions which she ever appeared so solicitous to prevent. Monimia then attended. Orlando treated her as a stranger, whom he was slightly acquainted with; and Mrs. Rayland did not appear to have the remotest suspicion that he had any particular regard for her: so friendly to him, as it happened, had been the mistakes and interpretations which the jealousy of Pattenson had put upon those circumstances that had so frequently threatened to betray him.

He had settled with Monimia the preceding night, to stay supper with his father, and return to their usual rendezvous; and their stolen glances during the half hour that they were together, in the presence of the two old ladies, confirmed this appointment.

Early in the evening, then, Orlando took leave of Mrs. Rayland, and went back to the house of his father, whose uncommon good spirits had diffused more than usual gaiety among his family. Mrs. Somerive and Selina were particularly cheerful—the mother, because she saw her husband for a moment happy, and forgetting the concern he continually felt about Philip, in looking forward to the prosperity of his brother—while Selina, who had trembled for the teasing persecution she apprehended for Orlando, was delighted to find that her father would forbear to urge him on such a subject, and had acquired new confidence in the future intentions of Mrs. Rayland.

Isabella, whose marriage was now within a week to take place, and who had just received from London some of those elegant clothes which her father had ordered for her, as well as some magnificent presents from the General, was the least gay of the party; amidst all her endeavours to persuade herself that she was happy, she had of late, and particularly since she had possessed these fineries, often enquired of herself whether they had really any power to bestow happiness. She had tried on her diamond ear-rings, and a valuable pearl neck-lace; but she could not discover that she looked at all handsomer in them than when she wore nothing but a simple ribband. The General's valet de chambre had dressed her hair: but she thought the mode unbecoming to her face, and the beautiful dark auburn hue, which had been so much admired, was no longer distinguishable. As for her intended husband, he was so far from having made any progress in her affections since he had been received as such, that her contempt was converted into disgust. His servants had been talking among those of Somerive, of his gallantries, and, above all, of the sudden desertion of the lady who lived with him; of all which Isabella had heard from her maid, and the longer she listened to, or thought of the anecdotes thus collected, the greater became her repugnance; and yet she knew not how to retract, and was not always sure that she wished it.

Her gravity was easily accounted for, as the day approached that was to divide her from her family; and she was suffered, after some gentle raillery, to be silent and pensive amidst the cheerful conversation of the rest.

It was a lovely evening in early May. Orlando, having dispatched his letter, dismissed Dr. Hollybourn and the disagreeable heiress from his mind, and gave it up only to pleasurable impressions and flattering hopes. In a happier frame of mind than he almost ever was in before, he joined his family in their evening walk. When they reached the house, they stopped in the court before it, to admire the beauty of the moon, and to listen to the nightingale, who seemed to be addressing to that beautiful planet her plaintive orisons. Orlando wished himself with Monimia; and thought with delight that within two hours he should be so, and should relate the unpleasant alarm of the day, only to tell her it was over, and had eventually been fortunate in drawing from Mrs.

Rayland declarations more than ever favourable to his future hopes.

The whole party sat down to supper in this cheerful disposition. The General, like a happy lover, was particularly animated; and the younger girls were much amused by some anecdotes he was relating, when a servant entered hastily, and said that a gentleman who was just come post from London desired to speak to General Tracy.

"To me!" cried the General, changing countenance: "Impossible! I know no business any one can have with me that should give him that trouble. Pray, enquire his name, or send my servants to enquire."

"I will go myself, General," said Orlando. "I thank you," cried Tracy, affecting great unconcern; "but I dare say it is nothing worth your troubling yourself to go out for."

Orlando, however, went out, and instantly returned bringing with him Captain Warwick.

Surprise was visible on the faces of all the party, but that of General Tracy expressed consternation—*Why* Warwick came he could not conjecture; but he felt it to be extremely disagreeable to him that he came at all. Warwick was covered with dust, and had that wild and fatigued look that announces tumult of spirit from an hot and rapid journey. The person, however, that nature had given him, was such as no disadvantageous circumstance could obscure. He looked like a young hero just returned unhurt from the field to recount its triumphs.

After addressing his uncle, and being introduced to Mr. and Mrs. Somerive, he turned gaily to Orlando, and, shaking him by the hand, said, "I don't know, my friend, how you can ever forgive the man whose fortune it is to announce to you that you must quit immediately such a circle of friends as I now find you in!"

"Quit them!" exclaimed Mrs. Somerive. "Quit us! leave us!" cried her husband.—"Yes, indeed!" answered Warwick with less vivacity: "That part of our regiment which is in England, consisting of two companies, is ordered to join the troops that are going thither, and are to sail from Portsmouth next week. The moment I was sure of this, which was not till late last night, I thought it best to come down myself; because the time is so short that my friend here, the young ancient,[1] had better proceed immediately from hence to Portsmouth."

Never was a greater, a more sudden change, than these few words made in the dispositions of all present—except Tracy, whose only distress was the appearance of Warwick, where he so little wished to see

---

[1]   Ensign. [CS]

him. Mrs. Somerive, struck to the heart by the cruel idea of losing Orlando, retired in silent tears; and her daughters, little less affected, followed her. Somerive bore this painful intelligence with more apparent fortitude; but he felt it with even greater severity, and with something like a prepossession that he should never see Orlando again if he left England. He stifled, however, his emotions, and endeavoured to do the honours of his house to his unexpected visitor; but the effort was too painful to be long supported, and in a few moments he left the room, saying to Orlando, that as the General and Captain Warwick might perhaps have some business, they would leave them together.

CHAP. IX.

Mr. Somerive threw himself into a chair, and, clasping his hands eagerly together, exclaimed, "Good God! what is to be done now?"

"Nothing, my dear Sir," replied Orlando, "can or ought to be done, but for me to obey the orders I have received; and, I beseech you, do not suffer a matter so much in course, or which might have been so easily foreseen, to make you unhappy!"

"What will become of me," cried Somerive wildly, "when you, Orlando, are gone?—And your brother, your unhappy brother! is a misery rather than a protection to your sisters, to your mother...!"

"They will want no protector, Sir," said Orlando, much affected by his father's distress, "while you live—and...!"

"That will be but a very little while, my son! the cruelty of your brother has broken my heart! While you were all that could make me amends, the wound, however incurable, was not immediately mortal; but now—!"

He put his hands on his heart, as if he really felt there the incurable wound he described bleed afresh. Orlando, concealing his own concern as well as he could, endeavoured to sooth his father, by representing to him that this was always likely to happen, and that probably a few months would restore him to his family.—Somerive listened to nothing but his own overwhelming apprehensions, and cast his thoughts around to every remedy that might be applied to so great an evil. The assurance General Tracy had given him that there was no likelihood Orlando should be sent abroad, now appeared a cruel deception, which had betrayed him into such folly and rashness as sending into the army that son on whom rested all the dependence of his family.—Bitterly repenting what he could not now recall, he caught at the hope that Mrs. Rayland might interpose to prevent her favourite's being exposed to the dangers of an American campaign—"You cannot go," cried Somerive, after a moment's pause; "Mrs. Rayland will never suffer it—it will be renouncing all the advantages she offers you."

"I must then renounce them, Sir," said Orlando; "because I must otherwise renounce my honour.—What figure, I beseech you, would a man make, who having in December accepted a commission, should resign it in May because he is ordered abroad? My dear Sir, could you wish such an instance should happen in the person of your Orlando?"

The unhappy father could not but acknowledge the truth of what Orlando said; but his heart, still unable to resist the pain inflicted by the idea of losing him, clung involuntarily to the hope that the attachment of Mrs. Rayland might furnish him with an excuse for withdrawing from the army, and the greatness of the object for which he staid justify his doing so to the world.—Orlando in vain contended that this could not be, and besought his father not to give to his mother any expectations that it could—"Consider, Sir," said he, "that my mother will suffer enough; and let us try rather to soften those sufferings than to aggravate them by suspense, and by those fallacious hopes which will serve only to irritate her concern: when my going to whither my duty calls me is known to be inevitable, my mother, with all her tenderness of heart, is too reasonable either fruitlessly to oppose or immeasurably to lament it—she would despise a young man who shrunk from his profession because there was danger in it, and, I am sure, affectionate as she is, would rather see her son dead with honour, than living under the stigma of cowardice!"

"I believe you are right, Orlando," replied Somerive; "and I will endeavour, my son, to conquer this selfish weakness.—But Mrs. Rayland, it is necessary you immediately see her."—"I shall go thither to-night, Sir," said Orlando, "that I may wait upon her early in the morning; but do not, I entreat you, harbour an idea that Mrs. Rayland will even *wish* to prevent my departure."

Somerive now, at the earnest entreaty of Orlando, promised to compose himself before he went to his wife and daughters, and not to encourage their want of fortitude, by shewing himself wholly deficient in it. He then wished him good night, saying, that he would speak a few words to Captain Warwick, and then go to the Hall.

Somerive retired with an oppressed heart; and Orlando entreated Warwick to walk with him part of the way. He then heard that he must go to Portsmouth within two days; and Warwick, who spoke of it with all the indifference of a soldier long used to these sudden orders, proceeded to talk of other matters.—"Do you know," said he, "that I am in love with all your sisters, my friend; but particularly with my future aunt?—Orlando, I shall be a very *loving* nephew.—What eyes the rogue has!—Egad, I shall be always commending the Portuguese fashion of marrying one's aunt—that is, if our old boy should have the conscience to make an honourable retreat."

"You are a happy man, Warwick," answered Orlando: "How lightly you can talk of what would depress half the young fellows in England—the chance of losing such a fortune as the General's marriage may deprive you of!"

"Oh, hang it!" replied Warwick, "'tis not the fortune I mind, for I suppose I shall have some of it at last, unless some little cousins should have the ill nature to appear against me; but I hate that such a lovely girl as this Isabella of yours should be sacrificed to my poor old uncle, whom, if you could see him in the morning, before he is, like Lord Ogleby,[1] wound up for the day, you would vote to be much fitter for flannels and a good old nurse, than for a husband to a girl of nineteen[2]—and such a girl! upon my soul, she is a little divinity!"

"Not half so interesting in my mind," said Orlando, "as the soft, sensible Selina."

"You are no judge of your sisters—Selina, that is I suppose the second, is a beautiful Madonna; but Isabella, my most respectable aunt, is a Thalia, a Euphrosyne.[3]—I have a great notion, Somerive, that she would prefer the nephew to the uncle—I have half a mind to try."

---

1 In *The Clandestine Marriage* (1766) by George Colman the Elder and David Garrick, the valet Brush mocks his master Lord Ogleby: "What with qualms, age, rheumatism, and a few surfeits in his youth, he must have a great deal of brushing, oiling, screwing, and winding-up, to set him a-going for the day" (II.i). The play's plot mirrors *The Old Manor House* in several ways, although characters and plotlines are conflated: the young hero Lovewell secretly marries the heroine Fanny. Lord Ogleby and his nephew Sir John Melvil also fall in love with Fanny. Like Orlando, Lovewell secretly visits Fanny's bedroom. The play, and Smith's allusions to it, turn on the misunderstandings, and risks to a woman's reputation, resulting from a secret marriage.

2 As Ehrenpreis notes (540, n. to p. 324), Warwick's description of Isabella as nineteen contradicts other descriptions in the novel where she is variously "not of age" (i.e., not yet twenty-one), twenty-one, and older than Orlando, who is twenty (see note 1, p. 175). Either Warwick romanticizes Isabella's age, or Smith is once again careless with her characters' ages.

3 Warwick suggests that Selina's beauty is divine and maternal—that is, disembodied—while Isabella's is more embodied; Thalia and Euphrosyne are two of the three Graces, famously sculpted (1815–17) as nude figures by Antonio Canova.

"There is hardly time for the experiment, I fear," answered Orlando; who made an effort to be as unconcerned as his friend.

"Not time!" cried Warwick. "Yes, there is time enough for a soldier accustomed to carry every point by a *coup de main*—I own, indeed, for an approach by sap I should be too much limited.—Orlando, shall I try my military skill? have I your leave?—Or should you object to exchange the intended grave Governor for the Soldier of fortune?"

"Not I, indeed," answered Orlando; "you have my permission, Warwick—and so now I will wish you good night; for, if I take you any farther, you will not find your way back."[1]

"Trust that to me, Orlando," answered his friend; "I am used to reconnoitre in all lights, from the golden rays of Phoebus to the accommodating beams of the paper lantern of an apple-woman at the corner of the street in a country town.—But whither art going, my friend? for that is a question which I set forth without asking."

"To the Hall," replied Orlando.

"To the Hall!—and to the turret of that Hall!—Oh! you happy dog!—

Monimia—my angel!—It was not kind
To leave me like a turtle here alone![2]

Hah, my friend! has your sweet nymph of the enchanted tower no para-nymph that you could introduce me to? It will be horribly flat for me to go back, to go to my solitary couch, and envy you here, and my prosperous uncle there—I shall hang myself before morning."

Orlando, hurt at this light way of naming Monimia, answered rather coldly, "Your spirits are really enviable, Warwick! but do no let them hurry you into a persuasion that I am happy enough now to be amused with them, pleasant as they are!"

---

[1] The ease with which Orlando gives Warwick "permission" to assail Isabella's emotional battlements once again points out his inadequacy—here, as a brother—and also gives Smith another chance to weave anti-romance into her "history."

[2] The quotation is from Otway's *The Orphan* (II.i.323–24). Warwick exclaims lines (indicated by the dashes and exclamation mark) that are otherwise rather subdued in the play. His assumption that Monimia is Orlando's lover (based on her servant status) further undercuts the reliability of a romantic approach to life. Warwick's subsequent allusions to Hero and Leander, Romeo and Juliet, and Gray's "Ode" illustrate that Orlando's handling of his love affair is clichéd and trite.

"Why, what the devil's the matter with you?" answered Warwick; "you are not going to turn parson, I trow? But really so dolorous a tone is fit only for the pulpit of a methodist.—Why, what makes you *unhappy*, when such a girl as you describe Monimia"—

Orlando interrupted him warmly—"You are determined to mistake me, Captain Warwick! Whatever confidence I have reposed in you in regard to Monimia, surely I have never said any thing that should authorise you to speak thus lightly of her. It is true that I love her passionately, that her heart is mine; but if you suppose—"

"Pooh, pooh! I suppose nothing—Pr'ythee do not be so grave about your little Hero, my dear Leander!"[1]—Then assuming a more serious tone, he added:"But upon my soul, I mean nothing offensive, my friend; and rattled as much to disguise my own heaviness as to divert yours, for I have left people with whom I should much rather have remained a little longer, and that without having time to attempt consoling the gentle heart that is breaking for me." He then communicated to Orlando an intrigue in which he had engaged after he left him. Orlando represented to him all the cruelty and folly of his conduct.—"Oh! yes," cried Warwick;"all that you say is very wise and very true, and it must be owned that it comes with peculiar propriety from you, my most sage friend!—Now that we are within sight of the Hall, for, if I mistake not, that great building which is before us is the abode of the sybil whose rent-roll exceeds in value the famous leaves of antiquity,[2] and of the fair vestal, who—"

"Nay, nay!" cried Orlando, "you are beginning again; I will not stay to hear you."

"Only let me go with you to the next rise," answered Warwick;"only shew me the light from the turret, and I will be content:

It is the East—and Juliet is the sun![3]

And then I will go back like a miserable wretch as I am, and try to dream of my future aunt."

---

[1] Hero and Leander suffer a tragic love in which Leander drowns while attempting to cross the Hellespont at night to reach Hero; she subsequently drowns herself in despair. Warwick consistently makes light of Orlando's romantic pretensions, as the following few notes also show.

[2] The Sybil was a prophet whose "leaves"—that is, books—of prophecies were sought by those who desired the truth.

[3] *Romeo and Juliet*, II.ii.3.

"Rather try not to dream of her," said Orlando; "upon my honour, Warwick, this *gaieté de coeur* of yours excites at once my envy and my fear."

"Oh! a soldier, and afraid!—What, do you think I shall release the General's fair prisoner, and, like an undutiful nephew, escape from the garrison with the old boy's prize?"

"No, no, Warwick, I have no such apprehensions; but"—"But what? Egad, my friend, considered in a political light, it is clear to me that this is the very best thing I could do.—But behold the venerable towers of Rayland Hall!

Ye distant spires, ye antique towers,
That crown the woody glade,
Where fond Orlando still adores
The sweet imprison'd maid!

Give me a moment's time," added Warwick, pausing—"but a moment, and I will make for you a parody on the whole." [1]

"You are intolerable, Warwick," cried Orlando, "and I positively will endure you no longer!"—"Yes, a little longer," said Warwick; "let me finish my parody; I tell you I am in a fortunate vein.—You, Orlando, who are yourself a poet, would you be tasteless enough to check a man inspired?—Listen, I am going on—"

"Nay, but this is a sad trifling, my dear Warwick! and what is worse, you will really be heard from the house, which will not be a trifling inconvenience. Besides, upon my honour, your returning late across the park is unsafe; for, when the old butler has no reasons of his own to have them kept up, there are three fierce blood-hounds let loose to range over it all night, and they would not fail to seize any stranger."

"D—n your blood-hounds!—Pr'ythee, Orlando, do you think I am not accustomed to guards of all sorts, and have encountered the mastiff dog, and the dragon aunt, in twenty scrambling adventures?"

"I do not doubt your prowess," replied Orlando; "but here, as there is no reward, why should you exert it?"

"*Mais seulement pour me tenir en haleine, mon ami, et pour passer le tems*[2]—But, however, if it is seriously inconvenient to you, I will go.— Come, now, be serious—at what time to-morrow shall you be at your father's?"

---

[1]   Gray's Ode on a distant Prospect of Eton College. [CS]

[2]   "But only to keep me breathing [ie, amuse myself], my friend, and to pass the time."

"Long before you are awake probably, for you know you never are very alert in a morning."

"Not when I have nothing to do; but, pray, are your family early risers? At what hour may I ask, by anticipation, the blessing of my blooming aunt?"

"That you must discover, for it is very uncertain—and now, Warwick, once more good night!"

"Good night! O most fortunate and valorous Orlando of the enchanted castle!"

Orlando then gave his light-hearted friend directions to find his way back, and when he left him, advanced slowly towards the house, from which he was not above three hundred yards distant.

His mind, which had been at first distracted by the distress of his father, and since harrassed by the ill-timed raillery of his friend, now returned to those bitter reflections which arose from the certainty of his being immediately to take a long leave of Monimia, and under the cruel necessity of telling her so. But a few hours since he looked forward to the pleasure of meeting Monimia with only tidings of satisfaction and hope; now, he was to meet her, only to tell her that they were to part so soon, never perhaps to meet again!

He now entered his Study (for one of the servants sat up to let him in), and endeavoured to collect himself enough to communicate what he had to say to Monimia, without too much shocking her. But when he thought that their next meeting might be the last they should ever have, his own courage forsook him, and he dreaded lest he should be quite unable to sustain hers.

The hour soon came when he knew she expected him; and he trembled as he led her down the stairs. At length, since it was impossible to disguise from her those emotions which agitated his mind, he related to her all the occurrences of the eventful day, and the necessity there was for his preparing himself the next day, and taking leave of this part of the country the day following.

Monimia could not shed tears; her heart seemed petrified by the greatness and suddenness of the blow, which fell with more force, because their last interview had been so little embittered by fears or broken by alarms. When, however, Orlando explained to her, that his honour would be irreparably injured if he even expressed any reluctance to enter on the active parts of the profession he had engaged in, and that to attempt disengaging himself now would be a blemish on his character from which he could never recover, her good sense, and her true tenderness for him, gave her some degree of composure, and even of resolution. As he declared that he felt nothing so severely as leaving her—leaving her unprotected, and almost alone in the world, she nobly struggled to conceal her own anguish, that she might not aggravate his; and, since his going was inevitable, endeavoured not to depress, by her fears, that spirit with which it was necessary for him to go.

Orlando, as much charmed by her sense as her affection, became ashamed of betraying less tender resolution than a timid uninformed girl. She taught him how to repress his concern; and this interview, instead of increasing his regret, fortified his mind against it. Monimia remained with him a less time than usual—with faltering lips he entreated her to meet him again the next night because it would be the last.—Monimia, unable to articulate, assented only by a broken sigh! and Orlando retired to his bed, where sleep absolutely refused to indulge him with a few hours of forgetfulness till towards morning.

When he had told Warwick that he should be at his father's house early in the morning, he forgot that he should be detained by the necessity he was under to attend Mrs. Rayland. He sent up for permission to wait upon her at breakfast, which was immediately granted; and he opened to her, as soon as he was admitted, the reason of this early visit, and the necessity he was under to take leave of her the next day to join his regiment in America.

Mrs. Rayland expressed more surprise than concern at this information: accustomed, from early impressions, to high ideas of the military glory of her ancestors, and considering the Americans as rebels and round-heads, to conquer them seemed to her to be not only a national cause, but one in which her family were particularly bound to engage.—She had contemplated the honours, and thought little of the dangers of war. The trophies that surrounded the picture of her warlike grandfather Sir Orlando, and the honourable mention that was made of his prowess in the family annals, seemed to her ample compensation for a wound in his leg, which had made him a little lame for the rest of his life. Of Orlando's personal danger, therefore, she had, as he expected, no apprehensions, and was rather desirous he should justify her partiality to him, by emulating the fame of the heroes of her family, than afraid of what might happen in the experiment.

Mrs. Rayland parted from him in high good humour, desired he would give her as much time as he could the next day, and set out from the Hall rather than from West Wolverton, when he went to

Portsmouth; all which Orlando readily promised, and then, with a heavy heart, went to the house of his father.

That capricious fate which seemed to be weary of the favours she had long been accumulating on the head of General Tracy, appeared now determined to discard him, as she is often said to do her ancient favourites. A more malicious trick than she now meditated, could hardly befall any of them—The General had long kept off, by art, an attack of the gout, a disease to which he did not allow himself to be supposed liable; but whether it was the long walk of the preceding evening, or the tumult of his spirits on his approaching nuptials, or the sudden sight of his nephew, that occasioned an unlucky revulsion, certain it is that, in the middle of the night, he was awakened by this most inexorable disease peremptorily telling him, in more than one of his joints, that the visit would be more oppressive by having been so long delayed. His valet de chambre was hastily summoned, with such applications as, however dangerous, had sometimes repelled its attacks; but it was to no purpose the unfortunate General would have risked his life to preserve his activity; the morning found him a cripple, compelled to yield, with whatever reluctance, to the old remedies of patience and flannel. This circumstance, so very mal-apropos, appeared yet more terrible to the General, when he reflected that Warwick, the formidable handsome Warwick, had now an opportunity of entertaining Isabella: and the pain of his mind irritating and increasing his bodily sufferings, Mr. Somerive, instead of a man of the church, who was within three days to have attended on his guest, thought it more expedient to send for a physician.

Tracy, however, considered of nothing so earnestly as getting Warwick away—It was true, indeed, that he was to go away the next day, or at farthest the day after that, which depended upon the letters he received from Portsmouth; but, that he should be under the same roof with Isabella was not to be endured. After many plans, therefore, adopted and rejected, the General at last determined that he would make some pretence to send Warwick to London which he could not evade, and imagined that he should then be able to say,

"Being gone—I am myself again!"[1]

For this purpose he ordered his nephew to be called to his bed-side; and when Orlando arrived at the house, they were in close conference.

---

[1]   *Macbeth*, III.iv.106–07. Smith misquotes slightly: "Why so, being gone, / I am a man again."

The three girls were at work in the parlour when their brother entered it. He observed something very unusual in the manner of Isabella, who spoke little; while all his questions were answered by one of his youngest sisters. He enquired for Warwick; and, in a moment, heard him come down stairs. He went to him in the Hall, and Warwick hastily said—"Orlando, will you come out with me? I have something to say to you."

They went together into the avenue: Warwick walked fast, but appeared lost in thought; and Orlando, oppressed with his own sorrows, had no inclination to speak first.

At length Warwick, as if he had found the expedient he wanted, exclaimed suddenly—"By Heaven it will do?—it must do!—it shall do!"

"Indeed!" said Orlando; "may I know what?"

"Tell me, my friend," cried Warwick with vehement warmth—"tell me if you love Monimia—if it is not death to part with her?"

"To what purpose is such a question? You know I exist but for her—you know I should prefer death to this separation, because my mind will be torn to pieces by anxiety for what may befall her in my absence!"

"Well, then, I may trust you—I may ask what you would do for *that* friend who should not only prevent your parting with her, but give you your Monimia for ever!"

"Do not trifle with me, Warwick," said Orlando mournfully, "I cannot bear it!"

"By all that is sacred!" replied Warwick, "I never was more in earnest in my life; and, if you do not trifle with yourself, Monimia may be yours immediately, and it will be beyond the power of fortune to divide you!"

"Explain yourself then—but it is impossible, and your wild imagination only—"

"Say rather," retorted Warwick, "that your cold prudence will destroy what my *imagination* would realize.—I tell you, it is in your own power to be happy; but before I reveal how, swear to me, upon the honour of a soldier and a gentleman, that if you do not *approve* my plan you will not betray it."

"Surely, there is little need," said Orlando, more and more amazed, "of my giving you an oath that I will not betray my friend, especially when he meditates how to serve me."

"Pardon me," cried Warwick; "I desire, Orlando, to serve you; but I am not quite so disinterested as not to think a little of myself, at the same time—"

"I may venture to swear, Warwick, that I will never betray you," said Orlando gravely; "but put an end to these riddles."

"You swear then, upon the honour of a soldier and a gentleman, that you will not mar my plan if you will not make yourself a party in it— you have sworn."

"I have," answered Orlando, "sworn; but if it relates—"At that moment an idea of the truth occurred to him.

"If it relates to your sisters, you were going to say, the oath is not binding—Well it *does* relate to Isabella!"

"To Isabella?"

"Yes, to Isabella. It matters not, nor have I time to relate, how I have contrived, even in this short interval, to persuade your lovely sister that a young fellow of three-and-twenty, with only *one* thousand pounds in the world, and his commission, is more to her taste than an old one of three-and-sixty, who is a General, and worth about an hundred and fifty times that sum.—I told you, I always carried my object by a *coup de main*.—To be brief, I am madly in love with Isabella, and she is as much in love with me as she dares to own on so short an acquaintance.—My uncle is in love with her too; but she is not at all in love with him; and as she prefers the nephew with his knap-sack to the uncle with his money-sack, she shall not be sacrificed to him; but I will marry her, and take her with me to America."[1]

"Marry her!" cried Orlando in extreme surprise.

"Why, you may well wonder, to be sure, because I believe she is the only girl in the world that could have made me take so extraordinary a resolution."

"But how is it possible? How is there time to execute it?"

"Oh, my friend! it is a matter that takes up very little time when the parties are agreed."

"But Isabella is not of age; she cannot be married here."

"She may in Jersey, though,"

"In Jersey?"

"Yes; and it is very possible to go from Portsmouth to Jersey, and be back again time enough for the sailing of the squadron we must proceed with to America."

"And has Isabella consented to all this?"

"No, because I have not directly proposed it to her; nor did I, till since the conversation I have had with my uncle, know that I should

---

[1] Shadowing the romance of Orlando and Monimia is the "real" romance of Warwick and Isabella, which conforms much more closely to generic convention. Orlando's romance seems incapable of living up to its generic ideal.

have the means of performing it, which (I thank him) his anticipating jealousy has put into my hands." Warwick then took out of his pocket-book a draft of the General's to him for a thousand pounds, payable at sight in London.—"My grave old uncle," cried he, "for whom I think fortune has interfered, to prevent his being ridiculous in his old age, is just now more miserable because *I* am in the house, than because the gout is in his toe; and he has found out, that instead of staying till to-morrow or next day to go to Portsmouth with you, it will be better for me to set out as soon as I can, to do some business for him in London, which, though he never thought of it before, he now says admits of no delay; and that I may have no excuse to stay afterwards on my own business, or to return hither, he has given me a bank note of an hundred for my immediate expences, and this draft for a thousand—the douceur he promised me on his marriage."

"Well!"

"Well! and so we shall not want money, which would have been an almost invincible impediment. I shall now, as soon as I have settled our proceedings with my angelic Isabel, which I have not the least doubt of doing, make the best of my way to London, execute the imaginary business which my most profoundly politic uncle has given me, and then—"

"I do not yet understand you," said Orlando; "how is my sister to be of this party, or how ..."

"Nothing so easy," answered Warwick; "I thought, my friend, you were enough in love yourself to suppose every thing possible, and not to hesitate between quitting your mistress, perhaps for ever, and taking her with you as your wife.—I go from London to Portsmouth—Is there any difficulty in your meeting me there with my Isabella and your Monimia? You know there is not; and whatever scruples your sister may have, or as you perhaps think ought to have, to taking such a journey to me on the acquaintance of the day, will be obviated by your going with her, and by her having a female companion.—My purse is yours, and its present condition will enable us to do well enough till something or other happens in our favour—*I am determined*, if Isabella consents, which I am now going to try; and so I leave you, Orlando, to consider of my proposal: you must, however, resolve quickly; for I shall set out almost as soon as dinner is over for London, as I have promised my uncle."

Warwick then walked away towards the house, leaving Orlando in a state of mind difficult to be conceived or described. To have the power of taking with him his adored Monimia, secure of a present support for her, and certain that with him she would be happy in any country, was a temptation it was almost impossible to resist: when he considered on the other hand, the pain of being separated from her, for a long, perhaps an eternal absence, and of leaving her to the mercy of such a woman as Mrs. Lennard, who might, either by withdrawing her protection, or rendering it an intolerable bondage, drive the lovely orphan alone and friendless into a cruel world; other means of saving her he had none, and neither the laws of God or man were against those which were now so unexpectedly offered him.

But his father, already broken-hearted by the desertion of one of his children, would be hurried to the grave by thus being deceived by two others. His mother would be rendered wretched, and he should perhaps accuse himself of being accessary to the death of both his parents:—the thought was not to be borne. He determined for a moment to renounce every happiness which must be purchased by their misery, and not only to fly himself from this almost irresistible temptation, but to prevent Isabella from yielding to it. But this resolution was hardly formed, before the image of Monimia weeping in solitude her desolate fate, complaining to him, who was too far off to hear—ill-treated or abandoned by her aunt—exposed to the insults of the profligate, and the contempt of the fortunate—came with all its pathetic interest to win him from his duty; and then, the happiness of calling her his—of knowing that only death could divide them! the contest was dreadful; and he knew that when he saw Monimia it would be worse.—Once or twice he determined to put an end to it, by telling his father; but to this desperate expedient was opposed the honour he had given to Warwick not to betray, if he would not participate, the intended flight of his sister; nor did he imagine that her going off with Warwick would be a very distressing circumstance to his father.—However enraged the General might at first be, his pride would not suffer him finally to abandon his nephew. In every point but that of present fortune, Warwick must have the preference; and Orlando thought that he had often seen, by his father's countenance as he looked at Isabella, that he regretted the sacrifice he was induced by his own circumstances to promote.— But with himself it was quite otherwise; and the rash step he was thus strongly tempted to take, would blast at once all those hopes his father now so fondly cherished in regard to the Rayland estate (for it was certain Mrs. Rayland would never forgive him); and, by acceding to Warwick's proposal, he must deeply aggravate every pang of that separation which his father seemed already unable to endure.

CHAP. X.

Torn by these distracting contests between love and duty, Orlando continued for some moments to traverse the place where Warwick had left him. His two younger sisters appeared to interrupt without relieving this painful debate. He learned from them that Captain Warwick and Isabella were gone together for a walk, and that the former had sent them to him, as he wanted to speak with them. A new doubt now arose in the mind of Orlando—Ought he to communicate to Selina what was going forward, of which she appeared to be ignorant? or conceal within his own bosom what he could not prevent, or entirely disapprove? After a little consideration he thought it would be best not to make Selina a party: and he endeavoured to dissemble as well as he could the conflict of passions which were preying on his heart. His father, pale and dejected, with a slow and languid step, soon after joined them: he bade the two girls go to their mother, and then taking Orlando's arm, they walked together to a greater distance from the house.

"You go then to-morrow, Orlando?" said Somerive: "there are no hopes of any favourable reverse to this cruel sentence? Mrs. Rayland, I find,"—he hesitated—"does not wish to interfere, Sir," replied Orlando. "On the contrary, she seems to think that a young man of my age and profession cannot be so well employed as in the actual service of his country."

Somerive answered only with a deep sigh; and after a short pause Orlando went on:

"I beseech you, my dearest Sir, not to make yourself thus unhappy. Consider that, notwithstanding this temporary parting, my prospects are infinitely better than I had any right to expect, and—"

"They might, however, have been better," said his father in his turn interrupting him—"at least they might have been more permanently assured, if you had listened to the proposals we heard yesterday: instead of quitting your family, you might then have been settled near it in affluence."

"Let us not, my dear father," answered Orlando, "discuss that any more; I would not marry Miss Hollybourn, if she could give me a kingdom."

"Nor give up your boyish fancy for that girl at the Hall to save your family, to save your father!"

Orlando started as if he had trod on a serpent: this was a string that jarred too much, it threatened to destroy all the virtuous resolutions which he had been labouring to adopt; for it seemed to be cruelty and injustice to his father to reproach him; and, conscious of the sacrifice he hoped to have fortitude enough to make, it appeared too hard that he was at that moment blamed for not making more.

"No, Sir," said he, "I will not give up my fancy for the girl at the Hall, as you are pleased to term her; but I see not how my affection for her can injure my family, nor how my resigning her could save them— For God's sake, do not embitter the few hours we are to pass together, either by reproaches which indeed I do not deserve, or by concern which the occasion does not demand. Believe me, your son suffers enough, without the additional misery of seeing you either displeased with him or grieving for him."

Orlando, then fearful that any farther conversation with his father, in the humour he seemed to be in, would serve only to give pain to them both, and wishing to be alone for a few minutes before he again saw Warwick, went another way; and on his return to the house he found an official letter directing him to repair immediately for Portsmouth, where the captain of his company was assembling his men in order to embark immediately for America.

Thus certain that he must set out the next day, and that he had only a few moments before he must meet Warwick and give his answer, he hid himself in the least frequented part of the shrubbery that adjoined to the house, and again considered of the tempting offer that was made him. Fascinating as it was, and though his excessive affection for Monimia was often on the point of overbalancing every other consideration whatever; his pride and his duty, his affection for his father, and his respect for himself, united at length to conquer his inclination. How could he bear to plunge a dagger into the heart of his father, who had little other hope on earth but in him? or, if he could determine on that, and fortify himself against the reproaches his conscience might make him, how could he submit to be obliged for his support, for the support of Monimia, to Warwick? There was something repugnant to the generous feelings of Orlando, in Warwick's using the very money his uncle had given him, as the means of disappointing his benefactor. But, whatever apology Warwick might make to himself for this, Orlando thought there could be none for him if he were to participate in money thus acquired. He knew that, accustomed to expence and indulgencies as his friend was, a thousand pounds would be no very permanent resource when Isabella was to share it: and he could not bear that *he* should be supposed to connive at her flight, only to become with Monimia a burthen to her and Warwick. On the slender pay of an ensign it were madness to think he could support a wife, however humble might be her wishes; and his marriage would cut him off for ever from all hopes of that assistance from Mrs. Rayland, which his father, even though he should forgive, had not the power to afford him. Could he then endure to expose his beloved Monimia to the inconveniencies of following a camp, without having the means of procuring her such alleviations as it allowed? He might die in the field, and leave her exposed to hazards infinitely greater than those which could befall her in England. This last consideration determined him—It decided his wavering virtue, and he resolved to give Warwick a positive refusal immediately before he should relapse, and to conceal the almost invincible temptation he had been under from his Monimia, lest her weaker, softer heart yielding to it, he should again find himself unable to resist it.

He now hastened to find Warwick; and fortunately met him at the entrance of the house, whither they were summoned to dinner. Warwick enquired with great eagerness on what he had resolved. "To be miserable," answered Orlando, "in abstaining from what is wrong. I should be miserable if I agreed, Warwick, to your proposal; and I have determined, since either way I must be unhappy, to be so with integrity rather than self-reproach."

"What the devil!" said Warwick, "you won't go then my way?"

"No, I will not."

"But you will not, I hope, Sir," cried Warwick half angry—"you will not think it necessary to prevent your sister?"

Orlando, who did not greatly relish the peremptory manner in which this was said, answered coldly, "You have my honour, Captain Warwick, and any other question is an affront."

"Forgive me, my friend," replied Warwick, resuming his usual good humour—"forgive me for doubting you. I cannot live without Isabella, nor do I intend to try at it—I have prevailed upon her, not without difficulty I assure you, to consent to meet me at Portsmouth.—You know how much happiness your going with Monimia would have given to us all!—But I have not a moment to argue the matter with you.—You say you are determined—So am I; and all I ask of you is, that you will not rob me of my happiness, upon the same false, cold sort of reasoning system to which you are sacrificing your own."

A servant now coming out to say that dinner waited, they went into the house. A melancholy and silent meal was soon concluded. The General's horse was brought to the door, on which Warwick was to go to the next post town: and he rose to take leave of the family, which he did with a composure that amazed Orlando, who had no idea how a man could so conceal the feelings which must on such an occasion naturally arise. Isabella was far from appearing so tranquil; but all the rest were too much engaged with their own sensations to remark those which her countenance betrayed, though to Orlando her confusion was evident.

Warwick went up to receive the last orders of his uncle, and then prepared to mount his horse; when Orlando took his arm, and begged he would send the servant on with the horses, and give him a few moment's attention as they walked on after them.

Warwick readily agreed, in hopes that he had changed his mind; but Orlando soon put an end to such expectations by asking him in what way Isabella was to meet him.—"I have given you my honour, Warwick," said he, "not to betray you: but I must have yours in return that my sister shall be exposed to no improper adventures. How is she who never was from home in her life, but for a few days with her mother in London, to find her way to Portsmouth?"

"Ridiculous!" exclaimed Warwick, "to find her way to Portsmouth! One would really think she was to take a flight to the extreme parts of the earth, instead of hardly five-and-thirty miles.—My poor friend, thou hast not been used, I see, to these little adventures—I have an aid-de-camp, who, in the absence of his commander, can secure a little deserter for him.—Isabella is determined to trust me; and it may suffice you to know that I love her too well not to take every possible precaution for her safety."

"No," said Orlando, "it may *not* suffice—Though I have promised not to interfere, it is only on condition that I am sure my sister will not suffer either in her person or her reputation. Give me therefore the particulars."

Warwick then related, that his servant, on whom he could depend, was on the evening they should appoint to be ready with a post-chaise and four at some place they could fix upon; where after supper Isabella, instead of retiring to her room, should meet it—"Nothing is more easy, I suppose," said Warwick, "or less dangerous, than for your sister to do this; and, when she is once off in the chaise, relays of horses being ordered at the two stages between this and Portsmouth, my servant, following on horseback, will escort her thither in less than four hours: there I shall have a vessel ready to carry us to Jersey—Money, my dear boy! Money, contrivance and courage are all that are necessary.—I have found the two first, and have given the last to the only person that wanted it.—I have convinced Isabella that, if she follows my directions, she may be at Portsmouth before she is missed, and married before any one can guess where to look for her.—Well, Orlando, you now have my whole plan; and I trust to your honour not to render it abortive."

"And I," replied Orlando, "trust my sister to yours, not without reluctance and remorse—We shall probably meet at Portsmouth?"

"Probably," answered Warwick; "for the two companies are to embark at the same time; and I only trust to some private interest, which I have prevailed upon my uncle to make for me, to procure leave to embark in whatever vessel is most convenient.—The captain of one of the frigates is my particular friend, and I shall probably get a birth with him instead of going in a transport." Orlando, to whom the whole scheme appeared easily practicable, now again felt all the disposition to join in it which he had before combatted: but again his reason came to his aid, and he saw Warwick depart without betraying any symptoms of that struggle which still tore his heart.

Once more, however, he subdued it; and recalled his resolution to go through the trying scene which was to wait him on his return to the house, where he was early in the evening to bid adieu to all his family, in order to sup with Mrs. Rayland as she had desired; and then! the last cruel parting with Monimia, more dreadful than any of his former sufferings, was to embitter his last moments at Rayland-Hall.

The last adieu between a father so affectionate and unhappy and a son so beloved, need not be described—it would indeed be difficult to do it justice. As his mother and his sisters hung weeping about him, he could not help addressing some words to Isabella, however unfavourable the time, which she seemed perfectly to understand—though she shrunk from them, and had carefully avoided giving him any opportunity of speaking to her alone. At length Orlando tore himself away; and not daring to look behind him, yet hardly feeling the ground beneath him, he hurried to the Hall.

Mrs. Rayland received him with as much calmness as if he only came on a usual visit. Of the violent emotions which agitated him she had no idea. Time and uninterrupted prosperity had so blunted the little sensibility nature had given her, that she was utterly incapable of participating or comprehending the acute feelings of her young favourite: yet in her way she was extremely kind to him; and, after giving him another course of excellent advice, which lasted near two hours, she told him, that as his first equipment might have taken a good part of her former present, she had another note of fifty pounds at his service. This present was extremely acceptable to Orlando, who had not above sixty left of her preceding bounty. Mrs. Rayland, detaining Orlando an hour longer than he expected, at length dismissed him with her blessing; and Orlando shed tears of gratitude on her hand, which he kissed, and, without being able to speak, left her.

He then took leave of the servants; but gave to Mrs. Lennard, with whom he desired to speak in her own room, more time than to the rest;

and desirous of doing what he could to soften the situation of his Monimia, he determined to speak to her aunt on her behalf.

"You know, Madam," said he, "that on my last departure you spoke to me of your niece: let me now speak to you of her. My absence may satisfy you as to those suspicions, that I know not why you entertained of me—but let me entreat you to be kind to my lovely young friend, for whom I scruple not to avow to you a very great regard."

"What!" cried Mrs. Lennard, "has she ever then been such an ungrateful girl as to say I was unkind to her?"

"Never," said Orlando:—"in the conversations we have accidentally had, your niece has always spoken of you with gratitude and respect: but, after what you once said to me about her, I should be remiss were I to quit the house without trying to obviate any little lurking prejudice which may at some future time be remembered to her disadvantage: allow me therefore to intercede with you, not only to forget any of these circumstances which may prejudice your mind against her, but to increase that tenderness for her, which does so much honour to your heart."

"Thank you, Sir," said Mrs. Lennard, "but I hope I do not want your advice, nor any body's, to do my duty to the girl, since she is left upon my hands."

Orlando never felt so great an inclination as at that moment, to take Monimia off her hands; and, as he found little was to be hoped for from his solicitations in her favour, he took leave of Mrs. Lennard, and endeavoured, when alone, to collect all his resolution for this final adieu with Monimia; to drive from his recollection the offer of Warwick, which still recurred to tantalize and torment him; to conceal from her that it had ever been made, and to fortify her mind for their long separation while he felt his own sinking under it.

Among other things it occurred to him, that if death or caprice deprived Monimia of the cold and reluctant protection her aunt now afforded her, she might be not only desolate but pennyless. He determined, therefore, to leave with her one of the banker's notes he had just received, of five-and-twenty pounds, and to pass these last moments in arming her against every possible contingency which might happen during his absence, and, as far as he could, instructing her how to act if they occurred.

Monimia, with swollen eyes, from which the tears slowly fell notwithstanding her endeavours to restrain them, listened in silence, as with a faltering tone and in disjointed sentences he went through this mournful task. She promised in a voice hardly articulate to attend to all he desired, and to keep a journal of her life; "though what will it be," said she, "but a journal of sufferings and of sorrow?"

"But when that sorrow, those sufferings are over, my Monimia," cried Orlando, trying to speak cheerfully, "with what transport shall we look back on this journal, and compare our past anxieties with our actual happiness!—Let that idea encourage you amidst the heavy days that are to intervene before we meet again. Whatever you suffer, remember that your Orlando will return to dry your tears! And take care of your precious health, my Monimia, preserve it for him."

She could only answer by a deep drawn sigh; while Orlando, cruel as the scene was, could not determine to put an end to it. Day already dawned; and as he did not mean to go to bed, but had ordered the under-keeper to attend him with the horses as soon as it was light, he knew that he should soon be called by Jacob: yet could he not determine to lead Monimia back to her turret till he heard the man at the door, who, tapping at it, informed him the horses were ready, and the hour passed at which he ordered himself to be called.

Monimia then arose and said—"Farewell then, Orlando!" He had no power to answer her; but led her silently through the chapel, round the court, and to her turret. The moment that tore him from her could not be delayed; he took the last embrace, and hastily bade her shut the door, lest he should fall into such a paroxysm of anguish as might render him unable to leave her at all. Monimia, who could not have supported the pain she endured much longer, with feeble and trembling hands obeyed him; but as slowly he descended the stairs, he heard her loud sobs, and was on the point of returning again to snatch her to his bosom, and declare it impossible to part with her.

The loud noise of a whip, which Jacob impatient of his long delay now sounded around the house, roused him once more.

He started from the dangerous reflection he was indulging, that it was yet in his own power to take Monimia with him, or at least to secure her following him with his sister; and again recovering his courage, he descended the stairs, left for the last time the beloved turret, and in a few moments mounted his horse, and rode almost at full speed through the park. He was soon on the high-road to the first post-town towards Portsmouth; and having ascended an high down that afforded him the last view he could have of Rayland Hall, he stopped on the top of it, and, turning his horse's head, fixed his eyes on the seat of all his past happiness, of all his future hopes, and thought how much he probably had to suffer before he should revisit it again, how probable it was that he should never see it more!

Jacob, who had but little notion of all this, yet supposed the captain, as he was now called at the Hall, was sorry to leave all his friends and Miss Monimmy, and hunting and shooting, and such like, to go to the wars, now thought it might be kind to console him: but Orlando heeded not the very eloquent harangue, which had lasted near a quarter of an hour, but suddenly turned his horse, and set out as speedily as before.

He took a post horse at the town, and put his portmanteau into a Portsmouth diligence[1] that was passing; then dismissing his favourite horse, which he would take no farther, and recommending him particularly to Jacob, who promised to attend to him while he fed at liberty in the park, he made the servant a handsome present, and on the hack which was ready he proceeded as if was pursued; for the speed with which he rode seemed to give him something like relief. A very short time brought him to Portsmouth; where he found his baggage from London just arrived; and learned that some of the soldiers were already embarked, that the wind was fair, and that new orders for the greatest expedition were arrived that day to the commander of the reinforcement going to America.

CHAP. XI.

Exhausted by the fatigue of body and mind, Orlando would now probably have lost the painful recollection of what had passed within the last eight-and-forty hours by transient forgetfulness; but even this was not permitted him: the orders for immediate embarkation were so strict, and the commander of the squadron which was to convoy the transports so impatient to execute the directions of Government, that every thing was hurry and confusion; and Orlando, far from being allowed time to think of what he had left, found the care of the company devolve almost entirely upon him: the men were for the most part raw recruits; the captain, the younger son of an illustrious house, already raised to that rank (though not so old as Orlando), was not come down; and the lieutenant, a man near fifty, was almost incapacitated from attending his duty by the agonies of his wife and a family of several children, who, as they had been in lodgings in a neighbouring town ever since his return from America the preceding year, now assembled around him to bid to their only protector and support a last farewell.

---

[1]   A public stage-coach.

The short notice he had received of his departure had prevented his settling many things for them which were now indispensable; the moment therefore Orlando arrived, this officer (whom he had not before seen) related to him his situation; and Orlando, in generously endeavouring to alleviate his troubles by taking as much business from him as he could, found his additional fatigue well repaid by the necessity it laid him under to detach his mind from his own regret and anxiety. At the first dawn of day he was at the Point—embarking the men and baggage; and the scene of distracting hurry that now presented itself, the quarrels and blasphemy with which the beach resounded, the confusion among the soldiers and sailors, the rage of the commanders and the murmurs of the commanded, the eager impatience of those who had articles to buy for their voyage, and the unfeeling avarice of others who had them to sell, formed altogether a scene as extraordinary as it was new to Orlando, who had never been from the neighbourhood of the Hall except for a few weeks, which were either passed in pleasure in London or in a quiet country town: he heard therefore, with a mixture of wonder and disgust, the human tempest roar in which he was engaged, and for the first time enquired of himself what all this was for?

This was not a place or hour when such a question, however naturally it occurred, could be answered—He was to act, not to speculate; and hardly had he a moment to reflect that, hurried as he was to be, he should not have the satisfaction (if satisfaction it might be called) of seeing Isabella and Warwick before he went himself on board; after which it would be impossible to know what became of them, at least not til his arrival in America. Amid the tumult that surrounded him, this gave him infinite disquiet. A thousand fears for his sister crowded on his mind; he apprehended she might by some accident be prevented in such a place meeting Warwick; he trembled lest, if she did, his conduct towards her, when she was entirely in his power, might be dishonourable. Such were the distressing reflections of Orlando in every momentary pause the confusion of the scene allowed him. But whatever uneasiness he felt, the time permitted him to have no mitigation; and, in the evening of the day after his arrival at Portsmouth, he found himself on board a transport with the greater part of that company to which he belonged, and about an equal number of dragoons with their horses.[1] The wind, though violent, blew down the channel; and at night-fall, all previous

---

[1] Dragoons: the cavalry; cornet: fifth commissioned officer in a cavalry troop, who carried the colours; minority: the state of being underage (i.e. under twenty-one).

orders being given, they obeyed the signal for getting to sea. It was not till they were many miles at sea that Orlando had time to consider his situation: then, the tumult having a little subsided, he saw himself in a little crowded vessel, where nothing could equal the inconvenience to which his soldiers were subjected, but that which the miserable negroes endure in their passage to slavery. Indifferent to this so far as it merely related to himself, he could not see the sufferings to which the men were likely to be exposed without concern. All of them were young and new to the service; and the captain was too attentive to his own delicacy to have time to give the poor fellows all the alleviation their condition allowed them; and, on the second day of their voyage, he found his own situation so unpleasant, that he went in a boat on board one of the frigates, the commander of which was distantly related to him, and obtained of him for the rest of the voyage a birth more suitable to a man of fashion than a crowded transport could afford him.[1]

Orlando, the lieutenant (who was half broken-hearted), and a cornet of horse were left in charge of the men; and it was perhaps fortunate for the former, that he was so incessantly called upon to attend to his duty that he had hardly a moment to command but for repose, and, occupied about others, could think but little of himself.

They had now been so long at sea, that the fresh-water sailors had conquered the first uneasy sensations given by that element, except the young cornet, who was the only son of a very opulent family and heir to an immense fortune: during a very long minority his mother had so humoured him, that even his request to enter the army, though extremely opposite to her wishes, could neither be evaded nor denied. The smart uniform of a light horseman appeared to him extremely desirable; and the possibility of danger in such a service never occurred to him, nor would he listen to it when it was represented by others. He had hardly put on this seducing attire, and provided himself with a very beautiful horse, before he was ordered abroad; and now sick and desponding, this unhappy child of foolish affluence wanted a nurse much more than a broad sword—No puling girl just out of the nursery was ever more helpless; and Orlando at once despised and pitied him; but found that, having been friendly enough to offer him his assistance, his new acquaintance soon leaned entirely upon him; and that,

---

[1] It has lately been alledged in defence of the Slave Trade, that Negroes on board Guineamen are allowed *almost* as much room as a Soldier in a Transport.—Excellent reasoning! [CS]

having been used to have every one around him at his command, he received every friendly attention which compassion extorted from others, as matters of course.

The fleet had now passed Madeira, without however touching at it, and were launched into the great Atlantic Ocean. Hitherto their voyage had been prosperous and quick; and a short time promised to terminate it: but the heat of the weather, operating on the crowds of men and of horses stowed in such a vessel, now began to be severely felt. A fever of the malignant kind broke out; and within a week five men sickened of it, of whom three died; and the other two, more like spectres than living creatures, seemed by their partial recovery only to be reserved for more lingering sufferings.

Nor was that the worst; for the disease, after a cessation of a few days, broke out afresh, and Orlando saw his men depressed and dispirited, sinking around him its easy victims. Contrary winds, or sullen calms which allowed them to make very little way, added to the hopelessness of their situation, and the other transports could afford them little assistance; for in some the same cruel distemper had begun its ravages, and those who were yet free from it dreaded the infection. It was now that Orlando felt the justice of that pathetic description, given by Thomson, of the mortality at sea before Carthagena, where he addressed the admiral, as witnessing

> "The deeply racking pang, the ghastly form,
> The lip pale quivering, and the beamless eye
> No more with ardour bright—
> —The groans
> Of agonizing ships—"

and as having then heard

> "Nightly plunged amid the sullen waves,
> The frequent corse."[1]

From such a scene, whenever the distresses of his men (whom in despite of the danger of infection he attended with paternal kindness) or the terrors of the little effeminate cornet would allow him a moment's respite, he escaped as much as he could by passing the evenings on deck;

---

[1] Thomson, *The Seasons*, "Summer," ll. 1044 *passim*.

for the heat below was more dreadful to him than even the want of sleep or any other inconvenience. He frequently took the night watch; and at other times wrapped himself in a great coat, and lay down where he might at least have air. On these occasions sleep would not always befriend him; and then all he had left, his Monimia, his family, the Hall, the rural happiness he had enjoyed in his native country, forcibly presented themselves in contrast to the wretchedness around him; and when he considered a number of men thus packed together in a little vessel, perishing by disease; such of them as survived going to another hemisphere to avenge on a branch of their own nation a quarrel, of the justice of which they knew little, and were never suffered to enquire; he felt disposed to wonder at the folly of mankind, and to enquire again *what all this was for?*

He sometimes, however, endeavoured to persuade himself that it was for glory: he had been taught to love glory—What so sacred as the glory of his country? To purchase it no exertion could be too great—to revenge any insult on it, no sacrifice should be regretted. If, for a moment, his good sense arose in despite of this prejudice, and induced him to enquire if it was not from a mistaken point of honour, from the wickedness of governments, or the sanguinary ambition or revenge of monarchs, that so much misery was owing as wars of every description must necessarily occasion; he quieted these doubts by recurring to history—our Henries and our Edwards, heroes whose names children are taught to lisp with delight, as they are bid to execrate the cruel Uncle[1] and the bloody Queen Mary; and he tried to believe that what these English Kings had so gloriously done, was in their descendants equally glorious, because it went to support the honour of the British name.—Then Alexander, Caesar, and all the crowned murderers of antiquity—they were heroes too whom his school-studies had taught him to admire, and whom his maturer reflection had not yet enabled him to see divested of the meteor glare which surrounded them. There was something great in their personal valour, in their contempt of death; and he did not recollect that their being themselves so indifferent to life was no reason why, to satisfy their own vanity, they should deluge the world with human blood. There were, indeed, times when the modern directors of war appeared to him in a less favourable light—who incurred no personal danger, nor gave themselves any other trouble than to raise money from one part of their subjects, in order to enable them to destroy another, or the subjects of some neighbouring potentate. Nor

---

[1]   Richard the Third. [CS]

had he, after a while, great reason to admire the integrity of the subordinate departments, to whom the care of providing for troops thus sent out to support the glory of their master was entrusted. The provisions on board were universally bad; and the sickness of the soldiers was as much owing to that cause as to the heat of the climate. Musty oatmeal, half-dried pease, and meat half spoiled before it had been salted down, would in any situation have occasioned diseases; and when to such defective food, their being so closely stowed and so long on board was added, those diseases increased rapidly, and generally ended fatally. But it was all for *glory*. And that the ministry should, in thus purchasing glory, put a little more than was requisite into the pockets of contractors, and destroy as many men by sickness as by the sword, made but little difference in an object so infinitely important; especially when it was known (which, however, Orlando did not know) that messieurs the contractors were for the most part members of parliament, who under other names enjoyed the profits of a war, which, disregarding the voices of the people in general, or even of their own constituents, they voted for pursuing. Merciful God! can it be thy will that mankind should thus tear each other to pieces with more ferocity than the beasts of the wilderness? Can it be thy dispensation that kings are entrusted with power only to deform thy works—and in learning politics to forget humanity?

Orlando, embarked in a cause of which he had hardly ever thought till he was called upon to maintain it, was insensibly visited by reflections like these; but whenever they recurred he drove them from him as much as he could, and endeavoured to cherish the fond hope that all might yet be well; that Isabella, about whom he was haunted with a thousand fears, was in some of the vessels which were now all assembled in one fleet—for the slowness of their progress had enabled those ships which last sailed to overtake them; and that on his landing he should meet Warwick and his sister, and anticipate with them the fortunate hour of his return to England.

As the perilous situation of Isabella occupied his thoughts, whenever he could a moment detach them from the scene before him, he made several efforts to learn, if she was in any of the vessels near which he often found himself; but in none of them could he gain information of an officer of the name of Warwick. He then contrived to send a message to the captain of the frigate, one of the convoy, with whom Warwick had told him he was acquainted; but this officer, to the infinite disappointment of Orlando, told him in answer to his letter, that it was true his friend Warwick had sent some of his baggage on board, and a negro servant; but that, after waiting for him till the last moment, it became absolutely necessary for him to sail without him. This account only served, therefore, to increase the uneasiness of Orlando, who now feared that, instead of being able on his landing in America to write instantly to his father with an account both of himself and his sister, he should only add to the disquiet which he believed her flight must have occasioned to her family: nor was he at all satisfied that Warwick's dishonourable conduct to her was not the cause of their not being in the fleet, which he was now almost persuaded they were not.

If at any time he had obtained a short interval of repose, these cruel images haunted him; but as the voyage was prolonged, and the discomforts of his condition became more severe, he found abundant reason to rejoice that he had resisted the alluring temptation offered to him by Warwick, and had not exposed his Monimia to difficulties and distresses, under which many around him had sunk: and in this self-congratulation he found the first reward of virtue; a sensation which soothed all his sorrows, and enabled him to support the accumulated evils which now pressed upon him.

The fleet was now within four days sail of New-York; or at least the sailors, though it was a dead calm, declared that they had no doubt but before the end of that time they should get in thither. The sick men revived a little with the intelligence; and the rest bore with less dejection the funeral of the dead (for two days had not for some time passed without a funeral) and the loss of the horses, of which a third had already perished. Orlando, to escape the intolerable smells below, now always passed the night on deck, and was sleeping on it when the noise occasioned by a sudden change of the weather awakened him: he got up, as well to be out of the way, as to assist the sailors, who were soon all busily employed; for in a few moments it blew a hurricane. The darkness of the night and the violence of the storm were horrors, greatly increased by the apprehension the seamen expressed, that they should be driven against some of the other vessels and sunk: and this appeared extremely probable; for, by the flashes of lightning, the transports in company were seen driven about, sometimes within a few yards of each other—guns of distress were heard, but none were in a condition to assist the rest; nor was it possible for a boat to live in a sea that ran mountains high, and threatened to overwhelm even the men of war which formed the convoy.

Orlando, to whom as a novice in maritime adventures the danger seemed even greater than it was, imagined that death was inevitable, because it had never appeared to him so near before. He thought, however, not so much of the event, as of the effect the intelligence of it would have on those infinitely dearer to him than himself—He heard the agonising shrieks of his mother, the more silent but more destructive anguish of his father, the tears of his sisters, unable to suppress their own grief while they attempted to administer comfort to their parents, and above all the sufferings of his gentle Monimia, sufferings more acute because she dared not complain. Yet, when the vessel strained so much that the seamen declared they every moment expected the timbers to part, Orlando again thanked God that Monimia was not with him. The despair of the lieutenant was solemn and silent;—he believed that the hour was come when he was to leave his family destitute in a world where, with all his exertions, his want of interest had not afforded him the means of supporting them by that perilous profession to which he had dedicated his life. But he bore this certainty (for there seemed not the least hope of escape) like a soldier and a man: he assisted the sailors; he encouraged the soldiers; and endeavoured, with a calmness of mind which gave Orlando an exalted opinion of him, to inspire others with that hope he did not himself feel. To Orlando only he declared his opinion that they must perish; and he spoke in approbation of the fortitude with which so young a man, and one so unaccustomed to look on danger and death, bore this intelligence: but with the little cornet he could not keep his temper, who, half dead with terror, lamented himself aloud in terms unmanly and ridiculous; and who, though he declared himself too much affected by the violent heaving of the ship to keep the deck a moment, ran up continually to ask puerile questions of the seamen, and to distract their attention by his complaints and clamours.

Morning at length appeared, but the wind rather increased than abated; and the light of day served only to shew the horrors of their situation, and of some of their companions in distress, who were still in sight, for the men of war were no longer visible; and of the three transports who were near them, one was dismasted, and another without her rudder was driven about a wreck upon the waves, under bare poles. From this vessel, which the first dawn of day discovered close to them, they heard repeated signals of distress. Whenever the mountainous waves afforded them a view of her, they saw the people, among whom were two or three women, appearing on her deck, apparently in all the agonies of despair. Orlando was suddenly struck with the idea that this vessel might contain his sister; and with dreadful solicitude he watched it, till, in the confusion of his thoughts, he fancied he really discerned her— All care for his own safety was then at an end; and he entreated the commander of the ship he was in to allow him to attempt in a boat to go on board, in the hopes of administering some help; but this the man positively refused, giving very loud and short reasons, in terms which Orlando did not understand, why such an attempt would be fatal to whoever undertook it, without being of the least use to those for whom it was undertaken. More and more impressed with the idea that Isabella was among the women, whose terrors he saw distinctly on the deck of the other vessel, he now hardly possessed his senses, and was on the point of plunging into the waves, tremendous as they were—when, as his eyes were fixed wildly and eagerly on it, he saw it sink, and the sea bury all it contained!—There was hardly time to utter an exclamation of horror, when some of the unhappy people appeared so near the ship, that the sailors, though so likely to share the same fate, endeavoured to save them; but two only, stout men who swam strongly, were snatched from the raging element. The rest soon disappeared, never to rise again!

The force of the wind was now somewhat lessened, and the men were inspired by some degree of hope to greater exertions. About ten o'clock the storm was so much abated that the master was able to take an observation; and he found himself many leagues out of his course. No ship remained in sight but one transport at a great distance, and the vessel yet drove too much to allow them to attempt altering her course. Their immediate danger, however, gradually diminished; and every man on board, who was able to work, laboured, in despite of the fatigue they had undergone, to repair their rigging, and remedy the damages the hull had sustained. The sick, who had for many hours been neglected, were now visited; and one soldier was found dead. As to the horses that remained, they had all been thrown overboard during the most imminent peril, as their weight occasioned the ship to labour so much more than she would do without them. The dead soldier was committed to the waves; and as Orlando, with glazed eyes, saw him deposited in his watery grave, and recollected all the horrors of the preceding night, he again involuntarily enquired of himself, whether such things were to be accounted the dispensations of Heaven—or, if they were the works of man, why were they permitted? The terrible idea that Isabella had perished in that ship he saw sink still haunted him, and redoubled by imaginary sorrow all that he saw or suffered. The poor fellows who had been taken up were so terribly bruised, and had swallowed so much water, that they were not yet sensible. As soon as they were, however, Orlando eagerly questioned them as to the females whom he had, through the obscurity of the dark and dashing waves, discovered on the deck; and he learned, to increase his misery, that one of them was a young lady, whose husband was an officer of foot, and who was himself either in the fleet, or coming with the next convoy. The sailor who gave him this information knew not which, nor did he know the lady's name, or to what regiment her husband belonged. The other women, he said, were, one of them the lady's servant, and the other the wife of a sergeant in Orlando's regiment: which seemed to add to the probability that the young person who had perished was Isabella. There hardly needed this sad conjecture to add to the despondency which, in despite of all his steady courage, now took possession of Orlando—despondency which he found it extremely difficult to conceal. Strong as his constitution was, it yielded, at length, to the united power of malignant infection, uneasiness, and fatigue; and when, after beating about above ten days, the vessel at length reached the harbour of New-York, he was taken on shore in a state of insensibility, from the fever which had attacked him; and his friend, the old lieutenant, saw him accommodated as well as the circumstances the place was under would admit; and, feeling for him the affection of a father, shed over the blasted hopes of a youth so promising tears, which his own misfortunes had never extorted from him.[1]

CHAP. XII.

By the care of this excellent man, aided by the medical skill of the surgeon of the regiment, Orlando in about a fortnight arose as it were from the grave. His sense returned long before his strength, and with them all the sad recollection of his disastrous voyage:—almost the first use he made of his returning reason, was to implore the lieutenant to enquire for Captain Warwick, of whom he found, with inexpressible sorrow, that no intelligence had been received, and that he was believed by his brother officers to be in one of those transports that had gone to the bottom. In a few days a negro servant enquired for Ensign Somerive, and Orlando in a moment recollected that it was Perseus, the man who had served Warwick some years.—He now hoped to have heard some account of his sister and his friend that might have quieted his extreme uneasiness: but the sight of Perseus only served to increase it; for he

---

[1]   Orlando arrives in America in July 1777 feverish and already unfit for active duty. This time Smith uses physical frailty to suggest Orlando's defectiveness.

learned from him that Captain Warwick arrived at Portsmouth the evening the first transports sailed, and that, by his interest with the captain of the frigate in which the negro embarked, and some persons still higher in power, that ship was delayed for some days, at the end of which Warwick promised to appear; but as he did not, nor even at the end of some hours longer than the time he required, the captain would have incurred too great a risk by waiting longer; and therefore got under weigh with so strong and favourable a wind, that they overtook the rest of the fleet two days before they made the Pike of Teneriffe. This circumstance, however, Perseus said, was the only one that gave him hope; for he knew his master, thus missing his passage, would hire a vessel to convey him, which would probably not only take up some days, but hardly sail as they did; and therefore there was reason to hope that he might have escaped the storm in which they suffered, and it was improbable that the lady whom Orlando had seen perish, and afterwards heard was the wife of an officer of foot, was his sister.

On being questioned farther, the negro, who was very intelligent, said, that Captain Warwick had ordered him, with a great part of his baggage, on board; and that he knew his master expected a lady to go with him— but he knew not whom. The baggage was landed, and put into Orlando's lodging, where Perseus desired leave to wait upon him; and where the attention of this faithful fellow, and the hopes he gave him that Isabella and her husband were safe, contributed greatly to his recovery.

A fortnight had now elapsed since his landing, and no news of his sister reached him, nor had he a single line from England as he had been taught to expect. The sad scene at home, where he feared Isabella's elopement had created insupportable sorrow, cruelly tormented him; and the image of Monimia in continual tears and hopeless solitude, pursued him incessantly. A thousand times during the paroxysms of his fever he had insisted upon having pen and ink to write to her and to his family; and he began many letters to his father, recommending Monimia to his protection, and apologising for his conduct in regard to his sister; but the Lieutenant, Mr. Fleming, had never sent any of these incoherent letters.—Orlando had now strength of body and of mind enough to look them over; but, circumstanced as he was about Isabella, he now hardly knew better than he did then, what to say that should not aggravate all the pain he lamented: something, however, it was necessary to write, as ships were now daily returning to England; and not to send some intelligence of himself would be more distressing to his friends, than the ignorance he must avow as to the fate of his sister.

Another idea however struck him, that some discovery, or even her own fears, as the moment arrived when she was to leave her father's house, might have prevented the departure of Isabella from home; and that even her intention of doing so might be unknown.—This made him hesitate whether to name her at all; and at length he determined he would not, since it would be only giving to his father an exchange, but not an alleviation of uneasiness.

He wrote then these unsatisfactory letters to his family; and afterwards one to Monimia.—He gave in all of them the best account he could of himself, described his voyage as tedious and stormy; and said, slightly, that he had been ill on his first landing; but was now recovered, and should soon proceed to join the body of his regiment with the northern army under Burgoyne.[1]—But such was the agitation of his spirits while he was writing, from the lively idea he had of the sensations his letters would give to those whom they were addressed, that it brought on an access of fever, and he was confined for a few days: nor had he quite recovered his usual health, when the commander of the two companies, despairing of seeing the men who were missing arrive, was ordered to muster all that remained of the two companies; and, with a party of dismounted dragoons, to find their way to the army, which was now on its march from Canada to Albany, in order to form a junction, or at least to open a communication between that army and New York. The whole body, thus destined to force its way through an enemy's country, consisted, including American volunteers, of about two hundred and fifty men; but they were not incumbered with artillery, and were almost all young men, eager for actual service, and in haste to join an army, of whose brilliant success they formed the greatest expectations.

It was on the 6th of August that this small party left New York; and now Orlando, who had hitherto been in garrison, began to perceive all the horrors and devastations of war. The country lately so flourishing, and rising so rapidly into opulence, presented nothing but the ruins of houses, from whence their miserable inhabitants had either been driven entirely, or murdered!—or had, of the burnt rafters and sad relics of their former

---

[1] General John Burgoyne first arrived in America in 1775, but soon returned to Britain where he helped persuade the government that war with the colonies was necessary. In spring 1777, having returned to America, he led the attempted British invasion of New York from Canada, which dragged on through the summer and autumn. Orlando leaves New York to join his regiment on 6 August 1777, almost exactly two months before Burgoyne's engagement with American troops on 7 October 1777, which leads to Orlando's capture by the Iroquois.

comfortable dwellings, constructed huts on their lands, merely because they had no where else to go.—Even from these wretched temporary abodes they were often driven, to make way for the English soldiers; and their women and children exposed to the tempest of the night, or, what was infinitely more dreadful, to the brutality of the military. In a war so protracted, and carried on with such various success, these scenes of devastation had occurred so often, that the country appeared almost depopulated, or the few stragglers, who yet lingered round the places most eagerly contended for, had been habituated to suffer till they had almost lost the semblance of humanity. The party had now marched about seventy miles; and as they carried their provisions with them, which it was not possible to do in a great quantity, it became necessary for them to encamp, and send out foraging parties to obtain a supply before it was actually wanted. It was on the edge of one of those morasses which are called by the natives savannahs,[1] encircled on all sides by woods, that they formed this small camp; where the Colonel, to whom the conduct of this expedition was entrusted, fortified it as well as such a situation would admit; but Lieutenant Fleming, whose attachment to Orlando a long intercourse of mutual kindness had now greatly strengthened, pointed out to him, in confidence, the defects of the station thus chosen; and declared that if any body of American troops, or rebels as they were then called, was in the country, they must be surrounded, and either compelled to surrender or fight their way through. It happened, however, that for many days they remained unmolested—some recruit of provisions was obtained, and the plan of their future march settled. The parties who went out saw no enemies to oppose them; and Orlando had now an opportunity of observing this wonderful country, so extremely unlike England, that it appeared to him to be indeed a new world.

Every object seemed formed upon a larger scale. The rivers, more frequent than in England, were broader than the most boasted of ours, even on their approach to the sea; and the woods, larger than the oldest European forests, even those that Kings have reserved for their pleasure in France or England, consisted often of trees of such magnitude and beauty as must be seen before a perfect idea can be formed of them. What Orlando had often seen cherished in English gardens as beautiful shrubs, here rose into plants of such majestic size and foliage as made the

---

[1] Ehrenpreis speculates that Smith is indebted for her description of the savannahs and forests to William Bartram's *Travels through North and South Carolina, Georgia, East and West Florida* (Philadelphia, 1791) (p. 541), and through ignorance of the North American landscape, allowed such semi-tropical plant life to flourish even in upstate New York and Canada.

British oak poor in comparison; and under them innumerable shrubs, of many of which he knew not the names, grew in profusion. These woods, however, had in many places suffered like the rest of the country; and in some had been set on fire—in others the trees had been felled, as means of temporary defence.—And Orlando, whose early and ingenuous philanthropy had of late been often injured by a painful sensation of disgust, could not help remarking with a sigh, that man seemed not only a creature born to consume the fruits of the earth, but to wound and deform the bosom of that earth! and he found himself almost involuntarily assenting to some of the most gloomy aphorisms of Rousseau.[1]

But he was yet a novice; and had only of late understood, as well as a partial representation of the cause by his otherwise candid friend Fleming would let him understand, the origin of the quarrel in which he had drawn his sword.

The scenes however he had already been witness to, were, *he* thought, not to be justified by *any* cause: but his fellow soldiers seemed to see them in a very different light; and to consider the English Americans as men of an inferior species, whose resistance to the measures, whatever those might be, of the mother country, deserved every punishment that the most ferocious mode of warfare could inflict; and even the brave and generally humane Fleming endeavoured to convert Orlando, whose scruples as to the justice of the war became greater the more he heard of its origin.—He assured him that a soldier never thought of examining into such matters—"It is," said he, "our business to fight; never to ask for what—for if every man, or even every officer in the service were to set about thinking, it is ten to one if any two of them agreed as to the merits of the cause. A man who takes the King's money is to do as he is bid, and never debate the matter. For my part, I have heard while I was in England a great deal of clamour upon the subject; and it has been called a war upon the people, and therefore an unpopular war.—I am no politician, nor do I desire to enter into a discussion about taxation and representation, which these fellows have made the ground for their resistance. There is no end of the nonsense that may be talked in favour of their rebellion, nor the pleas of the ministerial party. For myself, as I was brought up in the army, I have always cut the matter very short—the sword is my argu-

---

[1] Rousseau held that modern civilization, instead of encouraging the spread of enlightenment, actually promoted inequality, corruption, and idleness; he advocated a return to nature and celebrated the "noble savage." In light of this it is interesting that Smith portrays the Iroquois as both "noble" and "savage."

ment; and I have sold that to my King, and therefore must use it in his service, whatever and wherever it may be pointed out to me."

This way of settling the matter was, however, so far from being convincing to Orlando, that it gave him new cause for reflection. He had always been told, that the will of the people was the great resort in the British Government; and that no public measure of magnitude and importance could be decided upon, but by the agreement of the Three Estates.[1] Yet the present war, carried on against a part of their own body, and in direct contradiction of the right universally claimed, was not only pursued at ruinous expence, but in absolute contradiction to the wishes of the people who were taxed to support it. Orlando did not comprehend how this could be—he could not, however, though so often assured that it was no part of his business, help thinking about it; and an American prisoner, who was brought to their little camp by a scouting party just before it broke up, assisted very much to clear up his ideas on this subject. He was a man in middling life, and had kept a store at New York; but having taken part with his own country-men, had been sent by them to Congress, where, being a man of strong plain understanding, he had joined heartily in all the measures of resistance, and afterwards gone into the field for the same purpose: but hearing that his wife, an English woman, whom he passionately loved, and his only son, a boy of seven years old, were arrived at New York from England, whither they had gone two years before, he had obtained leave to quit his command for a short time, and had set out alone, and in disguise, in the intention of reaching the neighbourhood of New York; where, at the house of one of his temporising friends, he had appointed his wife and child to meet him—in the hope of conveying them himself, through a country abounding in perils, to a place of present safety.

But when he was within an hundred miles of the place he wished to reach (a distance that in America is reckoned a trifle), he had been met by a party of Indians, whom the British commanders had lately let loose upon the Americans; and having narrowly escaped being scalped, by promises, and some deceptions very allowable in such a situation, he was brought by the red warriors to the small camp of their allies the English, of which they had just received intelligence. As this unfortunate

---

[1]   The Three Estates consisted of the clergy, the aristocracy, and the military. While Orlando thinks in terms of the British government, it is significant that Smith uses this terminology: the French Revolution was set in motion with the assembly of the Estates-General (the Three Estates) in May 1789, followed by the storming of the Bastille in July 1789.

American immediately disclosed to the commanding officer who he really was, and for what purpose going to New York, he was deemed of consequence enough to be sent thither a prisoner, and till this could be done, he was alternately guarded by the British officers:—a circumstance that gave Orlando an opportunity he never before had of hearing the American party tell their own story, which served only to excite his pity for them, and a pity not unmixed with respect; while his astonishment increased as he considered the infatuation of the British Cabinet, or rather the easy acquiescence of the British People.

If his concern was called forth by witnessing the anguish of mind endured by his new acquaintance when he thought of his wife and child—anguish with which Orlando well knew how to sympathise—his surprise and curiosity were not less awakened by the appearance of the native American auxiliaries who had been called to the aid of the English. They consisted of a party of near forty, most of them young men; and headed by a celebrated veteran warrior, who was distinguished by a name which expressed in their language, "The bloody Captain!" Their savage appearance, and the more savage thirst of blood which they avowed—that base avidity for plunder, with an heroic contempt of danger, pain, and death, made them altogether objects of abhorrence, mingled with something like veneration: but the former sentiment altogether predominated when Mr. Jamieson (the prisoner) informed him, that among all the unfair advantages which the Colonists complained of in the manner of carrying on the war, there was none that seemed so unjustifiable as that of sending forth the Indians[1] against them. And when

---

[1] "Several nations of savages were induced to take up arms as allies to his Britannic Majesty. Not only the humanity, but the policy of employing them was questioned in Great Britain. The opposers of it contended, that Indians were capricious, inconstant, and intractable; their rapacity insatiate, and their actions cruel and barbarous. At the same time their services were represented as uncertain, and that no dependence could be placed on their engagements. On the other hand, the zeal of the British *Ministers* for reducing the revolted Colonies was so violent as to make them, in their excessive wrath, forget that their adversaries were men. They contended that, in their circumstances, every appearance of *lenity*, by inciting to disobedience, and thereby increasing the objects of punishment, was eventual cruelty. In their opinion, *partial severity* was *general mercy*; and the only method of speedily crushing the rebellion was to envelop its abettors in such complicated distress, as, by rendering their situation intolerable, would make them willing to accept the proffered blessings of peace." Ramsay's History of the American Revolution.—The happy effects of this barbarous policy never appeared. Of the tragical scenes it occasioned, the reader, if he or she delight in studying circumstance in this war redounding to the honour of British humanity, is referred to the Annual Register for 1779, where an account is given of the expedition of sixteen hundred men, among whom one fourth were Indians, the rest British Americans in the interest and service of Government

Orlando saw in the hands of the Bloody Captain eleven scalps, some of them evidently those of women and children, others of very old, and consequently defenceless men; many of them fresh, which he said, with an air of triumph, he had taken from the enemies of the King of England within three weeks—the young unhardened Englishmen shuddered with horror, and blushed for his country!

He could not help speaking warmly on this subject to Fleming, who answered calmly, it was very true that arming the Indians was a very severe measure—"and their cruelty what we ourselves," said he, "so loudly complained of in the last war:—but after all, my friend, in war every advantage is taken by both sides; and our Government has considered, that if by this dreadful sort of warfare they can the sooner conquer the rebels and reduce them to obedience, it is in fact best for them."[1] Orlando, still unable to digest or approve such doctrine, could never hear of the ferocity with which these red warriors treated their prisoners without disgust. With some of the younger among them, however, who were less inured to blood, he formed some kind of acquaintance, and learned some of their words. One of these he had distinguished from the rest, by remarking his more open countenance—his more gentle manners; and by hearing that he had, at the risk of his own life, saved a woman from the fury of his relation the Bloody Captain, when he was on the point of killing her with his tomahawk. This woman, whom they had found wandering in the woods, whither she had been driven by the British troops who had burned her little farm and killed her husband, the young Indian, who was known by the

---

(these Americans were then called Tories), to the forts Kingston and Wilkesborough, in the settlement of Wyoming on the Susquehanna. Those who have so loudly exclaimed against a whole nation struggling for its freedom, on account of the events of the past summer (events terrible enough, God knows!), are entreated to recollect how much the exploits of this expedition (even as related by our own historian) exceed any thing that happened on the 10th of August, the 2d of September, or at any one period of the execrated Revolution in France—and own, that there are savages of all countries—even of our own! [CS]

Ehrenpreis glosses Smith's note as follows: "David Ramsay, *The History of the American Revolution* (Philadelphia, 1789), ii. 26; *Annual Register*, 1779, 8–14" (540, n. to p. 360). Smith's reference to the events of the French Revolution in August and September 1792, which took place as she was writing the first volumes of *The Old Manor House*, show how closely the American and French revolutions were associated in her mind, and how clearly readers may take her criticisms of the British handling of the American war to be veiled critiques of its approach to the French Revolution.

[1] The same sort of sophistry was used by the monster Catherine de Medicis, to urge her son, the infamous Charles the Ninth, to the massacre of the Protestants in 1572.—"What pity," said she, "do we not shew in being cruel!—What cruelty would it not be to have pity!" [CS]

name of the Wolf-hunter, had conducted in safety to a fort garrisoned by her own countrymen—again hazarding his own life to preserve hers.

The secret sympathy between generous minds seems to exist throughout the whole human kind; for this young warrior became as soon as much attached to Orlando as his nature allowed him to be to any body; and when they left their camp, and continued with their march (after having dispatched their prisoner to New York with as strong an escort as they could spare), the Wolf-hunter constantly marched by the side of his new friend; and between the little English he had picked up, and Orlando's unusual aptness to learn languages, which had however been little exercised till now, he contrived to acquire a good deal of the customs of the Indians of North America, of which he hitherto had known but little: but in regard to their wars, the more he heard of them the more unpardonable it seemed to him to be in the managers of the war at home to authorise them to take up the hatchet.

After a very fatiguing march of many days, during which their Indian associates were eminently useful to them in guiding their way through woods and morasses, where they were least likely to meet parties of the Colonists superior to their own, they reached the place of rendezvous, where there was a probability of their finding the army they were to join; but it had pushed forward with so much celerity, that they found themselves three days behind it: its track, however, was sufficiently marked by smoking ruins—by the corn destroyed on the ground—and by the bodies of the dead with whom they could not either encumber themselves, or always stay to bury. The heart of Orlando sickened at the sight; but he had little time for contemplation—for a strong detachment of Americans, who had harrassed the rear of the British army, were now returning northward; and meeting this body of British, an engagement ensured, in which the Provincials were repulsed with some loss—but at the expence of nine men killed and eleven wounded—among the latter was Lieutenant Fleming: his wound, however, was not dangerous, and Orlando had the satisfaction of shewing, by his unwearied attendance on him, some part of the gratitude he felt for his former friendship. But the care necessary to the wounded, and the difficulties that their own people, in order to prevent their being followed by the enemy, had every where thrown in the way of the march, made it so tedious and so dangerous, that they often despaired of effecting their purpose; and when they at length arrived, quite worn down with fatigue, had the mortification to find the forces they joined in a situation very different from what they had been taught to expect—while the main body was equally disappointed that a stronger reinforcement was not sent them from New York, and a supply of provisions, of which they began to apprehend the want. At the same time the march of such a small body of men, for so many hundred miles, through a country every where in arms against them, was a matter of wonder; and in the detail of their expedition given by the commanding officer to the General, the conduct of Orlando was spoken of in such high terms, that he was desired to make him a compliment on the occasion. Orlando, from his ignorance of the country, had entertained a faint hope that he might find Warwick already arrived in the northern army; but he had the mortification not only to discover that this hope was groundless, but his brother officers, who knew him best, were unanimously of opinion that he had perished at sea, from Orlando's account—They were sure, they said, that nothing but some such disaster would have prevented their friend Warwick from coming back with his company; and Orlando, with increased anguish of heart, assented apparently to this, and forbore to say the reasons he had to feel, that though this might not be exactly the truth, the absence of Warwick was every way to him a subject of uneasy conjecture and bitter regret.

CHAP. XIII.

The increasing difficulties to which the British army, under the command of General Burgoyne, were at this period exposed, have been so often described, and so largely insisted upon, that they need not here be repeated. Deserted by the Canadians and other Americans, who were discouraged by their perilous situation—in want of necessary provisions, and seeing themselves likely to be surrounded—it was determined that, if the assistance they had been taught to expect from New York did not arrive before the expiration of another fortnight, they must give up all hopes of defence. In the mean time, however, a movement was resolved upon by a chosen body of fifteen hundred men, which brought on a general attack from the Americans, who carried part of the British lines, and night only put an end to the combat, in which a great number of brave men fell, as well English as Germans. Among the slain was Orlando's respectable friend Fleming, who, though hardly recovered of his former wound, had hurried without orders to defend the lines, and was shot through the lungs as he was leading on his men to repulse a party of the enemy with the bayonet.—Orlando, who was only a few paces from him, saw him fall; and, amid the impetuosity of the action, he ran towards him, exhorting the men to proceed.—Fleming, as he lifted him up, knew him, and, wringing his hand, said—"Go, my dear boy! don't waste a moment upon me—I am killed! but I die contented if those scoundrels are driven off.—If you return to England, be a friend to my poor wife—to my poor little ones!" He spoke these last words with extreme difficulty, as the blood choked him. Orlando saw his noble spirit depart, and hastily ordering the black servant (who had belonged to Warwick, and now attended on him) to carry off the body, he plunged with a degree of desperation into the thickest of the battle; which lasted, however, only a few moments longer, because, as it was by that time too dark to distinguish friends from foes, each party found it necessary to retreat. The British passed the rest of the night in the melancholy employment of ascertaining their loss, which was very considerable in killed and prisoners, particularly in officers, of whom some that had been brought off the field were mortally wounded. Orlando, with concern that superseded every thought for himself, made it his first care to visit the body of his gallant friend, in a sort of lingering hope that he might yet live; but this hope was immediately at an end; and Orlando had no other comfort than in recollecting that he died gloriously, and shared an honourable grave with many other brave officers who ended a career of honour in this fatal field. The interval between this action and the removal of the British camp by night, from a situation no longer tenable, was short, but dreadful. Fatigue and famine, great as those evils were, seemed less terrible to the minds of the English, than the certainty that they must very soon surrender to an enemy whom they at once abhorred and contemned. The officers still endeavoured to encourage their men, and keep up the spirits of each other—they recollected other occasions in which armies, in a condition equally desperate, had broken through their enemies, and conquered those who hoped to have destroyed them: but the commander himself knew the fallacy of these hopes, and saw that, unless succours arrived in very few days, the surrender of his army was inevitable.

They had now, however, a messenger from New York, with information that three thousand men were advancing to their assistance up Hudson's River; but this expedition had been so delayed, or was, after it was undertaken, so managed, that there appeared not the least probability of their arriving in time to save the necessity of a surrender the devoted army. The same messenger, however, who had with infinite difficulty made his way to the English camp from New York, brought a few letters to the British officers—and among them, Orlando, with a beating heart, and with hands so tremulous that he could hardly break the seal, opened a packet from his sister Selina. It contained a short letter from her, the comfortless purport of which, in regard to his family, was repeated in what follows from Monimia herself, whose letter Selina had inclosed:

Rayland Hall, 28th June 1777.

"Though I know it is yet impossible for me to hear from you, every moment now seems to me an age.—Alas! Orlando, how little satisfactory was the short letter I received from Portsmouth! yet I know you could not write more, hurried as you were. You have now been gone six long—long weeks, and that is only a very small portion of the time you are to be absent, though to me it seems already a thousand years.

"I do not love, Orlando, to say much of myself, unless I could tell you any thing that would make you happy, which Heaven knows I cannot! unless it is merely that I am as well as so unhappy a being can be. It would be some comfort to me, if what I cannot tell you of myself, I could relate of your dear family: but Selina will tell you, if I do not, that your father's health is still in a very precarious state, and that all your friends have suffered greatly by Isabella's going from them, and by their not knowing what is become of her; for though she wrote to them from Portsmouth, desiring their forgiveness, and informing them that she had gone off to be married to Captain Warwick, and that her unconquerable aversion to General Tracy was partly the reason of her doing so; yet they have never heard that she was really married, nor have any of Captain Warwick's friends, of whom your father has made constant enquiries, had any intelligence of him. It is concluded that he is gone with your sister to America; but not knowing it certainly, is a continual source of distress both to Mr. and Mrs. Somerive; sadly aggravated, I fear, by their hearing but too much of your brother, who is known to be living in London in great splendour, which it is said he supports by gaming. Your poor mother went up with Selina about ten days since, in hopes of seeing him, and persuading him to return to his family. Selina described the meeting to me, and half broke my heart by the description. All your mother could obtain was, a sort of half promise that he would come down to West Wolverton in August or September, with which she has endeavoured to console your father; and I find has kept to herself the greatest part of what passed, and has no hope of changing his conduct.

"The poor old General has never recovered the shock and mortification of Isabella's defection. He left West Wolverton as soon afterwards as the gout allowed him to move; and, it is said, has disinherited Captain Warwick, and given his whole fortune to his brother's son, whose title I cannot now recollect—However, he does not seem to resent Isabella's desertion of him towards the rest of your family; for I understand that it was by his means your mother procured an interview with your brother; and that he was very obliging to her and Selina while they were in London. I have, though with a heavy heart, Heaven knows! rallied my dear Selina upon this; and told her, that perhaps the gallant General, who always admired her, may have an intention of transferring his affections to her; but she assures me, and I easily believe it, that were he emperor of the world she would not accept them.

"And now, Orlando, must I talk to you of your poor Monimia—Ah! it is reluctantly I do it; for I can tell you nothing but what will make you unhappy. Mrs. Rayland seems to regret your absence very much; she speaks of you every day, and appears to me to be sorry she ever suffered you to depart. Judge, dear Orlando! whether I do not execute the little offices about her, which now she will suffer no other person to do, with redoubled pleasure, when I hear her thus speaking of you like a tender mother! I wonder how I ever disliked her and thought her severe. Ah! I wish Mrs. Lennard had half as much kindness; yet has her Lady had much to disturb her lately, and my aunt reason to be in good humour. Mr. Harbourne, the gentleman who has so long managed the business of the Rayland estate, is dead; and within these last ten days my aunt has prevailed upon Mrs. Rayland to replace him with a Mr. Roker, who she tells me is a relation of hers, and a relation of mine, which may be; but of all the disagreeable men I ever beheld, he is to me the most disagreeable—He has, however, got every thing into his hands through the influence of my aunt; and his nephew, a creature as odious as himself, is put into the house at North Park End, where Mr. Harbourne used to be for a month or two; which is fitting up quite in an elegant style, as to new papering, painting, &c. I hope when it is done he will be less at this house than he is now; for, at present, he passes every day here, and very often the night; though I never could observe that his hateful cringing manners pleased Mrs. Rayland, who does not know, I believe, that he has taken possession of your room.—Oh! how different a possessor from what it ought to have! I meant, Orlando, to have said as little of this disagreeable change as I could; but my unconquerable aversion to these two men has betrayed me into saying more about them than I intended; yet I find from Selina, that your father is uneasy at their introduction to the management of the Rayland estate, and says that Roker is a man of the worst character of any attorney in the country.

"Perhaps you will impatiently exclaim, Why does Monimia talk to me about these attorneys when she began with saying she would mention herself! It is, Orlando, because they have had more influence already in injuring my peace than you would suppose likely. This Roker (the nephew), were he not young enough almost to be her grandson, I should really fancy was a lover of my aunt Lennard's. He is a great raw-boned fright of a man, I think, with two eyes that look I know not how, but particularly horrible to me—a wide mouth, full of great teeth, that are only the more hideous for being white, because his face is so red that, when he grins, the contrast makes him seem ready to devour one; then he has a red beard, and a great bushy head of carroty hair: but all this my aunt says is handsome; and that this giant-looking monster, who is not, I think, above eight-and-twenty, is a fine manly figure. The man returns, or rather earns, this her good opinion of him, by flattery so fulsome that really I blush for my aunt when I hear it; which, however, she takes care I shall do as little as possible, for she is almost always out of humour with me on some pretence or other when he comes into the room where I am, and generally contrives some excuse to send me away; and before her the disagreeable monster affects not to notice me: but if ever I meet him by accident in the house, which I avoid as much as I can, he speaks to me so impertinently that I have often been provoked to tears; indeed I am convinced he would be more insolent if I did not threaten that I would acquaint my aunt.

"I pass every moment of the time that Mrs. Rayland does not want me, in my own room; and you know how little I should regret never leaving it, if I could there possess quiet, and read the books you left me directions to go through. But even these comforts are denied your poor girl! and while my very soul sickens to tell you how, because you will in one respect fancy yourself the cause of it, it is necessary that I adhere to my promise, Orlando, and conceal nothing from you.

"You recollect, my dear friend, the pain we both endured, and the risk you incurred (of which I cannot now think without trembling), in consequence of that unlucky meeting with Sir John Belgrave.—This person, you know, left the country soon after, and went into Scotland with your brother; and I remember your telling me afterwards, that he was gone abroad for his health—Would to Heaven he had staid there, that I might never have heard again a name I could never hear without terror!

"It is to-day a week since, Mrs. Rayland being extremely well, which she had not been for some days before, my aunt desired leave to go out to dinner with Mr. Roker's family, who were on a visit at Great

Wolverton, at farmer Stepney's.—She accordingly had the coach, and set out in great form, leaving me strict orders not to quit her mistress. After tea the evening was so warm, and Mrs. Rayland felt herself so well, that she had an inclination to get into the park chair; and for Pattenson to lead the old pony in it round the park slowly, that she might see the alterations and repairs which she had been persuaded to order for the accommodation of the nephew and deputy of her new steward at North Park; and after she was seated by the footman safely in this low carriage, which you know she has not been in for almost two years, she said she found it very pleasant, and was sure she could bear to go quite up to the lodge; but, lest she should be faint, she ordered me to walk by the side of the chair with her drops. Pattenson did all he could to persuade her that the distance would be too great for her; but she spoke to him more sharply than ever I heard her do before—saying, that she was the best judge of that; and we set out, the carriage being drawn only a foot pace, so that I found no difficulty in keeping up with it. As we went along, we saw your horse lying under the chesnut trees in the long walk; for it was a very hot evening, and he had gone there for shade. Mrs. Rayland called to me, and pointed him out to me—"Poor creature!" said she, "he looks melancholy, as if he missed his master; and he is quite solitary too in the park." Then speaking to Pattenson, she asked if he was well taken care of?—While I, with a sigh, *could* have answered her remark, by saying—Ah, Madam! there are other beings who miss Orlando yet more than that beloved animal, and who are more solitary and undone than he is.—But I affected to be at ease; and hope my countenance did not betray how much my heart was otherwise.—Indeed there was the less danger of this, because Pattenson's answer, which was very surly, and signified that she had better ask about your horse of Jacob, with whom it was left in charge, if she had any doubts about it, diverted Mrs. Rayland's attention from me, and fixed it upon Pattenson, towards whom she expressed her displeasure. Indeed he has seemed to me for some time to be losing ground in her favour. At length we reached the north lodge; and as the workmen were putting up a new door, which you know is next the high road from Carloraine Castle to Wolverton and other villages, and putting on a new coat of stucco on that side, Mrs. Rayland ordered Pattenson to lead the chaise round thither, and stopped some moments there, while she talked to the carpenter and plasterer, who were just going from their work. She kindly said to me—"If you are tired, Mary, sit down at my feet and rest yourself."—I assured her I was not; but she bade me get her a glass of water out of the house, and give her a few drops, lest she should find the ride too much before she got home. There was not a glass in the house; so I ran across the way to James Carter's cottage, which is, you know, about fifty yards beyond the lodge, on the opposite side. His wife went out with the water, and I followed her; when a gentleman, attended by two servants, rode up so very fast, that his horse almost trampled on me before I could cross the road. He checked it, however, when he saw me, and exclaiming with a great oath—"My lovely little wood-nymph! By all that's sacred she shall not now escape me!" He then alighted from his horse, and (as I conclude, not seeing Mrs. Rayland and her servants, who were concealed partly by the projection of the lodge on that side, and partly by the slight turning in the road) rudely seized me.—I shrieked aloud; and the woman, who was but a few paces before me, began to remonstrate with him— I hardly knew, so great was my terror and confusion, what either of them said; but upon Pattenson's advancing with Robert, who had also accompanied the chaise, he let me go, saying, "You are still at the Hall then; I shall see you again, for I find your gallant defender has resigned his post." He said this as he mounted his horse, and as I, almost senseless, was led by Carter's wife towards Mrs. Rayland, who, hearing from her how the gentleman had behaved, expressed great indignation; and as he was by this time past her, she ordered Pattenson to follow him, and let him know that she desired to speak to him. I would have prevented this if I had retained breath or recollection enough to speak; but I sat down on the foot-stool of the chaise, unable to utter a word to prevent Pattenson's waddling away after Sir John, to whom, as there were no hopes of his overtaking him, he hallooed—Sir John stopped his horse, and Pattenson, puffing and blowing with hurry and anger, delivered, and I suppose in no very complaisant terms, his Lady's message—I did not hear it, but I distinguished Sir John's answer, which was—

"Come to your Lady, good fellow? No; she will excuse me—my business is with young ladies; I have too much respect for the old ones to intrude upon them. My service to the ancient gentlewoman of the Hall, good Mr. favourite butler, and tell her, if she has any commands for me, she must employ one of her pretty handmaids (*that* I saw just now, if she pleases); and she will not fail to find for her embassy a more favourable reception than I think it necessary to give your worship." Sir John then laughing aloud at his own wit, in which his two servants accompanied him, put his horse into a gallop, and was out of sight in an instant; long before Pattenson, whom rage and indignation did not render more active, had reached Mrs. Rayland, and repeated this message, not without some additions of his own, to his Lady. I think I never saw Mrs. Rayland so much disturbed as at the general brutality of this rude stranger. I however soon recovered of my alarm, when I found that this very disagreeable scene had ended without bringing on any conversation as to what had formerly passed; and I hoped and believed I should hear no more of Sir John Belgrave. Mrs. Rayland, from the agitation of spirits this insult had thrown her into, was quite ill when she got back to the Hall; but the next day, after she had given vent to her displeasure, by talking about it to my aunt Lennard, and every one who approached her, she seemed to recover; and the bustle that this ridiculous man had occasioned gradually died away. It happened on Friday, and on the following Sunday I had promised to meet Selina, whom I had never had an opportunity of seeing after her return from London till now. We were equally eager to meet each other; and as I have now no difficulty in obtaining leave to walk in the park when my aunt is with her Lady, I got her permission to go out on this evening, and passed with our dearest Selina an hour, the most delightful and yet the most melancholy that I have known since your departure. Selina was afraid of being missed, as she told me her father was never easy when she was out of his sight; and now only stole out while he was asleep after dinner. She left me therefore sooner than either of us wished; but after she was gone I sat some time weeping where she had left me. It was the bench, Orlando, in the fir grove, by the boat-house, where we sat all together when you made us promise to meet there, and talk of you when you should be gone. All your sister had told me of what passed in London between your mother and your brother, and of your father's dejected spirits and declining health, had affected me more than I can describe: but after I had indulged my tears some time, I recollected your charge to me to keep up my spirits, and I endeavoured to conquer this depression. The sun was nearly set, and I went over the pond-head by the great cascade, in order to go home the nearest way. I had just passed through the high plantation, and was entering the park, when I saw this hateful Sir John Belgrave approaching me.—Had I met him in the path of the plantation, it would have been impossible for me to have escaped him; but now, as the park was open before me, I ran the instant I observed him the opposite way. He pursued me for some time, intreating me to stop, and assuring me that he meant only to beg my pardon for his behaviour two days before, with a great deal of other nonsense; which I did not however, hear much of, for I was almost in a moment within sight of the house, and I saw him turn back. I arrived quite out of breath, and sadly terrified, but I dared not complain. After I recovered myself, my greatest concern was to think that I could never meet Selina without fearing a repetition of this disagreeable adventure; but I had now nobody to listen to my complaints or to relieve me from my sorrows. I thought the sermon of that evening the most tedious and uninteresting I had ever read; and both the old ladies were certainly particularly ill humoured, my aunt more especially, who was snappish and peevish to such a degree that she almost quarrelled with Mrs. Rayland: but, as she could not vent all her spleen on her, it fell upon me; and I went to bed in more than usual wretchedness, and for the first time wished that the younger Roker might return to the Hall—for to his having been two days absent I imputed the irritability of my poor aunt's temper.

"Ah! Orlando, how dreary now seemed my own room, to which, when you were here, I used to retire with so much delight from all the discomforts of my lot! It was a lovely moon-light night, and yet early when I went to the turret. From the window I looked into the park, with sensations how different from those I used to feel when I expected to see you cross it! I was restless and wretched, and knew I could not sleep if I went to bed; or, if I did, I feared I should dream of Sir John Belgrave's pursuing me. I wished for some book I never had read, for you have often told me that nothing so soon quieted the mind, and led the troubled spirit away from its own sad reflections, as some amusing or instructive author; but I had none in my room but those books of your own that you gave me, which I had read over and over again; and since this Mr. Roker has occasionally been in possession of your apartment next the study, and I once met him as I was going thither, I have never had the courage to venture down after the books as I used to do. Some of the poems however, Orlando, that you gave me, I am never, never weary of reading, though I can say them almost by heart; and therefore, when I was tired of looking at the moon, I took up that little volume of Gray, and read that beautiful ode to Adversity which you have so often bade me admire; and indeed I thought, Orlando, that we, though suffering under its "iron scourge and torturing hour," were yet in a situation more really happy than the prosperous worthless Sir John Belgrave, who was unable to enjoy every luxury of life, while you were wandering about the world in danger and in sorrow. Alas! these thoughts, however consoling at first, brought on a train of others, and fears, the most terrible fears for your precious life assailed me. My fancy conjured up a thousand horrid visions, and dwelt on a thousand terrible possibilities, till at length I found myself unable to bear the wretchedness I had thus created for myself, and I determined to attempt at least to lose it in sleep; and was, from mere fatigue of spirits, beginning to doze, when I was startled by a rap at the door at the back of the bed. I believed it to be a dream, too well recollecting that you were not there. When I listened a moment, and the noise was repeated, never, among all the terrors I have suffered, did I feel any alarm like this—I had not courage to speak, nor to move: my first idea was to run into my aunt's room; but then I must have discovered to her what we have so anxiously concealed; and of which, I believe, she never had the least notion; for whatever might be her suspicions of our meeting, she never seemed to guess how. While I deliberated in the most fearful agitation what it would be best to do, the noise was made a third time, louder than before; and a voice called, in a half whisper, Miss! Miss!

"For God's sake, who is there?" cried I, hastening to dress myself. "You cannot have any business there, whoever you are, and I will call my aunt and the servants."

"No, no, Miss!" cried a man's voice aloud! "don't do that, for you will only betray yourself; I mean you no harm, but, on the contrary, good.— Lord, Miss, 'tis only me; and I would not have frightened you so at this time o'night if I could have met you by day. I have got a letter for you."

"I now knew, by the voice, that it was Jacob, the under game-keeper; and though I trembled still with fear, it was mixed with a sensation of joy, for I hoped the letter was from you. "A letter!" said I: "Oh, pray give it me instantly." Yet I recollected as instantly, that it was foolish to open the door. The man said eagerly, "But make haste then, Miss, and take it."—"No," answered I; "leave it at the door, or put it under it; I cannot open the door, for it is nailed up."—"Ah! Miss! Miss!" cried the man; "it did not used to be nailed up when I know who was here." This speech, though I know not why, increased again the terror which had a little subsided; and his manner of speaking of you gave me a confused idea that the letter was not from you. "Where did you get the letter, Jacob?" said I; "and who is it from?"—"Never mind that," replied he, "it is a letter that will please you, I can tell you."—"I will not receive it," answered I, "unless I know whom it is from."—"Pooh pooh! what a to do is here?" said the man, in a very impertinent manner—"Well, then, if you are so squeamish all of a sudden, I'll leave the letter, and will come to-morrow up the stairs the same way for an answer."

"Jacob then seemed to go down; and I thought I heard him shut the door of the lower turret room after him; but, for the world, I could not have opened that of my room. Oh, Orlando! consider what I must have suffered, from supposing there might be a letter lying without it; and that only a few pieces of half-decayed board were between me and the first intelligence I had received from you! Yet it was also possible that it might be from some other person, though I could not conjecture who should write to me: but there was something of impertinent assurance in the manner of the game-keeper that shocked me; and I well recollected that you once thought of our corresponding through his means, yet afterwards determined not to hazard it, and seemed sorry that you had entrusted him so far. I will not attempt to describe the state of mind in which I passed the night. It was not, luckily for me, very long; but the sun had risen some time before I could acquire courage enough to open the door, and even then I trembled. But my hopes vanished, or rather were exchanged for the most alarming fears, the moment I saw that, if the letter contained any news of you, it was not from yourself. I know not how I opened it, for I expected now nothing but tidings of despair; when, casting my eyes on the name that concluded it, for I could not read the contents at that moment, I saw that of Sir John Berkely Belgrave; and though I instantly comprehended the insult it contained, I was relieved to find that it was not written by some friend of yours, to tell me what you were unable to write yourself.

"I will not, Orlando, copy this ridiculous billet; but as I was determined neither to answer it, nor to give the officious Jacob any excuse to come up the stairs to my room, I thought, after some consideration, that the best thing I could do would be to speak to this letter-carrier, though nothing could be more disagreeable to me, unless it was his coming for an answer. As soon as breakfast was over, I summoned all the courage I could, and went out to the stable yard, where I knew it was most likely I should meet him. As soon as he saw me, he came eagerly towards me; and none of the other men within hearing, he said, "I hope you have got an answer for Sir John to give me, Miss?"

"No," I answered; "I neither have an answer, nor ever intend to give one to so impertinent a letter; and I beg you, Mr. Jacob, not to disturb me any more with messages so very improper; for if you do, it will oblige me to complain to Mrs. Lennard."

"The fellow had the impertinence to say, that if I would not give him an answer, Sir John would come for one himself; but I hope and believe I shall hear no more of it, as it is now Thursday, and I have had no more visits. I have fastened the door as well as I am able, and would secure that below if I knew how: but it is not possible for me to do it myself; and were I to ask any other person, it would put whoever it was in possession of the secret which we have so much reason to regret was ever divulged.

"But do not, ever dear Orlando, be uneasy—I am persuaded Sir John is satisfied with his frolic, and that I shall hear no more of it; indeed I believe he has left the country; but I own I am uncomfortable at being so much in the power of such a man as this game-keeper—However, I now leave half open the door into the passage that leads to my aunt's room; and, upon the least alarm, I would fly to her, and rather own the truth, than subject myself to a repetition of such visits, either from this worthless servant or his employer. Do not, therefore, I again entreat you, my dear friend, be uneasy.

"What a letter have I written, Orlando! and how little pleasure will any one sentence in it give to you! I, who would die to procure you the smallest satisfaction, am destined to be the cause of your unhappiness. Sometimes I am so wretched when I think of this, that I wish we had never met, or resisted, in its beginning, an attachment likely to make all your days uneasy; yet I feel that were I without this tender affection my life would be a blank, and my existence not worth having.

"I will not conjure you to remember your poor Monimia! I must indeed end a letter which I have made so very long, that I am afraid Selina will not be able to send it in her packet. Oh! how hard it is to say adieu! yet my tears fall so fast that it is quite time—God bless you, my dear, dear friend!"

Orlando, during the perusal of this letter, was so entirely occupied by it, that he forgot where he was. The Hall and all its inhabitants were present to him; and he started up to demand instant satisfaction of Sir John Belgrave, and to chastise the mercenary and insolent servant, when he found himself, by the distance of many thousand miles, deprived of all power of protecting his Monimia, under marching orders to remove he knew not whither, and cut off from all communication with her. He stamped about the tent in a turbulence of mind little short of phrensy—cursed with ineffectual vengeance the objects of his indignation, whom he could not reach; and was awakened from this dreadful state, only by a message from his Colonel that he must that moment attend him.—Hardly knowing what he did or said, he followed the serjeant who brought these orders; and was directed, instead of preparing to go with the camp, to make himself ready, with another officer, the negro Perseus, and three rank and file, for an expedition to New York, where it was hoped so small a party might arrive unobserved; and as the men were chosen who were the fittest for so perilous an exploit, Orlando was named, from the experience his commanding officer had in his first march of his patience, prudence, and resolution. Orlando cared not whither he went or what became of him—he obeyed, as soon as possible, the orders he had received; and that night, at eleven o'clock, began his excursion with his five companions, and crossed Hudson's River.

CHAP. XIV.

The small party dispatched on this hazardous adventure, having crossed the river, penetrated a wood near it, where they rested till the light of the morning should afford them assistance to pass through it. One of the soldiers, who had a knowledge of the country, made light of the difficulties of their undertaking; and the whole party were in some degree cheerful, except Orlando, who, far from attending to the perils that surrounded himself, was lost in thinking of those to which Monimia was exposed; and in meditating schemes of vengeance against her persecutors, which he forgot that it was impossible for him to accomplish.[1] In the midst of an immense American forest, surrounded with almost every species of danger, and suffering, if not actual hunger, a great deficiency of nourishment (for the whole army had been some days on short allowance) he felt nothing but that Monimia was liable to the insults of Sir John Belgrave; perhaps already the victim of his infamous designs—an idea that stung him almost to madness. The painful news he had heard from his father's house added to the anguish of his spirit; and perhaps never was a mind more distracted with a variety of tormenting apprehensions, not one of which he had the means of alleviating. As soon as it was light, the party renewed their journey, but had not proceeded half a quarter of a mile towards the thickest part of the wood before the war-whoop burst forth; and a shower of bullets fell among them, wounding some, and killing one of their small party. The Indians rushed forward the moment the English had at random fired through the trees, and Orlando saw no more; a violent blow on the head deprived him of his senses, and to all appearance of his life.

When he recovered his recollection, he found himself lying on the ground in one of those temporary huts which the Indians erect in their

---

[1] Orlando's frenzy and his inability to distinguish fantasy from reality function in two ways: they again show his constitutional weakness, but they also show the dehumanizing, maddening effects of war. Smith does not allow battle and war to be glorious.

hunting parties. It was night, and he heard them in loud conversation near him—He found he was their prisoner, and concluded he was reserved for those horrid tortures of which he had heard so many terrific descriptions. Death appeared to him most desirable; and his great hope was that he should by death escape them—for the pain from the wound in his head was so excessive, that he doubted not but that his scull was fractured, and of course his dissolution near.

He attempted to rise; not with any hope of escape, for that was impossible, but with a sort of confused desire to accelerate his fate; when an Indian entered the hut with a light, in whom Orlando discovered his former acquaintance the Wolf-hunter.

This young savage approached and spoke kindly to him, telling him, that though his brothers had killed and scalped the rest of the party, he had saved him, and was his sworn friend—that no harm should come to him, and that the chief had promised him his life.

Orlando in a faint voice thanked him for his kindness, which he said was too late, as he felt the wound in his head to be mortal. He then enquired why the Indian warriors had fallen upon a party of their allies and brethren, the soldiers of the king of England?

The Wolf-hunter replied, that the English had not dealt fairly with them—that they were promised provisions, rum, and plunder, instead of which they got nothing in the English camp, but had lost some of their best men in defending the lines; and that, the English having thus deceived them, they were no longer their allies, but were going home to their own lands, determined to plunder the stragglers of whatever party they might meet in their way, to make themselves amends for the loss of time, and the heavier loss of brave warriors that had perished by believing the promises of the great English Captain.

Orlando's generous heart bled for his comrades thus inhumanly sacrificed; and he lamented that they, as well as himself, had not fallen like his friend Fleming in the field. He asked if all the men who were with him had perished. His Indian friend answered, All but two—a white man and a negro—who had escaped while they were plundering the rest.

Orlando heard this with a sigh of deeper concern; for he knew that, unless these unfortunate men could again cross the river and regain the camp, they would probably die in the woods of hunger and fatigue. The Wolf-hunter then enquired of Orlando, if he thought he could march with them in the morning?—To which he answered, he hoped so; but at the same time imagined that he should long before that time be released from all his sufferings. He knew, however, that to complain would not only be fruitless, but injure him in the opinion of his host, who made light of the wound he had received; and telling Orlando he would cure it, he cut off the hair, washed it with rum, and then laid on it a pledget of chewed leaves. An Indian blanket was thrown over him, for his own clothes were taken away; and the young savage giving him a drink, such as they had themselves been merry over, of rum, water and honey, desired him to sleep, and in a few moments set him the example.

Giddy and disturbed as was the unhappy Orlando from the effects of the blow, he now began to awaken to a sense of his condition; and in believing the injury he had received was not of so fatal a nature as he had on the first sensation of pain imagined, he felt infinitely more miserable in supposing that he should live in such insupportable anguish as his fears for Monimia and his family would inflict upon him— condemned probably as long as his life lasted, to drag on a wretched existence among the savage tribes of the American wilderness, and cut off from all communication with his country.

In such reflections on his own wretchedness he passed this miserable night, his Indian protector soundly sleeping in the same hut. Before the dawn of day they began to move; as the chief, or leader of the party, was anxious to escape, with the plunder they had already got, to the Iroquois country, from which they came. Orlando, contrary to his expectations, found he could walk; and his friend the Wolf-hunter, pleased with the resolution he exerted, sometimes assisted him when he appeared on the point of failing in this rapid and difficult march, through a country known and accessible only to Indians. His shoes and stockings had been taken from him, and his feet bled at every step: but he went on in a sort of desperation, hoping that the more severe his sufferings were, the sooner they would end; nor was it the least of these, that, on the first dawn of morning, he saw the scalps of his unfortunate comrades triumphantly carried by the chief of the party, whose title was the Wild Elk.

New scenes of horror awaited him on his way. As plunder was now the avowed purpose of this party of Iroquois,[1] which consisted of near forty men, they attacked the defenceless villages of the English Americans,

---

[1]   The classic study of the Iroquois civilization is Lewis Henry Morgan's *League of the Iroquois* (1851; New York: Corinth, 1969). The Iroquois are commended for their "hardihood, courage and sagacity." The author also notes that their success at establishing a federation (the Five Nations) also resulted in "a universal spirit of aggression" and "a thirst for military glory and political aggrandizement" (8). While this description postdates *The Old Manor House* by more than fifty years, it does suggest some interesting parallels between the Iroquois, the British, and the nascent Americans.

whose men were out with the army; and destroyed the women and children, or led them away to captivity infinitely worse than death. Some few the Wolf-hunter, who was the second in power, was influenced by the entreaties of Orlando to spare; but even these were, he feared, reserved only for a more lingering and deplorable fate; and in fact many hundreds of the unhappy people, thus driven from their dwellings in the course of the war, perished by famine in the woods and gullies.

Orlando was now nearly recovered of the wound in his head, notwithstanding so rude a method of cure; but, in fact, the skull had not been injured. The blow was given with the butt end of a musket, and not with a tomahawk, which are almost always mortal. His friend the Wolf-hunter had equipped him like an Indian warrior. His fine hair was cut off, all but a long lock on the crown of his head—and he was distinguished from an Iroquois by nothing but his English complexion. In these circumstances, after a long and fatiguing march of eleven days, he arrived with his protector at the camp or rendezvous of those Indians who had taken up the hatchet as allies to the king of England, where they halted and held a general council. A party who had just arrived before them, brought intelligence of the convention of Saratoga,[1] so fatal to the British, and their German allies: in consequence of this, one body of the Indians returned again towards the seat of war, on a scheme of general depredation; and the other, in which was the Wolf-hunter, who carried every where with him his English friend, went to the town of their district, with an intention of recruiting their numbers, and falling upon the back settlements while they were in their present defenceless state.

The ground was now every where frozen; and their way seemed to lay over sharpened flints—so impenetrable it was become. Orlando was inured to every personal suffering: but those of the unhappy victims of this war—victims that every day seemed to multiply around him, and very few of whom he could save, were a continual source of torment to him; while, at every pause of these horrors, the fears of what might happen, perhaps had already happened at home, were even more dreadful than his actual miseries. He found that Perseus, Warwick's black servant that had attended

---

[1]   In order to surrender to the American General Gates "honorably"—that is, avoiding an unconditional surrender—General Burgoyne proposed instead that "the royal army would lay down its arms and be permitted to sail to England, with the stipulation that none of its members would serve again in America during the war." Gates accepted and on 17 October 1777 Burgoyne surrendered; see note 1, p. 391. For more information, see John Richard Alden, *The American Revolution, 1775–1783* (New York: Harper and Row, 1954), pp. 148–49.

him, was among those who escaped from his unfortunate party: if he did not fall a victim to hunger, or failed of being destroyed by some other wandering horde of savages, he might, as he was a stout man, inured to hardship, and of good courage, find his way to New-York, and from thence to England, where he would undoubtedly report to Mr. Somerive and his distracted family, that he saw Orlando die under the hands of an Indian. The wretchedness that such news would inflict on his friends, on his Monimia, there was no likelihood of his being able to remove; for, in his present situation, there was no means of conveying a letter with any hope of its ever reaching the place of its destination. He tried to prevail on his savage friend to let him go with the party who were returning towards Boston, in hopes that he might escape from them, and find his way alone to some fort, either of English Americans or English: but this, for reasons which Orlando did not altogether comprehend, the Wolf-hunter refused, and even expressed some resentment that it was proposed.

By the time they had reached the Indian village, it was the end of November; and the winter set in with such severity that the Indians, however eager after plunder, felt but little disposed to encounter its rigour. Orlando then saw that the dreary months between November and April he must be condemned to pass among these barbarians, deprived of all human intercourse, and in a kind of living death. Even if he could have forced his mind from the consideration of his own disastrous situation, to contemplate the wonderful variety which Nature exhibits, and to have explored these wild scenes, this resource was denied him; for the whole country was a wide waste of snow, and every thing around him seemed cold and hopeless as his own destiny.

The booty which the Indians had divided at their camp comprised, among other articles, a small port folio of his, a memorandum book, his pocket book, and a writing case: these had fallen to the share of his friend the Wolf-hunter, who was very willing to restore to Orlando things of so little use to himself. This was the only alleviation the unhappy Orlando found to his sorrows; yet it was a melancholy one, to write letters which he could hardly expect would ever be read, to make for his father a journal of occurrences so mournful, and to feel, while he wrote it, that it was too probable the eye for which it was intended was closed for ever.

The sufferings of Orlando were such as time, the great softener of most affliction, served only to aggravate. What would he have given for even a hope of hearing from England! and how many conjectures were continually passing through his mind, each more distressing than another! In his dreams he often saw his Monimia pursued by Sir John Belgrave entreating his protection, and he started up to chastise the inhuman persecutor of her innocence. At other times fancy, more favourable, represented her as she used to appear in the early days of their attachment—cheerful, because unconscious of having erred—and tenderly trusting to him, even when she discovered that their clandestine meetings were contrary to the strict line of duty and propriety. He heard her voice, he admired her simple beauty, her innocent tenderness, the strength and candour of her uncultivated understanding—and supposed himself engaged, as he used to be, in the delightful task of improving it. Dreary was the contrast between his real situation and these soothing visions; and he often preferred such as gave him sleeping torment, to such as by flattering with happiness tendered more insupportable the despair which consumed him.

Five weeks, five miserable and dreary weeks had now crept away; when something like a change of ideas was offered by the arrival of two French Canadians and a party of Indians from that country, who had travelled across the snows and frozen lakes to the Indian village.

It was some comfort to the desolate Orlando to hear a European language; and though he could speak but little French, he could read it extremely well. But with these men he now constantly conversed, and soon found himself able to speak it fluently; from whence he was encouraged to hope that he might contrive to get to Quebec, and that from thence a passage to Europe might easily be obtained.

> "The miserable have no other medicine
> But only hope"——
> MEASURE FOR MEASURE.[1]

—and of this the young soldier of late had so little, that the least glimpse of more restored his dejected spirits; which, when all the evils he felt or feared are remembered, it will be acknowledged that nothing but a temper naturally sanguine, and a constitution unusually strong, could have enabled him so long to support.

On sounding his savage protector, who was extremely attached to him, he found it seemed not very unlikely that he might go himself with five or six young warriors to Quebec to trade early in the spring, hunting or fighting on their way as occasion might offer. His Canadian friends encouraged this plan: and Orlando ventured to promise a considerable present of spirits from the governor of Quebec, as an acknowledgement for the restoration

---

[1]   *Measure for Measure*: III.i.2–3.

of an English officer; and made many promises to the Wolf-hunter, of sending him from England what should give him a great superiority over all his countrymen, if he would release him, and promote his return to Europe. The means of conciliating this his Indian master, and procuring his consent to a scheme that he formerly seemed so averse to, were suggested to him by his new Canadian friends, and promised to be successful.

Thus relieved by hope, the months of January, February, and March, passed less heavily. The spring, which in America approaches not gradually as it does in England, but appears at once, surprised him by the sudden change which it produced. The snow was gone; and in a very few days, the whole country was covered with verdure and burst into bloom. A thousand birds filled the extensive forests, as gay in their plumage as exquisite in their song; and, whichever way Orlando looked, a new Eden seemed to be opening around him.

On the 20th of April 1778, Orlando, the French Canadians, and the Wolf-hunter leading a party of five-and-twenty Indian warriors, set out for Quebec—the Indians carrying great quantities of furs, the spoils of the animals they had taken during the winter. Of these Orlando carried his share; and now, re-animated by the soothing expectation of being restored to his country, he endeavoured to conform himself to the modes of his savage hosts, and was indeed become almost as expert an hunter, in their own methods, as the most active among them.

They had travelled some hundred miles, and were within a few days journey of Quebec, when it was resolved by the Wolf-hunter to encamp for some days, in a spot particularly favourable to hunting. This determination, however unpleasing to Orlando, he knew was not to be disputed; and though every delay was death to him, he was compelled to submit to what no remonstrance would avert.

The camp, therefore, was formed; and if any local circumstance could have reconciled him to the procrastination of a journey on which all the hopes of his deliverance from this wretched and tedious captivity depended, it was the very uncommon beauty of the scenery amid which these huts were raised.

This was on the banks of the river St. Lawrence, at a spot where it was about a mile and a quarter over. The banks where they encamped were of an immense height, composed of lime-stone and calcined shells; and an area of about an hundred yards was between the edge of this precipice, which hung over the river, and a fine forest of trees, so magnificent and stately as to sink the woods of Norway into insignificance. On the opposite side of the river lay an extensive savannah, alive with cattle, and coloured with such a variety of swamp plants, that their colour, even at that distance, detracted something from the vivid green of the new sprung grass: beyond this the eye was lost in a rich and various landscape, quite unlike any thing that European prospects offer; and the acclivity on which the tents stood sinking very suddenly on the left, the high cliffs there gave place to a cypress swamp, or low ground, entirely filled with these trees; while on the right the rocks, rising suddenly and sharply, were clothed with wood of various species; the ever-green oak, the scarlet oak, the tulip tree, and magnolia, seemed bound together by festoons of flowers, some resembling the convolvuluses of our gardens, and others the various sorts of clematis, with vignenias, and the Virginian creeper; some of these already in bloom, others only in the first tender foliage of spring: beneath these fragrant wreaths that wound about the trees, tufts of rhododendron and azalea, of andromedas and calmias, grew in the most luxuriant beauty; and the straw-berries already ripening, or even ripe, peeped forth among the rich vege-tation of grass and flowers. On this side all was cheerful and lovely—on the other mournful and gloomy, the latter suited better with the disposi-tion Orlando was in, and he reared his little hut on that side next the cypress swamp, and under the covert of the dark fir trees that waved over it. They had been here three days, when, with the usual capriciousness of his country, the Wolf-hunter determined to recommence their journey—a circumstance that gave Orlando some satisfaction; and he went to his couch of bear-skin with more disposition to sleep than he had felt for some time, and, contrary to his usual custom, soon sunk to repose; and his dreams were of his Monimia, soothing and consolatory.

There is in America a night hawk,[1] whose cry is believed by the Indians always to portend some evil to those who hear it. In war, they affirm that, if a chief falls, the funereal cry of this bird announces it to his distant survivors. Ignorance, the mother of superstition, has so deeply impressed this on the minds of the Indians, that it is an article of their faith, and Orlando had seen some of the most courageous and fierce among them depressed and discouraged by hearing the shriek of this bird of woe near their tents.

From the most delicious dream of Rayland Hall, and of Monimia given to him by the united consent of Mrs. Rayland and his father, he was suddenly awakened by the loud shriek of this messenger of supposed ill tidings; piercing, and often repeated, it was echoed back from the woods;

---

[1] Supposed to be the Caprimulgus Americanus: the bird that is called by the Anglo-Americans "Whip poor Will," because his notes or cry seem to express those words. [CS]

and Orlando, once roused to a comparison between his visionary and his real situation, was alive to the keenest sensations of sorrow. The hateful noise still continued, and he went out of his tent, for he knew any farther attempt to sleep would be vain—Alas! the turrets of Rayland Hall were no longer painted on his imagination—instead of them he looked perpendicularly down on a hollow where the dark knots of cypress seemed, by the dim light of early morning, which threatened storms, to represent groups of supernatural beings in funereal habits; and over them he saw, slowly sailing amid the mist that arose from the swamp, two or three of the birds which had so disturbed him. Great volumes of heavy fog seemed to be rolling from the river, and the sun appeared red and lurid through the loaded atmosphere. Orlando endeavoured to shake off the uncomfortable sensations, which, in despite of his reason, hung about him; but he rather indulged than checked them, in throwing upon paper the following

S O N N E T.[1]

ILL omen'd bird! whose cries portentous float
O'er yon savannah with the mournful wind,
While as the Indian hears your piercing note
Dark dread of future evil fills his mind—
Wherefore with early lamentations break
The dear delusive visions of repose?
Why from so short felicity awake
My wounded senses to substantial woes?
O'er my sick soul, thus rous'd from transient rest,
Pale Superstition sheds her influence drear,
And to my shuddering fancy would suggest,
Thou com'st to speak of every woe I fear—
But aid me, Heaven! my real ills to bear,
Nor let my spirit yield to phantoms of despair.

END OF THE THIRD VOLUME.

---

[1] This sonnet appears in Smith's *Elegiac Sonnets*, subtitled "supposed to have been written in America," and the last two lines read "Ah! Reason little o'er the soul prevails,/ When, from ideal ill, the enfeebled spirit fails!" Smith notes in the *Sonnets* that the poem was "first inserted in the Novel called The Old Manor House," but as the changed couplet suggests, the poem's persona undergoes a different sort of despair than that suffered by Orlando.

VOL. IV.

J'ai beaucoup souffert; j'ai vu souffrir d'avantage; que d'infortunés j'ai vu mourir! et moi, je les ai survécu.[1]

[1] Rousseau, *La Nouvelle Heloise* (1761), Pt. IV, letter 3. "I have suffered much; I have seen suffering even more; I have seen the death of so many unfortunates! and I, I have survived them" (translation by John Rignall).

CHAP. I.

In a very few days after leaving this temporary settlement, Orlando arrived at Quebec.—He there found means to convince his Indian friend, that to permit him to go would be much more to his interest than to detain him.—But he was without money, and without clothes.—His Canadian acquaintance, however, persuaded him that, on proper application to the Governor, he would be furnished with necessaries as a British officer:—and, after encountering a few difficulties of office, he had an opportunity of submitting his situation to the then Governor; who being convinced, notwithstanding his present appearance, that he was the person whom he described himself to be, gave orders for his being received and treated as an officer in the service of his Britannic Majesty. Orlando referred himself to his Excellency for orders.—He had now no longer a regiment to return to, as that to which he belonged was one of those that had surrendered at Saratoga[1]—Though he was not actually among those who suffered there the humiliation of laying down their arms, having been sent away with dispatches two days before, he knew not how far he was included in their captivity, or might consider himself freed by it to serve in any other regiment, or to return to Europe.

The Governor advised him to proceed to New-York, there to receive the orders of the Commander in Chief of the British forces. A small vessel was preparing to sail in about a fortnight; and in this Orlando, once more restored to the appearance of an Englishman (though much changed by the hardships he had undergone, and by the loss of his hair, which had been remarkably fine), embarked five weeks after his arrival at Quebec. He took leave of his Iroquois protector, with a thousand protestations of gratitude for all the services he had rendered him, and promised to remit him a present of such articles as were most acceptable, to Quebec, as soon as he returned to England, or arrived in any port where they could be obtained; and these promises he meant religiously to fulfil.

The vessel on board of which the luckless adventurer hoped to make his way to New York, was a small sloop sent with dispatches from the Governor of Quebec to the Commander in Chief; and the master, who knew the importance of his commission, took every precaution to secure the execution of it. But all were fruitless; for at some leagues

---

[1]   General Burgoyne surrendered at Saratoga in October 1777.

distance from the mouth of the Delaware, he was seen and chased by two French frigates dispatched from the fleet of Count D'Estaing;[1] and though he was an excellent seaman, and his vessel sailed well, he found it impossible to escape.—His dispatches, however, were thrown overboard; but the sloop immediately surrendered to force which it would have been folly to have resisted, and Orlando was once more a prisoner.

His captivity was, however, much less terrible than that he had formerly sustained. He received from the French officers all those attentions which, among civilized nations, ought to soften the horrors of war. Nor was he sorry to learn that the Fleur de Lys, in which he was, was to return to the fleet from which she was detached, only for her last orders, and then proceed to France.—The Chevalier de Stainville, who commanded her, made a point of testifying, by his behaviour to Orlando, his regard and respect for the English nation; divested, by the candour of his mind, and the strength of his understanding, of all national prejudice, he conceived an esteem for Orlando the moment he conversed with him; and agreed most willingly to give him his parole[2] as soon as he arrived in France (that he should not serve during the present war, either against America or France), and to assist him in returning to England, which he thought no military engagement now prevented his doing with a perfect adherence to duty and propriety.

The Fleur de Lys, after receiving her dispatches for the Court of Versailles from Count D'Estaing, proceeded with a fair wind; and in six weeks Orlando saw himself once more on European ground. He landed at Brest, and felt such sensations as are only known to those who, after having resigned all hope of ever being restored again to their friends and country, see themselves almost within reach of all they hold dear on earth. France, contrasted with his banishment in America, seemed to him to be part of his country, and in every Frenchman he saw, not a *natural* enemy, but a brother.

Had the Chevalier de Stainville been really so, he could not have behaved to Orlando with more generosity, or more kindness. He was himself under the necessity of going immediately to Paris:—but he placed his English friend in the house of a merchant, whom he

---

[1] France allied with America in February 1778. The Comte d'Estaing arrived in New York on 11 July 1778 with a fleet of 17 ships. In August his fleet engaged with the British garrison at Newport, Rhode Island, but a storm scattered the ships. Orlando is taken prisoner by a member of the fleet off the mouth of the Delaware river. Smith is careful to anchor Orlando's American adventures in real events.

[2] One's promise or word of honour.

commissioned to supply him with every thing he might want; and recommending him also to the protection of his second captain while he remained in Brest, this generous captor took leave with regret of his interesting English prisoner—not, however, without procuring him a proper passport, giving him a certificate, and taking his parole. Orlando, eager and anxious as he was to return to his own country, had now a wish that went farther; it was to have an opportunity of renewing his acquaintance, and testifying his gratitude to this amiable officer.

He staid only a few days after him at Brest, when, taking from the merchant who was ordered to supply him, as much money as he supposed would be requisite for his journey, he set out by the diligence for St. Malo, where, he was told, he might perhaps get a conveyance to Jersey or Guernsey. The name of those islands brought afresh into his mind all his fears concerning the fate of his sister Isabella: eighteen months had nearly elapsed since her departure with Warwick; and the mention made of her in Monimia's letter, dated in the following June, was the only intelligence he had received of her. Nor was this the sole mournful recollection to which Orlando was subject in his journey—It was, alas! almost as long since he had received any information relating to the destiny of his Monimia. As to the situation of his family—Gracious Heaven! how many events might in that time have occurred, any one of which would embitter, with eternal regret, his return to his native country.

At St. Malo he could not find the conveyance he sought, and therefore journeyed along the coast in as cheap a manner as he could to Havre; but, there being no open communication now between France and England, he found the accommodation he wanted extremely difficult to obtain, and it was not till almost the end of October[1] that he found means to engage a large fishing-bark, which under that pretence was employed in smuggling on the coast, to land him at Southampton; and this bargain was made at the price of all the money he had, with a promise of a farther reward if he arrived safely at an English port, where he doubted not but that, upon making himself known, he should find friends who would enable him to fulfil his promises. There was considerable hazard to his conductors in attempting to land at any port of Hampshire, when so many vessels lay at Portsmouth; an hazard which

---

[1]   Orlando arrives back in England in late October 1778, having spent more than a year in America, Canada, and France. On his return, he finds that no one recognizes him, and that vast changes have taken place. Smith uses the passage of time, and his experience of war, to "Gothicize" Orlando—that is, to make him strange, his return uncanny, and his personality even more unstable than before he left.

they took care to insist with great vehemence, after they had got their passenger on board. Orlando, who had infinitely rather have been landed on the coast of Sussex, proposed to them to make for some part of that country; but even this proposal did not seem to please them, and two of three men appeared to be very surly and savage.

They agreed, however, to go up the Channel; and the wind, though very high, served them for the purpose. It was already night when they adopted this resolution. With the dawn of morning Orlando saw the white cliffs for which his heart had so long languished. It was, the Frenchmen told him, the back of the Isle of Wight; and Orlando whose impatience to touch English ground was redoubled, entreated them there to put him on shore; but this they refused, as they alleged that their bark would there be in the most imminent danger of being seen and seized by the vessels cruizing round the island; and their only way was to haul off the English coast, and affect to be fishing. Orlando, supposing them practised in these sort of deceptions, and having no remedy even if he had not approved of their plan, submitted to do whatever they thought safest.

They kept, therefore, as near their own coast as if they had intended landing there; but towards evening, the wind being still strong and favourable, they stretched away for the Sussex coast, and Orlando saw the land where all his hopes were reposed!—He was little disposed to dispute with these men any terms they now wished to impose upon him; but he began to think them very unreasonable, when they told him that, as he must land at night, and on the open coast, he could not pay them the farther reward he had promised them on his getting safely on shore; and, therefore, they expect that he would make up to them that failure, by giving up part of his baggage. This was so little, after the casual supplies he had received at Quebec and at Brest, that, as he was now within a few miles of his home, it appeared to him no object. But if he had more tenaciously intended to preserve his little wardrobe, it could not have been attempted without rashness. He was alone, and unarmed, in the boat with three very stout fellows, who were answerable for his life to nobody, and who might, with safety to themselves, have thrown him overboard. He yielded, therefore, to this robbery with as good a grace as he could; and at sunset, in a stormy evening at the beginning of November, he was set on shore between Shoreham and Worthing, with two pieces of twelve sous in one pocket, which had escaped the rapacity of his piratical conductors, and a shirt in the other; his sword, which he had got at Quebec, and which was returned to him immediately by De Stainville on his being captured, his high and romantic spirit might have been unwilling to surrender to those rapacious wretches; but fortunately perhaps both for them and for himself, this his only weapon had slipt from under his arm as he was violently staggered by a sudden tossing of the boat, and to the vexation of his guides, who meant to make it their prize, it fell overboard and was irrecoverably lost. All the other articles of his little property, which they coveted, he granted them very readily: with these petty acquisitions they hurried from the English coast, and were very soon out of sight. Orlando, who had waded through a heavy surf to the land, kissed the beloved soil the moment he reached it; and was unconscious that he was half drowned, and knew not where to lay his head. To be on English ground, to be within a few miles of his native place, was happiness he so little expected ever to have enjoyed, that the tumult of his spirits would not give him leave for some time to think of any thing else. He was, however, so breathless, and so much agitated by his bodily exertion, and the various sensations of his mind, that he sat down a moment to recollect and compose himself.

It was not yet so dark but that he knew nearly where he was; but it was necessary to proceed along the shore to some town or village, where he might procure an horse, on which he meant to hasten instantly to the Hall. The village of Worthing was the nearest to the place where he wished to be. He walked therefore along the sands: but a storm from the south-west, which had been long threatening, now came on with such violence that he took the first shelter he could find, in a little alehouse built under the low cliffs, and serving as a receptacle for the inferior contraband trader, or those of even a more humble description.

A light, however, invited him into a place than which nothing could be more dreary and desolate, and the group he found around a fire in a miserable little room black with smoke, and filled with the fumes of tobacco and gin, did not contribute to give him a more favourable idea of this receptacle: but he had lived near ten months among the Iroquois; and evil is only by comparison. He saw that his entrance very much disturbed the people who were assembled here. Some took him for a Frenchman, and some for an Exciseman; two beings extremely obnoxious, it seems, to some or other of the party. All agreed that he was a spy, and heartily wished him away.

Orlando now spoke to the landlady, and begged of her to give him something to eat; for he had fared very ill on board the fishing-boat. To this, and to his request that he might be allowed to dry his clothes by her fire, she answered in a way which convinced Orlando she doubted his power of paying for the accommodation he desired. To remove an objection so natural, and so incontrovertible, he put his hand into his pocket, and produced two pieces, which the hostess, not a novice in the value of French money, knew was hardly equal in amount to an English shilling. This (and Orlando had actually forgotten that it was all he possessed) was, however moderate, enough to pay for the coarse repast he expected: but the woman seemed more discontent than before, and the people surveyed him with eyes more severely scrutinizing; being convinced he was a French spy, or some person whose appearance there boded them no good: and these their suspicions, now that they found he was poor, they very openly professed; and the landlady, telling him "she never took no French money, not she—nor let folks bide in her house as she know'd nothing of, because as why? it made her liable to lose her license," desired him to walk out: a request with which, though the storm continued with some violence, Orlando found it necessary to comply; and, fatigued as he was, determined to attempt finding his way through the darkness and the tempest to Shoreham, where he thought there must be some person who would believe his story, and assist him for so short a journey as he had to perform.

In this resolution he set out to go back the way he came; but mortified that such brutish inhospitality as what he had just experienced could exist in British bosoms, and lamenting that there were Englishmen less humane than the rude savages of the wilds of America.

Cold, hungry, wet, and fatigued, he pursued his walk: it was soon so extremely dark that he could not distinguish the cliff, on which he was walking, from the beach over which it hung. The rain, driven by violence, almost blinded him, and the roaring of the wind and sea deafened him. Hardly able to stand against the tempest, he frequently stopped, debating whether he had not better wait the return of morning before he attempted to proceed.

His impatience, however, to get to Rayland Hall, conquered every idea of present danger—and he went on, contending against the united opposition of darkness and storm. After a walk of above a mile, he was nearly overcome with fatigue and cold, when lights, which he thought he distinguished through the comfortless gloom, animated him to new exertions, and he went on.

His hope did not deceive him; but, in the eagerness to pursue it, he forgot the precaution with which he had walked before, and fell headlong from the top to the bottom of the cliff, which fortunately for him was not at this place above ten or twelve feet deep, and he reached the bottom, without breaking any of his limbs, at the expence of some contusions. Recovering immediately from the surprize, he found himself able to walk; and kept along the cliff till he reached the town, which was not till between twelve and one.

It was then with some difficulty that he discovered a house of public entertainment; and when he did, it was with more difficulty still he obtained admittance. At length, after telling his story, which the man who heard it did not seem to believe, he was suffered to enter the kitchen of an abode between an inn and an alehouse; where some embers of fire were renewed, and where, though suspicion evidently appeared to be very unfavourable to him, the man who had let him in brought him some cold meat, beer and bread, none of it of a very promising appearance, but such as his hunger made extremely welcome. This being appeased, he enquired if he might have a bed, as he could go no farther that night. There either was no bed, or the person to whom he spoke thought him a traveller whom it was unsafe to admit to one; for this man answered drily, that they made up no beds in that house; but that he might go into the stable, where there was plenty of clean straw. There seemed to be no alternative, as the man objected to his proposal of sitting by the fire all night. To the stable, therefore, the unhappy wanderer was led, and in his wet cloths threw himself down on the straw in one of the stalls; where, in despite of his uncomfortable situation, extreme fatigue gave him up to sleep.

The noise of men entering to take care of their horses awakened him at the early dawn of the morning; and awakened him to such a sense of pain, from the bruises he had received, and the damp clothes in which he had lain, that it was with some difficulty he was able to move from his straw into the kitchen, where he had been the night before. Two sailors were drinking there, who, having nothing else to do, began questioning the stranger. Orlando related in a few words his melancholy adventures, and saw that these honest fellows not only believed him, but pitied his distress, and wished to contribute to his relief. His sufferings were now so acute from the bruises received in his fall, that all his fortitude could not conceal them. One of his new friends went to get him "something comfortable," which in his opinion was a large glass of spirits; while the other assisted him in drying his clothes, which were still wet; and as during his operation Orlando surveyed himself in a little looking-glass stuck against the wall, he found, in the appearance he made, some excuse for the coldness of his reception the night before.

His face was covered with blood and dirt, for his nose had bled from the fall; an old hat, which his pirate-fishermen had given him in place of a very good one they took, had been torn at the same time, and seemed only half a hat; his great coat was gone, and his coat was French; his waistcoat being the only part of his dress that was the same as he brought from Quebec. He had no buckles in his shoes, for the fishermen had desired them; and his hair, which had not had time to grow long since his coiffure, was in the mode of the Iroquois, and now presented what is called a shock head. Having amended his appearance as much as he could, he enquired if he could have an horse? but he was told that none were let there, nor did they know of any to be had in the town. By this time several other men were assembled in the kitchen; and the same enquiry being renewed, one of them said, that he could let him have a horse for fifteen shillings: but then how was it to come back? and besides, he must be paid for it upon the spot. This Orlando at once confessed his inability to do, and the *reasonable* man who offered it made no farther attempt to accommodate him.

Orlando then determined to set out on foot. The very little money he had in his pocket was insufficient to pay for even such entertainment as he had had, and he proposed leaving the shirt he had in his pocket as a pledge for the rest, when the two honest seamen offered to discharge his reckoning between them, and even to lend him each a shilling to carry him homeward—an offer he without hesitation accepted; made a memorandum of their names, as he doubted not of having an immediate opportunity, not only of repaying them, but of returning their kindness fourfold; and then he set out on foot, notwithstanding the pain he suffered, taking leave of the honest tars with many acknowledgements, and giving them his address at Rayland Hall. He was told that a stage would pass along about eleven o'clock; which, if he did not miss it by getting out of the high road, would carry him some part of the seventeen or eighteen miles that was between him and the place where he wished to be. This route was farther about; but he determined to pursue it, because he found himself unable to walk with his usual activity; nor could any less forcible inducement than the excessive impatience he felt to be at the Hall, have supported him in such an undertaking, worn out as he was with the fatigue he had sustained, and his limbs almost dislocated by the injuries he had received the night before.

His progress was slow; and when at length the stage, by which he had been promised a conveyance part of the way, overtook him, he found it carried only so small a part of his way that he had then seven miles to walk. He knew that by going over the downs, he could reach Rayland Hall by a nearer way than continuing along the turnpike highroad; and therefore, quitting the vehicle, he again proceeded on foot.

So little was he able to walk as he used to do, that as the days were now short, it was almost dusk before he reached the top of an high chalky down—the same where, on his departure, he had taken a last look of the place that contained all that was dear to him—and he again beheld it, its antique grey towers rising among the fading woods; he distinguished the turret; and recollecting that so long a space had intervened since he left there the object so dear to his soul, and how many distressing circumstances might have occurred within that time to destroy all his happiness, he became breathless through excess of agitation, and was under the necessity of sitting down on the turf to recover himself.

Beyond the Hall, which was within a mile and a half of the foot of the hill, he distinguished the country round West Wolverton:—the house was concealed: but a wood, or rather shrubbery, on a rising ground behind it, and some part of the offices, were clearly discernible. With sensations of mingled dread and delight he surveyed the well known spot. "Dear paternal house," cried he, "in what a situation do I return to your asylum!—but of how little consequence is that if your beloved inhabitants are well!—Oh, my father! are you now thinking of your Orlando, unconscious that he is within a few miles of you? The son whom you perhaps regret as dead is returning—a beggar indeed but not dishonoured—to your arms, and to find in the bosom of his family ample consolation for all his misfortunes."

When, in indulging these mixed sensations, Orlando had a little recovered his breath and his resolution, he descended the hill; and was soon, by crossing the nearest way the few fields that intervened, at one of those gates at Rayland park where there was no lodge. He found it locked; but there was a stile near it, and he was soon under those well-known shades where he had passed the pleasantest hours of his life. Every thing seemed just as it had been left about the park. With a heart almost throbbing through his bosom, he approached the house, and wondered to see no servants round it; nor the dogs who were usually running out on the approach of strangers. All was mournfully silent; and most of the windows were shut. Certain of not being known, he was unable to resist the temptation he felt, to try the door of the lower turret—It was locked and he proceeded round the house to the stable-yard. There was no person to be seen where formerly there had been four or five servants: there was no appearance of horses; no poultry pecking about; all was still as death, and the grass had grown up among the pavement. Orlando's heart sunk within him; yet he knew not what to fear! the approach of the evening lent new gloom to the desolate appearance of all that he beheld.

CHAP. II.

An apprehension of the truth, vague as it was, was infinitely more terrible than any certainty. With trembling hands, and breathless fear, Orlando now attempted to open the great door of the passage that led to the kitchen and servants' hall; but this too was locked. He called aloud: his voice echoed round the old buildings that surrounded the court where he now stood; but no answer was returned. After waiting and repeating again and again the names of the servants who lived with Mrs. Rayland when he went away, he rapped at the doors, and then at the windows: the lower windows on this side of the house, having strong iron bars, were not shut within. He looked through them into the servants' hall, and the passage leading to it; all was apparently deserted and dark!

He could not longer doubt but that Mrs. Rayland was dead—But where was Monimia? what was become of all her domestics? to whom did the mansion now belong, that it was thus forsaken? New horrors beset him at every step; but now, in a desperate determination to know the worst, or rather to indulge the mournful propensity he had to traverse these dreary rooms, and to visit the turret, he went round to the other part of the house. He tried the chapel-door, which had so often befriended him in happier days; he found it broken, and off the hinges:— he entered the chapel, which appeared more ruinous and neglected than it used to be; he would have enquired if the remains of his benefactress slumbered in the vault beneath it, but no trace remained that could inform him:—he approached the door that led from the chapel to his former apartment, but that was strongly fastened on the inside.

He then, while the only sound he heard was that of the owls from the neighbouring woods, or the night jar as it flitted before him near the house, again traversed the park around it, and went to the opposite side, or principal front in the middle of which was the door of the great hall;—that too was fastened; but over it was the achievement of Mrs. Rayland, the family-arms in a lozenge:—Mrs. Rayland then was undoubtedly no more.

Whither could the weary, the wretched Orlando go for information? and how sad the information he must ask! for it was but too certain that, if Mr. Somerive, or any part of his family, had possessed the Hall, it could not have been thus desolate.

Orlando meditated a moment; if he could be said to meditate, whose heart felt petrified by the shock. He recollected, that the old and long-deserted summer parlour near the library had a glass door which opened into the park, and which was formerly left unlocked. He tried it: it was fastened; but it was yet light enough for him to distinguish that the key was in it, within. He broke a pane of the glass without hesitation, and, putting his hand through, unlocked the door, and entered this parlour.

Melancholy were the observations he made, as, by the little light he had, he traversed this room. The wainscot had fallen down, and the boards were rotted away: the study, of which the door was open, had only half its books left; and the tapestry hung in fragments from the walls. Orlando could not bear the cold chill that struck on his heart. A low hollow gust of wind rushed through the deserted rooms: it seemed loaded with the groans of all he had ever loved, or revered—Yet he proceeded along the passage, which was quite dark—and, hardly knowing to what purpose, went through the great hall, and up the principal stair case—He entered the long north gallery, where, in the April days of their juvenile affection, he had nearly betrayed his innocent partiality for Monimia, by throwing the cricket-ball against the window.—Hideous spectres seemed to beckon to him from the other end of it, and to menace him from the walls; though he knew that they were the portraits of his family in their black doublets, their armour, or their flowing night-gowns:—he stopped, however, in terror he was ashamed of feeling, and, listening a moment, thought he heard a door shut in some distant part of the house—Were there then inhabitants? or was it only the wind which flung-to one of the doors he had left open?—He listened again; but all was still, and he began to consider what he should do next.—Fatigued and worn out as he was, and almost incapable of going farther, he felt a momentary inclination to take possession of a bed. He opened the door of one of the bed-chambers: the old high testered green silk bed looked like a mausoleum—it seemed black, and Orlando could have fancied that the corpse of Mrs. Rayland lay on it: the whole room appeared so damp that he resigned his half-formed project, and returned into the gallery with an intention of going out of the house, and repairing to some of the neighbouring cottages, when he heard again a door shut towards the kitchen, and thought he distinguished a human voice.

He then went down a back stair-case across the apartment where Mrs. Rayland generally sat, and shuddering, as he now almost felt his way, he walked towards the kitchen. This was a room quite in the old-fashioned English style; and such as gave an immediate conviction, by the size of every utensil, of old English hospitality. It was such as Pope describes in his letter to the Duke of Buckingham, where the peasantry suppose the infernal spirits hold their sabbath; but upon a still larger scale.[1]—As Orlando came near the door, he was convinced that he heard the murmuring sound of some person speaking as if in discontent. The door was not shut close; he pushed it gently open, and saw a female figure blowing the fire: he advanced towards her, and remarked, by the flashing light of the flame which rose as she blew, that she was bent double with age, and in coarse dress of the lowest peasantry.—Instead of turning or speaking to him, she continued to mutter and mumble to herself, of which Orlando could distinguish no more than, "Why a plague did you not come sooner? about no good, I warrant ye ... at this time o'night! and stalking about instead of helping ..." Orlando now appeared before her, and spoke to her, enquiring for Mrs. Rayland; when the beldam, suddenly looking up, let fall the bellows, and, uttering a shriek or rather yell, hobbled towards the nearest door, crying out, "Thieves! murder! thieves!"

Orlando, following, attempted to pacify her: he assured her he was no thief, but the son of Mr. Somerive, the nearest relation of the late owner of that house, who was lately come from abroad, and did not know but what she still owned it.—His voice seemed to have some effect in appeasing the fears of the old woman; but upon surveying him, they again returned—"You 'squire Somerive's son!" exclaimed she— "Will you persuade me of that? Didn't I know 'em both—Oh Lord! oh Lord! I shall be murder'd, that's for certain, and our Ralph's not come back—Oh! What shall I do?—what shall I do?" It was in vain Orlando renewed his protestations that he meant her no harm; she continued to insist on his leaving the house, and he remained resolutely bent not to go till he had obtained some information as to whom it now belonged. The contest lasted some minutes, when at last an halloo was heard without, and the woman exclaimed, "Oh! thank the good Lord, there's our Ralph." She went out to the passage, opened the door, and a stout surly-looking clown followed her into the kitchen, to whom she had related

---

[1]   In his letter, Pope writes, "The Kitchen is built in form of the Rotunda, being one vast Vault to the Top of the House; where one overture serves to let out the smoak [sic] and let in the light. By the blackness of the walls, the circular fires, vast cauldrons, yawning mouths of ovens and furnaces, you would think it either the forge of Vulcan, the cave of Polypheme, or the temple of Moloch. The horror of this place has made such an impression on the country people, that they believe the Witches keep their Sabbath here, and that once a year the Devil treats them with infernal venison, a roasted Tiger stuff'd with ten-penny nails." (cited by Ehrenpreis, p. 541: *Correspondence*, ed. George Sherburn [1956], i. 510). It is interesting to note that what Pope calls "the horror of this place," Smith sees as "the old-fashioned English style" and "old English hospitality." Of course, Orlando's reception belongs more in the realm of the supernatural: he is seen as a revenant.

that a strange man had got into the house, had been walking all about it, and now would not go out—"I thoft, Lord help me! it was you; and there sat I blowing the fire, and wondering what a dickins you could be prancing about up stairs for."

The sturdy peasant surveyed his new visitor with evident marks of displeasure, while Orlando told him who he was, and desired to know to whom Rayland Hall now belonged.

"I don't believe 'tis any business of yours," replied the churl, "and I'm sure you have nothing to do here; for, let it belong to who 'twill—'tis no place for travellers and wagabons—Come, master, troop! mother and I we be put in this here Hall to look ater it, and we can't not answer it to our employers to let in no strangers nor wayfaring people."

"I only ask," said Orlando, "who *are* your employers? surely you can have no objection to tell me that."—"Why, master archdeacon Hollybourn is *my* employer, then, if you must know; and this house and premises belongs now to our bishop and dean; and the archdeacon Hollybourn—"

"Good God! and how long has Mrs. Rayland been dead?"

"How long? Why eight months or there away—But, come, master, I've answered your question civilly, though I don't know no right you have got to ask it, and now I desire you to walk out; and I hope there's no more on you about the premises; for, if there is, I must carry you before the Justice—and so, look'e, I've got a gun here" (and he reached one down from over the chimney) "that will do more sarvis in case of need besides hitting a rook."

Orlando, unarmed and defenceless as he was, and finding no success in his attempts to gain credit, was now compelled to leave this once hospitable mansion, where he had formerly been encouraged to dream of passing in it the noon of his life with his beloved Monimia—after whom, or her aunt Lennard, he enquired fruitlessly. With despair in his heart he left the house (not however for the last time, though it was now the property of the good bishop and his dean and chapter), being determined to return the next day, for the mournful delight of survey-ing the apartment of Monimia, where he almost wished to expire. Yet he had hardly given way a moment to this unmanly despondence, than he was ashamed of it: his father and his family were yet ready to receive him, and he quickened his pace through the gloom; for it was now quite dark, and a strong south-west wind brought on a heavy driving rain.

How very mournful were the reflections of Orlando as he followed the well-known foot-path to West Wolverton!—How different was his situation from that he fondly thought to have been in when he last took a reluctant leave, in this very path, of his Monimia!—Accustomed to associate poetry with all his ideas, his present condition, opposed to that which his sanguine imagination had flattered him with, brought to his mind that sublime ode, "the Bard" of Gray,

> "Fair laughs the morn, and soft the zephyr blows;
> While proudly riding o'er the azure realm,
> In gallant trim the gilded vessel goes,
> Youth on the prow, and pleasure at the helm;
> Regardless of the sweeping whirlwind's sway,
> That, hush'd in grim repose, expects his evening prey."[1]

In such mournful meditations, and by dint of habit, or rather of his perfect recollection of every shrub and tree about the place, so that he could have found his way even had it been darker than it was, Orlando reached the upper plantation, and descended on the other side, the almost perpendicular path that led down over the pond head. The roar of the water, which murmured hollow in the blasts of wind, and the sullen noise of the mill, well-known sounds which Orlando had so often listened to, brought back, in all their force, the recollection of the evening walks he used to have from Wolverton to the Hall to visit his Monimia. He went over the foot-bridge that arched the cascade now swollen with the rain, and entered the old fir-grove, where he fancied, in some former fits of despondence, that he heard, in every hollow wind, "Orlando will revisit this place no more!" Yet he did revisit it; but how? How fallen from all those dreams of happiness that had so often flattered him, and, in contradiction to this gloomy impression of his pensive moments, had said—"Orlando will be the master of these scenes!"

Yet, if he found his father living and rejoiced at his return—if he once more felt the maternal tear of his beloved mother wet his cheek—if his sisters were well—if news had been received of Isabella—and if Selina, as he fondly hoped, could give him certain intelligence where he might fly to Monimia, all would be well; and, though he should regret his kind benefactress, regret the severe disappointment to his family, there was yet happiness, much happiness, to be hoped for.

It was so perfectly dark within the wood, that Orlando, not being

---

[1]   *The Bard* (1757), by Thomas Gray (1716–71), a Pindaric Ode and an exploration of the sublime.

able with all his knowledge of the place to find his path, went out to the edge of it, and continued his way along the pond side. He saw a light glimmering at a distance upon the water, which he perceived was reflected from the mill. The storm becoming more violent, he determined to go thither. The miller was one of Mrs. Rayland's tenants, who had not long before Orlando's departure for America granted him a very great favour in regard to the renewal of his lease, in consequence of Orlando's intercession. From this man, therefore, he doubted not of an hospitable reception, and the information relative to Mrs. Rayland which at the Hall he had been denied.

He soon arrived; and, with a short stick he carried with him, rapped loudly at the door. A woman soon after looked out of the window from whence the light had proceeded, and enquired in apparent alarm, "Who is there?"

Orlando answered, "Is it Mrs. Whitly who speaks?"

"Mrs. Whitly, friend!" replied the female voice: "Lord! I cannot think what you want here at this time o'night; why, master's a-bed, and the men folk too—I'm sure I wish you'd go about your business."

"My business," said Orlando, "is with Mr. Whitly—Tell him it is Orlando Somerive, his old friend."

The woman then retired from the window as if to speak to somebody, and, presently returning, cried, "Master says how he knows no such person—Young 'squire Orlando is dead a long while ago in parts beyond sea; and you must be an impostor—for 'tis well known the young man's not alive, and all his family were in mourning for un before they went out of this country."

The woman would then have shut the window; but Orlando, rendered half frantic by her last expression, conjured her with so much vehemence to hear him, that she delayed it a moment.—He implored her to tell him what she meant by saying that the Somerive family had left the country.—"Why, 'tis plain," answered she, "that you don't belong to none of them—for, if you did, you'd know that the old 'squire have been dead ever so long—a matter of two or three months before old Madam at the Hall; and that the young one, he as was always so wild like, have sold the house and farms and all to the great 'squire at the castle, and that the rest on 'em have left the country."

Orlando could hear no more—his fortitude and his senses forsook him together—and weakness, from fatigue and want of food, disabled him from resisting any longer these repeated and overwhelming strokes of affliction—He staggered a few paces, and fell against the door of the house.

The woman, who perceived him by the light of the candle from the casement, began to think he must be, in some way or other, interested for the Somerive family, since he was thus so affected; and, communicating his situation to her husband, who was in bed in the room from the window of which she had spoken, the miller, not without some grumbling and swearing, got up, and, looking out, saw Orlando lying on the ground, and apparently insensible. He then feared that he might "get into trouble," to use the expression of the country, if a man was found dead at his door, without his having assisted him; and calculating, rather than yielding to the impulse of humanity, he ordered his wife to go call up one of the men, and go down with him to see what was the matter with the fellow; and, if he was only drunk, or sick, to give him a dram, and to haul him away to a hovel full of straw in the yard—all which he thought less trouble than might be given him by the Coroner's Inquest, if the man should be found dead at his door in the morning.

His wife obeyed—and, taking a servant man with her, who had lived many years at the mill, they opened the door.—Orlando was insensible, and the man pronounced him dead;—but had not half a second held the candle to his face, before he exclaimed with a great oath, that it was either Orlando Somerive, or his ghost! That it was not his ghost, but himself, though sadly changed both in countenance and appearance, the miller's man was convinced, when Orlando, awakened from his trance by being moved, opened his eyes, while with a deep sigh, and wildly staring about him, he wrung the man's hand, and conjured him, in incoherent terms, to tell him if it was true that his father was dead, and all his family dispersed—or if it were only a hideous dream.

The old man, who had known him from his infancy, was moved by the melancholy situation in which he saw him; and, helping him into the house, put him into a chair, and made him swallow some coarse kind of spirits—Orlando submitting to receive his assistance, but still passionately imploring him to say if what he fancied he heard was real, while the man with tears in his eyes continued silent. By this time, however, the miller himself, Mr. Whitly, having been assured by his wife of Orlando's identity, came down; and Orlando renewing to him his eager adjurations, he began a long consolatory discourse, in which he attempted to prove that, as every body must die, none should be immeasurably grieved when an event so common happened to their friends.

Orlando with glazed eyes and contracted brows appeared to listen to his discourse; but, in fact, heard not a word of it beyond those that confirmed his misfortune. With wildness in his voice and manner, he now desired to go to the house that was his father's, to go to the parish-church where he was buried. He demanded eagerly where his mother was? where were his sisters? His host answered, that they had gone a long time to London; and that as to talking of going to West Wolverton house or such-like, or for to go for to think of going into the church at such a time, why it was quite out of reason; but he advised him to go to bed where he was for the night, saying very coldly (which coldness Orlando did not however remark), that he was welcome to a spare bed they had for one night or so; and the old servant plying him with spirits as liber-ally as his master did with advice, and believing his remedy the most effi-cacious of the two, fatigue and weakness soon overcome by the power of this application, he suffered himself, almost in a state of insensibility, to be led to a room where was a bed, on which, without taking off his clothes, he threw himself, and forgot a little while all his sorrows.

Alas! they recurred in the morning with severer poignancy—He did not, on his first recovering his senses, recollect where he was, and stared wildly about him; but too soon the sad remembrance of his irreparable calamities rushed upon him, and he had need of all his reason and all his fortitude to enable him to bear this terrible conviction like a man. He went down stairs, determined to visit West Wolverton and the church, and then to set out for London; but he had only eighteen-pence in his pocket, the remainder of what the sailors had lent him at Shoreham, and his clothes were such as would prevent him from obtaining credit on the road. He hoped that at the neighbouring town he might, when he was known, obtain credit for such an equipment as would prevent his terrifying his family by his appearance; and, perhaps, a small supply of money from Mr. Whitly, to whom, as soon as he saw him, he opened without hesitation the reduced state of his finances, and desired he would lend him a guinea or two to bear his expences to London. This man, who was grown very rich by the excellent bargain he held under Mrs. Rayland, and by being a great proficient in the secrets of his trade, had, like many other rich men, an invincible aversion to the poor, or to any who might be accidentally reduced to the necessity of borrowing; and to Orlando, coming under both these descriptions, he gradually became more and more reserved as his present situation was explained; and when he ended by desiring a temporary assistance, the miller, with a very sagacious look, replied, that he was very sorry, to be sure, that things were as they were—"For my own part," said he, "I have a family of my own; nevertheless, I'm sure I would do a kind thing by a neighbour's son as soon as another—But the thing is this—Here's a will, d'ye see, of old Madam's, dated a good many years ago, which gives all her landed property to the bishop of this here diocese, his dean and chapter for purposes therein mentioned, and then legacies"— Orlando would here have interrupted him with questions; but the affluent Miller, opining, like most other affluent men, that a borrower ought to have no sentiments of his own, waved his hand to silence him, and continued—"Well, well, but hear me out, and then I'll hear you—I say, that being the case, why the will is disputed; because as why? Your brother Phill, d'ye see, says he's heir at law, and so there's a Chancery law-suit about it—But we knows that a will's a will, and the longest purse will carry the day.—Well! the upshot of all is, that heir at law, or no heir at law, your brother, if he can carry on the suit, which folks be pretty dubious about, will never get no part of it."—"And, therefore," said Orlando sharply, "you will not lend me what I asked?—It is well—I wish you a good morning, and desire to pay for what I have had at your house, which I think cannot exceed a shilling in value." He then threw down a shilling on the table; and, without attending to Mr. Whitly any farther, left his house; and hardly knowing what he did, he went towards the house of his father. The ingratitude and selfishness of the man whom he had left gave him an additional pang; but it was only momentary, for grief of a more corrosive nature overwhelmed him; and when he arrived at the door of the house he proposed entering, his knees trembled under him; his looks were wild and haggard; and he was incapable of considering that the house was now in possession of strangers. He passed into the yard, which was surrounded by the offices; but all was changed; and he stood in the stupefaction of despair, without having any precise idea of what he intended to do, till he was roused from this torpid state by a maid-servant, who, hearing the dogs bark, came out and enquired what he did there.

Orlando answered incoherently that it was his father's house—that he came to look for his father.—The girl in terror left him; and, believing him either a madman or a robber, but rather the former, ran in to her mistress, and, carefully locking the kitchen door, informed her that there was a crazy man in the yard. This young woman, who was the mistress of one of Stockton's friends to whom he had lent the house, wanted neither understanding nor humanity, however deficient she might be in other virtues;[1] and knowing the natural propensity of the

---

[1]   It is important to note that Smith does not follow the convention that disallowed virtue of any sort to a "fallen" woman; this young woman is the most humane and helpful of all those, stranger and putative friend, that Orlando encounters. It is equally important, however, that Smith never calls her "lady," but instead uses the more ambiguous terms of "person" and "woman."

vulgar to terrify themselves and others, she called to a man, who was at work in the garden, to follow her, and then went to speak herself to the person whom her servant had represented as a lunatic.

She found the unhappy young man seated on a pile of wood near the door, his arms resting on his knees and concealing his face. The noise of her opening the door and approaching him seemed not to rouse him from his mournful reverie: but she spoke gently to him; and Orlando, looking up, shewed a countenance on which extreme agony of mind was strongly painted, but which was still handsome and interesting, and appeared to belong to one who had seen better days:—"Is there any thing, Sir, you wish to know? Can I be of any service to you?" These few words, spoken in a pleasing female voice, had an immediate effect in softening the heart of Orlando, petrified by affliction. He burst into tears; and rising said—"Ah, Madam! forgive my intrusion, forgive me, who am a stranger where I had once a home. This house was my father's!—Here I left him when seventeen months since I went to America—Here I left my father, my mother, and three sisters—and all, all are gone!" He lost his voice, and leaned against a tree near him.

The young person, extremely affected by the genuine expression of grief, and convinced that he was no madman, now invited him into the parlour; and Orlando, unknowing what he did, followed her.

Every object that he saw was a dagger to his heart. As Philip had sold to Stockton every thing as it remained at his father's death, a great part of the furniture was the same. Startled at every step he took by the recollection of some well-known object, he entered the parlour more dead than alive, and pale as a corpse, and with quivering lips, he attempted to speak, but could not. The young woman saw his agitation, and pouring him out a large glass of wine, besought him to drink it and to compose himself, again repeating her offers of kindness. He put back the glass—"I thank you, Madam, but I cannot drink—I cannot swallow.—That picture," added he, fixing his eyes wildly on a landscape over the chimney—"that picture belonged to my father; he used, I remember, to value it highly—I beg your pardon, Madam—I know not what I proposed by coming hither, unless it were to procure a direction to my mother and sisters. Where my father is I know too well, though I believe," continued he, putting his hand to his forehead, "that I said when I first came into the court-yard, that I looked for him—Can you, Madam, tell me where I can find the part of my family that does survive?"

The young woman, with increasing interest, told him that she had been there only a few weeks, and was quite a stranger in the country;

but that, if he could recollect any person thereabouts likely to be better informed, she would send a servant to fetch them, or with any message he might direct.

CHAP. III.

After a pause, sufficiently expressive of the difficulty with which he thought, Orlando said, that there was at the neighbouring town an Attorney with whom his father had been long connected; and who at his setting out in life had received many favours from the family of Somerive.—To him he wished to send—"or rather I will go to him, Madam—for why should I be longer troublesome to you?" He then got up; but the young person with great gentleness and good nature, said, "You are not able, I am sure, to walk so far—if you are not too much wounded by the recollections that surround you here to stay, I beg you to take some refreshment, while I send a servant to the gentleman; he shall go on horse-back, and will soon be back." As Orlando did indeed doubt whether he was able to walk so far as the town, and an idea struck him, that while the messenger was gone, he could visit the family vault, in the church of West Wolverton, where the remains of his father were deposited, he accepted, after a slight apology, of the obliging offer of his hostess; who bringing him pen and ink, he wrote with an uncertain and trembling hand—"Mr. O. Somerive being returned from America, and quite ignorant till his arrival here of the many alterations in this neighbourhood, will esteem it a favour if Mr. Brock will oblige him with his company for half an hour—at the house formerly his father's at West Wolverton.—"

Having sent away this note, and being prevailed upon to take the refreshment he had at first refused; he told his new acquaintance, that he had a wish to visit two or three places in the adjoining village, and would, with her permission, return to the house in time to meet Mr. Brock, if he were so obliging as to attend upon his message.

The servant being sent away, Orlando set forth to visit the tomb of his father.—He knew well the spot: it was in the chancel of the church, and the entrance was marked with a stone, with the arms of Somerive and Rayland quartered upon it. The sexton, who at first appeared to have lost all recollection of him, gave him the keys as soon as he knew him—and the unhappy wanderer, throwing himself on the ground, gave way to that grief which he had hitherto checked.—Now it was, however, that he felt the reward of his dutiful conduct; for he was conscious that, except in the single instance in regard to his sister Isabella, he had never wilfully disobeyed his father; and he felt too, that if by taking Monimia with him, or by any other act of disobedient ingratitude, he had felt himself accessary to that affliction which he too well understood had hastened the death of his parent, that sorrow, which was now unmixed with self-reproach, would then have driven him to distraction.—As he kissed and took a last leave of this deposit of the ashes of his family, he recollected, that his affection to the lost friend whom he deplored would be shewn rather by his tenderness and duty towards his mother and sisters, than by giving himself up to useless despair.—Roused by this reflection to more manly thoughts, he arose from the ground, and his heart having been relieved by the indulgence he had thus given to his grief, he quitted the church with a deep sigh, and determined to walk as quickly as he could round Rayland park—having an unconquerable desire to visit the turret of Monimia, which he thought he might do in the day time, by letting himself in through the same door where he had entered before; and as he knew every part of the house, finding his way thither without alarming the vigilance of the old woman who kept the house. In this intention he traversed the outside of the park paling very hastily, when the sight of the north lodge and the cottage near it, brought to his mind the circumstances of Monimia's letter; who there described her meeting with Sir John Belgrave; and he thought the woman of the cottage might give him some particulars, which he hitherto had not been able to learn.—Entering therefore, and making her, not without much difficulty, recollect him; he was forced to bear all her wondering, and all her enquiries, before he could prevail upon her to give him the following particulars:

"Lord, Sir! why now I tell you as well as I can all how these bad things have come to pass.—In the first place, after you was gone, somehow there seemed no content at the Hall—I heard say, that Madam began to droop as 'twere a fortnight or two afterwards; and was never pleas'd with nothing that could be done for her—And there came out a story about Pattenson—the rights of the matter, my husband says, never were cleared up; but however, to the surprise of every body, my Lady she believed some story about him; and though 'twas reported he tried to turn the tables upon Madam Lennard, sure enough he was dismissed from the Hall for good; but for certain not like a disgraced servant; for Madam gave him a power of good things, and his farm as he took was stocked from the Hall; and sure enough he had feather'd his nest well one way or another; for he died worth a mort of money."—

"Pattenson is dead then?" said Orlando.

"Lord help you, yes!" answered the good woman—"Why he died of the gout in his stomach just afore my Lady—But if you'll have a little patience I'll go on with my story. So Pattenson went away; and after that Madam Lennard seem'd somehow to govern my Lady more than ever; yet folks said, that it was not so much she, as them there Rokers, uncle and nephew, that was put in by her as stewards; and to be sure there was for a long time strange talk—and they said, that Madam Lennard was jealous of young Roker, he as she afterwards married—and so sent away her niece's daughter, that sweet pretty young creature that you remember at the Hall."

"And what is become of her?" cried Orlando eagerly—"Whither was she sent?"

"Why that nobody knew nothing about at the time, as every body saw Madam Lennard was shy of speaking of her; but folks *have* said since, that she was gone up to London, with some Lord or Baron Knight; for my part, as I says to my husband, I don't care to give credit to such scandalous stories upon mere hearsay.—However, to go on with my story:—By then Madam Lennard had sent this poor young thing away, every body thought how the affair would go—at least folks about the house says, they saw it plain enough—So then, your poor father, who had been ailing a long time, he was taken sick, and when all the doctors had given him over, he sent to beg Mrs. Rayland would come to him; and though Mrs. Lennard she did, as I've heard say, all she could to hinder my Lady's going, she went; and though nobody knows what passed, because nobody was in the room but Madam Somerive, your good mother, yet every body said, that the 'squire got a power better after he had seen the old lady, and said his mind was easy; and then every body thought he would recover—and it was given out, that the 'squire had seen my Lady's will, or, however, that she had told him the contents, and that she had made you her heir."

"Me?" said Orlando—"alas! no!"—

"Well, but that was the notion of the country, and I am sure, there's nobody in all this here part of our county but heartily wishes it had been true—Well, and so 'Squire Somerive he went on for a little while, getting better and better; till something fresh broke out, about your brother, Mr. Philip; and so upon that, he grew worse again, and died in a few days. Oh! what sad affliction all the family was in! but Madam, at the Hall, was more kind to them than she used to be; for she sent to fetch them up to the Hall the day of the funeral, and kept them there three or four days, till the young 'squire hearing how his father was dead, came down—then your mother and sisters went back to their house: but alack-a-day!—he soon began to make sad alterations, and was driving a bargain for the sale of the estate to 'Squire Stockton, almost, folks said, before his father was cold in his grave."—

Orlando clasped his hands eagerly together, and drew a convulsed sigh; but he was unable to interrupt the narration, and the woman went on—

"So, Sir, just about that time Madam Rayland she was taken ill—yet it did not seem, somehow, that there was much the matter with her; but she drooped, and drooped, and pined, and pined—and people said, as saw her sometimes, that is, the footmen who waited before she took to her bed, and the maids as sat up with her, especially Rachel, that she honed so after you, and used to send every day to your mother to know if she had heard of you; and sent for her to come to her, and gave her letters for you to desire you would come back; for she mistrusted, some-how, that Lennard had never sent the letters she wrote to you before; and all the people said, that Lennard, with all her art, had not been able to keep matters so snug, about her lover, but that her lady had an inkling of the matter—And they said, too, that Madam was not half so fond of her as she used to be; but that she had been used to her so long, and had been so in the custom of letting her do what she would, that now, as she was so old, and sick, and feeble, and out of spirits, she had not resolution to speak her mind.—Well, Madam died, and then—Good Lord, what a work there was at Hall!"—

"How do you mean?" said Orlando.

"Why, your brother Philip sent to take possession of every thing as heir at law; but old Roker and his nephew would not let him or his people come in; as they said they had a will of Mrs. Rayland's, and he must come and hear it read.—Your mother tried, as I heard say, to pacify your brother; because she knew, or however believed for certain, that your honour's self was the heir—So with that, upon a day appointed by these Rokers, who had possession of the house, your poor mother, and your two sisters, and the young 'squire your brother, they went to the Hall, and there, as I heard say, was the two Rokers and Madam Lennard, and the servants, all assembled; and so young Roker took upon him to read the will, though your brother took a young lawyer with him from London, one Counsellor Staply; and there the will was read; and instead of leaving you the heir, it was a will made ever so long before, when Madam Rayland was out of humour with Mr. Somerive: and so there, it seems, that she gave five thousand pounds to Pattenson if he outlived her, but he was dead, and there was an end of that; and two thousand to the old coachman, who is as rich as a jew already—and a matter of ten thousand to Mrs. Lennard—And not only so, but all her clothes—and ever so many pieces of fine plate; and a diamond ring—and the Hampshire farms, which ben't worth so little as four hundred pounds a year—And then, all Madam's fine laces, and sattin gowns, and her sister's too, for none of them had ever been given away—They say that 'twas not so little as six or seven hundred pounds worth of clothes and laces; and all the fine household linen—Such beautiful great damask tablecloths and napkins—and such great chests full of sheets; besides a mort of things that I cannot remember not I—But the great house, and all the noble estates in this county, she gave to the Bishop, as I suppose you know, and to the Dean and Chapter, for charitable uses, and to build a sort of alms-house—But it's very well known that the greatest part of it will go into their own pockets—and I cannot think, for my share, and my husband he says the same, why a-deuce Madam gave her money to them there parsons, when they always take care to have enough out of the farmers and poor men, let who will go without."

A deep sigh was again extorted from Orlando, and the good gossip remarking it, said: "Ah, Sir, to be sure you may well sigh!—Such a fine estate! and so justly your right by all accounts; and then after promising your father so faithfully too!—Poor Madam Somerive, your good mother, was in very sad trouble—Philip he raved and ranted, and made a sad to-do, but there was no remedy; them two Rokers had got possession of the house, and after the funeral, I reckon, they thought to have kept it, as stewards to the new owners; but whip! the parsons come upon them, and packed them off; and they've put in old Betty Grant and her son just to look after it, and open the windows—But, Lord! I'm sure the place looks so mollencholy as makes my very heart ach to pass it.—But, however, to go on with my story of all the troubles of your poor dear mother—After this, a week or so, news came by a negur man as went with that young captain as your sister Belle ran away with, that he and miss were drowned or cast away, at some place beyond sea—I can't remember rightly the name of it; but, however, that they were lost, and that you were killed in battle by the wild Ingines; this man told my husband he saw you dead with his own eyes, and your skull cleft with one of their swords"—

"And where," said Orlando, "is this man now?"—"Why, Madam took him," replied the woman, "and when the family left the country, he went up to London with them"—

"And how long have they been gone?"

"Nigh two months, as well as I can remember; poor dear ladies! I'm sure we poor folks miss them sadly, and so we do the Hall."—

"And my brother," enquired Orlando, "what is become of my brother?"

"Oh, as for that," answered the woman, "nobody knows; and I must say this, 'squire, that if you'd a been like him, nobody would have been so sorry as they were, that Madam gave her money elsewhere; for would you think it?—at the very time he came down here to take possession of his house, after the poor gentleman his father's death, and when all the family was in such affliction—what did he do, but bring down that nasty flaunting hussey Bet Richards, that was took from the parish work-house to be housemaid at the Hall—whom he have kept in London all's one as a lady, and dressed her up better than any of his sisters—and she's as impudent and proud!—I'd have all such wicked toads sent to beat hemp[1]— and every body has said 'twas a thousand pities she was not in her old place the work-house again, instead of prancing about as she did, to break poor dear Madam Somerive's heart; who, though she seemed to bear it all with patience, and to take no notice, was quite as I may say, sunk and weighed down with one sorrow's falling so fast upon another—and, at last, when she found the house and estate and all the goods were sold, and that she and her daughters must leave it, and then, just afterwards, when the negur's news came, she seemed to be quite, quite gone!—and I heard say, her health was in a bad state after she got to London."

Dreadfully affected by this account of his mother, all of whose sufferings he felt, however coarse and simple the relation of them, Orlando now again enquired of his informer, if she knew where his mother and sisters lived in town?—She said, No; there was a neighbour's daughter gone up lately to London to live with them as a servant; whose friends knew the direction, and to them she would send if he would stay. Orlando thanked her—and then expressed some wonder that his mother, who had always disliked London, should fix there. To which the woman said, "Why, Sir, I've heard say, that the reason of that was, that Madam's brother, the London Merchant, insisted upon it; and another reason was, because she thought that if she was not always at his elbows, your brother would go after his pleasures and that; and so neglect the great law-suit."

---

[1]   Bridewell was a house of correction for prostitutes, and other outcasts from society. Its inhabitants were given menial and repetitive jobs such as beating hemp, that is, beating the rotted stems of hemp so as to detach the fibre, which was then used to make rope, cord, and stout fabrics. See note 1, p. 110; Betty achieves her desire to be a "fine lady."

"What law-suit?"—said Orlando, who had forgotten at that moment the vague information he had received from the miller.

"Why you must know, Sir," replied the woman, "that when first my Lady died, there was a great talk about the country, that there was some black doings about the will; for from what she had said to your father, and from a great many other things she had said, and from her having Lawyers from London come down about three years and a half ago, when folks thought she made a new will in your favour; there were those, and in the house too, who didn't scruple to say, that the real will was made away with by them Rokers, and that an old will was proved— So your brother he was advised by counsellor Staply to go to law;— but he said if there was another will, it was in your favour, not in his; and he'd as lieve the Parsons, or the Devil, had the estate as you.— However, when a little while after news came of your death, then he went to law directly; because, he said, if there was such a will, he was your heir-at-law, and the old woman's too:—and so he is suing the Rokers; that is, Mrs. Lennard and her husband; for you know the old soul took to herself a young husband at last."

Orlando expressing his surprise at this, enquired where they lived— "Oh!" answered she, "when they found they were bit as to continuing in the stewardship, and the Archdeacon Hollybourn had provided another for my Lord Bishop and the Parsons, and was to overlook the estate himself, Mr. and Mrs. Roker went away to live in Hampshire, upon the estate my Lady gave them there; and there, I understand, they live quite like great people, and are visited and noticed by all the quality; only Madam I hear is terribly jealous;—and they say her young husband is not over and above good-humoured to her, though he got such a great fortune by her."

The good woman seemed never weary of talking; but having at length exhausted all she could recollect, and promising to procure a direction from her neighbour, and send it down in a few minutes to West Wolverton, Orlando took his leave. And as, just as he left the cottage, the clock in it struck three, he was afraid of intruding upon the benevolence of his new friend, at the house once his father's, if he left her long with the lawyer whom he had sent for; and therefore, instead of going then to make his mournful visit to the turret, he returned to West Wolverton, where he found the man sent to the town had been some time returned, and had brought from his father's former friend, the attorney, a note to this purport—

"Mr. Brock's compts: imagines some mistake—has not the honor to know any gentleman of the name of Somerive, except Philip S. Esq; late of West Wolverton—hopes to be excused, being particularly engaged."

This note completed the distress of Orlando, who saw that he should now be taken for an impostor where he was, and obtain no credit where he expected it to carry him to London, where he now most earnestly wished to be, because there only could he hope to see his family, or to have any explanation of the hints so darkly given by the labourer's wife—hints, which among the complicated misfortunes which surrounded him, gave him the most insupportable pain.—"Gone with some lord!" Impossible—Yet the very idea was distraction. He was believed dead. He regretted that he had not asked whether Monimia heard of his death, not at the moment recollecting that his informer's knowledge hardly went so far; and that, by her account, Monimia was gone before the death of Mrs. Rayland, and before the arrival of the intelligence brought by Perseus the negro: yet again he recollected, that if Selina and Monimia still corresponded, she must immediately have known it; and thus by all he loved in the world he was considered as dead.

To undeceive them as soon as he could was what appeared most necessary; but how to do that he knew not. He could not bear to beg of any of the neighbouring gentlemen—indeed he knew none of them but Stockton (who was the last man in the world he desired to meet), for all the rest were at a great distance, and the elder Somerive had never sought their acquaintance: some were too expensive for him, and others too ignorant to afford him any pleasure in their society. By the richest he was contemned as a petty gentleman; and by the rest envied as the future possessor of Rayland Hall—and therefore very little intercourse had ever passed between them and the family at West Wolverton. While Orlando, whom his hospitable acquaintance had the consideration to leave by himself, was meditating on his wretched and forlorn situation, a young man was introduced into the room, in whom he immediately recollected a clerk to the lawyer to whom his unsuccessful note was written; who, immediately acknowledging him, changed as he was, related, that Mr. Brock having shewn him the note, and declaimed against it as an imposition, it being, he said, perfectly well known that Orlando Somerive was dead—the young man thought he recollected his hand, there having been formerly some degree of intimacy between them; and unwilling to dispute the point with Brock, who was, he told him, Solicitor in the depending cause between the Bishop and the Somerive family, he had made some excuse of business, and came to see himself whether it was his old friend, or some one wishing to represent him.

All the difficulties which Orlando had to encounter as to going to London were now removed at once—This young man, Mr. Dawson, offered not only to supply him with money but clothes; and they agreed to proceed together to the town in the dusk, as Orlando did not wish to be known, nor indeed to be seen, in his present condition. This being settled, Orlando would immediately have taken leave of his humane hostess; but she entreated both him and his friend to stay dinner, with a frankness and good humour which Dawson was less disposed than Orlando to resist. As soon as it was nearly dark she ordered him to be accommodated with a horse, and sent a servant with him to bring it back.

With a thousand grateful acknowledgments Orlando took his leave; and with an agonizing sigh left, as he believed for ever, the paternal house and the neighbourhood of the Hall, without having been able to indulge his melancholy by visiting the turret.

His friend, though he could give him very little information more than he had already received, and none about Monimia, yet soothed and consoled him; and, having equipped him with a coat, hat, and linen of his own, as they were nearly of a size, he put five guineas into his hand; and, desiring to hear from him, saw him into the stage-coach, which, at six every morning, set out from the town where they were for London.

CHAP. IV.

The variety of uneasy emotions which passed through the mind of Orlando, as he journeyed towards London, would be difficult to describe, since he himself could hardly discriminate them; but each, though not distinct, was acutely painful. In what a situation did he return to his family! in what a situation did he find it! How should he, while his mind was yet enfeebled from the cruel disappointments he had experienced on his arrival in England, be able to bear the tears of his mother, the sorrow of his two sisters? how console them for the loss they had sustained? how strengthen by his example their more tender minds, to endure what he feared the dissolute folly of his brother might yet bring upon them; while his own heart recoiled from the idea of meeting that brother, and was bleeding with the dreadful wounds inflicted by the uncertainty of what was become of Monimia; which, had he not entertained some hopes of hearing of her from his sister Selina, would have driven him to distraction! Of his sister Isabella he thought too with great concern; and when the reflection, which alone brought some comfort to his mind, occurred to him, that he had resisted the temptation Warwick threw in his way, and had not, to gratify himself, plunged another dagger in the heart of his father—even this consolatory testimony of his conscience was embittered by the enquiry that conscience immediately made, whether he had not acted wrong in not discovering the design of Warwick, and had not sacrificed his real duty to a mistaken point of honour. As he approached London, the agitation of his mind became greater. As his mother believed him dead, his sudden appearance might have the most fatal effects—That even if he was put down at a coffee-house, and sent a note to inform her of his arrival, the sight of his hand-writing might equally affect a mother and sisters, who had long lamented him as consigned to a grave on the banks of Hudson's River.

There was one expedient that occurred, which, though extremely disagreeable to him, he at length determined to adopt—which was, to go on his reaching London to Mr. Woodford's, and consult with him on the properest way of discovering to his family his unexpected arrival.

Though he was aware that he should have only insulting pity or coarse raillery to sustain from his uncle, he thought the dread of such transient and inconsequential evils, should yield to the important point of not injuring the health of a parent so beloved; and as soon as the stage in which he travelled reached Westminster Bridge, he got into an hackney coach and ordered it to be driven to the house of Mr. Woodford.

On his reaching this place, and enquiring for him, he was told by a maid that opened the door, that Mr. Woodford's family had been removed some months from that house, and resided in King's Street, St. James's Square, at an house of which the maid gave him the number, and whither he immediately repaired.

It was easily found—two lamps at the door, and the appearance of the house, which had been lately refitted in a style of uncommon elegance, seemed to say to Orlando, that he would find his uncle in increasing affluence.

A very smart powdered footman opened the door, who, upon being asked if Mr. Woodford was at home, answered shortly, No; and surveying the hackney coach with contempt, seemed disposed to close the half-opened door, without attending to any farther enquiries.

But Orlando, putting his head out of the coach, called to the servant, and enquired at what time that evening he could see Mr. Woodford, with whom he had business that admitted of no delay.

"He can't be seen to-night," said the servant; "he is engaged for the evening."

"If you will tell me where then," replied Orlando, "I will go to him, for I must see him immediately."

The man, who seemed afraid of venturing out to the coach door, lest he should soil his shoes, or lose the powder from his hair, still held the door only partly open, and said very sullenly—"You must leave your business, and call again—my master will do no business with any body to night; he expects company to dinner; and I am sure he won't be disturbed."

Orlando now got out of the coach, and said to the servant, that as he was Mr. Woodford's nephew, he was sure he would see him. The man then, though with apparent reluctance, opened the door of a back parlour, and, while he stood at it himself, as if he was afraid Orlando would steal something, called to another footman to go and inform his master that his nephew desired to see him below.

At the same moment loud rapping was heard at the door, and the man, in visible distress, said, "I shall be blamed for letting any body in— here's the company come; I wish, Sir, you'd call any other time—there's my Lord and Sir Richard and Lady Wiggin, and Sir James and Lady Penguin—it's quite impossible, Sir, for my master to see you."

Orlando had not time to answer, before the other footman returned, and said very roughly, that his master desired the person, whoever he was, to walk out—for he must be an impostor, because he acknowledged no nephew.

Orlando, imagining Mr. Woodford supposed him to be his brother, and therefore would not see him, had only to quit the house, and desist from his design of speaking to his uncle that evening; or to convince him that he had yet a nephew living, whom he had at least no reason to disclaim: he resolved on the latter, and putting back with his hand the servants who would have opposed his passage, he went up stairs. The door of the dining-room was yet open, for the visitors had hardly settled themselves, and some were standing near it till Sir Richard and Lady Wiggin had paid their compliments. Orlando, notwithstanding the abusive and insolent efforts of the servants, who had followed him up stairs to stop him, entered the room, and going up to Mr. Woodford, who stared at him as a perfect stranger, made himself immediately known to him. Mr. Woodford expressed more surprise than pleasure.

But he could not help acknowledging his nephew, whom he slightly named to his guests, and coldly asked him to sit down and stay dinner.

Orlando, not much flattered by his reception, answered, that as he had not seen his mother, he must hasten to her, and meant no farther to intrude upon Mr. Woodford, than to consult with him on the properest way of breaking to his mother, news the joy of which might overpower her.

"Oh!" cried Woodford, "if that be all, I fancy, you may venture to take your own way—I never heard that joy killed any body; and I don't imagine you have much good fortune to relate (added he, surveying him) to turn the brains of your family."

Lady Wiggin, a squat figure, most sumptuously dressed, now surveyed Orlando, as he stood talking to his uncle before the fire, and then whispered to a younger woman who sat next her, whom he had not till then observed, but in whom, under the disguise of the most preposterous extremity of the fashion, with a very high head, and cheeks of the last Parisian dye, he discovered his elder cousin, to whom he bowed; while she slightly bowing in return, bit the end of her fan, and screwing herself into an attitude which she seemed to have studied, replied with half shut eyes to the whisper of her titled neighbour.

Woodford seemed glad that Orlando declined dining with him, yet was unwilling to take the trouble of interfering in his first introduction to his mother. Pre-determined not to be discouraged by the unfeeling raillery, or repressed by the coldness of his uncle, he enquired again in a low voice, if he could be allowed to speak to him alone—"I have much to say to you, Sir," said he, "which it is not proper to discourse upon now. You may imagine I am very impatient to see my mother and my sisters—I will not detain you long—only let me for five minutes ask your attention below."

The great man, who was no longer a wine merchant in the Strand soliciting the custom of the great, but their pompous entertainer, who was enabled, by the advantages of a great contract obtained by the favour (and perhaps by yielding to the participation) of one of them, to vie in splendour with his patrons, seemed to be made very restless by this demand—"I'd go down into my study with you, with all my heart," said he, in the same low tone; "but my Lord and Sir James are not come, and my son not being here to receive them, I should be sorry ... but however ... you had better stay and dine perhaps, and then ..." Another loud rap at the door relieved him from this embarrassment; it wanted but a quarter to seven, and my Lord was announced. In the bustle to receive so eminent a personage, with what Woodford thought politeness, but what appeared to Orlando the most cringing servility he had ever witnessed, his worthy uncle seemed totally to have forgotten him; and before the ceremony of this reception, and that of Sir James, who followed the peer as one of his satellites, was over, dinner was announced; and the company proceeded down stairs; while Orlando, finding that his uncle had as little taste for poor relations as if he had been born himself a great man, instead of having suddenly become so, by means which Orlando wondered at, rather than understood, took the opportunity of opening the street door himself, and returned to his hack, which was driven into the square, to make room for the splendid equipages which had since arrived at the door.

He stepped in; but when the coachman asked him whither to drive, he knew not what to reply. He knew nobody: nor did he recollect one friend in this immense town, to whom he could in such an exigence apply.—The small house his mother had taken, was in Howland-Street; and he thought he had better drive to some coffee-house in the neighbourhood, where he might consider how he could first speak to Selina. As he proceeded to a coffee-house in Oxford Street, which the coachman named to him upon his enquiring for one, he could not help reflecting on the strange vicissitudes of fortune, and the strange way in which her gifts are divided. It was only a few months since he had an almost undoubted prospect of succeeding to the great estates of Mrs. Rayland; he was now not only deprived of all those hopes, but was literally a beggar—and going home, not to assist his ruined family, but to add to it another indigent member, and to weep with them all the mournful changes that had happened during his absence.

He had not yet determined how he should introduce himself to the dear dejected group, when he arrived at the coffee-house, where he discharged his coach, and called for a private room. He then, since no better expedient occurred to him, desired a pen, ink, and paper, and in an hand which he attempted to disguise (and he trembled so as to aid the deception) he wrote these few words to Selina—"Your brother Orlando is living, and in England—have the presence of mind not to betray this secret, which will I think give you great pleasure, to your mother too suddenly; and when he knows he can come without too much surprising your mother, he will be at your door."—He had hardly finished and directed this note, in which he tried to alter his hand only that the sight of it might not so suddenly strike his sister as to render his precaution useless, he recollected, that as Perseus the negro was now his mother's servant, he had better go himself to the door of the house; discover himself to that faithful fellow; and contrive by his means to speak to Selina first.

This scheme appeared to him so much better than the first, that he determined to put it into immediate execution. However, he put the note he had written into his pocket, that if Perseus happened not to be at home, he might still proceed as he had at first intended.

With a beating heart he approached the door, and hesitated with apprehension before he could determine to knock at it. At length he gave a loud single rap, and Perseus appeared.—"Do you know me, Perseus?" said Orlando, in a low voice. "Know you," answered the negro, who spoke pretty good English, and without much of the negro accent—"No! how should I know you?" "Have you forgot," said Orlando, "the morning we passed together in the wood, on the banks of Hudson's River?" While he thus spoke, Perseus held the candle, which he had set down in the passage, to his face, and with a sudden exclamation letting it fall, he ran as fast as he could back into the kitchen, declaring to the two maids, as trembling he threw himself into a chair, that he had seen a ghost.

The elder of these women, a stout peasant from the weald of Sussex, who had no notion of ghosts, huffed the affrighted negro for his folly, and said, "I wonder what you mean, Perseus—why sure you are not in your right wits? A ghost quotha! I hope you have not left the door open, with your ghosts."

"I cannot tell," cried Perseus—"but you better see—I see master Orlando's ghost, and I'll go no more."

Orlando, foreseeing that from the poor fellow's terror, all the risk would be incurred which he had wished to avoid, now walked into the house, in the hope of preventing his mother and sisters from being alarmed by the folly of the servants; and when Hannah ascended to secure the door, which she had been strictly enjoined never to leave of an evening without a chain, she met Orlando on the top of the stairs. Struck with equal terror, though from a different cause, she now screamed and returned to the kitchen, where, as well as her fright would let her, she declaimed against the folly of Perseus, who being afraid of a ghost, had let in a man.

Orlando, provoked by the ridiculous fears of both, now went into the kitchen; and not without difficulty convinced the negro that he was alive; and the maid, that he had no intention to rob the house: but all the clamour that these mistakes had excited, could not be unheard in the room where Mrs. Somerive was sitting with her daughters; and the bell had rung violently several times, before the assurance of Orlando's identity had restored to Perseus courage enough to obey the summons.

Orlando entreated of him to go up, to account for the noise below as well as he could, and to beckon, or by some other means contrive to get his sister Selina out of the room. Perseus, trembling with his former apprehensions and his present joy, undertook to do this, and hastened up stairs. At the door of the dining-room Selina stood, and asked him if any thing was the matter below; and Mrs. Somerive eagerly repeated the question, saying—"Perseus, is any thing wrong below? who was at the door?"—He advanced to the table near which his mistress was sitting, and saying to Selina in an half whisper as he passed her—"'Tis your brother, miss, you go see him," he answered to the questions Mrs. Somerive asked him—"No, Ma'am—no bad matter—only that I thought, that I ... that Hannah ... she say—"His confusion was the more evident, the more he attempted to conceal it; nor did his dark skin conceal the emotion of his spirits; while Selina, who believed it was her elder brother, and who felt only terror at his name, approached the table paler than death; and Mrs. Somerive, convinced that something was the matter below, though she could not conjecture what, arose from her seat, and taking a candle said, "What can have happened? Selina, my child—if you know it, for God's sake tell me!—Alas!" added she recollecting all that had happened to her within so short a space—"after all I have suffered, what can I have to fear?"

She now approached the door, while neither Selina nor the servant had courage to stop her.—But in the passage she was met by Hannah, whom Orlando, mistrusting the skill of his first messenger, had sent up while he waited himself at the foot of the stairs. Mrs. Somerive, more convinced from the appearance of the maid, that some alarming circumstance had happened, was struck with the idea of fire, and calling to her two daughters to follow her, said, "The lower part of the house is on fire—let us, if it is so, make our escape.—Selina! Emma! my children! let me at least have something."[1]

"Dear ma'am," exclaimed Hannah, "how you do fright yourself!— Lord! there's no fire below, I assure you: I'm sure if there was, we should not stand staring here; but don't be frighted, pray, ma'am! nothing at all

---

[1]   Mrs. Somerive's overwrought response and immediate thoughts of disaster show her to be as unstable in the face of adversity as the rest of her family—and a signal contrast to Smith herself.

is the matter, but very good news—Come, ma'am; pray go back into the room and sit down, and make yourself easy; you can't imagine, I'm sure, as that I would go for to deceive you."

Mrs. Somerive, hardly knowing what to believe, returned into the room; and Hannah following her, said—"Now, ma'am, as you be so calm I'll tell you, it is the young captain, ma'am, your son—he is not dead, thank God."

"Not dead!" cried Mrs. Somerive, "my Orlando alive! Oh! it is impossible; don't be so inhuman as to awaken such hopes, only to aggravate my misery. He is dead, and I shall never see him more!" "No, no," said Perseus, "young captain's alive." "He is indeed, ma'am," cried Hannah. "Where?" said Selina, "where is my brother?" "He is below, miss," said she, in a low voice.—Selina rushed out of the room, and Orlando caught her in his arms. Emma, divided between her fears for her mother, who rested almost insensible on the arm of the servant, and the anxious desire to see her brother, trembled and wept a moment; and then seeing him actually enter, Selina resting on his arm, she uttered a faint shriek, and flew back towards her mother, at whose feet Orlando kneeling, besought her to recollect and compose herself. She threw her arms round him, but convulsive sobs were the only signs she gave of recollection; while the servant was bathing her temples, and her two daughters entreating her, for their sakes, to assume a composure, which their own extreme agitation proved they did not themselves possess.

The scene was too painful, though produced by excess of happiness, to last long. The certainty that her son, her beloved Orlando, was living, was joy to which the mind of Mrs. Somerive, long weighed down by affliction, could not sustain without feeling what almost approached to a momentary deprivation of reason; but the manly tenderness of Orlando, who argued with her, and the lively sensibility of her two girls, who hung around her, and entreated her not to destroy herself, now that they were so blest as to have their brother restored to them, at length called her to a greater serenity of mind; yet as she looked at Orlando, she started, she trembled, she seemed to doubt whether she was awake; and when she spoke to him of his father, she relapsed into such inarticulate expressions of agonizing sorrow, that her children, looking in consternation at each other, dreaded the consequence, so much had she in those moments the appearance of a person about to lose her reason.

There was another topic which had not during the first hour of their incoherent conference been touched; and Orlando, who dreaded it, endeavoured to avoid it. This was the loss of his sister Isabella; for that she had perished at sea, in their ill-starred voyage to America, he now more than ever believed. He tried therefore to call off the attention of his mother from what she had lost; and to convince her, that not merely her son was restored to her, but restored to her as affectionate, and as much attached to his family, as when in an evil hour he quitted it.

Mrs. Somerive, feeling herself unequal to some kind of conversation that evening, confined herself, when she was able to do more than gaze at her son, to questions that related wholly to himself. She observed how very much he was altered—that his hair, of which in his infancy and youth she had been so vain, was grown much darker, and had been cut close to his head. Orlando, to escape from subjects which he thought would be from their catastrophes more painful to her, gave her, or rather attempted to give her, a short history of his adventures, from his leaving New-York till his return to England; but when he came to speak of the wounds he had received, and of his being carried up the country by the Iroquois, she became so extremely faint, that Selina advised her, and she consented to desist from any farther enquiries, till she was better able to bear the relation of Orlando's sufferings. At the request of her children she consented to go early to rest, where Emma was to remain with her till she became more calm; and when Selina had seen her in bed, and left her in much quieter spirits, she returned to Orlando, who was in an agony of impatience to enquire about Monimia, which in his mother's presence he had not dared to alleviate or betray.

When his sister returned to him, they both sat down by the fire; and the soft-tempered Selina yielded to those emotions, which during her mother's alarming situation she had struggled to suppress. Orlando, his eyes overflowing, tenderly kissed her hand, and said—"Are these tears, my own Selina, given to past sorrows? or are they excited by your knowledge of tidings yet to come, that will wound the heart of your brother worse than any of the accumulated miseries which he has told you he has collected since his landing in England?—Monimia! what is her fate, Selina? Where is she? am I completely miserable?" ... He could not go on, nor could his sister immediately answer him—"You do not speak, Selina," cried he eagerly ... "I can hear nothing worse than my fears suggest, nor can any torment equal this horrid suspense."

"Indeed," answered Selina, in a tremulous voice—"indeed I know no reason to believe that you ought to be in despair about her, but"—"But!" exclaimed he—"but what?—You believe—you don't know? Have you not *seen* her then, Selina? Is it possible you can have been so cruel to her, and to me, as to have abandoned her, because she was abandoned by all the rest of the world, because you thought me dead...? Oh, Selina! should you not therefore have cherished, with redoubled tenderness, her who was so very dear to me?"

"Have patience with me, my dear brother," replied Selina—"pray, have patience with me; and do not, do not condemn me unheard, nor suppose that I would willingly neglect or forsake her whom you loved, and whom I loved too ... But ..."

"You have however forsaken her! you do not know where she is now?"

"No indeed, I do not," answered Selina—"nor have I heard of her for many months."

"Well," cried Orlando, with a deep sigh, "I have patience, you see, Selina—I do not beat my breast, nor dash myself against the wall. I am wretched, my sister; but I will believe you could do nothing in performance of your solemn promise, nothing to avert such extreme wretchedness, and I will not reproach you."

"You will have no cause," replied the weeping Selina; "indeed, Orlando, you will have none, when you have heard all I have to say—Oh! if you did but know all we have suffered!"

"Poor Monimia!" sighed Orlando, "she too has suffered, and in this general wreck I have lost her—You do not even know then," continued he, "you do not even know if she yet lives? I would rather hear of her death, than of her being exposed to all the dangers I dread for her, perhaps to disgrace, to shame, to infamy ..." This idea was too horrible; he started from his chair, wildly traversed the room; and it was some time before Selina could persuade him to listen quietly to the relation he yet continued to demand of her.

CHAP. V.

"When you left us, my brother," said Selina, "we hardly thought it possible that any sorrow could exceed what your departure and the apparent estrangement of Philip inflicted on us all; yet in a very few days we learned that, heavy as these evils were, they were only the beginning of that long train of calamity which was about to overtake us. Isabella disappeared within two days, and left a letter to say that she was gone with Captain Warwick to America."

"And pray tell me," said Orlando, interrupting her, "was my poor father extremely hurt at her elopement?"

"Not so much at her elopement, as at her having deceived him; for I do not believe, Orlando, that my father ever thought of Isabella's marrying General Tracy without pain and doubts of her future happiness. But it grieved him severely to reflect that Isabella was capable of deception, which, notwithstanding the rashness of her going away with a man she hardly knew, must have been meditated for some days."

"Did my father believe me to have been a party in this deception?"

"Of that he sometimes doubted: yet, after dwelling on those doubts a moment, he would say, "No—Orlando could never be acquainted with the plan of these two young people;—Orlando would not have concealed their intentions from me—Orlando never in his life deceived me—He is all integrity and candour—"

"And in this persuasion my father died?"

"Yes; and never spoke of you, Orlando, but as the hope and reliance of us all."

Orlando sighed deeply, reflecting that he had not deserved in this single instance the confidence of his father; yet he rejoiced that, believing him ignorant of his sister's flight, this opinion of his integrity had not been impaired where it could have done no good to have known the truth, and would only have inflicted another wound on his father's heart. Selina proceeded.

"We received your letter from Portsmouth, and some days afterwards another from Isabella—I believe it was near a fortnight afterwards—She was about to embark for America with her husband, who had hired a small vessel for that purpose, having missed his passage.—This, in some degree, quieted the apprehensions of my father about my sister; though, as General Tracy almost immediately disinherited his nephew, we had the mortification of knowing that Isabella had married in what is called a very indiscreet way.—However, as nothing could be objected to Captain Warwick, but his conduct towards his uncle, and his consequent want of fortune; and as the young people seemed to be passionately attached to each other, my father seemed gradually to lose his anger, and to recover his spirits; when a new instance of Philip's cruel disregard for us all threw him into an illness of so dangerous a nature, or rather so hastened the progress of that which uneasiness about him had first brought on, that he was soon given up by the physicians. It was then that, believing himself dying, and feeling more concern for the state in which he was about to leave us than for his own dissolution, he sent to Mrs. Rayland to come to him—a step which, he said, was very hazardous, but which he could not satisfy himself without taking. She came; we were none of us present at the conversation—but my father told us, as soon as she was gone, that his mind was now quite easy, and that he should die content, at least as far as related to pecuniary affairs; for Mrs. Rayland had assured him, that in her last will she had given you the Rayland estate, and entailed it all upon your posterity, on condition of your taking the name and bearing the arms of Rayland only; that she had set apart a sum for the purchase of a baronet's title; and that was the only money, except legacies to her servants to the amount of eight thousand pounds in the whole, which she had appropriated—having given you all the rest of her real and personal estate; and my father said that the latter had accumulated much more than he was aware of.

"I am sure, said he, when he had told us this—I am sure that Orlando will use, as he ought to do, the power that is thus put into his hands to secure the provision for you, my love (speaking to my mother), and for our dear girls—Nay, that, if our poor unhappy Philip should, as my fears prognosticate, utterly dissipate his paternal fortune, that he too will find a resource in the fraternal affection of his younger brother. In this persuasion my father became much easier, and, we hoped, grew much better: but a discovery that he very unluckily made by opening a letter intended for my brother, which, from the names being alike, he thought was his own—a discovery that Philip was actually in treaty with Stockton for the sale of his future interest in the estate at West Wolverton, quite undid the good effects of Mrs. Rayland's generosity, and in less than a fortnight we lost our dear father—who, alas! Orlando, died of a broken heart!

"I will not distress you with a description of the terrible scene—I mean that of his last hours; for, though he died calmly, recommending us to your protection and to that of Heaven, the distraction of my mother is not to be described; and I never think of it but my heart sinks within me.—When the first shock was a little over, my mother reflected on the necessity of her living for us, unprotected and helpless as we were, and she became more tranquil; though I am sorry to say that the presence of my brother Philip, who came down as soon as he heard of my father's death, did not serve to assist her in the recovery of her spirits.—On the contrary, his evident wish that we might soon remove from the house, and his bringing down a mistress, whom he seemed impatient to put into it, were far from being cordials to a mind so oppressed with her recent loss.—The only hope that sustained her was your return and succeeding to the Rayland estate: but even this comfortable hope was diminished and embittered by a thousand fears:—days, and weeks, and months, were passed, and we had not heard of your arrival at New-York; but learned that the fleet of transports, with which you sailed, was dispersed by a storm, and some of the vessels lost. This I heard, for ill news is always communicated early; but I kept it from my mother till Mrs. Rayland's impatience, who sent continually for news of you, and at length expressed her fears for you, in consequence of the accounts she saw in the newspapers, discovered it; and added to all the sufferings of my poor mother, doubts of your safety, which were more dreadful than any.—

"Mrs. Rayland, who had always disliked my mother, and, as I thought, us till now, seemed much more disposed than she used to be to shew us all kindness, and really seemed concerned for my father's death. She made us all a present for mourning; and used to invite us often to the Hall, and I believe would have taken us to live there if Mrs. Lennard would have let her. But that good for nothing old woman, who had her own purposes to answer by it, would never leave any of us a moment alone with Mrs. Rayland—who often seemed to have an inclination to speak to my mother, and to be checked in what she intended to say by the presence of Lennard, who, in proportion as the old lady became more feeble through age, and as her mind became weaker, seemed to acquire over her more power: though it often appeared to me that Mrs. Rayland submitted to it rather from habit than from choice, and had not resolution to throw off a yoke she had been accustomed to so many years—"

"But, my Selina," cried Orlando, "you have not all this while said a word of Monimia."

"We contrived to meet," replied Selina, "every Monday, according to your injunction; except when my poor father lay so dangerously ill, and after his death. And though these short interviews were passed almost always in tears on both sides, they were the only pleasure we either of us tasted; and we have often said, that the consolation of the rest of the week was, that Monday would return at the beginning of the next!

"I missed meeting Monimia for three weeks, for the melancholy reason I have assigned; and on the fourth I hastened, at the usual hour, to the place of our appointment, the bench near the boat-house, where I saw Monimia waiting for me. If my mourning and dejected looks struck her with concern, I was not less shocked to see her look so very pale, thin, and dejected—We could neither of us speak for some time, for our tears choked us, till at length she recovered voice enough to say, with deep sobs that seemed almost to burst her heart, that she should never see me more; that even this little comfort of meeting by stealth was denied her; for that her aunt had determined to send her away, and to put her apprentice to a person who kept an haberdasher's and milliner's shop at Winchester, who had agreed to take her for a small premium, and that she was to go in two days.

"Amazed and distressed by this intelligence, I enquired why her aunt would do this? and she told me, that the importunity of Sir John Belgrave, and his perpetual attempts to see her by the same means by which you had formerly found access to her room, compelled her, in order to avoid him, to tell her aunt of the door in the turret; and after enduring a great deal of very cruel usage, and having been repeatedly threatened with Mrs. Rayland's displeasure and with being turned out of the house, her aunt first removed her into her room; and then, finding that inconvenient, had the door in the lower room at the bottom of the stairs bricked up, and Monimia returned to her former apartment— from whence she was hardly ever suffered to stir out but for a walk in the park, and even then was ordered not to go out of sight of the house. So that it had always been at a great risk that, while we did meet, she used to run as far as the fir-wood on those mornings.—"My aunt," said poor Monimia as she told me all this, "my aunt was always very cruel to me; but now she was much more so than ever; for the strange and ridiculous fancy she had taken to Roker, who now lived almost always in the house, though Mrs. Rayland did not know it, made her jealous of every body, but particularly of me, who detested the man so much that I was quite as desirous to avoid him, as she was that I should not meet him— while the odious fellow affected to be jealous of her attachment to me, though all the time he took every opportunity of speaking to me very impertinently; but between my aunt's watchfulness that I should never be in the room with him, and my own to shun him, I escaped tolerably well from his insolent speeches, and never regretted my confinement, unless when I feared, my dear Selina, it would prevent my seeing you.— Now, however, for some reason or other, my aunt has taken it into her head that I shall not stay at the Hall any longer.—I cannot guess why I am more obnoxious to her than formerly, as she seems to have settled to marry and secure her dear Mr. Roker to herself, unless it is because Mrs. Rayland seems lately to grow more fond of me; and as my aunt is engaged with her lover more than with her mistress, I have been more about her, and she seems always satisfied with my services—which makes Mrs. Lennard quite in a rage with me sometimes; and often of late she tells me I am a sly, deceitful girl, and she'll blow me up with her lady— such is her expression, if I dare to fancy that I have any interest with her.

This she has repeated so often lately, that knowing as I do that the discovery she has made of my meeting Orlando would entirely ruin him with Mrs. Rayland, I think that, however dreadful it is, Selina, for me to leave this place, where only I can have an opportunity of weeping with you and talking of him, I had much better do so than hazard, by my stay, incurring my aunt's unreasonable displeasure, since it may so much hurt Orlando;—and as she told me again, about ten days since, that she was determined to send me off to Winchester, and had given her lady such good reasons for it that she advised it, and had promised to give me the apprentice fee, I answered, that I had rather go than be burthensome to her.—So she wrote immediately, and the answer came yesterday, which fixes my departure next Thursday." Thus, my dear brother, our dear injured Monimia related to me the circumstances which had produced this resolution, so distressing to me. Some of them indeed, particularly what related to that hateful Sir John Belgrave, I had heard before; for he used not only to persecute poor Monimia with attempts to speak to her by means of a servant—Jacob I think she called him—who was unluckily let into the secret, but wrote to her continually letters which, from the high promises they contained, might have tempted many young women so uncomfortably situated as she was"—"Eternal curses light on him!" exclaimed Orlando; "he shall feel, the scoundrel shall feel, that she is not now so unprotected as to suffer him to make his insulting proposals with impunity."

Alarmed by his vehemence, Selina repented that she had said so much; yet, by way of palliation, added—"The last letter Monimia shewed me ..."

"Why did she open—why receive his d——d letters?" cried Orlando.

"They were forced upon her," answered his sister, "in a thousand ways, which I hope she will one day have an opportunity of telling you herself, though it would take up too much time were I to do it now.—However, I am sure that when she related to me how she was beset with them, I saw no cause at all to blame her; and as for the last letter, of which I was going to speak, it was sent in form under cover of one to her aunt, and contained a proposal of marriage."

"Of marriage!"

"Yes, indeed, and even offered settlements—and begged pardon for his former ill behaviour: it was after Monimia was obliged to complain to Mrs. Lennard of his behaviour, and was removed to her room. And one great cause of her aunt's displeasure afterwards was, that Monimia positively refused to marry Sir John, which her aunt insisted that, if he was in earnest, she should do. Monimia, however, wrote to him a refusal, in the most positive terms we could invent together; and after that she heard no more of him till she left the Hall."

"Well," said Orlando; "but for Heaven's sake tell me! has she heard of him then since she left the Hall?—and where is she now?"

"Would to God, my dearest brother," replied Selina, "that I could tell you!—We settled to correspond, not without some difficulty, because, though my mother herself, if I had dared to tell her the truth, would not I am sure have refused to let me write to and hear from her, yet as I did not dare, and she knows I have no correspondents but my sister Philippa, who now and then writes me from Ireland, it is very natural for her to ask what letter I receive. However, I contrived it, and did for you, Orlando, what worlds should not bribe me to do for myself; I mean, deceive my mother, or rather act without her knowledge; yet I hope it was innocent."

"Not only innocent, but meritorious," said Orlando warmly; "but you still do not answer me, Selina, where is Monimia now?"

"Alas! Orlando, have I not already undergone the pain of telling you that I do not know?"

"Not know!"

"Indeed, I do not.—Amidst all the wretched scenes I passed through upon Mrs. Rayland's death—our very cruel disappointment in reading a will, so unlike what we were taught to expect—and Philip's horrible conduct, which drove us from the country, and from our father's house, now sold, with every thing almost in it, to Mr. Stockton:—amidst all the exertions I was compelled to make to support my poor mother, who seemed to be sinking under our complicated misfortunes; misfortunes rendered almost insupportable, by the dreadful increase of our fears for your life:—believe me, Orlando, amidst all this, I never forgot to write punctually, according to our agreement, to our beloved Monimia; and for some time she punctually answered my letters:—but for these last five weeks never having any letter from her, I grew very uneasy, and last week wrote to the person with whom her aunt had placed her, and a few days since I had an answer."

"What answer?" enquired Orlando, with breathless eagerness.

"None from the person herself to whom my sweet friend was bound, but from a relation of hers, who informed me that Mrs. Newill had, in consequence of some embarrassment in her affairs, left Winchester, and was gone to London, with her apprentice, where she was under the necessity of remaining concealed till her affairs were settled; and then proposed going into business in London, if she could find friends to set her up."

"Distraction and death!" cried Orlando, striking his hands together, and starting from his chair, "I shall be driven to phrensy!—And is it to a person thus situated that my poor Monimia is entrusted? and, under the pretence of becoming an apprentice, is she given up to a mean servitude? or perhaps sold to that detestable Belgrave, by her necessitous mistress? But I will pursue him to the end of the world.—Good God!" added he, walking quickly about the room, "if something very dreadful had not happened to her, she would have written to you—surely, Selina, she would have written, wherever situated."

"Perhaps," replied Selina, still more apprehensive of the effects of that despair he seemed to feel at this account—"perhaps her not having written may have been owing to her having never received that letter of mine, which contained a direction whither to write to me."

"What direction?" asked Orlando.

"To this house," replied his sister, "where we have only been about a month; having got it cheap of a gentleman who was obliged to go abroad, and was glad to let it on reasonable terms, for the few remaining months of his lease. We were before in lodgings in Holles-Street, and I knew nothing of our removal hither till a few days before it happened. The moment I did, I wrote to Monimia; but that letter was among those she never received."

This conversation, in which the impatient anguish of Orlando only found increase, was now interrupted by the entrance of his youngest sister, who came down to tell him and Selina that Mrs. Somerive, hearing them talk below, and supposing the melancholy account Selina had to give Orlando might affect him too much, entreated him to put off any farther conversation till the next day, but for the present to take some refreshment and go to bed.

Orlando, vexed that the agitation of his mind had betrayed him into vehemence which had alarmed and distressed his mother, promised to obey; and endeavouring to stifle his torments, he consented to sit down to supper, and requested that he might see his mother, and endeavour to calm the inquietude she expressed for his health. She desired he would come up to her; but when he approached the bed, he could not speak to her—he could only take the hand she gave him, and bathe it with tears, in spite of his endeavours to check them, as he pressed it to his lips. In a broken voice, however, he at length collected resolution to assure her, in answer to her tender enquiries, that it was true he had been much affected by the detail his sister had at his own request given him, yet that he was now recovered, and after a night's rest should regain fortitude enough to consider his own situation, and what it was best to do, without shrinking from any task, by executing which he would contribute to her comfort. His mother blessed him—and, expressing the utmost solicitude about his health, said—"Make yourself, dear Orlando, easy about me; for, after so great, so unexpected, and I fear so undeserved a blessing as having you restored to me, and to your dear sisters, I should be unthankful and unworthy of such happiness if I dared to murmur."

As the repose of Mrs. Somerive would not, Orlando thought, be much promoted by the continuance of this affecting conversation, he shortened it as much as he could, and, in pursuance of his promise, went, in hopes of transient forgetfulness, to his bed.

CHAP. VI.

If Orlando had known Monimia was in safety—if he had known where, after this cruel absence, he might find her, and assure her of the sentiments of an heart more fondly than ever devoted to her, all the cruel circumstances that had happened in his absence would have been supportable; but when, in addition to the death of his father, and the dispersion of his family, his loss of the Rayland estate, and the ruin of his brother (for, being now utterly undone, and unable to carry on the law-suits he had begun, he had for some time disappeared, and no one knew what was become of him)—when to all these distracting certainties was added his fear of finding Monimia, or finding her innocent, lovely, and devoted to him, as he had left her; he was no longer able to check the violence of his apprehension; nor could he, for some hours after awaking from his short and disturbed sleep, collect his thoughts enough to form any plan for his future conduct.

Two things, however, were immediately necessary: one was, to find some method of tracing his lost Monimia; and the other, to find the means of subsisting, not only without being a burthen to his mother, whose income was so very small, but to endeavour if possible to make hers and his sister's situation more comfortable. This he knew the slender pay of an ensign would not enable him to do; and, while he knew that nothing could be more dreadful to his mother than the idea of his going abroad again, he felt that few means of passing his time would to him be so disagreeable as that of remaining unoccupied, and disarmed as he was by his parole, while he yet called and considered himself a soldier.

He at length determined to enquire how far, as his commission was given to him, he could dispose of it; and if that could be done, to put the money it would produce into some business. But even this arrangement was secondary to his ardent desire to gain some intelligence of Monimia. He wrote as soon as he arose in the morning to the relation of the person with whom she lived at Winchester, entreating a direction to that person, and assuring her to whom he wrote, that his enquiry was not meant to do any injury, but rather might produce some advantage to the person under inconvenient circumstances. He then, after some deliberation, determined to write to Mrs. Lennard, or, as she was now called, Mrs. Roker;—and, as he now had no longer any thing to fear from the resentment of his benefactress, he openly avowed to Mrs. Roker the purpose of his enquiry; informing her that, if her niece was unmarried, and still retained for him her former affection, he intended to offer her his hand.

Having thus taken all the means which his anxiety immediately suggested, he joined his mother and sisters at breakfast with some degree of apparent composure, and gave them, as he found his mother now better able to bear it, a sketch of his adventures upon the road; at which they were so much affected, that he soon found it necessary to drop the conversation; and saying he should walk out till dinner, he took his way to a coffee-house much frequented by military men, near St. James's, where he hoped to hear something of Warwick, as well as to learn whether the General (whom he dared not mention to his mother lest it should occasion enquiries about Isabella which he could not answer) had consoled himself with some other young woman for his cruel mortification in regard to Isabella, and revenged himself by disinheriting his nephew for the loss of his intended bride.

He met several of his old acquaintance; one of whom very willingly gave him all the information he wanted about his commission; but told him that he could not, he thought, dispose of it without applying to General Tracy, from whose hands he had received it. This Orlando determined to do; and as he was impatient to be at some certainty, he went immediately to his house in Grosvenor-Place.

It happened that the General, who was now almost always a martyr to the gout, had given orders to be denied to every body who might chance to call, except two persons whom he named, and for one of whom the man who opened the door, and who had only lately come into the house, mistook Orlando, who was therefore ushered up stairs, where, in a magnificent room, the General sat in a great chair, supported by pillows, and his limbs wrapped in flannel. Orlando was much altered, and the General was near-sighted; so that he was obliged to approach, and announce himself. Forgetting for a moment his disabled limbs, Tracy almost started out of his chair; but then recollecting probably that a man of fashion should never suffer himself to appear discomposed at any thing, he recovered himself, and coldly desired Orlando to sit down.

Orlando, affected by seeing a man whom he had last seen as a guest of his father, gave, in a mild and low voice, into a little history of his adventures; the parole he had given, which precluded him from serving during the present war; and his wish therefore to transfer his commission to some one who might not be under the same disadvantages.

General Tracy heard him with repulsive indifference, and then said—"Well, Sir, the commission is yours, and you are perfectly at liberty to keep or to dispose of it.—I am very far from meaning to trouble you with my advice; but as your expectations of Mrs. Rayland's fortune are all disappointed, I should have supposed a profession might have been found useful to you. However, Sir, you are the best judge. The commission is yours—I am sorry I am too much indisposed to have the pleasure of your company longer, and I wish you a good day." He then rang, and his valet appearing, he bade him open the door.

Orlando, thus dismissed, retired in anger, which he had no means of venting; and went back to the coffee-house, where his friend waited for him, to whom he forbore, however, to speak of Tracy's behaviour; because he could not but feel that if he believed him, as he probably did, concerned in the elopement of Isabella with Warwick, he had some grounds for his resentment—a resentment which, when Orlando reflected on his humiliation, and his being now tormented by bodily infirmities, he was too generous not to forgive. His friend, a lieutenant in the 51st, now went with him to the office of an agent, to treat about his commission; and, as they went, related to him, that it was believed at the War-office, Warwick had perished at sea, as there never was an instance of a man's missing for so many months; and that, had he been taken prisoner by an American or French privateer, and carried to some of their places of rendezvous, he would before now have written home, or he would have been exchanged. This appeared to be but too probable; but still Orlando, in recollecting how he had been situated himself, entertained a faint hope that they might yet hear of his friend and his sister, though the dangers and difficulties to which the latter might have been exposed made him tremble. Having put his business in the proper train, he returned home, meditating, as he went, on all the strange and disagreeable occurrences that had happened since he used to traverse these streets with Warwick, who had lodgings in Bond-Street.—All the scenes he had passed through arose in lively succession in his mind, and that for the first time since his landing in England; for the shocks he received on his arrival at Rayland Hall, and by hearing of the death of his father, had for a while absorbed all other recollections.—He now considered that, when his commission was disposed of, his whole fortune would be only between three and four hundred pounds; yet, with the sanguine spirit of a young man, which his former severe disappoint-ments had not checked, he believed that, with a sum so moderate, he could, by dint of perseverance and industry, find some reputable employ-ment, by which he might not only be enabled to assist his mother, but to keep a wife—as he was resolved, the moment he could find Monimia, to marry her; and in this only he thought he might be forgiven for not consulting his mother—to his duty and affection towards whom he never meant that any other attachment should be injurious.

He had not yet had time to talk to Selina, of the law-suit which he heard Philip had instituted for the recovery of the Rayland estate; but he had in the evening an opportunity of talking about it to Selina, and heard that it now languished, partly for want of money, and partly through Philip's neglect, who had of late again disappeared, and there-fore nothing was likely to be made of the suit.

Orlando enquired against whom, and on what grounds it was begun?—and learned, though Selina did not very clearly understand the terms, that it was against the reverend body who claimed the estate, one of whom (Doctor Hollybourn) had administered as executor; because the will nominated to that office the dean of the diocese for the time being, to which the doctor had succeeded a few days only before Mrs. Rayland's death; and that there was not only a suit at common law, but in chancery.[1]

As there was great reason to believe that there was another will entirely in his favour, which had been either secreted or destroyed, Orlando deter-mined to attempt discovering this, and got a recommendation from his friend the lieutenant (for he was too much disgusted by the reception he met with from Mr. Woodford to trouble him again) to a young attorney,

---

[1] Before the Judicature Act of 1873, which created the High Court of Justice, the court of Chancery consisted of the ordinary court of common law, and the extraordinary court of equity. The court of equity moderated the common law and acted as an appeals court. The lawsuit over the will thus challenges both its legality (i.e. its legitimacy) and its moral-ity (i.e. that it is wrong to will property away from the heir-at-law).

before whom he laid the affair, and who gave him great encouragement to pursue it.

But the occupation in which this engaged him, or in which he was engaged by the sale of his commission, that was now within a few days of being completed, could not for a moment detach his mind from those fears which continually haunted him for Monimia.—He waited with anxiety for the answer he expected from Winchester, which he had hoped to have, as he had very earnestly pressed for it, by the return of the post; but that, and another, and another post arrived without any letter; and he wrote again, waited again three days, and was again disappointed of an answer.—He now determined to go down himself, and find out the woman from whom Selina had received the information of Monimia's removal; but, the day on which he had hired an horse, and was on the point of setting out for that place, he was visited by a man of between fifty and sixty, who sent in his name, in great form, as Mr. Roker.

If a painter had occasion to put upon his canvas a figure that should give an horrible idea of the worst, meanest, and most obnoxious passions—and to represent the most detestable character in Pandaemonium, where, on the brow, villany sits enjoying the misery it occasions—where every rascal vice, concealed by cowardice and cunning, are mingled with arrogance, malice, and cruelty—where a nose, the rival of Bardolph's, depends over a mouth "grinning horribly a ghastly smile,"—and scornful eyes, askance, seemed to be watching, with inverted looks, the birth of chicanery in the brain—this fiend-like wretch would have been a fine study. His shambling figure appeared to have been repaired with straw and rags, since it had suffered depredations on a well-earned gibbet—A figure more adapted to the purpose of scaring crows, was never exhibited in former days as Guy Vaux, the Pope, or the Pretender.[1]

Orlando was somewhat surprised to behold this strange being, who, strutting up close to him, put his nose almost in his face, and then, in a sonorous voice, said—

"Your name, Sir, is Somerive?"

---

[1] The quotation is from *Paradise Lost*, ii. 846, slightly misquoted: "grinn'd horrible a ghastly smile." Mr. Roker serves as an instance of the "natural Gothic": that is, although in terms of plot a real person, his physique and his manner of speech are as monstrous as any demon's. He is an embodiment of Smith's intense distrust of lawyers. This dense paragraph also alludes to Hell as described by Milton ("Pandemonium"), Shakespeare ("Bardolph," a ne'er-do-well companion of Falstaff's in *Henry IV Parts 1 and 2* and *The Merry Wives of Windsor*), and the more mundane scarecrow effigy (here, Guy Fawkes; the Pope, a symbol of Catholicism and hence corruption; and the Pretender to the English throne, James I).

"I suppose you know it is," replied Orlando, "since you come to seek me by it."

"You wrote, Sir, to my nephew's wife, Mrs. Rachel Roker—"

"Well, Sir, and I expected Mrs. Rachel Roker would have answered my letter."

"No, Sir—*We* make it a rule never to put our hands to any thing—We desire to know, Sir, your reasons for writing—I call, Sir, in behalf of Mrs. Rachel Roker—You ask after a young woman, Sir, whom she kept out of charity—Now, Sir, though we never do give answers to matters so irrelevant, my client, that is my niece, Mrs. Rachel Roker, does hereby inform you, that she the said Rachel—"

Orlando, anxious as he was, and trembling in the expectation of hearing something of Monimia, could not check his indignation and impatience—"Your niece! your client!—What is all this to me?" said he.

"Sir," cried the fiend, "have patience if you please—I go on in this matter according to the due course, and such as I always observe in all my business, whether it relates to Sir John Winnerton Weezle, Baronet, my very worthy client, or any other. Now, Sir—Nay, Sir—(seeing Orlando about to speak)—nay, Sir, hear me! and when I have done, Sir, you shall speak in turn—"

"You will be pleased then," said Orlando, "to be brief, as patience is not my forte."

He felt much disposed to prove this assertion by turning the fellow down stairs; but, recollecting that he might thus lose all trace of Monimia, which her aunt might otherwise afford him, he checked himself: and the man proceeded in an harangue of some length, tending to give an high opinion of his abilities, and of his skill in conducting causes; laying much stress on the confidence with which he was treated by Sir John Winnerton Weezle, Baronet, and his brother Thomas Weezle, Esquire, who seemed to have taken, from their rank, great hold on his imagination: and he at length concluded with saying, that the girl Orlando enquired after had behaved most ungratefully, to his niece Mrs. Rachel Roker, and had contemptuously refused to marry advantageously, to a Baronet, a man of great rank, Sir John Berkely Belgrave, Baronet;—an acquaintance of his client, and very good friend, Sir John Winnerton Weezle, Baronet, and Thomas Weezle, Esquire, his brother:—wherefore Mrs. Rachel Roker had discarded her; and the person to whom she was bound apprentice was now a prisoner for debt in some of the London prisons, and this girl had left her for another service, nobody knowing whither she was gone.

This account almost drove Orlando to distraction. From the man's coming himself on a message with which he had so little to do; and from several other observations he made while he was talking, it seemed as if he had some particular reason for wishing to put an end to all farther enquiry on the part of Orlando—who now, stifling his detestation, asked if he could not see Mrs. Roker, formerly Mrs. Lennard? The attorney said, No! that she was not only at a great distance from London, but kept her bed, and saw nobody. In the course of these enquiries, which he now insisted upon some answer to, he found that this Roker and his nephew were employed by the reverend body of clergy to defend their right to the Rayland estate against Philip Somerive; and it was easy to see, that the arrival of Orlando in England was the thing in the world these worthy gentlemen the least expected and the least wished.—

When this hateful being was gone, Orlando, after a moment's reflection, resolved upon visiting all those receptacles of misery in London where poverty is punished by loss of liberty, and where, in a land eminent for its humanity, many thousands either perish, or are rendered by confinement and desperation unfit to return to society—where vice and misfortune are confounded, and patient wretchedness languishes unpitied, unrelieved, unknown—while villany shows that, if there is money to support it, it will triumph in despite of punishment.

Selina knew the name of the person—Mrs. Newill, to whom Monimia had been consigned; and Orlando, making a memorandum of it in his pocket-book, with such other circumstances as might lead to a discovery, set out on his melancholy search.

He had now been near a fortnight in London, and had in a great measure recovered his looks—so that he was no longer a stranger to the few acquaintance he had: and his mother beheld with satisfaction the same Orlando, on whose fine figure and ingenuous countenance she had formerly so fondly prided herself.

His first visit was to the Fleet-prison—He enquired of every one likely to inform him, if the person whom he named to them was there? But mistrust seemed universal in that scene of legal wretchedness; and, with an heart bleeding at the thoughts of there being such complicated miseries, and that man had the power to inflict them on his fellow-creatures, he almost wished himself again among the cypress swamps and pathless woods of uncultivated America, that he might fly from the *legal* crimes[1]

---

[1] That Orlando's encounters with lawyers throw up only one humane specimen (Carr) accords with Smith's description of "*legal* crimes," a common refrain throughout her prose and poetical works.

to which such scenes were owing; when, indulging this mournful train of thought, he quitted the prison, and walked slowly up Holborn Hill.

There was a crowd just before he reached St. Andrew's church, and several coaches stood at the door of an haberdasher's shop. In making his way by them, a female figure, very smartly and somewhat tawdrily drest, took his arm and cried—"Ah, Sir! your name is Mr. Orlando Somerive?" "It is, indeed," replied Orlando; "but I do not know, Madam, how I deserve the honour of your being acquainted with it."

"What! have you forgot me then?' said the lady: "Lord! how soon old acquaintance are forgot!"

Orlando then thought he knew the voice, and had some recollection of the face; but he still hesitated, unable to remember where he had heard or seen either.—"Have you far to go?" said she, still detaining him:—"I have a carriage here, and can put you down—Lord! why, have you really forgot Betsy Richards?"

Orlando now immediately recollected his former acquaintance, and what he had heard of her being entertained as a mistress by Philip occurred to him: as he had been very solicitous ever since his return to see his brother, he now eagerly enquired where he was. "Ah, Lord!" cried the girl, shaking her head, "I have but very so so news to tell you about him, that's the truth—But, dear! one can't talk of them sort of things in the street—why, I shan't bite you, Sir—you may as well get into the coach with me." Orlando, though unwilling to be seen with such a companion, yet, on finding she could give him some information of his brother, determined to accept the offer; and the lady, who called herself Mistress Filmer, then ordered her carriage to advance: and Orlando seated himself by her, in an hired chariot with a black boy in a turban and feathers behind.

Though he was persuaded nobody knew him, he was very much ashamed of the equipage; but, applying himself immediately to learn of his fair companion what he so much wished to know, he listened to her very attentively—and, after some circumlocution in a style peculiar to herself, he learned with inexpressible concern that his brother Philip was a prisoner, for a debt of an hundred and twenty pounds, in the place he had just been visiting; and that Mrs. Filmer, though now under the protection of another person, yet retained so much recollection of her first seducer, and so much gratitude for the sums he had lavished upon her, that she had that morning been to visit him, and only stopped in Holborn to make some purchases before she went to her lodgings in Charlotte-Street.

Orlando could not bear to hear that his unhappy brother was in such a place, without going immediately to him. He staid only, therefore, a moment longer to enquire of Mrs. Filmer, if she had, when she was in the country with his brother (for they had not long before, she said, been down at Stockton's together), heard what was become of Monimia. She would have rallied him on his constancy, but he could not a moment endure to be trifled with; and, finding she knew nothing of importance, he said he recollected some material business in the city, whither he must return.—Then, stopping the chariot, he wished her a good day, and hastened back to the Fleet-prison.

On enquiry for the person he wanted, he still found some difficulty in being admitted to him: but, on signifying that he was brother to Mr. Somerive, which his resemblance to him immediately confirmed, a turnkey, to whom he gave a shilling, walked before him to the apartment where Philip was confined.

On his entrance, the neglected and altered figure of his brother struck him with the deepest concern—He was sitting at piquet with another prisoner, on a dirty table, where some empty porter pots seemed to signify that they had lately taken their dinner. Philip hardly looked up; and Orlando stood a moment unnoticed, till the man who was with him cried—"Why, 'squire, here's your honour's brother."

"The devil it is!" replied Philip—"By the Lord, though, but—let me see—It is he!—why, hast had a resurrection, my honest Rowland?—Thou wert killed and scalped, I thought, by the Cherokees."

"I almost wish I had, Philip," answered Orlando, "for I think I should have preferred death to what I now see."

"Why, to be sure, pleasanter sights may be seen if a man is in luck—For example, it would have been pleasanter for thee to have come home master of Rayland Hall—Eh! Sir Knight!"

"Good God!" exclaimed Orlando, "will you never, my brother, be reasonable? Will you never believe that, notwithstanding your repeated unkindness to me, I can never consider you otherwise than my brother, and can have no motive in coming hither but to do you good?"

"And what good canst do me? Canst let me out of this cage? Hast brought any money from the Yankies? any plunder, my little soldier? Canst lend me the ready to pay this confounded debt?"

The person who was with Orlando, now supposing they might be upon business, left them together; and Philip finding from the generous earnestness of Orlando, that though he had very little money (in fact no more than the price of his commission, which he was to received in a few days), he was willing to pay his debt, and to share with him all that he should then have left, began to grow more civil to his brother, and

did not refuse to lay before him, though his pride seemed cruelly mortified as he did it, the state of his affairs.

CHAP. VII.

The unfortunate brother of Orlando now related to him, that though
his actual debts were very great, the sum he was at present confined for
was not much above ninety pounds; and his arrest was at the suit of the
very attorney whom he had been persuaded by Stockton to employ—
a young and inexperienced man; who having, without knowing what
he was about, led his client into very heavy expences, had been, as it
seemed, bribed by Roker to abandon him; and now, without returning
his papers, had arrested him. Orlando, inexperienced as he still was in
the miserable chicane with which our laws are disgraced and counter-
acted, yet knew that this could not be right, and that some means might
be found to procure at least the papers such a man detained—This he
promised his brother he would do, and take every necessary measure
for his speedy release. He then gave Philip all the money he had in his
pocket; and, leaving him with an heavy heart, returned home, not only
disappointed in his search after Monimia, but that disappointment
embittered by the discovery he had made of his brother's situation,
whom, now that he was in distress and in prison, Orlando forgave for
all the calamities he had brought on his family, and for all the ill offices
which jealousy had excited him to be guilty of against himself.

Yet, to his mother he dared not speak of Philip; for, though she at present suffered extreme anguish in believing her son had forsaken her, after
having so largely contributed to the dispersion and ruin of his family, she
would, he knew, be quite overwhelmed by the intelligence that he was
in prison. She had already in bitterness of heart experienced—

"How sharper than a serpent's tooth it is
To have a thankless child."[1]

But still that half-broken heart had all the tenderness of a mother
within it for this her eldest child, on whom, during his early years, her
fondest affections were fixed—and Orlando well knew that the misery

---

[1] *King Lear*, I.iv.265–66.

he had thus brought upon himself would add an incurable wound to those which his mother had already received.

But, though he endeavoured to conceal the extreme dejection of his spirits on his return, his mother immediately perceived that something had more than usual disturbed him. He told her, however, in answer to her anxious enquiries, that he had been embarrassed by the delays of office in regard to the sale of his commission; and as soon as he could quit her without exciting anew her apprehensions, he left the house, and set out to execute, as far as he could that evening, his promise to his brother, telling his mother and his sisters that he should not be at home to supper.

Baffled in his first attempt to find Mrs. Newill, who was the only person from whom he could hope to hear any intelligence of Monimia, new terrors assailed him; and he thought that, amidst the most dreary hours he had passed in the wilds of America, and among men who have little more rationality than the animals of their desert, he had never suffered such wretchedness as he now felt; for, then, though he was exposed to almost every personal inconvenience, and uncertain whether he should ever again revisit his native country, he fancied Monimia was in safety; but now, every evil that could surround defenceless innocence, and unprotected beauty, was incessantly represented to his imagination; and, in proportion as time elapsed without his being able to gain any intelligence of her, his despair became intolerable—Yet other duties, indispensable duties, demanded his attention, and interrupted his pursuit, which alone could relieve his mind, by keeping alive his hopes of finding her.

His new friend, the young attorney, whose name was Carr, told him that he would instantly set about procuring the release of his brother Philip; and if, as he believed, any illegal proceeding had occurred in his confinement, Fisherton, the attorney who was the cause of it, would perhaps be compelled by a little spirit to lower his demands—"I know this man well," said Carr, "and know that nothing but his impudence can equal his ignorance. *That other honour to our profession*, Roker, is well versed in chicane, and knows more of the law, or rather of its abuse, than an honest man would wish to know; but Fisherton is so ignorant that, while his lavish expences continually reduce him to necessities that drive him into bold attempts at robbery, his skill in managing them is so inferior that he is almost always baffled, and has been more than once exposed."

"How then does he contrive to live?" said Orlando: "I learn from Philip that he has a house in town, another in the country, and entertains his clients splendidly at both; and that, in his common discourse, he talks as if he was a man of great property."

"Oh! as to that," answered Mr. Carr, "he has had a contested election for a Western borough to carry on for a Nabob; and since, a process to defend for the same worthy personage in Doctors Commons[1]—This comfortable client has been supposed his principal support for some time; and it is wonderful how his wild boasting, in which there is not a syllable of truth, imposes upon the world—He is such a man as Shakespeare somewhere describes—

'A gentleman who loves to hear himself talk, and will speak more in an hour than he'll stand to in a month.'[2]

—I am heartily sorry your brother has got into the hands and into the debt of this yelping fellow; who, even if he could prevail upon himself to be honest, is always from ignorance on the wrong scent. However, we must get him out of so sad a scrape as well as we can; and as all your elder brother's proceedings have been wrong and will only mar ours since that wretched Roker has purchased his *Solicitor* (for every pettyfogging fellow is now, not an attorney, but a solicitor), we must begin again, and file a bill of discovery against the younger Roker and his wife."

Orlando then pressed his friend (whom he thought a man of talents, and who had all the appearance of being honest without professing it) to set about the release of his brother immediately.—This he willingly agreed to, and said he would instantly go about it to one of the persons concerned, who lived also in Clement's Inn—"I shall not be gone a quarter of an hour," said Carr: "Perhaps you would like to stay till my return—here is a newspaper, if you will amuse yourself with that; but books I have none, but law books, which I suppose you have no taste for."—Orlando assured him that his mind was not in a state to receive amusement from any of the usual resources: and entreated him to go instantly about Philip's business, and allow him to wait in his chambers till his return.

Carr departed; and Orlando sat for a moment, his eyes fixed on the fire, in sad contemplation, of which Monimia was the principal object. The clerk brought him in candles (for he and Carr had conversed by fire light)

---

[1] "Doctors Commons" is slang for the complex of law courts near St. Paul's, London, from 1565–1858. Of the three courts it held, the courts of civil law, which handled matrimonial and civil cases, is the most likely venue for Fisherton's client. The other two courts were ecclesiastical and Admiralty (*The Oxford Companion to British History*, ed. John Cannon. Oxford: Oxford UP, 1997, p. 299).

[2] *Romeo and Juliet*, II. iii.133–34. Romeo actually says "A gentleman, nurse, who loves to hear himself talk, and will speak more in a minute than he will stand to in a month."

and the newspaper; but he was too much occupied by his private distresses to be able to attend to public occurrences, interesting as they were at that period to every Englishman, and particularly to one who had seen what Orlando had seen, of the war then raging with new violence in America.

He read, however, in a lingering expectation of hearing of Warwick, which never wholly forsook him, the list of the killed and wounded in an engagement or rather skirmish which was related in that paper; and when he read that the American soldiers, fighting in defence of their liberties (of all those *rights* which his campaign as a British officer had not made him forget were the most sacred to an *Englishman*), had marked their route with the blood which flowed from their naked feet in walking over frozen ground, his heart felt for the sufferings of the oppressed and for the honour of the oppressors.[1]

But from the contemplation of both, his private miseries recalled him—In laying down the newspaper on a long desk that was in the room, he cast his eyes accidentally on some of the bundles of papers that were ranged on it, tied with red tape, and saw on one—Bagshaw v. Fleming. The name of Fleming instantly brought to his mind his regretted friend the lieutenant, and his heart as instantly reproached him with breach of promise, and want of gratitude, in not having sooner enquired after the family of the lieutenant, who had with his last breath recommended them to his friendship. Nor could he forgive himself for his neglect; though a mind of less generous sensibility might easily have found excuses in the multiplicity of more immediate claims and family distresses which had overwhelmed him on his return to England.

When Carr returned, he gave to Orlando a more favourable account of his mission than he had expected; and as soon as they had agreed upon what was to be done the next day to hasten the liberation of Philip Somerive, Orlando asked him if he had a client of the name of Fleming? Carr replied that he had, and that she was a widow who was under very melancholy circumstances: "Her husband," added he, "was a lieutenant, killed in America, and she has nothing or very little more than her pension to live upon, with five children, all young; and is besides involved in a suit by the villany of some of her husband's relations, which I am defending for her."

---

[1]   The perusal of the history of the American Revolution, of Ramsay, is humbly recommended to those Englishmen who doubt whether, in defence of their freedom, any other nation but their own will fight, or conquer. [CS]

    At this point in the war, November/December 1778, the British were experiencing some success; in December, for instance, Georgia was taken.

"Good God!" cried Orlando, "it is the widow of my dear old friend, whose last breath left his gallant bosom as he, grasping my hand while I knelt on the ground stained with the blood which flowed in torrents from his breast, bade me be a friend to his poor wife, to his orphan children—And I have neglected this, shamefully neglected it! and have selfishly suffered my own sorrows to absorb me quite. —Where do Mrs. Fleming and her family live?—Where can I see them?—If they are in town I will go to them this evening."

Carr smiled at the vehemence of his young friend, and said, "What pity it is, Somerive, that such an heart as yours should ever lose this amiable warmth, and become hackneyed in the ways of men!"

"I trust," answered Orlando, "that it never will; but Carr, you do not answer my question—does Mrs. Fleming reside in London?"

"No," replied Carr; " she is at present near Christchurch in Hampshire, where a friend has lent her a cottage, for she is by no means in a situation to pay rent for such a house as her family requires." Orlando then taking an exact direction, determined to see the widow of his deceased friend as soon as he had visited the other prisons of the metropolis in search of Mrs. Newill.

The following day, therefore, after passing some time with his brother, who appeared satisfied with the prospect of his immediate release, he went to the King's-Bench prison, and, his enquiry there being fruitless, to the other receptacles of the unhappy debtor; but no such person as a Mrs. Newill was to be heard of, and Orlando returned in deeper despair than ever.

In two days the spirit and assiduity of Mr. Carr had been so effectually exerted that Philip Somerive was released, but at the expence to Orlando of somewhat upwards of an hundred pounds, including the fees which are on these occasions paid to the satellites of our most excellent law; nor would the sum have been so moderate, but from the exertions of Carr, and his threats of exposing the conduct of Fisherton. Orlando fetched his brother away in a hackney-coach to a lodging he had provided for him; where he supplied him with present money, and where he hoped he should be able to support him till something (though he knew not what) should happen to give a fortunate turn to the affairs of their family.

Philip was pensive, silent, and, as Orlando hoped, penitent. He had not as yet spoken of him to his mother; and though the circumstances that would have most sensibly afflicted her were now at an end, Orlando, who saw his mother in that state of spirits which even the sudden opening of a door, or any unexpected noise were sufficient to overset, dared not yet ask her to receive and to forgive a son, who, though she still loved him, had given her so much cause of complaint— as well since, as before his father's death.

The whole fortune of Orlando was now reduced to about two hundred and fifty pounds; for his commission did not produce him quite four. On this fortune, however, he was still bent on marrying Monimia, if he could find her; and of trusting to Providence for the rest.

A few more mornings were still passed in fruitless research. It was now the beginning of January;[1] and this beginning of Term his bill was to be filed against the persons who were supposed to have any knowledge of Mrs. Rayland's having made another, and a subsequent will. It was in search of these people, of the servants who had lived with her at the time of her death, and of the lawyers who had made the will, that he was now compelled for many days longer to employ himself; every hour increasing the agony of mind with which he thought on the fate of Monimia, while all the consolation he had was in talking of her to Selina, if he could at any time steal an hour with her alone. On these occasions he wearied himself with conjecture as to what was become of her; repeated the same questions on which he had already been often satisfied; and imagined new means of tracing her, which when he pursued, served only to renew his disappointment and regret.

At length—having learned that the lawyer who made the will was dead, and his clerk who had accompanied him to Rayland Hall settled at a town in Wiltshire—he resolved, by the advice of Carr, to go thither in search of him, and then to visit the village near Christchurch, where Mrs. Fleming and her family resided. He communicated this scheme to his mother, who, while she allowed the necessity of his finding a person whose evidence might be so very material to him, could hardly prevail upon herself to let him go for ten days from her; for so long he imagined it would be before he could return.

At length he fixed the day with her approbation, hired an horse for the journey, and took leave of his mother and his sisters. He then visited Philip, whom he found in a very silent, and, as he thought, somewhat sullen mood. He gave him a ten pound bank note, as he complained of being without money; and, in depressed spirits, with hardly a glimpse of hope to cheer his melancholy way, he began his journey.

The weather was severe; but on the first night of his journey, a deep snow threatened to render his progress more slow, and compelled him to

---

[1]   That is, January 1779.

stay till a late hour of the day, that the road might be beaten, for all was now a pathless plain, and he was a stranger to the road. About one o'clock, however, he left the town where he had passed the night, and went slowly on. He was inured to the cold by his abode in America; and in no haste to get to his inn, where nothing awaited him but a solitary supper and mournful reflections.

Again he ran over in his mind every possible circumstance that could rob him of Monimia—and awakened in his breast all the scorpions of distrust, dread, and jealousy; for, whatever attempts he made to conquer so horrible an apprehension, it was to Sir John Belgrave, and to the success of his cruel artifices, that his fears most frequently pointed; and there were moments in which he thought, that, were a person before him who could tell him all he so solicitously desired to know, he should not have courage to ask; for, should he hear that Monimia was lost by the infamous seduction of such a man, he believed he should die on the spot, or lose his reason in the greatness of his sorrow.

It was between ten and eleven o'clock in the evening of his second day's journey, that, in a wild and moory country, where extensive heaths seemed to spread without end before him, he began to think it time to seek a lodging for the night. All around was dreary and silent; and blank, he thought, as his destiny. Yet he wished the torpid sensation that being long exposed to the cold had given to his limbs could reach his heart, which was too acutely sensible! In the midst of the uniform waste stood a small village, the rustic inhabitants of which had long since retired to their hard beds; and every thing was as quiet in their houses as it was around the little church that rose beyond them. Orlando would have enquired the distance to the next post-town, but no human creature appeared, and he passed on; his thoughts (as he compared their peaceful slumbers with the state of his own troubled mind) assuming a poetical form, in the following

SONNET.[1]

While thus I wander, cheerless and unblest,
And find, in change of place, but change of pain;

---

[1] This sonnet appears as "Sonnet LXII: Written on passing by moon-light through a village, while the ground was covered with snow," in Smith's *Elegiac Sonnets* (1797), with small changes. Smith does not note that the sonnet appeared first in *The Old Manor House*, suggesting that this time she wants to reclaim the sonnet from Orlando. Indeed, the sonnet is key to understanding Smith's *Sonnets* persona, and bears comparison with Wordsworth's "The Discharged Soldier," reprinted in Appendix D.

In tranquil sleep the village labourers rest,
And taste repose, that I pursue in vain.
Hush'd is the hamlet now; and faintly gleam
The dying embers from the casement low
Of the thatch'd cottage; while the moon's wan beam
Lends a new lustre to the dazzling snow.
—O'er the cold waste, amid the freezing night,
Scarce heeding hither, desolate I stray:
For me! pale eye of evening! thy soft light
Leads to no happy home; my weary way
Ends in dark vicissitude of care:
I only fly from doubt—to meet despair.

After being near an hour longer on his horse, he arrived at Chippenham, where the lawyer lived from whom he expected information; and going extremely fatigued to an inn, he sent, at an early hour the following morning, to the person in question, who immediately came; and, inviting him to his house for a farther discussion of the business, he received him there with hospitality, and answered him with candour.

This gentleman, whose name was Walterson, informed him that it was very true he, being then clerk to a Mr. Lewes, accompanied his principal to Rayland Hall, where Mr. Lewes was closetted two days with Mrs. Rayland; after which he was called upon with another person, who he thought was a tenant, or son to a tenant of Mrs. Rayland's, to witness it: but he did not hear the contents, nor know what was afterwards done with the will: relative to which every thing was conducted with great secrecy—That he was employed to engross some other writings about one of Mrs. Rayland's farms; but that he never copied the will, nor knew more of its contents than what passed in conversation afterwards between him and Mr. Lewes—who, as they travelled together to London, afterwards said, in going through the park, out at the north lodge, that he thought Rayland Hall one of the finest old places he had ever seen; and added, speaking of the Somerive family, "And I am very glad that the old lady has determined to give it to the right heirs—because Mr. Somerive is a very worthy man, and that younger son of his a fine young fellow."—That, on some farther questions from him, Mr. Walterson, Mr. Lewes spoke as if the bulk of the fortune was given to Mr. Orlando Somerive.

Orlando made minutes of what Mr. Walterson said, who assured him he would be ready at any time to give his testimony in a court of law—

He in vain endeavoured to recollect the name of the person who was witness with him to the will, and whose information he advised Orlando by all means to procure; but he described him as a stout man, between thirty and forty, with a very florid complexion and dark straight hair, who was dressed like a substantial farmer. Orlando, having thanked Mr. Walterson for all his civilities, and received gratefully his advice for the conduct of the business, mounted his horse and proceeded towards Salisbury, meditating sometimes on the hopes he had of obtaining restitution of the Rayland estate; but oftener on Monimia, for whose sake more than his own he wished to possess it.

His journey, almost across the whole country of Wilts, was long, and rendered particularly tedious by the vicissitudes of frost and thaw that had prevailed for some days—which had made the roads, where the snow half dissolved had been again suddenly frozen, so dangerous, that he was often under the necessity of leading his horse for many miles together, he proposed, after visiting Mrs. Fleming, to cross the country to Rayland Hall; and, whatever pain it might cost him to revisit those scenes of his former happiness, to discover, if possible, the person whom Walterson described as having with him witnessed Mrs. Rayland's will.—He suddenly recollected that, in his way, he should be within a few miles of the residence of Mrs. Lennard—for so he called her, forgetting at that moment her change of name; and that it could at least do no harm if he saw her, and endeavour to find in her conversation, if not from her candour, something which might lend him a clue for the discovery of Monimia.

CHAP. VIII.

At Salisbury Orlando determined to make some slight alteration in his plan, and instead of going from thence to Christchurch, to go first into the more eastern part of Hampshire, to the residence of Mrs. Roker; for though this would make his journey considerably longer, yet, having now seized the idea that by this visit some intelligence might be obtained of Monimia, every other consideration yielded to that hope.— Somewhat cheered by it, remote and uncertain as it was, he traversed the dreary flat of Salisbury plain, and by the evening arrived at Winchester, where he vainly enquired for that relation of Mrs. Newill (the person with whom Monimia was placed) who had given his sister Selina all the intelligence she had ever received of her. Nobody knew, or wished to aid his search after an obscure woman who had probably been only a lodger in the place; and with an heart sinking under the disappointments he had already experienced, and those he yet feared, he proceeded to Alresford, near which town was situated the estate which Mrs. Rayland had given her old companion, and which she had so worthily bestowed on Mr. Roker the younger.

It was about one o'clock when Orlando found the place; a red brick house with a court before it, and a garden walled behind, on the banks of the Itching. This had been a farm-house, but had been smartened and new cased by Mr. Roker, who, assuming all the dignity of a man of landed property, was no longer the assistant steward, or the humbly assiduous attorney, but a justice of the peace, and an esquire—a title which he held the more tenaciously, as he suspected that it was believed by other esquires that he had no right to it. He was not indeed very eminent either for *morals* or *manners*; but he was a man of property, and a thriving man in the world, and his neighbours were not therefore disposed to trouble themselves either with one or the other. As he still practised the law he was usually in London in the winter; and of late it was observed, that his ancient spouse was always by indisposition prevented from accompanying him when he accepted the invitations to dinner, which were frequently given to them both by the neighbouring families; and some stories were in circulation not much to the honour of his conjugal affection: but whatever were his domestic faults, he was every where received and considered as a respectable man, because he had every appearance of becoming a rich one.

When Orlando arrived at the outward gate, he left his horse, and proceeded up a gravel walk that led to the door of the house, at which he tapped; a maid servant looked out at the parlour window, of which the shutters were before shut, and said, "Master be'nt at home."

"It is not your master," said Orlando, "that I want, but your mistress."—"Mistress be'nt well," answered the girl, "and you cannot see her."

"Is she confined to her bed then?" enquired Orlando.

"Aye," cried the girl, "confined enough for matter of that."

"I should be very much obliged to you," said Orlando, "if you could procure me only a few minutes conversation with her. I have some very particular business with her—it really is very material to me, and I will not be ungrateful if you will oblige me so far." He then took out half a guinea, and said, "Perhaps this may be some small acknowledgment for your taking the trouble to oblige me."

"Half a guinea!" cried the girl—"Ecollys I haven't a no objection to that, sure enough; for 'tis a sight as we don't often see at our house; but, Lord, I wish I dared! but, no, I mawn't."

"Why not?" said Orlando eagerly—"Pray, my dear, do, and I'll make this half guinea a whole one!"

"Will you by George!" answered the peasant girl, who was quite a rustic from the fields—"what! gi me a whole entire guinea?"

"Yes," said Orlando—"Here, this very guinea."

"A bran new one, as I hope to live!" exclaimed the girl; "but I'll tell you, master, if I does, and I should be found out, I shall lose my place."

"I'll get you a better place," cried Orlando.

"He! he!" said the girl with an ideot laugh—"what would mother say?"

"Tell me, pray," cried Orlando, "why you would lose your place for letting me see your mistress?"

"Why, Lord! don't you know? Mistress is gived out to be mad, thof she's no mad nor I be—and so when master e'ent at home, ye see, his sister keeps watch over her, and never lets nobody see her; and when we be hired, we be told never to let no strangers in to see mistress upon no account whatever; for master and his sister, and his nasty old uncle as comes here sometimes, they will all have it that mistress she's out of her mind, and that strangers makes her worse; and so she's locked up stairs, and have a been ever so long; though, poor old soul! she's tame enough for aught I ever see, and I'm sure repents her many a time as she have got into their clutches—But, hark! oh Gemini! our Tyger barks! I warrant you Miss Sukey is coming home."

"Who is she? pray hasten to tell me, and take your money."—"Oh, the Lord!" answered the girl, "Miss Sukey is our master's sister, a nasty cross old maid—She've been to Alresford this morning, or else, mun, I shouldn't have talked here so long—and now if she catches me—"

Orlando, into whose mind a thousand confused ideas now rushed, of the cause of Mrs. Roker's confinement, now dreaded lest the only opportunity he should have of hearing of or seeing Mrs. Lennard should escape him—"Can you not give your mistress a letter," said he, "if you think she is in her senses, and bring me an answer this evening?"—"I'll try," answered the girl; "but you'll give me the guinea then—and where shall I get the letter, and how will you get the answer?—Lord, Sir! it must be at night, after Miss Sukey is a-bed; and I must get out of our pantry-window, as I gets off the hooks every now and tan—for the bar on't is loose, so I takes it out." "That will do," said Orlando; "I'll go write my letter;—where will you come for it?"

"Down to the hovel," answered the girl, "there, close along the gert barn—I'll slip down there when I goes a milking; and then if Madam will gi an answer, why you must stay there till ater our folks be all a-bed; but God a bless you go now! for I sees Miss Sukey coming along."

"Take your money," said Orlando, giving her the guinea that had so tempted her, "and be punctual to the place—You mean that red-roof'd barn on the edge of the turnip field?"

"Yes, yes," answered the girl—"Go, pray, now! and as you'll run bump up against our Miss Sukey, tell her as how you wanted master, and I wouldn't let you in."

Orlando, not without somewhat admiring the talent for intrigue, of which even this rude peasant girl had so considerable a share, walked back along the gravel walk; and at the wicket gate, which opened at the end of it to the road, he was accosted by a short, thick, red-faced woman, dressed in a yellow-green riding habit, faced with orange colour, and trimmed with silver, and a hat with green and black feathers in it. Her whole face was the colour of bad veal; the shade towards her nose rather more inveterate, and two goggle grey eyes, surmounted by two bushy carrotty eye-brows, gave to her whole countenance so terrific an air, that Orlando absolutely started back when his eyes first distinguished it; while this amiable figure, stepping in the gate-way, and putting one hand on her hip, while the other held a cane, said in a loud and masculine voice to Orlando—"Who are you friend? and what is your business here?"

Orlando answered as he had been directed, that he wished to speak to Mr. Roker, but found he was not at home.

"You may leave your business with me," said Miss Sukey. Orlando answered, "No; that there was no haste, and he would call again." He then passed by this person, who gave him an idea of a fury modern-ized; and observed that she surveyed him with scrutinizing looks, and watched him till he was out of sight.

He hastened back to the inn he had left, and sat down to compose his letter to Mrs. Roker, in which he found much more difficulty than he had at first been aware of.

If she was confined by her husband under pretence of madness, as he thought was very probably the case, in order to prevent her testi-mony being received, or her discovering what it was supposed Roker had insisted on her continuing to conceal, she would probably still be deterred, by her fears and her shame, from declaring the truth; and if she was indeed mad, his letter to her would avail nothing, or perhaps be prejudicial, by falling into the hands of her keepers. There was also a third possibility, which was, that she might still retain so much affection for her young husband, as to resent the interference of any one who supposed her ill used, even though they offered her the means of escaping from her tyrant. However, as no other chance seemed to offer, he determined to hazard this measure; and wording his letter as cautiously as he could, so as not to offend her, he offered, if she was in any degree unpleasantly situated, to send her the means of escaping, and entreated her to tell him where Monimia was, and all she knew of Mrs. Rayland's affairs at the time of her death; assuring her, in the most solemn manner, that if he ever recovered the estate, and by her means, he would not only enter into any agreement she should dictate to secure to her all she now possessed, but would if she had given all up to her husband, settle upon her for life a sum that should make her more rich and independent that she had been before she gave herself to Mr. Roker; and that she should inhabit her own apartments at the Hall, or any house on the estate which she might choose. He ended with some professions of personal regard to her, as well on account of their long acquaintance, as because she was the relation, and had been the benefactress of his beloved Monimia.

This letter being finished, he again set out on foot; and as it was nearly dusk, concealed himself in the hovel which the servant girl had directed him to, where he had not waited many minutes before his emissary arrived, breathless with her fears of being discovered. He gave her the letter; with which she hurried away, charging him to stay there till she returned to him, though it should be twelve o'clock at night. He promised her a farther reward if she succeeded in procuring him an answer; and then, as the hovel was not in very good repair, and the cold extremely severe, he opened a door in it, made for the purpose of throwing straw out of the adjoining barn, and took shelter in the barn itself—repeating those lines of Shakespeare where Cordelia describes her father; and, in recollecting all that had of late befallen him, all that he had lost, and the cruel uncertainty of his future destiny, as he applied to himself those descriptive lines,

To "hovel him with swine and rogues forlorn,
In short and musty straw,"

he remembered the preceding exclamation,

"Alas! alas!
'Tis wonder that thy life and wits at once
Had not concluded all."[1]

Thus, in meditations more moral than amusing, Orlando passed two or three tedious hours, sheltered by pease-halm and straw, which he gathered around him, and leaning against the boards of the barn, that he might not fail to hear when the ambassadress entered the out-house adjoining to it. About ten o'clock, as he guessed by the time he had been there, he heard a rustling among the wood and refuse of the hovel; and eagerly listening, in expectation of being called by his female Mercury,[2] he heard a deep sigh, or rather groan, and a voice, very unlike a female voice, lamenting in very bitter and somewhat coarse terms the cruelty of fate: the person soon after made his way through the same door by which Orlando had found entrance, and going farther into the barn, he heard this unwelcome guest make a noise which he knew was striking a light, and, putting a candle into a lantern, which he seemed to have hid, he set it down by him, and began to eat his miserable supper, consisting of scraps and dry crusts.—Orlando, peeping over his fortification, contemplated for a moment this forlorn outcast, whose head, shaded by a few white locks, was on the crown and temples quite bald, and otherwise resembled him who is described as the occasional visitor of the simple village priest:

"The long remember'd beggar was his guest,
Whose beard descending, swept his aged breast."

He resembled too the "Broken Soldier" of the same admirable poem;[3] for he had lost one leg, and wore the remnant of a coat that had once been scarlet.[4] As the faint and dull light of a small candle through a thick horn lantern fell upon the furrowed countenance of this unhappy wanderer, Orlando contemplated it with pity, which for an instant detached him from the recollection of his own miseries; and he said to himself—"How unworthy, how unmanly are my complaints, when I compare my own situation with that of this poor old man, who, trembling on the verge of

---

[1]   *King Lear*, IV.vii.39–42. What Smith calls the "preceding exclamation" actually follows the lines she initially quotes.

[2]   Mercury was the Roman messenger god, but also the god of eloquence, skill, and thieving; Smith makes use of the "messenger" status but the other meanings are implicit.

[3]   Goldsmith's Deserted Village. [CS]

[4]   Again, a comparison with Wordsworth's "Discharged Soldier" is illuminating.

life, seems to have none of its common necessaries; yet perhaps has been disabled from acquiring them by having lost his limb in the service of what is called his country, that is, in fighting the battles of its politicians; and having been deprived of his leg to preserve the balance of Europe, has not found in the usual asylum a place of rest, to make him such amends as can be made for such a misfortune!" All the horrors of which he had been a witness in America now returned to his recollection; and the madness and folly of mankind, which occasioned those horrors, struck him more forcibly now than when his spirits were heated by having been a party in them. In a few moments, however, he recollected, that though he wished to give some relief to the distressed veteran before him, it would not be at all convenient that he should hear the purport of his conversation with his emissary; but before he had time to consider how this might be prevented, he heard her enter the hovel; and, without farther consideration, his eagerness to know if she had a letter for him, induced him to rush out and meet her.

"Speak softly!" said he, as soon as he found it was really his messenger—"there is a beggar in the barn who will hear you; have you a letter for me?"

"Lord, yes!" answered the girl; "and such a twitter as I be in surely!"

"Give me the letter," cried Orlando, trembling with haste; "and pray speak softly, lest the old man within should betray us!"

"'Tis only old Thomas," answered the girl, "I dare say; for he lies every night all winter long in our barns; and I'll warrant you he'll tell no tales—for in the first place he knows how he'd get no more of our broken victuals if he did; and in the next place he's as deaf as a post."

Orlando, whose impatience to read the letter was quite insupportable, then thought he might safely avail himself of the convenience of the old man's lantern to read it by. The girl assured him he might, and they entered the barn together for that purpose; but there was no longer any light, and all was silent. The girl, however, at the earnest entreaties of Orlando, called aloud to her old acquaintance, and assuring him in a very elevated voice that it was only Pat Welling who wanted him to do a message for her at town the next day—a grumbling assent was soon after heard, and at her request he struck a light, relighted his candle, and brought it to the gentleman, who, eagerly tearing open the billet, read these lines:

"Dear Sir,

"I have received yours. I do not know what is become of the girl you enquire for, as she chose to quit the worthy person I put her to, after perversely and wickedly refusing a great and high match with Sir John Belgrave, Bart. the which I doubt not but she has reason to repent of before now; though I do heartily beseech the Lord that she may not have taken to wicked courses, as there is great reason to fear; but my conscience is clear thereon. I assure you, if I know where she is to be found, I will let you know, if you please to leave your direction with Martha Welling the bearer hereof:—at the same time, as to myself, thanking you for your kind offers, have no need to trouble you at present; and know of no such thing as you are pleased to name, in regard to my late dear friend, deceased, Mrs. Rayland. Must beg to have no applications of like nature notwithstanding, because interference between married people is dangerous, generally making matters worse; and if any little disagreements, which I wonder that you should have heard, have passed, it is no more than I have heard happens between the happiest couples; and I am sure Mr. Roker really has an affectionate regard for me, and I am willing to impute all that seems to the contrary to his family, who are very disagreeable people, and such as I confess I should be glad to be out of their way, if so be as it could be done without offending Mr. Roker, whom I must love, honour and obey till death, as in duty bound. Same time should be glad to do you any service not inconsistent with that; and, as I said before, would be glad of your direction, who am, dear Sir,

Your humble servant,

Rachel Roker.

Lessington House, near Alresford,
Hants, 10th January 1779.
P.S. Mrs. R. hopes that Mr. S. will be cautious in mentioning having received these few lines, as it would be disagreeable to Mr. R——."

Orlando thought that in this letter he saw the struggle of its writer's mind, between something which she fancied was love, with shame and revenge. She had been too much flattered at first by the very unexpected acquisition of a young husband, to own now, without reluctance, that he was a savage who had robbed her under pretence of marrying her, and who now confined her, that she might not either discover his amours, of which he was said to have a great number, or be tempted through resentment of them, or her natural ill humour, to declare the conduct she had at his persuasion adopted; while her asking for Orlando's direction, and not seeming offended at his letter, persuaded him that she was pleased with the opportunity it gave her, to gratify the revenge which was always in her power, while she knew where to apply to one so much interested in the discovery she could make.

Orlando now determined, since the servant assured him there was no chance of his being admitted to see her, to write to her again, and await her answer at the inn the next day. He thought there was an opening for suggesting to her much that he had before omitted, and he had at all events assured himself by the letter he was now in possession of, that she was not mad; a plea which he perfectly understood her husband meant to set up against the evidence she might otherwise be brought to give.

It was not difficult to engage the old beggar to become his messenger on this occasion, nor to prevail on Patty to give him the next letter she should get from her mistress, on the condition however that her profits should not be lessened. He gave her another present; comforted the beggar with an earnest of his future generosity; and bidding him come by day-break the next morning for the billet he intended to send to Mrs. Roker, he took leave for that time of his two newly acquired acquaintance, whom he left much better content with the events of the day than he was—since, whatever reason he had to believe that he might recover his property, he felt with increase of anguish that he had no nearer prospect of recovering Monimia. Determined however to lose no opportunity of continuing his correspondence, he sat down the moment he came to the inn, and composed a very long letter, in which he enlarged on the ill treatment of her husband, whose gallantries he touched upon, affirming they were the more unpardonable when compared with her merit, and the obligations she had conferred upon him; he hinted at the consequence of her being compelled to appear, to answer upon oath to what she knew, and entreated her to save him the pain of calling into court as a party in secreting a will, a person for whom he had so much regard and respect; and he concluded with renewed offers of kindness in case of her coming voluntarily forward to do him justice.

His wandering messenger was the next morning punctual to his appointment; Orlando sent him away with his letter; and notwithstanding his age and his having but one leg, he returned again in about two hours—but, to the infinite mortification of Orlando, with a verbal message, which, though it had passed through the memory of Mrs. Patty, was very clearly delivered, and was to this effect—"That Madam had got the gentleman's letter; and being prevented from writing at this present time, begged him of all love to leave the country for fear of accidents, and he might depend upon hearing of her shortly." Not satisfied with this, Orlando now paid his bill at the inn, and went down to the barn, where he sent his vagabond ambassador to seek for the maid to whom he owed the little progress he had made. With some difficulty he found her, and prevailed upon her to revisit the place of rendezvous, where she informed Orlando that Miss Sukey had been watching about old mistress more than ordinary, and that the poor woman was frightened out of her wits lest Orlando's having written to her should be known; wherefore, as Miss Sukey seemed to suspect something, old Madam did entreat the 'squire not to stay thereabouts; because she should in that case be more strictly confined, and never should be able to write to him, which she now promised to do, if he would only leave the country. As this was all the intelligence the disappointed Orlando could now procure, he was compelled to obey this unwelcome injunction, lest he should lose all future advantage; and engaging by renewed presents the fidelity and future assistance of his two emissaries, he remounted his horse, and took the road to Winchester. He now fell again into melancholy reflections: every hour added to his despair about Monimia, and without her, life was not in his opinion worth having. From these thoughts a natural transition led him to consider the wonderful tenacity with which those beings clung to life, whose existence seemed to him only a series of the most terrible sufferings:—beings, who exposed to all the miseries of pain, poverty, sickness and famine; to pain unrelieved, and the feebleness of age unassisted, yet still were anxious to live; and could never, as he at this moment found himself disposed to do—

"Reason thus with life:
If I do lose thee, I do lose a thing
Which none but fools would keep." [1]

Yet he had seen many die in the field, who neither seemed to fear nor feel the stroke of that destiny which miserable age still recoiled and crept away from. The poor maimed wanderer, whose daily wants he had for a little while suspended, was an instance that the fear of death makes the most wretched life supportable. In pursuing this train of thought he arrived at Winchester, where he intended to remain till the next day.

---

[1] *Measure for Measure*, III.i.6–8.

CHAP. IX.

Early on the following morning Orlando left Winchester; but it was between three and four o'clock before he arrived at that part of the New Forest which is near Christchurch, and the frost, now set in with great severity, had made the roads very difficult for an horse, especially the way which he was directed to pursue, through the forest to the residence of Mrs. Fleming.—It was a deep, hollow road, only wide enough for waggons, and was in some places shaded by hazle and other brushwood; in others, by old beech and oaks, whose roots wreathed about the bank, intermingled with ivy, holly, and evergreen fern, almost the only plants that appeared in a state of vegetation, unless the pale and sallow mistletoe, which here and there partially tinted with faint green the old trees above them.

Orlando, as slowly he picked his way over the rugged road, whose poached surface, now hardened by the frost, hardly allowed a footing to his horse, recollected the hunting parties in the snow, which had amused him in America; but the scene on each side of him was very different. The scanty appearance of foliage was quite unlike an American forest, where, in only a few hours after the severest weather, which had buried the whole country in snow, burst into bloom, and presented, beneath the tulip tree and the magnolia, a more brilliant variety of flowers than art can collect in the most cultivated European garden. Orlando, however, loved England, and had early imbibed that fortunate prejudice, that it is in England only an Englishman can be happy; yet now he thought, that were he once sure Monimia was lost to him (and his fears of finding it so became every hour more alarming), he should be more wretched in his own country than in any other, since every object would remind him of their cruel separation. In this disposition, trying to accustom himself to reflect on a circumstance which now distracted him, he made a sort of determination, that if all his endeavours to find Monimia were baffled, as they had hitherto been, he would remain only to see the termination of the suit relative to the Rayland estate, in hopes of leaving his mother, brother, and sisters, in a more fortunate situation; and reserving for himself only as much as would support him in the itinerant life he should embrace, to wander alone over Europe and America. While he pursued these contemplations, the way became almost impassable; for a small current of water filtering through the rocky bank, had spread itself over the road, and formed a sheet of ice, on which his horse was every moment in danger of falling, though the precaution had been taken to turn the shoes.—He had before dismounted, and now contrived to get his horse up the least steep part of the hollow, and then, still leading it by the bridle, he followed the foot-path which led along its edge.

The tufts of the trees and thick underwood now became more frequent; and though it was a fine, clear evening, the winter sun, almost sunk beneath the horizon, lent only pale and cold rays among the intervening wood.—Orlando supposing, that if he were benighted, he should no longer distinguish the path, quickened his pace; and the path he followed, diverging a little from the horse road, brought him to a place where the inequalities of the ground, half shaded with brush-wood, shewed that beneath it were concealed more considerable fragments of ruins, than what appeared above among the trees, from whence the masses of stone were so mantled with ivy, they could hardly be distinguished. The path which Orlando continued to pursue, wound among them, and led under broken arches and buttresses, which had resisted the attacks of time and of violence, towards an old gateway, whose form was yet entire.

Every thing was perfectly still around; even the robin, solitary songster of the frozen woods, had ceased his faint vespers to the setting sun, and hardly a breath of air agitated the leafless branches. This dead silence was interrupted by no sound, but the slow progress of his horse, as the hollow ground beneath his feet sounded as if he trod on vaults. There was in the scene, and in this dull pause of nature, a solemnity not unpleasing to Orlando, in his present disposition of mind.—Certain that the path he was pursuing must lead to some village or farm-house, and little apprehensive of the inconvenience that could in this country befall a man accustomed to traverse the deserts of America, he stopped a moment or two indulging a mournful reverie, before he began to remove, in order to make a passage for his horse, a kind of bar, or rather broken gate, which, with thorns, and a faggot or two piled under it, passed from one side to the other of the broken arch, and made here, with an hedge that was carried among the ruins, a division of the forest, or perhaps one of its boundaries.

As he meditated here, he heard, not far from him, human voices, which seemed to be those of children; and, leaning over the bar, to see if he could discern the persons who spoke, he observed a female figure seated on a mass of fallen stone, and apparently waiting for two girls, one about nine, the other seven years old, who were prattling together, as they peeped about in search of something among the fern-stacks and low tufts of broom that were near. The woman, whose face was turned towards them, seemed lost in thought—Her straw bonnet was tied down close to her face, and she was wrapped in a long black cloak; a little basket stood by her, and her appearance, as well as that of the children, was such as seemed to denote, that though they were not of the peasantry of the country, they were as little to be ranked among its most affluent inhabitants.

Orlando, apprehending that the approach of a stranger, in such a place, and at such a time, might alarm so defenceless a party, proceeded with as little noise as possible to unfasten the bar; but, on his approach, the young woman arose, and in apparent hurry said, "Come, my loves! you forget how late it is, and that your mama will expect us."

The voice riveted Orlando to the spot for a moment; he then involuntarily stepped forward, and saw—Monimia![1]

He repeated her name wildly, as if he doubted whether he possessed his senses; and as he clasped her to his bosom, and found it was indeed his own Monimia, she was unable, from excess of pleasure and surprise, to answer the incoherent questions he asked her. Half frantic with joy as he was, he soon perceived that the suddenness of this meeting had almost overwhelmed her. Silent, breathless, and trembling, she leaned on his arm, without having the power to tell him, what he at length understood from the two little girls, who had been at first frightened, then amazed at the scene—That Monimia, or, as they called her Miss Morysine, was now, and had been for some time, under the protection of that very Mrs. Fleming, the widow of his gallant friend, whom he was now going to visit. Neither of them knew how they arrived at her humble retirement, a cottage among the woods, fitted up and enlarged with two additional rooms by a sea officer, the distant relation of Fleming, who was now in America, and who had lent this pleasant, solitary house as a shelter to his widow and her children.—Nor was it for some time possible for Orlando properly to explain to Mrs. Fleming who he was, or how different those motives were, which induced him now to see her, from any hope of finding, in the pious office of visiting the family of his deceased friend, the sole happiness of his life.

When at length, amid this disjointed and broken conversation, Mrs. Fleming was brought not only to recollect the young man, who, on her husband's embarkation for America, had taken so much pains to be useful to him, in the trying moment of separation from his family, but

---

[1]   Orlando's discovery of Monimia takes the reader back to the land of romance, but it also again shows Orlando's inability to control himself (as, indeed, his frenzied reaction to Monimia's story in the subsequent scenes make plain): the two little girls are "frightened, and then amazed at the scene."

to acknowledge him who had actually received his last breath, and now brought her his dying blessing; her own afflictions, to a lively sense of which Orlando's account of Fleming's death had awakened her, prevented her, for some time, from attending to the unexpected happiness of her young friends. Unable to hear, with composure, the account which Orlando held himself bound to give, yet solicitously asking questions, the answers to which made her heart bleed afresh, Mrs. Fleming at length requested leave to retire; and taking her children with her, Monimia was left at liberty to give to the impatient Orlando the account he so eagerly desired to hear, of what had happened to her since the date of the only letter he had ever received from her, which was written not more than six weeks after his departure.—She doubted of her own strength to give, and of his patience to hear this recital: but he appeared so very solicitous, that she determined to attempt it; and while his eyes were ardently fixed on her face, and watched every turn of her expressive features, which, though she was pale and thin, Orlando thought more lovely than ever, she thus in a soft and low voice began:

"As well as I can recollect, Orlando, I related to you, in my long letter, the troublesome and impertinent intrusion of Sir John Belgrave; and Selina has told you since, that, as he carried his persecutions so far as to come into the house, and endeavour to force his way into my room, I was under the necessity of telling my aunt how he found admittance, and of betraying a secret I had so many reasons to wish might never have been discovered.—Alas! Orlando, how much did I not suffer from the bitterness of her reproaches! sufferings which were sharpened by my being compelled to acknowledge, that I had in some measure deserved them, by having carried on a correspondence contrary to what I knew was my duty.—Indeed the punishment I now underwent, from day to day, seemed sometimes much heavier than the crime deserved; especially when my aunt, to whom my moving was inconvenient (though certainly, in that great house, there was room enough for me without interfering with her), began to make the discovery, I had thus been compelled to make, an everlasting theme of reproach to me; to say, that such a cunning, intriguing creature was not fit to be in any house; and to threaten me continually to ruin you, Orlando, with Mrs. Rayland, by blowing us up, as she was pleased to term it. All this I bore, however hard it was to bear, with silence, and, I hope, with patience, flattering myself, my dear friend! that the anger we had perhaps mutually deserved would thus be exhausted on me, and that I alone should be the victim, if a victim were required: yet, when my cruel aunt, unmoved by my resignation and submission, seemed so desirous of getting rid of me, that I believe she would have been glad to have sold me to Sir John Belgrave; and when she insisted upon my consenting to marry him, though I do not believe he ever intended it, and only made that a pretence for getting me into his power; I own there were moments, when, in absolute despair, I thought it would hardly have been criminal to have put an end to a life so very insupportable; nor could I, I think, have lived, if some of those books you taught me to read, and to understand, had not instructed me, that it was impious to murmur, or resist the dispensations of Providence, who knew best what we were able to bear.—Perhaps too, the hope, the dear hope of living in your affection, and of being beloved by you, however hard my lot, lent me a portion of fortitude, for which, surely, nobody ever had more occasion; for in proportion, Orlando, as Mrs. Lennard became attached to that odious Roker, the little affection she had ever shewn me declined, and was changed into dislike and hatred.— She was sometimes so much off her guard, as to suffer her excessive and ridiculous attachment to him to diminish her attention to her mistress, and on these occasions, I used to supply her place;—yet then, if Mrs. Rayland seemed pleased with my attendance, she would quarrel with me for attending, and say, that she supposed the next thing such an artful slut would think of, would be to supplant her with her lady; and then again she would threaten to blow you up.—Indeed, I believe, that no situation could be less enviable than that of my poor aunt was at this time; for though certainly, at her age, one would have thought she might have been exempt from suffering much pain from love, she did really appear so tormented for her excessive passion for Roker, and her fears of losing him, that she was an object of pity.—If I was below with her lady, while she was with him, then she was afraid of my getting into favour with Mrs. Rayland; and if I was above, and he was in the house, she was in terror lest so intriguing a creature should carry off her lover. When I so firmly resisted all the insidious offers of Sir John Belgrave, she doubted whether this detestable Mr. Roker was not the cause of it; and even when he happened to come into the room where I was, though she was present, she turned pale with jealousy, and I suppose, tormented the man, who, though one of the most horrid-tempered monsters existing, commanded himself so much, that he bore it all with an apparent increase of affection; and pretending, in his turn, to be jealous, said, that he could not bear to divide her affections even with me.

"I saw that they were determined to get rid of me, but could not immediately settle how; for though Roker, from time to time, started some plan for that purpose, the lady, always suspecting that he liked me, was fearful lest he should only divide me from her, to secure me to himself."

"Execrable villain!" cried Orlando, starting up—"he dared not think of it."

"Be patient, Orlando, or I shall never have courage to go on.—I know not what was in his imagination, though certainly he took every opportunity of making very improper speeches to me; but detestable as I believe his morals are, his avarice is greater than any other of his odious passions; and this he found he might gratify, when the success of any other was uncertain; and therefore he affected to be as anxious as my aunt was, to remove me from Rayland Hall.

"Ah, my dear friend, what an autumn was that I passed there! yet my fate, dreary as it appeared to me, was not then at the worst; I had still some sweeteners of my melancholy existence; for I sometimes met Selina, and wept with her; and sometimes, when I was convinced Sir John Belgrave no longer lingered about the park (where for many weeks I could never go without being insulted by him), I used to get out alone; and stealing away to some of those places we used to visit together, I would lean my head against a tree, or hide my face with my hands, and listening, with closed eyes, to the sounds that were then familiar to us, used to fancy I heard your footsteps among the leaves, or your voice whispering in the air that sighed among the trees. Once, at the old seat on the Hurst hill, I saw your name, so lately cut as the very day before you went away; and could I have wept on the letters, I believe the tears I afterwards shed there would have worn them out.—I took a fancy to the place, which nobody else ever thought of frequenting; and often, as autumn came on, and the days grew short, I staid till I was frightened at being out so late, and have run home terrified at every noise.—If a pheasant flew up, or an hare darted across the path, they threw me into such terrors, that I could hardly reach the house. On these occasions, all was well if my aunt's Adonis[1] was with her; but if it happened that he was out when I was, she took it into her head that we were together, or that we might meet, and then she was, I really believe, out of her senses. Very unluckily for me, I came in one evening later than usual, breathless with my foolish fears, and found my poor aunt in terrible agitation, because Mr. Roker had promised her to be in at tea-time, and he was not yet arrived.—She questioned me sharply where I had been; and I said in the mill wood, which was the truth; for I had that evening met Selina. She asked me, with still more asperity, if I had

---

[1] That is, a beautiful young man: even Monimia now engages in sarcasm.

not met somebody? The consciousness that I had, made me blush, I believe, very deeply, and I faltered as I said No!—In a moment Roker came in, half drunk, and the poor old lady flew at him like a turkey-cock, and asked him, which way he came? As he was less upon his good behaviour than usual, he said, "Came! why I came by the mill; which way should I come from the place where I have been?"—This confirmed, she thrust me out of the room, and ordering me to go up stairs to bed that moment, she threw herself into a fit, as Rebecca told me afterwards. I do not know how Mr. Roker contrived to appease her—she was reconciled to him the next day; but I was the victim, and was, after that time, forbidden to go out without her leave. This, hard as it was, I could still have borne, because it was just at that time Mrs. Rayland seemed to grow particularly kind to me; and to have even a degree of pleasure in talking to me of you. It was now time to expect to hear from you, and I observed her anxiety every day increase.—She often sighed when she spoke of you; and once said, that her house seemed to have lost all its cheerfulness since you had left it;—and often she would look at an old enameled picture of Sir Orlando, her grandfather, and, comparing his features with yours, admire the likeness—then, again, regret your absence, and sink into low spirits. Indeed her health seemed every day to decline: and I sometimes thought she was discontented with Mrs. Lennard, though from long habit she was more entirely governed by her than ever. Patterson's having dealt so largely in smuggled goods, and having even made her house a receptacle for them, was discovered by his not being able or willing to bribe a new officer who succeeded some of his old friends, and who, upon that Jonas Wilkins's turning informer, came one night to the Hall, and made a seizure of about two hundred pounds worth of spirits, tea, and lace; a thing that offended Mrs. Rayland extremely, as she thought it derogatory to her dignity, and a profanation of her cellars, which, as we know (and Monimia faintly smiled), are immediately adjoining to the family vault of the Raylands. This, and other things, particularly some of his amours, which now came to her knowledge, had occasioned her to dismiss Patterson, and to think higher of you for the pains Patterson had taken to prejudice her against you: but the dismission, and soon afterwards the death of Patterson, and the disgrace of the old coachman, who was a party concerned in this contraband business (and who had besides displeased Mrs. Rayland by setting up a whisky,[1] and dressing his daughters in the most expensive fash-

---

[1]   A light two-wheeled one-horse carriage common in the late eighteenth/early nineteenth century.

ion), threw the old lady more than ever into the power of my aunt; though, how she escaped being included in the charge, I never could imagine: I know she was acquainted with, and I believe she was concerned in the clandestine trade which had for so many years been carried on at Rayland Hall; but probably Patterson dared not impeach her, lest, though he might ruin her, he should at the same time provoke her to discover some things in his life which would have effectually cut him off from that portion of favour he still possessed with Mrs. Rayland; who, angry as she was with him, stocked the farm he retired to, furnished his house, and continued to him almost every advantage he enjoyed at the Hall, except the opportunity of making it a receptacle for smuggled goods.

"However that was, my aunt certainly continued to have great influence over Mrs. Rayland, though I often thought it was more through habit than love; and I am persuaded that, if she had not always guarded against the inclination which Mrs. Rayland at times betrayed to take your mother and sisters into favour, they would by degrees have acquired that ascendancy over her from their own merit, which Mrs. Lennard had now only from habit—But my aunt was too cunning to give them an opportunity; and that, I believe, was partly the reason why she was so afraid of my being taken into Mrs. Rayland's kindness, since nothing was more natural than for me to speak in their favour. She need not, however, have dreaded this; for, however willing or anxious I might be, my awe of Mrs. Rayland was too great for me to aspire to the character of her confident: and she looked upon me as a mere child.—Probably our ages differed too much to allow any great sympathy between us— and I could give her no other pleasure than by attending to the stories she used to love to repeat, of the days of her youth.—But Mrs. Lennard, though by no means desirous of being herself the auditor, and never easy but when she could remain unmolested with her dear Mr. Roker, was still jealous lest her lady should feel any degree of kindness for me; and, I believe, by imputing to me faults which Mrs. Rayland took her word for, contrived gradually to get her consent to my going apprentice, under the idea of my being enabled to get my own bread honestly in business; while she obviated the inconvenience of my departure by introducing a new servant to be about her lady, who was entirely devoted to her own interest—and kept away the old cook as much as she could, whom Mrs. Rayland never would part with, but whom my aunt feared and disliked, because she was an honest blunt creature, who never feared speaking her mind, and was particularly a friend of yours, as you may I am sure recollect. Latterly she became more than usually disagreeable to my aunt and

Roker, because she used to rejoice in the thought that her dear young captain would one day or other be master of the Hall; and when Lennard angrily asked her how she dared talk of any one's being master of the Hall while her lady lived? she replied, that she dared talk so, because Madam herself had told her so."

"And where, my Monimia, is this good old friend of mine now?" said Orlando—"Her evidence may be of great importance to us."—"Alas!" replied she, "I know not: I only heard from your sister, that Dr. Hollybourn, who acted as executor to the only will that was produced, immediately discharged all the servants, giving to each of them a present above the two years wages which Mrs. Rayland had in that will given to each of the inferior ones; and, with many good words, got as many as he could of them into other services, at a distance from the country— But I recollect that the cook had relations in the neighbourhood of the Hall, of whom, I dare say, intelligence about her may be procured.

"Ah, dear Orlando! if the account I have already given you of my unhappy life after your departure has affected you, what will you feel when I relate what passed afterwards, to which all my preceding sufferings were nothing!—It is true that, as I lay listening of a night to the howling of the wind in the great melancholy room at the end of the north gallery, where I was locked up every night, I have frequently started at the visions my fancy raised; and as the dark green damask hangings swelled with the air behind them, I have been so much terrified as to be unable to move or to summon to my recollection all the arguments you were wont to use against superstitious fear—Then too I have been glad even to hear the rats as they raced round the skirting boards, because it convinced me there were some living creatures near me, and helped me to account for the strange noises I sometimes heard. As winter came on, my misery in this great room became worse and worse; and such was my terror, that I could hardly ever sleep—I once contrived to get candles, and set up a light in my room; but this only served to shew me the great grim picture over the chimney, of one of the Rayland family in armour, with a sword in his hand: and I was indeed, besides this, effectually cured of wishing for a light on the second night I tried it—for a party of my friendly rats, perceiving the candle, which was to them a delicate treat, took it very composedly out of the socket, and began to eat the end of it which was not alight.— This compelled me to leave my bed to put it out, and them to flight; while the terror I suffered was only increased by this attempt to mitigate it.—Good God! how weak I was to add imaginary horrors to the real calamities of my situation; rather than try to acquire strength of mind to bear the evils from which I could not escape!

"It was at this time that Sir John Belgrave, who, on finding his insulting proposals treated with the contempt they deserved, had left the country for some time, returned thither; and as Jacob, his confident, could no longer find means to put his letters in my way, or to harass and alarm me by coming to the door of my turret, he changed his plan, and pretended that his views were highly honourable. In a letter to my aunt he entreated her interest with me, and that she would prevail upon me to see him: and then it was, Orlando, that my sufferings were almost beyond the power of endurance."

"What!" exclaimed Orlando, "was the infamous woman base enough then to betray you to this villain?"

"Have patience, I entreat you, Orlando!—She betrayed me then, so far as to insist upon my seeing Sir John, and hearing what he had to say."

"Eternal curses blast them both!" exclaimed Orlando:—"but I terrify you, my angel!"

"You do, indeed," answered Monimia; "and I shall never, Orlando, conclude my mournful narrative, if you will not be more calm."

"I will," replied he; "at least I will try at it—Pray go on."

"I resisted this proposal of seeing Sir John Belgrave for many days; till my aunt, enraged at what she called my stupid idiotism, declared to me that, if I persisted to behave so senselessly, she would relate to Mrs. Rayland all my clandestine meetings with you, and then turn me out of the house to take my own courses.—I would willingly have left the house, and, rather than have undergone one day longer the misery I hourly experienced, I would have begged my way to you in America (Orlando sighed and shuddered); but when my cruel aunt threatened to take such means as I knew would ruin you, and blast all those hopes on which alone I lived, of seeing you return to happiness and independence, I own I could not bear to hazard it, and at length consented to see this detested suitor—not without some hope that my peremptory refusal repeated (for I had already given it to him in writing) might put an end to all his hateful pretensions. A day therefore was fixed: but Sir John, either repenting that he had gone so far, or from some caprice, wrote to my aunt to say he was that day sent for express to London, to attend a dying relation, from whom he expected a great acquisition of fortune. This might be true—I cared not whether it was or no, but blessed the fortunate relief from persecution. In the interim your father, who was taken ill some time before, died.—Oh! how much did I see

Selina suffer during his illness—how much did I suffer myself! and all was aggravated to an indescribable degree of wretchedness, by our believing that you, Orlando, were lost in your passage to America!—If I thought my former condition insupportable, what was the increase of my sorrows now, when torn from the last consolation I had left, that of weeping sometimes with Selina!—My aunt, almost as soon as Sir John Belgrave had left the country, informed me that she had found a person at Winchester willing to take me for a small premium, and that I was to go the following Thursday.—I never knew how all this was settled; but very, very certain it is, that it was arranged between her, her lover Mr. Roker, and Sir John Belgrave. She was impatient to have me gone; and sent the old cook, to take care of me, as far as Havant, where Mrs. Newill, to whom I was consigned, met me, and conducted me to a little miserable apartment, which, with a small bow-windowed shop, she inhabited at Winchester, and where she was to teach me a business which I soon found she did not know herself.

"Mrs. Newill was said to have been well brought up; but, if she were, her having long associated with people in very inferior life had considerably obliterated the traces of a good education; and the inconvenient circumstances to which she had been exposed, in consequence of having had a brutal and extravagant husband, seemed at once to have soured her temper, and relaxed her morals.—She had some remains of beauty, and was fonder of talking of its former power than I thought redounded much to her honour.—Her husband had possessed a place in the dock-yard at Portsmouth, from whence he had been dismissed for some heavy offences, and lived now upon the wide world; while his wife was, by the assistance of her friends, trying to get into business to support herself; their only son, a young man of twenty, was in the navy.—The greatest personal hardship I endured on this my change of abode, was sleeping in the same bed with Mrs. Newill, which I did for the first week:—but, fortunately for me, though it was probably much otherwise to her, her husband, believing she had money, for he had heard of her taking an apprentice, came suddenly to her house, or rather lodging, and I was dismissed to a little closet in a garret with a truckle bed: but it was paradise compared with my share of Mrs. Newill's; for now I could weep at liberty, and pray for you!

"The arrival of such a man as Mr. Newill did not much contribute to the prosperity of his wife's business—Those who, from their former knowledge of her, were willing to promote her welfare, grew cold when they found their bounty served only to support her husband in drunkenness, and her distress became very great, of which I was a sharer; but I endeavoured to do all I could to continue her business, which was now almost entirely neglected.

"This went on for six weeks, when a regiment came thither to assist in guarding the prisoners at the castle; and Sir John Belgrave suddenly made his appearance, protesting to me, that he knew nothing of my being there, and only came down on a visit to some of his friends in the newly arrived corps.

"I did not believe this, and found every day more cause to suppose that Mrs. Newill's necessities had driven her to the inhuman expedient of betraying me to him. Though I had often ridiculed the stories in novels where young women are forcibly carried away, I saw great reason to believe some such adventure might happen to me, for I was totally unprotected, and I believe, absolutely sold."

Orlando, starting up, traversed the room; nor could, for some time, the soothing voice of Monimia restore him to sufficient composure to attend to her narrative.

At length his anxiety to know what he yet trembled to hear obliged him to reassume his seat, and she thus proceeded:

"Surely, Orlando, you do not suppose that any distress, any misery, could have induced me to listen to Sir John Belgrave, though, instead of the advantages he affected to offer me, he could have laid empires at my feet.—It is true that I now suffered every species of mortification, and even much personal inconvenience; but my heart felt only the horrid tidings I received from Selina. Mrs. Rayland's death, and the total disappointment of your family's hopes, were very melancholy; but when Perseus arrived, and your death, Orlando, was confirmed by the testimony of a man who had seen you fall, my wretchedness so much exceeded all that I believed it possible to bear, that I became stupified and insensible to every thing else, and walked about without hearing or seeing the objects around me. I never slept, but with the aid of laudanum—I could not shed a tear, and my heart seemed to be turned to marble. I had nobody to hear my complaints, and therefore I did not complain; and the only circumstance that roused me from this state of mind, was the renewal of Sir John Belgrave's visits, who, after an absence of seven or eight days, returned with new proposals, and dared to triumph in the knowledge that his rival, as he insolently called you, was no longer in his way.

"It was now, Orlando, that a new method was pursued. He contrived, what was not indeed very difficult, to gain over Mrs. Newill to his interest.—I was now treated with great respect—A room was hired for me in the same house, and Mrs. Newill offered me credit for any clothes I chose to have. I, who was hardly conscious of my existence, who mechanically performed the business of the day, and cared not whether I ever again saw the light of the sun, refused her offers, and desired nothing but that I might be protected from the affront of Sir John Belgrave's visits. If I sat at work in the shop, he was there:—if I quitted it, he came into the work-room, under pretence of speaking to Mrs. Newill. I found that Newill was a wretch who would have sacrificed a daughter of his own for a few guineas, with which to purchase his favourite indulgences; and Sir John Belgrave scrupled not to say, that, since I had refused his honourable offers, he held it no dishonour to compel me, by any means, to exchange my present wretched dependence, for affluence and prosperity—that I could not now have the pretence of constancy to you, and that his excessive love for me would in time induce me to return it.—Such were the terms in which he pressed his suit, giving me at the same time to understand that I was in his power.

"But, liberal as I have reason to believe he was to Mr. Newill, his debts were too numerous and extensive to be so settled; and, in consequence of one of these, to the amount of five hundred pounds, he was arrested in London, and sent for his wife to attend him in the King's-Bench.[1]

"This the unhappy woman prepared to do in two or three days; and, in that time, made over the little stock for sale to one of her friends, who had advanced money for her.—But what was to become of me?—As she had no longer a business, she could have no occasion for an apprentice, and I could be only a burthen to her; but I soon found that it was her husband's directions that she should take me with her, and I determined at all events not to go.

"I now again wrote to my cruel aunt, who though she almost immediately after Mrs. Rayland's death settled within twelve miles of the town whither she had sent me, had never taken any other notice of me than to send me a small supply of clothes and two guineas, together with a verbal message, that the reason she had not answered any of my former, nor should answer any of my future letters, was, that she would not encourage in her perverseness a person so blind to her own interest, and that, till I knew how to behave to Sir John Belgrave, I should find no friend in her. It was in vain I wrote to her, urging every plea that I

---

[1]   Debtors are imprisoned in the King's Bench, where their wives and families may join them; Smith lived with her husband in the King's Bench for seven months in 1783–84, and it was there that she first put together her *Elegiac Sonnets*.

thought might move her, and soliciting her pity and protection, as the only friend I had in the world. She either hardened her heart against me, or perhaps never got my letters. The business that detained Mrs. Newill at Winchester, could not be settled so expeditiously as she expected. In the mean time, what a situation was mine! I had nothing to hope but death, and death only could deliver me from the fear of evils infinitely more insupportable. Orlando, how earnestly did I pray to join you in heaven! how often did I invoke you to hear me! and casting towards the west my swollen eyes (for I was now able to weep in repeating your name), how often have I addressed the setting sun, which, as it sunk away from our horizon, might illuminate, I thought, that spot in the wilderness of America where all my happiness was buried!"

Orlando kissed away the tears that now fell on her lovely cheeks, and mingled his own with them; when Monimia after a little time recovered her voice, and went on—"It was to indulge such meditations, the only comfort I had, that I stole out whenever I could be secure that my persecutor was with his military friends; and as I dared not go far, the churchyard on that side of the cathedral where the soldiers did not parade, or sometimes the cathedral itself, were the only places where there was a chance of my not being molested; and there, if I could ever procure quiet for a quarter of an hour, the daws that inhabited the old buildings, and who were now making their nests (for it was early spring), recalled to my mind, by the similarity of sounds, Rayland Hall; and when I compared my present condition with even the most comfortless hours I passed there, I reproached myself for my former discontent, and envied all who were at peace beneath the monumental stones around me.—Later than usual one evening I returned from this mournful walk, and, making my way with some difficulty through the crowds who were assembling in the streets to celebrate some victory or advantage in America (and at the very name of America my heart sickened within me), I was overtaken near the door of Mrs. Newill's lodging, by the person whom I most dreaded to meet—Sir John Belgrave, evidently in a state of intoxication, with three officers in the same situation, who insisted on seeing me home. I was within a few yards of the door, and hastened on to disengage myself from them; but they followed me, or rather Sir John Belgrave with one arm round my waist hurried me on, talking to me in a style of which I was too much terrified to know more than that it was most insulting and improper.

"In this way, however, while I remonstrated, and trembled, and entreated in vain, I was forced into a little room behind the shop, where Mrs. Newill usually sat, where, instead of her, there sat by the side of a small fire (for the weather was yet cold) a young man in the naval uniform, who starting up on the abrupt entrance of such a party, stood amazed a moment at the language of Sir John Belgrave and his friends, and then, fiercely demanding what business they had in that house, ordered them to leave it; and, taking my hand, he said—"I am ashamed, gentleman, of your treatment of this young woman—Don't be alarmed, miss—I will protect you."

"I most willingly put myself into the protection he offered, when Belgrave, enraged at being thus addressed by a person whom he considered as so much his inferior, uttered a great oath, and said—"And, pray, fellow, who are you?—and what the devil have you to do with this girl?"—"Master of my mother's apartment," replied the young sailor, who I now understood was Mrs. Newill's son—"and an Englishman! As the first, I shall prevent any ruffian's insulting a woman here; as the second, I shall defend her from insult any where."—"You be d——d!" cried Belgrave; "you impudent puppy, do you think that black stock[1] makes you on a footing with a gentleman?" Belgrave's companions had by this time wisely retired; for, as I was not *their* pursuit, they saw no occasion to incur the danger of a quarrel in it. The only answer the stranger gave to this additional insolence of Belgrave was a violent blow, which drove the aggressor against the side of the wainscot, that in so narrow a room prevented his falling; and then young Newill, seizing him by the collar, with a sudden jerk threw him out of the room, and shut the door. The noise all this made brought Mrs. Newill down stairs, who demanded of her son what was the matter? He answered, that some brutal officers, very drunk, had insulted a young lady who had taken shelter in that room, and whom he had rescued from their impertinence by turning them out of it. His mother, in additional consternation, then turned to me, "What!" said she, "it was you, miss, was it? And I suppose the gentleman was Sir John Belgrave—Fine doings! And so, William, this is the way you affront my friends?"

"I care not whose friends I affront," replied he: "if they behave like brutes to a woman, I would affront them if they were emperors." His mother, who I am afraid had been solacing herself above stairs with some of those remedies to which she often applied for consolation, now began to cry and lament herself; and, in her pathetic complaints, bemoaned her ill luck that had given her an apprentice that, so far from being an

---

[1]   A stiff, close-fitting neckcloth, part of the military uniform, but also at the time worn by men in general.

assistant, was only a trouble to her, and did nothing but offend her customers. Young Newill then, for the first time, understood that I was this apprentice; and as I sat weeping in a corner, I saw he pitied me—"Come, come, Madam," said he to his mother, "no more of this, if you please—nobody has offended your customers; but, on the contrary, your customers, as you call them, have offended me; let us look a little after this good friend of yours, perhaps he may have some farther commands for me—it is unhandsome to sink such a fine fair-weather jack, without lending a hand to heave him up." He then, in spite of his mother's entreaties, opened the door; but no Sir John Belgrave appeared, and the sailor observed that he had set all his canvas and scudded off. "So now, dear mother," said he, "pr'ythee let's have no more foul weather; but let us sit down to supper, for I'm sure this young woman must be glad of something after her fright—poor little soul, how she trembles still!—and you should remember that I have rode from Portsmouth since dinner, and a seaman just come from a two months cruise must eat." Mrs. Newill still however appearing to think more of Sir John Belgrave than her son, he became presently impatient; and going out to a neighbouring inn, he ordered a supper and some kind of wine or punch; which being soon brought, Mrs. Newill consented to partake of it, though she still behaved to me with such rude reserve, that I would immediately have retired, if young Newill had not insisted on my sitting down to supper with them, and I was too much obliged to him to refuse."

"You were certainly obliged to him," said Orlando in a hurried voice; "but after such a scene I wonder you were able to remain with these people—What sort of a man is young Newill? Is he a well-looking man?"

"Yes," replied Monimia, "rather so; but I hardly knew then how he looked—and in the scene I have described, I rather recollected it afterwards, than attended to it at the time."

"Pardon me," interrupted Orlando, with quickness—"you must have attended to it at the time, or you could not have recollected it afterwards. Have you often seen this Mr. Newill since? What is become of him now?"

"He is gone to sea," replied Monimia.

"You have not seen him since?"

"Yes, certainly I have—I saw him the next day."

"Where?" cried Orlando, impatiently.

"I was obliged," answered Monimia, "because Mrs. Newill was now going immediately to join her imprisoned husband, to be up early to pack up some things in the shop for the person who had brought them;

and while I did it, all my sorrows pressing with insupportable weight on my mind, and above all, your loss, Orlando—I wept as I proceeded in my task of tying up band-boxes and parcels, and yet I hardly knew I wept; when young Newill entered the place where I was, and offered to help me—"Good God!" said he, "you are crying!" He took my hand, it was wet with tears."

"And he kissed them off," cried Orlando, again wildly starting from his chair, "I know he did—yes! this stranger, infinitely more dangerous than Belgrave ..."

"Oh! dear Orlando," said Monimia, with a deep and tremulous sigh, "what is it you suspect me of? Do not, I beseech you, destroy me as soon as we have met, by suspicions, which indeed, if you will hear me with patience ..."

"Go on, Monimia," said he, recovering himself—"go on, and I will be as patient as I can—but this Newill"—"Always," said Monimia, "behaved to me like the tenderest brother, and it is to him alone I am indebted for the safety and protection I have found. Yet it is true, Orlando, and I will not attempt to conceal it from you, that young Newill in this first interview professed himself my lover; but when I assured him that all my affections were buried with you, that it was out of my power to make him any other return to the regard he expressed for me, than gratitude; and if he would be so much my friend as to influence his mother, either to prevail upon my aunt to receive me, or to let me remain with any creditable person in the country, instead of taking me to London (where I had too much reason to believe I was to be exposed anew to the persecutions of Sir John Belgrave), I should be eternally indebted to him—this he promised to undertake, and seemed to acquiesce in my refusal of his addresses, which had I been capable of listening to them, it would have been very indiscreet on his part to have pursued; for he was possessed of nothing but the pay of a midshipman, and out of that little had often contributed to relieve the distresses of his parents; and now on hearing of his father's confinement, immediately after his return from a cruise, in which the frigate he was on board had taken two small prizes, he hastened to their assistance; and bearing with sailor-like philosophy all present evils, and never considering those of the future, he was treating for the advance of his pay for the next half year, in order to enable his mother to discharge some debts for which her creditors were very clamorous, before she left the town. Yet did he, under such circumstances, think very seriously of a wife—I believe that he supposed the dejection of my spirits was rather owing to my forlorn situation, than to an attachment which he had no notion of as existing after the death of its object, and that I should gradually be induced to listen to his love."

"Yet," cried Orlando warmly, "yet you talk of the brotherly and of the disinterested regard of this new friend of yours."

"It was so in effect, Orlando, and I did not too minutely enquire into the motive of his conduct. Allow me to go on and you will own that we are both much obliged to him. When he fully understood the nature of my situation, my invincible aversion to Sir John Belgrave, and my fears, which, mortifying as they must be to him, I could not help expressing, lest his father should prevail on Mrs. Newill to betray me entirely into his power—he expressed in his rough sea language so much pity for me, and so much indignation at the conduct of his family, that I became persuaded I might trust him. But, alas! I had nothing to entrust him with—no means of escape from the evils I dreaded to propose to him—except Mrs. Roker, I had no friend or relation in the world.—I had written three letters to Selina, but I received no answer—and she too had, I feared, by the troubles of her own family, been compelled to appear for a while unmindful of her unhappy Monimia. —Young Mr. Newill desired a few hours to consider what he could do for me; and in that time he talked to his mother of her ungenerous and base conduct in regard to me, with so much effect, that, after a struggle between her necessities and her conscience, she promised her son to receive no more the bribes of Sir John Belgrave, and even to let me quit her, if I insisted upon it. Having obtained thus much, he returned to me, and I was then to determine whither I would go. Oh! how gladly would I then have accepted of the lowest service! But who would take a creature apparently so slight as not to be able to do any kind of household work; and from such a woman as Mrs. Newill, who was but little esteemed either for her morals or her œconomy? In this distress I wrote again to Selina, entreating her to enquire for a place for me; but no answer came in the usual course of the post, and Newill's leave of absence expiring in three days, it became necessary to determine on something. Fruitless as every written application had hitherto been to Mrs. Roker, I could think of nothing better than to address her in person; and as I dared not go so far alone, being ever in apprehension of meeting Sir John Belgrave, Mr. Newill offered to go with me, and ..."

"How did you go?" said Orlando, interrupting her.

"In the stage to Alresford," replied Monimia; "and from thence we walked to the house, where, however, I was refused admittance by a sister of Roker's, who told me her poor dear sister-in-law was in a bad state of health; that nobody could be admitted to see her; and advised me by all means not to depend upon any thing she could do for me, since her condition put all attention to business out of the question; and Miss Roker was sorry indeed to remind me, that my perverse undutiful behaviour had not a little contributed to derange the faculties of my worthy relation. I could have answered, that her faculties were certainly deranged when she married Mr. Roker; but I had no opportunity to make this observation if I had had courage enough—for the woman shut the door in my face, repeating in very rude terms, "that any visits there would be to no purpose."

"Thus driven from the habitation of my only relation, I returned more broken-hearted than I set out to Winchester."

"And your protector, I suppose, renewed his solicitations by the way?" said Orlando.

"No indeed," answered Monimia, "he had too much sensibility; and whatever he might intend for the future, he too much respected the grief into which this cruel repulse had plunged me. The next day but one he was to go back to his duty, with a young shipmate who was visiting his mother then at Southampton, who was to call upon him, that they might return together. While I was yet undetermined what to do, time passed away, and this comrade of Mr. Newill's arrived. It was young Fleming, the eldest son of your friend, whom his mother's relation, an old captain of a man of war, had taken from Winchester college at eighteen, and adopted at his father's death upon condition of his becoming a sailor—a condition which Mrs. Fleming, who had so recently lost her husband, lamented, but dared not oppose. War had just deprived her of her first support; yet him on whom she next relied she was compelled to part with for the same dreadful trade, because her pension, as a lieutenant's widow, which was almost her sole dependence, was very insufficient for the support of her four other children; the two little girls you saw with me last night, another yet younger, and her second boy, whom her relation partly supports at an academy, intending him also for the sea—and who would have been so much offended, had she thwarted him in regard to taking the eldest son from college, that he would have renounced the whole family.

"To this young man, who was his most intimate friend, Newill communicated, but not without first asking my permission, the difficulties I was under; concealing however those circumstances that seemed to reflect so much disgrace on his mother. They consulted together what I could do ..."

"Excellent and proper counsellors truly!" exclaimed Orlando impatiently.

"Less improper than you imagine," replied Monimia. "Fleming had not, like Newill, been so long at sea as to acquire that steadiness of mind which enables men of that profession to look on all personal danger with indifference, and on moral evil as a matter of course. But yet, recollecting not only his classics, but the romances he had delighted in at school, he had that natural and acquired tenderness of mind which made him sensible at once of all the discomforts of my situation. He saw in me a poor, deserted heroine of a novel, and nothing could be in his opinion so urgent as my relief.—Accustomed in all emergencies to apply to his mother, to whom he is the most affectionate and dutiful of sons ..."

"What is become of this Fleming?" enquired Orlando, "is he often at home with his mother?"

"No; he went almost immediately after my first becoming acquainted with her, to the East-Indies—but your impatience, Orlando, will not let me conclude my sad story. Fleming seeing the affair in the light I have described, settled with his friend Newill that the latter should return alone to the ship—make some excuse for Fleming's being absent two days longer, while he would return to his mother, and endeavour by her means to find some proper asylum for me. The readiness with which Newill consented to this plan, convinced me of his disinterestedness; though I own I had little hope of its success. I supposed that Mrs. Fleming would have suspected the zeal of so young a man for a woman of my age, in distress, and would decline interfering for a person of whom she could know nothing. But the generosity of my young advocate rendered him eloquent; and she to whom he pleaded was not only naturally of the most candid and humane disposition, but her own sorrows had so softened her heart, that calamity never pleaded to her in vain, though her circumstance are such as do not always enable her to relieve it, as her heart dictates.

"This excellent woman reflected, that there must be something remarkable in the situation which had made so great an impression of her son; and that even if I was a young woman whom necessity had reduced to a discreditable mode of life, her kindness might yet save me from deeper destruction. With this human persuasion, and remembering always the maxim of doing as she would be done by, she came herself to Winchester, to enquire what she could do for me—thinking, as she has since told me, that she ought to do this, if she hoped for the mercy of Heaven towards her own girls, who might, by so likely an event as her death, be as desolate and friendless as I was. I am too much exhausted, Orlando, to be particular now in relating our first interview. We shall, I hope, have frequent opportunities of admiring the simplicity of character, the goodness of heart, and the attractive manners of my benefactress, who, from your description of your mother, is almost her counterpart. It is sufficient if I tell you that Mrs. Fleming not only implicitly believed my melancholy story, but, as nothing immediately occurred to her for my permanent relief, determined to take me home with her, till some eligible situation could be found. When she had been a little accustomed to me, she would not part with me; I have been so happy as to make myself useful to her and her children; and in acquitting myself as far as I could of my debt of gratitude, I have found the best and only defence against that regret and anguish which devoured me. She had sorrows enough of her own; I forbore therefore to oppress her with mine, and I tried to be calm when I could not be cheerful; but when the conversation turned on the loss she had sustained in her husband, I mingled my tears with hers, and wept for Orlando."

Orlando, forgetting in this tender confession the little jealousies he had felt, while he considered her liable to the addresses of a rival, now pressed her fondly to his heart; and seeing her quite overcome by the fatigue of relating so long a narrative, and the violence of those emotions she had so lately experienced, consented to leave her, and they parted for the night; though Orlando could not wish her good night without protesting to her that he would never again consent to be separated from her, even for a day; for that if ever he was absent from her again, the insolent Sir John Belgrave would incessantly pursue her in imagination, and he should believe her exposed again to dangers and insults which it almost drove him to madness to recollect she had already endured.

CHAP. X.

In retiring to the room Mrs. Fleming had ordered to be prepared for him, Orlando attempted not to sleep: but his imagination was busied in considering how, since he had so unexpectedly found Monimia, he might escape the misery of ever again parting with her. Poor as he was, he had long since determined, that if she was restored to him, he would marry her, and trust to Providence, and his own exertions, for her support:—and since he had heard all the dangers, trials, and insults, to which her unprotected and desolate situation had made her liable, he could not bear to think of ever quitting her again, even for a day.

Yet, circumstanced as he was, their immediate union was attended with innumerable difficulties: his mother would, he feared, be secretly averse, though she might not openly oppose it; and as to deceiving her, he would not think of it.

Monimia, being under age, could not be married without the consent of her aunt, her only near relation, which he knew it would be impossible to obtain; and all the other impediments were in the way which occur in regard to a minor, and which there seemed no ways of obviating but by a journey to Scotland.[1] Yet the business of the disputed will, so very important to him, was to come on, as he believed, the ensuing Term, and it was to begin in a few days; a consideration that, added to the expence of such a journey, out of his little fortune, which was reduced within an hundred and fifty pounds, made him hesitate concerning an expedition so distant and expensive. After long debates with himself, he recollected that Warwick had been married to Isabella at Jersey or Guernsey; and as he was so near the coast, from whence a passage to those islands might be obtained, he resolved to propose such an excursion to Monimia, and to procure the consent of the friend to whose kindness she was so much indebted.

This was not difficult; for Mrs. Fleming, prejudiced in favour of Orlando, on account of the friendship her husband had for him, and believing that his mind possessed all those virtues his ingenuous countenance and liberal manners expressed;—knowing too how truly her young friend was attached to him, imagined that she must be happy in such a union, whatever might be their pecuniary difficulties. Monimia had no will but his; and no anxiety now hung on the mind of Orlando, but in regard to his mother.—He doubted whether he ought not to consult her before he married; yet as her disapprobation would only render him and Monimia unhappy, without changing his resolution, he concluded it would be best to trust to her affection for him, and the impression which Monimia's beauty and innocence could not, he thought, fail to make in her favour, when he presented her to his mother, as his wife. Very little preparation was necessary for their short voyage.—Mrs. Fleming gave her blessing to the weeping Monimia as

---

[1]   Since Scotland had a lower age of consent than England, many eloping couples journeyed to Gretna Green (the first town over the border) in order to marry without a parent or guardian's consent.

she parted with her, and gave it with a tenderness and fervency not always found in the friends who surround the brides of higher fortune.—It was agreed that the young couple should return to her as soon as they were married, and go from thence to London.

Orlando found no difficulty in procuring a vessel to transport them to Guernsey.—Notwithstanding the season of the year, the weather was mild, and the wind favourable. Within ten days from their departure, Orlando brought back his wife to Mrs. Fleming's solitude, secure that death alone could divide them.

They remained with their respectable friend only two days. It was now time for Orlando to be in London, and they hastened thither, too happy to reflect on what was to become of them, and with no other solicitude on their minds, than what arose from the idea of their first meeting with Mrs. Somerive.—And this dwelt more on the spirits of Orlando, than he chose to communicate to his wife.

On their arrival in town, he ordered the chaise to the chambers of his friend Carr, as he would not abruptly introduce Monimia to his mother. He went alone to procure a lodging in the neighbourhood of his family; which being easily found, they took possession of it in the evening—as Orlando required yet some time to prepare himself for disclosing a secret, which he still feared, manage it how he would, might give pain to his mother.

About one o'clock, however, the following morning he went to Howland-street. His mother, who had been very uneasy at his long absence, received him with even more than her usual affection; but her expressions of pleasure at seeing him, were mingled with tears. All that had happened to his brother, had come to her knowledge; and to his excessive concern, he heard that Philip, after applying to his mother for money, with which she could not supply him, had again disappeared, and was, as they had reason to believe, again imprisoned.

In beholding his mother under such depression of mind, he could not determine to inform her of what might possibly add to it; but instead of speaking to her of Monimia, as he intended, he endeavoured to appease the agony of her mind about Philip, whom he promised to find, and gave her hopes that they should succeed in the recovery of the Rayland estate. To Selina alone he communicated his recent marriage; and found with additional concern, that she dreaded the effect this intelligence would have on her mother, who was already overwhelmed with anxiety for her eldest son, and whose maternal grief had been lately awakened by having heard that her daughter Isabella was certainly living in one of the American islands with her husband, long after they had been given over for lost:—yet, as she concluded that her daughter, if yet living, was totally estranged from her family, or regardless of their distress; a reflection not less bitter than it was to consider her as dead. The doubt of what was really her fate, proved perhaps more distressing than any certainty. With all this, were Orlando's marriage to be discovered to her, while she was continually expressing her anxiety how he would himself be supported, Selina dreaded the consequence of her uneasiness; and therefore entreated Orlando to defer the discovery at least for a few days, in hopes that something favourable might happen; while she herself expressed the warmest solicitude to see and embrace Monimia, as her beloved sister; and they agreed that Orlando should find some pretence to take her the next day out with him, and carry her to his lodgings for that purpose.[1]

With an heavy heart he now returned to Monimia, who anxiously expected him.—A poor dissembler, he could not conceal from her the state of his mind; but he led her to believe it was rather owing to the new distress occasioned by Philip's disappearance, than to any doubts as to her reception by his mother. Her gentle and soothing conversation was the only balm for his wounded heart; and while he felt himself unhappy, he considered how much less so he was now, than when, in addition to the calamities of his family, he had the loss of his Monimia to lament, and the dread of all those evils to which her desolate state exposed her.

As soon as he had dined, he set out, in pursuance of his promise to his mother, to find Philip; but while Carr sent his clerk, and went himself to some of the places where it was but too probable he was to be found, Orlando himself visited another; but when they met at night at Carr's chambers, all their enquiries were found equally fruitless; and they agreed, that if this unhappy young man was, as there was too much reason to believe, in confinement, he had taken precautions not to be discovered. With this unsatisfactory intelligence, Orlando, late as it was, went back to his mother; but, assuring her he would never rest till he had found out, and relieved his brother, he told her, that as he must now be constantly engaged with Mr. Carr in arranging the business of the law-suit, and must be at his chambers early in a morning, he had taken

---

[1]   Orlando's secret marriage, and his later ability to see Monimia "always busy" without asking her what with (and thus allowing her to "add a little to the slender stock on which depended their existence" "without shocking his tenderness or his pride"), shadow his romantic elopement with "anti-romance": Smith shows the risks inherent in romance while also questioning Orlando's claim to the status of "hero."

a lodging near him, the time of going so far as from Howland-street to the inn of court being more than he could now spare. This accounted for his absence tolerably well; yet his heart smote him for this temporary deception, which was however, considering his circumstances at this juncture, only a pious fraud.

Another, another, and another day passed away without any news of Philip; and, to add to the vexation of Orlando, he found new difficulties likely to arise in his suit. Old Roker, to whom subornation of perjury was familiar, and every other infamous device which an unprincipled villain could be guilty of, had not only taken the usual method of gaining time by artificial delays, but was, it was feared, putting it out of Mrs. Roker's (Lennard's) power to give her testimony against the will that had been proved, by making her a lunatic; he was infamous enough to have taken still more decisive means of quieting both her conscience and her evidence, if they had not been rendered less eligible by the circumstance of great part of her income having been left her for her life only.

Carr, who had all the zeal of a young man for his client, and was perfectly convinced, from the substance of Mr. Walterson's report, that there had been another will, was yet doubtful of their success against the impudence and chicane of the Rokers; supported by two such powerful motives, as their own interest, and the purse of a rich body of clergy. Orlando therefore saw with anguish of mind his own little fund dwindling away, without any certainty that such part of it as went to the payment of law expences would ever be repaid him: and the sad idea of Monimia in as great poverty as that from which he had rescued her, continually corroded his heart; while she, from his long delay in presenting her to his mother, and from the knowledge she had of his little fortune, perceived but too clearly, in a depression of spirits which he could not always disguise, what were his fears. These she tried to dissipate, by assuming herself an air of cheerfulness—"I have always been used to work, Orlando," said she—"you know that I never was brought up to any other expectation—where then will be the difficulty or hardship of my employing myself to assist in our mutual support? and surely it will be better to begin now, than to wait till our necessities become more pressing. Since I shall not disgrace your family by it; since I am unknown to every body but Selina, who has too much sense to love me less, why should I not directly engage in what sooner or later I must, I ought to have recourse to?"—Orlando, who thought that all the world ought to be at the feet of a creature whose mind seemed to him even more lovely than her person, was so hurt and mortified whenever she thus expressed herself, that she by degrees ceased to repeat it; but as he was now very much out with Carr, she contrived in his absence to apply to a very considerable linen warehouse in the neighbourhood, the proprietors of which at first trusted her with articles of small value to make; by degrees she acquired their confidence! and, by the neatness and punctuality of her performance, entered soon into constant employment.—Orlando saw her always busy; but he made no remarks on what occupied her; and without shocking his tenderness or his pride, she was thus enabled to add a little to the slender stock on which depended their subsistence. Thus in continual combats with himself, whether he ought not to acquaint his mother with his situation, in fruitless enquiries after his brother, and in hopes and fears about the event of his suit, passed the first six weeks of his marriage.—Term was now over, and the discovery of the true will of Mrs. Rayland did not seem to be at all nearer than when he first undertook it.

Encouraged, however, by his friend Carr, to proceed, though he often trembled at the proofs that came to his knowledge, of the successful villany of Roker, Orlando failed not to pursue such means as his solicitor thought most requisite; and, amid all the fatigue and disappointments of the law's delay, which often baffled him where he most sanguinely hoped for advantage, the tenderness, the sweetness of Monimia soothed and tranquillized his troubled spirits; and when he returned to her of an evening, wearied with the contradictory opinions of counsel, or tormented by trifling and unnecessary forms, he seemed to be transported from purgatory to paradise, and forgot that, if some favourable event did not soon occur, he should be unable to support this adored being, to whom he was more fondly attached as an husband than he had been as a lover.

His mother, who had been at first satisfied with his reasons for absenting himself from her house, now began (since his law-business was she thought for a while suspended) to express her uneasiness that he no longer resided with her. To the expression of this discontent she was particularly excited by her brother, Mr. Woodford, whose boisterous manners, though softened even to mean obsequiousness before his superiors, were still exerted to keep in subjection the mild and timid spirit of his sister, who considered herself besides as obliged to him, because he had afforded her some small pecuniary assistance, rather to preserve his own pride from being wounded, than to oblige and serve her.

Orlando, extremely disgusted by the reception he met with at the house of his uncle on his arrival in London, had never again visited him; and had avoided, as if by accident, meeting him at his mother's; where he did not indeed often visit, being become a much richer, and consequently a much greater man, since he had been the *ostensible* possessor of a very lucrative contract, which he held to so much advantage as reconciled him to the necessity of relinquishing a seat in parliament for a Cornish borough, with which he had obliged some of his powerful friends. He was not therefore a *representative of twenty or thirty electors, who had been paid for their suffrages at so much a head*; but such were now his qualifications of purse and of pride, that he was admitted to the cabals of those who had the distinction of an M.P. after their names; and was often closeted with the secretaries of yet greater men, consulted on loans, let into the secret of stocks, and was accommodated with scrip and other douceurs with which those who *deserve well of government* are gratified; he was besides a director of an opulent company, and received, in addition to the salary of the office, considerable presents from those who had favours to request. Mrs. Woodford waddled about in the most valuable shawls; mandarins and josses nodded over her chimneys; and pagodas and japans ornamented her rooms. The two young ladies were both married; the elder to a merchant, who was a sharer in some of the fortunate adventures of his father-in-law, and besides in a flourishing business. His lady was one of the elegant and fashionable women on the other side Temple-bar: but the little circumstance of her being compelled to live on that other side, continually embittered her good fortune: having been accustomed to see people who are called of rank, in the early part of her life, she was so much flattered by having acquired admission to some few now, that she talked of nothing but lords. If she related what happened at the opera, Lord Robert was sitting by her at the time, and said so and so; if she spoke of her losses or successes at cards, Lady Frances or Lady Louisa were her party; and sometimes Sir James or Sir George betted on her side: but whenever this equestrian order were introduced, she took care to impress upon the minds of her audience, that she spoke of men who really bore the arms of Ulster, and not of any paltry city knight;[1] whom, together with every thing in the city, she held in sovereign contempt; having quite forgotten herself, and desiring that every body else should forget the preceding years, when she was a wine-merchant's daughter in the Strand, and glad of an hackney-coach to a benefit play; or supremely happy to be acquainted with any one who kept their own carriage, and would take her "to the other end of the town."

---

[1] Like Mrs. Rayland, Mrs. Woodford only believes in the worth of birth: a "paltry city knight" is newly-created rather than hereditary.

The acquaintance and notice of General Tracy had been almost their first step towards emerging from middling life to the confines of fashion; therefore the lady now in question, and her sister, who was become the wife of a counsellor in Lincoln's-inn-fields, were never able to forgive the Somerive family, for having first fascinated the uncle, and then the nephew, whose notice they had always coveted, because he was among the first of those who had obtained the name of "a fashionable man about town," and one whose approbation was decisive in determining on the beauty and elegance of the female candidates for general admiration.

Young Woodford too, though he had failed of marrying the rich young Jewess, either because of his indifference towards her, or of the preference she gave at the time he was first acquainted with her to Orlando, had since married the daughter of a great underwriter, and was in high affluence. The whole of the Woodford family, being thus circumstanced, looked down with contempt on the remains of that of Somerive; and, under the semblance of pity, enjoyed their depression, particularly that of Orlando, of whom, in talking of him to his mother, Mr. Woodford affected to speak with great concern.

"'Tis of no use," said he, "to remember what is passed, since to be sure it only serves to vex one; but I must say, it was a thousand pities, sister Somerive, that you suffered this young man to refuse the advantageous offer that I made him. If I had taken him into my house, only think how differently he would have been situated from what he is now!—God bless my soul, I declare 'tis a sad thing!—In the first place, he would have been now as well off as Martin my partner is now, which, let me tell you, is no bad thing; besides that as *my* nephew, and in partnership with *me*, he might have married, let me tell you, any woman of fortune in the city, and might now be a man of the first consideration; nay, in parliament for aught I know.—Instead of that, what is the case now?—First of all, there was waiting upon and coaxing that foolish, proud old woman, who after all did nothing for him; but saw him set off with a brown musket, to be shot at for half-a-crown a day, or whatever it is; and then forsooth left her estate to a parcel of fat-gut parsons, as if that would do her old squeezy soul any good in t'other world—For my part, I don't desire to vex you—what is done, why, it cannot be helped: only I must say that 'tis a devilish kettle of fish altogether. Here, instead of this young fellow's being an help to you, he is like, for what I can see, to be a burthen. Since things are as they are, I see no reason why he should be humoured in idleness now, and, under the pretence of following up this law-suit, lounge away any more of his time: as to the recovery of the

Rayland estate, you may as well sue for so many acres in the moon; take my word for it, sister Somerive."

This brutish speech being answered only by the sighs and tears of the dejected auditor, her consequential brother stopped a moment for breath, and then proceeded:

"However, don't be cast down: you know that though my opinion has always gone for nothing, I am always willing to serve you, sister; and so I wish you would, before 'tis too late, and before your youngest son goes the way of your eldest, think a little of making him do something to get himself on in the world:—for my part, and I'm sure every body as knows any thing of life and human nature, will agree with me, that the boy will be undone if he goes on as he does at present; and I give you warning, that in a little time there won't be a pin to choose between him and that hopeful youth, 'squire Philip."

This was almost too much for poor Mrs. Somerive, who however commanded her tears and sobs so far as to ask her brother what reason he had to think so.

He then communicated to her, as he assured her in perfect friend-ship, that there was great reason to suppose Orlando kept a mistress, and was lavishing on her the small remains of the money his commission had sold for; and upon her beseeching him to tell her what reason he had to believe so, he informed her that not only it was false that Orlando had taken a lodging near the inns of court in order to be near Carr, but that he actually lived within two streets of his mother's house, with a young woman who had of late been frequently met with him of an evening, leaning on his arm, and whom, on enquiry, he was found to have brought with him from the country.

Thunderstruck with intelligence which Orlando's general air of absence and impatience when he was with his family gave her too much reason to believe was true, and dreading lest she had lost the sole stay on which she depended for the protection of her two girls in case of her death, the unhappy mother gave herself up to tears, nor could the rough hand of her cruel brother succeed in drying them. Distressed so cruelly, she caught eagerly at whatever had the appearance of reliev-ing her, and therefore promised to adhere to the advice Mr. Woodford gave her. He recommended it to her to press Orlando's return to her house: "by which," said he, "you will soon find out, if you don't believe it yet, that your pious good boy is not a whit better than t'other. And let me also desire you'll not let him go on helter skelter in this law-suit, with no better advice than a whiffled-headed fellow such as Carr can give him or get for him; but send him to Mr. Darby, my son-in-law, a man I can tell you that knows what he's about, and is a thriving man in the law. He shall not charge any thing upon your account for his advice; so you'll save five or ten guineas at once. I'll speak to Mr. Darby; and in the mean time, d'ye see, do you have some serious conversation with your son. Let him find out that we are not so easily to be gull'd; and that 'twont do to take old birds with chaff."

Mrs. Somerive then promised to do as he dictated; and he left her, after this conversation, one of the most miserable beings on earth.

Orlando, the next time he saw his mother, found the effects of his uncle's ungenerous interference. She received him with an air of constraint to which he was little accustomed, and which seemed to be attended with extreme pain to herself: she questioned him in a tone she had never taken up before; seemed dissatisfied with his answers, which certainly were embarrassed and contradictory; and ended the conversation with telling him that, unless he would extremely disoblige her, he must lay the whole state of the question as to the Rayland estate before Mr. Darby, his cousin's husband. This Orlando promised to do, being very desirous of obliging his mother wherever he could do it without betraying a secret which he thought it would distress her to know; and, desirous to end as soon as he could a conversation so painful, he agreed to go directly to Carr, and procure a proper state of the affair for the opinion of counsel; and to wait on Mr. Darby the next morning, against which time Mrs. Somerive was to give him notice, by Mr. Woodford, of the application of this client.

Orlando owed too much to the good nature, integrity, and industry of his friend Carr, not to use the greatest precaution against offending him; but the moment he opened his business, and told him what his mother had insisted upon, Carr very candidly offered to promote this application without prejudice to those he had already made; and the case, and steps already taken in the business, having been prepared, Orlando waited the next day on Mr. Darby according to his own appointment, and for the first time was introduced to him at once as his cousin and his client. The lady, formerly Miss Eliza Woodford, "kept her state;"[1] and Orlando, instead of being shewn into her dressing-room to wait till Mr. Darby should be at liberty to speak to him, as he would naturally have been if he had fortunately been a rich relation, was shewn into a back room, surrounded by books that seemed more for shew than use, and desired to wait.

---

[1] *Julius Caesar*, I.ii.161.

Here he remained more than half an hour, before his relation learned in the law appeared. He was a tall, awkward, raw-boned man, with a pale face, two small wild grey eyes, and a squirrel-coloured riding-wig; who, having coldly saluted his new acquaintance, took his case, and, looking slightly over it as Orlando explained his situation, he said (drawing in his breath at every word, and doubling in his lips so that they disappeared)— "Hum, had; hum—I see ... Hum, hum, hum; I observe a!—Hum a!—I perceive a!—Yes a—Hum!—dean and chapter—hum; so a—Doctor Hollybourn a, hum—I know him—hum a—know him a little ..." Then rubbing his forehead, added, "a respectable—hum! a—man, a—a Doctor Hollybourn—man of very considerable, hum, a—property, a—hum, a—"

Orlando, marvelling how this man, with his inverted lips, and the hum-a's that broke every second word, could be reckoned to make a respectable figure at the bar, now began, as the eloquent counsel was silent, another explanatory speech; which, however, he was not allowed to finish, for Mr. Darby, again assuring him that Doctor Hollybourn was very rich, and of course very respectable, said, he could not think that—hum, a—the doctor, so worthy a man as he was, would be accessary in—hum a, injuring any one, or keeping the right heir out of his estate; but, hum a—hum a—there must be some misrepresentation: but that, however, he was engaged that morning with two briefs, of the utmost importance; therefore, he would consider the thing at his leisure, and let him know in a few days—hum a—. Orlando, then leaving his compliments to Mrs. Darby, hastened away, rather repenting of his visit, and having gained, he thought, nothing by it, but what was likely to end in a hum a!

On his return to Carr's chambers, his friend accosted him with an enquiry how he liked the special pleader?—"A special pleader d'ye call him?" cried Orlando; "for Heaven's sake, wherefore?"

"Because it is our name," replied Carr, "for a particular branch of our profession."

"Curse the fellow!" cried Orlando—"A special pleader! why he cannot speak at all—with his hum a, and hum a."

"That would not signify so much," said Carr, "if the man was honest; but I may say to you, that, under the most specious professions of honesty, I don't believe there is a more crafty or mercenary head in Westminster Hall, than that orange tawny caxon of his covers. The hesitation and embarrassment of his oratory was at first the effect of stupidity; but by degrees, as acquired chicane supplies the place of natural talent, he has continued it, because it is a sort of excuse for never giving an immediate or positive answer; and while he is hum a-ing and haw a-ing, he is often considering how he may best make his advantage of the affairs confided to him."

"Good God!" exclaimed Orlando, "and why, then, would you let me apply to such a man?"

"Nay," replied Carr, "how could I pretend to engage you to decline a reference recommended by your mother? Besides, you know, my friend, that in our profession we make it a rule never to speak as we think. What? would you have an apothecary declaim against a physician in whose practice it is to occasion the greatest demand for drugs?"

"Hang your simile!" said Orlando: "I am afraid you are all rogues together."

"More or less, my good friend—some of more sense than others, and some a little, little more conscience—but, for the rest, I am afraid we are all of us a little too much professional rogues; though some of us, as individuals, would not starve the orphan, or break the heart of the widow—but in our vocation, Hal![1] labouring in our vocation, we give all remorse of that sort to the winds."

"Would your profession were annihilated, then!" cried Orlando.

"Why, I do not believe," answered Carr, "that the world would be much the worse if it were; but, my friend, not to be too hard upon *us*, do reflect on the practices of other professions. The little, smirking fellow, with so smiling an aspect, and so well-powdered a head, whom you see pass in his chariot, administers to his patient the medicines a physician orders, though he knows they are more likely to kill than cure; and, in his account at night, thinks not of the tears of a family whom he has seen in the greatest distress, but of the bill he shall have for medicines and attendance. The merchant, who sits down in his compting-house, and writes to his correspondent at Jamaica, that his ship, the Good Intent of Liverpool, is consigned to him at Port-Royal with a cargo of slaves from the coast of Guinea, calculates the profits of a fortunate adventure, but never considers the tears and blood with which this money is to be raised. He hears not the groans of an hundred human creatures confined together in the hold of a small merchantman—he ..."

"Do," cried Orlando, "dear Carr, finish your catalogue of human crimes, unless you have a mind to make me go home and hang myself."

"No man would do that," answered Carr, "who had such a lovely wife as you have—she would reconcile me to a much worse world than this is."

---

[1] *1 Henry IV*, I.ii.92. In the play, Falstaff's "vocation" is robbery.

The friends then parted; Orlando very far from being satisfied with his visit to his cousin learned in the law—and very uneasy, on his arrival at his mother's, to observe, in her behaviour to him, increased symptoms of that discontent he had observed the day before.

CHAP. XI.

Nearly six weeks more now passed; another Term was almost wasted in those contrived delays which destroy all the boasted energy and simplicity of the British laws; when Mr. Carr advised Orlando to see Dr. Hollybourn himself; which, however disagreeable it was to him, he at length consented to do, at the earnest and repeated request of one who he believed had his real interest much at heart. Orlando had lately suffered so much uneasiness at the deception he had been and was still guilty of towards his mother, that he found it almost impossible for him to continue it; but he was continually withheld from the avowal he wished to make, by the tears of Selina, and by his fears for the effect that a reluctant, or even an affectionate reception might have on the timid spirits of his wife, whose situation increased his tenderness and anxiety; while his reduced finances filled him with the most painful solicitude, as he reflected that, when they were quite exhausted, he should have nothing to support his Monimia and the infant he expected she would give him.[1]

Sacrificing to the remotest hope of benefiting objects so precious to him, his own reluctance to make a very disagreeable visit, he repaired to the residence of Dr. Hollybourn, at an hour when he was told the reverend Divine was most likely to be at home.

On his arrival, however, he heard the Doctor was out: but as a coach was waiting at the door, he doubted this: and, while he was yet speaking to the footman at the door, another from the top of the stairs called out, "Let counsellor Darby's coach draw up!"—Orlando then stepped forward into the hall, telling the servant that he had very particular business with Dr. Hollybourn, and could not call again; therefore that he must see him:—at the same moment Mr. Darby himself hurried down stairs, and Orlando met him in the hall.—The lawyer seemed in as

---

[1] It is now April or May 1779; Monimia is pregnant after only a few months of marriage (she should be about eighteen; Orlando is either about twenty-three or twenty-one).

much confusion when he met him, as such a lawyer is capable of being: slightly bowing, and muttering something of haste as he passed, he hurried into his coach; while Orlando, without waiting for the return of the footman, who was gone up to announce him to the Doctor, walked up stairs, and entered a very elegant room, where the worthy Doctor, looking more than ever like the uncle of Gil Blas,[1] was squatted on a sopha, with some papers before him, which, on the appearance of Orlando (whom he was ordering his servant to dismiss), he huddled away in some confusion.

Orlando now approached, and in few words opened his business, laying some stress upon the hardships he had suffered in being deprived of an estate to which his father was undoubtedly next heir, while it went to enrich a body who had no manner of occasion for such an acquisition of wealth.

The divine professor of humility and charity—he who some months before offered his most accomplished daughter to the then fortunate Orlando, now deigned not to ask him to sit; but, cocking up his little red nose, and plumping down again on his cushion, he began to snuffle forth his wonder at this application. He said, "God forbid, young man, that I, as executor to the late worthy lady of Rayland Hall, whose soul is now with the blessed, should defraud you or any man! But that pious woman, the last remains of an ancient, honourable, and religious family, to be sure knew best what would most contribute to the glory of the Lord, and the good of his creatures; among the poor and needy of whom she left her noble fortune to be divided, and I shall take care most sacredly to perform her worthy wish, and to sanctify her estate to the holy purposes she intended it for."

Orlando, who could not command the indignation he felt against this canting hypocrite, now very loudly and peremptorily demanded to know, "Whether Doctor Hollybourn was not well apprised, that there was another will made by Mrs. Rayland, after that under which his society claimed the estate? and whether two persons had not declared, at Rayland Hall, that they knew it to be so, whose evidence Roker had since been employed to stifle?"—To this the Doctor said, "He understood he was to reply upon oath in putting in his answer to the bill in chancery, and therefore he should now say nothing: but if you, young man, have any thing more to say, you know where to find

---

[1] "A little fellow, three feet and a half high, as fat as you can conceive, with a head sunk between his shoulders." *Gil Blas*, trans. Smollett, I.i.

Mr. Roker, my solicitor; to him I refer you.—Here—Richard!—Peter!—John!—shew this person down!"—Orlando, by no means disposed to submit to this cavalier treatment, though the age and profession of the Doctor protected him from the effects of the resentment he felt, began however a severe remonstrance; which the Doctor not being disposed to listen to, rose from his sopha, and with the grace of a terrier bitch on the point of pupping, he waddled into the next room, and shut the door. Orlando then finding his attempts to argue such a sordid and selfish being into any sense of justice totally useless, left the house, and, returning to his friend Carr, related his adventures; where he had the mortification to have his suspicions confirmed by Carr, that, so far from his application to Mr. Darby being likely to produce any good, there was every appearance that he had entered the lists on the other side—"And this," said Carr, "has been a frequent practice with him; it being with this worthy man an invariable maxim, inherited I believe from his father, that no man is poor, but from his own faults and follies—for which, though no man has been guilty of more than he has in the former part of his life, he professes to have no pity—And as to the law, he is not much out, nor was your honest friend the miller, in saying, that he who has the longest purse is in this country the most frequently successful."

Orlando, with an heart not much lightened by the transactions of the day, returned to his lodgings to a late dinner.—Monimia was ill, a circumstance that added to the gloom that hung over him:—she made light of it however, and endeavoured to restore to him that cheerfulness, of which, she observed with great uneasiness, he had been some time deprived; but it is difficult to communicate to others sensations we do not feel ourselves.—She smiled, but tears were in her eyes—She assured him she suffered nothing; but he saw her pale and languid, and now was confirmed in what he had long fancied, that the air of London did not agree with her; and it was with inexpressible anguish he reflected, that now, when the tenderest attention to her health was necessary, he was deprived of the means of procuring her country air, which, as spring advanced, she seemed to languish for.—London, where she had never been before, was at first unpleasant, and now disgusting to her; but she never betrayed this but by accident, and wished Orlando to believe that with him every place was to her a heaven.

He now more seldom went to his mother's than he used to do; because, since her dialogue with Mr. Woodford, all her tenderness for him did not prevent her teasing him with questions, and very earnestly pressing him to return to his usual apartment in her house. This some-what estranged him from his family: but in absenting himself, he found no peace; for though he saw less of his mother and sisters than he used to do, he was as fondly attached to them as ever: and while he thought he saw, in the conduct of his mother, new reasons to adhere to that secrecy which it had already given him so much pain to observe, he imputed it all to the influence of the unfeeling and mercenary Mr. Woodford, and, in his most gloomy moods, wished that so unhappy a being as he was had never been born. A thousand times he repented of his having ever left Rayland Hall, to which unfortunate absence all his subsequent disappointments were owing; and sometimes lamented, though he could not repent, that he had married his Monimia, without being able to shield her, as his wife, from the poverty of her former lot.

Nothing gave him more mortification, than to find that his mother was not satisfied with his conduct in regard to Mr. Darby; and would not be persuaded that it was the affluence of his opposers, and not his doubts about the cause, that prevented his engaging it. Mr. Woodford, taking advantage of the faith his sister reposed in him as understanding business, had so harassed her with representations of Orlando's neglect, the inexperience of Carr, and the want of skill in the counsel he employed, that Mrs. Somerive now often pressed him to leave the management of the whole to his uncle, and to withdraw it from Carr; and wearied by these importunities, and by the delays which the adverse party seemed determined still to contrive, Orlando was sometimes half tempted to give up the pursuit, and, with the little money he yet had left, to retire to some remote village, where, wholly unknown, he might work at any certain, though laborious business, for the support of his wife and child:—but, when he saw the tears that his mother shed in speaking to him of his brother Philip, who had entirely deserted his family, after having, as far as he could, undone it, he could not deter-mine to plunge her into equal, perhaps greater uneasiness on his account; and he then resolved rather to suffer any pain himself, than to fail in those duties which he felt he ought to fulfil.

It was in one of the most melancholy moods, which the increasing difficulties of his situation inspired, that Orlando, sitting alone in the little dining room of his lodgings, when Monimia's indisposition confined her to her bed, that he composed a little ode to Poverty, which he had hardly put on paper, when Carr came in, to whom he carelessly shewed it. Carr, who had a taste for poetry, desired a copy of it; to which Orlando replied, "that he was too idle to copy it, but that he might have the original, for he should himself perhaps never look at it again." Carr put it into his pocket, and, asking "if he might do what he would with it?" Orlando answered, "Yes," and thought no more about it.

Carr had often told Orlando, as they talked over his situation together, "that he had literary talents, which might be employed to advantage;" and he said, "he should get acquainted with some of the writers of the day, who were the most esteemed, or at least the most fashionable, who would help him into notice."

"Nay," said Orlando, "if what I write will not help me into notice, I am afraid, my friend, the trade of authorship, which will not do without recommendation, will be but little worth following."

"It is not certainly," replied his friend, "the very best trade that can be followed in any way, but yet is not so despicable as you suppose:— for example, if you could write a play now, and get it received by the managers; and if it should be successful ..."

"Dear Carr," cried Orlando, "how many ifs are here!—I have no dramatic talents; nor, if I had, do I know one of the managers; or could I conquer, by dint of attendance, the difficulties which, I have heard you say, they throw in the way of authors—I should probably not be successful."

"And yet," said Carr, "there have been very successful authors, who have not the natural turn to poetry which you seem to me to have; indeed, who have none; but who have contrived, by bringing together a few scenes without any plot, a scattering of equivocal expressions, and some songs (which, being set to pretty music, we do not discover are not even rhyme), have really had wonderful success; and those who have succeeded once, get into fashion, and succeed in a second piece, because they have done so in the first."

"They must, however," said Orlando, "have more genius than you are willing to allow them."

"You shall judge, if you will," said Carr, "of them, as far as conversation will enable you to judge.—A relation of mine is a constant attendant at the conversations of one of our celebrated authoresses—I have sometimes gone thither with him, and have been often invited to go, since my first introduction, either with him, alone, or with any literary friend. The lady is never so well pleased as when her room is crowded with men, who either are, or fancy they are men of genius. She professes to dote upon, to adore genius in our sex; though, in her own, she will hardly allow it to any body but herself."

Orlando hesitated, at first, whether it was worth while to give up Monimia's company for an evening, for the sake of being introduced into this society, of which he did not form any very great expectations; but Carr, who saw how much his spirits were depressed, urged him to try the experiment. "The assembly is not, I own," said he, "the very first of the kind in London; for, to the first, neither my relation or I have any chance of being admitted; but, I assure you, the lady of whom I speak is celebrated for her wit, and for the novelty of her poetry, if not for that of her plays; and you will find some people there, who may be worth being acquainted with."

Orlando consented to go on the following Friday, and Carr attended him accordingly.

He was introduced to a little ill-made woman,[1] with a pale complexion, pitted with the small-pox; two defects which her attachment to literature did not prevent her from taking all possible pains to conceal: there was in her air a conviction of self-consequence, which predominated over the tender languor she affected—Indeed it was towards the gentlemen only that this soft sensibility was apparently exhibited: Ladies, and especially those who had any pretence to those acquirements in which she believed herself to excel, were seldom or never admitted; and she professed to hold them in contempt.

Though no longer young, she believed herself still an object of affection and admiration; and that the beauties of her mind were irresistible to all men of taste.—They were indeed of a singular cast: but as there are collectors of grotesque drawings, and books, no otherwise valuable than because they are old; so there were minds who contemplated hers with some degree of admiration; who thought her verses were really poetry, and that her dramas (the productions of writers of the sixteenth and seventeenth centuries modernized) had really merit. As she was by no means insensible to perfection, if it appeared in the form of a young man, she was immediately struck with the figure and address of Orlando; and, amidst the something which was called wit and literary conversation that now began, she addressed herself particularly to him—enquired into his studies, and his taste in poetry—besought him to favour her with some of his productions, and seemed disposed to elect him to emulate, if not to rival, the Florios and Philanders with whom she held a tender correspondence in the news-papers.

Orlando, naturally of a gay temper, and easily seizing the ridiculous, entered at once into this singular character; and before he had been half

---

[1]   As Ehrenpreis persuasively argues, Mrs. Manby is based on the poet and playwright Hannah Cowley (542–43, n. to p. 507).

an hour in the company of this modern Centlivre,[1] she declared in a loud whisper to Carr, whom she beckoned across the room to come to her, "that he was the most divine creature she had ever conversed with." A gentleman was now announced by the name of Mr. Lorrain, at whose arrival the lady of the house expressed great pleasure; and said to Orlando, "Oh, Mr. Somerive! I shall now have an opportunity of introducing you to one of the most sublime geniuses of the age—a man of the warmest fancy, of the most exquisite wit."—Orlando looked towards the door where this phaenomenon was expected to enter, and saw, to his utter astonishment, a gentleman who seemed to him to be—Warwick.

He remained riveted to his chair, gazing on the stranger, who approached the lady of the house without noticing her guests. After he had however paid her some very extravagant compliments on her looks, and received her answers, which were designed to be at once tender and spirited, she desired to introduce him to a newly-acquired friend of hers; and Mr. Lorrain, turning his eyes to the young man who sat next her, discovered immediately, by the wonder expressed in his looks, that in this new acquaintance of hers, he had found an old acquaintance of his own.

A few confused words were all that either the one or the other was at first able to utter. Orlando, not much pleased with a change of name, which he thought boded no good to his sister, enquired very earnestly after her:—his brother-in-law, in increased confusion, which he seemed endeavouring to conquer, answered, "that she was well;" and then, as he found Orlando in no humour to connive at the deception, which for some reason of other he chose to practice, as to his name and situation, he took him by the arm, and begged he would walk with him to the other end of the room, where he told him, in a hurried way, "that he was but lately come to England, after a variety of distresses, and being afraid of his creditors, and for other reasons which he would hereafter give him, he had changed his name for the present;" of which he desired him not to speak in the company they were then in. "But my sister, Sir," said Orlando, "where is my sister?—has *she* too changed her name?"[2]—"Of course," replied Warwick, who seemed hurt at the vehemence with which he spoke.—"Well, Sir; but by whatever name you choose to have her called, you will allow me immediately to see her— Is she in town?"

---

[1] "This modern Centlivre": reference to Susannah Centlivre, Restoration and early eighteenth-century playwright (?1667–1723).

[2] When Orlando asks if Isabella has "changed her name," he is asking if Warwick has married her, thus calling into question both Warwick's and his sister's honour.

"Yes," said Warwick coldly; "here is a card that will direct you to her—All I request is your silence this evening in regard to my change of name; a matter that surely cannot be material to any one here."

Orlando assented to this, and they returned together towards Mrs. Manby, the lady of the house, to whom Warwick, after assuming again the name of Lorrain, said, in a careless way, "that he now owed her another obligation, by having been introduced by her means, to an old friend, for whom, ever since his arrival in London, he had been enquiring in vain." The conversation then became general. Some other visitors arrived, some departed; and Orlando, impatient to have some private conversation with Warwick, asked "if he would accompany him and his friend Carr?"—to this he assented; but Mrs. Manby would not release them till they had promised to visit her again the following week.

Carr, as soon as he learned from Orlando who Warwick really was, took leave of him, under pretence of business in another part of the town; and as the evening was fine, Orlando and his brother-in-law walked homewards together.

As soon as they were alone, the former expressed his surprise at meeting thus unexpectedly, and under another name, one who had so long been given up for lost; and his still greater wonder, that it was possible for his sister to be in London, without having seen or made any enquiry after her mother and sisters, or her family.

"Suspend your astonishment, Somerive," said Warwick, "or at least suspend your blame: when you hear all we have suffered, and all we have contended with, you will find at least no occasion for the latter; and though I own it appears extraordinary that my wife had not yet sought her family, that circumstance will seem less so, when you know that it is not above three weeks since we came out of Scotland; and that, after our long detention in America, we returned to Europe, without being able to return to England—and have been in Spain, in Portugal, in Ireland, and at length in Scotland.—When I can relate to you in detail all these adventures,[1] you will find more to pity, than to reproach us for."

---

[1] Which may perhaps appear in a detached work [CS]. This appeared as *The Wanderings of Warwick* in January 1794, some time after it had been promised. The publisher, J. Bell, prefaced the volume with the following "Advertisement": "so long a period having elapsed since the *speedy* publication of THE WANDERINGS OF WARWICK in *two volumes* was announced, the Publisher conceives he should be wanting in that respect which he owes to the Public, were he now silently to publish the work in *one*, without stating his own exculpation, that both the delay, and the promising it in two volumes, are imputable solely to the Author—to whom he leaves the task of justifying her own conduct" (*The Wanderings of Warwick*, London: J. Bell, 1794).

"But, my dear Warwick," said Orlando, who already forgave what he had before thought there was cause to resent, "will not our Isabella see her mother now?—Will not she give this inexpressible comfort to a tender parent, who has never ceased to regret her loss?"

"You must settle that with her, my friend, to-morrow, when I beg you will breakfast with us. Your sister has two little boys to present to you, and will be delighted I know to see you, but it must not be without some preparation." Orlando promised to be with them at breakfast; and on Warwick's expressing a wish to hear how he was himself situated, he gave a brief detail of all that had happened from their last parting at Rayland Hall to the present time.

Warwick heard him with attention, and then said, "So, my dear boy! it does not appear that thy piety has succeeded better than my rashness:—I have been disinherited and bedeviled by my uncle for marrying a girl I liked—and you, who sacrificed your own inclinations to your virtue, have been disinherited, for these orthodox fellows in their cauliflower wigs and short aprons—Why, you could not have been worse served, if you had taken off your little nymph with you to America, as I took off mine."

"Yes, surely," replied Orlando, "I should have been worse off; for I should not have what is now, and will be, in whatever extremity I may be, my greatest consolation, the consciousness that I have never, to gratify myself, given pain to those who had a claim to my duty; and that if I am unfortunate, I have at least not deserved my ill fortune."

"Bravo!" cried Warwick—

"'Tis not in mortals to command success;
But we'll do more, Sempronius—we'll deserve it."[1]

I wish you joy, my young Cato; but for my part, I find I have no qualms of conscience about bilking the old boy in Grosvenor Place—I rather think I have done him a kindness, and perhaps one day or other he may find it out."

"In the mean time, however, I suppose General Tracy remains inexorable."

"Faith!" answered Warwick, "I have never tried; and one reason of my

---

[1] Joseph Addison (1672–1719), *Cato* (1713), I.ii.43–44, a tragedy with contemporary political resonance. Smith slightly changes the punctuation: "'Tis not in mortals to command success,/ But we'll do more, Sempronius; we'll deserve it."

taking another name was, that he might not know I was in England."

They were now arrived at a street where, as Warwick's lodgings were near Leicester Square, and those of Orlando in a street near Oxford street, it was necessary for them to part for the evening. Orlando, whose affection for Isabella was already revived, sent her a thousand kind remembrances; and Warwick, in return, told him, "he longed to be introduced to the nymph of the inchanted tower," whom he never had an opportunity of seeing at Rayland Hall. Orlando, after he had left him, considered with astonishment the volatility of his temper.—His person was a little altered by change of climate; but his spirits were not at all depressed by a change of situation so great as between being the heir of General Tracy, and a wandering adventurer, for he did not conceal from his friend that such was his present situation; that it was in consequence of his having written something for the news-papers, that he had become acquainted with Mrs. Manby, who had answered them; and that he was now soliciting the managers to accept of a play he had finished. The humiliating attendance which he owned this pursuit seemed likely to render necessary, was added to the reasons he had already given Orlando why he wished to be known at present only as Mr. Lorrain.

CHAP. XII.

On his return home, Orlando related to his wife his extraordinary meeting with Warwick; and though he expressed great delight in knowing that his sister was living and well, he could not but feel concern for the situation in which he found her. He knew not whether Warwick did not, notwithstanding his apparent gaiety and carelessness, repent him of his precipitate marriage; and he feared, that, by a man of so volatile a temper, the evils of narrow circumstances would not be softened to Isabella.

He hastened to her the next morning, and she received him with blended emotions of joy and distress particularly affecting. It was not till some time after Warwick left them together, that Isabella had courage to ask the circumstance of her father's death; yet she was consoled by hearing, that *her* elopement did not appear to have hastened it. Orlando then entreated her to determine on seeing her mother immediately, and she left it to him to manage it as he would. He embraced her two lovely children with affection, and could not behold them, without representing to her how necessary it was to think of some means to reconcile Warwick to General Tracy.

Isabella answered, "that they had come to London with that intention; but that Warwick's pride, and his uncle's having certainly made a will in favour of his brother's son, had combined to throw difficulties in the way of a reconciliation; and she now despaired of Warwick's pursuing his hopes of it, or of their being crowned with success if he did.—His change of name," she said, "had been made partly to avoid his creditors, who now believed him dead, till he could find means of paying them; and partly that General Tracy might not be informed of his being in London, till he could know whether there was a likelihood of his being forgiven." The vivacity of Isabella seemed subdued, but she was not dejected; and after she had wept over the account of her father's death, her brother's misconduct, and the dispersion of her family, she recovered some degree of cheerfulness, and seemed to prepare herself for an interview with her mother, with more resolution than, from all that had happened, Orlando thought it possible for her to assume.

This formidable meeting was fixed for the next day; and when Orlando left his sister, he began to consider if he might not, at the same time, acknowledge his own marriage, and put an end, at once, to the state of uneasiness, and consciousness of violated integrity which he now was in.

When he rapped at his own door, he was told by the maid who opened it, "that the porter whom he saw in the passage had been waiting for him some time with a letter, which he was directed to deliver into no hands but his own." He opened it with precipitation, and found these words written in a hand hardly legible:

"DEAR ORLANDO,

"If my having left you so long ignorant of what is become of me, has not entirely estranged you from me—come to me at the place the bearer will shew you, and perhaps it will be the last trouble you will ever receive from

"Yours,

"P. SOMERIVE."

Orlando, shocked and surprised, enquired of the man, who stood by, "where he had left the gentleman who sent him?"—The man replied, "that he had orders not to answer, but to shew him the way:—that the gentleman was ill in bed, and given over by the doctor." Still more alarmed by this account, he bade the man wait a moment, while he went up to speak to Monimia, in order to account for his being so much longer absent, and then hastened with his conductor to an obscure street leading from the Strand to Covent Garden; where, in an attic room, very dirty and ill furnished, Orlando found his unhappy brother, in an illness which seemed to be the last stage of a rapid decline, brought on by debauchery and excess.

It might give too tragic a colouring to the conclusion of this narrative, were the scenes of some days to be minutely described—it may therefore suffice to state, that Orlando could not conceal from his mother the situation of her eldest son, who, conscious of his approaching end, and conscious too of all his offences towards her, implored her pity and forgiveness. In his repentance, however late, his mother forgot his errors, and as solicitously tried to save him as if he had never offended her.— With difficulty he was removed to her own house, where she constantly attended him, with Orlando, and where there were for some days, hopes of his recovery.—It was in this interval that Orlando, who could not bear to be so constantly separated from Monimia, and whose heart continually reproached him with the deception he was guilty of towards his mother, concerted with Selina the means of declaring both his marriage, and the return of Isabella to London. Mrs. Somerive, on the point of losing one of her children, embraced, with transport, the daughter she had so long believed lost; and though she trembled for the consequence of Orlando's marriage, when there seemed so little probability of his finding a support for a family, she acknowledged that Monimia, of whom she soon became passionately fond, was an apology for his indiscretion. With the tenderest assiduity, Monimia shared the fatigue of attending on the dying brother of her husband; and in despite of the remonstrances and displeasure of Mr. Woodford, who did all he could to irritate his sister against Orlando, and who mingled the pecuniary favours which she was obliged to owe him, with admonitions and reproaches that destroyed all their value, Mrs. Somerive not only forgave Orlando, but seemed to love him more fondly than ever. That cruel want of money, which too often divides families, and estranges even the child from the parent, served only to unite this family more closely. The pride of Warwick alone kept him at a greater distance than the rest; and unable, under his present circumstances, to appear as he once did, he could not bear to appear at all before those, who had once seen him so differently situated. He avoided therefore going to the house, when he thought there was a probability of his meeting any of the Woodford family; none of them indeed but Woodford himself were very likely to be there; but from him Warwick would have flown with more apprehension than from the rest, not only on account of his coarse jokes, but because of his connection with General Tracy.

But Isabella, though equally desirous of escaping the unfeeling raillery or cold remonstrance of her uncle, was, without meeting him, constantly with her family, and was, with Monimia and Selina, the support of the unhappy Mrs. Somerive, when, after lingering about a fortnight after his removal, her eldest son expired in the arms of Orlando.

There is a degree of folly, and of vice, which gradually dissolves the tenderest affections, weans the friend from the beloved companion of youth, and renders the ties of blood the most galling and insupportable chains. To this point of irreclaimable misconduct Philip Somerive had long since arrived. He had too plainly evinced, that to his own selfish gratifications he would always sacrifice the welfare, and even the subsistence of his family; yet, in his repentance on the bed of pain and languor, his mother forgot and forgave all she had suffered from him; and when he died, she wept for him as the child of her early affection, whose birth and infancy had once formed her greatest felicity.—In shedding tears over an object once so beloved by her husband, she seemed a second time to have lost him; and the first subject to which she attended, was to have his remains deposited with those of his father, in the family vault at West Wolverton.

In this Orlando determined that she should at all events be gratified, whatever inconvenience might in their present narrow circumstances arise from the expence: he gave therefore directions accordingly; when he found that Mr. Woodford took upon him to oppose this wish of his mother, in a way so rude and savage, that after very high words had passed between him and his uncle (in which Woodford reproached Orlando with all the pecuniary favours he had bestowed upon his family, and ridiculed his beggarly marriage), Orlando at the last part of his conversation entirely lost his temper, and desired the unfeeling man of consequence to leave the house.

He had then the additional difficulty of concealing this disagreement from his mother, and of finding the means to supply that deficiency which this cruelty of his uncle would create.—The little sum left of his commission, after paying some late expences of his brother's and for his own lodgings, was reduced within thirty pounds, in which consisted his whole fortune. His uncle, who had till now contributed yearly to the support of his mother and his sisters, now protested that he would do no more. From his eldest sister married in Ireland, who had a family of her own, very trifling assistance only could be expected; and Warwick could not provide for his own family. Thus Orlando saw, that on an income of hardly an hundred a year, his mother and two unmarried sisters were to live; and that Monimia and her family, whom he could not think of suffering to be any additional burthen to them, could have no other dependence than on his exertions; yet into what way of life to enter, or where to seek the means of providing for them, he knew not.[1]

Sad were his reflections on the past, on the present, and on the future, when he set out with the melancholy procession that was to convey the remains of his deceased brother to the last abode of the Somerive family; and little was the correspondence between his internal feelings and the beauty of the season, which gave peculiar charms to the country through which he passed.—The tears of the family he had left, of which Monimia was during his absence to be a part, seemed to have deprived him of the power of shedding a tear; but with eyes that gloomily surveyed the objects around him, without knowing what he saw, he reached at the close of the second day's journey West Wolverton; and at a little alehouse, the only one in the village, the funeral stopped that night, while Orlando went out alone to direct what yet remained of the necessary preparations.

It was a beautiful still evening, towards the end of May; but the senses of the unhappy Orlando were shut to all the pleasures external objects could bestow.—When he had visited the church, and spoken to the curate, he walked back towards the house once his father's. The grass was grown in the court, and half the windows were bricked up: the greater part of the shrubs in the garden were cut; and the gates out of repair and broken. All wore an appearance of change and of desolation, even more deplorable, in the opinion of Orlando, than the spruce alterations, and air of new-born prosperity, which, on his former visit, he had remarked as the effect of Mr. Stockton's purchase.

Pain, and even horrors, were grown familiar to Orlando; and he seemed to have a gloomy satisfaction in the indulgence of melancholy. He opened, therefore, the half fallen gate, that led from a sort of lawn, that surrounded the house, to the shrubbery and pleasure ground, and entered the walk which he had so often traversed with his father, and where he had taken his last leave of him on his departure for America.—The moon, not yet at its full, shed a faint light on every

---

[1]   This provides an interesting contrast to Orlando's confidence that a young man of twenty with all his faculties could easily support a family; see Chapter IV, Volume II.

object: he looked along a sort of vista of shrubs, which seemed to have been left merely because they were not yet wanted as firing; and the moonlight, at the end of this dark avenue of cypress and gloomy evergreens, seemed partially to illuminate the walk, only to shew him the spectre of departed happiness. He remembered with what pleasure his father used to watch the growth of these trees, which he had planted himself; and with what satisfaction he was accustomed to consider them, as improving for Philip.—Sad reverse!—The father, who thus fondly planned future schemes of felicity for his son, long since mouldered in the grave, whither that son himself, after having been but too accessary to the premature death of this fond parent, was now, in the bloom of life, precipitated by his own headlong folly.

A temper so sanguine as that of Orlando, possesses also that sensibility which arms with redoubled poignancy the shafts of affliction and disappointment. He felt, with cruel acuteness, all the calamities which a few short years had brought upon his family:—all their hopes blasted—their fortune gone—their name almost forgotten in the country—and strangers possessing their habitations. He now remembered that he used to think, were he once blessed with Monimia, every other circumstance of life would be to him indifferent; yet she was now his— she was now more beloved, as his wife, than she had ever been as his mistress; and the sweetness of her temper, the excellence of her heart, the clearness of her understanding, and her tender attachment to him, rendered her infinitely dearer to him than that beauty which had first attracted his early love. But far from being rendered indifferent to every other circumstance, he felt that much of his present concern arose from the impossibility he found of sheltering his adored creature from the evils of indigence; and that the romantic theory, of sacrificing every consideration to love, produced, in the practice, only the painful consciousness of having injured its object.

It was late before the unhappy wanderer returned to the place where he was to attempt to sleep; but the mournful ceremony of the next day, added to the gloomy thoughts he had been indulging, deprived him of all inclination to repose; and as he saw the sun arise which was to witness the interment of his brother—how different appeared its light now, from what it used to do, when from the same village, in the house of his father, he beheld it over the eastern hills, awakening him to hope and health—to the society of a happy cheerful family—and to the prospect of meeting his little Monimia, then a child, who innocently expressed the delight she felt in seeing him!

But to indulge these painful reflections appeared to him unmanly, while they were likely to disable him from the exercise of the melancholy duties before him. These at length over, he found himself, in despite of all his philosophy, so much depressed, that he could not determine to return that night towards London; but sending away the undertaker's people, and retaining for himself the horse on which one of them had rode, he resolved to pass the rest of the day in gratifying the strange inclination he had long felt, to wander about Rayland Park, to visit the Hall, and take a last leave of that scene of his early happiness, the turret once inhabited by Monimia.

This plan would detain him from her another day; but he felt an invincible inclination to make this farewell visit, which he knew Monimia herself would wish him to indulge. Having therefore disengaged himself from the gloomy duties of the day, and sent a few lines to his mother and Monimia, to account for his absence, if the man who carried it should arrive in town before him, he set out towards evening for the Hall, flattering himself that, as he was now known, and made a better appearance than on his former visit, he should without difficulty obtain admittance to the house.—In this, however, he was mistaken: he found many of the windows bricked up, the œconomy of the present possessors not allowing them to pay so heavy a window tax;[1] the old servants hall below was entirely deprived of light; and hardly a vestige remained of inhabitants, in the grass-grown courts and silent deserted offices.

Orlando, after waiting for some time at the door, before he could make any one hear, saw at length the same sturdy clown he had before spoken to, who asked him in a surly tone his business.—Orlando replied, that he desired to be allowed to see the house. The man answered, that he had positive orders from Dr. Hollybourn to shew the house to nobody; and he shut the door in his face.

Thus repulsed, Orlando only felt a more determined resolution to gratify himself by a visit to the library, the chapel, and the turret; and he went round the house with an intention to enter without permission by the door that opened near the former out of the summer parlour—Here, however, he was again disappointed: this door, as well

---

[1]   Beginning in 1696, a tax was imposed on windows, which were seen as a luxury in a dwelling. Interestingly, the window tax was abolished on houses with fewer than seven windows in 1792, the year before *The Old Manor House* was published (only to be reintroduced in 1797 at a much higher rate due to the war with France). However, in the 1770s the tax was still firmly in place (see *Dictionary of British History*, ed. J.P. Kenyon, London: Secker and Warburg, p. 364).

as the windows in the same line with it, was nailed up, and boarded on the inside; and while Orlando, thus baffled, was examining the other wing of the house, to see if he could not there obtain entrance, the man who guarded it looked from a window above, and told him, that if any body was seen about the house he should fire at them, for that "nobody had no business there."

From the savage brutality of his manner, Orlando had little doubt but that he would act as he said; yet, far from fearing his fire-arms, he told him that he would see the house at all events, and that opposition would only serve to give more trouble, but not deter him from his purpose. He then attempted to bribe this guardian of the property of the church, and offered him a handful of silver:[1] but his answer was, that he should fetch his blunderbuss.

Orlando now thought that it would be better to return to West Wolverton, and to write to a lawyer in the neighbourhood, employed by Dr. Hollybourn in the management of the estate, requesting leave to see the house; though he foresaw that it would be difficult to make such a man comprehend the sort of sensations that urged him to this request—and that it was possible he might impute his desire of visiting the Hall to motives that might make him refuse his permission.— Resolved however to try, he returned slowly and disconsolate through the park; and observed, as he reached the side of it next the lake, that in the copse that clothed the hill many of the large trees were felled, and some others marked for the axe.—His heart became more heavy than before; and when he reached the seat near the boat-house in the fir-wood, which was now indeed broken down, he rested a moment against the old tree it had once surrounded, to recover from the almost insupportable despondence which oppressed him.

Absorbed in the most melancholy thoughts, every object served to increase their bitterness—He listened to sounds once so pleasing with anguish of heart bordering upon despair, and almost wished that he had been drowned in this water when a boy, by the accident of falling from a boat as he was fishing on the lake, from whence his father's servant had with difficulty saved him.

In such contemplations he remained for some time, with his eyes fixed on the water, when he saw reflected in its surface the image of some object moving along its bank.—The figure, from the gentle

---

[1]   The reference is to the thirty pieces of silver for which Judas betrayed Jesus. Orlando is clearly not in his creator's favour at this point.

waving of the water as it approached the shore, was not distinct; and its motion so slow and singular, that the curiosity of Orlando was somewhat awaked. As it came nearer to him, therefore, he stepped forward, and saw advancing with difficulty on his crutches the old beggar whom he had met in a barn in Hampshire four months since, when he waited for communication with Mrs. Roker.

However surprised Orlando was at the appearance of this person, the man himself seemed to have expected to meet him; for, advancing towards him as speedily as his mutilated frame would allow, he exclaimed, "Ah! my dear master! well met: I have found you at last."

"Have you been looking for me then, my old friend?"

"Aye, marry have I—and many a weary mile have my leg and my crutches hopped after your honour—Why, mun, I've been up at London after you; and there, at the house where you give me a direction to, I met a Neger man, who would not believe, like a smutty-faced son of a b— -h as he is, that such a poor cripple as I could have to do to speak with you—and so all I could get of him was telling me that you were come down here—I knows this country well enough; and so I e'en set off, and partly one way, and partly another, I got down and have found you out."

Orlando, not guessing why this wandering veteran had taken so much trouble—was about, however, to ask what he could do for him, when the old man, putting on an arch look, and feeling in the patched pocket of what had once been a coat, said—

"And now, master, since we be met, I hopes with all my heart I brings you good news—There—There's a letter for you from Madam Roker—A power of trouble, and many a cold night's waiting I had to get it: but let an old soldier alone—Egad, when once I had got it, I was bent upon putting it into no hands but yours, for fear of more tricks upon travellers."

Orlando, in greater emotion that a letter from such a lady was likely to produce, took it, and unfolding two or three dirty papers in which it was wrapped, he broke the seal, and read these words:

"Dear Sir,
"I am sorry to acquaint you that Mr. Roker is by no means so grateful to me as I had reason to expect from the good fortune I brought him, and indeed from his assurances when I married him of his great regard and affection for me. I cannot but say that I am cruelly treated at present. As to Mr. Roker, he passes all his time in London, and I have too much cause to fear that very wicked persons are enjoying too much of the

money which is mine—a thing so wicked, that, if it was only for his soul's sake, I cannot but think it my duty to prevent: but, to add to my misfortune herein, his relations give out that I am *non compos mentis*; which to be sure I might be reckoned when I bestowed my fortune on such an undeserving family, and made such sacrifices for Mr. Roker, as I am now heartily sorry for.—Sir, I have read in Scripture, that it is never too late to repent; and I am sure, if I have done you a great injury, I do repent it from the bottom of my soul, and will make you all the reparation in my power: and you may believe I am in earnest in my concern, when I hereby trust you with a secret, whereon perhaps my life may depend: for, besides that I don't know how far I might be likely to be punished by law for the unjust thing Mr. Roker persuaded me to consent to—against my conscience I am sure—I know that he would rather have me dead than to speak the truth; and 'tis for that reason, for fear I should be examined about the will of my late friend, Mrs. Rayland, that he insists upon it I am at this time a lunatic, and keeps me under close confinement as such.

"Oh! Mr. Orlando, there is a later will than that which was proved, and which gave away from you all the Rayland estate—and with shame and grief I say, that when my Lady died I read that copy of it she gave to me; and finding that I had only half as much as in a former will, I was over-persuaded by Mr. Roker, who had too much power over me, to produce only the other, and to destroy in his presence that copy which my Lady had given to me to keep, charging me to send it, if any thing happened to her, to your family.—I did not then know the contents, which she had always kept from me: and I am sure I should never have thought of doing as I did but for Mr. Roker—I hope the Lord will forgive me!—and that you, dear Sir, will do so likewise, since I have not only been sincerely repentant of the same, but have, luckily for us both, kept it in my power to make you, I hope, reparation.

"After the decease of my late dear Lady, Mr. Roker had the other will proved; and Dr. Hollybourn and he agreed together in all things. Mr. Roker, to whom I was married, was very eager after every box of papers, and almost every scrap belonging to Mrs. Rayland; but I thought him, even in those early days, a little too much in a hurry to take possession of all the jewels, and rings, and effects, of which I had the care; and did not see why, as they were mostly mine, I should give them entirely up to him; seeing that I had already given him my fortune—and that such things belong to a woman, and in no case to her husband.—This being the case, I own, I did not put into his hands some of these things, nor a small rose-wood box of my Lady's, in which she always kept some lockets, and miniature pictures, and medals, and other such curiosities, and some family papers. Mr. Roker never saw this box, nor did I ever have the keys of it, for there are two belonging to it with a very particular lock; my late Lady always kept them in her purse; and it was only after her decease that they came into my possession; and thereupon opening the box, which Mr. Roker knew nothing of, I found a paper sealed up and dated in my Lady's own hand, and indorsed—"Duplicate of my last Will and Testament, to be delivered to Orlando Somerive, or his Representative."—I assure you that I had repented me before of the thing I had done in destroying the will, and now resolved to keep it in my power always to make you amends, by taking care of this; which I, knowing I could not do if I had it in my own possession, put therefore into this box again, with the medals and family papers, and some jewels of no great value, but which I thought would be no harm to make sure of—because, as the proverb observes, things are in this world uncertain at best; and we all know where we eat our first bread, but none can tell where they shall eat their last. Mr. Roker was at that time a fond and affectionate husband; but men are but fickle, even the very best, and none can tell what may befall; by bad people especially, who are so wicked to meddle and interfere between man and wife, to destroy all matrimonial comfort, as is too often the case.

"Mr. Roker thought then of residing at the Hall as steward for the Bishop, &c.; but Dr. Hollybourn not being agreeable thereto, it was settled otherwise: only Mr. Roker and I were to go once a year to the Court holding for Manors, and to overlook the premises till they were disposed of, according to the will of my Lady which was proved, which the worthy Divines seemed not to be in a great hurry to do— Whereupon, as I did not choose for many reasons to carry this small box about with me, I put it into a place of safety in the house.

"If you have not forgot old times, Mr. Orlando, you know very well that Rayland Hall, which belonged to such famous cavaliers in the great rebellion, has a great many secret stair-cases, and odd passages, and hiding-places in it; where, in those melancholy times, some of my late Lady's ancestors, who had been in arms for the blessed Martyr and King, Charles the Second,[1] were hid by others of the family after the

---

[1] As Ehrenpreis notes (p. 543), this is an error for Charles the First. Given Smith's knowledge of British history, as displayed in this novel and much of her poetry, it is odd that she makes this slip. It may well be that it is Mrs. Lennard (now Roker) who does not know her history.

fight at Edgehill, &c.—which I have heard my Lady oftentimes recount: but, nevertheless, I do not know that she herself knew all those places.

"By the side of my bed, in that chamber hung partly with scarlet and gold printed leather, and partly with painting in pannels, where there is a brown mohair bed lined with yellow silk, you may remember a great picture of Lady Alithea, second wife of the first Sir Hildebrand Rayland, with her two sons and a dog—She was an Earl's daughter, and a celebrated beauty, and great great grandmother to my late Lady. The picture is only a copy from that in the great gallery, and done, as I have heard my Lady say, by some painter of that time when he was a young man—so that, as there was another, this was not hung in the gallery. Close under that picture there seems to be a hanging of gilt leather: but this is only fastened with small hooks: and under it is a sliding oak board, which gives into a closet where there is no light—but a very narrow stair-case goes from it through the wall, quite round to the other side of the house, and into other hiding-places, where one or two persons might be hid for years, and nobody the wiser.

"Now, Sir, in a sort of hollow place about three feet wide, made like an arch under the thick wall in this closet, is a tin box with a padlock—and in that box this inlaid rose-wood box or casket. There you will find the real will of my Lady, and I hope all you wish and expect in it; and what I desire of you in return is, that you will take means to convince the world that I am not to blame; and that I am not a lunatic; and you have so much honour, that I rely upon your promises not to injure me if it should be in your power; but to make me amends for what I thus lose for your sake and the sake of justice—as in your letter you faithfully promise.

"For that poor unfortunate young woman, the daughter of my deceased kinswoman, I do assure you that, if I knew what was become of her, I would give you notice. But she has never been heard of that I know of for a great many months—and I am afraid, from her flippant ways with my Mr. Roker before I was forced to send her away, has taken to courses very disgraceful, and which have made her unworthy of your farther thoughts. God forgive me if I judge amiss herein!—We must be charitable one towards another, as the Scripture says, poor sinful mortals, who have so much to answer for ourselves, as to be sure all of us have!

"And now, dear Sir, I take my leave, having been four days writing this long letter by fits and snatches, when Mr. Roker's sister, who even sleeps in my room, has been out of the way; for she watches me like a jailor, and I am quite a prisoner: and have not pen and ink but by stealth. If I were to attempt to send this to the post, all would be lost: so I have trusted it to old Hugh March[1] the beggar, by means of the servant girl, and I have given the old man the three keys. Heartily wishing you health and happiness I recommend myself to your prayers, as mine are for your success, and remain, dear Sir,

      Your affectionate humble servant,
          RACHEL ROKER."

      "P.S. Pray let me hear speedily by the bearer."

Orlando read this strange confession, this avowal of iniquity so black, mingled with appeals to Heaven, and sentences of religion, with such a palpitating heart, that, when he had finished it, he looked around him to discover whether he was alive—The objects about him seemed real—He saw the old man before him, who, after a long search in his other pocket, produced the three keys; and then pulling off the relics of an hat from his grey head, bowed with an air of much humility, and cried, "Well, and what says my young master?—Does his lame messenger bring him bad news or good?—Ah, your honour is a noble gentleman, and will reward your old soldier!"

"That I will, my honest fellow! to the utmost of your wishes, as soon as I have discovered whether all this is real; but it seems to me at present that I am in a dream."

"Wide awake, depend upon it," answered the beggar;—"so come, dear young gentleman! will you go back to yon ale-house, and let us see what the good news will do for us?—I do not very well know, indeed, what it is; but I know that I was promised that you could do me a power of good, if I delivered the letter and the keys safe.—You know I had promised afore to serve you by night and by day, and so I have." "Serve me a little longer, my brave old man!" said Orlando; "by preserving in the place we are going to the secrecy I desire of you, without which all may yet be lost.—Here, I will share my purse with you—Go back to the ale-house, order whatever you like, and shew them that you have money to pay for it.—Do not make use of my name, nor say a word about Mrs. Roker till I return.—I must go to the next town, to consult a friend I have there on the best steps to be

---

[1]   The name of the old beggar, here called Hugh March but earlier named "Old Thomas" by Pat Welling (vol. IV, chapter VIII), raises again the question of Smith's inaccuracies with names and ages. As noted in the introduction, Smith wrote much of the novel under difficult pressures of time, and may simply be making mistakes. On the other hand, it is possible that her inconsistencies work to destabilize reader and novel alike, and in that way add to the overall sense of a vitiated genre. Even the narrator is implicated.

taken; in which if I succeed, I will make thee the very prince of old soldiers."

Orlando then put some guineas into his hand, and saw him take the way to the ale-house, less rejoiced at his future hopes of reward, than at the power of immediate gratification. He somewhat doubted his discretion, but thought that very few hours would put it out of the power of any indiscretion to mar the happy effects of Mrs. Roker's repentance:—and to set about securing this advantage, he hastened to his friend Dawson, as he saw that too many precautions could not be taken in an affair so unusual and so important.

CHAP. XII.

The young man to whom Orlando now applied, was very sincerely his friend, and possessed an acute and penetrating mind.—He saw at once all the importance of the business, and the hazard Orlando would incur by the smallest delay. Mrs. Roker's letter evidently expressed a mind fluctuating between resentment towards her husband, and unwillingness to acknowledge the folly she had committed in marrying him; and as no great dependence could be placed on the repentance of a person under the influence of such a contrariety of passions, there was reason to fear, that her love, or what she fancied so, her pride, her avarice, and her fear, might unite to conquer the compunction she had shewn, and to make her discover the steps she had taken to her husband.

Dawson advised therefore an immediate application to a justice of peace, for a warrant to search the house that night; and as there was none resident in the town, Orlando set out with him in a post-chaise for the house of a magistrate, about seven miles distant, who had formerly been much acquainted with the Somerive family, and had been always full of professions of regard for them.

To this man, now in much higher affluence than formerly, by the acquisition of the fortunes of some of his relations, Dawson opened the business on which they came.

But here he had occasion to remark the truth of that observation,[1] which, whoever has seen many vicissitudes of fortune, must have too

---

[1]   Of La Rochefoucault. [CS]

Jonathan Swift (1667–1745) uses these lines, in French, as the epigraph to his poem "Verses on the Death of Dr. Swift" (1739), which popularized the saying in Britain. François de la Rochefoucauld (1613–80) was famed for his sardonic wit.

often beheld, as a melancholy evidence of the depravity of our nature, "That in the misfortunes of our best friends, there is something not displeasing to us."—Far from appearing to rejoice at the probability which now offered itself, that the son of his old friend would be restored to the right of his ancestors, and from depressing indigence be raised to high prosperity, this gentleman seemed to take pains to throw difficulties in his way:—he doubted the letter from Mrs. Roker; he doubted the legality of his granting a warrant; and it was not till after considerable delay, and long arguments, that he was at length prevailed upon to lend to Orlando the assistance of the civil power, without the immediate exertion of which, it seemed possible that his hopes might be again baffled.

Orlando was not without apprehensions, that this worthy magistrate might send immediate information of what was passing to Dr. Hollybourn; and he determined, late as it was, to go to Rayland Hall that night. He set forward, therefore, attended by Dawson, two other young men of the same town, who were eager for his success, and the persons who were to execute the warrant. It was midnight when they arrived at the Hall—All was profoundly silent around it, and it had no longer the appearance of an inhabited house. The summons, however loud, was unanswered. As the men rapped violently at the old door of the servants hall, the sullen sounds murmured through the empty courts, and to their call only hollow echoes were returned. These attempts to gain admittance were repeated again and again without effect, and they began to conclude, that there was nobody within the house; but at length some of them going round to another part of the house, the man who had the charge of it looked out of a window, and demanded their business.

Upon hearing there was a warrant and a constable, the fellow, who had deeply engaged in the same sort of business as that which used to be carried on by Pattenson and Company, imagined immediately that he had been informed against: but as there was no remedy, he came down with fear and trembling to open the door; and it was a great relief to him to learn, that it was only for a paper, which might occasion the house to change its master, but not for any of his effects that the intended search was to be made. The posse now proceeded to the place indicated by the letter of Mrs. Roker—the constable, a most magisterial personage, marching by the side of Orlando, while Dawson and his friends followed, with candles in their hands; and as silently they ascended the great stair-case, and traversed the long dark passages that led towards the apartment in question, Orlando could not, amid the anxiety of such a moment, help fancying, that the scene resembled one of those so often met with in old romances and fairy tales, where the hero is by some supernatural means directed to a golden key, which opens an invisible drawer, where a hand or an head is found swimming in blood, which it is his business to restore to the inchanted owner.[1] With a beating heart, however, he saw the picture of Lady Alithea removed, and the sliding board appears. On entering the closet, the tin box, covered with a green cloth, was discovered. The key which Orlando possessed opened it, and the casket was within it; which he unlocked, in presence of all the persons present, and saw the important paper, exactly as it had been described by Mrs. Roker.

He now debated whether he should open it; but at length, with the advice of his friend Dawson, determined not to do so till his arrival in London. Replacing every thing else as it was found, and securing the closet and the room that led to it, he now hastened to reward the persons who had attended him on this search—and without resting, set out post with Dawson for London, where they arrived at nine o'clock the next morning.

Orlando hastened immediately to the house of his mother, with sensations very different from those which he had quitted it.—He found Monimia alone in the dining room, pensively attentive to the two children of Isabella, who were playing on the carpet.—She received him with that degree of transport which shewed itself in tears; nor could he prevail upon her for a moment or two to be more composed, and to answer his enquiries after his mother and his sisters.—She at length told him, that Mrs. Somerive had been so much affected by the visits her brother had made during his absence, by his reproaches for her false indulgence to both her sons, and by his total dislike to the marriage of Orlando (which he had represented as the most absurd folly, and as the utter ruin of his nephew) and by the disposition he (Mr. Woodford) shewed to withdraw all assistance from her and her two youngest daughters, if she did not wholly with draw all countenance both from Orlando and Isabella, that Mrs. Somerive was actually sinking under the pain such repeated instances of cruelty had inflicted; and had determined, rather than continue to be obliged to a brother who was capable of thus empoisoning the favours her circumstances obliged her to accept, to quit London, discharge all but one servant, and to retire to

---

[1] Smith here makes the artifice of her Gothicisms plain, by calling attention to the imaginary nature of such supernatural scenes. It is only Orlando who can anticipate such an eventuality.

some cheap part of Wales or Scotland, where the little income she possessed might be more sufficient to their support.

Orlando, who felt that some precaution was necessary, in revealing to Monimia the fortunate reverse that now presented itself, was considering how to begin this propitious discovery, when his mother, who eagerly expected him, having learned from the servants that he was arrived, sent down Selina to beg to see him.

She put back the curtain as he came into the room; and held out her hand to him, but was unable to speak.—The mournful particulars she expected, which however she had not courage to ask, filled her heart with bitterness, and her eyes with tears.

Orlando, affected by the looks and the pathetic silence of his mother, kissed with extreme emotion the hand she gave him—He thanked her, after a moment's silence, for her goodness to Monimia during the few days of his absence; and entreated her to be in better spirits. He then gradually discovered to her, by a short and clear relation of what had happened, the assurance he now had, which the transactions of that evening would, he hoped, confirm, of a speedy change in their circumstances.

The heart of Mrs. Somerive, so long accustomed only to sorrow and solicitude, was no longer sensible of those acute feelings which agitate the warm and sanguine bosom of youth; but to hear that her children, for whom only she wished to live, were likely to be at once rescued from the indigence which impended over them, and secured in affluence and prosperity, could not be heard with calmness. At length both herself and her son acquired composure enough to consider of the proper steps to be taken. Every person interested was summoned to attend that evening at the house of Mrs. Somerive, who found herself animated enough to be present at the opening of the will, at which all who were sent for were present, except Doctor Hollybourn (who sent his attorney) and the Rokers. The elder only sent a protest against it by his clerk; and the younger thought it safer immediately to disappear.

It was found on the perusal of this important paper, and the codicils belonging to it, that, with the exception of five thousand pounds, and two hundred a year for her life, to her old companion Lennard, Mrs. Rayland had given every thing she possessed, both real and personal, to Orlando, without any other restriction than settling the whole of the landed estate of the Rayland family on his male heirs, and appropriating a sum of money to purchase the title of a Baronet, and for an act to enable him to take and bear the name and arms of Rayland only.

The subsequent proceedings were easy and expeditious. Against a will so authenticated all opposition was vain; and within three weeks Orlando was put in possession of his estate, and Doctor Hollybourn obliged, with extreme reluctance, not only to deliver up all of which he and his brother had taken into their hands, but to refund the rents and payments for timber; which operation went to the poor Doctor's heart. There are some men who have such an extreme affection for money, even when it does not belong to them, that they cannot determine to part with it when once they get possession of it. Of this order was the worthy Doctor; who, with charity and urbanity always in his mouth, had an heart rendered callous by avarice, and a passion for the swinish gratifications of the table, to which the possession of Rayland Hall, the gardens and hot-houses of which he alone kept up, had lately so considerably contributed, that he could not bear to relinquish them; and actually suffered so much from mortification that he was obliged to go to Bath to cure a bilious illness, which vexation and gluttony contributed to bring on.

Orlando lost no time in rescuing the unfortunate Mrs. Roker from the hands of her tyrant; who, in order to incapacitate her from giving that testimony which he knew was in her power, and with which she often had threatened him, had taken out against her a commission of lunacy. It was superseded on the application of Orlando, who himself immediately conducted Mrs. Roker to Rayland Hall; where he put her in possession of the apartments she had formerly occupied; and employed her to super-intend, as she was still active and alert, the workmen whom he directed to repair and re-furnish the house, and the servants whom he hired to prepare it for the reception of its lovely mistress. He forbore to pursue Roker himself, as he might have done; having no pleasure in revenge, and being rather solicitous to give to those he loved future tranquillity, than to avenge on others those past misfortunes, which perhaps served only to make him more sensible of his present felicity.

Fortune, as if weary of the long persecutions the Somerive family had experienced, seemed now resolved to make them amends by showering her favours upon every branch of it. Warwick had hardly rejoiced a week in the good fortune of Orlando, when he received a summons to attend General Tracy; who, quite exhausted by infirmity, saw the end of his life approaching, and sacrificed his resentment, which time had already considerably weakened. He was not, however, yet able to see Isabella; but his pride had been alarmed by the accounts he had received of Warwick's distressed circumstances, and above all, of his having a play coming forward at one of the theatres; which, though it was to pass as the work of an unknown young author, with a suppositious name, was well known to be, and publicly spoken of as his. That *his* nephew—that the nephew of an Earl should become an author and write for support, was so distressing to the haughty spirit of the old soldier, that though he saw many examples of the same thing in people of equal rank, he could not bear it; and the very means his brother's family took to irritate him against Warwick, by informing him of this circumstance, contributed more than any thing else to the resolution he formed of seeing his nephew, and restoring him to his favour. Warwick immediately agreed to withdraw his play. His uncle burnt the will by which he had been disinherited, and died about five months afterwards, bequeathing to his two boys by Isabella, all his landed estates, after their father, who was to enjoy them, together with his great personal property, for his life.

In the mean time the happy Orlando had conducted his lovely wife, his mother and his sisters, to Rayland Hall; where, without spoiling that look of venerable antiquity for which it was so remarkable, he collected within it every comfort and every elegance of modern life. With what grateful transports did he now walk with Monimia over the park, and talk with her of their early pleasures and of their severe subsequent sufferings! and how sensible did these retrospects render them both of their present happiness!

Orlando was only a few weeks in undisputed possession of his estate, before he presented to each of his sisters five thousand pounds; and to add to his power of gratifying his mother, it happened that very soon after his arrival at Rayland Hall Mr. Stockton died, the victim of that intemperance which exorbitant wealth and very little understanding had led him into. As he had no children, his very large property was divided among distant relations, his joint-heirs; Carloraine Castle was sold, pulled down by the purchaser, and the park converted into farms; and in this division of property, the house and estate at West Wolverton, formerly belonging to the Somerive family, were to be sold also. This his paternal house had been inhabited by farmers, under tenants of Stockton, when Orlando's last melancholy visit was paid to it. He now purchased it; and putting it as nearly as he could into the same state as it was at the death of his father, he presented it to his mother with the estate around it; and thither she went to reside with her two youngest daughters, though they all occasionally paid visits to the Hall, particularly Selina, of whom Orlando and his Monimia were equally fond.

Incapable of ingratitude, or of forgetting for a moment those to whom he had once been obliged, Orlando was no sooner happy in his restored fortune, than he thought of the widow of his military friend

Fleming. To Fleming himself he owed it, that he existed at all;—to his widow, that an existence so preserved, had not been rendered a curse by the estrangement or loss of Monimia.

One of the first uses therefore that he made of his assured prosperity, was, to remove from this respectable protectress of his beloved Monimia, the mortifications and inconveniencies of very narrow circumstances. He wrote to her, entreating to see her at the Hall with her children, and that she would stay there at least till after the accession of happiness he was to expect in the autumn. Towards the middle of September, Mrs. Fleming and her younger children arrived; and in a few days afterwards Monimia's gallant young friend the sailor, to whom she owed her providential introduction to Mrs. Fleming, unexpectedly made his appearance. He returned from a very successful cruize; he was made a lieutenant, and had obtained leave of absence for ten days, to comfort with these tidings the heart of his widowed mother; when, not finding her at her usual habitation in the New Forest, he had followed her to Rayland Hall, where he was a most welcome guest.

This young man, who was in disposition and in figure the exact representative of his father, could not long be insensible of the charms of the gentle Selina; and he spoke to Orlando of the affection he had conceived for her, with his natural sincerity. Orlando, who never felt the value of what he possessed, so much as when it enabled him to contribute to the happiness of his friends, seized with avidity an offer which seemed so likely to constitute that of his beloved sister; and he had the happiness in a few days of discovering that the old sea officer, Fleming's relation and patron, was so well pleased with his gallant behaviour in the engagement he had lately been in, that he had determined to make him his heir, and most readily consented to make a settlement upon him more than adequate to the fortune Orlando had given his sister; and it was settled that Selina and Lieutenant Fleming should in a few months be united.

Orlando was very soon after made completely happy by the birth of a son,[1] to whom he gave his own name, and who seemed to render his charming mother yet more dear to all around her. Every subsequent hour of the lives of Orlando and his Monimia was marked by some act of beneficence; and happy in themselves and in their connections, their gratitude to Heaven for the extensive blessings they enjoyed, was shewn in contributing to the cheerfulness of all around them.

---

[1] Orlando's son is born in September, nine months after his marriage to Monimia. The action thus closes in September 1779, having begun in the summer of 1775.

In the number of those who felt the sunshine of their prosperity, and prayed for its continuance, no individual was more sincere in his joy, or more fervent in repeated expressions of it, than the useful old military mendicant, whose singular services Orlando rewarded by making him the tenant for life of a neat and comfortable lodge in his park—an arrangement that gratified both the dependent and his protector.— Orlando never passed through his own gate without being agreeably reminded, by the grateful alacrity of this contented servant, of his past afflictions, and his present felicity.

F I N I S.

Appendix A: Reviews and Notices of The Old Manor House

[This section contains excerpts from several reviews of the novel and biographical accounts of Smith. Here and in the subsequent appendices original spellings and punctuation have been retained.]

1. *The Analytical Review*, 16 (May 1793): 60–63.

If it were inquired what is the principal excellence of novel writing, the greater number of readers would perhaps place it in novelty of story, variety of incident, and an arrangement happily contrived to awaken, and to keep alive curiosity. Others, who have naturally a high degree of sensibility, or who are at that period of life in which the heart is most susceptible of tender emotions, would be inclined to pronounce those the best novels, which most successfully touch the strings of sentiment and passion; and would estimate the merit of a story, by its power of calling forth the sympathetic tear. Whilst a third class of readers, who, even in the perusal of a novel, look further than to the present momentary amusement of fancy or gratification of feeling, will value a fictitious tale in proportion as it exhibits a true picture of men and manners; and, in judging of the merit of any work of this kind, will, first of all, inquire what characters it describes, and with what degree of accuracy and strength it delineates them.

Disposed as we are to rank ourselves in the last class of novel readers, we give the ingenious author of the Old Manor House, to whom the public has been indebted for some other similar productions, great credit for her talents as a novelist. In the present novel, she has not, indeed, been particularly fortunate in her story. Some leading circumstances are scarcely reconcileable with probability; particularly the daily and nightly interviews of the two lovers, residing so long in the same mansion, all the while kept secret from the rest of the family. Sometimes the narrative is clogged by collateral incidents, which produce little effect: the whole amour of the old general with the sister of Orlando might have been omitted without much loss. With respect to sentiment and passion, the reader's mind is throughout agreeably interested, rather than powerfully agitated. But, as an exhibition of characters, the piece has considerable merit. They are taken from different classes of life, marked with distinct features, illustrated by happily associated incidents, and furnished with suitable sentiments and language. Among these, the principal persons, Orlando and Monimia, are patterns, the former of ardent and unalterable affection, courage, generosity, and gratitude, the latter of simplicity, modesty, and tenderness. Mrs. Rayland, the mistress of the mansion, is family-pride, personified. Her old *femme de charge*, Mrs. Lennard, is a starch prude, severe and suspicious with respect to others, but very indulgent to herself. General Tracy is a great master of the polite art of appearing to be what a man is not. Dr. Hollybourn is a pompous, but fawning, canting priest, capable of any meanness, or baseness, to serve his interest. Several of the less important characters, both in high and low life, are equally well drawn; and the piece, on the whole, is a gallery of portraits, of which it would not be difficult to find the originals in real life....

2. *The Critical Review*, 8 (May 1793): 44–54.

Among the various productions of literary genius, there is, perhaps, none that has a more legitimate claim to an ascendency over the human mind than a well written novel. There is, moreover, no species of writing whatever better calculated for conveying, in the most engaging manner, useful instruction and moral truths to a numerous description of readers, who, either averse from the labour of serious application, or unqualified for the office of abstruse investigation, turn with alacrity from the dry and thorny paths of science, to scenes where passion awakes amidst natural events, and imagination sports amidst probable vicissitude. To the man of genuine taste, genius, and information, a finer field cannot open for a display of literary talents; to a proper and a well cultivated mind, a more favourable theatre cannot present itself for an exhibition of whatever is great, and good, and amiable in human nature. But as the execution of this species of writing requires a happy combination of parts and acquirements very rarely conjoined in the same person; and as the usual limits which bound and divide mental abilities are seldom over-stepped, so do we find that the number of those who have arrived at excellence in this walk of polite literature has been but small. The creative powers of invention may indeed furnish plot and incident, and the suggestions of a tender and a susceptible mind produce occasionally circumstances to interest and affect the heart. But he who aspires to pre-eminence as a novelist, or looks forward with fond expectations to future applause, must possess very superior qualifications, both mental and acquired, before he can obtain that celebrity which can secure him a temporary fame, or recommend him to the attention of posterity. To conduct a series of familiar events so as to rouse and preserve attention, without a violation of nature and probability; to draw and support the different characters necessary for an animated and varied drama in just and glowing colours; to hold up the mirror of truth in the moment of youthful intemperance, and to interweave amidst the web of fable, pictures to instruct, and morals to reform, requires such strength of genius; such stores of wit, humour, and original fancy; such nice discrimination of character, and such intimate and universal knowledge of the world, as very seldom fall to the lot of humanity in the same individual. In support of these assertions, and in vindication of our opinions relative to the difficulties annexed to what is called *novel writing*, we need only appeal to facts, and by a single coup d'œil[1] distinguish, amidst innumerable competitors for fame, those who by a rare and happy combination of talents have succeeded in this species of composition. We mean not to be invidious by a comparative view of living authors, or by giving a marked preference to any. We may, however, with some safety and confidence assert, that in the course of two centuries, and during the æra of polite learning in Europe, the number of novelists who have arrived to that degree of fame which will entitle their labours to the admiration of posterity is extremely limited, in which number, for the farther information of those concerned, we include a Cervantes, a Le Sage, a Rousseau, and a Voltaire.[2]

We have been led to these animadversions by the perusal of the work immediately under our inspection, and as it is the avowed production of a lady who has already furnished the public with several ingenious performances, and who has obtained a very considerable share of public approbation; we conceived ourselves called upon to deliver our sentiments at some length on a subject to which we seldom dedicate so large a portion of our Review. We shall now take a general view of the merits of Mrs. Smith's last production, compared with the requisites which we have already specified, and which we conceive indispensible in the formation of a good novel.

After a perusal of these four volumes we are forced to confess, that though we have found much to commend, we have also found much to disapprove. From the name of Mrs. Charlotte Smith we certainly were led to expect something above the common love cant of novels; some novelty in the delineation of character; some new and interesting description; some artful concealment of plot; some happy and ingenious developement and design.—At all events, we fully persuaded ourselves we should not wander long in search of what is exemplary and amiable in the eye of virtue; and that, whatever deficiencies might appear in regard to taste or invention, the picture of moral rectitude would never be defaced, nor the colouring of honourable sentiment ever obscured. How much we were disappointed in these expectations may be collected from the following leading circumstances in the Old Manor House.

---

[1] To take in the general view at a glance.

[2] Miguel de Cervantes (1547–1616): author of *Don Quixote* (1605 and 1613). Alain-René Le Sage (1668–1747): author of *Gil Blas* (1715–35). Jean-Jacques Rousseau (1712–78): author of *Julie, ou la Nouvelle Héloïse* (1761) and *Emile* (1762). Voltaire, pseudonym of François-Marie Arouet (1694–1778): author of *Candide* (1759).

A young man of family, education, and great expectations becomes violently enamoured of a young girl of low birth, illiterate, and poor, who acts as a kind of upper servant in the Old Manor House, and who is niece to Mrs. Lennard, housekeeper to the proprietor, Mrs. Rayland. As the rigid severity and caution of the aunt precludes all possibility of interviews between the two lovers during the day, Orlando (the hero of the piece), tries every expedient to obtain interviews by night; but as the fair Monimia is regularly locked up by the implacable aunt in a remote turret of the Old Manor every night at an early hour, Orlando finds all his invention fruitless, till accident discovers an old back-door, which had been long shut up and concealed from view, and which, on removing some wood and forcing open, he finds, to his inexpressible transport, leads to a stair-case which terminates at another door, against which no barrier presents itself than the head of Monimia's bed. This trifling impediment (as the bed runs on castors), the prudent and timid Monimia quickly removes; and, after a rapturous scene, it is agreed upon between the lovers, that, to prevent discovery, and to enjoy each other's society without restraint, Monimia, after all the family retire to rest, is to be conducted by Orlando every night, from her turret through an old chapel which leads to his apartment at the other extremity of the Old Manor House, unoccupied by any of the family but himself. Here the lovers nightly meet and exchange mutual vows of everlasting constancy, till an alarming circumstance induced them for some time to change the place of interview to Monimia's *bed-room in the turret.*—As this incident is described with considerable effect, and is among the most interesting events in the work, we with pleasure break off our narrative to lay it before our readers, as a specimen of Mrs. Smith's powers in exciting emotions of terror ...

[Review quotes from Volume I, Chapter 10: Monimia and Orlando hear noises in the chapel]

... Matters continue in this train till colonel Tracey, an old beau of sixty-five, enamoured of Orlando's sister Isabella, comes on a visit to Mr. Somerive, her father, with a determined purpose to seduce and carry her off. Finding that a youth of Orlando's spirit and high sense of honour was likely to impede his plan, he suggests to his father the impropriety of his son's consuming his time, inactively, at Rayland-hall, makes an offer of his interest, and finally procures him a commission in the army. Frustrated in his attempts of seduction, and becoming daily more captivated with Isabella's charms, the old colonel makes honourable proposals, and the young lady, after a faint struggle between interest and dislike, determines to take to her arms, a man old enough to have been her grandfather. Previous to the intended marriage, the colonel and Orlando go to London, where the latter is introduced to a captain Warrick, nephew to the colonel, and presumptive heir to his fortune. After some time spent in London, the colonel returns to the country with a view of celebrating his nuptials, whither Orlando, panting for another turret interview, accompanies him. The old colonel is attacked by a severe fit of the gout which confines him to his room, and Warrick arriving to intimate orders for the immediate embarkation of Orlando's regiment for America, becomes instantly enamoured of his intended aunt, and in less than forty-eight hours procures her consent to abscond with him to Portsmouth, whither he is obliged to go to attend his duty. This ungrateful and scandalous scheme, which at once repays an uncle's former kindness with villany, and involves a virtuous family in affliction, is communicated by Warrick to the honourable and dutiful Orlando; who, instead of taking any step to counteract a plan so pregnant with mischief and immorality, contents himself with simply disapproving, and promises with inviolable secrecy to favour the escape of the lovers. Orlando embarks for America, where he experiences a variety of disastrous fortune, and returning to England, finds nothing but disappointment, misery, and distress. Mrs. Rayland, on whom his chief hopes depended, is dead—The estate of Rayland Hall, which, previous to his departure, he had every reason to expect by succession, made over to a person altogether unconnected with the late proprietor—The mansion house deserted—Monimia gone, and no intelligence to be obtained of her place of abode—His father dead—The family estate sold—His brother in prison; and his mother and sisters gone to live on a scanty subsistence in London. He sells his commission for 400l.—Relieves his worthless brother from gaol—Goes in quest of Mrs. Lennard, now Mrs. Roker—Meets unexpectedly with Monimia, and hurried on by the ardour of his love, and with no other visible provision than 250l. in defiance of prudence, duty, and impending want, married her instantly.

Having thus briefly enumerated a few of the exceptionable parts of this drama, we now pause to ask Mrs. Smith, or any novel writer or reader, what possible benefit can accrue to society, and to youth in particular, from a perusal of scenes so repugnant to decorum and virtue? To draw characters where the follies, the passions, and the vices of mankind are finally productive of calamity is proper painting; because, from the ill success and punishment of imprudence and criminality, an excellent moral is deduced. But is this the colouring of Mrs. Smith's pictures? No such thing. On the contrary we find, that while youthful thoughtlessness and intemperance are crowned with success, ingratitude and the most complicated villany remain unpunished. The old colonel is reconciled to Warrick, and leaves him his whole fortune.—The infamous Rokers, and their accomplice the bishop, are only obliged to refund what they had procured by fraud, and Mrs. Lennard, the grand instrument of evil to the Somerive family, and the tyrant of poor Monimia, is taken home and placed in her former station in Rayland-hall, where she is cherished and caressed by those whom she strove by the blackest arts to ruin. With regard to *character* in this novel, we find little that can be said to leave a clear and distinct image on the mind.—We sometimes think we see Philip Somerive, and his unhappy father—but the one, the authoress has kept so much in the back ground of the piece as to be seldom visible; and the other, who unquestionably is the most respectable and amiable personage in the group, she has thought it expedient to put out of the way by making him die of a broken heart. We are afraid we can say little of *plot*, for there seems to be none but the *concealment of a will*, and still less of the *denouement*, which, in our opinion, is 'most lame and impotent.' Why did not Mrs. Lennard, when she dipped so deep in treachery, burn the real will; and what at the time of her apostacy could have been her motives for preserving that which could alone detect the infamy of the transaction?— The conclusion is wound up in such a hasty and improbable manner; and every thing is so instantaneously reversed, that it reminds us of those pantomimical entertainments where the whole scenery is changed by a stroke of harlequin's sword. We were in expectation, that, as an apology for Orlando's misplaced affection, and as an explanation of Mrs. Lennard's unaccountable harshness to Monimia, the heroine of the piece would have turned out a very different personage—but no; she still remains the obscure niece of Mrs. Lennard, and Orlando's conduct is, of course, held up as an example for all young gentlemen of family and fortune to marry any pretty servant maid they chuse.

To deny Mrs. Smith merit in other respects would be unjust. She certainly possesses in no inferior degree the power to arrest and command attention, by a happy description of circumstances and objects awful, terrific, and sublime; and discovers such fertility of imagination, as often to multiply incident on incident, even when there appears no necessity for it. The pathetic, or the tender, we do not think is Mrs. Smith's forte; but the bold, the manly, the intrepid, and the dignified sentiments of the human breast are touched with no unskilful hand. The work is likewise, on the whole, written in an easy flowing style, and except a few *prettinesses*, such 'books never disturbed in their long slumber'—'a tear blistered the paper'—'iron prudery'—'massive dignity'—'infant April', &c. is free from that affectation and turgidity which of late have disgraced modern compositions of this kind. The letters between old Mr. Somerive and Orlando, relative to the impending duel, are elegant examples of epistolary writing ...

...The whole of the story might have been comprised in *two* volumes. Were novelists a little more merciful to their readers, perhaps we Reviewers, who are obliged to read *all* they write, would be more patient.—But when we find the most ordinary and trivial occurrences in life drawn out to whole chapters, and the eternal theme of love and sentiment spun out to *thirteen hundred pages*, can it be wondered at if we sometimes yawn, and exclaim in the words of Hotspur, "Oh! it is as tedious as a tired horse or a scolding wife?"[1]

3. *The Monthly Review*, 11 (May 1793): 150–53.

Mrs. Smith's talents for novel-writing are already well known to the public; and we have had repeated occasions to acknowlege her merit in a species of composition, which, when executed with judgment and ability, in a moral view, is useful, as well as pleasant to those who read only for amusement: it is therefore the less necessary for us to undertake an elaborate examination of the present work: but we shall not dismiss it without giving a brief outline of its plan.

The principal scene of the tale is one of those spacious antient halls, or manor houses, which fill the warm imagination with romantic ideas, and which at once invite and favour adventure. The possessor of the mansion is an ancient maiden lady, the sole heiress of a great family. A favourite kinsman, a youth of seventeen, whose family resides in the neighbourhood, is permitted to visit the hall; and, when winter arrives, to sleep in a little tapestry room, next to the old library, in a wing of the house far remote from the division inhabited by the female part of the family. The confidential servant, or companion of the old lady, had been permitted to take into the house an orphan niece, nearly of the same age with the young hero of the tale, and the apartment allotted to her is in a turret which terminates one wing of the house. This young pair, Orlando and Monimia, who find opportunities for frequent interviews, entertain a tender and innocent attachment for each other. The principal business of the piece is to exhibit the embarrassments which attend their concealed passion during Orlando's residence at home, and the difficulties and distresses through which they afterward pass. The main plot is diversified with many collateral occurrences, which all contribute to give unity to the whole. The narrative, if not in every particular guided by probability, is however too well filled up with incident to suffer the reader's attention to flag. The characters are drawn with strength and discrimination, and speak their own appropriate language.

This novel particularly contains many very successful imitations of the ordinary language of people in different classes of the inferior ranks, which may in some instances remind the reader of that great painter of manners, Henry Fielding.[2] Several humourous scenes in higher life are also represented ...

---

[1] Shakespeare, *Henry IV, Part I* III:1:158–59, slightly misquoted ("Oh! He's as tedious as a tired horse; a railing wife").

[2] Henry Fielding (1707–54): author of *Joseph Andrews* (1742) and *Tom Jones* (1749).

...The reader is not to infer, from this specimen, that the novel is entirely, nor chiefly, of the humorous kind. In many parts it is sentimental; sometimes, though not frequently, it becomes pathetic; and once or twice, but very sparingly, political ideas and opinions are introduced, and the author takes occasion to express that generous spirit of freedom, which is displayed more at large in her "*Desmond.*" In fine, though we cannot say that we think the present novel *superior* to those which Mrs. S., has formerly produced, yet it discovers, in a considerable degree, facility of invention, knowlege of life, and command of language.

4. From Walter Scott, "Charlotte Smith," *Miscellaneous Prose Works*, 4 (Edinburgh: Cadell, 1834): 124–25.

...The *chef-d'œuvre*[1] of Mrs. Smith's works is, according to our recollection, the *Old Manor-House*, especially the first part of the story, where the scene lies about the ancient mansion and its vicinity. Old Mrs. Rayland is without a rival; a Queen Elizabeth in private life, jealous of her immediate dignities and possessions, and still more jealous of the power of bequeathing them. Her letter to Mr. Somerive, in which she intimates rather than expresses her desire to keep young Orlando at the Hall, while she is so careful to avoid committing herself by any direct expression of her intentions with respect to him, is a masterpiece of diplomacy, equal to what she of Tudor could have composed on a similar occasion. The love of the young people thrown together so naturally, its innocence and purity, and the sort of perils with which they are beset, cannot fail deeply to interest all those who are interested by this peculiar species of literature. The unexpected interview with Jonas the smuggler, furnishes an opportunity for varying the tale with a fine scene of natural terror, drawn with a masterly hand.

In the *Old Manor-House* there are also some excellent sketches of description; but such are indeed to be found in all Mrs. Smith's works; and it is remarkable that the sea-coast scenery of Dorset and Devon, with which she must have been familiar, is scarce painted with more accuracy of description, than the tower upon a rugged headland on the coast of Caithness, which she could only become acquainted with by report—so readily does the plastic power of genius weave into a wreath materials, whether collected by the artist or by other hands. It may be remarked, that Mrs. Smith not only preserves in her landscapes the truth and precision of a painter, but that they sometimes evince marks of her own favourite

---

[1] Masterpiece.

pursuits and studies. The plants and flowers are described by their Linnean names,[1] as well as by their vulgar epithets; and in speaking of the denizens of air, the terms of natural history are often introduced. Something like this may be observed in Mr. Crabbe's poems;[2] but neither in these nor in Mrs. Smith's novels does it strike the reader that there is pedantry in such details; an objection which certainly would occur, were such scientific ornaments to be used by a meaner hand.

The most deficient part of Mrs. Smith's novels, is unquestionably the plot, or narrative, which, in general, bears the appearance of having been hastily *run up*, as the phrase goes, without much attention to probability or accuracy of combination. This was not owing to any deficiency of invention; for when Charlotte Smith had leisure, and chose to employ it to the purpose, her story, as in the *Orphan of the Castle*, is conducted with unexceptionable ingenuity. But she was too often summoned to her literary labours by the inexorable voice necessity, which obliged her to write for the daily supply of the press, without having previously adjusted, perhaps without having even rough-hewn, the course of incidents which she intended to detail. Hence the hurry and want of connexion which may be observed in some of her stories, and hence, too, instances, in which we can see that the character of the tale has changed, while it was yet in the author's imagination, and has in the end become different from what she herself had originally proposed. This is apt to arise either from the author having forgotten the thread of the story, or her having, in the progress of the narrative, found it more difficult to disentangle it skilfully than her first concoction of the tale had induced her to hope. This desertion of the story is, no doubt, an imperfection; for few of the merits which a novel usually boasts are to be preferred to an interesting and well-arranged story. But then this merit, however great, has never been considered as indispensable to fictitious narrative. On the contrary, in many of the best specimens of that class of composition—Gil Blas, for example, Peregrine Pickle, Roderick Random,[3] and many others of the first eminence—no effort whatever is made to attain the praise belonging to a compact system of adventure, in which the volumes which succeed the first, like the months of summer maturing the flowers and fruit which have germinated in spring, slowly conduct the tale to the maturity at which it arrives upon its conclusion, as

---

[1] Linnaeus: Carl Linné (1707–78): founder of the binomial system by which plants and animals are named.

[2] George Crabbe (1754–1832): poet whose work concentrated on realistic portraits of rustic life and the rural landscape.

[3] All characters in eighteenth-century picaresque novels: *Gil Blas* (see note 1, p. 183), *The Adventures of Peregrine Pickle* (1751) and *The Adventures of Roderick Random* (1748), the latter two by Tobias Smollett (1721–71).

autumn gathers in the produce of the year. On the contrary, the adventures, however delightful in themselves, are but

"Like orient pearls at random strung,"[1]

and are not connected together, otherwise than as having occurred to one individual, and in the course of one man's life. In fine, whatever may be the vote of the severer critics, we are afraid that many of the labourers in this walk of literature will conclude with Bayes by asking, "What is the use of the plot but to bring in fine things?"[2] And truly, if the fine things really deserve the name, we think there is pedantry in censuring the works where they occur, merely because productions of genius are not also adorned with a regularity of conception, carrying skilfully forward the conclusion of the story, which we may safely pronounce one of the rarest attainments of art.

The characters of Mrs. Smith are conceived with truth and force, though we do not recollect any one which bears the stamp of actual novelty; and indeed, an effort at introducing such, unless the author is powerfully gifted with the inventive faculty, is more likely to produce monsters than models of composition. She is uniformly happy in supplying them with language fitted to their station in life; nor are there many dialogues to be found which are at once so entertaining, and approach so nearly to truth and reality. The evanescent tone of the highest fashionable society is not easily caught, nor perhaps is it desirable it should be, considering the care which is taken in these elevated regions to deprive conversation of every thing approaching to the emphasis of passion, or even of serious interest. But of every other species of dialogue, from the higher to the lower classes of her countrymen, Mrs. Smith's works exhibit happy specimens; and her portraits of foreigners, owing to her long residence abroad, are not less striking than those of Britons.

There is yet another attribute of Mrs. Smith's fictitious narratives, which may be a recommendation, or the contrary, as it affects readers of various temperaments, or the same reader in a different mood of mind. We allude to the general tone of melancholy which pervades her composition, and of which every one who has read the preceding Memoir can no longer be at a loss to assign the cause. The conclusions of her novels, it is true, are generally fortunate, and she has spared her readers, who have probably enough arising out of their own concerns to make them anxious and unhappy, the uncomfortable feeling of having wasted their hour of leisure upon making themselves yet more sad and uncomfortable than before, by the unpleasant

---

[1] From *A Persian Song of Hafiz*, by Sir William Jones (1746–94).
[2] Bayes, a character in George Villiers, Duke of Buckingham's (1628–87) burlesque *The Rehearsal* (1672), commonly thought to parody John Dryden.

conclusion of a tale which they had taken up for amusement. The sky, though it uniformly lours upon us through Mrs. Smith's narrations, breaks forth on the conclusion, and cheers the scene when we are about to part from it. Still, however, we long for a few sunny glimpses to enliven the landscape in the course of the story, and with these we are rarely supplied; so that the general influence of melancholy can scarce be removed by the assurance, that our favourites are at length married and prosperous. The hasty and happy catastrophe seems so inconsistent with the uniform persecutions of Fortune, through the course of the story, that we cannot help doubting whether adversity had exhausted her vial, or whether she had not farther misfortunes in store for them after the curtain was dropped by the Authoress. Those who have few sorrows of their own, as Coleridge beautifully expresses it, love the tales which call forth a sympathy for which their own feelings give little occasion; while others, exhausted by the actual distresses of life, relish better those narratives which steal them from a sense of sorrow. But every one, whether of sad or gay temperament, must regret that the tone of melancholy which pervades Mrs. Smith's compositions, was derived too surely from the circumstances and feelings of the amiable Authoress. We are indeed informed by Mrs. Dorset that the natural temper of her sister was lively and playful; but it must be considered, that the works on which she was obliged, often reluctantly, to labour, were seldom undertaken from free choice. Nothing saddens the heart so much as that sort of literary labour which depends on the imagination, when it is undertaken unwillingly, and from a sense of compulsion. The galley-slave may sing when he is unchained, but it would be uncommon equanimity which could induce him to do so when he is actually bound to his oar. If there is a mental drudgery which lowers the spirits and lacerates the nerves, like the toil of the slave, it is that which is exacted by literary composition, when the heart is not in unison with the work upon which the head is employed. Add to the unhappy author's task, sickness, sorrow, or the pressure of unfavourable circumstances, and the labour of the bondsman becomes light in comparison.

Before closing a rough attempt to discharge the debt we owe in acknowledgment of many pleasant hours derived from the perusal of Mrs. Smith's works, we cannot but remark the number of highly-talented women, who have, within our time of novel-reading, distinguished themselves advantageously in this department of literature. Besides the living excellence of Mrs. D'Arblay, and of Maria Edgeworth, of the Authoress of *Marriage* and the *Inheritance*, and of Mrs. Opie, the names arise on us of Miss Austen, the faithful chronicler of English manners, and English society of the middling, or what is called the genteel class; besides also Mrs. Radcliffe, Miss Reeves, and others, to whom we have endeavoured to do some justice in these sheets. We have to thank Mrs. Inchbald, the authoress of *Frankenstein*, Mrs. Bennet, too, and many other women of talents for the amusement which their works have afforded; and we must add, that we think it would be impossible to match against these names the same number of masculine competitors, arising within the same space of time.[1] The fact is worthy of notice; although, whether it arises from mere chance; whether the less marked and more evanescent shades of modern society are more happily painted by the finer pencil of a woman; or whether our modern delicacy, having excluded the bold and sometimes coarse delineations permitted to ancient novelists, has rendered competition more easy to female writers, because the forms must be veiled and clothed with drapery.— is a subject which would lead us far, and which, therefore, it is not our present purpose to enter into.

---

[1] Scott names and alludes to many of the most important female novelists of the time. Mrs. D'Arblay: Frances Burney (1752–1840), author of, most famously, *Evelina* (1778), *Cecilia* (1782), and *Camilla* (1796). Maria Edgeworth (1768–1849), author of *Castle Rackrent* (1800), *Belinda* (1801), *Moral Tales* (1801), *Popular Tales* (1804), *Patronage* (1814), and other novels. She is, along with Walter Scott, credited with developing the regional novel. The author of *Marriage* (1818) and *The Inheritance* (1824) was Susan Ferrier (1782–1854); she also wrote *Destiny* (1831). Mrs. Opie: Amelia Opie (1769–1853), author of *Adeline Mowbray* (1805). Miss Austen: Jane Austen (1775–1817), author of *Sense and Sensibility* (1811), *Pride and Prejudice* (1813), *Mansfield Park* (1814), *Emma* (1816), and *Northanger Abbey* and *Persuasion* (both 1818). Mrs. Radcliffe: Ann Radcliffe (1764–1823), author of *The Mysteries of Udolpho* (1794) and *The Italian* (1797), among others: a leading figure in Gothic writing. Miss Reeves [sic]: Clara Reeve (1729–1807), author of *The Old English Baron* (1778), one of the first Gothic novels. Mrs. Inchbald: Elizabeth Inchbald (1753–1821), playwright and novelist; author of *A Simple Story* (1791) and the English translation of Kotzebue's *Lovers' Vows* (1798), which features prominently in Austen's *Mansfield Park*. The author of *Frankenstein* (1818) is Mary Wollstonecraft Shelley (1797–1851), who also wrote other novels, literary biographies, and short stories. Mrs. Bennet is probably Anna Maria Bennett (?1750–1808), author of, among other novels, *The Beggar-Girl and her Benefactors* (1797), a satire.

Appendix B: The Genre Debate

[*The Old Manor House* straddles several genres: it is a novel and a romance, with realist and Gothic thematics. During the late eighteenth century, readers were concerned to define the style and type of literature they were reading. The texts in this section show various commentators engaging with the idea of genre and how it can be defined, as well as how the act of reading affects those who read.]

1. Anna Letitia Barbauld and John Aiken, "An Enquiry into Those Kinds of Distress which Excite Agreeable Sensations" (1773), *Miscellaneous Pieces in Prose* (London: J. Johnson, 1792): 190–214.

It is undoubtedly true, though a phænomenon of the human mind difficult to account for, that the representation of distress frequently gives pleasure; from which general observation many of our modern writers of tragedy and romance seem to have drawn this inference, that in order to please, they have nothing more to do than to paint distress in natural and striking colours. With this view, they heap together all the afflicting events and dismal accidents their imagination can furnish; and when they have half broke the reader's heart, they expect he should thank them for his agreeable entertainment. An author of this class sits down, pretty much like an inquisitor, to compute how much suffering he can inflict upon the hero of his tale before he makes an end of him; with this difference, indeed, that the inquisitor only tortures those who are at least reputed criminals; whereas the writer generally chooses the most excellent character in his piece for the subject of his persecution. The great criterion of excellence is placed in being able to draw tears plentifully; and concluding we shall weep the more, the more the picture is loaded with doleful events, they go on, telling

> ———of sorrows upon sorrows
> Even to a lamentable length of woe.[1]

A monarch once proposed a reward for the discovery of a new pleasure; but if any one could find out a new torture, or non-descript calamity, he would be more entitled to the applause of those who fabricated books of entertainment.

But the springs of pity require to be touched with a more delicate hand; and it is far from being true that we are agreeably affected by every thing

---

[1]   Verse unidentified.

that excites our sympathy. It shall therefore be the business of this essay to distinguish those kinds of distress which are pleasing in the representation, from those which are really painful and disgusting.

The view or relation of mere misery can never be pleasing. We have, indeed, a strong sympathy with all kinds of misery; but it is a feeling of pure unmixed pain, similar in kind, though not equal in degree, to what we feel for ourselves on the like occasions; and never produces that melting sorrow, that thrill of tenderness, to which we give the name of pity. They are two distinct sensations, marked by very different external expression. One causes the nerves to tingle, the flesh to shudder, and the whole countenance to be thrown into strong contractions; the other relaxes the frame, opens the features, and produces tears. When we crush a noxious or loathsome animal, we may sympathize strongly with the pain it suffers, but with far different emotions from the tender sentiment we feel for the dog of Ulysses, who crawled to meet his long-lost master, looked up, and died at his feet. Extreme bodily pain is perhaps the most intense suffering we are capable of, and if the fellow-feeling with misery alone was grateful to the mind, the exhibition of a man in a fit of the tooth-ach, or under a chirurgical operation, would have a fine effect in a tragedy. But there must be some other sentiment combined with this kind of instinctive sympathy, before it becomes in any degree pleasing, or produces the sweet emotion of pity. This sentiment is love, esteem, the complacency we take in the contemplation of beauty, of mental or moral excellence, called forth and rendered more interesting, by circumstances of pain and danger. Tenderness is, much more properly than sorrow, the spring of tears; for it affects us in that manner, whether combined with joy or grief; perhaps more in the former case than the latter. And I believe we may venture to assert, that no distress which produces tears is wholly without a mixture of pleasure. When Joseph's brethren were sent to buy corn, if they had perished in the desert by wild beasts, or been reduced (as in the horrid adventures of a Pierre de Vaud[1]) to eat one another, we might have shuddered, but we should not have wept for them. The gush of tears breaks forth when Joseph made himself known to his brethren, and fell on their neck, and kissed them. When Hubert prepares to burn out prince Arthur's eyes, the shocking circumstance, of itself, would only affect us with horror; it is the amiable simplicity of the young prince, and his innocent affection to his intended murderer, that draws our tears, and excites that tender sorrow which we love to feel, and which refines the heart while we do feel it.[2]

---

[1] Jeanne de la Pierre of Vaud (?)—condemned as a werewolf April 22, 1602 for kidnapping and eating a child (note courtesy Colleen Franklin).

[2] The reference is to Shakespeare's *King John* (1596): IV.i.

We see, therefore, from this view of our internal feelings, that no scenes of misery ought to be exhibited which are not connected with the display of some moral excellence, or agreeable quality. If fortitude, power, and strength of mind are called forth, they produce the sublime feelings of wonder and admiration: if the softer qualities of gentleness, grace, and beauty, they inspire love and pity. The management of these latter emotions is our present object.

And let it be remembered, in the first place, that the misfortunes which excite pity must not be too horrid and overwhelming. The mind is rather stunned than softened by great calamities. They are little circumstances that work most sensibly upon the tender feelings. For this reason, a well-written novel generally draws more tears than a tragedy. The distresses of tragedy are more calculated to amaze and terrify, than to move compassion. Battles, torture and death are in every page. The dignity of the characters, the importance of the events, the pomp of verse and imagery interest the grander passions, and raise the mind to an enthusiasm little favourable to the weak and languid notes of pity. The tragedies of Young[1] are in a fine strain of poetry, and the situations are worked up with great energy; but the pictures are in too deep a shade: all his pieces are full of violent and gloomy passions, and so over-wrought with horror, that instead of awakening any pleasing sensibility, they leave on the mind an impression of sadness mixed with terror. Shakespeare is sometimes guilty of presenting scenes too shocking. Such is the trampling out of Gloster's eyes; and such is the whole play of Titus Andronicus.[2] But Lee, beyond all others, abounds with this kind of images.[3] He delighted in painting the most daring crimes, and cruel massacres; and though he has shewn himself extremely capable of raising tenderness, he continually checks it course by shocking and disagreeable expressions. His pieces are in the same taste with the pictures of Spagnolet,[4] and there are many scenes in his tragedies which no one can relish who would not look with pleasure on the slaying of St. Bartholomew. The following speech of Marguerite, in the massacre of Paris, was, I suppose, intended to express the utmost tenderness of affection.

> Die for him! that's too little; I could burn
> Piece-meal away, or bleed to death by drops,
> Be flay'd alive, then broke upon the wheel,

---

1   Edward Young (1683–1765), poet. His most famous poem, *Night Thoughts* (1742–45), popularized what is known as the Graveyard School of poetry.

2   Gloucester loses his eyes in Shakespeare's *King Lear* (1604–05), III.vii. *Titus Andronicus* (1594) is one of Shakespeare's most violent tragedies.

3   Nathaniel Lee (?1649–92), whose popular tragedies relied on overwrought sensationalized imagery.

4   Lo Spagnuolo: Guiseppe Maria Crespi (1665–1747), noted for his satirical paintings and use of heavy chiaroscuro.

Yet with a smile endure it all for Guise:
And when let loose from torments, all one wound,
Run with my mangled arms and crush him dead.[1]

Images like these will never excite the softer passions. We are less moved at the description of an Indian tortured with all the dreadful ingenuity of that savage people, than with the fatal mistake of the lover in the Spectator, who pierced an artery in the arm of his mistress as he was letting her blood. Tragedy and romance-writers are likewise apt to make too free with the more violent expressions of passion and distress, by which means they lose their effect. Thus an ordinary author does not know how to express any strong emotion otherwise than by swoonings or death; so that a person experienced in this kind of reading, when a girl faints away at parting with her lover, or a hero kills himself for the loss of his mistress, considers it as the established etiquette upon such occasions, and turns over the pages with the utmost coolness and unconcern; whereas real sensibility, and a more intimate knowledge of human nature, would have suggested a thousand little touches of grief, which though slight, are irresistible. We are too gloomy a people. Some of the French novels are remarkable for little affecting incidents, imagined with delicacy, and told with grace. Perhaps they have a better turn than we have for this kind of writing.

A judicious author will never attempt to raise pity by any thing mean or disgusting. As we have already observed, there must be a degree of complacence mixed with our sorrows to produce an agreeable sympathy; nothing, therefore, must be admitted which destroys the grace and dignity of suffering; the imagination must have an amiable figure to dwell upon; there are circumstances so ludicrous or disgusting, that no character can preserve a proper decorum under them, or appear in an agreeable light. Who can read the following description of Polypheme without finding his compassion entirely destroyed by aversion and loathing?

—————— His bloody hand
Snatch'd two unhappy of my martial band,
And dash'd like dogs against the stony floor,
The pavement swims with brains and mingled gore;
Torn limb from limb, he spreads his horrid feast,
And fierce devours it like a mountain beast,
He sucks the marrow, and the blood he drains,
Nor entrails, flesh, nor solid bone remains.

---

[1] Lee, *The Massacre of Paris* (1679–81): III.i.23–28. The play, extremely anti-Catholic, was banned at first but finally performed after the 1688 Revolution, in 1689.

Or that of Scylla,

> In the wide dungeon she devours her food,
> And the flesh trembles while she churns the blood.[1]

Deformity is always disgusting, and the imagination cannot reconcile it with the idea of a favourite character; therefore the poet and romance-writer are fully justified in giving a larger share of beauty to their principal figures than is usually met with in common life. A late genius, indeed, in a whimsical mood, gave us a lady with her nose crushed for the heroine of his story;[2] but the circumstance spoils the picture; and though in the course of the story it is kept a good deal out of sight, whenever it does recur to the imagination we are hurt and disgusted. It was an heroic instance of virtue in the nuns of a certain abbey, who cut off their noses and lips to avoid violation; yet this would make a very bad subject for a poem or a play. Something akin to this is the representation of any thing unnatural; of which kind is the famous story of the Roman charity, and for this reason I cannot but think it an unpleasing subject for either the pen or the pencil.

Poverty, if truly represented, shocks our nicer feelings; therefore, whenever it is made use of to awaken our compassion, the rags and dirt, the squalid appearance and mean employments incident to that state must be kept out of sight, and the distress must arise from the idea of depression, and the shock of falling from higher fortunes. We do not pity Belisarius as a poor blind beggar; and a painter would succeed very ill who should sink him to the meanness of that condition.[3] He must let us still discover the conqueror of the Vandals, the general of the imperial armies, or we shall be little interested. Let us look at the picture of the old woman in Otway:

> ——————A wrinkled hag with age grown double,
> Picking dry sticks, and muttering to herself;
> Her eyes with scalding rheum were gall'd and red;
> Cold palsie shook her head; her hands seem'd wither'd;
> And on her crooked shoulder had she wrapt
> The tatter'd remnant of an old strip'd hanging,

---

[1] Both passages are from Alexander Pope's (1688–1744) translation of Homer's *The Odyssey* (1725–26): Book IX: 341–49 and Book XII: 306–07.

[2] Barbauld refers to Amelia in Henry Fielding's novel of the same name (1752), who has a nose "beat all to pieces."

3 Belisarius was a great general under Justinian (see note 3, p. 561), who defeated the Vandals in Africa, occupied Rome, and defeated the Goths in Italy.

Which serv'd to keep her carcase from the cold;
So there was nothing of a piece about her.[1]

Here is the extreme of wretchedness, and instead of melting into pity, we should turn away with disgust, if we were not pleased with it, as we are with a Dutch painting, from its exact imitation of nature. Indeed the author only intended it to strike horror. But how different are the sentiments we feel for the lovely Belvidera![2] We see none of those circumstances which render poverty an unamiable thing. When the goods are seized by an execution, our attention is turned to *the piles of massy plate, and all the ancient, most domestic ornaments*, which imply grandeur and consequence; or to such instances of their hard fortune as will lead us to pity them as lovers: we are struck and affected with the general face of ruin; but we are not brought near enough to discern the ugliness of its features. Belvidera ruined, Belvidera deprived of friends, without a home, abandoned to the wide world—we can contemplate with all the pleasing sympathy of pity; but had she been represented as really sunk into low life, had we seen her employed in the most servile offices of poverty, our compassion would have given way to contempt and disgust. Indeed, we may observe in real life, that poverty is only pitied so long as people can keep themselves from the effects of it. When in common language we say *a miserable object*, we mean an object of distress which, if we relieve, we turn away from at the same time. To make pity pleasing, the object of it must not in any view be disagreeable to the imagination. How admirably has the author of Clarissa managed this point?[3] Amidst scenes of suffering which rend the heart, in poverty, in a prison, under the most shocking outrages, the grace and delicacy of her character never suffers even for a moment; there seems to be a charm about her which prevents her receiving a stain from any thing which happens; and Clarissa, abandoned and undone, is the object not only of complacence, but veneration.

I would likewise observe, that if an author would have us feel a strong degree of compassion, his characters must not be too perfect. The stern fortitude and inflexible resolution of a Cato[4] may command esteem, but does not excite tenderness; and faultless rectitude of conduct, though no rigour be mixed with it, is of too sublime a nature to inspire compassion. Virtue has a kind of self-sufficiency; it stands upon its own basis, and cannot be injured by any violence. It must therefore be mixed with something of helplessness

---

[1] Barbauld quotes from Thomas Otway's play *Venice Preserv'd* (1682). Otway also wrote *The Orphan* (1680), from which Monimia draws her "fanciful" name.

[2] The tragic heroine of *Venice Preserv'd*, who dies of a broken heart.

[3] Samuel Richardson (1689–1761), who published *Clarissa* to great acclaim in 1747–49.

[4] The subject of a tragedy (1713) by Joseph Addison (1672–1719). Cato kills himself rather than submit to a dictator's oppression.

and imperfection, with an excessive sensibility, or a simplicity bordering upon weakness, before it raises, in any great degree, either tenderness or familiar love. If there be a fault in the masterly performance just now mentioned, it is that the character of Clarissa is so inflexibly right, her passions are under such perfect command, and her prudence is so equal to every occasion, that she seems not to need that sympathy we should bestow upon one of a less elevated character; and perhaps we should feel a livelier emotion of tenderness for the innocent girl whom Lovelace[1] calls his Rose-bud, but that the story of Clarissa is so worked up by the strength of colouring, and the force of repeated impressions, as to command all our sorrow.

Pity seems too degrading a sentiment to be offered at the shrine of faultless excellence. The sufferings of martyrs are rather beheld with admiration and sympathetic triumph than with tears; and we never feel much for those whom we consider as themselves raised above common feelings. The last rule I shall insist upon is, that scenes of distress should not be too long continued. All our finer feelings are in a manner momentary, and no art can carry them beyond a certain point, either in intenseness or duration. Constant suffering deadens the heart to tender impressions; as we may observe in sailors, and others who are grown callous by a life of continual hardships. It is therefore highly necessary, in a long work, to relieve the mind by scenes of pleasure and gaiety; and I cannot think it so absurd a practice as our modern delicacy has represented it, to intermix wit and fancy with the pathetic, provided care be taken not to check the passions while they are flowing. The transition from a pleasurable state of mind to tender sorrow is not so difficult as we imagine. When the mind is opened by gay and agreeable scenes, every impression is felt more sensibly. Persons of a lively temper are much more susceptible of that sudden swell of sensibility which occasions tears, than those of a grave and saturnine cast: for this reason women are more easily moved to weeping than men. Those who have touched the springs of pity with the finest hand, have mingled light strokes of pleasantry and mirth in their most pathetic passages. Very different is the conduct of many novel-writers, who, by plunging us into scenes of distress without end or limit, exhaust the powers, and before the conclusion either render us insensible to every thing, or fix a real sadness upon the mind. The uniform stile of tragedies is one reason why they affect us so little. In our old plays, all the force of language is reserved for the more interesting parts; and in the scenes of common life there is no attempt to rise above common language: whereas we, by that pompous manner and affected solemnity which we think it necessary to preserve through the whole piece, lose the force of an elevated or passionate expression where the occasion really suggests it.

---

[1] Lovelace pursues, abducts, and finally rapes Clarissa, who eventually dies from shame.

Having thus considered the manner in which fictitious distress must be managed to render it pleasing, let us reflect a little upon the moral tendency of such representations. Much has been said in favour of them, and they are generally thought to improve the tender and humane feelings; but this, I own, appears to me very dubious. That they exercise sensibility, is true; but sensibility does not increase with exercise. By the constitution of our frame our habits increase, our emotions decrease, by repeated acts; and thus a wise provision is made, that as our compassion grows weaker, its place should be supplied by habitual benevolence. But in these writings our sensibility is strongly called forth without any possibility of exerting itself in virtuous action, and those emotions, which we shall never feel again with equal force, are wasted without advantage. Nothing is more dangerous than to let virtuous impressions of any kind pass through the mind without producing their proper effect. The awakenings of remorse, virtuous shame and indignation, the glow of moral approbation— if they do not lead to action, grow less and less vivid every time they recur, till at length the mind grows absolutely callous. The being affected with a pathetic story is undoubtedly a sign of an amiable disposition, but perhaps no means of increasing it. On the contrary, young people, by a course of this kind of reading, often acquire something of that apathy and indifference which the experience of real life would have given them, without its advantages.

Another reason why plays and romances do not improve our humanity is, that they lead us to require a certain elegance of manners and delicacy of virtue which is not often found with poverty, ignorance and meanness. The objects of pity in romance are as different from those in real life as our husbandmen from the shepherds of Arcadia:[1] and a girl who will sit weeping the whole night at the delicate distresses of a lady Charlotte, or lady Julia, shall be little moved at the complaint of her neighbour, who, in a homely phrase and vulgar accent, laments to her that she is not able to get bread for her family. Romance-writers likewise make great misfortunes so familiar to our ears, that we have hardly any pity to spare for the common accidents of life: but we ought to remember, that misery has a claim to relief, however we may be disgusted with its appearance; and that we must not fancy ourselves charitable, when we are only pleasing our imagination.

It would perhaps be better, if our romances were more like those of the old stamp, which tended to raise human nature, and inspire a certain grace and dignity of manners of which we have hardly the idea. The high notions of honour, the wild and fanciful spirit of adventure and romantic love, elevated the mind; our novels tend to depress and enfeeble it. Yet there is a species of this kind of writing which must ever afford an exquisite pleasure to persons of taste and sensibility; where noble sentiments are mixed with

---

[1]   The shepherds of Arcadia occupied an idealized pastoral landscape.

well-fancied incidents, pathetic touches with dignity and grace, and invention with chaste correctness. Such will ever interest our sweetest passions....

2. From John Moore, "A View of the Commencement and Progress of Romance," *The Works of Tobias Smollett. With Memoirs of His Life*, I (London: B. Law, 1797): xci–xcv.

.... Dr. Smollett,[1] in the Continuation of his History of England, observes, that towards the end of the reign of George II. and about the beginning of that of his present majesty,[2] "genius in writing spontaneously arose; and though neglected by the great, flourished under the culture of a public which had pretensions to taste, and piqued itself on encouraging literary merit." He proceeds to enumerate the most distinguished writers in the various branches of literature at that period, and gives his suffrage to the great talents of one who pursued the same line with himself, in the following words: "The genius of Cervantes was transfused into the novels of Fielding, who painted the characters and ridiculed the follies of life with equal strength, humour, and propriety."

The success of Richardson, Fielding, and Smollett, in this species of writing, produced, what great success generally does produce, a prodigious number of imitators: but by far the greater part of them, like Hamlet's players, imitated abominably; and instead of representing the manners of the age, exhibited men and women, neither having the manners of Christians nor Pagans, and who seemed to have been made by the least expert of Nature's journeymen. There were, for a considerable time, so many novels written of this description, and with so few exceptions, that the very words Romance of Novel conveyed the idea of a frivolous or pernicious book. Even this, however, did not diminish the number, though it made many people at pains to declare, that for their part they never read novels; a declaration sometimes made by persons of both sexes, who never read any thing else. This is being by much too cautious. They might, with equal prudence, declare, that they never would read any book, because many books are silly or pernicious. The truth is, that the best romances always have been, and always will be, read with delight by men of genius; and with the more delight, the more taste and genius the reader happens to have. Nothing can be so interesting to man as man. The modern romances are or ought to be a representation of life and manners in the country where the scene is placed. Had works of this nature existed in the flourishing ages of the Greek and Roman republics, and had

---

[1] Tobias Smollett (1721–71). *The Continuation of the Complete History of England* appeared in 1760.

[2] George II reigned from 1727–60; the "present majesty" is George III (1760–1820).

some of the best of them been preserved, how infinitely would they be relished at present! as they would give a much more minute and satisfactory picture of private and domestic life than is found in history, which dwells chiefly on war and affairs of state. This species of writing may also be made most subservient to the purposes of instruction; but even those which afford amusement only, provided they contain nothing immoral, are not without utility, and deserve by no means to be spoken of with that contempt which they sometimes are, by their most intimate acquaintance. These gentlemen ought to recollect in what manner they usually employ that portion of their time which they do not pass in reading what they so much affect to despise: they ought to recollect how many languid intervals there are in their journey through life; how often they fill them up in a more pernicious way; and if a novel or romance should now and then help them to jog along with more innocence and less yawning, they ought to be a little more grateful.

It may be said, that such people had much better study books of science, or read moral essays or sermons. Unquestionably they had: but unfortunately they will not: for although some authors have shewn that it is possible to write sermons so that they shall be as much or more read than the best romance, yet this talent is extremely rare: and it is often lamented that sermons and moral essays, containing much good instruction, are less universally perused than many novels, more inelegantly written. What does this prove, but that there is something so peculiarly attractive in this species of writing, that performances, which would have been neglected in any other form, find readers in this?

Some very respectable authors have even insinuated, that romances are more entertaining than history itself, and that they thereby breed a dislike to that useful study. I fear this is not a likely argument to prevail on mankind to quit romances for history; and therefore, even if I were of that opinion, which is not the case, I should not publish it.

But it is universally known, that books of pure science and instruction, which require much thought, are not studied spontaneously by any but those who have already a considerable degree of steadiness of mind and desire of knowledge. Persons of dissipated minds, incapable of attention, who stand most in need of instruction, are the least willing to receive it; they throw such books down the moment they perceive their drift. But a romance in the highest degree entertaining, may be written with as moral an intention, and contain as many excellent rules for the conduct of life, as any book with a more solemn and scientific title. This, however, not being suspected by the persons above alluded to, they continue to read in the confidence of meeting with amusement only, and fearless of any plot or plan for their instruction or improvement; they find folly ridiculed in a pleasant manner, vice placed in a degrading light, and a variety of instructive lessons so interwoven with an interesting story, that they cannot satisfy their curiosity until they have received impressions of a useful or virtuous nature, and thus acquire something infinitely more valuable than what they were in pursuit of....

3. From Walter Scott, "Romance," *Miscellaneous Prose Works,* 4 (Edinburgh: Cadell, 1834): 30–31; 50–51.

Dr. Johnson has defined Romance, in its primary sense, to be "a military fable of the middle ages; a tale of wild adventures in love and chivalry." But although this definition expresses correctly the ordinary idea of the word, it is not sufficiently comprehensive to answer our present purpose. A composition may be a legitimate romance, yet neither refer to love nor chivalry— to war nor to the middle ages. The "wild adventures" are almost the only absolutely essential ingredient in Johnson's definition. We would be rather inclined to describe a *Romance* as "a fictitious narrative in prose or verse; the interest of which turns upon marvellous and uncommon incidents;" being thus opposed to the kindred term *Novel,* which Johnson has described as a "smooth tale, generally of love"; but which we would rather define as "a fictitious narrative, differing from the Romance, because the events are accommodated to the ordinary train of human events, and the modern state of society." Assuming these definitions, it is evident, from the nature of the distinction adopted, that there may exist compositions which it is difficult to assign precisely or exclusively to the one class or the other; and which, in fact, partake of the nature of both. But, generally speaking, the distinction will be found broad enough to answer all general and useful purposes.

The word Romance, in its original meaning, was far from corresponding with the definition now assigned. On the contrary, it signified merely one or other of the popular dialects of Europe, founded (as almost all these dialects were) upon the Roman tongue, that is, upon the Latin. The name of Romance was indiscriminately given to the Italian, to the Spanish, even (in one remarkable instance at least) to the English language. But it was especially applied to the compound language of the Franks, the Celtic of the ancient Gauls, and the classical Latin, formed the ingredients. Thus Robert De Brunne:

> "All is calde geste Inglis,
> That in this language spoken is—
> Frankis speech is caled *Romance,*
> So sayis clerkis and men of France."[1]

---

[1] Robert Mannyng of Brunne (Bourne, in Lincolnshire) (1288–1338). He is known only for his two poems *Handlyng Synne* (1303–38) and *Chronicle of England* (finished 1338), from which this excerpt is probably taken. Scott mistakes the year, as Mannyng was not yet born in 1150.

At a period so early as 1150, it plainly appears that the Romance language was distinguished from the Latin, and that translations were made from the one into the other; for an ancient Romance on the subject of Alexander, quoted by Fauchet,[1] says it was written by a learned clerk,

> "Qui de *Latin* la trest, et *en Roman* la mit."

That is, "who translated the tale from the Latin, and clothed it in the *Romance* language." The most noted metrical tales or chronicles of the middle ages were usually composed in the Romance or French language, which, being spoken both at the Court of Paris and that of London, under the kings of the Norman race, became in a peculiar degree the speech of love and chivalry. So much is this the case, that such metrical narratives as are written in English always affect to refer to some French original, which, usually at least, if not in all instances, must be supposed to have had a real existence. Hence the frequent recurrence of the phrase,

> "As in romance we read;"

Or,

> "Right as the romaunt us tells;"

and equivalent terms, well known to all who have at any time perused such compositions. Thus, very naturally, though undoubtedly by slow degrees, the very name of *romaunt*, or *romance*, came to be transferred from the language itself to that peculiar style of composition in which it was so much employed, and which so commonly referred to it. How early a transference so natural took place, we have no exact means of knowing; but the best authority assures us, that the word was used in its modern and secondary sense so early as the reign of Edward III.[2] Chaucer, unable to sleep during the night, informs us, that, in order to pass the time,

> "Upon my bed I sate upright,
> And bade one rechin me a boke,
> A ROMAUNCE, and it me took
> To read and drive the night away."

---

[1] Alexander the Great: Alexander III of Macedonia (356–323 BC). Claude Fauchet (1529–1601) wrote *Antiquités gauloises et françoises* (1579–99) and *Recueil de l'origine de la langue et poésie françoise, rime et romans* (1581).

[2] Edward III reigned from 1327–77.

The book described as a Romance contained, as we are informed,

> "Fables
> That clerkis had, in old tyme,
> And other poets, put in rhyme."

And the author tells us, a little lower,

> "This boke ne spake but of such things,
> Of Queen's lives and of Kings."[1]

The volume proves to be no other than Ovid's Metamorphoses; and Chaucer, by applying to that work the name of Romance, sufficiently establishes that the word was, in his time, correctly employed under the modern acceptation.

Having thus accounted for the derivation of the word, our investigation divides itself into three principal branches, though of unequal extent. In the FIRST of these we propose to inquire into the general History and Origin of this peculiar species of composition, and particularly of Romances relating to European Chivalry, which necessarily form the most interesting object of our inquiry. In the SECOND, we shall give some brief account of the History of the Romance of Chivalry in the different states of Europe.[2] THIRDLY, We propose to notice cursorily the various kinds of Romantic Composition by which the ancient Romances of Chivalry were followed and superseded, and with these notices to conclude the article.

I. In the views taken by Hurd, Percy,[3] and other older authorities, of the origin and history of romantic fiction, their attention seems to have been so exclusively fixed upon the Romance of Chivalry alone, that they appear to have forgotten that, however interesting and peculiar, it formed only one species of a very numerous and extensive genus. The progress of Romance, in fact, keeps pace with that of society, which cannot long exist, even in the simplest state, without exhibiting some specimens of this attractive style of composition. It is not meant by this assertion, that in early ages such narratives were invented, as in modern times, in the character of mere fictions, devised to beguile the leisure of those who have time enough to read and

---

[1]   Geoffrey Chaucer (1340–1400): the quotation is from *The Book of the Duchess* (1369–72): ll. 46–49, 52–54, 57–58.

[2]   Here omitted.

[3]   Scott refers to prominent eighteenth-century antiquarians: Bishop Richard Hurd (1720–1808) and his *Letters in Chivalry and Romance* (1762) and Thomas Percy (1729–1811), famous for his *Reliques of Ancient English Poetry* (1765, 3 vols).

attend to them. On the contrary, Romance and real history have the same common origin. It is the aim of the former to maintain as long as possible the mask of veracity; and indeed the traditional memorials of all earlier ages partake in such a varied and doubtful degree of the qualities essential to those opposite lines of composition, that they form a mixed class between them; and may be termed either romantic histories or historical romances, according to the proportion in which their truth is debased by fiction, or their fiction mingled with truth ...

... III. We should now say something on those various kinds of romantic fictions which succeeded to the Romance of Chivalry. But we can only notice briefly works which have long slumbered in oblivion, and which certainly are not worthy to have their slumbers disturbed.

Even in the time of Cervantes, the Pastoral Romance, founded upon the *Diana* of George of Monté Mayor,[1] was prevailing to such an extent as made it worthy of his satire. It was, indeed a system still more remote from common sense and reality than that of chivalry itself. For the maxims of chivalry, high-strained and absurd as they are, did actually influence living beings, and even the fate of kingdoms. If Amadis de Gaule was a fiction, the Chevalier Bayard was a real person.[2] But the existence of an Arcadia, a pastoral region in which a certain fantastic sort of personages, desperately in love, and thinking of nothing else but their mistresses, played upon pipes, and wrote sonnets from morning to night, yet were supposed all the while to be tending their flocks, was too monstrously absurd to be long credited or tolerated.

A numerous, and once most popular, class of fictions, was that entitled the *Heroic Romance of the Seventeenth Century.*

If the ancient *Romance of Chivalry* has a right to be called the parent of those select and beautiful fictions, which the genius of the Italian poets has enriched with such peculiar charms, another of its direct descendants, *The Heroic Romance of the Seventeenth Century*, is, with few exceptions, the most dull and tedious species of composition that ever obtained temporary popularity. The old Romance of Heliodorus, entitled Theogenes and Chariclea,[3] supplied, perhaps, the earliest model of this style of composition; but it was from the Romances of Chivalry that it derives its most peculiar character-

---

[1] Jorge de Montemayor (1519–61), was a Portuguese writer, whose *Diana* (?1559) relocates Arcadia to Spain. It was translated into English in 1598.

[2] The Chevalier de Bayard, Pierre du Terrail (c. 1473–1524), was a heroically brave captain in the French army during the wars waged with Italy by Charles VIII, Louis XII, and François I. He was known as the "chevalier sans peur and sans reproche" (the chevalier without fear and beyond reproach).

[3] Heliodorus of Emesa lived in the third century AD. His romance *Aethiopica* was translated into English in 1569.

istics. A man of a fantastic imagination, Honoré d'Urfé, led the way in this style of composition.[1] Being willing to record certain love intrigues of a complicated nature which had taken place in his own family, and amongst his friends, he imagined to himself a species of Arcadia on the banks of the Lignon, inhabited by swains and shepherdesses, who live for love and for love alone. There are two principal stories, said to represent the family history of D'Urfé and his brother, with about thirty episodes, in which the gallantries and intrigues of Henry IV's[2] court are presented under borrowed names. Considered by itself, this is but an example of the Pastoral Romance; but it was so popular, that three celebrated French authors, Gomberville, Calprenede, and Madame Scuderi,[3] seized the pen, and composed in emulation many interminable folios of Heroic Romance. In these insipid performances, a conventional character, and a set of family manners and features, are ascribed to the heroes and heroines, although selected from distant ages and various quarters of the world. The heroines are, without exception, models of beauty and perfection; and so well persuaded of it themselves, that to approach them with the most humble declaration of love was a crime sufficient to deserve the penalty of banishment from their presence; and it is well if the doom were softened to the audacious lover, by permission, or command to live, without which, absence and death were to be accounted synonymous. On the other hand, the heroes, whatever kingdoms they have to govern, or other earthly duties to perform, live through these folios for love alone; and the most extraordinary revolutions which can agitate the world are ascribed to the charms of a Mandane or a Statira[4] acting upon the crazy understanding of their lovers. Nothing can be so uninteresting as the frigid extravagance with which these lovers express their passion; or, in their own phrase, nothing can be more freezing than their flames, more creeping than their flights of love. Yet the line of metaphysical gallantry which they exhibited had its date, and a long one, both in France and England. They remained the favourite amusement of Louis XIV's court, although assailed by the satire of Boileau.[5] In England they continued to be read by our grandmothers during the Augustan age of English, and while Addison was amusing the world with his wit, and Pope by his poetry, the

---

[1] Honoré d'Urfé (1567–1625), author of the prose romance *L'Astreé* (in 4 parts: 1607, 1610, 1619, 1627).

[2] Reigned from 1399–1413.

[3] All were writing in the seventeenth century and based their romances on classical tales of heroes and heroines. "Madame Scuderi" is more familiar as Madame de Scudery.

[4] Famous classical romance heroines.

[5] Louis XIV (1638–1715; reigned 1643–1715), known as the Sun King (le Roi Soleil). Nicolas Boileau-Despréaux (1636–1711), esteemed for his unassailable literary taste, and a major voice in the development of neo-classical theory.

ladies were reading *Clelia, Cleopatra,* and the *Grand Cyrus.* The fashion did not decay till about the reign of George I.;[1] and even more lately, Mrs. Lennox, patronized by Dr. Johnson, wrote a very good imitation of Cervantes, entitled, The Female Quixote, which had those works for its basis.[2] They are now totally forgotten.

The Modern Romance, so ennobled by the productions of so many master hands, would require a long disquisition. But we can here only name that style of composition in which De Foe rendered fiction more impressive than truth itself, and Swift could render plausible even the grossest impossibilities.[3]

---

[1] Reigned from 1714–27.

[2] Charlotte Lennox (1720–1804) published *The Female Quixote* in 1752, which sharply satirized the older style of romance Scott has been describing.

[3] Daniel Defoe (1660–1731), author of *Robinson Crusoe* (1719); Jonathan Swift (1667–1745), author of *Gulliver's Travels* (1726).

Appendix C: Blackstone's Views on the Laws of Property

[William Blackstone's (1723–1780) magisterial *Commentaries on the Laws of England* became the standard work defining and clarifying the law. This section lays out the laws of property, inheritance, and conveyancing: the passing of property from one owner to another. Smith's reliance on the laws of property and wills in *The Old Manor House* anchors the plot and allows for Orlando's eventual claiming of Rayland Hall.]

I. From William Blackstone, "The Rights of Things" (1766). *Commentaries on the Laws of England*, 4 vols. (Oxford: Clarendon, 1765–69), II: 10–14, 45–46, 53–57, 103–05, 234–36, 376–79, 501–02.[1]

From Chapter I: "Of Property, in General"

... The most universal and effectual way, of abandoning property, is by the death of the occupant; when, both the actual possession and intention of keeping possession ceasing, the property, which is founded upon such possession and intention, ought also to cease of course. For, naturally speaking, the instant a man ceases to be, he ceases to have any dominion: else, if he had a right to dispose of his acquisitions one moment beyond his life, he would also have a right to direct their disposal for a million of ages after him; which would be highly absurd and inconvenient. All property must therefore cease upon death, considering men as absolute individuals, and unconnected with civil society: for then, by the principles before established, the next immediate occupant would acquire a right in all that the deceased possessed. But as, under civilized governments which are calculated for the peace of mankind, such a constitution would be productive of endless disturbances, the universal law of almost every nation (which is a kind of secondary law of nature) has either given the dying person a power of continuing his property, by disposing of his possessions by will; or, in case he neglects to dispose of it, or is not permitted to make any disposition at all, the municipal law of the country then steps in, and declares who shall be the successor, representative, or heir of the deceased;

---

[1] All legal terms and Latin phrases are from *Ballentine's Law Dictionary*, 3rd. ed., ed. William S. Anderson (Rochester, N.Y.: Lawyers Co-operative Publishing Co., 1969). All legal figures cited are identified in *The Sovereignty of the Law*, ed. Gareth Jones (London: Macmillan, 1973).

that is, who alone shall have a right to enter upon this vacant possession, in order to avoid that confusion, which it's becoming again common would occasion. And farther, in case no testament be permitted by the law, or none be made, and no heir can be found so qualified as the law requires, still, to prevent the robust title of occupancy from again taking place, the doctrine of escheats is adopted in almost every country; whereby the sovereign of the state, and those who claim under his authority, are the ultimate heirs, and succeed to those inheritances, to which no other title can be formed.

The right of inheritance, or descent to the children and relations of the deceased, seems to have been allowed much earlier than the right of devising by testament. We are apt to conceive at first view that it has nature on it's side; yet we often mistake for nature what we find established by long and inveterate custom. It is certainly a wise and effectual, but clearly a political, establishment; since the permanent right of property, vested in the ancestor himself, was no *natural*, but merely a *civil*, right. It is true, that the transmission of one's possessions to posterity has an evident tendency to make a man a good citizen and a useful member of society: it sets the passions on the side of duty, and prompts a man to deserve well of the public, when he is sure that the reward of his services will not die with himself, but be transmitted to those with whom he is connected by the dearest and most tender affections. Yet, reasonable as this foundation of the right of inheritance may seem, it is probable that it's immediate original arose not from speculations altogether so delicate and refined; and, if not from fortuitous circumstances, at least from a plainer and more simple principle. A man's children or nearest relations are usually about him on his death-bed, and are the earliest witnesses of his decease. They became therefore generally the next immediate occupants, till at length in process of time this frequent usage ripened into general law. And therefore also in the earliest ages, on failure of children, a man's servants born under his roof were allowed to be his heirs; being immediately on the spot when he died. For we find the old patriarch Abraham expressly declaring, that "since God had given him no seed, his steward Eliezer, one born in his house, was his heir."

While property continued only for life, testaments were useless and unknown; and, when it became inheritable, the inheritance was long indefeasible, and the children or heirs at law were incapable of exclusion by will. Till at length it was found, that so strict a rule of inheritance made heirs disobedient and headstrong, defrauded creditors of their just debts, and prevented many provident fathers from dividing or charging their estates as the exigence of their families required. This introduced pretty generally the right of disposing one's property, or a part of it, by *testament*; that is, by written or oral instructions properly *witnessed* and authenticated, according to the *pleasure* of the deceased; which we therefore emphatically stile his *will*. This was established in some countries much later than in others. With us in England, till modern times, a man could only dispose of one third of his moveables from his wife and children: and, in general, no will was permitted of lands till the reign of Henry the eighth;[1] and then only of a certain portion: for it was not till after the restoration that the power of devising real property became so universal as at present.

Wills therefore and testaments, rights of inheritance and successions, are all of them creatures of the civil or municipal laws, and accordingly are in all respects regulated by them; every distinct country having different ceremonies and requisites to make a testament completely valid: neither does any thing vary more than the right of inheritance under different national establishments. In England particularly, this diversity is carried to such a length, as if it had been meant to point out the power of the laws in regulating the succession to property, and how futile every claim must be that has not it's foundation in the positive rules of the state. In personal estates the father may succeed to his children; in landed property he never can be heir, by any the remotest possibility: in general only the eldest son, in some places only the youngest, in others all the sons together, have a right to succeed to the inheritance: in real estates males are preferred to females, and the eldest male will usually exclude the rest; in the division of personal estates, the females of equal degree are admitted together with the males, and no right of primogeniture is allowed.

This one consideration may help to remove the scruples of many wellmeaning persons, who set up a mistaken conscience in opposition to the rules of law. If a man disinherits his son, by a will duly executed, and leaves his estate to a stranger, there are many who consider this proceeding as contrary to natural justice: while others so scrupulously adhere to the supposed intention of the dead, that if a will of lands be attested by only *two* witnesses instead of *three*, which the law requires, they are apt to imagine that the heir is bound in conscience to relinquish his title to the devisee. But both of them certainly proceed upon very erroneous principles: as if, on the one hand, the son had by nature a right to succeed to his father's lands; or as if, on the other hand, the owner was by nature intitled to direct the succession of his property after his own decease. Whereas the law of nature suggests, that on the death of the possessor the estate should again become common, and be open to the next occupant, unless otherwise ordered for the sake of civil peace by the positive law of society. The positive law of society, which is with us the municipal law of England, directs it to vest in such person as the last proprietor shall by will, attended with certain requisites, appoint; and, in defect of such appointment, to go to some

---

1   Reigned from 1509–47.

particular person, who, from the result of certain local constitutions, appears to be the heir at law. Hence it follows, that, where the appointment is regularly made, there cannot be a shadow of right in any one but the person appointed: and, where the necessary requisites are omitted, the right of the heir is equally strong and built upon as solid a foundation, as the right of the devisee would have been, supposing such requisites were observed ...

From Chapter IV: "Of the Feudal System"

...The constitution of feuds had it's original from the military policy of the northern or Celtic nations, the Goths, the Hunns, the Franks, the Vandals, and the Lombards,[1] who all migrating from the same *officina gentium*,[2] as Crag very justly entitles it, poured themselves in vast quantities into all the regions of Europe, at the declension of the Roman empire. It was brought by them from their own countries, and continued in their respective colonies as the most likely means to secure their new acquisitions: and, to that end, large districts or parcels of land were allotted by the conquering general to the superior officers of the army, and by them dealt out again in smaller parcels or allotments to the inferior officers and most deserving soldiers. These allotments were called *feoda*, feuds, fiefs, or fees; which last appellation in the northern languages signifies a conditional stipend or reward. Rewards or stipends they evidently were; and the condition annexed to them was, that the possessor should do service faithfully, both at home and in the wars, to him by whom they were given; for which purpose he took the *juramentum fidelitatis*, or oath of fealty: and in case of the breach of this condition and oath, by not performing the stipulated service, or by deserting the lord in battle, the lands were again to revert to him who granted them.

Allotments thus acquired, naturally engaged such as accepted them to defend them: and, as they all sprang from the same right of conquest, no part could subsist independent of the whole; wherefore all givers as well as receivers were mutually bound to defend each others possessions. But, as that could not effectually be done in a tumultuous irregular way, government, and to that purpose subordination, was necessary. Every receiver of lands, or feudatory, was therefore bound, when called upon by his benefactor, or immediate lord of his feud or fee, to do all in his power to defend him. Such benefactor or lord was likewise subordinate to and under the command of his immediate benefactor or superior; and so upwards to the prince or general himself. And the several lords were also reciprocally bound, in their respective gradations, to protect the possessions they had

---

[1] Blackstone refers to the original inhabitants of modern Europe.
[2] "The workshop of nations."

given. Thus the feodal connection was established, a proper military subjection was naturally introduced, and an army of feudatories were always ready enlisted, and mutually prepared to muster, not only in defence of each man's own several property, but also in defence of the whole, and of every part of this their newly acquired country: the prudence of which constitution was soon sufficiently visible in the strength and spirit, with which they maintained their conquests ...

...The grand and fundamental maxim of all feodal tenure is this; that all lands were originally granted out by the sovereign, and are therefore holden, either mediately or immediately, of the crown. The grantor was called the proprietor, or *lord*; being he who retained the dominion or ultimate property of the feud or fee: and the grantee, who had only the use and possession, according to the terms of the grant, was stiled the feudatory or *vasal*, which was only another name for the tenant or holder of the lands; though, on account of the prejudices we have justly conceived against the doctrines that were afterwards grafted on this system, we now use the word *vasal* opprobriously, as synonymous to slave or bondman. The manner of the grant was by words of gratuitous and pure donation, *dedi et concessi*; which are still the operative words in our modern infeodations or deeds of feoffment. This was perfected by the ceremony of corporal investiture, or open and notorious delivery of possession in the presence of the other vasals, which perpetuated among them the æra of the new acquisition, at a time when the art of writing was very little known: and therefore the evidence of property was reposed in the memory of the neighbourhood; who, in case of a disputed title, were afterwards called upon to decide the difference, not only according to external proofs, adduced by the parties litigant, but also by the internal testimony of their own private knowledge.

Besides an oath of *fealty*, or profession of faith to the lord, which was the parent of our oath of allegiance, the vasal or tenant upon investiture did usually *homage* to his lord; openly and humbly kneeling, being ungirt, uncovered, and holding up his hands both together between those of the lord, who sate before him; and there professing that "he did become his *man*, from that day forth, of life and limb and earthly honour:" and then he received a kiss from his lord. Which ceremony was denominated *homagium*, or *manhood*, by the feudists, from the stated form of words, *devenio vester homo*.[1]

When the tenant had thus professed himself to be the man of his superior or lord, the next consideration was concerning the *service*, which, as such, he was bound to render, in recompense for the land he held. This, in pure, proper, and original feuds, was only twofold: to follow, or do *suit* to, the lord in his courts in time of peace; and in his armies or warlike retinue,

---

[1] "I become your man."

when necessity called him to the field. The lord was, in early times, the legislator and judge over all his feudatories: and therefore the vasals of the inferior lords were bound by their fealty to attend their domestic courts baron, (which were instituted in every manor or barony, for doing speedy and effectual justice to all the tenants) in order as well to answer such complaints as might be alleged against themselves, as to form a jury or homage for the trial of their fellow-tenants; and upon this account, in all the feodal institutions both here and on the continent, they are distinguished by the appellation of the peers of the court: *pares curtis*, or *pares curiae*.[1] In like manner the barons themselves, or lords of inferior districts, were denominated peers of the king's court, and were bound to attend him upon summons, to hear causes of greater consequence in the king's presence and under the direction of his grand justiciary; till in many countries the power of that officer was broken and distributed into other courts of judicature, the peers of the king's court still reserving to themselves (in almost every feodal government) the right of appeal from those subordinate courts in the last resort. The military branch of service consisted in attending the lord to the wars, if called upon, with such a retinue, and for such a number of days, as were stipulated at the first donation, in proportion to the quantity of the land.

At the first introduction of feuds, as they were gratuitous, so also they were precarious and held at the *will* of the lord, who was the sole judge whether his vasal performed his services faithfully. Then they became certain, for one or more *years*. Among the antient Germans they continued only from year to year; an annual distribution of lands being made by their leaders in their general councils or assemblies. This was professedly done, lest their thoughts should be diverted from war to agriculture; lest the strong should incroach upon the possessions of the weak; and lest luxury and avarice should be encouraged by the erection of permanent houses, and too curious an attention to convenience and the elegant superfluities of life. But, when the general migration was pretty well over, and a peaceable possession of their new-acquired settlements had introduced new customs and manners; when the fertility of the soil had encouraged the study of husbandry, and an affection for the sports they had cultivated began naturally to arise in the tillers; a more permanent degree of property was introduced, and feuds began now to be granted for the *life* of the feudatory. But still feuds were not yet *hereditary*; though frequently granted, by the favour of the lord, to the children of the former possessor; till in process of time it became unusual, and was therefore thought hard, to reject the heir, if he were capable to perform the services: and therefore infants, women, and professed monks, who were incapable of bearing arms, were

---

[1] Both phrases mean "peers of the court."

also incapable of succeeding to a genuine feud. But the heir, when admitted to the feud which his ancestor possessed, used generally to pay a fine or acknowledgement to the lord, in horses, arms, money, and the like, for such renewal of the feud: which was called a relief, because it re-established the inheritance, or, in the words of the feodal writers, "*incertam et caducam hereditatem relevabat.*"[1] This relief was afterwards, when feuds became absolutely hereditary, continued on the death of the tenant, though the original foundation of it had ceased.

For in the process of time feuds came by degrees to be universally extended, beyond the life of the first vasal, to his *sons*, or perhaps to such one of them, as the lord should name; and in this case the form of the donation was strictly observed: for if a feud was given to a man and his *sons*, all his sons succeeded him in equal portions: and as they died off, their shares reverted to the lord, and did not descend to their children, or even to their surviving brothers, as not being specified in the donation. But when such a feud was given to a man, and his *heirs*, in general terms, then a more extended rule of succession took place; and when a feudatory died, his male descendants *in infinitum*[2] were admitted to the succession. When any such descendant, who thus had succeeded, died, his male descendants were also admitted in the first place; and, in defect of them, such of his male collateral kindred as were of the blood or lineage of the first feudatory, but no others. For this was an unalterable maxim in feodal succession, that "none was capable of inheriting a feud, but such as was of the blood of, that is, lineally descended from, the first feudatory." And the descent, being thus confined to males, originally extended to all the males alike; all the sons, without any distinction of primogeniture, succeeding to equal portions of the father's feud. But this being found upon many accounts inconvenient, (particularly, by dividing the services, and thereby weakening the strength of the feodal union) and *honorary* feuds (or titles of nobility) being now introduced, which were not of a divisible nature, but could only be inherited by the eldest son; in imitation of these, *military* feuds (or those we are now describing) began also in most countries to descend according to the same rule of primogeniture, to the eldest son, in exclusion of all the rest ...

From Chapter VII: "Of Freehold Estates, of Inheritance"

...The next objects of our disquisitions are the nature and properties of *estates*. An estate in lands, tenements, and hereditaments, signifies such interest as the

---

[1] "It freed the uncertain and fallen inheritance"; that is, it cleared up any confusion over rightful inheritance.
[2] "To infinity": without end or limit.

tenant hath therein: so that if a man grants all *his estate* to another, every thing that he can possibly grant shall pass thereby. It is called in Latin, *status*; it signifying the condition, or circumstance, in which the owner stands, with regard to his property. And, to ascertain this with proper precision and accuracy, estates may be considered in a threefold view: first, with regard to the *quantity of interest* which the tenant has in the tenement: secondly, with regard to the *time* at which that quantity of interest is to be enjoyed: and, thirdly, with regard to the *number* and *connexions* of the tenants.

First, with regard to the *quantity of interest* which the tenant has in the tenement, this is measured by it's duration and extent. Thus, either his right of possession is to subsist for an uncertain period, during his own life, or the life of another man; to determine at his own decease, or to remain to his descendants after him: or it is circumscribed within a certain number of years, months, or days: or, lastly, it is infinite and unlimited, being vested in him and his representatives for ever. And this occasions the primary division of estates, into such as are *freehold*, and such as are *less than freehold*.

An estate of freehold, *liberum tenementum*, or franktenement, is defined by Britton to be "the *possession* of the soil by a free man."[1] And St. Germyn tells us, that "the *possession* of the land is called in the law of England the franktenement or freehold."[2] Such estate therefore, and no other, as requires actual possession of the land, is legally speaking freehold: which actual possession can, by the course of the common law, be only given by the ceremony called livery of seisin, which is the same as the feodal investiture. And from these principles we may extract this description of a freehold; that it is such an estate in lands as is conveyed by livery of seisin; or, in tenements of an incorporeal nature, by what is equivalent thereto. And accordingly it is laid down by Littleton, that where a freehold shall pass, it behoveth to have livery of seisin.[3] As therefore estates of inheritance and estates for life could not by common law be conveyed without livery of seisin, these are properly estates of freehold; and, as no other estates were conveyed with the same solemnity, therefore no others are properly freehold estates.

Estates of freehold then are divisible into estates of *inheritance*, and estates *not of inheritance*. The former are again divided into inheritances *absolute* or fee-simple; and inheritances *limited*, one species of which we usually call fee-tail.

---

[1] The exact identity of Britton is unknown, but the name commonly refers to a text written around 1290 and based on Henry de Bracton's (d. 1268) *De Legibus et Consuetudinibus Angliae*.

[2] St. Germyn: Christopher Saint-German (?1460–1540), whose treatise *Doctor and Student* (1523) was frequently cited.

[3] Sir Thomas Littleton (1422–81), whose *Tenures* was commentated on by Coke (see note 5, p. 560).

I. Tenant in fee-simple (or, as he is frequently stiled, tenant in fee) is he that hath lands, tenements, or hereditaments, to hold to him and his heirs for ever; generally, absolutely, and simply; without mentioning *what* heirs, but referring that to his own pleasure, or to the disposition of the law. The true meaning of the word fee (*feodum*) is the same with that of feud or fief, and in it's original sense it is taken in contradistinction to *allodium*; which latter the writers on this subject define to be every man's own land, which he possesseth merely in his own right, without owing any rent or service to any superior. This is property in it's highest degree; and the owner thereof hath *absolutum et directum dominium*,[1] and therefore it is said to be seised thereof absolutely in *dominico suo*, in his own demesne. But *feodum*, or fee, is that which is held of some superior, on condition of rendering him service; in which superior the ultimate property of the land resides. And therefore sir Henry Spelman defines a feud or fee to be the right which the vasal or tenant hath in lands, to *use* the same, and take the profits thereof to him and his heirs, rendering to the lord his due services; the mere allodial *propriety* of the soil always remaining in the lord.[2] This allodial property no subject in England has; it being a received, and now undeniable, principle in the law, that all the lands in England are holden mediately or immediately of the king. The king therefore only hath *absolutum et directum dominium*;[3] but all subjects' lands are in the nature of *feodum* or fee; whether derived to them by descent from their ancestors, or purchased for a valuable consideration; for they cannot come to any man by either of those ways, unless accompanied with those feodal clogs, which were laid upon the first feudatory when it was originally granted. A subject therefore hath only the usufruct,[4] and not the absolute property of the soil; or, as sir Edward Coke expresses it, he hath *dominium utile*, but not *dominium directum*.[5] And hence it is that, in the most solemn acts of law, we express the strongest and highest estate, that any subject can have, by these words: "he is seised thereof *in his demesne, as of fee*." It is a man's demesne, *dominicum*, or property, since it belongs to him and his heirs for ever: yet this *dominicum*, property, or demesne, is strictly not absolute or allodial, but qualified or feodal: it is his demesne, *as of fee*; that is, it is not purely and simply his own, since it is held of a superior lord, in whom the ultimate property resides ...

---

[1] "Sole and direct dominion" or control.

[2] Sir Henry Spelman (?1564–1641), whose works include *Tenures by Knight Service*.

[3] I.e., only the king has the right to sole and direct dominion.

[4] Usufruct: the right to the use, enjoyments, profits, and avails of property belonging to another.

[5] *Dominium utile*: equitable or beneficial ownership of property; *dominium directum*: absolute control over property. Sir Edward Coke (1552–1634), one of the most influential English lawyers before Blackstone; he wrote the *Institutes of the Laws of England*.

From Chapter XIV: "Of Title by Descent"

...The seventh and last rule or canon is, that in collateral inheritances the male stocks shall be preferred to the female; (that is, kindred derived from the blood of the male ancestors shall be admitted before those from the blood of the female)—unless where the lands have, in fact, descended from a female.

Thus the relations on the father's side are admitted *in infinitum*, before those on the mother's side are admitted at all; and the relations of the father's father, before those of the father's mother; and so on. And in this the English law is not singular, but warranted by the examples of the Hebrew and Athenian laws, as stated by Selden, and Petit;[1] though among the Greeks, in the time of Hesiod, when a man died without wife or children, all his kindred (without any distinction) divided his estate among them.[2] It is likewise warranted by the example of the Roman laws; wherein the *agnati*, or relations by the father, were preferred to the *cognati*, or relations by the mother, till the edict of the emperor Justinian abolished all distinction between them.[3] It is also conformable to the customary law of Normandy, which indeed in most respects agrees with our law of inheritance.

However, I am inclined to think, that this rule of our laws does not owe it's immediate original to any view of conformity to those which I have just now mentioned; but was established in order to effectuate and carry into execution the fifth rule or canon before laid down; that every heir must be of the blood of the first purchasor. For, when such first purchasor was not easily to be discovered after a long course of descents, the lawyers not only endeavoured to investigate him by taking the next relation of the whole blood to the person last in possession; but also, considering that a preference had been given to males (by virtue of the second canon) through the whole course of lineal descent from the first purchasor to the present time, they judged it more likely that the lands should have descended to the last tenant from his male than from his female ancestors: from the father (for instance) rather than from the mother; from the father's father, rather than the father's mother: and therefore they hunted back the inheritance (if I may be allowed the expression) through the male line; and gave it to the next relations on the side of the father, the father's father, and so upwards; imagining with reason that this was the most probable way of continuing it in the line of the first purchasor. A conduct much more rational than the preference of the *agnati* by the Roman laws: which, as they

---

[1] John Selden (1584–1654), jurist and antiquarian, whose collected works were published posthumously in 1726. "Petit": unidentified.

[2] Hesiod: early Greek poet, c. 8th century BC.

[3] Justinian: Roman emperor at Constantinople, AD 527–65.

gave no advantage to the males in the first instance or direct lineal succession, had no reason for preferring them in the transverse collateral one: upon which account this preference was very wisely abolished by Justinian.

That this was the true foundation of the preference of the *agnati* or male stocks, in our law, will farther appear if we consider, that, whenever the lands have notoriously descended to a man from his mother's side, this rule is totally reversed, and no relation of his by the father's side, as such, can ever be admitted to them; because he cannot possibly be of the blood of the first purchasor. And so, *e converso*,[1] if the lands descended from the father's side, no relation of the mother, as such, shall ever inherit. So also, if they in fact descended to John Stiles from his father's mother Cecilia Kempe; here not only the blood of Lucy Baker his mother, but also of George Stiles his father's father, is perpetually excluded. And in like manner, if they be known to have descended from Frances Holland the mother of Cecilia Kempe, the line not only of Lucy Baker, and of George Stiles, but also of Luke Kempe the father of Cecilia, is excluded. Whereas when the side from which they descended is forgotten, or never known, (as in the case of an estate newly purchased to be holden *ut feudum antiquum*[2]) here the right of inheritance first runs up all the father's side, with a preference to the male stocks in every instance; and, if it finds no heirs there, it then, and then only, resorts to the mother's side; leaving no place untried, in order to find heirs that may by possibility be derived from the original purchasor. The greatest probability of finding such was among those descended from the male ancestors; but, upon failure of issue there, they may possibly be found among those derived from the females.

This I take to be the true reason of the constant preference of the agnatic succession, or issue derived from the male ancestors, through all the stages of collateral inheritance; as the ability for personal service was the reason for preferring the males at first in the direct lineal succession. We see clearly, that, if males had been perpetually admitted, in utter exclusion of females, the tracing the inheritance back through the male line of ancestors must at last have inevitably brought us up to the first purchasor: but, as males have not been *perpetually admitted*, but only *generally preferred*; as females have not been *utterly excluded*, but only *generally postponed* to males; the tracing the inheritance up through the male stocks will not give us absolute demonstration, but only a strong probability, of arriving at the first purchasor; which, joined with the other probability, of the wholeness of entirety of blood, will fall little short of a certainty ...

---

[1]   "Conversely."
[2]   "As an ancient feud": i.e., although newly purchased, the estate is considered equivalent to one inherited from an ancestor.

From Chapter XXIII: "Of Alienation by Devise"[1]

...With regard to devises in general, experience soon shewed how difficult and hazardous a thing it is, even in matters of public utility, to depart from the rules of the common law; which are so nicely constructed and so artificially connected together, that the least breach in any one of them disorders for a time the texture of the whole. Innumerable frauds and perjuries were quickly introduced by this parliamentary method of inheritance: for so loose was the construction made upon this act by the courts of law, that bare notes in the hand writing of another person were allowed to be good wills within the statute. To remedy which, the statute of frauds and perjuries, 29 Car. II. c. 3. directs, that all devises of lands and tenements shall not only be in writing, but signed by the testator, or some other person in his presence, and by his express direction; and be subscribed, in his presence, by three or four credible witnesses. And a similar solemnity is requisite for revoking a devise.

In the construction of this last statute, it has been adjudged that the testator's name, written with his own hand, at the beginning of his will, as, "I John Mills do make this my last will and testament," is a sufficient signing, without any name at the bottom; though the other is the safer way. It has also been determined, that though the witnesses must all see the testator sign, or at least acknowlege the signing, yet they may do it at different times. But they must all subscribe their names as witnesses *in his presence*, lest by any possibility they should mistake the instrument. And, in a case determined about twenty years ago, the judges were extremely strict in regard to the credibility, or rather the competency, of the witnesses: for they would not allow any legatee, nor by consequence a creditor, where the legacies and debts were charged on the real estate, to be a competent witness to the devise, as being too deeply concerned in interest not to wish the establishment of the will; for, if it were established, he gained a security for his legacy or debt from the real estate, whereas otherwise he had no claim but on the personal assets. This determination however alarmed many purchasors and creditors, and threatened to shake most of the titles in the kingdom, that depended on devises by will. For, if the will was attested by a servant to whom wages were due, by the apothecary or attorney whose very attendance made them creditors, or by the minister of the parish who had any demand for tithes or ecclesiastical dues, (and these are the persons most likely to be present in the testators last illness) and if in such case the testator had charged his real estate with the payment of his debts, the whole will, and every disposition therein, so far as related to real property, were

---

[1] I.e., transferring property by will.

held to be utterly void. This occasioned the statute 25 Geo. II. c. 6. which restored both the competency and the credit of such *legatees*, by declaring void all legacies given to witnesses, and thereby removing all possibility of their interest affecting their testimony. The same statute likewise established the competency of *creditors*, by directing the testimony of all such creditors to be admitted, but leaving their credit (as well as that of all other witnesses) to be considered, on a view of all the circumstances, by the court and jury before whom such will shall be contested. And in a much later case the testimony of three witnesses, who were creditors, was held to be sufficiently credible, though the land was charged with the payment of debts; and the reasons of the former determination were adjudged to be insufficient.

Another inconvenience was found to attend this new method of conveyance by devise; in that creditors by bond and other specialties, which affected the heir provided he had assets by descent, were now defrauded of their securities, not having the same remedy against the devisee of their debtor. To obviate which, the statute 3 & 4 W. & M. c. 14. hath provided, that all wills, and testaments, limitations, dispositions, and appointments of real estates, by tenants in fee-simple or having power to dispose by will, shall (as against such creditors only) be deemed to be fraudulent and void: and that such creditors may maintain their actions jointly against both the heir and the devisee.

A will of lands, made by the permission and under the controll of these statutes, is considered by the courts of law not so much in the nature of a testament, as of a conveyance declaring the uses to which the land shall be subject: with this difference, that in other conveyances the actual *subscription* of the witnesses is not required by law, though it is prudent for them so to do, in order to assist their memory when living and to supply their evidence when dead; but in devises of lands such subscription is now absolutely necessary by statute, in order to identify a conveyance, which in it's nature can never be set up till after the death of the devisor. And upon this notion, that a devise affecting lands is merely a species of conveyance, is founded this distinction between such devises and testaments of personal chattels; that the latter will operate upon whatever the testator dies possessed of, the former only upon such real estates as were his at the time of executing and publishing his will. Wherefore no after-purchased lands will pass under such devise, unless, subsequent to the purchase or contract, the devisor re-publishes his will ...

From Chapter XXXII: "Of Title by Testament, and Administration"

... As to written wills, they need not any witness of their publication. I speak not here of devises of lands, which are entirely another thing, a conveyance by statute, unknown to the feodal or common law, and not under the same jurisdiction as personal testaments. But a testament of chattels, written in the testator's own hand, though it has neither his name nor seal to it, nor witnesses present at it's publication, is good; provided sufficient proof can be had that it is his hand-writing. And though written in another man's hand, and never signed by the testator, yet if proved to be according to his instructions and approved by him, it hath been held a good testament of the personal estate. Yet it is the safer, and more prudent way, and leaves less in the breast of the ecclesiastical judge, if it be signed or sealed by the testator, and published in the presence of witnesses; which last was always required in the time of Bracton;[1] or, rather, he in this respect has implicitly copied the rule of the civil law.

No testament is of any effect till after the death of the testator. "*Nam omne testamentum morte consummatum est; et voluntas testatoris est ambulatoria usque ad mortem.*"[2] And therefore, if there be many testaments, the last overthrows all the former: but the republication of a former will revokes one of a later date, and establishes the first again.

Hence it follows, that testaments may be avoided three ways: 1. If made by a person labouring under any of the incapacities before-mentioned: 2. By making another testament of a later date: and, 3. By cancelling or revoking it. For, though I make a last will and testament irrevocable in the strongest words, yet I am at liberty to revoke it: because my own act or words cannot alter the disposition of law, so as to make that irrevocable, which is in it's own nature revocable. For this, saith lord Bacon, would be for a man to deprive himself of that, which of all other things is most incident to human condition; and that is, alteration or repentance[3] ...

---

[1] See note 1, p. 559.

[2] "For every testament is consummated by death, and the will of the testator is revocable up to his death."

[3] Francis Bacon (1561–1626), philosopher and writer; Solicitor-General (1607) and Attorney-General (1613).

Appendix D: War and Its Effects

1. Poetic Responses

[Poets such as Smith and William Wordsworth were concerned to portray the results of war on the people of Britain, especially the working classes on whose shoulders much of the burden fell. Smith's poem *The Emigrants* charts her reaction to the French clergy and aristocrats who chose exile over certain death. Wordsworth's fragment "The Discharged Soldier" describes the plight of a soldier abandoned by the same army that has rendered him unfit to return to society.]

a. From Charlotte Smith, *The Emigrants*, Book I, 296–382 (1793). *The Poems of Charlotte Smith*, ed. Stuart Curran (Oxford: Oxford UP, 1993).

.... Poor wand'ring wretches, whosoe'er ye are
That hopeless, houseless, friendless, travel wide
O'er these bleak russet downs, where, dimly seen
The solitary shepherd shiv'ring tends
His dun discoloured flock (shepherd unlike
Him whom in song the poet's fancy crowns
With garlands, and his crook with vi'lets binds)—
Poor vagrant wretches! Outcasts of the world
Whom no abode receives, no parish owns,
Roving, like nature's commoners, the land
That boasts such general plenty—if the sight
Of wide-extended misery softens yours
Awhile, suspend your murmurs, here behold
The strange vicissitudes of fate, while thus
The exiled nobles from their country driven,
Whose richest luxuries were theirs, must feel
More poignant anguish than the lowest poor,
Who, born to indigence, have learned to brave
Rigid Adversity's depressing breath!
Ah, rather Fortune's worthless favourites
Who feed on England's vitals—pensioners
Of base corruption, who, in quick ascent
To opulence unmerited, become
Giddy with pride, and as ye rise, forgetting
The dust ye lately left, with scorn look down

On those beneath ye (though your equals once
In fortune, and in worth superior still,
They view the eminence on which ye stand
With wonder, not with envy, for they know
The means by which ye reached it, have been such
As in all honest eyes degrade ye far
Beneath the poor dependent, whose sad heart
Reluctant pleads for what your pride denies)—
Ye venal, worthless hirelings of a court!
Ye pampered parasites whom Britons pay
For forging fetters for them!—rather here
Study a lesson that concerns ye much,
And, trembling, learn that if oppressed too long
The raging multitude, to madness stung,
Will turn on their oppressors and no more
By sounding titles and parading forms
Bound like tame victims, will redress themselves!
Then swept away by the resistless torrent
Not only all your pomp may disappear,
But in the tempest lost, fair Order sink
Her decent head, and lawless Anarchy
O'erturn celestial Freedom's radiant throne—
As now in Gallia,[1] where Confusion, born
Of party rage and selfish love of rule,
Sully the noblest cause that ever warmed
The heart of patriot virtue.[2] There arise
The infernal passions: Vengeance, seeking blood,
And Avarice, and Envy's harpy fangs
Pollute the immortal shrine of Liberty,
Dismay her votaries, and disgrace her name.
Respect is due to principle, and they
Who suffer for their conscience have a claim,
Whate'er that principle may be, to praise.
Those ill-starred exiles then who bound by ties
To them the bonds of honour, who resigned
Their country to preserve them, and now seek
In England an asylum, well deserve
To find that (every prejudice forgot

---

[1] Archaic name for France.
[2] This sentiment will probably *renew* against me the indignation of those who have an inter-
     est in asserting that no such virtue anywhere exists [Smith's note].

Which pride and ignorance teaches) we for them
Feel as our brethren, and that English hearts
Of just compassion ever own the sway
As truly as our element, the deep,
Obeys the mild dominion of the moon.
This they *have* found, and may they find it still!
Thus mayst thou, Britain, triumph! May thy foes
By Reason's gen'rous potency subdued,
Learn that the God thou worshippest delights
In acts of pure humanity! May thine
Be still such bloodless laurels, nobler far
Than those acquired at Cressy or Poictiers—[1]
Or of more recent growth, those well bestowed
On him who stood on Calpe's[2] blazing height
Amid the thunder of a warring world,
Illustrious rather from the crowds he saved
From flood and fire, than from the ranks who fell
Beneath his valour! Actions such as these,
Like incense rising to the throne of Heaven,
Far better justify the pride that swells
In British bosoms, than the deafening roar
Of victory from a thousand brazen throats,
That tell with what success wide-wasting war
Has by our brave compatriots thinned the world.

b. William Wordsworth, "The Discharged Soldier" (composed January-March 1798).[3] *Selected Poetry*, ed. Stephen Gill and Duncan Wu (Oxford: Oxford UP, 1997).

        ... I love to walk
Along the public way when for the night,
Deserted in its silence, it assumes
A character of deeper quietness
Than pathless solitudes. At such a time
I slowly mounted up a steep ascent

---

[1] Battles fought by Edward III in 1346 and 1356 in his bid to win the throne of France.

[2] Duncan Wu (*Romantic Women Poets: An Anthology*, p. 99, n. 41) identifies "him" as George Augustus Eliott, 1st Baron Heathfield (1717–90, and adds "[he] maintained British rule of Gibraltar throughout a four-year siege, by sea and land, from the Spanish (1779–83)." "Calpe": archaic name for Gibraltar.

[3] This poem, not published separately in Wordsworth's lifetime, was later incorporated into *The Prelude* (1805) iv: 364–504, with some revisions.

Where the road's watry surface to the ridge
Of that sharp rising glittered in the moon
And seemed before my eyes another stream
Stealing with silent lapse to join the brook
That murmured in the valley. On I passed
Tranquil, receiving in my own despite
Amusement, as I slowly passed along,
From such near objects as from time to time
Perforce disturbed the slumber of the sense
Quiescent, and disposed to sympathy,
With an exhausted mind worn out by toil
And all unworthy of the deeper joy
Which waits on distant prospect, cliff or sea,
The dark blue vault, and universe of stars.
Thus did I steal along that silent road,
My body from the stillness drinking in
A restoration like the calm of sleep
But sweeter far. Above, before, behind,
Around me, all was peace and solitude
Speak to my eye, but it was heard and felt.
Oh happy state! What beauteous pictures now
Rose in harmonious imagery—they rose
As from some distant region of my soul
And came along like dreams, yet such as left
Obscurely mingled with their passing forms
A consciousness of animal delight,
A self-possession felt in every pause
And every gentle movement of my frame.
While thus I wandered, step by step led on,
It chanced a sudden turning of the road
Presented to my view an uncouth shape
So near that, stepping back into the shade
Of a thick hawthorn, I could mark him well,
Myself unseen. He was in stature tall,
A foot above man's common measure tall,
And lank, and upright. There was in his form
A meagre stiffness. You might almost think
That his bones wounded him. His legs were long,
So long and shapeless that I looked at them
Forgetful of the body they sustained.
His arms were long and lean; his hands were bare;
His visage, wasted though it seemed, was large

In feature; his cheeks sunken; and his mouth
Shewed ghastly in the moonlight. From behind
A mile-stone propped him, and his figure seemed
Half-sitting and half-standing. I could mark
That he was clad in military garb,
Though faded yet entire. His face was turned
Towards the road, yet not as if he sought
For any living thing. He appeared
Forlorn and desolate, a man cut off
From all his kind, and more than half detached
From his own nature.

                He was alone,
Had no attendant, neither dog, nor staff,
Nor knapsack—in his very dress appeared
A desolation, a simplicity
That appertained to solitude. I think
If but a glove had dangled in his hand
It would have made him more akin to man.
Long time I scanned him with a mingled sense
Of fear and sorrow. From his lips meanwhile
There issued murmuring sounds as if of pain
Or of uneasy thought; yet still his form
Kept the same fearful steadiness. His shadow
Lay at his feet and moved not. In a glen
Hard by a village stood, whose silent doors
Were visible among the scattered trees,
Scarce distant from the spot an arrow's flight.
I wished to see him move, but he remained
Fixed to his place, and still from time to time
Sent forth a murmuring voice of dead complaint,
A groan scarce audible. Yet all the while
The chained mastiff in his wooden house
Was vexed, and from among the village trees
Howled never ceasing. Not without reproach
Had I prolonged my watch, and now confirmed,
And my heart's specious cowardice subdued,
I left the shady nook where I had stood
And hailed the Stranger. From his resting-place
He rose, and with his lean and wasted arm
In measured gesture lifted to his head
Returned my salutation. A short while
I held discourse on things indifferent

And casual matter. He meanwhile had ceased
From all complaint—his station had resumed,
Propped by the mile stone as before, and when erelong
I asked his history, he in reply
Was neither slow nor eager, but unmoved,
And with a quiet uncomplaining voice,
A stately air of mild indifference,
He told a simple fact: that he had been
A Soldier, to the tropic isles had gone,
Whence he had landed now some ten days past;
That on his landing he had been dismissed,
And with the little strength he yet had left
Was travelling to regain his native home.
At this I turned and through the trees looked down
Into the village—all were gone to rest,
Nor smoke nor any taper light appeared,
But every silent window to the moon
Shone with a yellow glitter. "No one there,"
Said I, "is waking; we must measure back
The way which we have come. Behind yon wood
A labourer dwells, an honest man and kind;
He will not murmur should we break his rest,
And he will give you food if food you need,
And lodging for the night." At this he stooped,
And from the ground took up an oaken staff
By me yet unobserved, a traveller's staff,
Which I suppose from his slack hand had dropped,
And, such the languor of the weary man,
Had lain till now neglected in the grass,
But not forgotten. Back we turned and shaped
Our course toward the cottage. He appeared
To travel without pain, and I beheld
With ill-suppressed astonishment his tall
And ghostly figure moving at my side.
As we advanced I asked him for what cause
He tarried there, nor had demanded rest
At inn or cottage. He replied, "In truth
My weakness made me loth to move, and here
I felt myself at ease and much relieved,
But that the village mastiff fretted me,
And every second moment rang a peal
Felt at my very heart. There was no noise,

Nor any foot abroad—I do not know
What ailed him, but it seemed as if the dog
Were howling to the murmur of the stream."
While thus we travelled on I did not fail
To question him of what he had endured
From war and battle and the pestilence.
He all the while was in demeanor calm,
Concise in answer: solemn and sublime
He might have seemed, but that in all he said
There was a strange half-absence and a tone
Of weakness and indifference, as of one
Remembering the importance of his theme,
But feeling it no longer. We advanced
Slowly, and ere we to the wood were come
Discourse had ceased. Together on we passed
In silence through the shades gloomy and dark,
Then turning up along an open field
We gained the cottage. At the door I knocked,
And called aloud, "My Friend, here is a man
By sickness overcome; beneath your roof
This night let him find rest, and give him food—
The service if need be I will requite."
Assured that now my comrade would repose
In comfort, I entreated that henceforth
He would not linger in the public ways
But at the door of cottage or of inn
Demand the succour which his state required,
And told him, feeble as he was 'twere fit
He asked relief or alms. At this reproof
With the same ghastly mildness in his look
He said, "My trust is in the God of heaven,
And in the eye of him that passes me."
By this the labourer had unlocked the door,
And now my comrade touched his hat again
With his lean hand, and in a voice that seemed
To speak with a reviving interest
Till then unfelt, he thanked me. I returned
The blessing of the poor unhappy man,
And so we parted ...

2. The American Revolution

[Since Smith sets her novel during the American Revolution, it is useful to have some background on how this war came about and why it was fought. The following excerpts illustrate the British attitude towards taxing the distant colonists and Britain's opinion that war was justified (a, b, c, and d), and the revolutionaries' distrust of, and appeal for neutrality to, the Native Americans who were also drawn into the conflict (e and f). The source for these excerpts is *Major Problems in the Era of the American Revolution, 1760–1791*, ed. Richard D. Brown (Lexington, MA: D.C. Heath, 1992): 96–97, 148, 198–99, 260–61, 261–65.]

a. The Repeal Act, March 18, 1766.[1]

Whereas an Act was passed in the last session of Parliament entitled, An Act for granting and applying certain stamp duties, and other duties in the British colonies and plantations in America towards further defraying the expenses of defending, protecting, and securing the same; and for amending such parts of the several Acts of Parliament relating to the trade and revenues of the said colonies and plantations as direct the manner of determining and recovering the penalties and forfeitures therein mentioned; and whereas the continuance of the said Act would be attended with many inconveniencies, and may be productive of consequences greatly detrimental to the commercial interests of these kingdoms; ... be it enacted by the king's most excellent Majesty, by and with the advice and consent of the Lords spiritual and Temporal, and Commons ... that ... the above-mentioned Act ... is ... hereby repealed.

b. The Declaratory Act of March 18, 1766.[2]

Whereas several of the houses of representatives in his Majesty's colonies and plantations in America, have of late, against law, claimed to themselves, or to the general assemblies of the same, the sole and exclusive right of imposing duties and taxes upon his Majesty's subjects in the said colonies and plantations; and have, in pursuance of such claim, passed certain votes, resolutions, and orders, derogatory to the legislative authority of Parliament, and inconsistent with the dependency of the said colonies and plantations upon the Crown of Great Britain: may it therefore ... be declared ... in this present Parliament assembled ... that the said colonies and plantations in America have been, are, and of right ought to be, subordinate unto, and

---

[1] Parliament repeals the Stamp Act.
[2] Parliament asserts its authority to govern the colonies unchallenged.

dependent upon the imperial Crown and Parliament of Great Britain; and that the ... Parliament assembled, had, hath, and of right ought to have, full power and authority to make laws and statutes of sufficient force and validity to bind the colonies and people of America, subjects of the Crown of Great Britain, in all cases whatsoever.

II. And be it further declared and enacted by the authority aforesaid, that all resolutions, votes, orders, and proceedings, in any of the said colonies or plantations, whereby the power and authority of the Parliament of Great Britain, to make laws and statutes as aforesaid, is denied, or drawn into question, are, and are hereby declared to be, utterly null and void to all intents and purposes whatsoever.

c. The American Prohibitory Act, 1775.[1]

Whereas many persons in the colonies of New Hampshire, Massachusetts Bay, Rhode Island, Connecticut, New York, New Jersey, Pennsylvania, the three lower counties on Delaware, Maryland, Virginia, North Carolina, South Carolina, and Georgia, have set themselves in open rebellion and defiance to the just and legal authority of the king and Parliament of Great Britain, to which they ever have been, and of right ought to be, subject: and have assembled together an armed force, engaged his Majesty's troops, and attacked his forts; have usurped the powers of government, and prohibited all trade and commerce with this kingdom and the other parts of his Majesty's dominions; for the more speedily and effectually suppressing such wicked and daring designs, and for preventing any aid, supply, or assistance being sent thither during the continuance of the said rebellious and treasonable commotions, be it therefore declared and enacted ... that all manner of trade and commerce is and shall be prohibited with the colonies of New Hampshire, Massachusetts Bay, Rhode Island, Connecticut, New York, New Jersey, Pennsylvania, the three lower counties on Delaware, Maryland, Virginia, North Carolina, South Carolina, and Georgia; and that all ships and vessels of or belonging to the inhabitants of the said colonies, together with their cargoes, apparel, and furniture, and all other ships and vessels what soever, together with their cargoes, apparel, and furniture, which shall be found trading in any port or place of the said colonies, or going to trade, or coming from trading, in any such port or place, shall become forfeited to his Majesty, as if the same were the ships and effects of open enemies ...

...And, for the encouragement of the officers and seamen of his Majesty's ships of war, be it further enacted, that the flag officers, captains,

---

[1]   Parliament effectively declares an embargo on American trade; the British navy is free to capture American ships for profit.

commanders, and other commissioned officers in his Majesty's pay, and also the seamen, marines, and soldiers on board shall have the sole interest and property of and in all and every such ship, vessel, goods, and merchandise, which they shall seize and take ...

d. Speech by General John Burgoyne, 1777.

The forces entrusted to my command, are designed to act in concert, and upon a common principle, with the numerous armies and fleets which already display in every quarter of America, the power, the justice, and, when properly sought, the mercy of the king.

The cause in which the British arms is thus exerted, applies to the most affecting interests of the human heart; and the military servants of the crown, at first called forth for the sole purpose of restoring the rights of the constitution, now combine with love of their country, and duty to their sovereign, the other extensive incitements, which form a due sense of the general privileges of mankind. To the eyes and ears of the temperate part of the public, and the breasts of suffering thousands, in the provinces, be the melancholy appeal, whether the present unnatural rebellion has not been made a foundation for the completest system of tyranny that ever God, in his displeasure, suffered for a time to be exercised over a forward and stubborn generation.

Arbitrary imprisonment, confiscation of property, persecution, and torture, unprecedented in the inquisition of the Romish church, are among the palpable enormities that verify the affirmative. These are inflicted, by assemblies and committees, who dare to profess themselves friends to liberty, upon the most quiet subjects, without distinction of age or sex, for the sole crime, often for the sole suspicion, of having adhered in principle to the government under which they were born, and to which, by every tie, divine and human, they owe allegiance. To consummate these shocking proceedings, the profanation of religion is added to the most profligate prostitution of common reason, the consciences of men are set at nought; and multitudes are compelled not only to bear arms, but also to swear subjection to an usurpation they abhor ...

... The intention of this address is to hold forth security, not depredation to the country. To those, whom spirit and principle may induce to partake the glorious task of redeeming their countrymen from dungeons, and re-establishing the blessings of legal government, I offer encouragement and employment; and, upon the first intelligence of their association, I will find means to assist their undertakings. The domestic, the industrious, the infirm, and even the timid inhabitants, I am desirous to protect, provided they remain quietly at their houses; that they do not suffer their cattle to be removed, nor their corn or forage to be secreted or destroyed;

that they do not break up their bridges or roads; nor by any other act, directly or indirectly, endeavor to obstruct the operations of the king's troops, or supply or assist those of the enemy.

Every species of provision, brought to my camp, will be paid for at an equitable rate, and in solid coin.

In consciousness of christianity, my royal master's clemency, and the honor of soldiership, I have dwelt upon this invitation, and wished for more persuasive terms to give it impression. And let not people be led to disregard it, by considering their distance from the immediate situation of my camp. I have but to give stretch to the Indian forces under my direction— and they amount to thousands—to overtake the hardened enemies of Great Britain and America. I consider them the same, wherever they may lurk.

If, not withstanding these endeavors, and sincere inclinations to effect them, the phrenzy of hostility should remain, I trust I shall stand acquitted in the eyes of God and men in denouncing and executing the vengeance of the state against the wilful outcasts. The messengers of justice and of wrath await them in the field: and devastation, famine, and every concomitant horror, that a reluctant, but indispensable prosecution of military duty must occasion, will bar the way to their return.

e. Letter from John Adams.[1]

Phyladelphia June 7, 1775

Dear Sir

We have been puzzled to discover, what we ought to do, with the Canadians and Indians …

…Whether We Should march into Canada with an Army Sufficient to break the Power of Governor Carlton,[2] to overawe the Indians, and to protect the French has been a great Question. It Seems to be the general Conclusion that it is best to go, if We can be assured that the Canadians will be pleased with it, and join.

The Nations of Indians inhabiting the Frontiers of the Colonies, are numerous and warlike. They seem disposed to Neutrality. None have as yet taken up the Hatchet against us; and We have not obtained any certain Evidence that Either Carlton or Johnson[3] have directly attempted to persuade them to take up the Hatchet. Some Suspicious Circumstances there are.

---

[1] To an unknown correspondent. John Adams (1735–1826), was President of the United States from 1796–1800.

[2] Governor Guy Carlton of Quebec (Richard Brown's note).

[3] Guy Johnson, superintendent of Indians in the northern department (Brown's note).

The Indians are known to conduct their Wars, So entirely without Faith and Humanity, that it would bring eternal Infamy on the Ministry throughout all Europe, if they should excite these Savages to War. The French disgraced themselves last War, by employing them. To let loose these blood Hounds to scalp Men, and to butcher Women and Children is horrid. Still it [is] Such Kind of Humanity and Policy as we have experienced, from the Ministry.

f. A Speech to the Six Confederate Nations, Mohawks, Oneidas, Tuscaroras, Onandagas, Cayugas, Senecas, from the Twelve United Colonies, convened in Council at Philadelphia (1775).[1]

Brothers, Sachems, and Warriors! We, the Delegates from the twelve United Provinces ... now sitting in General Congress at *Philadelphia*, send this talk to you our Brothers. We are sixty-five in number, chosen and appointed by the people throughout all these Provinces and Colonies, to meet and sit together in one Great Council, to consult together for the common good of the land, and speak and act for them.

Brothers! In our consultation we have judged it proper and necessary to send you this talk, as we are upon the same island, that you may be informed of the reasons of this great Council, the situation of our civil Constitution, and our disposition towards you our *Indian* brothers of the *Six Nations* and their allies.

Brothers and Friends, now attend! When our fathers crossed the great water and came over to this land, the King of *England* gave them a talk, assuring them that they and their children should be his children, and that if they would leave their native country and make settlements, and live here, and buy and sell, and trade with their brethren beyond the water, they should still keep hold of the same covenant chain and enjoy peace; and it was covenanted, that the fields, houses, goods and possessions which our fathers should acquire, should remain to them as their own, and be their children's forever, and at their sole disposal.

Trusting that this covenant should never be broken, our fathers came a great distance beyond the great water, laid out their money here, built houses, cleared fields, raised crops, and through their own labour and industry grew tall and strong ...

... *Brothers and Friends, open a kind ear!* We will now tell you of the quarrel

---

[1] The Continental Congress in Philadelphia drafted this address to the Six Nations (a Native American tribal council) to entreat their neutrality in the conflict with Britain. *The Old Manor House* portrays the Iroquois (who are not a member of the Six Nations, but rather established their own federation, the Five Nations) as firstly in league with, and then against, the British.

betwixt the Counsellors of King *George* and the inhabitants and Colonies of *America*.

Many of his Counsellors are proud and wicked men. They persuade the King to break the covenant chain, and not to send us any more good Talks. A considerable number have prevailed upon him to enter into a new covenant against us, and have torn asunder and cast behind their backs the good old covenant which their ancestors and ours entered into, and took strong hold of.

They now tell us they will slip their hand into our pocket without asking, as though it were their own; and at their pleasure they will take from us our Charters, or written Civil Constitution, which we love as our lives; also our plantations, our houses and goods, whenever they please, without asking our leave; that our vessels may go to this island in the sea, but to this or that particular island we shall not trade any more; and in case of our non-compliance with these new orders, they shut up our harbours.

Brothers, this is our present situation; thus have many of the King's Counsellors and servants dealt with us. If we submit, or comply with their demands, you can easily perceive to what state we will be reduced. If our people labour on the field, they will not know who shall enjoy the crop. If they hunt in the woods, it will be uncertain who shall taste of the meat, or have the skins. If they build houses, they will not know whether they may sit round the fire, with their wives and children. They cannot be sure whether they shall be permitted to eat, drink, and wear the fruits of their own labour and industry.

Brothers and Friends of the Six Nations, *attend!* We upon this island have often spoke and entreated the King and his servants the Counsellors, that peace and harmony might still continue between us; that we cannot part with or lose our hold of the old covenant chain which united our fathers and theirs; that we want to brighten this chain, and keep the way open as our fathers did; that we want to live in peace with them as brothers, labour, trade, travel abroad, eat and drink in peace. We have often asked them to love us, and live in such friendship with us as their fathers did with ours.

We told them again that we judged we were exceedingly injured, that they might as well kill us, as take away our property and the necessaries of life. We have asked why they treat us thus? What has become of our repeated addresses and supplications to them? Who hath shut the ears of the King to the cries of his children in *America*? No soft answer, no pleasant voice from beyond the water has yet sounded in our ears.

Brothers, thus stands the matter betwixt old *England* and *America*. You *Indians* know how things are proportioned in a family—between the father and the son—the child carries a little pack. *England* we regard as the father; this island may be compared to the son.

The father has a numerous family—both at home and upon this island. He appoints a great number of servants to assist him in the government of his family. In process of time, some of his servants grow proud and ill-natured; they were displeased to see the boy so alert and walk so nimbly with his pack. They tell the father, and advise him to enlarge the child's pack; they prevail; the pack is increased; the child takes it up again—as he thought it might be the father's pleasure—speaks but few words—those very small—for he was loth to offend the father. Those proud and wicked servants, finding they had prevailed, laughed to see the boy sweat and stagger under his increased load. By and by, they apply to the father to double the boy's pack, because they heard him complain; and without any reason, said they, he is a cross child; correct him if he complains any more. The boy entreats the father; addresses the great servants in a decent manner, that the pack might be lightened; he could not go any farther; humbly asks, if the old fathers, in any of their records, had described such a pack for the child; after all the tears and entreaties of the child, the pack is redoubled; the child stands a little while staggering under the weight, ready to fall every moment. However, he entreats the father once more, though so faint he could only lisp out his last humble supplication; waits a while; no voice returns. The child concludes the father could not hear; those proud servants had intercepted his supplications, or stopped the ears of the father. He therefore gives one struggle and throws off the pack, and says he cannot take it up again; such a weight would crush him down and kill him, and he can but die if he refuses.

Upon this, those servants are very wroth; and tell the father many false stories respecting the child; they bring a great cudgel to the father, asking him to take it in his hand and strike the child.

This may serve to illustrate the present condition of the King's *American* subjects or children.

Amidst these oppressions we now and then hear a mollifying and reviving voice from some of the King's wise Counsellors, who are our friends, and feel for our distresses; when they heard our complaints and our cries, they applied to the King; also told those wicked servants, that this child in *America* was not a cross boy; it had sufficient reason for crying, and if the cause of its complaint was neglected, it would soon assume the voice of a man, plead for justice like a man, and defend its rights and support the old covenant chain of the fathers.

Brothers, listen! Notwithstanding all our entreaties, we have but little hope the King will send us any more good Talks, by reason of his evil Counsellors; they have persuaded him to send an army of soldiers and many ships-of-war, to rob and destroy us. They have shut up many of our harbours, seized and taken into possession many of our vessels; the soldiers have struck the blow; killed some of our people; the blood now runs of the *American* children. They have also burned our houses and Towns, and taken much of our goods.

Brothers! We are now necessitated to rise, and forced to fight, or give up our Civil Constitution, run away, and leave our farms and houses behind us. This must not be. Since the King's wicked Counsellors will not open their ears, and consider our just complaints, and the cause of our weeping, and hath given the blow, we are determined to drive away the King's Soldiers, and to kill and destroy all those wicked men we find in arms against the peace of the twelve United Colonies upon this island. We think our cause is just; therefore hope God will be on our side. We do not take up the hatchet and struggle for honour and conquest; but to maintain our Civil Constitution and religious privileges, the very same for which our forefathers left their native land and came to this Country.

Brothers and Friends! We desire you will hear and receive what we have now told you, and that you will open a good ear and listen to what we are now going to say. This is a family quarrel between us and *Old England.* You *Indians* are not concerned in it. We don't wish you to take up the hatchet against the King's Troops. We desire you to remain at home, and not join on either side, but keep the hatchet buried deep. In the name and behalf of all our people, we ask and desire you to love peace and maintain it, and to love and sympathize with us in our troubles; that the path may be kept open with all our people and yours, to pass and repass, without molestation.

Brothers! We live upon the same ground with you. The same island is our common birthplace. We desire to sit down under the same tree of peace with you; let us water its roots and cherish its growth, till the large leaves and flourishing branches shall extend to the setting sun, and reach the skies.

Brothers, observe well! What is it we have asked of you? Nothing but peace, notwithstanding our present disturbed situation; and if application should be made to you by any of the King's unwise and wicked Ministers to join on their side, we only advise you to deliberate with great caution, and in your wisdom look forward to the consequences of a compliance. For, if the King's Troops take away our property, and destroy us, who are of the same blood with themselves, what can you, who are *Indians*, expect from them afterwards?

Therefore, we say, Brothers, take care; hold fast to your covenant chain. You know now our disposition towards you, the *Six Nations* of *Indians*, and your allies. Let this our good Talk remain at *Onondaga*, your central Council-House. We depend upon you to send and acquaint your allies to the northward, the seven Tribes on the River *St. Lawrence*, that you have this Talk of ours at the Great Council Fire of the *Six Nations.* And when they return, we invite your great men to come and converse farther with us at *Albany*, where we intend to rekindle the Council Fire, which your and our ancestors sat round in great friendship.

Brothers and Friends! We greet you all farewell.

Brothers! We have said we wish you *Indians* may continue in peace with one another, and with us the white people. Let us both be cautious in our behaviour towards each other at this critical state of affairs. This island now trembles; the wind whistles from almost every quarter; let us fortify our minds and shut our ears against false rumours; let us be cautious what we receive for truth, unless spoken by wise and good men. If any thing disagreeable should ever fall out between us, the twelve *United Colonies*, and you, the *Six Nations*, to wound our peace, let us immediately seek measures for healing the breach. From the present situation of our affairs, we judge it wise and expedient to kindle up a small Council Fire at *Albany*, where we may hear each other's voice, and disclose our minds more fully to each other.

Ordered, That a similar Talk be prepared for the other *Indian* Nations, preserving the tenour of the above, and altering it so as to suit the *Indians* in the several Departments.

3. The French Revolution.

[Although Smith sets *The Old Manor House* during the American Revolution, it is published at the height of the French Revolution, just before Britain and France go to war. It is possible to read her turn to the past as a way of disguising her critical stance on the British Government's actions towards France. The following excerpts show a variety of responses to the events in France and indicate the political climate of the 1790s. The source for these excerpts is *The Debate on the French Revolution, 1789–1800*, ed. Alfred Cobban (London: Adam & Charles Black, 1963): 55–56, 92–94, 273–74.]

a. From *The Analytical Review* (1789).

What are the machinations of despots, or the intrigues of worthless statesmen, when compared to the object now before us? A nation of 24 millions of people raising their unanimous voice in favour of liberty, and the rights of human nature! ... As men, and as Britons, we most sincerely wish them success; and pray that no dissentions amongst themselves may obscure the glorious prospect before them. We are confident, indeed, that it cannot long be obscured ... There are some who are of opinion that if the French become a free and commercial people, it will be much against the interest of this country; but for our part we declare this a narrow and ill-grounded idea ... The emancipation of France may be followed by a restoration of their ancient rights to the Austrian Netherlands; and in time, by the emancipation of Spain and other countries of Europe. We seem to be advancing to a great aera in the history of human affairs. The papal power, that scourge of nations, is declining ... More liberal ideas, both in politics and religion, are everywhere gaining ground ... The Genius of Commerce is gone forth amongst the nations of the earth; everywhere carrying Peace and Plenty, and Freedom in her train.

b. From James Mackintosh, *Vindicae Gallicae: Defence of the French Revolution, and its English Admirers, against the accusations of The Right Hon. E. Burke* (1791).

The three Aristocracies, Military, Sacerdotal, and Judicial, may be considered as having formed the French Government. All attempts to improve them would have been little better than (to use the words of Mr. Burke) "mean reparations on mighty ruins."[1] They were not perverted by the accidental depravity of their members. They were not infected by any transient passion, which new circumstances would extirpate. The fault was in the essence of the institutions themselves, which were irreconcilable with a free Government. But it is objected, these institutions might have been gradually reformed. The spirit of Freedom would have silently entered. The progressive wisdom of an enlightened nation would have remedied, in process of time, their defects, without convulsion.

To this argument I confidently answer, *that these institutions would have destroyed LIBERTY, before Liberty had corrected their SPIRIT.* Power vegetates with more vigour after these gentle prunings. A slender reform amuses and lulls the people; the popular enthusiasm subsides, and the moment of effectual reform is irretrievably lost. No important political improvement was ever obtained in a period of tranquillity. The corrupt interest of the Governors is so strong, and the cry of the people so feeble, that it were vain to expect it. If the effervescence of the popular mind is suffered to pass away without effect, it would be absurd to expect from languor what enthusiasm had not obtained. If radical reform is not, at such a moment, procured, all partial changes are evaded and defeated in the tranquillity which succeeds. The gradual reform that arises from the presiding principle exhibited in the specious theory of Mr. Burke, is belied by the experience of all ages. Whatever excellence, whatever freedom is discoverable in Governments, has been infused into them by the shock of a revolution, and their subsequent progress has been only the accumulation of abuse. It is hence that the most enlightened politicians have recognized the necessity

---

[1]   Mackintosh quotes from Edmund Burke (1729-1797), *Reflections on the Revolution in France* (1790).

of frequently recalling Governments to their first principles; a truth equally suggested to the penetrating intellect of Machiavel, by his experience of the Florentine democracy, and by his research into the history of ancient Commonwealths.[1]— Whatever is good ought to be pursued at the moment it is attainable. The public voice, irresistible in a period of convulsion, is contemned with impunity, when dictated by that lethargy into which nations are lulled by the tranquil course of their ordinary affairs. The ardour of reform languished in unsupported tediousness. It perishes in an impotent struggle with adversaries, who receive new strength from the progress of the day. No hope of great political improvement (let us repeat it) is to be entertained from tranquillity, for its natural operation is to strengthen all those, who are interested in perpetuating abuse. The National Assembly seized the moment of eradicating the corruptions and abuses, which afflicted their country. Their reform was total, that it might be commensurate with the evil, and no part of it was delayed, because to spare an abuse at such a period was to consecrate it; because the enthusiasm which carries nations to such enterprises is short-lived, and the opportunity of reform, if once neglected, might be irrevocably fled.

c. Royal Proclamation Against Seditious Writings, 21 May 1792.

George *R.*

Whereas divers wicked and seditious writings have been printed, published, and industriously dispersed, tending to excite tumult and disorder, by endeavouring to raise groundless jealousies and discontents in the minds of our faithful and loving subjects, respecting the laws and happy constitution of government, civil and religious, established in this kingdom; and endeavouring to vilify and bring into contempt the wise and wholesome provisions made at the time of the glorious revolution, and since strengthened and confirmed by subsequent laws for the preservation and security of the rights and liberties of our faithful and loving subjects. And whereas divers writings have also been printed, published, and industriously dispersed, recommending the said wicked and seditious publications to the attention of all our faithful and loving subjects. And whereas we have also reason to believe that correspondences have been entered into with sundry persons in foreign parts, with a view to forward the criminal and wicked purposes above mentioned ...

  ...We, therefore, being resolved, as far as in us lies, to repress the wicked and seditious practices aforesaid, and to deter all persons from following so

---

[1] Mackintosh refers to Niccolò Machiavelli's (1469-1527) famous treatise on courtly politics and statecraft, *The Prince* (1513).

pernicious an example, have thought fit, by the advice of our privy council, to issue this our royal proclamation, solemnly warning all our loving subjects, as they tender their own happiness, and that of their posterity to guard against all such attempts which aim at the subversion of all regular government within this kingdom, and which are inconsistent with the peace and order of society; and earnestly exhorting them at all times, and to the utmost of their power, to avoid and discourage all proceedings, ending to produce riots and tumults; and we do strictly charge and command all our magistrates in and throughout our kingdom of Great Britain, that they do make diligent inquiry in order to discover the authors and printers of such wicked and seditious writings as aforesaid, and all others who shall disperse the same.

It being our determination, for the preservation of the peace and happiness of our faithful and loving subjects, to carry the laws vigorously into execution against such offenders as aforesaid.

Given at our court at the Queen's House, the 21st day of May, 1792 in the 32nd year of our reign.

Select Bibliography

Aiken, John, and Anna Letitia Barbauld. *Miscellaneous Pieces in Prose*. London: J. Johnson, 1792.

Analytical Review, The. "The Old Manor House." 16 (May 1793): 60–63.

Barbauld, Anna Letitia. "Introduction to *The Old Manor House*." *The British Novelists, with an Essay and Prefaces Biographical and Critical*. 50 vols. London: 1810.

Bartolomeo, Joseph. "The Subversion of Romance in *The Old Manor House*." *Studies in English Literature* 33 (1993): 645–57.

———. "Charlotte to Charles: *The Old Manor House* as a Source for *Great Expectations*." *Dickens Quarterly* 8 (1991): 112–20.

Blackstone, William. "The Rights of Things." *Commentaries on the Laws of England*. 4 vols. Oxford: Clarendon, 1765-69.

Bonwick, Colin. *English Radicals and the American Revolution*. Chapel Hill: U of North Carolina P, 1977.

Brydges, Samuel Egerton. "Memoir of Mrs. Charlotte Smith." *Censura Literaria, Containing Titles, Abstracts and Opinions of Old English Books*. 10 vols. London: Longman, 1815. 242–55.

Burke, Edmund. *Edmund Burke on Government, Politics, and Society*. Ed. B. W. Hill. Sussex: Harvester Press, 1975.

Butler, Marilyn, ed. *Burke, Paine, Godwin and the Revolution Controversy*. Cambridge: Cambridge UP, 1984.

Clay, Christopher. "Property Settlements, Financial Provision for the Family, and Sale of Land by the Greater Landowners, 1660–1790." *Journal of British Studies* 21 (1981): 18–38.

Cobben, Alfred, ed. *The Debate on the French Revolution, 1789–1800*. London: Adam and Charles Black, 1960.

Conway, Alison. "Nationalism, Revolution, and the Female Body: Charlotte Smith's *Desmond*." *Women's Studies* 24 (1995): 395–409.

Critical Review, The. "The Old Manor House." 8 (May 1793): 44–54.

Curran, Stuart, ed. *The Poems of Charlotte Smith*. Oxford: Oxford UP, 1994.

Derry, John. *English Politics and the American Revolution*. London: J.M. Dent, 1976.

Donoghue, Bernard. *British Politics and the American Revolution: The Path to War, 1773–75*. London: Macmillan, 1964.

Ehrenpreis, Anne Henry, ed. *The Old Manor House*. Oxford: Oxford UP, 1969.

Fletcher, Loraine. *Charlotte Smith: A Critical Biography*. Basingstoke: Macmillan, 1998.

———. "Charlotte Smith's Emblematic Castles." *Critical Survey* 4 (1992): 3–8.

Forbes, Joan. "Anti-Romantic Discourse as Resistance: Women's Fiction 1775–1820." *Romance Revisited*. Eds. Lynne Pearce and Jackie Stacey. London: Laurence and Wishart, 1995. 293–305.

Habbakuk, John. "The Rise and Fall of English Landed Families, 1600–1800." *Transactions of the Royal Historical Society*, 5th ser., 29 (1979): 187–207.

Hays, Mary. "Mrs. Charlotte Smith." *British Public Characters*. Ed. Richard Phillips. Vol. 3. London: 1800–01. 43–65.

Labbe, Jacqueline M. "'Every Poet Her Own Drawing Master': Charlotte Smith, Anna Seward, and *ut pictura poesis*." *Early Romantics: Perspectives in British Poetry from Pope to Wordsworth*. Ed. Tom Woodman. Basingstoke: Macmillan, 1998. 200–14.

——. "Charlotte Smith: *Beachy Head*." *The Blackwell Companion to Romanticism*. Ed. Duncan Wu. Oxford: Blackwell, 1998. 204–10.

——. "Selling One's Sorrows: Charlotte Smith, Mary Robinson, and the Marketing of Poetry." *The Wordsworth Circle* XXV (1994): 68–71.

——. "The Exiled Self: Images of War in Charlotte Smith's 'The Emigrants'". *Romantic War: Studies in Conflict and Culture, 1789–1815*. Ed. Philip Shaw. London: Scolar Press, 2000. 37–56.

——. "'Transplanted into more congenial soil': Footnoting the Self in the Poetry of Charlotte Smith." *Mar(k)ing the Text: The Presentation of Meaning on the Literary Page*. Eds. Joe Bray, Miriam Handley, and Anne Henry. London: Scolar Press, 2000. 71–86.

Lady's Monthly Museum, The. "Mrs. Charlotte Smith." 2 (May 1799): 336–41.

Monthly Review, The. "*The Old Manor House*." 11 (May 1793): 150–53.

Paine, Thomas. *Political Writings*. Ed. Bruce Kuklick. Cambridge: Cambridge UP, 1989.

Perry, Keith. *British Politics and the American Revolution*. Basingstoke: Macmillan, 1990.

Rogers, Katherine M. "Romantic Aspirations, Restricted Possibilities: The Novels of Charlotte Smith." *Re-Visioning Romanticism*. Eds. Carol Shiner Wilson and Joel Haefner. Philadelphia: U of Pennsylvania P, 1994. 72–88.

Scott, Walter. "Charlotte Smith." *Miscellaneous Prose Works*. 4 vols. Edinburgh: Cadell, 1834. 58–70.

Smith, Charlotte. *The Old Manor House*. London: Pandora, 1987.

Stanton, Judith. "Introduction." *The Old Manor House*. Ed. Anne Henry Ehrenpreis. Oxford: Oxford UP, 1989.

——. "Charlotte Smith's 'Literary Business': Income, Patronage, and Indigence." *The Age of Johnson* 1 (1987): 375–401.

Turner, Rufus Paul. "Charlotte Smith (1749–1806): New Light on her Life and Literary Career." Diss. U of Southern California, 1966.

Ty, Eleanor. *Unsex'd Revolutionaries: Five Women Novelists of the 1790s*. Toronto: U of Toronto P, 1993.

Wikborg, Eleanor. "Political Discourse versus Sentimental Romance: Ideology and Genre in Charlotte Smith's *Desmond.*" *English Studies* 78 (1997): 522–31.

Wollstonecraft, Mary. *Political Writings.* Ed. Janet Todd. London: William Pickering, 1993.